American Short Stories
Since 1945

D0727875

American
Short Stories
Since 1945

Edited with an Introduction by
JOHN HOLLANDER

A Perennial Classic
Harper & Row, Publishers, New York

AMERICAN SHORT STORIES SINCE 1945
Introduction and compilation
copyright © 1968 by John Hollander.
Printed in the United States of America.
All rights reserved.
All sources and acknowledgments appear on pages vi through viii.
First edition: PERENNIAL CLASSICS, 1968, Harper & Row, Publishers, Incorporated, 49 East 33rd Street, New York, N.Y. 10016.
Library of Congress Catalog Card Number: 68–57375.

Contents

Acknowledgments

"The Facts of Life," by Paul Goodman, from *The Facts of Life*, Vanguard Press, 1945, with revisions by the author, 1968. Originally appeared in *The Partisan Review*, 1940. Reprinted by permission of the author.

"Lions, Harts, Leaping Does," by J. F. Powers, from *Prince of Darkness and Other Stories*, Doubleday & Company, Inc. Copyright 1943 by J. F. Powers. Reprinted by permission of the publisher.

"Miriam," by Truman Capote, was first published in *Mademoiselle* magazine, June 1945. It is reprinted by permission of the author.

"The Interior Castle," by Jean Stafford. Reprinted by permission of Farrar, Straus & Giroux, Inc. from *Children Are Bored on Sunday*, by Jean Stafford, copyright 1946 by Jean Stafford; originally published in *The Partisan Review*, Nov.–Dec. 1946.

"The Lottery," by Shirley Jackson, reprinted by permission of Farrar, Straus & Giroux, Inc. from *The Lottery*, by Shirley Jackson, copyright 1948, 1949 by Shirley Jackson. Originally published in *The New Yorker*, June 26, 1948.

"Pages from Cold Point," by Paul Bowles. Originally published in *New Directions* in 1949. Reprinted from *The Delicate Prey and Other Stories*, published by Random House, Inc. Copyright 1945, 1946, 1947, 1948, 1949, 1950 by Paul Bowles.

"Heartburn," by Hortense Calisher, from *In the Absence of Angels*, by Hortense Calisher, Little, Brown and Company. Copyright 1951 by Hortense Calisher. Originally published in the *New American Mercury*, January 1951.

"The Heart of the Artichoke," by Hubert Gold. Originally published in *The New Republic*, 1951. Reprinted from *Love*

Introduction

John Hollander

This collection aims to show the major shapes taken by shorter fiction in America since the end of World War II. I almost find myself writing "since the War" here, and perhaps the slip is not totally trivial—certainly for all but perhaps the two youngest authors represented here, "the end of the war" was some kind of private event as well as one of the "genuine dates" of institutional history. It would have to be so in order to serve as a significant boundary on any map of the imagination's terrain. For such a mapping, too, the natural conformations are always rather unwilling to be ruled in or out of any geometric frame, and most anthologists would have to confess to some deep suspicions if literary history in fact seemed to fit their categories too neatly. And so it is with my starting point, for in order to show some continuities I have had to violate others, and it will be seen that in my title I have used "since" in a special sense. There are certainly several important authors whose inclusion I myself, looking over this list for the first time, would miss, and two of them, whose influence on so much of the American short story in the last two decades cannot be minimized, have continued to write during that time themselves. Eudora Welty began to be known just before the postwar late 'forties which was the seed–time of this period (her direct influence may be seen in Truman Capote's story, "Miriam"); John O'Hara had been well established considerably earlier, and even though his longer, rambling stories of the past fifteen years have shown the effects of his own reiterated attempt at the comprehensive *Bildungsroman,* he cannot be said to have emerged as a creative presence since the war. On the other hand, the initial versions of the first two stories in the collection actually appeared in print during the war, but Paul Goodman and J. F. Powers must certainly count as writers of the present age.

However, several other exclusions appear to me to be significant for a very different reason: I am thinking of some of the most distinguished novelists of the postwar period who cannot be considered writers of short stories. William Styron's *The Long March* is as clearly a novella in scope as John Phil-

lips' "The Engines of Hygeia," which appeared in a similar
format within a year or so, is a longish short story. It is even
more startling to note that in the case of William Gaddis and
Ralph Ellison (whose *The Recognitions* and *Invisible Man* I
think from time to time to be the two most important American novels since Faulkner) there has come as yet no subsequent novel, let alone a rush of short stories of impressive
quality. And this is perhaps as it should be, for the American
novel of any pretension looms like a mountain peak above the
imaginative ambitions of the writer. A short story can yet remain a discrete task in the best sense of the word, but that is
not to say that there are not realms of contemporary American experience which have only been adequately confronted
by novels. Wright Morris' magnificient handling, in some of
his earlier books, of the war between men and women in
some of its classical mid–western campaigns, is certainly a
case in point.*

In addition, I have not wanted to include short fictions
that were in fact pieces of novels. In the instance of Thomas
Pynchon's "Under the Rose," we have a totally self–contained digressionary tale, one of several such episodes from
that problematic and brilliant book, *V.*, whose structure was
dominated by such episodes rather than by its more conven-
tionally picaresque frame story, or even by its central theme,
reminiscent of Gaddis' symbol of art forgery, of the mechanical simulation of life. Had there been room, I might have
also added the improbable narrative of Williaus, La Vas and
Pendastrava from Harry Mathews' profoundly artificial,
Borgesian fiction, *The Conversions*. But aside from these
cases of actual short stories encapsulated in novels, the differences in range and scale between the two forms seemed to
me to show up most strongly in the very idea of the episodic
itself. It is almost as if every good story were in some sense a
chunk cut out of an otherwise unwritten novel, but in such a
way that all of the lacunae, ellipses, précis, condensations,
and so forth were visionary rather than editorial. Fiction allows us to peep into the windows of an occupied apartment
whose layout and occupancy we can only guess at from our
limited glimpses into separate windows; short stories are like
a single night of watching, but novels are more like spending
weeks or months of regular but slightly obsessed life with the

* And so Saul Bellow, John Barth, and others are not represented.
John Cheever and J. D. Salinger ("A Perfect Day for Banana-
fish") refused permission.

world across the way, perhaps enriched by occasional additional research. A piece of a novel, then, is most emphatically not a story: no fragment could give us a sense of what Saul Bellow's Augie March or Henderson were really about, nor how, as protagonists, they generated their respective fictional worlds. There is no part of Thomas Berger's wonderful *Reinhart in Love* which would properly frame the moral vision of that fine, fat comic hero who "never forgot his mission to bear witness to the principal phenomena," thereby typifying the perspective of so many of the writers represented here.

If not all the major postwar American fiction show up in the short story, certain principal planes and lines within it are quite apparent. In many ways, Paul Goodman's *The Facts of Life*, which opens this collection, strikes a keynote for what will follow it in time. The last twenty years have seen the development of an explicit concern, in American imaginative literature, with the exploration of sexual identity as well as with racial particularity. To have suggested in 1946 to a tired, hopeful national consciousness that to be an American was to be hyphenated in some way, or that the most serious fiction would seek to digest and transform many of the elements of outright pornography would have sounded irrelevant and shrill. And yet Goodman's extremely parochial story, illuminated by what seemed at the time to be the unnecessarily sectarian concerns of eclectic anarchism and Reichian psychology, was pointing out areas of significance which Europeans still have difficulty in recognizing as characteristic of the American consciousness.

As far as the theme of sexuality is concerned, it became so important and so specifically treated that it ceased, in a sense, to be a subject for a story in its own right. Ernest Hemingway's earliest story, "Up in Michigan," was the straightforward, if yet a bit elliptical, record of the sexual initiation of a midwestern farm girl, narrated in the third person but from the girl's point of view. It started lowering the threshold of explicitness in such description on a course which is only beginning to slacken off now that a minimal point has almost been reached. Even in Norman Mailer's powerful and extravagant "The Time of Her Time," which certainly increased the slope of that course, the primary task seems to be the rendering of the personality of its narrator; the minute particulars of the developing sexual relationship in the story are chronicled with all the solemnity of a spiritual journal. In another instance, the diarist of Paul Bowles' "Pages from Cold Point" avoids all expressionistic devices and actually soft–pedals what in another age would have approached the Gothic in its nastiness; the confessional torpor in which the boy's seduction of his father is revealed is part of the atmosphere of moral nullification typical of the author's exploration in tropical fringes of modern life. (How much more genuinely horrific is the casual revelation occasioned by discursive permissiveness than, for instance, the cheesy melodrama with which the merely banal is revealed in Maugham's "Rain." And how much more morally universal is the imaginative treatment of the socially unique.) Even the various satirical modes in which aspects of contemporary homosexual life are represented in the stories by Gore Vidal and James Purdy depend to a good degree for effects upon a sense of the reader's sophistication. Postwar literature in America brought with it an urbanization of the very sexual frontiers toward which it originally pointed.

But it is not only the sexual localities from which imaginative literature seeks to survey the larger terrain. The leap from the grotesque, even the pathological, to the universal has been the primary moral mechanism of much important American fiction for over a century, exemplifying one aspect of romantic poetic tradition as much as a novelistic one. The great monuments in English of the "naturalistic" sketch at which so many short stories of the 'thirties aimed are in Joyce's *Dubliners*, and yet recent criticism has been showing more and more how those model slices of life were actually molded and shaped with a poet's hand. The American novel has often been part poem; the American short story, less concerned with developing a formal structure that would accommodate greater length and range, has aimed in recent decades at the compact intensities that modernist criticism was discovering in the language of certain short lyric poems. Perhaps the younger writers represented here may have been partially influenced by the climate of academic literary criticism as it was applied to college teaching—a kind of analogue of the influence that blow–ups, on slides for G.I. Bill art–history classes, of select patches of Velasquez, may have had on the overall format of some abstract expressionist painting in New York in the 'forties and 'fifties. Certainly freshman English classes in which a Hemingway story and a poem of Donne would be compared with respect to the way they exhibited a quality called "tension" (popular among English professors at the time) taught young writers to read in a variety of ways the models they themselves selected. Very few of the stories in this collection are clearly molded in the forms of the avowed masterpieces which, in other ways, lie behind them. Perhaps the most "old fashioned" story from this point of view, "The Engines of Hygeia," is characterized by the touch of F. Scott Fitzgerald.

The movement from the intimately particular to the general in these stories is also exemplified by a new aspect of regionalism. The total breakdown of traditional American isolationism in World War II somehow made a feeble joke of the older notion of "local color." By the mid–fifties, one could point to three writers whose stories typified the finest energies of American writing at the time, all of whom were most successful in their short fiction, and all of whom confined their work to one milieu. The New York Jews of Bernard Malamud, the Catholic priests of J. F. Powers' sad and seedy midwestern rectories, the ludicrous and nasty south of Flannery O'Connor, lit up always with the imminence of first and last things—all these seemed to be instances, rather than merely interesting special cases, of an America whose destiny was already beginning to darken. These three writers are quite unlike each other, but their respective visions of the immediate and the possibility of transcendence all seem to operate in the same imaginative scale.

The increased scope of comic writing in America since the war is, I think, worthy of mention in this context. The tradition of "humor" in the 'twenties and 'thirties tended to create a genre of book or essay virtually sealed off from the most ambitious and serious fiction. Nevertheless, some of the most profound influences exerted in both America and England by pre–war authors came from S. J. Perelman, James Thurber, and, to a lightly lesser degree, Dorothy Parker (for her merciless eye, ear, and tongue which schooled so many younger writers in the ways of camp archness). In films, the deep satirical misanthropy of W. C. Fields and the wild rearrangements of reality for the sake of a gag or a routine by the Marx Brothers also contributed dimensions to the new space in which seriousness was to create its worlds. But Perelman in particular remains one of the under–acknowledged masters and teachers; among other things, he seems to have made the comic regions of *Ulysses* accessible to a whole generation which had begun to come to terms with the undeniable sanctity and sublimity of low comedy. Henry Miller, whom everyone read in suppressed editions in the 'forties, was pointing out the Rabelaisian directions toward which multitudes would later flock; his influence on the comical treatment of explicit sexual description over about a decade was so general that Norman Mailer felt moved, he said, in "The Time of Her Time" to try to make the sex not be funny. Almost half of the stories here are in good measure comical and their range of attitudes is quite remarkable, from broad picaresque to the fragility of James Schuyler's feeling for the world of the schoolchildren in "Current Events," whose utter seriousness, like that of the children in his splendid and, alas, unobtainable novella, *Alfred and Guinevere*, is reverently portrayed.

The handling of pain and disease in these stories is again, I think, interesting in the light of previous modern literature. While illness is used symbolically to stand for far more general spiritual conditions in what were school texts for the postwar generation (*The Waste Land*, "Death in Venice"), one can observe the extreme personalization of pain, in Jean Stafford's almost intolerable "The Interior Castle," and the intimacies of long dying in "The Engines of Hygeia." In both cases, the surgical hardware and the mechanisms of human relationships that surround and threaten and hurt help to mark out the definition of a self, enclosed and authentic, but totally vulnerable. One's own hurting, in short, can be nobody else's business, ever; there will always be something false about the intrusion of others into such privateness. Even in Philip Roth's grotesque perspective of military life in "Novotny's Pain," the affliction in question comes more and more to seem like the concretization of that metaphorical intrusion on the psyche, "a pain–in–the–ass." But in no way is there any attempt to use disease itself to stand for a decay in the quality of life in society. In the erotic overtones of the surgical probing in Jean Stafford's story there is no trace of philosophical generalization, none of aphoristic Sade, nor of oceanic *Liebestod*. Again we are confronting the clarity and energy of the particular as a source of illumination of the landscape at large.

Four of these stories are remarkable for the way in which they approach the domain of fable without ever really violating some of modern fiction's inflexible boundaries. Perhaps the late James Agee's story of cattle, with its wonderful contained miniature epic, takes the most chances with credibility; but set against a background of human slaughter in the read-

er's consciousness, the relation of cow to calf transcends the
animal world of the story and takes on significance in the
realm of human generation of the cycle of perishable innocence and incomplete experience in which motherhood and
love continue always to serve as a beautiful, and hopeless,
bond. The late Shirley Jackson's "The Lottery" is a brilliant
tour–de–force of selectivity; the timelessness of the setting is
partially accomplished by means of the very details which
point to the localized world of the New England village. And
it is the constant interplay of the inevitable and the implausible (charting the land in which fable dwells, as
opposed to the vast continents of the more or less probable
in which novels are born) that allows this tale to show how
the most primitive of social forces lie close beneath the sur-
faces of civilization. The story uses a kind of trick played
upon normal pastoral expectations: the simpler and more
basic rural life becomes, the more unambiguously feral it is
seen to be.

In George P. Elliott's "Faq'" the author succeeds in repre-
senting, far more successfully than in his perhaps better–
known and certainly more complicated "Among the Dangs,"
a kind of utopian polarization of the roles of the sexes in
human society. The stark realignments of activity, passivity,
engagement, and contemplation perform some of the funda-
mentally satiric work with which all utopian models reveal
at once the richness and the poverty of the actual complexities of social organization. The tone, on the other hand, is far
from that at which satirical representation is usually pitched.
But it is in Hortense Calisher's fable of the crisis of belief
that traditional and experimental elements of romance are
most effectively combined. Somewhere between a quasi–
allegorical Hawthorne story and the kind of phenomenologi-
cal romance, reminiscent of contemporary French fiction,
which the author turned to many years later in her unaccountably neglected *Journal from Ellipsia,* this remarkable
tale mythologizes into actuality a strange sort of creature,
born of an otherwise incomprehensible union of doubt and
faith. Perhaps the small, rapidly transferred animal is a
poetic reification of what in the common idiom is "swallowed whole." In any event, even the title, in its systematic
ambiguity, bears witness to the kind of imaginative space the
story will inhabit: the mundane phenomena of hyperacidity
and the mythological valentine–shaped emblem of love are

equidistant, as metaphors, from the real, the throbbing organ. "Heartburn" is as much an exploration of the viability of certain traditional conceptions of the state of the human will as it is a representation of those conceptions themselves.

The farthest reaches of experiment in this collection, however, occur in the violations of narrative format in Donald Barthelme's own kind of gallows humor (despite its modishness, it reminds me of Bierce, of Stephen Crane's poetry, and of the almost surreal absurdity of some of Donald Ogden Stewart's nonsense pieces), and in the ways in which episodes are constructed in William Gass' story. Here the love story of the middle–aged man and the young girl (which by itself is coming to be something of a genre piece of the mid–sixties) is not so much submerged in the amazing attention which the prose turns upon a world of objects and sensations; instead, the relationship (or rather, more authentically, the *awareness* of a relationship) is revealed through the meditative blocks, what are almost the story's *stanzas* in the original Italian sense of "rooms." But far wider than this is the range of rhetorical variation among all the stories in the collection. Mailer, Phillips, Powers and Miss Stafford all, in their various ways, employ a kind of mandarin prose in which the power of exposition is always felt; so indeed does Peter Taylor, whose southern chronicling tone partakes of the learned and the unhurried. At another end of the spectrum is the pitching of narrative in modes beyond even that of talk: more submerged in Herbert Gold's taste–and–smell–dominated evocation of adolescence's realms of vegetable love, and more flagrant in a story like Jeremy Larner's kind of super–charged road comedy (and hasn't this become a postwar genre on its own? Between the rich man's plaything of the 'twenties and the dust–bowl refugee's flivver of the 'thirties, automobiles were not of much literary significance). The sound of the speaking voice has been important in American fiction from Twain and, in a way, Melville, on, but recent decades have led writers to mutter, shout, whimper, giggle, snarl, and bray, for example, not as a digression from narrative telling, but in order thereby to accomplish it. Frequently local, regional or ethnic dialect will play its part in shaping this new kind of eloquence, but it is never a matter of dialect for its own sake. Rather is it usually local speech as filtered through the ear of a developing consciousness of language as of life.

Finally, I think that the overall variety of style, subject, method, and milieu that we perceive in the short fiction of the postwar period, the variety even in the possible modalities of seriousness, derives from certain consequences of the intimate nature of the short story itself. For an author it is not only more personal a form than the novel, but tends to be more empirical as well; neither the pressures of novelistic convention nor the less frequently avowed but ever–present editorial forces exerted by publishers are so constantly at work. Periodicals ranging from relatively obscure quarterlies to popular magazines like *The New Yorker* and *Esquire* have proved, in the past two decades, surprisingly adaptive; new departures from the sketch, on the one hand, and the yarn or tale, on the other, have in the pages of these last two helped to expand many molds, if not actually to break them. Indeed, in the case of most of the stories collected here, even the extremely knowledgeable reader who did not happen to know would be hard put to guess in which magazine which piece originally appeared. And although book publishers are frequently wary of short stories they will frequently cultivate a writer of them in hopes that novels will sprout. And this in itself, in an age that is beginning to close a traditional and even hallowed gap between the Serious Writer and the Best–Selling Novelist, has some value; stories, by being slightly despised, can become imaginatively useful and thus perhaps truly precious.

And above all, the very brevity of a fiction may make it more memorable, in its entirety, than all but scenes or moments in novels. Stories are free of the "books" they inhabit in something of the way that poems are. This is why the general tendency, as seen in this selection, of the modern American short story to leave behind the tradition of the sketch, the fragment, and to experiment with a large repertory of kinds of closure, seems such a hopeful one. And it is interesting that in the current literary period of what might be called post–modernism, of the revision of the critical categories that in the 'twenties had heralded the literature of a new age as the continuation of a rather specially defined version of "the tradition," American stories and poems are starting to share more than merely the avowal of another, romantic tradition, never abandoned but only temporarily denied. The interplay of voice and form remains a central and energizing problem for American expression, whether in prose or verse. The supreme fictions will probably only appear in discrete glimpses. But in any event, a crumb of vision will in the end have been worth more than any *trenche de vie*.

Churchill College, Cambridge
July, 1968

The Facts of Life

Paul Goodman

(revised by the author, 1968)

CHILDISH Ronnie Morris has a wife Martha and a daughter Marcià, aged nine.

Ronnie is middle-aged, ten years older than ourselves, and he has invented a wonderful scheme to milk money from those who make $20,000 a year: he sells them Fine Editions with odd associations, as *The Golden Ass* bound in donkey's hide or *The New Testament* signed by the designer in the blood of a lamb. (He is childish enough to go through with such a profitable idea, instead of dismissing it like the rest of us fools.) He has a two-masted sailboat. In a business way, he knows Picasso and Thomas Benton, and is the expert at the Club in the trade-secrets of the Muses. In the acts of love, he is medium; he went to Dartmouth; but he is only moderately fixated on the period when he was fifth-oar, for he had had a period of lust, which has saved him for philosophy and the arts rather than the brokerage.

Martha Morris is an Andalusian type. When she arranges flowers she keeps them under control with wires. She drives at high speeds. Her relations with Ronnie are as usual; she is her little daughter's friend, and every Christmas she and Marcia design a gift-volume for Ronnie's clientèle. She is more political than her husband and her position dramatically to the left of the right wing of the liberal center: a group that finds no representation in Washington but used to have thirty seats in Paris. I could write ads about Martha's teeth as they flash under her nose. The rhythms are delightful of the description of the upper middle class.

I

Now little Marcia goes to the University Progressive School where many of her schoolmates have fathers in the embassies, but Marcia, too, has been to the Near East in search of that lamb. At school they are taught to express themselves freely, and Marcia is good at collages.

Marcia has a fight in school today with one of the little gentlemen, her contemporaries. He breaks her photographic plate. The fight is about the nature of chickens' eggs. She stamps on his foot. Being a girl, she still has an advantage in mental age and more words to say; she says a sentence in French. He can't punch her in the nose because it is ungentlemanly. He is inhibited from drawing on his best knowledge because it is dirty; but worse, it is gloomily indistinct, and even on these matters she seems to have more definite information and is about to mention it.

"Shut up!" he argues, "shut up! you're just an old-time Jew."

This perplexing observation, of which she understands neither head nor tail, brings her to a pause; for up to now, at least with Harry—though certainly not with Terry or Larry—she has maintained a queenly advantage. But he has stopped her by drawing on absolutely new information.

In this crisis she does a reckless thing: she dismisses his remark from her mind and launches into a tirade that devastatingly combines contempt and the ability to form complete sentences, till Harry goes away in order not to cry. A reckless, a dangerous thing: because what we thus dismiss enters the regions of anxiety, of loss and unfulfilled desire, and there makes strange friends. It is the prologue to fanatic interests and to falling in love. How new and otherwise real is this observation on its next appearance!

Marcia calls her mother sometimes Momsy and sometimes Martha.

"What did Harry mean," she asks her, "when he called me an old-time shoe?"

"Jew?"

"Yes, he stated I was just an old-time Joo."

Across the woman's face passes, for ever so many reasons, a perceptible tightening. "Oh oh!" feels Marcia along her ears and scalp; and now she is confirmed and doubly confirmed in the suspicions she did not know she had. When she now has to express herself with colored chalks, new and curious objects will swim into the foreground alongside the pool, the clock will become a grandfather's clock, and all be painted Prussian blue, even though Miss Coyle is trying to cajole especially the girls into using warm bright colors, because that is their natural bent.

"Well, he was right, you are a Jewess," says Martha. "It's nothing to be ashamed of."

"Said Joo, not Juice."

"A Jew is a boy; a Jewess is a girl."

"Oh! there are two kinds!"

It's worse and worse. She never thought that Harry was up on anything, but perhaps even his veiled hints conceal something. She feels, it seems inescapable, that boys have a power, surely not obvious in school—and the grownups even take it for granted! She sees it every day, that these same boys when they become men are superior to the women. Yet men's clothes don't *express* anything, and actresses are better than actors. But just this *contradiction* confirms it all the more, for the explanations of contradictions are in the indistinct region—and everything there is mutually involved. Marcia is already working on a system of the mysteries. Especially when Momsy now tries to tell her some reasonable anecdote about Jewesses and Jews, just like a previous astringent account of the chickens and the flowers.

Martha never happens to have told little Marcia that they are all Jews.

"Is Ronnie a Joo?"

"Of course."

"Are Louis and Bernie Joos?"

"Louis is a Jew but Bernie is a Gentile."

It's a lie, thinks Marcia; they are both the same. They are both effeminate. Why is Martha lying to her?

"What is ser-cum-si-zhum?" asks Marcia, calling the lie.

This inquisition has become intolerable to Martha. "Good night, Marcia," she explains.

"Is Rosina a Juice?" Marcia cries, asking about Ronnie's mistress.

"Marcia! I said good night!"

"Tell me! tell me! is Rosina Juice?"

"No."

"Ah!"

"Why 'Ah!'?"

"Good night, Momsy," says Marcia, kissing her.

Since the habits are formed speediest where there is necessity and yet conscious and deliberate adjustment is embarrassing or tedious, Martha has speedily and long ago learned the few adjustments belonging to Jews of a certain class of money. The other hotel; not on this list; the right to more chic and modernity, but please no associations with Betsy Ross in tableaux. Of course habits learned by this mechanism are subject to amazing breaches, when submerged desire suddenly asserts itself and the son of Jacob becomes Belmont or Ronnie becomes, as he is, an honorary colonel in the militia. But on the whole, since money is so exchangeable, there are very few special adjustments. They never even came to Marcia's keen perception, especially since none of the Jews whom she is so often with without knowing it, ever mentions them. But there are other meanings, archaically forgotten.

"Since you have to put up with the handicap whether you like it or not," decides Mrs. Ronnie Morris, "why not make an advantage of it, and be proud of it?" She is writing out a check for a subscription to *The Menorah Journal*, the *Harper's* magazine of reformed Jews.

"Never heard such a stupid argument in my life!" says Ronnie. He is very angry, like anyone who has played the game like a gentleman and then finds that the other side goes too far and calls his daughter an old-time Jew.

"What's the use of *pretending* you're a Jew, when you're *not* a Jew?" he shouts.

"We are Jews. Don't shout," says Martha.

"I'll go to school and punch that brat's nose."

"Don't."

"Do I pay three hundred dollars a year for him to tell Marcia that she's a Jew?"

"But we are Jews," says Martha, with a new loyalty.

"Since when?" says Ronnie scientifically. "To be a Jew means one of three things: It means first a certain race; but there isn't any Jewish race in anthropology. Look at me, do I look like a Jewish race?"

He looks like a highly brushed and polished moujik.

"No. Secondly: it means a nationality. But even if some Jews think they have a nationality, do I? I went to Jerusalem to pick out a Gentile lamb. Anyway, I can't speak the language. Hebrew isn't the same as Yiddish, you know, even though it looks the same; but I can't speak that either.

"Third: it's a religion. So you see," he concludes, "It's not a matter of not *wanting* to be a Jew or trying to *hide* that you're a Jew, but you *can't* be a Jew if you're *not* a Jew!"

"Don't be a fool," says Martha. "A person's a Jew if his grandparents were Jews; even one's enough sometimes, depending."

"What sense does that make?"

"Do you think it's by accident," says Martha flatly, "that your mama and papa came to marry Jews and we married Jews?"

She means, thinks Ronnie, when all desire is toward Gentiles, toward retroussé noses and moon-face Hungarians. Does she mean Rosina? She means Bernie.

"I'll ask Louis," says Ronnie; for though he holds sway at the luncheon club, all his ideas come from this poet.

"He's taking Marshy to the Picassos tomorrow."

"Let him tell her, then."

"What! are you going to let your daughter find out the facts from a stranger?"

Having slept on it all night, by morning the little girl

has contrived the following working theory:

In the beginning, of course, all babies are alike. Her deep-seated conviction on this point has never been in the least shaken by Momsy's anecdotes about the chickens, for it is plain to observe that all babies are alike. But then comes the moment when the thing is cut off the girls. When this takes place, is not yet clear; but it is planned from the beginning, because you can tell by the names; although sometimes even there is a change of names; with some names you still can't tell; and others are easy to change, like Robert and Roberta or Bernie and Bernice. All of this is an old story.

But now, there are some *chosen* ones, who are supposed to be cut but somehow they get off. Why? They are only *partly* cut—and this is ser-cum-si-zhum, because they use a scissors. These are Joos. For a moment, starting from "Louis," Marcia thinks that she can tell by the names, but then when she thinks of "Ronnie" and of "Terry" and "Larry," two boys in school whom she now knows are Joos (in fact, Terry is and Larry is not), she sees that she can't. The *last* names are connected with marrying and have nothing to do with ser-cum-si-zhum.

Now, she sees in a flash, it is *better* to be a Joo, for then you still have the secret power and the thing, but at the same time you can be cleverer like a girl. This is why Larry and Terry are always able to beat her, they have an unfair advantage; but Harry, the dope, is only a boy and not a Joo.

There are also differences among Joos; for instance, Louis is much smarter than Papa. But this *proves* it, for Louis is more like Martha; that is, they cut the *best* amount off him, but not so much from Papa. Anyway, she hates Louis and loves her poor papa. Suddenly an enormous love for poor Harry suffuses her and she begins to tremble and want to go to school; he has so much secret power.

But more important—still lying in bed, Marcia begins to tremble as she thinks about herself—what is a Juice? and besides all these, there are Gen-tiles. (1. [G—] Scrip. One not a Jew.) Martha and Marcia are Juice and

Bernie is a Gen-tile. Oh! what a mean thing to say about poor Bernie, that he is not even a Juice, but even worse than a girl; he is not even clever. It is nice of Louis to be so kind to him. So it seems that things go in the following order: Boys, Joos, Juices, Girls, Gen-tiles. Except that it is smartest to be a Joo. But what is it? What is it that they did to Marcia to be a Juice? As she lets her fingers move between her thighs, she breaks into a cold sweat. With a violent dismissal, she leaps from bed.

While she is eating breakfast, an awful emptiness for her boy Harry spreads within her, and she bursts into tears.

Louis, who is intelligent, often cannot resist being cruel and supercilious to Ronnie, so that Ronnie feels like punching him in the nose—but then suddenly, at a poignant touch, even suggested by his own monologue, he relapses into natural melancholia. "To me of course," says he, "your Jewish problem doesn't exist. My paternal parent twelfth removed was Joseph Karo, the author of the *Shulchan Aruch,* or *Table* of the observances; he had established the lineage back to Joseph son of Eli, so that according to the Gentile gospels, we go back to David the son of Jesse and further; but you're a Russian Jew. On my mother's side, I am related to the convert Leo the Hebrew; but that blood throughout is tainted by conversions; my three cousins, Georges de Duchesse, Georges Catala, and Georges Catala-de Duchesse were all converts of Maritain. My cousin Georges Catala-de Duchesse is the Abbot of St. Germain-des-Prés, an *idol*-worshiper, as I told him last summer. It ought to be clear by now, I said, that only Maimonides conceived the relation of God and Man in a way helpful to the Modern Age. This is my faith. "If every Jew would read the *Mishnah Torah,* he would become a perfect snob," says Louis Parigi with pride; "he would set tradition against tradition and not take the insults lying down or by appealing merely to good sense! In our poetry both the Parigis and the de Duchesses look for inspiration to the Prophets. My cousin

Georges de Duchesse, on the very eve of his baptism, wrote his rime royal *Habakuk*; 'Habakuk,' as Voltaire said, 'était capable de tout!' But in writing my *Anacreontics* I have drawn on the dipsomaniac rhythms of your Chassidim. By the way, my cousin Georges Catala was married to an eighth removed descendant of the Vilna Gaon, her suicide was the cause of his conversion, which goes to show what comes of marrying with the Ashkenazim. (Are you also related to the Vilna Gaon, like all the other Lithuanians?) On the National issue, I am, like Judah ha-Levi, an allegorical Zionist; but the pathetic desire of a temporal habitation—this destroys, as I see it, just our distincton from the *Goyim*"—(he pronounces *Go-yeem* as if he had stepped from a fastness in Aragon where never a foreign Jew had once set foot); —"but God said—but *God* said," says Louis, raising a forefinger, "Make *Succoth*, Booths." At this quotation, suddenly, he sinks into the deepest gloom. "But," he finishes airily, "except the purity of our Jewish morals, what defense do I have against adultery and sodomy?"

It is especially this breezy ending that makes Ronnie punch him in the nose—almost. It's hard to put up with somebody else's thing.

In the afternoon, in front of the impassive checker-board of *The Three Musicians*, the little girl again bursts into tears. Louis, who has with some skill been pointing out to her only such features of the difficult paintings as she is adequate to, an underfed and melancholy face, a marvelous mother bathed in rose, the fact that in 1920 the colors are no longer blended, and enveloping it all in fanciful anecdotes—he looks at her in stupefaction.

"It's not fair! It's not fair!" she sobs.

They are alone in the room.

"What's not fair dear?" says Louis.

"It's not fair 'cause it's a myst'ry, and I won't *ever* be able to understand it."

"Why you've been understanding it very well, Marcia. What you said about the colors I didn't see my-self, because you're a painter and I'm not."

"You're *lying* to me—'cause it's a secret myst'ry, and I won't ever be able to understand it 'cause I'm only a girl, even if I'm a Juice."

? ?

"I understand about the colors and the poor boy, but I can't understand it *all*, 'cause they cut my thing off when I was little and Picass' is a man— An' I have nothing left but to be a nurse or a ballerina."

He takes her hand, for the tears are rolling down her cheeks.

"—I won't ever be able to make 'em with a myst'ry if I live to be a million years old."

She hides her face in her other arm, and she cries with the pent-up anxiety of her third to her ninth years.

The guard hastily goes into the other gallery.

On the walls, the impassive objects stare from side to side.

The tears glisten in Louis's eyes. "This Holy Spirit," he says—he thinks he says—"is given to us and not made by us. It's not my fault if I cannot any more."

"Ah," she says (he thinks), "maybe if it weren't for the Bernies and the Jackies, the prophetic voice of the Lord of Hosts would not prove so disheartened at the third and fourth verse."

"What a despicable argument!" he cries (he thinks), "if I'm finally tired of that boy, why don't I think so right off and not need these thin arguments to bolster up my courage? Stop staring, you," says he to the unblinking middle Musician, "or I'll punch you in the nose."

"Look, Marshy," he says reasonably to the little girl whose hand he is holding tight, "you can't expect to make pictures right off! You have to develop your power. Just as when you learn to play the piano, you have to be-gin with finger exercises."

"Oh!" she cries and pulls her hand away. "How could he tell so quick?" she thinks in terror; "Momsy couldn't tell."

"See, this one is easy to understand," he says, pointing to those Three Musicians. "You see, this is an oboe."

"What's a Obo?"

"An oboe is a kind of wooden instrument with stops. This part is what the oboe looks like from underneath, which you can't ordinarily see. This is a guitar; he broke it into two pieces in order to make the pattern here with this red business.—"

"Can you, Louis?" she seizes his hand, "I mean, can you? Can you develop your power by finger exercises?" ? ?

"Can you? Can you?"

"Certainly. Every day you'll be able to paint a little better."

"Hurrah!"

Two women come in, tittering at a pyramidal creature that is like one of the works of the Six Days.

But the silence is twangling with the music of the guitars, with the guitars of Catalonia, with the cubist harmony by which the acrobats drift away.

On the school field, the fourth-year boys, in maroon sweatsuits, are playing the in-tra-mur-al ball game, while Mr. Donlin is umpiring and keeping order. From time to time some of the little boys have their minds on the game. When his side is at bat, Harry is sitting on the lowest bench of the stands and Marcia bounces pebbles on him from above. Outside the iron fence, Timmy and Page McCroskey, who go to Holy Name Academy, are staring at the clean and distinguished boys within. Mr. Donlin looks a perfect fool, full of manly baby-talk such as, "Gooood try!" or "C'mon *Terry,* let's see what you can do!" Sometimes he loses his temper. One of the bo s takes off his clothes and to the amazement of the Irish boys discloses his delicate limbs in another maroon uniform of shorts and a shirt with a big U. Amid a chorus of complaints, Mr. Donlin has to assert his authority to keep the children from exposing themselves to the cold air.

"Mr. Donlin, Mr. Donlin," mimic the two outside the bars, "kin I take off my drawers?"

A local merchant-prince, a great contributor to the University, has the exclusive franchise for the manufacture and sale of these many uniforms. Timmy and Page and their friends call the U-school the Jew-school. They are envious of the boundless wealth inside the bars and of the fact that the girls and boys go to school together. "Why doncha let the girls play with youse?" shouts little Timmy. Page, who is a year younger and much bolder, cries, "Mr. Donlin, kin I take off my drawers and show the girls my prick?"

On the large field, which is used for the high-school games, the baseball, thrown by weak arms and tapped by little bats, makes little hops and arcs. Terry, distracted by the remark from the fence, drops a little pop-fly and the runners stream across the plate. Mr. Donlin advances to the fence, shouting without profanity, go away or he'll punch them in the nose. From a little distance, they shout in chorus "Jew School, Jew School!" and some of the little scholars, who at other times announce proudly that they go to the University P'rgressive School (as if they went to college), now turn pink. "Play ball!" shouts Mrs. Donlin in a manly voice.

Now all the little feelings are afire.

Marcia and Harry, however, have heard nothing. They have now progressed from the first stage of touching-yet-not-touching by throwing things at each other, to the next stage of punching and pulling shoelaces.

To the Irish boys, so systematically kept in order by their father and by the priest and Brothers to whom even their mother defers, there is no way of doubting that non-Catholics enjoy a full sexual freedom. They *know*, in fact, that the Reformation began with fornication; and even more enviable are the Jews, as is proved by the anti-Semitism, otherwise incomprehensible, that forms so large a part of the instruction by the Brothers. And along with this yearning, they observe this wealth and beauty and privilege through the bars. So is consolidated that deep sentiment of inferiority which will tomorrow need firearms to soothe.

To the little rich boys, on the other hand, it is obvious that freedom lies outside the bars among those wild boys whose dirty language makes them tremble with terror and stirs unconquerable lust in each one when he is alone; who can stay out late and wear hats decorated with paper clips and beg for pennies from strangers. So even before the first clash, the rich boys feel physically and morally powerless and would like to be the slaves of the poor ones, and it will require all the machinery of the state to treat them with an iron hand.

But why should I make the case any simpler than is necessary? For Timmy also hates little Page, just as he hates the Brothers in school; and among the U-boys there are the families going up and the families falling down, and the case, for instance, of tubby Billy, whose parents are slipping and climbing at the same time, and who will tomorrow be satisfied and avenged by burning for a hustler if his name happens to be Woodrow, until with a sinking heart he one day learns that Woodrow isn't a family name, but a war name, after President Wilson.

Fascinated, Timmy is watching Marcia wrestling with Harry and pulling his hair, while he is trying to concentrate on his teammate at bat: "Make it be a good one! Make it be a good one!" he cries; and then he chases Marcia up the stands. Pressed between the bars till he is white, Timmy follows them with his stare, above him, through the stands. But she jumps down and runs across the field toward the building, and then they both disappear. Poor Timmy stares at the gray door which has just closed.—So in each heart are fixed the types of love, after the girls who seem to be easy, who have the reputation of being available, who are easy and available in idea though never in fact. The Jewish girls to the Irish boys like Timmy, and the Irish girls to the Jewish boys like Ronnie, and the sailors to Louis. But for the most part, it is just one's own kind that is really available (and really desirable, and deeply forbidden!), and that we live with in the end, as Ronnie with Martha, and Louis with Bernie; these are no doubt also types of love, but too few to give us any pleasure.

"Knock knock!" cries Page McCroskey.

"Play ball!" shouts Mr. Donlin.

"Knock knock, Mr. Donlin, knock knock!" he screams.

"Don't pay any attention, play ball," says Mr. Donlin.

"Who's there?" answered Larry.

"Cohen!"

"Don't pay any attention!" cries Mr. Donlin.

"Cohen who?" answers a voice.

"Who said it?" shouts Mr. Donlin authoritatively.

"Cohen fuck yourself!" cry Page and Timmy together.

One of the boys throws a stone at them.

"You cocksuckers!" says Timmy, casting his eyes about for some resource.

"Shut up, McCroskey," says Terry, "or I'll tell somethin' on you, but I don't want to make you shamed."

"Do you believe that pile o' shit that O'Hara said?" says Timmy wildly.

"Naw, I *saw* it!" says Terry.

"What did O'Hara say?" says Page.

A foul ball jumps out over the fence.

"H'yaann! H'yaann!" sing Page and Timmy and run down the block with the ball, grasping off their hats.

"Where's Harry Riesling? He's supposed to be coaching on first," says the beaten Mr. Donlin.

But Marcia and Harry are in one of the empty rooms where they have never been before (it is part of the high school), and she is telling him all about Picass'. He explains to her that he likes Terry and Larry swell, but he hates his big brother; but he promises just not to notice him any more. "He probably hates your papa as much as you hate *him*," Marcia observes judiciously, "so that's something you know on *him*." This insight, this knowledge, casts such an angel light on Harry's usually puzzled countenance that Marcia turns and stares at him. He explains to her that he likes geography and history, but Miss Jensen doesn't make it interesting the way Mr. Bee used to, and that's why he's not smart. When Marcia tells

him that she was in Egypt and the Near-East (as opposed
to the Far-East), he is struck with admiration. But different now is his admiration and his pleasure and pride in
her ability to form complete sentences, as if she were a
teacher whom he can kiss and lick and not even have
to stand up and recite, from the animosity he felt yesterday when she was so goddamned smart. She draws
on the blackboard the dolphins playing on the *Ile de
France*'s prow.

"There are geniuses in every race," says Ronnie passionately, with all the energy of his desire for Rosina;
"but both per capita and absolutely there are more of
them among the Jews."

"I thought you said there was no Jewish race?"

"There's not, but facts are facts, and you can't get
around it. Einstein, Ehrlich, Freud."

"Yes, the Jews are always going in for syphilis or psychoanalysis or the fourth dimension," says Martha.

"Picasso—"

"Ha, the same thing!"

"Proust—"

"There you have it!" says Martha triumphantly. "I'm
not saying the Jews are not geniuses, but they're *queer*,
they're just queer, that's all."

"What about Dali? He's not a Jew."

"Will you please tell me what you're trying to prove
by that? I thought you were trying to prove that all the
Jews, including yourself, were geniuses."

"No, but you said that Proust and Picasso were Jews."

"*I* said it? *I* said it?"

"I didn't say you said it especially; they *are* Jews, *half-*
Jews."

"Oh, don't be a fool."

Ronnie says nothing.

"And let me tell you another thing," says Martha, "you
Jews are not doing yourselves any favor by putting yourselves forward so much. If Felix Frankfurter is so smart
as he's supposed to be, he knows that especially just now
there's no place for another Jew on the Supreme Court

bench. Every Jew that gets on the Supreme Court makes it just so much harder for us and Marcia. Where do you think I'm going to be able to send her to college?"

"That's a fine way of looking at it!" cries Ronnie. "It's true enough," he thinks; but Martha has always been ahead of him on national and international affairs.

"You're a Jew, so all right!" says Mrs. Ronnie Morris née de Havilland. "It's nothing to be ashamed of. But why bring it up in public? Who asks you?"

"Who?" says Ronnie, bewildered.

"But trust a Jew to put himself forward as if he were something peculiar! If it weren't for the Jews there wouldn't be any anti-Semitism."

"Who?" asks Ronnie.

Lions, Harts, Leaping Does

J. F. Powers

" 'Thirty-ninth pope. Anastasius, a Roman, appointed that while the Gospel was reading they should stand and not sit. He exempted from the ministry those that were lame, impotent, or diseased persons, and slept with his forefathers in peace, being a confessor.' "

"Anno?"

" 'Anno 404.' "

They sat there in the late afternoon, the two old men grown gray in the brown robes of the Order. Angular winter daylight forsook the small room, almost a cell in the primitive sense, and passed through the window into the outside world. The distant horizon, which it sought to join, was still bright and strong against approaching night. The old Franciscans, one priest, one brother, were left among the shadows in the room.

"Can you see to read one more, Titus?" the priest Didymus asked. "Number fourteen." He did not cease staring out the window at day becoming night on the horizon. The thirty-ninth pope said Titus might not be a priest. Did Titus, reading, understand? He could never really tell about Titus, who said nothing now. There was only silence, then a dry whispering of pages turning. "Number fourteen," Didymus said. "That's Zephyrinus. I always like the old heretic on that one, Titus."

According to one bibliographer, Bishop Bale's *Pageant of Popes Contayninge the Lyves of all the Bishops of Rome, from the Beginninge of them to the Year of Grace 1555* was a denunciation of every pope from Peter to Paul IV. However inviting to readers that might sound, it was in sober fact a lie. The first popes, persecuted and mostly martyred, wholly escaped the author's remarkable spleen and even enjoyed his crusty approbation. Father Didymus, his aged appetite for biography jaded by the orthodox lives, found the work fascinating. He usually referred to it as "Bishop Bale's funny book" and to the Bishop as a heretic.

Titus squinted at the yellowed page. He snapped a glance at the light hovering at the window. Then he closed his eyes and with great feeling recited:

"'O how joyous and how delectable is it to see religious men devout and fervent in the love of God, well-mannered—'"

"Titus," Didymus interrupted softly.

"'—and well taught in ghostly learning.'"

"Titus, read." Didymus placed the words in their context. The First Book of *The Imitation* and Chapter, if he was not mistaken, XXV. The trick was no longer in finding the source of Titus's quotations; it was putting them in their exact context. It had become an unconfessed contest between them, and it gratified Didymus to think he had been able to place the fragment. Titus knew two books by heart, *The Imitation* and *The Little Flowers of St. Francis*. Lately, unfortunately, he had begun to learn another. He was more and more quoting from Bishop Bale. Didymus reminded himself he must not let Titus read past the point where the martyred popes left off. What Bale had to say about Peter's later successors sounded incongruous—"unmete" in the old heretic's own phrase—coming from a Franciscan brother. Two fathers had already inquired of Didymus concerning Titus. One had noted the antique style of his words and had ventured to wonder if Brother Titus, Christ preserve us, might be slightly possessed. He cited the case of the illiterate Missouri farmer who cursed the Church in a forgotten Aramaic tongue.

"Read, Titus."

Titus squinted at the page once more and read in his fine dead voice.

"'Fourteenth pope, Zephyrinus. Zephyrinus was a Ro-

man born, a man as writers do testify, more addicted with
all endeavor to the service of God than to the cure of
any worldly affairs. Whereas before his time the wine in
the celebrating the communion was ministered in a cup
of wood, he first did alter that, and instead thereof
brought in cups or chalices of glass. And yet he did not
this upon any superstition, as thinking wood to be un-
lawful, or glass to be more holy for that use, but because
the one is more comely and seemly, as by experience it
appeareth than the other. And yet some wooden dolts
do dream that the wooden cups were changed by him
because that part of the wine, or as they thought, the
royal blood of Christ, did soak into the wood, and so it
can not be in glass. Surely sooner may wine soak into any
wood than any wit into those winey heads that thus both
deceive themselves and slander this Godly martyr.' "

"Anno?"

Titus squinted at the page again. " 'Anno 222,' " he
read.

They were quiet for a moment which ended with the
clock in the tower booming once for the half hour. Didymus got up and stood so close to the window his breath
became visible. Noticing it, he inhaled deeply and then,
exhaling, he sent a gust of smoke churning against the
freezing pane, clouding it. Some old unmelted snow in
tree crotches lay dirty and white in the gathering dark.

"It's cold out today," Didymus said.

He stepped away from the window and over to Titus,
whose face was relaxed in open-eyed sleep. He took Bishop
Bale's funny book unnoticed from Titus's hands.

"Thank you, Titus," he said.

Titus blinked his eyes slowly once, then several times
quickly. His body gave a shudder, as if coming to life.

"Yes, Father?" he was asking.

"I said thanks for reading. You are a great friend to
me."

"Yes, Father."

"I know you'd rather read other authors." Didymus
moved to the window, stood there gazing through the
tops of trees, their limbs black and bleak against the

sky. He rubbed his hands. "I'm going for a walk before vespers. Is it too cold for you, Titus?"

" 'A good religious man that is fervent in his religion taketh all things well, and doth gladly all that he is commanded to do.' "

Didymus, walking across the room, stopped and looked at Titus just in time to see him open his eyes. He was quoting again: *The Imitation* and still in Chapter XXV. Why had he said that? To himself Didymus repeated the words and decided Titus, his mind moving intelligently but so pathetically largo, was documenting the act of reading Bishop Bale when there were other books he preferred.

"I'm going out for a walk," Didymus said.

Titus rose and pulled down the full sleeves of his brown robe in anticipation of the cold.

"I think it is too cold for you, Titus," Didymus said.

Titus faced him undaunted, arms folded and hands muffled in his sleeves, eyes twinkling incredulously. He was ready to go. Didymus got the idea Titus knew himself to be the healthier of the two. Didymus was vaguely annoyed at this manifestation of the truth. *Vanitas.*

"Won't they need you in the kitchen now?" he inquired.

Immediately he regretted having said that. And the way he had said it, with some malice, as though labor *per se* were important and the intention not so. *Vanitas* in a friar, and at his age too. Confronting Titus with a distinction his simple mind could never master and which, if it could, his great soul would never recognize. Titus only knew all that was necessary, that a friar did what he was best at in the community. And no matter the nature of his toil, the variety of the means at hand, the end was the same for all friars. Or indeed for all men, if they cared to know. Titus worked in the kitchen and garden. Was Didymus wrong in teaching geometry out of personal preference and perhaps—if this was so he was —out of pride? Had the spiritual worth of his labor been vitiated because of that? He did not think so, no. No, he taught geometry because it was useful and eternally true, like his theology, and though of a lower order of truth it escaped the common fate of theology and the humanities, perverted through the ages in the mouths of dunderheads and fools. From that point of view, his work came to the same thing as Titus's. The vineyard was everywhere; they were in it, and that was essential.

Didymus, consciously humble, held open the door for Titus. Sandals scraping familiarly, they passed through dark corridors until they came to the stairway. Lights from floors above and below spangled through the carven apertures of the winding stair and fell in confusion upon the worn oaken steps.

At the outside door they were ambushed. An old friar stepped out of the shadows to intercept them. Standing with Didymus and Titus, however, made him appear younger. Or possibly it was the tenseness of him.

"Good evening, Father," he said to Didymus. "And Titus."

Didymus nodded in salutation and Titus said deliberately, as though he were the first one ever to put words in such conjunction:

"Good evening, Father Rector."

The Rector watched Didymus expectantly. Didymus studied the man's face. It told him nothing but curiosity —a luxury which could verge on vice in the cloister. Didymus frowned his incomprehension. He was about to speak. He decided against it, turning to Titus:

"Come on, Titus, we've got a walk to take before vespers."

The Rector was left standing.

They began to circle the monastery grounds. Away from the buildings it was brighter. With a sudden shudder, Didymus felt the freezing air bite into his body all over. Instinctively he drew up his cowl. That was a little better. Not much. It was too cold for him to relax, breathe deeply, and stride freely. It had not looked this cold from his window. He fell into Titus's gait. The steps were longer, but there was an illusion of warmth about moving in unison. Bit by bit he found himself duplicating every aspect of Titus in motion. Heads down, eyes just ahead of the next step, undeviating, they seemed peripatetic figures in a Gothic frieze. The stones of the walk were trampled over with frozen footsteps. Titus's feet were gray and bare in their open sandals. Pieces of ice, the thin edges of ruts, cracked off under foot, skittering sharply away. A crystal fragment lit between Titus's toes and did not melt there. He did not seem to notice it. This made Didymus lift his eyes.

A fine Franciscan! Didymus snorted, causing a flurry of vapors. He had the despicable caution of the comfortable who move mountains, if need be, to stay that way. Here he was, cowl up and heavy woolen socks on, and regretting the weather because it exceeded his anticipations. Painfully he stubbed his toe on purpose and at once accused himself of exhibitionism. Then he damned the expression for its modernity. He asked himself wherein lay the renunciation of the world, the flesh and the devil, the whole point of following after St. Francis today. Poverty, Chastity, Obedience—the three vows. There was nothing of suffering in the poverty of the friar nowadays: he was penniless, but materially rich compared to—what was the phrase he used to hear?—"one third of the nation." A beggar, a homeless mendicant by very definition, he knew nothing—except as it affected others "less fortunate"—of the miseries of begging in the streets. Verily, it was no heavy cross, this vow of Poverty, so construed and practiced, in the modern world. Begging had become unfashionable. Somewhere along the line the meaning had been lost; they had become too "fortunate." Official agencies, to whom it was a nasty but necessary business, dispensed Charity without mercy or grace. He recalled with wry amusement Frederick Barbarossa's appeal to fellow princes when opposed by the might of the medieval Church: "We have a clean conscience, and it tells us that God is with us. Ever have we striven to bring back priests and, in especial, those of the topmost rank, to the condition of the first Christian Church. In those days the clergy raised their eyes to the angels, shone through miracles, made whole the sick, raised the dead, made Kings and Princes subject to them, not with arms but with their holiness. But now they are smothered in delights. To withdraw from them the harmful riches which burden them to their own undoing is a labor of love in which all Princes should eagerly participate."

And Chastity, what of that? Well, that was all over for him—a battle he had fought and won many years ago. A sin whose temptations had prevailed undiminished through the centuries, but withal for him, an old man, a dead issue, a young man's trial. Only Obedience remained, and that, too, was no longer difficult for him. There was something—much as he disliked the term—to be said for "conditioning." He had to smile at himself: why should he bristle so at using the word? It was only contemporary slang for a theory the Church had always known. "Psychiatry," so called, and all the ghastly superstition that attended its practice, the deification of its high priests in the secular schools, made him ill. But it would pass. Just look how alchemy had flourished, and where was it today?

Clearly an abecedarian observance of the vows did not promise perfection. Stemmed in divine wisdom, they were branches meant to flower forth, but requiring of the friar the water and sunlight of sacrifice. The letter led nowhere. It was the spirit of the vows which opened the way and revealed to the soul, no matter the flux of circumstance, the means of salvation.

He had picked his way through the welter of familiar factors again—again to the same bitter conclusion. He had come to the key and core of his trouble anew. When he received the letter from Seraphin asking him to come to St. Louis, saying his years prohibited unnecessary travel and endowed his request with a certain prerogative— No, he had written back, it's simply impossible, not saying why. God help him, as a natural man, he had the desire, perhaps the inordinate desire, to see his brother again. He should not have to prove that. One of them must die soon. But as a friar, he remembered: "Unless a man be clearly delivered from the love of all creatures, he may not fully tend to his Creator." Therein, he thought, the keeping of the vows having become an easy habit for him, was his opportunity—he thought! It was plain and there was sacrifice and it would be hard. So he had not gone.

Now it was plain that he had been all wrong. Seraphin was an old man with little left to warm him in the world. Didymus asked himself—recoiling at the answer before the question was out—if his had been the only sacrifice. Rather, had he not been too intent on denying himself at the time to notice that he was denying Seraphin also? Harshly Didymus told himself he had used his brother for a hair shirt. This must be the truth, he thought; it hurts so.

The flesh just above his knees felt frozen. They were drawing near the entrance again. His face, too, felt the same way, like a slab of pasteboard, stiffest at the tip of his nose. When he wrinkled his brow and puffed out his cheeks to blow hot air up to his nose, his skin seemed to crackle like old parchment. His eyes watered from the wind. He pressed a hand, warm from his sleeve, to his exposed neck. Frozen, like his face. It would be chapped tomorrow.

Titus, white hair awry in the wind, looked just the same.

They entered the monastery door. The Rector stopped them. It was almost as before, except that Didymus was occupied with feeling his face and patting it back to life.

"Ah, Didymus! It must be cold indeed!" The Rector smiled at Titus and returned his gaze to Didymus. He made it appear that they were allied in being amused at Didymus's face. Didymus touched his nose tenderly. Assured it would stand the operation, he blew it lustily. He stuffed the handkerchief up his sleeve. The Rector, misinterpreting all this ceremony, obviously was afraid of being ignored.

"The telegram, Didymus. I'm sorry; I thought it might have been important."

"I received no telegram."

They faced each other, waiting, experiencing a hanging moment of uneasiness.

Then, having employed the deductive method, they

both looked at Titus. Although he had not been listening, rather had been studying the naked toes in his sandals, he sensed their eyes questioning him.

"Yes, Father Rector?" he answered.

"The telegram for Father Didymus, Titus?" the Rector demanded. "Where is it?" Titus started momentarily out of willingness to be of service, but ended, his mind refusing to click, impassive before them. The Rector shook his head in faint exasperation and reached his hand down into the folds of Titus's cowl. He brought forth two envelopes. One, the telegram, he gave to Didymus. The other, a letter, he handed back to Titus.

"I gave you this letter this morning, Titus. It's for Father Anthony." Intently Titus stared unremembering at the letter. "I wish you would see that Father Anthony gets it right away, Titus. I think it's a bill."

Titus held the envelope tightly to his breast and said, "Father Anthony."

Then his eyes were attracted by the sound of Didymus tearing open the telegram. While Didymus read the telegram, Titus's expression showed he at last understood his failure to deliver it. He was perturbed, mounting inner distress moving his lips silently.

Didymus looked up from the telegram. He saw the grief in Titus's face and said, astonished, "How did you know, Titus?"

Titus's eyes were both fixed and lowered in sorrow. It seemed to Didymus that Titus knew the meaning of the telegram. Didymus was suddenly weak, as before a miracle. His eyes went to the Rector to see how he was taking it. Then it occurred to him the Rector could not not know what had happened.

As though nothing much had, the Rector laid an absolving hand lightly upon Titus's shoulder.

"Didymus, he can't forgive himself for not delivering the telegram now that he remembers it. That's all."

Didymus was relieved. Seeing the telegram in his hand, he folded it quickly and stuffed it back in the envelope. He handed it to the Rector. Calmly, in a voice quite drained of feeling, he said, "My brother, Father Seraphin, died last night in St. Louis."

"Father Seraphin *from Rome?*"

"Yes," Didymus said, "in St. Louis. He was my brother. Appointed a confessor in Rome, a privilege for a foreigner. He was ninety-two."

"I know that, Didymus, an honor for the Order. I had no idea he was in this country. Ninety-two! God rest his soul!"

"I had a letter from him only recently."

"You did?"

"He wanted me to come to St. Louis. I hadn't seen him for twenty-five years at least."

"Twenty-five years?"

"It was impossible for me to visit him."

"But if he was in this country, Didymus . . ."

The Rector waited for Didymus to explain.

Didymus opened his mouth to speak, heard the clock in the tower sound the quarter hour, and said nothing, listening, lips parted, to the last of the strokes die away.

"Why, Didymus, it could easily have been arranged," the Rector persisted.

Didymus turned abruptly to Titus, who, standing in a dream, had been inattentive since the clock struck.

"Come, Titus, we'll be late."

He hastened down the corridor with Titus. "No," he said in agitation, causing Titus to look at him in surprise. "I told him no. It was simply impossible." He was conscious of Titus's attention. "To visit him, Seraphin, who is dead." That had come naturally enough, for being the first time in his thoughts that Seraphin was dead. Was there not some merit in his dispassionate acceptance of the fact?

They entered the chapel for vespers and knelt down.

The clock struck. One, two . . . two. Two? No, there must have been one or two strokes before. He had gone to sleep. It was three. At least three, probably four. Or five. He waited. It could not be two: he remembered the brothers filing darkly into the chapel at that hour. Disturbing the shadows for matins and lauds. If it was five —he listened for faint noises in the building—it would only be a few minutes. They would come in, the earliest birds, to say their Masses. There were no noises. He looked toward the windows on the St. Joseph side of the chapel. He might be able to see a light from a room across the court. That was not certain even if it was five. It would have to come through the stained glass. Was that possible? It was still night. Was there a moon? He looked round the chapel. If there was, it might shine on a window. There was no moon. Or it was overhead. Or powerless against the glass. He yawned. It could not be five. His knees were numb from kneeling. He shifted on them. His back ached. Straightening it, he gasped for breath. He saw the sanctuary light. The only light, red. Then it came back to him. Seraphin was dead. He tried to pray. No words. Why words? Meditation in the Presence. The perfect prayer. He fell asleep . . .

. . . Spiraling brown coil on coil under the golden sun the river slithered across the blue and flower-flecked land. On an eminence they held identical hands over their eyes for visors and mistook it with pleasure for an endless murmuring serpent. They considered unafraid the prospect of its turning in its course and standing on tail to swallow them gurgling alive. They sensed it was in them to command this also by a wish. Their visor hands vanished before their eyes and became instead the symbol of brotherhood clasped between them. This they wished. Smiling the same smile back and forth they began laughing: "Jonah!" And were walking murkily up and down the brown belly of the river in mock distress. Above them, foolishly triumphant, rippling in contentment, mewed the waves. Below swam an occasional large fish, absorbed in ignoring them, and the mass of crustacea, eagerly seething, too numerous on the bottom to pretend exclusiveness. "Jonah indeed!" the brothers said, surprised to see the bubbles they birthed. They strolled then for hours this way. The novelty wearing off (without regret, else they would have wished themselves else-

where), they began to talk and say ordinary things.
Their mother had died, their father too, and how old did
that make them? It was the afternoon of the funerals,
which they had managed, transcending time, to have
held jointly. She had seemed older and for some reason
he otherwise. How, they wondered, should it be with
them, *memento mori* clicking simultaneously within
them, lackaday. The sound of dirt descending six feet
to clatter on the coffins was memorable but unmen-
tionable. Their own lives, well . . . only half curious
(something to do) they halted to kick testingly a water-
logged rowboat resting on the bottom, the crustacea complaining and olive-green silt rising to speckle the surface
with dark stars . . . well, what *had* they been doing? A
crayfish pursued them, clad in sable armor, dearly de-
siring to do battle, brandishing hinged swords. Well, for
one thing, working for the canonization of Fra Bartolomeo, had got two cardinals interested, was hot after those
remaining who were at all possible, a slow business. Yes,
one would judge so in the light of past canonizations,
though being stationed in Rome had its advantages. Me,
the same old grind, teaching, pounding away, giving
Pythagoras no rest in his grave . . . They made an ir-
resolute pass at the crayfish, who had caught up with
them. More about Fra Bartolomeo, what else is there?
Except, you will laugh or have me excommunicated for
wanton presumption, though it's only faith in a faith-
less age, making a vow not to die until he's made a saint,
recognized rather—he is one, convinced of it, Didymus
(never can get used to calling you that), a saint sure as
I'm alive, having known him, no doubt of it, something
wrong with your knee? Knees then! The crayfish, he's
got hold of you there, another at your back. If you like,
we'll leave—only I do like it here. Well, go ahead
then, you never did like St. Louis, isn't that what you
used to say? Alone, in pain, he rose to the surface, part-
ing the silt stars. The sun like molten gold squirted him
in the eye. Numb now, unable to remember, and too
blind to refurnish his memory by observation, he waited
for this limbo to clear away. . . .

Awake now, he was face to face with a flame, blinding
him. He avoided it. A dead weight bore him down, his
aching back. Slowly, like ink in a blotter, his consciousness spread. The supports beneath him were kneeling
limbs, his, the veined hands, bracing him, pressing flat,
his own. His body, it seemed, left off there; the rest was
something else, floor. He raised his head to the flame
again and tried to determine what kept it suspended even
with his face. He shook his head, blinking dumbly, a
four-legged beast. He could see nothing, only his knees
and hands, which he felt rather, and the flame floating
unaccountably in the darkness. That part alone was a
mystery. And then there came a pressure and pull on his
shoulders, urging him up. Fingers, a hand, a rustling related to its action, then the rustling in rhythm with the
folds of a brown curtain, a robe naturally, ergo a friar,
holding a candle, trying to raise him up, Titus. The
clock began striking.

"Put out the candle," Didymus said.

Titus closed his palm slowly around the flame, un-
flinching, snuffing it. The odor of burning string. Titus
pinched the wick deliberately. He waited a moment, the
clock falling silent, and said, "Father Rector expects you
will say a Mass for the Dead at five o'clock."

"Yes, I know." He yawned deliciously. "I told him
that." He bit his lips at the memory of the disgusting yawn. Titus had found him asleep. Shame overwhelmed him, and he searched his mind for justification.
He found none.

"It is five now," Titus said.

It was maddening. "I don't see anyone else if it's
five," he snapped. Immediately he was aware of a light
burning in the sacristy. He blushed and grew pale. Had
someone besides Titus seen him sleeping? But, listening, he heard nothing. No one else was up yet. He was no
longer pale and was only blushing now. He saw it all
hopefully. He was saved. Titus had gone to the sacristy to
prepare for Mass. He must have come out to light the
candles on the main altar. Then he had seen the bereaved
keeping vigil on all fours, asleep, snoring even. What

did Titus think of that? It withered him to remember, but he was comforted some that the only witness had been Titus. Had the sleeping apostles in Gethsemane been glad it was Christ?

Wrong! Hopelessly wrong! For there had come a noise after all. Someone else was in the sacristy. He stiffened and walked palely toward it. He must go there and get ready to say his Mass. A few steps he took only, his back buckling out, humping, his knees sinking to the floor, his hands last. The floor, with fingers smelling of dust and genesis, reached up and held him. The fingers were really spikes and they were dusty from holding him this way all his life. For a radiant instant, which had something of eternity about it, he saw the justice of his position. Then there was nothing.

A little snow had fallen in the night, enough to powder the dead grass and soften the impression the leafless trees etched in the sky. Grayly the sky promised more snow, but now, at the end of the day following his collapse in the chapel, it was melting. Didymus, bundled around by blankets, sat in a wheel chair at the window, unsleepy. Only the landscape wearied him. Dead and unmoving though it must be—of that he was sure—it conspired to make him see everything in it as living, moving, something to be watched, each visible tuft of grass, each cluster of snow. The influence of the snow perhaps? For the ground, ordinarily uniform in texture and drabness, had split up into individual patches. They appeared to be involved in a struggle of some kind, possibly to overlap each other, constantly shifting. But whether it was equally one against one, or one against all, he could not make out. He reminded himself he did not believe it was actually happening. It was confusing and he closed his eyes. After a time this confused and tired him in the same way. The background of darkness became a field of varicolored factions, warring, and, worse than the landscape, things like worms and comets wriggled and exploded before his closed eyes. Finally, as though to orchestrate their motions, they carried with them a bewildering noise or music which grew louder and cacophonous. The effect was cumulative, inevitably unbearable, and Didymus would have to open his eyes again. The intervals of peace became gradually rarer on the landscape. Likewise when he shut his eyes to it the restful darkness dissolved sooner than before into riot.

The door of his room opened, mercifully dispelling his illusions, and that, because there had been no knock, could only be Titus. Unable to move in his chair, Didymus listened to Titus moving about the room at his back. The tinkle of a glass once, the squeak of the bookcase indicating a book taken out or replaced—they were sounds Didymus could recognize. But that first tap-tap and the consequent click of metal on metal, irregular and scarcely audible, was disconcertingly unfamiliar. His curiosity, centering on it, raised it to a delicious mystery. He kept down the urge to shout at Titus. But he attempted to fish from memory the precise character of the corner from which the sound came with harrowing repetition. The sound stopped then, as though to thwart him on the brink of revelation. Titus's footsteps scraped across the room. The door opened and closed. For a few steps, Didymus heard Titus going down the corridor. He asked himself not to be moved by idle curiosity, a thing of the senses. He would not be tempted now.

A moment later the keystone of his good intention crumbled, and the whole edifice of his detachment with it. More shakily than quickly, Didymus moved his hands to the wheels of the chair. He would roll over to the corner and investigate the sound. . . . He would? His hands lay limply on the wheels, ready to propel him to his mind's destination, but, weak, white, powerless to grip the wheels or anything. He regarded them with contempt. He had known they would fail him; he had been foolish to give them another chance. Disdainful of his hands, he looked out the window. He could still do that, couldn't he? It was raining some now. The landscape started to move, rearing and reeling crazily, as though drunken with the rain. In horror, Didymus damned his eyes. He realized this trouble was probably going to be chronic. He turned his gaze in despair to the trees, to the branches level with his eyes and nearer than the insane ground. Hesitating warily, fearful the gentle boughs under scrutiny would turn into hideous waving tentacles, he looked. With a thrill, he knew he was seeing clearly.

Gauzily rain descended in a fine spray, hanging in fat berries from the wet black branches where leaves had been and buds would be, cold crystal drops. They fell now and then ripely of their own weight, or shaken by the intermittent wind they spilled before their time. Promptly they appeared again, pendulous.

Watching the raindrops prove gravity, he was grateful for nature's, rather than his, return to reason. Still, though he professed faith in his faculties, he would not look away from the trees and down at the ground, nor close his eyes. Gratefully he savored the cosmic truth in the falling drops and the mildly trembling branches. There was order, he thought, which in justice and science ought to include the treacherous landscape. Risking all, he ventured a glance at the ground. All was still there. He smiled. He was going to close his eyes (to make it universal and conclusive), when the door opened again.

Didymus strained to catch the meaning of Titus's movements. Would the clicking sound begin? Titus did go to that corner of the room again. Then it came, louder than before, but only once this time.

Titus came behind his chair, turned it, and wheeled him over to the corner.

On a hook which Titus had screwed into the wall hung a bird cage covered with black cloth.

"What's all this?" Didymus asked.

Titus tapped the covered cage expectantly.

A bird chirped once.

"The bird," Titus explained in excitement, "is inside."

Didymus almost laughed. He sensed in time, however, the necessity of seeming befuddled and severe. Titus expected it.

"I don't believe it," Didymus snapped.

Titus smiled wisely and tapped the cage again.

"There!" he exclaimed when the bird chirped.

Didymus shook his head in mock anger. "You made that beastly noise, Titus, you mountebank!"

Titus, profoundly amused by such skepticism, removed the black cover.

The bird, a canary, flicked its head sidewise in interest, looking them up and down. Then it turned its darting attention to the room. It chirped once in curt acceptance of the new surroundings. Didymus and Titus came under its black dot of an eye once more, this time for closer analysis. The canary chirped twice, perhaps that they were welcome, even pleasing, and stood on one leg to show them what a gay bird it was. It then returned to the business of pecking a piece of apple.

"I see you've given him something to eat," Didymus said, and felt that Titus, though he seemed content to watch the canary, waited for him to say something more. "I am very happy, Titus, to have this canary," he went on. "I suppose he will come in handy now that I must spend my days in this infernal chair."

Titus did not look at him while he said, "He is a good bird, Father. He is one of the Saint's own good birds."

Through the window Didymus watched the days and nights come and go. For the first time, though his life as a friar had been copiously annotated with significant references, he got a good idea of eternity. Monotony, of course, was one word for it, but like all the others, as well as the allegories worked up by imaginative retreat masters, it was empty beside the experience itself, untranslatable. He would doze and wonder if by some quirk he had been cast out of the world into eternity, but since it was neither heaven nor exactly purgatory or hell, as he understood them, he concluded it must be an uncharted isle subscribing to the mother forms only in the matter of time. And having thought this, he was faintly annoyed at his ponderous whimsy. Titus, like certain of the hours, came periodically. He would read or simply sit with him in silence. The canary was there always, but except as it showed signs of sleepiness at twilight and spirit at dawn, Didymus regarded it as a subtle device, like the days and nights and bells, to give the lie to the vulgar error that time flies. The cage was small and the canary would not sing. Time, hanging in the room like a jealous fog, possessed him and voided everything except it. It seemed impossible each time Titus came that he should be able to escape the room.

" 'After him,' " Titus read from Bishop Bale one day, " 'came Fabius, a Roman born, who (as Eusebius witnesseth) as he was returning home out of the field, and with his countrymen present to elect a new bishop, there was a pigeon seen standing on his head and suddenly he was created pastor of the Church, which he looked not for.' "

They smiled at having the same thought and both looked up at the canary. Since Didymus sat by the window most of the day now, he had asked Titus to put a hook there for the cage. He had to admit to himself he did this to let Titus know he appreciated the canary. Also, as a secondary motive, he reasoned, it enabled the canary to look out the window. What a little yellow bird could see to interest it in the frozen scene was a mystery, but that, Didymus sighed, was a two-edged sword. And he took to watching the canary more.

So far as he was able to detect the moods of the canary he participated in them. In the morning the canary, bright and clownish, flitted back and forth between the two perches in the cage, hanging from the sides and cocking its little tufted head at Didymus querulously. During these acrobatics Didymus would twitch his hands in quick imitation of the canary's stunts. He asked Titus to construct a tiny swing, such as he had seen, which the canary might learn to use, since it appeared to be an intelligent and daring sort. Titus got the swing, the canary did master it, but there seemed to be nothing Didymus could do with his hands that was like swinging. In fact, after he had been watching awhile, it was as though the canary were fixed to a pendulum, inanimate, a piece of machinery, a yellow blur—ticking, for the swing made a little sound, and Didymus went to sleep, and often

when he woke the canary was still going, like a clock.
Didymus had no idea how long he slept at these times,
maybe a minute, maybe hours. Gradually the canary
got bored with the swing and used it less and less. In the
same way, Didymus suspected, he himself had wearied of
looking out the window. The first meager satisfaction
had worn off. The dead trees, the sleeping snow, like the
swing for the canary, were sources of diversion which
soon grew stale. They were captives, he and the canary,
and the only thing they craved was escape. Didymus
slowly considered the problem. There was nothing, obviously, for him to do. He could pray, which he did, but
he was not sure the only thing wrong with him was the
fact he could not walk and that to devote his prayer to
that end was justifiable. Inevitably it occurred to him his
plight might well be an act of God. Why this punishment, though, he asked himself, and immediately supplied the answer. He had, for one thing, gloried too much
in having it in him to turn down Seraphin's request to
come to St. Louis. The intention—that was all important, and he, he feared, had done the right thing for the
wrong reason. He had noticed something of the faker in
himself before. But it was not clear if he had erred.
There was a certain consolation, at bottom dismal, in this
doubt. It was true there appeared to be a nice justice in
being stricken a cripple if he had been wrong in refusing
to travel to see Seraphin, if human love was all he was
fitted for, if he was incapable of renunciation for the
right reason, if the mystic counsels were too strong for
him, if he was still too pedestrian after all these years of
prayer and contemplation, if . . .

The canary was swinging, the first time in several days.
The reality of his position was insupportable. There
were two ways of regarding it and he could not make up
his mind. Humbly he wished to get well and to be able
to walk. But if this was a punishment, was not prayer to
lift it declining to see the divine point? He did wish to
get well; that would settle it. Otherwise his predicament
could only be resolved through means more serious than

he dared cope with. It would be like refusing to see Seraphin all over again. By some mistake, he protested, he had at last been placed in a position vital with meaning and precedents inescapably Christian. But was he the man for it? Unsure of himself, he was afraid to go on trial. It would be no minor trial, so construed, but one in which the greatest values were involved—a human soul and the means of its salvation or damnation. Not watered-down suburban precautions and routine pious exercises, but Faith such as saints and martyrs had, and Despair such as only they had been tempted by. No, he was not the man for it. He was unworthy. He simply desired to walk and in a few years to die a normal, uninspired death. He did not wish to see (what was apparent) the greatest significance in his affliction. He preferred to think in terms of physical betterment. He was so sure he was not a saint that he did not consider this easier road beneath him, though attracted by the higher one. That was the rub. Humbly, then, he wanted to be able to walk, but he wondered if there was not presumption in such humility.

Thus he decided to pray for health and count the divine hand not there. Decided. A clean decision—not distinction—no mean feat in the light of all the moral theology he had swallowed. The canary, all its rocking come to naught once more, slept motionless in the swing. Despite the manifest prudence of the course he had settled upon, Didymus dozed off ill at ease in his wheel chair by the window. Distastefully, the last thing he remembered was that "prudence" is a virtue more celebrated in the modern Church.

At his request in the days following a doctor visited him. The Rector came along, too. When Didymus tried to find out the nature of his illness, the doctor looked solemn and pronounced it to be one of those things. Didymus received this with a look of mystification. So the doctor went on to say there was no telling about it. Time alone would tell. Didymus asked the doctor to recommend some books dealing with cases like

his. They might have one of them in the monastery library. Titus could read to him in the meantime. For,
though he disliked being troublesome, "one of those
things" as a diagnosis meant very little to an unscientific
beggar like him. The phrase had a philosophic ring to it,
but to his knowledge neither the Early Fathers nor the
Scholastics seemed to have dealt with it. The Rector
smiled. The doctor, annoyed, replied drily:

"Is that a fact?"

Impatiently Didymus said, "I know how old I am, if
that's it."

Nothing was lost of the communion he kept with the
canary. He still watched its antics and his fingers in his
lap followed them clumsily. He did not forget about himself, that he must pray for health, that it was best that
way—"prudence" dictated it—but he did think more of
the canary's share of their captivity. A canary in a cage,
he reasoned, is like a bud which never blooms.

He asked Titus to get a book on canaries, but nothing
came of it and he did not mention it again.

Some days later Titus read:

" 'Twenty-ninth pope, Marcellus, a Roman, was pastor
of the Church, feeding it with wisdom and doctrine.
And (as I may say with the Prophet) a man according to
God's heart and full of Christian works. This man ad-
monished Maximianus the Emperor and endeavored to
remove him from persecuting the saints——' "

"Stop a moment, Titus," Didymus interrupted.

Steadily, since Titus began to read, the canary had
been jumping from the swing to the bottom of the cage
and back again. Now it was quietly standing on one foot
in the swing. Suddenly it flew at the side of the cage
nearest them and hung there, its ugly little claws, like
bent wire, hooked to the slender bars. It observed them
intently, first Titus and then Didymus, at whom it continued to stare. Didymus's hands were tense in his lap.

"Go ahead, read," Didymus said, relaxing his hands.

" 'But the Emperor being more hardened, commanded
Marcellus to be beaten with cudgels and to be driven out

of the city, wherefore he entered into the house of one Lucina, a widow, and there kept the congregation secretly, which the tyrant hearing, made a stable for cattle of the same house and committed the keeping of it to the bishop Marcellus. After that he governed the Church by writing Epistles, without any other kind of teaching, being condemned to such a vile service. And being thus daily tormented with strife and noisomeness, at length gave up the ghost. Anno 308.' "

"Very good, Titus. I wonder how we missed that one before."

The canary, still hanging on the side of the cage, had not moved, its head turned sidewise, its eye as before fixed on Didymus.

"Would you bring me a glass of water, Titus?"

Titus got up and looked in the cage. The canary hung there, as though waiting, not a feather stirring.

"The bird has water here," Titus said, pointing to the small cup fastened to the cage.

"For me, Titus, the water's for me. Don't you think I know you look after the canary? You don't forget us, though I don't see why you don't."

Titus left the room with a glass.

Didymus's hands were tense again. Eyes on the canary's eye, he got up from his wheel chair, his face strained and white with the impossible effort, and, his fingers somehow managing it, he opened the cage. The canary darted out and circled the room chirping. Before it lit, though it seemed about to make its perch triumphantly the top of the cage, Didymus fell over on his face and lay prone on the floor.

In bed that night, unsuffering and barely alive, he saw at will everything revealed in his past. Events long forgotten happened again before his eyes. Clearly, sensitively, he saw Seraphin and himself, just as they had always been—himself, never quite sure. He heard all that he had ever said, and that anyone had said to him. He had talked too much, too. The past mingled with the

present. In the same moment and scene he made his first
Communion, was ordained, and confessed his sins for the
last time.

The canary perched in the dark atop the cage, head
warm under wing, already, it seemed to Didymus, without memory of its captivity, dreaming of a former freedom, an ancestral summer day with flowers and trees.
Outside it was snowing.

The Rector, followed by others, came into the room
and administered the last sacrament. Didymus heard
them all gathered prayerfully around his bed thinking
(they thought) secretly: this sacrament often strengthens
the dying, tip-of-the-tongue wisdom indigenous to the
priesthood, Henry the Eighth had six wives. He saw the
same hackneyed smile, designed to cheer, pass bravely
among them, and marveled at the crudity of it. They
went away then, all except Titus, their individual footsteps sounding (for him) the character of each friar. He
might have been Francis himself for what he knew then
of the little brothers and the cure of souls. He heard them
thinking their expectation to be called from bed before
daybreak to return to his room and say the office of the
dead over his body, become the body, and whispering
hopefully to the contrary. Death was now an unwel-
come guest in the cloister.

He wanted nothing in the world for himself at last.
This may have been the first time he found his will
amenable to the Divine. He had never been less himself
and more the saint. Yet now, so close to sublimity, or perhaps only tempted to believe so (the Devil is most wily
at the death-bed), he was beset by the grossest distrac-
tions. They were to be expected, he knew, as indelible
in the order of things: the bingo game going on under
the Cross for the seamless garment of the Son of Man:
everywhere the sign of the contradiction, and always.
When would he cease to be surprised by it? Incidents repeated themselves, twined, parted, faded away, came
back clear, and would not be prayed out of mind. He
watched himself mounting the pulpit of a metropolitan
church, heralded by the pastor as the renowned Francis-

can father sent by God in His goodness to preach this
novena—like to say a little prayer to test the microphone,
Father?—and later reading through the petitions to Our
Blessed Mother, cynically tabulating the pleas for a Catholic boy friend, drunkenness banished, the sale of real
estate and coming furiously upon one: "that I'm not pregnant." And at the same church on Good Friday carrying
the crucifix along the communion rail for the people to
kiss, giving them the indulgence, and afterwards in the
sacristy wiping the lipstick of the faithful from the image
of Christ crucified.

"Take down a book, any book, Titus, and read. Begin
anywhere."

Roused by his voice, the canary fluttered, looked
sharply about and buried its head once more in the
warmth of its wing.

" 'By the lions,' " Titus read, " 'are understood the ac-
rimonies and impetuosities of the irascible faculty,
which faculty is as bold and daring in its acts as are the
lions. By the harts and the leaping does is understood the
other faculty of the soul, which is the concupiscible—
that is——' "

"Skip the exegesis," Didymus broke in weakly. "I can
do without that now. Read the verse."

Titus read: " 'Birds of swift wing, lions, harts, leaping
does, mountains, valleys, banks, waters, breezes, heats
and terrors that keep watch by night, by the pleasant
lyres and by the siren's song, I conjure you, cease your
wrath and touch not the wall . . .' "

"Turn off the light, Titus."

Titus went over to the switch. There was a brief period
of darkness during which Didymus's eyes became accustomed to a different shade, a glow rather, which possessed
the room slowly. Then he saw the full moon had let down
a ladder of light through the window. He could see the
snow, strangely blue, falling outside. So sensitive was his
mind and eye (because his body, now faint, no longer
blurred his vision?) he could count the snowflakes, all of
them separately, before they drifted, winding, below
the sill.

With the same wonderful clarity, he saw what he had made of his life. He saw himself tied down, caged, stunted in his apostolate, seeking the crumbs, the little pleasure, neglecting the source, always knowing death changes nothing, only immortalizes . . . and still ever lukewarm. In trivial attachments, in love of things, was death, no matter the appearance of life. In the highest attachment only, no matter the appearance of death, was life. He had always known this truth, but now he was feeling it. Unable to move his hand, only his lips, and hardly breathing, was it too late to act?

"Open the window, Titus," he whispered.

And suddenly he could pray. *Hail Mary . . . Holy Mary, Mother of God, pray for us sinners now and at the hour of our death . . .* finally the time to say, *pray for me now—the hour of my death, amen.* Lest he deceive himself at the very end that this was the answer to a life-time of praying for a happy death, happy because pain-less, he tried to turn his thoughts from himself, to join them to God, thinking how at last he did—didn't he *now?*—prefer God above all else. But ashamedly not sure he did, perhaps only fearing hell, with an uneasy sense of justice he put himself foremost among the wise in their own generation, the perennials seeking after God when doctor, lawyer, and bank fails. If he wronged himself, he did so out of humility—a holy error. He ended, to make certain he had not fallen under the same old presump-tion disguised as the face of humility, by flooding his mind with maledictions. He suffered the piercing white voice of the Apocalypse to echo in his soul: *But because thou art lukewarm, and neither cold, nor hot, I will begin to vomit thee out of my mouth.* And St. Bernard, fiery-eyed in a white habit, thundered at him from the twelfth century: "Hell is paved with the bald pates of priests!"

There was a soft flutter, the canary flew to the window sill, paused, and tilted into the snow. Titus stepped too late to the window and stood gazing dumbly after it. He raised a trembling old hand, fingers bent in awe and sor-row, to his forehead, and turned stealthily to Didymus.

Didymus closed his eyes. He let a long moment pass

before he opened them. Titus, seeing him awake then, fussed with the window latch and held a hand down to feel the draught, nodding anxiously as though it were the only evil abroad in the world, all the time straining his old eyes for a glimpse of the canary somewhere in the trees.

Didymus said nothing, letting Titus keep his secret. With his whole will he tried to lose himself in the sight of God, and failed. He was not in the least transported. Even now he could find no divine sign within himself. He knew he still had to look outside, to Titus. God still chose to manifest Himself most in sanctity.

Titus, nervous under his stare, and to account for staying at the window so long, felt for the draught again, frowned, and kept his eye hunting among the trees.

The thought of being the cause of such elaborate dissimulation in so simple a soul made Didymus want to smile—or cry, he did not know which . . . and could do neither. Titus persisted. How long would it be, Didymus wondered faintly, before Titus ungrievingly gave the canary up for lost in the snowy arms of God? The snowflakes whirled at the window, for a moment for all their bright blue beauty as though struck still by lightning, and Didymus closed his eyes, only to find them there also, but darkly falling.

Miriam

Truman Capote

For several years, Mrs. H. T. Miller had lived alone in a pleasant apartment (two rooms with kitchenette) in a remodeled brownstone near the East River. She was a widow: Mr. H. T. Miller had left a reasonable amount of insurance. Her interests were narrow, she had no friends to speak of, and she rarely journeyed farther than the corner grocery. The other people in the house never seemed to notice her: her clothes were matter of fact, her hair iron-gray, clipped and casually waved; she did not use cosmetics, her features were plain and inconspicuous, and on her last birthday she was sixty-one. Her activities were seldom spontaneous: she kept the two rooms immaculate, smoked an occasional cigarette, prepared her own means and tended a canary.

Then she met Miriam. It was snowing that night. Mrs. Miller had finished drying the supper dishes and was thumbing through an afternoon paper when she saw an advertisement of a picture playing at a neighborhood theatre. The title sounded good, so she struggled into her beaver coat, laced her galoshes and left the apartment, leaving one light burning in the foyer: she found nothing more distrubing than a sensation of darkness.

The snow was fine, falling gently, not yet making an impression on the pavement. The wind from the river cut only at street crossings. Mrs. Miller hurried, her head bowed, oblivious as a mole burrowing a blind path. She stopped at a drugstore and bought a package of peppermints.

A long line stretched in front of the box office; she

took her place at the end. There would be (a tired voice groaned) a short wait for all seats. Mrs. Miller rummaged in her leather handbag till she collected exactly the correct change for admission. The line seemed to be taking its own time and, looking around for some distraction, she suddenly became conscious of a little girl standing under the edge of the marquee.

Her hair was the longest and strangest Mrs. Miller had ever seen: absolutely silver-white, like an albino's. It flowed waist-length in smooth, loose lines. She was thin and fragilely constructed. There was a simple, special elegance in the way she stood with her thumbs in the pockets of a tailored plum velvet coat.

Mrs. Miller felt oddly excited, and when the little girl glanced toward her she smiled warmly. The little girl walked over and said, "Would you care to do me a favor?"

"I'd be glad to if I can," said Mrs. Miller.

"Oh, it's quite easy. I merely want you to buy a ticket for me; they won't let me in otherwise. Here, I have the money." And gracefully she handed Mrs. Miller two dimes and a nickel.

They went into the theatre together. An usherette directed them to a lounge; in twenty minutes the picture would be over.

"I feel just like a genuine criminal," said Mrs. Miller gaily, as she sat down. "I mean that sort of thing's against the law, isn't it? I do hope I haven't done the wrong thing. Your mother knows where you are, dear? I mean she does, doesn't she?"

The little girl said nothing. She unbuttoned her coat and folded it across her lap. Her dress underneath was prim and dark blue. A gold chain dangled about her neck and her fingers, sensitive and musical-looking, toyed with it. Examining her more attentively, Mrs. Miller decided the truly distinctive feature was not her hair, but her eyes; they were hazel, steady, lacking any childlike quality whatsoever and, because of their size, seemed to consume her small face.

Mrs. Miller offered a peppermint. "What's your name, dear?"

"Miriam," she said, as though, in some curious way, it were information already familiar.

"Why, isn't that funny . . . my name's Miriam, too. And it's not a terribly common name either. Now, don't tell me your last name's Miller!"

"Just Miriam."

"But isn't that funny?"

"Moderately," said Miriam and rolled the peppermint on her tongue.

Mrs. Miller flushed and shifted uncomfortably. "You have such a large vocabulary for such a little girl."

"Do I?"

"Well, yes," said Mrs. Miller, hastily changing the topic to: "Do you like the movies?"

"I really wouldn't know," said Miriam. "I've never been before."

Women began filling the lounge; the rumble of the newsreel bombs exploded in the distance, Mrs. Miller rose, tucking her purse under her arm. "I guess I'd better be running now if I want to get a seat," she said. "It was nice to have met you."

Miriam nodded ever so slightly.

It snowed all week. Wheels and footsteps moved soundlessly on the street, as if the business of living continued secretly behind a pale but impenetrable curtain. In the falling quiet there was no sky or earth, only snow lifting in the wind, frosting the window glass, chilling the rooms, deadening and hushing the city. At all hours it was necessary to keep a lamp lighted, and Mrs. Miller lost track of the days: Friday was no different from Saturday and on Sunday she went to the grocery: closed, of course.

That evening she scrambled eggs and fixed a bowl of tomato soup. Then, after putting on a flannel robe and cold-creaming her face, she propped herself up in bed with a hot-water bottle under her feet. She was reading the *Times* when the doorbell rang. At first she thought it must be a mistake and whoever it was would go away.

But it rang and rang and settled to a persistent buzz. She looked at the clock: a little after eleven; it did not seem possible; she was always asleep by ten.

Climbing out of bed, she trotted barefoot across the living room. "I'm coming, please be patient." The latch was caught; she turned it this way and that way and the bell never paused an instant. "Stop it," she cried. The bolt gave way and she opened the door an inch. "What in heaven's name?"

"Hello," said Miriam.

"Oh. . . . why, hello," said Mrs. Miller, stepping hesitantly into the hall. "You're that little girl."

"I thought you'd never answer, but I kept my finger on the button; I knew you were home. Aren't you glad to see me?"

Mrs. Miller did not know what to say. Miriam, she saw, wore the same plum velvet coat and now she had also a beret to match; her white hair was braided in two shining plaits and looped at the ends with enormous white ribbons.

"Since I've waited so long, you could at least let me in," she said.

"It's awfully late. . . ."

Miriam regarded her blankly. "What difference does that make? Let me in. It's cold out here and I have on a silk dress." Then, with a gentle gesture, she urged Mrs. Miller aside and passed into the apartment.

She dropped her coat and beret on a chair. She was indeed wearing a silk dress. White silk. White silk in February. The skirt was beautifully pleated and the sleeves long; it made a faint rustle as she strolled about the room. "I like your place," she said. "I like the rug, blue's my favorite color." She touched a paper rose in a vase on the coffee table. "Imitation," she commented wanly. "How sad. Aren't imitations sad?" She seated herself on the sofa, daintily spreading her skirt.

"What do you want?" asked Mrs. Miller.

"Sit down," said Miriam. "It makes me nervous to see people stand."

Mrs. Miller sank to a hassock. "What do you want?" she repeated.

"You know, I don't think you're glad I came."

For a second time Mrs. Miller was without an answer; her hand motioned vaguely. Miriam giggled and pressed back on a mound of chintz pillows. Mrs. Miller observed that the girl was less pale than she remembered; her cheeks were flushed.

"How did you know where I lived?"

Miriam frowned. "That's no question at all. What's your name? What's mine?"

"But I'm not listed in the phone book."

"Oh, let's talk about something else."

Mrs. Miller said, "Your mother must be insane to let a child like you wander around at all hours of the night . . . and in such ridiculous clothes. She must be out of her mind."

Miriam got up and moved to a corner where a covered bird cage hung from a ceiling chain. She peeked beneath the cover. "It's a canary," she said. "Would you mind if I woke him? I'd like to hear him sing."

"Leave Tommy alone," said Mrs. Miller, anxiously. "Don't you dare wake him."

"Certainly," said Miriam. "But I don't see why I can't hear him sing." And then, "Have you anything to eat? I'm starving! Even milk and a jam sandwich would be fine."

"Look," said Mrs. Miller, arising from the hassock, "look . . . if I make some nice sandwiches will you be a good child and run along home? . . . It's past midnight, I'm sure."

"It's snowing," reproached Miriam. "And cold and dark."

"Well, you shouldn't have come here to begin with," said Mrs. Miller, struggling to control her voice. "I can't help the weather. If you want anything to eat you'll have to promise to leave."

Miriam brushed a braid against her cheek. Her eyes were thoughtful, as if weighing the proposition. She turned toward the bird cage. "Very well," she said, "I promise."

How old is she? Ten? Eleven? Mrs. Miller, in the kitchen, unsealed a jar of strawberry preserves and cut four slices of bread. She poured a glass of milk and paused to light a cigarette. *And why has she come?* Her hand shook as she held the match, fascinated, till it burned her finger: the canary was singing; singing as he did in the morning and at no other time. "Miriam," she called, "Miriam, I told you not to disturb Tommy." There was no answer. She called again; all she heard was the canary. She inhaled the cigarette and discovered she had lighted the cork-tip end and . . . oh, really, she mustn't lose her temper.

She carried the food in on a tray and set it on the coffee table. She saw first that the bird cage still wore its night cover. And Tommy was singing. It gave her a queer sensation. And no one was in the room. Mrs. Miller went through an alcove leading to her bedroom; at the door she caught her breath.

"What are you doing?" she asked.

Miriam glanced up and in her eyes there was a look that was not ordinary. She was standing by the bureau, a jewel case opened before her. For a minute she studied Mrs. Miller, forcing their eyes to meet, and she smiled. "There's nothing good here," she said. "But I like this." Her hand held a cameo brooch. "It's charming."

"Suppose . . . perhaps you'd better put it back," said Mrs. Miller, feeling suddenly the need of some support. She leaned against the doorframe; her head was unbearably heavy; a pressure weighted the rhythm of her heartbeat. The light seemed to flutter defectively. "Please, child . . . a gift from my husband . . ."

"But it's beautiful and I want it," said Miriam. "*Give it to me.*"

As she stood, striving to shape a sentence which would somehow save the brooch, it came to Mrs. Miller there was no one to whom she might turn; she was alone: a fact that had not been among her thoughts for a long time. Its sheer emphasis was stunning. But here in her own room in the hushed snow-city were evidences she could not ignore or, she knew with startling clarity, resist.

Miriam ate ravenously, and when the sandwiches and milk were gone, her fingers made cobweb movements over the plate, gathering crumbs. The cameo gleamed on her blouse, the blond profile like a trick reflection of its wearer. "That was very nice," she sighed, "though now an almond cake or a cherry would be ideal. Sweets are lovely, don't you think?"

Mrs. Miller was perched precariously on the hassock, smoking a cigarette. Her hair net had slipped lopsided and loose strands straggled down her face. Her eyes were stupidly concentrated on nothing and her cheeks were mottled in red patches, as though a fierce slap had left permanent marks.

"Is there a candy . . . a cake?"

Mrs. Miller tapped ash on the rug. Her head swayed slightly as she tried to focus her eyes. "You promised to leave if I made the sandwiches," she said.

"Dear me, did I?"

"It was a promise and I'm tired and I don't feel well at all."

"Mustn't fret," said Miriam. "I'm only teasing."

She picked up her coat, slung it over her arm, and arranged her beret in front of a mirror. Presently she bent close to Mrs. Miller and whispered, "Kiss me good-night."

"Please . . . I'd rather not," said Mrs. Miller.

Miriam lifted a shoulder, arched an eyebrow. "As you like," she said, and went directly to the coffee table, seized the vase containing the paper roses, carried it to where the hard surface of the floor lay bare, and hurled it downward. Glass sprayed in all directions and she stamped her foot on the bouquet.

Then slowly she walked to the door, but before clos-

ing it she looked back at Mrs. Miller with a slyly innocent curiosity.

Mrs. Miller spent the next day in bed, rising once to
feed the canary and drink a cup of tea; she took her temperature and had none, yet her dreams were feverishly
agitated; their unbalanced mood lingered even as she lay
staring wide-eyed at the ceiling. One dream threaded
through the others like an elusively mysterious theme in
a complicated symphony, and the scenes it depicted were
sharply outlined, as though sketched by a hand of gifted
intensity: a small girl, wearing a bridal gown and a
wreath of leaves, led a gray procession down a mountain
path, and among them there was unusual silence till a
woman at the rear asked, "Where is she taking us?" "No
one knows," said an old man marching in front. "But isn't
she pretty?" volunteered a third voice. "Isn't she like a
frost flower . . . so shining and white?"

Tuesday morning she woke up feeling better; harsh
slats of sunlight, slanting through Venetian blinds, shed
a disrupting light on her unwholesome fancies. She
opened the window to discover a thawed, mild-as-spring
day; a sweep of clean new clouds crumpled against a
vastly blue, out-of-season sky; and across the low line of
rooftops she could see the river and smoke curving from
tugboat stacks in a warm wind. A great silver truck
plowed the snow-banked street, its machine sound humming on the air.

After straightening the apartment, she went to the
grocer's, cashed a check and continued to Schrafft's,
where she ate breakfast and chatted happily with the
waitress. Oh, it was a wonderful day . . . more like a
holiday . . . and it would be foolish to go home.

She boarded a Lexington Avenue bus and rode up to
Eighty-sixth Street; it was here that she had decided to
do a little shopping.

She had no idea what she wanted or needed, but she
idled along, intent only upon the passers-by, brisk and
preoccupied, who gave her a disturbing sense of sepa-
rateness.

It was while waiting at the corner of Third Avenue that she saw the man: an old man, bowlegged and stooped under an armload of bulging packages; he wore a shabby brown coat and a checkered cap. Suddenly she realized they were exchanging a smile: there was nothing friendly about this smile, it was merely two cold flickers of recognition. But she was certain she had never seen him before.

He was standing next to an el pillar, and as she crossed the street he turned and followed. He kept quite close; from the corner of her eye she watched his reflection wavering on the shopwindows.

Then in the middle of the block she stopped and faced him. He stopped also and cocked his head, grinning. But what could she say? Do? Here, in broad daylight, on Eighty-sixth Street? It was useless and, despising her own helplessness, she quickened her steps.

Now Second Avenue is a dismal street, made from scraps and ends; part cobblestone, part asphalt, part cement; and its atmosphere of desertion is permanent. Mrs. Miller walked five blocks without meeting anyone, and all the while the steady crunch of his footfalls in the snow stayed near. And when she came to a florist's shop, the sound was still with her. She hurried inside and watched through the glass door as the old man passed; he kept his eyes straight ahead and didn't slow his pace, but he did one strange, telling thing: he tipped his cap.

"Six white ones, did you say?" asked the florist. "Yes," she told him, "white roses."

From there she went to a glassware store and selected a vase, presumably a replacement for the one Miriam had broken, though the price was intolerable and the vase itself (she thought) grotesquely vulgar. But a series of unaccountable purchases had begun, as if by prearranged plan: a plan of which she had not the least knowledge or control.

She bought a bag of glazed cherries, and at a place called the Knickerbocker Bakery she paid forty cents for six almond cakes.

Within the last hour the weather had turned cold again; like blurred lenses, winter clouds cast a shade over the sun, and the skeleton of an early dusk colored the sky; a damp mist mixed with the wind and the voices of a few children who romped high on mountains of gutter snow seemed lonely and cheerless. Soon the first flake fell, and when Mrs. Miller reached the brownstone house snow was falling in a swift screen and foot tracks vanished as they were printed.

The white roses were arranged decoratively in the vase. The glazed cherries shone on a ceramic plate. The almond cakes, dusted with sugar, awaited a hand. The canary fluttered on its swing and picked at a bar of seed.

At precisely five the doorbell rang. Mrs. Miller *knew* who it was. The hem of her housecoat trailed as she crossed the floor. "Is that you?" she called.

"Naturally," said Miriam, the word resounding shrilly from the hall. "Open this door."

"Go away," said Mrs. Miller.

"Please hurry . . . I have a heavy package."

"Go away," said Mrs. Miller. She returned to the living room, lighted a cigarette, sat down and calmly listened to the buzzer; on and on and on. "You might as well leave. I have no intention of letting you in."

Shortly the bell stopped. For possibly ten minutes Mrs. Miller did not move. Then, hearing no sound, she concluded Miriam had gone. She tiptoed to the door and opened it a sliver; Miriam was half reclining atop a cardboard box with a beautiful French doll cradled in her arms.

"Really, I thought you were never coming," she said peevishly. "Here, help me get this in, it's awfully heavy."

It was not spell-like compulsion that Mrs. Miller felt, but rather a curious passivity; she brought in the box, Miriam the doll. Miriam curled up on the sofa, not troubling to remove her coat or beret, and watched disinterestedly as Mrs. Miller dropped the box and stood trembling, trying to catch her breath.

"Thank you," she said. In the daylight she looked

pinched and drawn, her hair less luminous. The French doll she was loving wore an exquisite powdered wig and its idiot glass eyes sought solace in Miriam's. "I have a surprise," she continued. "Look into my box."

Kneeling, Mrs. Miller parted the flaps and lifted out another doll; then a blue dress which she recalled as the one Miriam had worn that first night at the theatre; and of the remainder she said, "It's all clothes. Why?"

"Because I've come to live with you," said Miriam, twisting a cherry stem. "Wasn't it nice of you to buy me the cherries—"

"But you can't! For God's sake go away . . . go away and leave me alone!"

"—and the roses and the almond cakes? How really wonderfully generous. You know, these cherries are delicious. The last place I lived was with an old man; he was terribly poor and we never had good things to eat. But I think I'll be happy here." She paused to snuggle her doll closer. "Now, if you'll just show me where to put my things . . ."

Mrs. Miller's face dissolved into a mask of ugly red lines; she began to cry, and it was an unnatural, tearless sort of weeping, as though, not having wept for a long time, she had forgotten how. Carefully she edged backward till she touched the door.

She fumbled through the hall and down the stairs to a landing below. She pounded frantically on the door of the first apartment she came to; a short, redheaded man answered and she pushed past him. "Say, what the hell is this?" he said. "Anything wrong, lover?" asked a young woman who appeared from the kitchen, drying her hands. And it was to her that Mrs. Miller turned.

"Listen," she cried, "I'm ashamed behaving this way but . . . well, I'm Mrs. H. T. Miller and I live upstairs and—" She pressed her hands over her face. "—It sounds so absurd. . . ."

The woman guided her to a chair, while the man excitedly rattled pocket change. "Yeah?"

"I live upstairs and there's a little girl visiting me, and

I suppose that I'm afraid of her. She won't leave and I can't make her and . . . she's going to do something terrible. She's already stolen my cameo, but she's about to do something worse . . . something terrible!"

The man asked, "Is she a relative, huh?"

Mrs. Miller shook her head. "I don't know who she is. Her name's Miriam, but I don't know for certain who she is."

"You gotta calm down, honey," said the woman, stroking Mrs. Miller's arm. "Harry here'll tend to this kid. Go on, lover." And Mrs. Miller said, "The door's open . . . 5A."

After the man left, the woman brought a towel and bathed Mrs. Miller's face. "You're very kind," Mrs. Miller said. "I'm sorry to act like such a fool, only this wicked child. . . ."

"Sure, honey," consoled the woman. "Now, you better take it easy."

Mrs. Miller rested her head in the crook of her arm; she was quiet enough to be asleep. The woman turned a radio dial; a piano and a husky voice filled the silence and the woman, tapping her foot, kept excellent time. "Maybe we oughta go up too," she said.

"I don't want to see her again. I don't want to be anywhere near her."

"Uh huh, but what you shoulda done, you shoulda called a cop."

Presently they heard the man on the stairs. He strode into the room frowning and scratching the back of his neck. "Nobody there," he said, honestly embarrassed. "She musta beat it."

"Harry, you're a jerk," announced the woman. "We been sitting here the whole time and we woulda seen . . ." she stopped abruptly, for the man's glance was sharp.

"I looked all over," he said, "and there just ain't nobody there. Nobody, understand?"

"Tell me," said Mrs. Miller, rising, "tell me, did you see a large box? Or a doll?"

"No, ma'am, I didn't."

And the woman, as if delivering a verdict, said, "Well, for cryinoutloud. . . ."

Mrs. Miller entered her apartment softly; she walked to the center of the room and stood quite still. No, in a sense it had not changed: the roses, the cakes, and the cherries were in place. But this was an empty room, emptier than if the furnishings and familiars were not present, lifeless and petrified as a funeral parlor. The sofa loomed before her with a new strangeness: its vacancy had a meaning that would have been less penetrating and terrible had Miriam been curled on it. She gazed fixedly at the space where she remembered setting the box and, for a moment, the hassock spun desperately. And she looked through the window; surely the river was real, surely snow was falling . . . but then, one could not be certain witness to anything: Miriam, so vividly *there* . . . and yet, where was she? Where, where?

As though moving in a dream, she sank to a chair. The room was losing shape; it was dark and getting darker and there was nothing to be done about it: she could not lift her hand to light a lamp.

Suddenly, closing her eyes, she felt an upward surge, like a diver emerging from some deeper, greener depth. In times of terror or immense distress, there are moments when the mind waits, as though for a revelation, while a skein of calm is woven over thought; it is like sleep, or a supernatural trance; and during this lull one is aware of a force of quiet reasoning: well, what if she had never really known a girl named Miriam? that she had been foolishly frightened on the street? In the end, like everything else, it was of no importance. For the only thing she had lost to Miriam was her identity, but now she knew she had found again the person who lived in this room, who cooked her own meals, who owned a canary, who was someone she could trust and believe in: Mrs. H. T. Miller.

Listening in contentment, she became aware of a double sound: a bureau drawer opening and closing; she

seemed to hear it long after completion . . . opening
and closing. Then gradually, the harshness of it was replaced by the murmur of a silk dress and this, delicately
faint, was moving nearer and swelling in intensity till
the walls trembled with the vibration and the room was
caving under a wave of whispers. Mrs. Miller stiffened
and opened her eyes to a dull, direct stare.

"Hello," said Miriam.

Interior Castle

Jean Stafford

PANSY Vanneman, injured in an automobile accident, often woke up before dawn when the night noises of the hospital still came, in hushed hurry, through her half-open door. By day, when the nurses talked audibly with the internes, laughed without inhibition, and took no pains to soften their footsteps on the resounding composition floors, the routine of the hospital seemed as bland and commonplace as that of a bank or a factory. But in the dark hours, the whispering and the quickly stilled clatter of glasses and basins, the moans of patients whose morphine was wearing off, the soft squeak of a stretcher as it rolled past on its way from the emergency ward—these suggested agony and death. Thus, on the first morning, Pansy had faltered to consciousness long before daylight and had found herself in a ward from every bed of which, it seemed to her, came the bewildered protest of someone about to die. A caged light burned on the floor beside the bed next to hers. Her neighbor was dying and a priest was administering Extreme Unction. He was stout and elderly and he suffered from asthma so that the struggle of his breathing, so close to her, was the basic pattern and all the other sounds were superimposed upon it. Two middle-aged men in overcoats knelt on the floor beside the high bed. In a foreign tongue, the half-gone woman babbled against the hissing and sighing of the Latin prayers. She played with her rosary as if it were a toy: she tried, and failed, to put it into her mouth.

Pansy felt horror, but she felt no pity. An hour or so

56

later, when the white ceiling lights were turned on and everything—faces, counterpanes, and the hands that groped upon them—was transformed into a uniform gray sordor, the woman was wheeled away in her bed to die somewhere else, in privacy. Pansy did not quite take this in, although she stared for a long time at the new, empty bed that had replaced the other.

The next morning, when she again woke up before the light, this time in a private room, she recalled the woman with such sorrow that she might have been a friend. Simultaneously, she mourned the driver of the taxicab in which she had been injured, for he had died at about noon the day before. She had been told this as she lay on a stretcher in the corridor, waiting to be taken to the X-ray room; an interne, passing by, had paused and smiled down at her and had said, "Your cab-driver is dead. You were lucky."

Six weeks after the accident, she woke one morning just as daylight was showing on the windows as a murky smear. It was a minute or two before she realized why she was so reluctant to be awake, why her uneasiness amounted almost to alarm. Then she remembered that her nose was to be operated on today. She lay straight and motionless under the seersucker counterpane. Her blood-red eyes in her darned face stared through the window and saw a frozen river and leafless elm trees and a grizzled esplanade where dogs danced on the ends of leashes, their bundled-up owners stumbling after them, half blind with sleepiness and cold. Warm as the hospital room was, it did not prevent Pansy from knowing, as keenly as though she were one of the walkers, how very cold it was outside. Each twig of a nearby tree was stark. Cold red brick buildings nudged the low-lying sky which was pale and inert like a punctured sac.

In six weeks, the scene had varied little: there was promise in the skies neither of sun nor of snow; no red sunsets marked these days. The trees could neither die nor leaf out again. Pansy could not remember another season in her life so constant, when the very minutes themselves were suffused with the winter pallor as they dropped from the moon-faced clock in the corridor. Likewise, her room accomplished no alterations from day to day. On the glass-topped bureau stood two potted plants telegraphed by faraway well-wishers. They did not fade, and if a leaf turned brown and fell, it soon was replaced; so did the blossoms renew themselves. The roots, like the skies and like the bare trees, seemed zealously determined to maintain a status quo. The bedside table, covered every day with a clean white towel, though the one removed was always immaculate, was furnished sparsely with a water glass, a bent drinking tube, a sweating pitcher, and a stack of paper handkerchiefs. There were a few letters in the drawer, a hairbrush, a pencil, and some postal cards on which, from time to time, she wrote brief messages to relatives and friends: "Dr. Nash says that my reflexes are shipshape (sic) and Dr. Rivers says the frontal fracture has all but healed and that the occipital is coming along nicely. Dr. Nicholas, the nose doctor, promises to operate as soon as Dr. Rivers gives him the go-ahead sign (sic)."

The bed itself was never rumpled. Once fretful and now convalescent, Miss Vanneman might have been expected to toss or to turn the pillows or to unmoor the counterpane; but hour after hour and day after day she lay at full length and would not even suffer the nurses to raise the head-piece of the adjustable bed. So perfect and stubborn was her body's immobility that it was as if the room and the landscape, mortified by the ice, were extensions of herself. Her resolute quiescence and her disinclination to talk, the one seeming somehow to proceed from the other, resembled, so the nurses said, a final coma. And they observed, in pitying indignation, that she might as well be dead for all the interest she took in life. Amongst themselves they scolded her for what they thought a moral weakness: an automobile accident, no matter how serious, was not reason enough for anyone to give up the will to live or to be happy. She had not— to come down bluntly to the facts—had the decency to be grateful that it was the driver of the cab and not she who had died. (And how dreadfully the man had died!)

She was twenty-five years old and she came from a distant city. These were really the only facts known about her. Evidently she had not been here long, for she had no visitors, a lack which was at first sadly moving to the nurses but which became to them a source of unreasonable annoyance: had anyone the right to live so one-dimensionally? It was impossible to laugh at her, for she said nothing absurd; her demands could not be complained of because they did not exist; she could not be hated for a sharp tongue nor for a supercilious one; she could not be admired for bravery or for wit or for interest in her fellow creatures. She was believed to be a frightful snob.

Pansy, for her part, took a secret and mischievous pleasure in the bewilderment of her attendants and the more they courted her with offers of magazines, crossword puzzles, and a radio that she could rent from the hospital, the farther she retired from them into herself and into the world which she had created in her long hours here and which no one could ever penetrate nor imagine. Sometimes she did not even answer the nurses' questions; as they rubbed her back with alcohol and steadily discoursed, she was as remote from them as if she were miles away. She did not think that she lived on a higher plane than that of the nurses and the doctors but that she lived on a different one and that at this particular time—this time of exploration and habituation—she had no extra strength to spend on making herself known to them. All she had been before and all the memories she might have brought out to disturb the monotony of, say, the morning bath, and all that the past meant to the future when she would leave the hospital, were of no present consequence to her. Not even in her thoughts did she employ more than a minimum of memory. And when she did remember, it was in flat pictures, rigorously independent of one another: she saw her thin, poetic mother who grew thinner and more peotic in her canvas deck-chair at Saranac reading *Lalla Rookh*. She saw herself in an inappropriate pink hat drinking iced tea in a garden so oppressive with the smell of phlox that the tea itself tasted of it. She recalled an afternoon in autumn in Vermont when she had heard three dogs' voices in the north woods and she could tell, by the characteristic minor key struck three times at intervals, like bells from several churches, that they had treed something: the eastern sky was pink and the trees on the horizon looked like some eccentric vascular system meticulously drawn on colored paper.

What Pansy thought of all the time was her own brain. Not only the brain as the seat of consciousness, but the physical organ itself which she envisaged, romantically, now as a jewel, now as a flower, now as a light in a glass, now as an envelope of rosy vellum containing other envelopes, one within the other, diminishing infinitely. It was always pink and always fragile, always deeply interior and invaluable. She believed that she had reached the innermost chamber of knowledge and that perhaps her knowledge was the same as the saint's achievement of pure love. It was only convention, she thought, that made one say "sacred heart" and not "sacred brain."

Often, but never articulately, the color pink troubled her and the picture of herself in the wrong hat hung steadfastly before her mind's eye. None of the other girls had worn hats and since autumn had come early that year, they were dressed in green and rusty brown and dark yellow. Poor Pansy wore a white eyelet frock with a lacing of black ribbon around the square neck. When she came through the arch, overhung with bittersweet, and saw that they had not yet heard her, she almost turned back, but Mr. Oliver was there and she was in love with him. She was in love with him though he was ten years older than she and had never shown any interest in her beyond asking her once, quite fatuously but in an intimate voice, if the yodeling of the little boy who peddled clams did not make her wish to visit Switzerland. Actually, there was more to this question than met the eye, for some days later Pansy learned that Mr. Oliver, who was immensely rich, kept an apartment in Geneva. In the garden that day, he spoke to her only once. He said, "My dear, you look exactly like something out of

Katherine Mansfield," and immediately turned and within her hearing asked Beatrice Sherburne to dine with him that night at the Country Club. Afterward, Pansy went down to the sea and threw the beautiful hat onto the full tide and saw it vanish in the wake of a trawler. Thereafter, when she heard the clam boy coming down the road, she locked the door and when the knocking had stopped and her mother called down from her chaise longue, "Who was it, dearie?" she replied, "A salesman."

It was only the fact that the hat had been pink that worried her. The rest of the memory was trivial, for she knew that she could never again love anything as ecstatically as she loved the spirit of Pansy Vanneman, enclosed within her head.

But her study was not without distraction, and she fought two adversaries: pain and Dr. Nicholas. Against Dr. Nicholas, she defended herself valorously and in fear; but pain, the pain, that is, that was independent of his instruments, she sometimes forced upon herself adventurously like a child scaring himself in a graveyard.

Dr. Nicholas greatly admired her crushed and splintered nose which he daily probed and peered at, exclaiming that he had never seen anything like it. His shapely hands ached for their knives; he was impatient with the skull-fracture man's cautious delay. He spoke of "our" nose and said "we" would be a new person when we could breathe again. His own nose was magnificent. Not even his own brilliant surgery could have improved upon it nor could a first-rate sculptor have duplicated its direct downward line which permitted only the least curvature inward toward the end; nor the delicately rounded lateral declivities; nor the thin-walled, perfectly matched nostrils.

Miss Vanneman did not doubt his humaneness nor his talent—he was a celebrated man—but she questioned whether he had imagination. Immediately beyond the prongs of his speculum lay her treasure whose price he, no more than the nurses, could estimate. She believed he could not destroy it, but she feared that he might

maim it: might leave a scratch on one of the brilliant
facets of the jewel, bruise a petal of the flower, smudge
the glass where the light burned, blot the envelopes,
and that then she would die or would go mad. While she
did not question that in either eventuality her brain
would after a time redeem its original impeccability, she
did not quite yet wish to enter upon either kind of eternity, for she was not certain that she could carry with
her her knowledge as well as its receptacle.

Blunderer that he was, Dr. Nicholas was an honorable enemy, not like the demon, pain, which skulked in
a thousand guises within her head, and which often she
recklessly willed to attack her and then drove back in
terror. After the rout, sweat streamed from her face and
soaked the neck of the coarse hospital shirt. To be sure,
it came usually of its own accord, running like a wild
fire through all the convolutions to fill with flame the
small sockets and ravines and then, at last, to withdraw,
leaving behind a throbbing and an echo. On these occasions, she was as helpless as a tree in a wind. But at the
other times when, by closing her eyes and rolling up the
eyeballs in such a way that she fancied she looked directly on the place where her brain was, the pain woke
sluggishly and came toward her at a snail's pace. Then,
bit by bit, it gained speed. Sometimes it faltered back,
subsided altogether, and then it rushed like a tidal wave
driven by a hurricane, lashing and roaring until she
lifted her hands from the counterpane, crushed her
broken teeth into her swollen lip, stared in panic at the
soothing walls with her ruby eyes, stretched out her legs
until she felt their bones must snap. Each cove, each narrow inlet, every living bay was flooded and the frail
brain, a little hat-shaped boat, was washed from its moor-
ing and set adrift. The skull was as vast as the world and
the brain was as small as a seashell.

Then came calm weather and the safe journey home.
She kept vigil for a while, though, and did not close her
eyes, but gazing pacifically at the trees, conceived of the
pain as the guardian of her treasure who would not let
her see it; that was why she was handled so savagely

whenever she turned her eyes inward. Once this watch
was interrupted: by chance she looked into the corridor
and saw a shaggy mop slink past the door, followed by
a senile porter. A pair of ancient eyes, as rheumy as an
old dog's, stared uncritically in at her and a toothless
mouth formed a brutish word. She was so surprised that
she immediately closed her eyes to shut out the shape of
the word and the pain dug up the unmapped regions of
her head with mattocks, ludicrously huge. It was the familiar pain, but this time, even as she endured it, she observed with detachment that its effect upon her was less
than that of its contents, the by-products, for example, of
temporal confusion and the bizarre misapplication of the
style of one sensation to another. At the moment, for example, although her brain reiterated to her that *it* was
being assailed, she was stroking her right wrist with her
left hand as though to assuage the ache, long since dis-
pelled, of the sprain in the joint. Some minutes after she
had opened her eyes and left off soothing her wrist, she
lay rigid experiencing the sequel to the pain, an ideal
terror. For, as before on several occasions, she was overwhelmed with the knowledge that the pain had been
consummated in the vessel of her mind and for the moment the vessel was unbeautiful: she thought, quailing,
of those plastic folds as palpable as the fingers of locked
hands containing in their very cells, their fissures, their
repulsive hemispheres, the mind, the soul, the inscrutable
intelligence.

The porter, then, like the pink hat and like her mother
and the hounds' voices, loitered with her.

II

Dr. Nicholas came at nine o'clock to prepare her for the
operation. With him came an entourage of white-frocked
acolytes, and one of them wheeled in a wagon on which
lay knives and scissors and pincers, cans of swabs and
gauze. In the midst of these was a bowl of liquid whose
rich purple color made it seem strange like the brew of
an alchemist.

"All set?" the surgeon asked her, smiling. "A little

nervous, what? I don't blame you. I've often said I'd
rather break a leg than have a submucous resection."
Pansy thought for a moment he was going to touch his
nose. His approach to her was roundabout. He moved
through the yellow light shed by the globe in the ceiling
which gave his forehead a liquid gloss; he paused by the
bureau and touched a blossom of the cyclamen; he looked
out the window and said, to no one and to all, "I couldn't
start my car this morning. Came in a cab." Then he came
forward. As he came, he removed a speculum from the
pocket of his short-sleeved coat and like a cat, inquiring
of the nature of a surface with its paws, he put out his
hand toward her and drew it back, gently murmuring,
"You must not be afraid, my dear. There is no danger,
you know. Do you think for a minute I would operate if
there were?"

Dr. Nicholas, young, brilliant, and handsome, was an
aristocrat, a husband, a father, a clubman, a Christian,
a kind counselor, and a trustee of his preparatory school.
Like many of the medical profession, even those whose
specialty was centered on the organ of the basest sense,
he interested himself in the psychology of his patients:
in several instances, for example, he had found that severe attacks of sinusitis were coincident with emotional
crises. Miss Vanneman more than ordinarily captured
his fancy since her skull had been fractured and her
behavior throughout had been so extraordinary that he
felt he was observing at first hand some of the results of
shock, that incommensurable element, which frequently
were too subtle to see. There was, for example, the matter of her complete passivity during a lumbar puncture,
reports of which were written down in her history and
were enlarged upon for him by Dr. Rivers' interne who
had been in charge. Except for a tremor in her throat
and a deepening of pallor, there were no signs at all
that she was aware of what was happening to her. She
made no sound, did not close her eyes nor clench her
fists. She had had several punctures; her only reaction
had been to the very first one, the morning after she had
been brought in. When the interne explained to her

that he was going to drain off cerebrospinal fluid which was pressing against her brain, she exclaimed, "My God!" but it was not an exclamation of fear. The young man had been unable to name what it was he had heard in her voice; he could only say that it had not been fear as he had observed it in other patients.

Dr. Nicholas wondered about her. There was no way of guessing whether she had always had a nature of so tolerant and undemanding a complexion. It gave him a melancholy pleasure to think that before her accident she had been high-spirited and loquacious; he was moved to think that perhaps she had been a beauty and that when she had first seen her face in the looking glass she had lost all joy in herself. It was very difficult to tell what the face had been, for it was so bruised and swollen, so hacked-up and lopsided. The black stitches the length of the nose, across the saddle, across the cheekbone, showed that there would be unsightly scars. He had ventured once to give her the name of a plastic surgeon but she had only replied with a vague, refusing smile. He had hoisted a manly shoulder and said, "You're the doctor."

Much as he pondered, coming to no conclusions, about what went on inside that pitiable skull, he was, of course, far more interested in the nose, deranged so badly that it would require his topmost skill to restore its functions to it. He would be obliged not only to make a submucous resection, a simple run-of-the-mill operation, but to remove the vomer, always a delicate task but further complicated in this case by the proximity of the bone to the frontal fracture line which conceivably was not entirely closed. If it were not and he operated too soon and if a cold germ then found its way into the opening, his patient would be carried off by meningitis in the twinkling of an eye. He wondered if she knew in what potential danger she lay; he desired to assure her that he had brought his craft to its nearest perfection and that she had nothing to fear of him, but feeling that she was perhaps both ignorant and unimaginative and that such consolation would create a fear rather than dispel one, he held his tongue and came nearer to the bed.

Watching him, Pansy could already feel the prongs of his pliers opening her nostrils for the insertion of his fine probers. The pain he caused her with his instruments was of a different kind from that which she felt unaided: it was a naked, clean, and vivid pain that made her faint and ill and made her wish to die. Once she had fainted as he ruthlessly explored and after she was brought around, he continued until he had finished his investigation. The memory of this outrage had afterward several times made her cry.

This morning she looked at him and listened to him with hatred. Fixing her eyes upon the middle of his high, protuberant brow, she imagined the clutter behind it and she despised its obtuse imperfection. In his bland unawareness, this nobody, this nose-bigot, was about to play with fire and she wished him ill.

He said, "I can't blame you. No, I expect you're not looking forward to our little party. But you'll be glad to be able to breathe again."

He stationed his lieutenants. The interne stood opposite him on the left side of the bed. The surgical nurse wheeled the wagon within easy reach of his hands and stood beside it. Another nurse stood at the foot of the bed. A third drew the shades at the windows and attached a blinding light that shone down on the patient hotly, and then she left the room, softly closing the door. Pansy stared at the silver ribbon tied in a great bow round the green crepe paper of one of the flower pots. It made her realize for the first time that one of the days she had lain here had been Christmas, but she had no time to consider this strange and thrilling fact, for Dr. Nicholas was genially explaining his anesthetic. He would soak packs of gauze in the purple fluid, a cocaine solution, and he would place them then in her nostrils, leaving them there for an hour. He warned her that the packing would be disagreeable (he did not say "painful") but that it would be well worth a few minutes of discomfort not to be in the least sick after the operation. He asked her if she were ready and when she nodded her head, he adjusted the mirror on his forehead and began.

At the first touch of his speculum, Pansy's fingers mechanically bent to the palms of her hands and she stiffened. He said, "A pack, Miss Kennedy," and Pansy closed her eyes. There was a rush of plunging pain as he drove the sodden gobbet of gauze high up into her nose and something bitter burned in her throat so that she retched. The doctor paused a moment and the surgical nurse wiped Pansy's mouth. He returned to her with another pack, pushing it with his bodkin doggedly until it lodged against the first. Stop! Stop! cried all her nerves, wailing along the surface of her skin. The coats that covered them were torn off and they shuddered like naked people screaming, Stop! Stop! But Dr. Nicholas did not hear. Time and again he came back with a fresh pack and did not pause at all until one nostril was finished. She opened her eyes and saw him wipe the sweat off his forehead and saw the dark interne bending over her, fascinated. Miss Kennedy bathed her temples in ice water and Dr. Nicholas said, "There. It won't be much longer. I'll tell them to send you some coffee, though I'm afraid you won't be able to taste it. Ever drink coffee with chicory in it? I have no use for it."

She snatched at his irrelevancy and, though she had never tasted chicory, she said severely, "I love it."

Dr. Nicholas chuckled. "De gustibus. Ready? A pack, Miss Kennedy."

The second nostril was harder to pack since the other side was now distended and this passage was anyhow much narrower, as narrow, he had once remarked, as that in the nose of an infant. In such pain as passed all language and even the farthest fetched analogies, she turned her eyes inward thinking that under the obscuring cloak of the surgeon's pain, she could see her brain without the knowledge of its keeper. But Dr. Nicholas and his aides would give her no peace. They surrounded her with their murmuring and their foot-shuffling and the rustling of their starched uniforms, and her eyelids continually flew back in embarrassment and mistrust. She was claimed entirely by this present, meaningless pain and suddenly and sharply she forgot what she had

meant to do. She was aware of nothing but her ascent to
the summit of something; what it was she did not know,
whether it was a tower or a peak or Jacob's ladder. Now
she was an abstract word, now she was a theorem of geometry, now she was a kite flying, a top spinning, a prism
flashing, a kaleidoscope turning.

But none of the others in the room could see inside
when the surgeon was finished, the nurse at the foot of
the bed said, "Now you must take a look in the mirror.
It's simply too comical." And they all laughed intimately
like old, fast friends. She smiled politely and looked at
her reflection: over the gruesomely fattened snout, her
scarlet eyes stared in fixed reproach upon her upturned
lips, gray with bruises. But even in its smile of betrayal,
the mouth itself was puzzled: it reminded her that something had been left behind, but she could not recall what
it was. She was hollowed out and was as dry as a white
bone.

III

They strapped her ankles to the operating table and put
leather nooses round her wrists. Over her head was a
mirror with a thousand facets in which she saw a thousand travesties of her face. At her right side was the table, shrouded in white, where lay the glittering blades
of the many knives, thrusting out fitful rays of light. All
the cloth was frosty; everything was white or silver and
as cold as snow. Dr. Nicholas, a tall snowman with silver
eyes and silver fingernails, came into the room soundlessly for he walked on layers and layers of snow that
deadened his footsteps; behind him came the interne, a
smaller snowman, less impressively proportioned. At the
foot of the table, a snow figure put her frozen hands
upon Pansy's helpless feet. The doctor plucked the packs
from the cold, numb nose. His laugh was like a cry on a
bitter, still night: "I will show you now," he called across
the expanse of snow, "that you can feel nothing." The
pincers bit at nothing, snapped at the air and cracked a
nerveless icicle. Pansy called back and heard her own
voice echo: "I feel nothing."

Here the walls were gray, not tan. Suddenly the face of the nurse at the foot of the table broke apart and Pansy first thought it was in grief. But it was a smile and she said, "Did you enjoy your coffee?" Down the gray corridors of the maze, the words rippled, ran like mice, birds, broken beads: Did you enjoy your coffee? your coffee? your coffee? Similarly once in another room that also had gray walls, the same voice had said, "Shall I give her some whisky?" She was overcome with gratitude that this young woman (how pretty she was with her white hair and her white face and her china-blue eyes!) had been with her that first night and was with her now.

In the great stillness of the winter, the operation began. The knives carved snow. Pansy was happy. She had been given a hypnotic just before they came to fetch her and she would have gone to sleep had she not enjoyed so much this trickery of Dr. Nicholas' whom now she tenderly loved.

There was a clock in the operating room and from time to time she looked at it. An hour passed. The snowman's face was melting; drops of water hung from his fine nose, but his silver eyes were as bright as ever. Her love was returned, she knew: he loved her nose exactly as she loved his knives. She looked at her face in the domed mirror and saw how the blood had streaked her lily-white cheeks and had stained her shroud. She returned to the private song: Did you enjoy your coffee? your coffee?

At the half-hour, a murmur, anguine and slumbrous, came to her and only when she had repeated the words twice did they engrave their meaning upon her. Dr. Nicholas said, "Stand back now, nurse. I'm at this girl's brain and I don't want my elbow jogged." Instantly Pansy was alive. Her strapped ankles arched angrily; her wrists strained against their bracelets. She jerked her head and she felt the pain flare; she had made the knife slip.

"Be still!" cried the surgeon. "Be quiet, please!"

He had made her remember what it was she had lost when he had rammed his gauze into her nose: she bustled like a housewife to shut the door. She thought, I must hurry before the robbers come. It would be like the time Mother left the cellar door open and the robber came and took, of all things, the terrarium.

Dr. Nicholas was whispering to her. He said, in the voice of a lover, "If you can stand it five minutes more, I can perform the second operation now and you won't have to go through this again. What do you say?"

She did not reply. It took her several seconds to re-member why it was her mother had set such store by the terrarium and then it came to her that the bishop's widow had brought her an herb from Palestine to put in it.

The interne said, "You don't want to have your nose packed again, do you?"

The surgical nurse said, "She's a good patient, isn't she, sir?"

"Never had a better," replied Dr. Nicholas. "But don't call me 'sir.' You must be a Canadian to call me 'sir.'"

The nurse at the foot of the bed said, "I'll order some more coffee for you."

"How about it, Miss Vanneman?" said the doctor. "Shall I go ahead?"

She debated. Once she had finally fled the hospital and fled Dr. Nicholas, nothing could compel her to come back. Still, she knew that the time would come when she could no longer live in seclusion, she must go into the world again and must be equipped to live in it; she banally acknowledged that she must be able to breathe. And finally, though the world to which she would return remained unreal, she gave the surgeon her permission.

He had now to penetrate regions that were not anes-thetized and this he told her frankly, but he said that there was no danger at all. He apologized for the slip of the tongue he had made: in point of fact, he had not been near her brain, it was only a figure of speech. He began. The knives ground and carved and curried and scoured the wounds they made; the scissors clipped hard gristle and the scalpels chipped off bone. It was as if a tangle of tiny nerves were being cut dexterously, one by one; the pain writhed spirally and came to her who was a pink bird and sat on the top of a cone. The pain was a pyramid made of a diamond; it was an intense light; it was the hottest fire, the coldest chill, the highest peak, the fastest force, the furthest reach, the newest time. It possessed nothing of her but its one infinitesimal scene: beyond the screen as thin as gossamer, the brain trembled for its life, hearing the knives hunting like wolves outside, sniffing and snapping. Mercy! Mercy! cried the scalped nerves.

At last, miraculously, she turned her eyes inward tranquilly. Dr. Nicholas had said, "The worst is over. I am going to work on the floor of your nose," and at his signal she closed her eyes and this time and this time alone, she saw her brain lying in a shell-pink satin case. It was a pink pearl, no bigger than a needle's eye, but it was so beautiful and so pure that its smallness made no difference. Anyhow, as she watched, it grew. It grew larger and larger until it was an enormous bubble that contained the surgeon and the whole room within its rosy luster. In a long ago summer, she had often been absorbed by the spectacle of flocks of yellow birds that visited a cedar tree and she remembered that everything that summer had been some shade of yellow. One year of childhood, her mother had frequently taken her to have tea with an aged schoolmistress upon whose mantelpiece there was a herd of ivory elephants; that had been the white year. There was a green spring when early in April she had seen a grass snake on a boulder, but the very summer that followed was violet, for vetch took her mother's garden. She saw a swatch of blue tulle lying in a raffia basket on the front porch of Uncle Marion's brown house. Never before had the world been pink, whatever else it had been. Or had it been, one other time? She could not be sure and she did not care. Of one thing she was certain: never had the world enclosed her before and never had the quiet been so smooth.

For only a moment the busybodies left her to her ecstasy and then, impatient and gossiping, they forced their way inside, slashed at her resisting trance with

questions and congratulations, with statements of fact
and jokes. "Later," she said to them dumbly. "Later on,
perhaps. I am busy now." But their voices would not go
away. They touched her, too, washing her face with
cloths so cold they stung, stroking her wrists with firm,
antiseptic fingers. The surgeon, squeezing her arm with
avuncular pride, said, "Good girl," as if she were a bright
dog that had retrieved a bone. Her silent mind abused
him: "You are a thief," it said, "you are heartless and
you should be put to death." But he was leaving, adjusting his coat with an air of vainglory, and the interne,
abject with admiration, followed him from the operating
room smiling like a silly boy.

Shortly after they took her back to her room, the
weather changed, not for the better. Momentarily the
sun emerged from its concealing murk, but in a few minutes the snow came with a wind that promised a blizzard.
There was great pain, but since it could not serve her,
she rejected it and she lay as if in a hammock in a pause
of bitterness. She closed her eyes, shutting herself up
within her treasureless head.

Heartburn

Hortense Calisher

THE light, gritty wind of a spring morning blew in on the doctor's shining, cleared desk, and on the tall buttonhook of a man who leaned agitatedly toward him.

"I have some kind of small animal lodged in my chest," said the man. He coughed, a slight, hollow apologia to his ailment, and sank back in his chair.

"Animal?" said the doctor, after a pause which had the unfortunate quality of comment. His voice, however, was practiced, deft, colored only with the careful suspension of judgment.

"Probably a form of newt or toad," answered the man, speaking with clipped distaste, as if he would disassociate himself from the idea as far as possible. His face quirked with sad foreknowledge. "Of course, you don't believe me."

The doctor looked at him noncommittally. Paraphrased, an old refrain of the poker table leapt erratically in his mind. "Nits"—no—"newts and gnats and one-eyed jacks," he thought. But already the anecdote was shaping itself, trim and perfect, for display at the clinic luncheon table. "Go on," he said.

"Why won't any of you come right out and say what you think!" the man said angrily. Then he flushed, not hectically, the doctor noted, but with the well-bred embarrassment of the normally reserved. "Sorry. I didn't mean to be rude."

"You've already had an examination?" The doctor was a neurologist, and most of his patients were referrals.

"My family doctor. I live up in Boston."

"Did you tell him—er . . . ?" The doctor sought gingerly for a phrase.

One corner of the man's mouth lifted, as if he had
watched others in the same dilemma. "I went through
the routine first. Fluoroscope, metabolism, cardiograph.
Even gastroscopy." He spoke, the doctor noted, with the
regrettable glibness of the patient who has shopped
around.

"And—the findings?" said the doctor, already sure of
the answer.

The man leaned forward, holding the doctor's glance
with his own. A faint smile riffled his mouth. "Positive."

"Positive!"

"Well," said the man, "machines have to be interpreted
after all, don't they?" He attempted a shrug, but the quick
eye of the doctor saw that the movement masked a slight
contortion within his tweed suit, as if the man writhed
away from himself but concealed it quickly, as one masks
a hiccup with a cough. "A curious flutter in the cardiograph, a strange variation in the metabolism, an alien
shadow under the fluoroscope." He coughed again and put
a genteel hand over his mouth, but this time the doctor
saw it clearly—the slight, cringing motion.

"You see," added the man, his eyes helpless and apologetic above the polite covering hand. "It's alive. It *trav-
els.*"

"Yes. Yes, of course," said the doctor, soothingly now.
In his mind hung the word, ovoid and perfect as a drop
of water about to fall. Obsession. A beautiful case. He
thought again of the luncheon table.

"What did your doctor recommend?" he said.

"A place with more resources, like the Mayo Clinic. It
was then that I told him I knew what it was, as I've told
you. And how I acquired it." The visitor paused. "Then,
of course, he was forced to pretend he believed me."

"Forced?" said the doctor.

"Well," said the visitor, "actually, I think he did believe
me. People tend to believe anything these days. All this
mass media information gives them the habit. It takes a
strong individual to disbelieve evidence."

The doctor was confused and annoyed. Well, "What then?" he said peremptorily, ready to rise from his desk in dismissal.

Again came the fleeting bodily grimace and the quick cough. "He—er . . . he gave me a prescription."

The doctor raised his eyebrows, in a gesture he was swift to retract as unprofessional.

"For heartburn, I think it was," added his visitor demurely.

Tipping back in his chair, the doctor tapped a pencil on the edge of the desk. "Did he suggest you seek help —on another level?"

"Many have suggested it," said the man.

"But I'm not a psychiatrist!" said the doctor irritably.

"Oh, I know that. You see, I came to you because I had the luck to hear one of your lectures at the Academy. The one on 'Overemphasis on the Non-somatic Causes of Nervous Disorder.' It takes a strong man to go against the tide like that. A disbeliever. And that's what I sorely need." The visitor shuddered, this time letting the *frisson* pass uncontrolled. "You see," he added, thrusting his clasped hands forward on the desk, and looking ruefully at the doctor, as if he would cushion him against his next remark, "you see—I am a psychiatrist."

The doctor sat still in his chair.

"Ah, I can't help knowing what you are thinking," said the man. "I would think the same. A streamlined version of the Napoleonic delusion." He reached into his breast pocket, drew out a wallet, and fanned papers from it on the desk.

"Never mind. I believe you!" said the doctor hastily.

"Already?" said the man sadly.

Reddening, the doctor hastily looked over the collection of letters, cards of membership in professional societies, licenses, and so on—very much the same sort of thing he himself would have had to amass, had he been under the same necessity of proving his identity. Sanity, of course, was another matter. The documents were all issued to Dr. Curtis Retz at a Boston address. Stolen, possibly, but something in the man's manner, in fact everything in it except his unfortunate hallucination, made the doctor think otherwise. Poor guy, he thought. Occupational fatigue, perhaps. But what a form! The Boston variant, possibly. "Suppose you start from the beginning," he said benevolently.

"If you can spare the time . . ."

"I have no more appointments until lunch." And what a lunch that'll be, the doctor thought, already cherishing the pop-eyed scene—Travis the clinic's director (that plethoric Nestor); and young Gruenberg (all of whose cases were unique), his hairy nostrils dilated for once in a *mise-en-scène* which he did not dominate.

Holding his hands pressed formally against his chest, almost in the attitude of one of the minor placatory figures in a *Pietà*, the visitor went on. "I have the usual private practice," he said, "and clinic affiliations. As a favor to an old friend of mine, headmaster of a boys' school nearby, I've acted as guidance consultant there for some years. The school caters to boys of above average intelligence and is run along progressive lines. Nothing's ever cropped up except run-of-the-mill adolescent problems, colored a little, perhaps, by the type of parents who tend to send their children to a school like that —people who are—well—one might say, almost tediously aware of their commitments as parents."

The doctor grunted. He was that kind of parent himself.

"Shortly after the second term began, the head asked me to come down. He was worried over a sharp drop of morale which seemed to extend over the whole school— general inattention in classes, excited note-passing, nightly disturbances in the dorms—all pointing, he had thought at first, to the existence of some fancier than usual form of hazing, or to one of those secret societies, sometimes laughable, sometimes with overtones of the corrupt, with which all schools are familiar. Except for one thing. One after the other, a long list of boys had been sent to the infirmary by the various teachers who presided in the dining room. Each of the boys had shown a marked debility, and what the resident doctor called

'All the stigmata of pure fright. Complete unwillingness to confide.' Each of the boys pleaded stubbornly for his own release, and a few broke out of their own accord. The interesting thing was that each child did recover shortly after his own release, and it was only after this that another boy was seen to fall ill. No two were afflicted at the same time."

"Check the food?" said the doctor.

"All done before I got there. According to my friend, all the trouble seemed to have started with the advent of one boy, John Hallowell, a kid of about fifteen, who had come to the school late in the term with a history of having run away from four other schools. Records at these classed him as very bright, but made oblique references to 'personality difficulties' which were not defined. My friend's school, ordinarily pretty independent, had taken the boy at the insistence of old Simon Hallowell, the boy's uncle, who is a trustee. His brother, the boy's father, is well known for his marital exploits which have nourished the tabloids for years. The mother lives mostly in France and South America. One of these perennial dryads, apparently, with a youthfulness maintained by money and a yearly immersion in the fountains of American plastic surgery. Only time she sees the boy . . . Well, you can imagine. What the feature articles call a Broken Home."

The doctor shifted in his chair and lit a cigarette.

"I won't keep you much longer," said the visitor. "I saw the boy." A violent fit of coughing interrupted him. This time his curious writhing motion went frankly unconcealed. He got up from his chair and stood at the window, gripping the sill and breathing heavily until he had regained control, and went on, one hand pulling unconsciously at his collar. "Or, at least, I think I saw him. On my way to visit him in his room I bumped into a tall red-headed boy in a football sweater, hurrying down the hall with a windbreaker and a poncho slung over his shoulder. I asked for Hallowell's room; he jerked a thumb over his shoulder at the door just behind him, and continued past me. It never occurred to me . . . I

was expecting some adenoidal gangler with acne . . .
or one of these sinister angel faces, full of neurotic sen-
sibility.

"The room was empty. Except for its finicky neatness,
and a rather large amount of livestock, there was nothing
unusual about it. The school, according to the current
trend, is run like a farm, with the boys doing the chores,
and pets are encouraged. There was a tank with a couple
of turtles near the window, beside it another, full of
newts, and in one corner a large cage of well-tended, brisk
white mice. Glass cases, with carefully mounted series of
lepidoptera and hymenoptera, showing the metamorphic
stages, hung on the walls, and on a drawing board there
was a daintily executed study of Branchippus, the 'fairy
shrimp.'

"While I paced the room, trying to look as if I wasn't
prying, a greenish little wretch, holding himself together
as if he had an imaginary shawl draped around him,
slunk into the half-dark room and squeaked 'Hallowell?'
When he saw me he started to duck, but I detained him
and found that he had had an appointment with Hallowell too. When it was clear, from his description, that
Hallowell must have been the redhead I'd seen leaving,
the poor urchin burst into tears.

" 'I'll never get rid of it now!' he wailed. From then
on it wasn't hard to get the whole maudlin story. It seems
that shortly after Hallowell's arrival at school he acquired
a reputation for unusual proficiency with animals and
for out-of-the-way lore which would impress the in-
genuous. He circulated the rumor that he could swallow
small animals and regurgitate them at will. No one actually saw him swallow anything, but it seems that in some
mumbo-jumbo with another boy who had shown cyni-
cism about the whole thing, it was claimed that Hallowell had, well, divested himself of something, and passed
it on to the other boy, with the statement that the latter
would only be able to get rid of his cargo when he in
turn found a boy who would disbelieve *him*."

The visitor paused, calmer now, and leaving the window sat down again in the chair opposite the doctor, re-

garding him with such fixity that the doctor shifted uneasily, with the apprehension of one who is about to be
asked for a loan.

"My mind turned to the elementary sort of thing we've
all done at times. You know, circle of kids in the dark,
piece of cooked cauliflower passed from hand to hand
with the statement that the stuff is the fresh brains of
some neophyte who hadn't taken his initiation seriously.
My young informer, Moulton his name was, swore however that this hysteria (for of course, that's what I thought
it) was passed on singly, from boy to boy, without any
such séances. He'd been home to visit his family, who
are missionaries on leave, and had been infected by his
roommate on his return to school, unaware that by this
time the whole school had protectively turned believers,
en masse. His own terror came, not only from his conviction that he was possessed, but from his inability to find
anybody who would take his dare. And so he'd finally
come to Hallowell. . . .

"By this time the room was getting really dark and I
snapped on the light to get a better look at Moulton. Except for an occasional shudder, like a bodily tic, which I
took to be the aftereffects of hard crying, he looked like
a healthy enough boy who'd been scared out of his wits.
I remember that a neat little monograph was already
forming itself in my mind, a group study on mass psy-
chosis, perhaps, with effective anthropological references
to certain savage tribes whose dances include a rite
known as 'eating evil.'

"The kid was looking at me. 'Do you believe me?' he
said suddenly. 'Sir?' he added, with a naive cunning
which tickled me.

" 'Of course,' I said, patting his shoulder absently. 'In a
way.'

"His shoulder slumped under my hand. I felt its tremor,
direct misery palpitating between my fingers.

" 'I thought . . . maybe for a man . . . it wouldn't
be . . .' His voice trailed off.

" 'Be the same? . . . I don't know,' I said slowly, for
of course, I was answering, not his actual question, but

the overtone of some cockcrow of meaning that evaded me.

"He raised his head and petitioned me silently with his eyes. Was it guile, or simplicity, in his look, and was it for conviction, or the lack of it, that he arraigned me? I don't know. I've gone back over what I did then, again and again, using all my own knowledge of the mechanics of decision, and I know that it wasn't just sympathy, or a pragmatic reversal of therapy, but something intimately important for me, that made me shout with all my strength—'Of course I don't believe you!'

"Moulton, his face contorted, fell forward on me so suddenly that I stumbled backwards, sending the tank of newts crashing to the floor. Supporting him with my arms, I hung on to him while he heaved, face downwards. At the same time I felt a tickling, sliding sensation in my own ear, and an inordinate desire to follow it with my finger, but both my hands were busy. It wasn't a minute 'til I'd gotten him onto the couch, where he drooped, a little white about the mouth, but with that chastened, purified look of the physically relieved, although he hadn't actually upchucked.

"Still watching him, I stooped to clear up the debris, but he bounded from the couch with amazing resilience.

" 'I'll do it,' he said.

" 'Feel better?'

"He nodded, clearly abashed, and we gathered up the remains of the tank in a sort of mutual embarrassment. I can't remember that either of us said a word, and neither of us made more than a halfhearted attempt to search for the scattered pests which had apparently sought crannies in the room. At the door we parted, muttering as formal a good-night as was possible between a grown man and a small boy. It wasn't until I reached my own room and sat down that I realized, not only my own extraordinary behavior, but that Moulton, standing, as I suddenly recalled, for the first time quite straight, had sent after me a look of pity and speculation.

"Out of habit, I reached into my breast pocket for my pencil, in order to take notes as fresh as possible. And then I felt it . . . a skittering, sidling motion, almost beneath my hand. I opened my jacket and shook myself, thinking that I'd picked up something in the other room . . . but nothing. I sat quite still, gripping the pencil, and after an interval it came again—an inchoate creeping, a twitter of movement almost *lackadaisical*, as of something inching itself lazily along—but this time on my other side. In a frenzy, I peeled off my clothes, inspected myself wildly, and enumerating to myself a reassuring abracadabra of explanation—skipped heartbeat, intercostal pressure of gas—I sat there naked, waiting. And after a moment, it came again, that wandering, aquatic motion, as if something had flipped itself over just enough to make me aware, and then settled itself, this time under the sternum, with a nudge like that of some inconceivable foetus. I jumped up and shook myself again, and as I did so I caught a glimpse of myself in the mirror in the closet door. My face, my own face, was ajar with fright, and I was standing there, hooked over, as if I were wearing an imaginary shawl."

In the silence after his visitor's voice stopped, the doctor sat there in the painful embarrassment of the listener who has played confessor, and whose expected comment is a responsibility he wishes he had evaded. The breeze from the open window fluttered the papers on the desk. Glancing out at the clean, regular façade of the hospital wing opposite, at whose evenly shaded windows the white shapes of orderlies and nurses flickered in consoling routine, the doctor wished petulantly that he had fended off the man and all his papers in the beginning. What right had the man to arraign *him*? Surprised at his own inner vehemence, he pulled himself together. "How long ago?" he said at last.

"Four months."

"And since?"

"It's never stopped." The visitor now seemed brimming with a tentative excitement, like a colleague discussing a mutually puzzling case. "Everything's been tried. Sedatives do obtain some sleep, but that's all. Purgatives. Even emetics." He laughed slightly, almost with pride.

"Nothing like that works," he continued, shaking his head with the doting fondness of a patient for some symptom which has confounded the best of them. "It's too cagey for that."

With his use of the word "it," the doctor was propelled back into that shapely sense of reality which had gone admittedly askew during the man's recital. To admit the category of "it," to dip even a slightly co-operative finger in another's fantasy, was to risk one's own equilibrium. Better not to become involved in argument with the possessed, lest one's own apertures of belief be found to have been left ajar.

"I am afraid," the doctor said blandly, "that your case is outside my field."

"As a doctor?" said his visitor. "Or as a man?"

"Let's not discuss me, if you please."

The visitor leaned intently across the desk. "Then you admit that to a certain extent, we *have* been—?"

"I admit nothing!" said the doctor, stiffening.

"Well," said the man disparagingly, "of course, that too is a kind of stand. The commonest, I've found." He sighed, pressing one hand against his collarbone. "I suppose you have a prescription too, or a recommendation. Most of them do."

The doctor did not enjoy being judged. "Why don't you hunt up young Hallowell?" he said, with malice.

"Disappeared. Don't you think I tried?" said his vis-à-vis ruefully. Something furtive, hope, perhaps, spread its guileful corruption over his face. "That means you do give a certain credence—"

"Nothing of the sort!"

"Well then," said his interrogator, turning his palms upward.

The doctor leaned forward, measuring his words with exasperation. "Do you mean you *want* me to tell you you're crazy!"

"In my spot," answered his visitor meekly, "which would you prefer?"

Badgered to the point of commitment, the doctor stared

back at his inconvenient Diogenes. Swollen with irrita-
tion, he was only half conscious of an uneasy, vestigial
twitching of his ear muscles, which contracted now as
they sometimes did when he listened to atonal music.

"O.K., O.K. . . !" he shouted suddenly, slapping his
hand down on the desk and thrusting his chin forward.
"Have it your way then! I don't believe you!"

Rigid, the man looked back at him cataleptically,
seeming, for a moment, all eye. Then, his mouth stretching in that medieval grimace, risorial and equivocal,
whose mask appears sometimes on one side of the stage,
sometimes on the other, he fell forward on the desk, with
a long, mewing sigh.

Before the doctor could reach him, he had raised himself on his arms and their foreheads touched. They recoiled, staring downward. Between them on the desk, as
if one of its mahogany shadows had become animate,
something seemed to move—small, seal-colored, and
ambiguous. For a moment it filmed back and forth,
arching in a crude, primordial inquiry; then, homing
straight for the doctor, whose jaw hung down in a rictus
of shock, it disappeared from view.

Sputtering, the doctor beat the air and his own person
wildly with his hands, and staggered upward from his
chair. The breeze blew hypnotically, and the stranger
gazed back at him with such perverse calm that already
he felt an assailing doubt of the lightning, untoward
event. He fumbled back over his sensations of the minute
before, but already piecemeal and chimerical, they eluded
him now, as they might forever.

"It's unbelievable," he said weakly.

His visitor put up a warding hand, shaking it fastidiously. "*Au contraire!*" he replied daintily, as though by
the use of another language he would remove himself
still further from commitment. Reaching forward, he
gathered up his papers into a sheaf, and stood up, stretching himself straight with an all-over bodily yawn of physical ease that was like an affront. He looked down at
the doctor, one hand fingering his wallet. "No," he said

reflectively, "guess not." He tucked the papers away. "Shall we leave it on the basis of—er—professional courtesy?" he inquired delicately.

Choking on the sludge of his rage, the doctor looked back at him, inarticulate.

Moving toward the door, the visitor paused. "After all," he said, "with your connections . . . try to think of it as a temporary inconvenience." Regretfully, happily, he closed the door behind him.

The doctor sat at his desk, humped forward. His hands crept to his chest and crossed. He swallowed, experimentally. He hoped it was rage. He sat there, waiting. He was thinking of the luncheon table.

The Lottery

Shirley Jackson

THE morning of June 27th was clear and sunny, with the fresh warmth of a full-summer day; the flowers were blossoming profusely and the grass was richly green. The people of the village began to gather in the square, between the post office and the bank, around ten o'clock; in some towns there were so many people that the lottery took two days and had to be started on June 26th, but in this village, where there were only about three hundred people, the whole lottery took less than two hours, so it could begin at ten o'clock in the morning and still be through in time to allow the villagers to get home for noon dinner.

The children assembled first, of course. School was recently over for the summer, and the feeling of liberty sat uneasily on most of them; they tended to gather together quietly for a while before they broke into boisterous play, and their talk was still of the classroom and the teacher, of books and reprimands. Bobby Martin had already stuffed his pockets full of stones, and the other boys soon followed his example, selecting the smoothest and roundest stones; Bobby and Harry Jones and Dickie Delacroix —the villagers pronounced this name "Dellacroy"— eventually made a great pile of stones in one corner of the square and guarded it against the raids of the other boys. The girls stood aside, talking among themselves, looking over their shoulders at the boys, and the very small children rolled in the dust or clung to the hands of their older brothers or sisters.

Soon the men began to gather, surveying their own

children, speaking of planting and rain, tractors and taxes. They stood together, away from the pile of stones in the corner, and their jokes were quiet and they smiled rather than laughed. The women, wearing faded house dresses and sweaters, came shortly after their menfolk. They greeted one another and exchanged bits of gossip as they went to join their husbands. Soon the women, standing by their husbands, began to call to their children, and the children came reluctantly, having to be called four or five times. Bobby Martin ducked under his mother's grasping hand and ran, laughing, back to the pile of stones. His father spoke up sharply, and Bobby came quickly and took his place between his father and his oldest brother.

The lottery was conducted—as were the square dances, the teen-age club, the Halloween program—by Mr. Summers, who had time and energy to devote to civic activities. He was a round-faced, jovial man and he ran the coal business, and people were sorry for him, because he had no children and his wife was a scold. When he arrived in the square, carrying the black wooden box, there was a murmur of conversation among the villagers, and he waved and called, "Little late today, folks." The postmaster, Mr. Graves, followed him, carrying a three-legged stool, and the stool was put in the center of the square and Mr. Summers set the black box down on it. The villagers kept their distance, leaving a space between themselves and the stool, and when Mr. Summers said, "Some of you fellows want to give me a hand?" there was a hesitation before two men, Mr. Martin and his oldest son, Baxter, came forward to hold the box steady on the stool while Mr. Summers stirred up the papers inside it.

The original paraphernalia for the lottery had been lost long ago, and the black box now resting on the stool had been put into use even before Old Man Warner, the oldest man in town, was born. Mr. Summers spoke frequently to the villagers about making a new box, but no one liked to upset even as much tradition as was represented by the black box. There was a story that the present box had been made with some pieces of the box that had preceded it, the one that had been constructed when the first people settled down to make a village here. Every year, after the lottery, Mr. Summers began talking again about a new box, but every year the subject was allowed to fade off without anything's being done. The black box grew shabbier each year; by now it was no longer completely black but splintered badly along one side to show the original wood color, and in some places faded or stained.

Mr. Martin and his oldest son, Baxter, held the black box securely on the stool until Mr. Summers had stirred the papers thoroughly with his hand. Because so much of the ritual had been forgotten or discarded, Mr. Summers had been successful in having slips of paper substituted for the chips of wood that had been used for generations. Chips of wood, Mr. Summers had argued, had been all very well when the village was tiny, but now that the population was more than three hundred and likely to keep on growing, it was necessary to use something that would fit more easily into the black box. The night before the lottery, Mr. Summers and Mr. Graves made up the slips of paper and put them in the box, and it was then taken to the safe of Mr. Summers' coal company and locked up until Mr. Summers was ready to take it to the square next morning. The rest of the year, the box was put away, sometimes one place, sometimes another; it had spent one year in Mr. Graves's barn and another year underfoot in the post office, and sometimes it was set on a shelf in the Martin grocery and left there.

There was a great deal of fussing to be done before Mr. Summers declared the lottery open. There were the lists to make up—of heads of families, heads of households in each family, members of each household in each family. There was the proper swearing-in of Mr. Summers by the postmaster, as the official of the lottery; at one time, some people remembered, there had been a recital of some sort, performed by the official of the lottery, a perfunctory, tuneless chant that had been rattled off duly each year; some people believed that the official of the lottery used to stand just so when he said or sang it, others believed that he was supposed to walk among the people, but years and years ago this part of the ritual had been allowed to lapse. There had been, also, a ritual salute, which the official of the lottery had had to use in addressing each person who came up to draw from the box, but this also had changed with time, until now it was felt necessary only for the official to speak to each person approaching. Mr. Summers was very good at all this; in his clean white shirt and blue jeans, with one hand resting carelessly on the black box, he seemed very proper and important as he talked interminably to Mr. Graves and the Martins.

Just as Mr. Summers finally left off talking and turned to the assembled villagers, Mrs. Hutchinson came hurriedly along the path to the square, her sweater thrown over her sholders, and slid into place in the back of the crowd. "Clean forgot what day it was," she said to Mrs. Delacroix, who stood next to her, and they both laughed softly. "Thought my old man was out back stacking wood," Mrs. Hutchinson went on, "and then I looked out the window and the kids was gone, and then I remembered it was the twenty-seventh and came a-running." She dried her hands on her apron, and Mrs. Delacroix said, "You're in time, though. They're still talking away up there."

Mrs. Hutchinson craned her neck to see through the crowd and found her husband and children standing near the front. She tapped Mrs. Delacroix on the arm as a farewell and began to make her way through the crowd. The people separated good-humoredly to let her through; two or three people said, in voices just loud enough to be heard across the crowd, "Here comes your Missus, Hutchinson," and "Bill, she made it after all." Mrs. Hutchinson reached her husband, and Mr. Summers, who had been waiting, said cheerfully, "Thought we were going to have to get on without you, Tessie." Mrs. Hutchinson said, grinning, "Wouldn't have me leave m'dishes in the sink, now, would you, Joe?," and soft laughter ran through the crowd as the people stirred back into position after Mrs. Hutchinson's arrival.

"Well, now," Mr. Summers said soberly, "guess we better get started, get this over with, so's we can go back to work. Anybody ain't here?"

"Dunbar," several people said. "Dunbar, Dunbar."

Mr. Summers consulted his list. "Clyde Dunbar," he said. "That's right. He's broke his leg, hasn't he? Who's drawing for him?"

"Me, I guess," a woman said, and Mr. Summers turned to look at her. "Wife draws for her husband," Mr. Summers said. "Don't you have a grown boy to do it for you, Janey?" Although Mr. Summers and everyone else in the village knew the answer perfectly well, it was the business of the official of the lottery to ask such questions formally. Mr. Summers waited with an expression of polite interest while Mrs. Dunbar answered.

"Horace's not but sixteen yet," Mrs. Dunbar said regretfully. "Guess I gotta fill in for the old man this year."

"Right," Mr. Summers said. He made a note on the list he was holding. Then he asked, "Watson boy drawing this year?"

A tall boy in the crowd raised his hand. "Here," he said. "I'm drawing for m'mother and me." He blinked his eyes nervously and ducked his head as several voices in the crowd said things like "Good fellow, Jack," and "Glad to see your mother's got a man to do it."

"Well," Mr. Summers said, "guess that's everyone. Old Man Warner make it?"

"Here," a voice said, and Mr. Summers nodded.

A sudden hush fell on the crowd as Mr. Summers cleared his throat and looked at the list. "All ready?" he called. "Now, I'll read the names—heads of families first —and the men come up and take a paper out of the box. Keep the paper folded in your hand without looking at it until everyone has had a turn. Everything clear?"

The people had done it so many times that they only half listened to the directions; most of them were quiet, wetting their lips, not looking around. Then Mr. Summers raised one hand high and said, "Adams." A man disengaged himself from the crowd and came forward. "Hi, Steve," Mr. Summers said, and Mr. Adams said, 'Hi, Joe." They grinned at one another humorlessly and nervously. Then Mr. Adams reached into the black box and took out a folded paper. He held it firmly by one corner as he turned and went hastily back to his place in the crowd, where he stood a little apart from his family, not looking down at his hand.

"Allen," Mr. Summers said. "Anderson. . . . Bentham."

"Seems like there's no time at all between lotteries any more," Mrs. Delacroix said to Mrs. Graves in the back row. "Seems like we got through with the last one only last week."

"Time sure goes fast," Mrs. Graves said.

"Clark. . . . Delacroix."

"There goes my old man," Mrs. Delacroix said. She held her breath while her husband went forward.

"Dunbar," Mr. Summers said, and Mrs. Dunbar went steadily to the box while one of the women said, "Go on, Janey," and another said, "There she goes."

"We're next," Mrs. Graves said. She watched while Mr. Graves came around from the side of the box, greeted Mr. Summers gravely, and selected a slip of paper from the box. By now, all through the crowd there were men holding the small folded papers in their large hands, turning them over and over nervously. Mrs. Dunbar and her two sons stood together, Mrs. Dunbar holding the slip of paper.

"Harburt. . . . Hutchinson."

"Get up there, Bill," Mrs. Hutchinson said, and the people near her laughed.

"Jones."

"They do say," Mr. Adams said to Old Man Warner, who stood next to him, "that over in the north village they're talking of giving up the lottery."

Old Man Warner snorted. "Pack of crazy fools," he said. "Listening to the young folks, nothing's good enough for *them*. Next thing you know, they'll be wanting to go back to living in caves, nobody work any more, live *that* way for a while. Used to be a saying about 'Lottery in June, corn be heavy soon.' First thing you know, we'd all be eating stewed chickweed and acorns. There's *always* been a lottery," he added petulantly. "Bad enough to see young Joe Summers up there joking with everybody."

"Some places have already quit lotteries," Mrs. Adams said.

"Nothing but trouble in *that*," Old Man Warner said stoutly. "Pack of young fools."

"Martin." And Bobby Martin watched his father go forward. "Overdyke. . . . Percy."

"I wish they'd hurry," Mrs. Dunbar said to her older son. "I wish they'd hurry."

"They're almost through," her son said.

"You get ready to run tell Dad," Mrs. Dunbar said.

Mr. Summers called his own name and then stepped forward precisely and selected a slip from the box. Then he called, "Warner."

"Seventy-seventh year I been in the lottery," Old Man Warner said as he went through the crowd. "Seventy-seventh time."

"Watson." The tall boy came awkwardly through the crowd. Someone said, "Don't be nervous, Jack," and Mr. Summers said, "Take your time, son."

"Zanini."

After that, there was a long pause, a breathless pause, until Mr. Summers, holding his slip of paper in the air, said, "All right, fellows." For a minute, no one moved, and then all the slips of paper were opened. Suddenly, all the women began to speak at once, saying, "Who is it?," "Who's got it?," "Is is the Dunbars?," "Is it the Watsons?" Then the voices began to say, "It's Hutchinson. It's Bill," "Bill Hutchinson's got it."

"Go tell your father," Mrs. Dunbar said to her older son.

People began to look around to see the Hutchinsons.

Bill Hutchinson was standing quiet, staring down at the paper in his hand. Suddenly, Tessie Hutchinson shouted to Mr. Summers, "You didn't give him time enough to take any paper he wanted. I saw you. It wasn't fair!"

"Be a good sport, Tessie," Mrs. Delacroix called, and Mrs. Graves said, "All of us took the same chance."

"Shut up, Tessie," Bill Hutchinson said.

"Well, everyone," Mr. Summers said, "that was done pretty fast, and now we've got to be hurrying a little more to get done in time." He consulted his next list. "Bill," he said, "you draw for the Hutchinson family. You got any other households in the Hutchinsons?"

"There's Don and Eva," Mrs. Hutchinson yelled. "Make *them* take their chance!"

"Daughters draw with their husbands' families, Tessie," Mr. Summers said gently. "You know that as well as anyone else."

"It wasn't *fair*," Tessie said.

"I guess not, Joe," Bill Hutchinson said regretfully. "My daughter draws with her husband's family, that's only fair. And I've got no other family except the kids."

"Then, as far as drawing for families is concerned, it's you," Mr. Summers said in explanation, "and as far as drawing for households is concerned, that's you, too. Right?"

"Right," Bill Hutchinson said.

"How many kids, Bill?" Mr. Summers asked formally.

"Three," Bill Hutchinson said. "There's Bill, Jr., and Nancy, and little Dave. And Tessie and me."

"All right, then," Mr. Summers said. "Harry, you got their tickets back?"

Mr. Graves nodded and held up the slips of paper. "Put them in the box, then," Mr. Summers directed. "Take Bill's and put it in."

"I think we ought to start over," Mrs. Hutchinson said, as quietly as she could. "I tell you it wasn't *fair*. You didn't give him time enough to choose. *Every*body saw that."

Mr. Graves had selected the five slips and put them

in the box, and he dropped all the papers but those onto the ground, where the breeze caught them and lifted them off.

"Listen, everybody," Mrs. Hutchinson was saying to the people around her.

"Ready, Bill?" Mr. Summers asked, and Bill Hutchinson, with one quick glance around at his wife and children, nodded.

"Remember," Mr. Summers said, "take the slips and keep them folded until each person has taken one. Harry, you help little Dave." Mr. Graves took the hand of the little boy, who came willingly with him up to the box. "Take a paper out of the box, Davy," Mr. Summers said. Davy put his hand into the box and laughed. "Take just *one* paper," Mr. Summers said. "Harry, you hold it for him." Mr. Graves took the child's hand and removed the folded paper from the tight fist and held it while little Dave stood next to him and looked up at him wonderingly.

"Nancy next," Mr. Summers said. Nancy was twelve, and her school friends breathed heavily as she went forward, switching her skirt, and took a slip daintily from the box. "Bill, Jr.," Mr. Summers said, and Billy, his face red and his feet over-large, nearly knocked the box over as he got a paper out. "Tessie," Mr. Summers said. She hesitated for a minute, looking around defiantly, and then set her lips and went up to the box. She snatched a paper out and held it behind her.

"Bill," Mr. Summers said, and Bill Hutchinson reached into the box and felt around, bringing his hand out at last with the slip of paper in it.

The crowd was quiet. A girl whispered, "I hope it's not Nancy," and the sound of the whisper reached the edges of the crowd.

"It's not the way it used to be," Old Man Warner said clearly. "People ain't the way they used to be."

"All right," Mr. Summers said. "Open the papers. Harry, you open little Dave's."

Mr. Graves opened the slip of paper and there was a general sigh through the crowd as he held it up and everyone could see that it was blank. Nancy and Bill, Jr., opened theirs at the same time, and both beamed and laughed, turning around to the crowd and holding their slips of paper above their heads.

"Tessie," Mr. Summers said. There was a pause, and then Mr. Summers looked at Bill Hutchinson, and Bill unfolded his paper and showed it. It was blank.

"It's Tessie," Mr. Summers said, and his voice was hushed. "Show us her paper, Bill."

Bill Hutchinson went over to his wife and forced the slip of paper out of her hand. It had a black spot on it, the black spot Mr. Summers had made the night before with the heavy pencil in the coal-company office. Bill Hutchinson held it up, and there was a stir in the crowd.

"All right, folks," Mr. Summers said. "Let's finish quickly."

Although the villagers had forgotten the ritual and lost the original black box, they still remembered to use stones. The pile of stones the boys had made earlier was ready; there were stones on the ground with the blowing scraps of paper that had come out of the box. Mrs. Delacroix selected a stone so large she had to pick it up with both hands and turned to Mrs. Dunbar. "Come on," she said. "Hurry up."

Mrs. Dunbar had small stones in both hands, and she said, gasping for breath, "I can't run at all. You'll have to go ahead and I'll catch up with you."

The children had stones already, and someone gave little Davy Hutchinson a few pebbles.

Tessie Hutchinson was in the center of a cleared space by now, and she held her hands out desperately as the villagers moved in on her. "It isn't fair," she said. A stone hit her on the side of the head.

Old Man Warner was saying, "Come on, come on, everyone." Steve Adams was in the front of the crowd of villagers, with Mrs. Graves beside him.

"It isn't fair, it isn't right," Mrs. Hutchinson screamed, and then they were upon her.

Pages from Cold Point

Paul Bowles

Our civilization is doomed to a short life: its component parts are too heterogeneous. I personally am content to see everything in the process of decay. The bigger the bombs, the quicker it will be done. Life is visually too hideous for one to make the attempt to preserve it. Let it go. Perhaps some day another form of life will come along. Either way, it is of no consequence. At the same time, I am still a part of life, and I am bound by this to protect myself to whatever extent I am able. And so I am here. Here in the Islands vegetation still has the upper hand, and man has to fight even to make his presence seen at all. It is beautiful here, the trade winds blow all year, and I suspect that bombs are extremely unlikely to be wasted on this unfrequented side of the island, if indeed on any part of it.

I was loath to give up the house after Hope's death. But it was the obvious move to make. My university career always having been an utter farce (since I believe no reason inducing a man to "teach" can possibly be a valid one), I was elated by the idea of resigning, and as soon as her affairs had been settled and the money properly invested, I lost no time in doing so.

I think that week was the first time since childhood that I had managed to recapture the feeling of there being a content in existence. I went from one pleasant house to the next, making my adieux to the English quacks, the Philosophy fakirs, and so on—even to those colleagues with whom I was merely on speaking terms. I watched the envy in their faces when I announced my departure by Pan American on Saturday morning; and the greatest pleasure I felt in all this was in being able to answer, "Nothing," when I was asked, as invariably I was, what I intended to do.

When I was a boy people used to refer to Charles as "Big Brother C.", although he is only a scant year older than I. To me now he is merely "Fat Brother C.", a successful lawyer. His thick, red face and hands, his back-slapping joviality, and his fathomless hypocritical prudery, these are the qualities which make him truly repulsive to me. There is also the fact that he once looked not unlike the way Racky does now. And after all, he still is my big brother, and disapproves openly of everything I do. The loathing I feel for him is so strong that for years I have not been able to swallow a morsel of food or a drop of liquid in his presence without making a prodigious effort. No one knows this but me—certainly not Charles, who would be the last one I should tell about it. He came up on the late train two nights before I left. He got quickly to the point—as soon as he was settled with a highball.

"So you're off for the wilds," he said, sitting forward in his chair like a salesman.

"If you can call it the wilds," I replied. "Certainly it's not wild like Mitichi." (He has a lodge in northern Quebec.) "I consider it really civilized."

He drank and smacked his lips together stiffly, bringing the glass down hard on his knee.

"And Racky. You're taking him along?"

"Of course."

"Out of school. Away. So he'll see nobody but you. You think that's good."

I looked at him. "I do," I said.

"By God, if I could stop you legally, I would!" he cried. jumping up and putting his glass on the mantel. I was trembling inwardly with excitement, but I merely sat and watched him. He went on. "You're not fit to have custody of the kid!" he shouted. He shot a stern glance at me over his spectacles.

"You think not?" I said gently.

Again he looked at me sharply. "D'ye think I've forgotten?"

I was understandably eager to get him out of the house as soon as I could. As I piled and sorted letters and magazines on the desk, I said: "Is that all you came to tell me? I have a good deal to do tomorrow and I must get some sleep. I probably shan't see you at breakfast. Agnes'll see that you eat in time to make the early train."

All he said was: "God! Wake up! Get wise to yourself! You're not fooling anybody, you know."

That kind of talk is typical of Charles. His mind is slow and obtuse; he constantly imagines that everyone he meets is playing some private game of deception with him. He is so utterly incapable of following the functioning of even a moderately evolved intellect that he finds the will to secretiveness and duplicity everywhere.

"I haven't time to listen to that sort of nonsense," I said, preparing to leave the room.

But he shouted, "You don't want to listen! No! Of course not! You just want to do what you want to do. You just want to go on off down there and live as you've a mind to, and to hell with the consequences!" At this point I heard Racky coming downstairs. C. obviously heard nothing, and he raved on. "But just remember, I've got your number all right, and if there's any trouble with the boy I'll know who's to blame."

I hurried across the room and opened the door so he could see that Racky was there in the hallway. That stopped his tirade. It was hard to know whether Racky had heard any of it or not. Although he is not a quiet young person, he is the soul of discretion, and it is almost never possible to know any more about what goes on inside his head than he intends one to know.

I was annoyed that C. should have been bellowing at me in my own house. To be sure, he is the only one from whom I would accept such behavior, but then, no father likes to have his son see him take criticism meekly. Racky simply stood there in his bathrobe, his angelic face quite devoid of expression, saying: "Tell Uncle Charley good night for me, will you? I forgot."

I said I would, and quickly shut the door. When I thought Racky was back upstairs in his room, I bade Charles good night. I have never been able to get out of his presence fast enough. The effect he has on me dates from an early period of our lives, from days I dislike to recall.

Racky is a wonderful boy. After we arrived, when we found it impossible to secure a proper house near any town where he might have the company of English boys and girls his own age, he showed no sign of chagrin, although he must have been disappointed. Instead, as we went out of the renting office into the glare of the street, he grinned and said: "Well, I guess we'll have to get bikes, that's all."

The few available houses near what Charles would have called "civilization" turned out to be so ugly and so impossibly confining in atmosphere that we decided immediately on Cold Point, even though it was across the island and quite isolated on its seaside cliff. It was beyond a doubt one of the most desirable properties on the island, and Racky was as enthusiastic about its splendors as I.

"You'll get tired of being alone out there, just with me," I said to him as we walked back to the hotel.

"Aw, I'll get along all right. When do we look for the bikes?"

At his insistence we bought two the next morning. I was sure I should not make much use of mine, but I reflected that an extra bicycle might be convenient to have around the house. It turned out that the servants all had their own bicycles, without which they would not have been able to get to and from the village of Orange Walk, eight miles down the shore. So for a while I was forced to get astride mine each morning before breakfast and pedal madly along beside Racky for a half hour. We would ride through the cool early air, under the towering silk-cotton trees near the house, and out to the great curve in the shoreline where the waving palms bend landward in the stiff breeze that always blows there.

Then we would make a wide turn and race back to the house, loudly discussing the degrees of our desires for the various items of breakfast we knew were awaiting us there on the terrace. Back home we would eat in the wind, looking out over the Caribbean, and talk about the news in yesterday's local paper, brought to us by Isiah each morning from Orange Walk. Then Racky would disappear for the whole morning on his bicycle, riding furiously along the road in one direction or the other until he had discovered an unfamiliar strip of sand along the shore that he could consider a new beach. At lunch he would describe it in detail to me, along with a recounting of all the physical hazards involved in hiding the bicycle in among the trees, so that natives passing along the road on foot would not spot it, or in climbing down unscalable cliffs that turned out to be much higher than they had appeared at first sight, or in measuring the depth of the water preparatory to diving from the rocks, or in judging the efficacy of the reef in barring sharks and barracuda. There is never any element of braggadoccio in Racky's relating of his exploits—only the joyous excitement he derives from telling how he satisfied his inexhaustible curiosity. And his mind shows its alertness in all directions at once. I do not mean to say that I expect him to be an "intellectual." That is no affair of mine, nor do I have any particular interest in whether he turns out to be a thinking man or not. I know he will always have a certain boldness of manner and a great purity of spirit in judging values. The former will prevent his becoming what I call a "victim": he never will be brutalized by realities. And his unerring sense of balance in ethical considerations will shield him from the paralyzing effects of present-day materialism.

For a boy of sixteen Racky has an extraordinary innocence of vision. I do not say this as a doting father, although God knows I can never even think of the boy without that familiar overwhelming sensation of delight and gratitude for being vouchsafed the privilege of sharing my life with him. What he takes so completely as a matter of course, our daily life here together, is a source of never-ending wonder to me; and I reflect upon it a good part of each day, just sitting here being conscious of my great good fortune in having him all to myself, beyond the reach of prying eyes and malicious tongues. (I suppose I am really thinking of C. when I write that.) And I believe that a part of the charm of sharing Racky's life with him consists precisely in his taking it all so utterly for granted. I have never asked him whether he likes being here—it is so patent that he does, very much. I think if he were to turn to me one day and tell me how happy he is here, that somehow, perhaps, the spell might be broken. Yet if he were to be thoughtless and inconsiderate, or even unkind to me, I feel that I should be able only to love him the more for it.

I have reread that last sentence. What does it mean? And why should I even imagine it could mean anything more than it says?

Still, much as I may try, I can never believe in the gratuitous, isolated fact. What I must mean is that I feel that Racky already has been in some way inconsiderate. But in what way? Surely I cannot resent his bicycle treks; I cannot expect him to want to stay and sit talking with me all day. And I never worry about his being in danger; I know he is more capable than most adults of taking care of himself, and that he is no more likely than any native to come to harm crawling over the cliffs or swimming in the bays. At the same time there is no doubt in my mind that something about our existence annoys me. I must resent some detail in the pattern, whatever that pattern may be. Perhaps it is just his youth, and I am envious of the lithe body, the smooth skin, the animal energy and grace.

For a long time this morning I sat looking out to sea, trying to solve that small puzzle. Two white herons came and perched on a dead stump east of the garden. They stayed a long time there without stirring. I would turn my head away and accustom my eyes to the bright sea-horizon, then I would look suddenly at them to see if they had shifted position, but they would always be in the same attitude. I tried to imagine the black stump without them—a purely vegetable landscape—but it was impossible. All the while I was slowly forcing myself to accept a ridiculous explanation of my annoyance with Racky. It had made itself manifest to me only yesterday, when instead of appearing for lunch, he sent a young colored boy from Orange Walk to say that he would be lunching in the village. I could not help noticing that the boy was riding Racky's bicycle. I had been waiting lunch a good half hour for him, and I had Gloria serve immediately as the boy rode off, back to the village. I was curious to know in what sort of place and with whom Racky could be eating, since Orange Walk, as far as I know, is inhabited exclusively by Negroes, and I was sure Gloria would be able to shed some light on the matter, but I could scarcely ask her. However, as she brought on the dessert, I said: "Who was that boy that brought the message from Mister Racky?"

She shrugged her shoulders. "A young lad of Orange Walk. He's named Wilmot."

When Racky returned at dusk, flushed from his exertion (for he never rides casually), I watched him closely. His behavior struck my already suspicious eye as being one of false heartiness and a rather forced good humor. He went to his room early and read for quite a while before turning off his light. I took a long walk in the almost day-bright moonlight, listening to the songs of the night insects in the trees. And I sat for a while in the dark on the stone railing of the bridge across Black River. (It is really only a brook that rushes down over the rocks from the mountain a few miles inland, to the beach near the house.) In the night it always sounds louder and more important than it does in the daytime. The music of the water over the stones relaxed my nerves, although why I had need of such a thing I find it difficult to understand, unless I was really upset by Racky's not having come home for lunch. But if that were true it would be absurd, and moreover, dangerous—just the sort of thing the parent of an adolescent has to beware of and fight against, unless he is indifferent to the prospect of losing the trust and affection of his offspring permanently. Racky must stay out whenever he likes, with whom he likes, and for as long as he likes, and I must not think twice about it, much less mention it to him, or in any way give the impression of prying. Lack of confidence on the part of a parent is the one unforgivable sin.

Although we still take our morning dip together on arising, it is three weeks since we have been for the early spin. One morning I found that Racky had jumped onto his bicycle in his wet trunks while I was still swimming, and gone by himself, and since then there has been an unspoken agreement between us that such is to be the procedure; he will go alone. Perhaps I held him back; he likes to ride so fast.

Young Peter, the smiling gardener from Saint Ives Cove, is Racky's special friend. It is amusing to see them together among the bushes, crouched over an ant-hill or rushing about trying to catch a lizard, almost of an age the two, yet so disparate—Racky with his tan skin looking almost white in contrast to the glistening black of the other. Today I know I shall be alone for lunch, since it is Peter's day off. On such days they usually go together on their bicycles into Saint Ives Cove, where Peter keeps a small rowboat. They fish along the coast there, but they have never returned with anything so far.

Meanwhile I am here alone, sitting on the rocks in the sun, from time to time climbing down to cool myself in the water, always conscious of the house behind me under the high palms, like a large glass boat filled with orchids and lilies. The servants are clean and quiet, and the work seems to be accomplished almost automatically. The good, black servants are another blessing of the islands; the British, born here in this paradise, have no conception of how fortunate they are. In fact, they do nothing but complain. One must have lived in the United States to appreciate the wonder of this place. Still, even here ideas are changing each day. Soon the people will decide that they want their land to be a part of today's monstrous world, and once that happens, it will be all over.

As soon as you have that desire, you are infected with the deadly virus, and you begin to show the symptoms of the disease. You live in terms of time and money, and you think in terms of society and progress. Then all that is left for you is to kill the other people who think the same way, along with a good many of those who do not, since that is the final manifestation of the malady. Here for the moment at any rate, one has a feeling of staticity—existence ceases to be like those last few seconds in the hourglass when what is left of the sand suddenly begins to rush through to the bottom all at once. For the moment, it seems suspended. And if it seems, it is. Each wave at my feet, each bird-call in the forest at my back, does *not* carry me one step nearer the final disaster. The disaster is certain, but it will suddenly have happened, that is all. Until then, time stays still.

I am upset by a letter in this morning's mail: the Royal Bank of Canada requests that I call in person at its central office to sign the deposit slips and other papers for a sum that was cabled from the bank in Boston. Since the central office is on the other side of the island, fifty miles away, I shall have to spend the night over there and return the following day. There is no point in taking Racky along. The sight of "civilization" might awaken a longing for it in him; one never knows. I am sure it would have in me when I was his age. And if that should once start, he would merely be unhappy, since there is nothing for him but to stay here with me, at least for the next two years, when I hope to renew the lease, or, if things in New York pick up, buy the place. I am sending word by Isiah when he goes home into Orange Walk this evening, to have the McCoigh car call for me at seven-thirty tomorrow morning. It is an enormous old open Packard, and Isiah can save the ride out to work here by piling his bicycle into the back and riding with McCoigh.

The trip across the island was beautiful, and would have been highly enjoyable if my imagination had not played me a strange trick at the very outset. We stopped

in Orange Walk for gasoline, and while that was being
seen to, I got out and went to the corner store for some
cigarettes. Since it was not yet eight o'clock, the store
was still closed, and I hurried up the side street to the
other little shop which I thought might be open. It was,
and I bought my cigarettes. On the way back to the
corner I noticed a large black woman leaning with her
arms on the gate in front of her tiny house, staring into
the street. As I passed by her, she looked straight into my
face and said something with the strange accent of the
island. It was said in what seemed an unfriendly tone,
and ostensibly was directed at me, but I had no notion
what it was. I got back into the car and the driver started
it. The sound of the words had stayed in my head, however, as a bright shape outlined by darkness is likely to
stay in the mind's eye, in such a way that when one shuts
one's eyes one can see the exact contour of the shape. The
car was already roaring up the hill toward the overland
road when I suddenly reheard the very words. And they
were: "Keep your boy at home, mahn." I sat perfectly
rigid for a moment as the open countryside rushed past.
Why should I think she had said that? Immediately I
decided that I was giving an arbitrary sense to a phrase I
could not have understood even if I had been paying
strict attention. And then I wondered why my subcon-
scious should have chosen that sense, since now that I
whispered the words over to myself they failed to connect with any anxiety to which my mind might have
been disposed. Actually I have never given a thought to
Racky's wanderings about Orange Walk. I can find no
such preoccupation no matter how I put the question to
myself. Then, could she really have said those words? All
the way through the mountains I pondered the question,
even though it was obviously a waste of energy. And soon
I could no longer hear the sound of her voice in my memory: I had played the record over too many times, and
worn it out.

Here in the hotel a gala dance is in progress. The abominable orchestra, comprising two saxophones and one
sour violin, is playing directly under my window in the

garden, and the serious-looking couples slide about on the waxed concrete floor of the terrace, in the light of strings of paper lanterns. I suppose it is meant to look Japanese.

At this moment I wonder what Racky is doing there in the house with only Peter and Ernest the watchman to keep him company. I wonder if he is asleep. The house, which I am accustomed to think of as smiling and benevolent in its airiness, could just as well be in the most sinister and remote regions of the globe, now that I am here. Sitting here with the absurd orchestra bleating downstairs, I picture it to myself, and it strikes me as terribly vulnerable in its isolation. In my mind's eye I see the moonlit point with its tall palms waving restlessly in the wind, its dark cliffs licked by the waves below. Suddenly, although I struggle against the sensation, I am inexpressibly glad to be away from the house, helpless there, far on its point of land, in the silence of the night. Then I remember that the night is seldom silent. There is the loud sea at the base of the rocks, the droning of the thousands of insects, the occasional cries of the night birds—all the familiar noises that make sleep so sound. And Racky is there surrounded by them as usual, not even hearing them. But I feel profoundly guilty for having left him, unutterably tender and sad at the thought of him, lying there alone in the house with the two Negroes the only human beings within miles. If I keep thinking of Cold Point I shall be more and more nervous.

I am not going to bed yet. They are all screaming with laughter down there, the idiots; I could never sleep anyway. The bar is still open. Fortunately it is on the street side of the hotel. For once I need a few drinks.

Much later, but I feel no better; I may be a little drunk. The dance is over and it is quiet in the garden, but the room is too hot.

As I was falling asleep last night, all dressed, and with the overhead light shining sordidly in my face, I heard the black woman's voice again, more clearly even than I did in the car yesterday. For some reason this morning there is no doubt in my mind that the words I heard are the words she said. I accept that and go on from there. Suppose she did tell me to keep Racky home. It could only mean that she, or someone else in Orange Walk, has had a childish altercation with him; although I must say it is hard to conceive of Racky's entering into any sort of argument or feud with those people. To set my mind at rest (for I do seem to be taking the whole thing with great seriousness), I am going to stop in the village this afternoon before going home, and try to see the woman. I am extremely curious to know what she could have meant.

I had not been conscious until this evening when I came back to Cold Point how powerful they are, all those physical elements that go to make up its atmosphere: the sea and wind-sounds that isolate the house from the road, the brilliancy of the water, sky and sun, the bright colors and strong odors of the flowers, the feeling of space both outside and within the house. One naturally accepts these things when one is living here. This afternoon when I returned I was conscious of them all over again, of their existence and their strength. All of them together are like a powerful drug; coming back made me feel as though I had been disintoxicated and were returning to the scene of my former indulgences. Now at eleven it is as if I had never been absent an hour. Everything is the same as always, even to the dry palm branch that scrapes against the window screen by my night table. And indeed, it is only thirty-six hours since I was here; but I always expect my absence from a place to bring about irremediable changes.

Strangely enough, now that I think of it, I feel that something *has* changed since I left yesterday morning, and that is the general attitude of the servants—their collective aura, so to speak. I noticed that difference immediately upon arriving back, but was unable to define it. Now I see it clearly. The network of common understanding which slowly spreads itself through a well-run household has been destroyed. Each person is by himself now. No unfriendliness, however, that I can see. They all behave with the utmost courtesy, excepting possibly Peter, who struck me as looking unaccustomedly glum when I encountered him in the kitchen after dinner. I meant to ask Racky if he had noticed it, but I forgot and he went to bed early.

In Orange Walk I made a brief stop on the pretext to McCoigh that I wanted to see the seamstress in the side street. I walked up and back in front of the house where I had seen the woman, but there was no sign of anyone.

As for my absence, Racky seems to have been perfectly content, having spent most of the day swimming off the rocks below the terrace. The insect sounds are at their height now, the breeze is cooler than usual, and I shall take advantage of these favorable conditions to get a good long night's rest.

Today has been one of the most difficult days of my life. I arose early, we had breakfast at the regular time, and Racky went off in the direction of Saint Ives Cove. I lay in the sun on the terrace for a while, listening to the noises of the household's regime. Peter was all over the property, collecting dead leaves and fallen blossoms in a huge basket and carrying them off to the compost heap. He appeared to be in an even fouler humor than last night. When he came near to me at one point on his way to another part of the garden I called to him. He set the basket down and stood looking at me; then he walked across the grass toward me slowly—reluctantly, it seemed to me.

"Peter, is everything all right with you?"

"Yes, sir."

"No trouble at home?"

"Oh, no, sir."

"Good."

"Yes, sir."

He went back to his work. But his face belied his words. Not only did he seem to be in a decidedly unpleasant temper; out here in the sunlight he looked positively ill. However, it was not my concern, if he refused to admit it.

When the heavy heat of the sun reached the unbear-able point for me, I got out of my chair and went down the side of the cliff along the series of steps cut there into the rock. A level platform is below, and a diving board, for the water is deep. At each side, the rocks spread out and the waves break over them, but by the platform the wall of rock is vertical and the water merely hits against it below the springboard. The place is a tiny amphitheatre, quite cut off in sound and sight from the house. There too I like to lie in the sun; when I climb out of the water I often remove my trunks and lie stark naked on the springboard. I regularly make fun of Racky because he is embarrassed to do the same. Occasionally he will do it, but never without being coaxed. I was spread out there without a stitch on, being lulled by the slapping of the water, when an unfamiliar voice very close to me said: "Mister Norton?"

I jumped with nervousness, nearly fell off the spring-board, and sat up, reaching at the same time, but in vain, for my trunks, which were lying on the rock practically at the feet of a middle-aged mulatto gentleman. He was in a white duck suit, and wore a high collar with a black tie, and it seemed to me that he was eyeing me with a certain degree of horror.

My next reaction was one of anger at being trespassed upon in this way. I rose and got the trunks, however, donning them calmly and saying nothing more mean-ingful than: "I didn't hear you come down the steps."

"Shall we go up?" said my caller. As he led the way, I had a definite premonition that he was here on an un-pleasant errand. On the terrace we sat down, and he of-fered me an American cigarette which I did not accept.

"This is a delightful spot," he said, glancing out to sea and then at the end of his cigarette, which was only partially aglow. He puffed at it.

I said, "Yes," waiting for him to go on; presently he did.

"I am from the constabulary of this parish. The police, you see." And seeing my face, "This is a friendly call. But still it must be taken as a warning, Mister Norton.

It is very serious. If anyone else comes to you about this it will mean trouble for you, heavy trouble. That's why I want to see you privately this way and warn you personally. You see."

I could not believe I was hearing his words. At length I said faintly: "But what about?"

"This is not an official call. You must not be upset. I have taken it upon myself to speak to you because I want to save you deep trouble."

"But I *am* upset!" I cried, finding my voice at last. "How can I help being upset, when I don't know what you're talking about?"

He moved his chair close to mine, and spoke in a very low voice.

"I have waited until the young man was away from the house so we could talk in private. You see, it is about him."

Somehow that did not surprise me. I nodded.

"I will tell you very briefly. The people here are simple country folk. They make trouble easily. Right now they are all talking about the young man you have living here with you. He is your son, I hear." His inflection here was sceptical.

"Certainly he's my son."

His expression did not change, but his voice grew indignant. "Whoever he is, that is a bad young man."

"What do you mean?" I cried, but he cut in hotly: "He may be your son; he may not be. I don't care who he is. That is not my affair. But he is bad through and through. We don't have such things going on here, sir. The people in Orange Walk and Saint Ives Cove are very cross now. You don't know what these folk do when they are aroused."

I thought it my turn to interrupt. "Please tell me why you say my son is bad. What has he done?" Perhaps the earnestness in my voice reached him, for his face assumed a gentler aspect. He leaned still closer to me and almost whispered.

"He has no shame. He does what he pleases with all the young boys, and the men too, and gives them a shilling so they won't tell about it. But they talk. Of course they talk. Every man for twenty miles up and down the coast knows about it. And the women too, they know about it." There was a silence.

I had felt myself preparing to get to my feet for the last few seconds because I wanted to go into my room and be alone, to get away from that scandalized stage whisper. I think I mumbled "Good morning" or "Thank you," as I turned away and began walking toward the house. But he was still beside me, still whispering like an eager conspirator into my ear: "Keep him home, Mister Norton. Or send him away to school, if he is your son. But make him stay out of these towns. For his own sake."

I shook hands with him and went to lie on my bed. From there I heard his car door slam, heard him drive off. I was painfully trying to formulate an opening sentence to use in speaking to Racky about this, feeling that the opening sentence would define my stand. The attempt was merely a sort of therapeutic action, to avoid thinking about the thing itself. Every attitude seemed impossible. There was no way to broach the subject. I suddenly realized that I should never be able to speak to him directly about it. With the advent of this news he had become another person—an adult, mysterious and formidable. To be sure, it did occur to me that the mulatto's story might not be true, but automatically I rejected the doubt. It was as if I wanted to believe it, almost as if I had already known it, and he had merely confirmed it.

Racky returned at midday, panting and grinning. The inevitable comb appeared and was used on the sweaty, unruly locks. Sitting down to lunch, he exclaimed: "Gosh! Did I find a swell beach this morning! But what a job to get to it!" I tried to look unconcerned as I met his gaze; it was as if our positions had been reversed, and I were hoping to stem his rebuke. He prattled on about thorns and vines and his machete. Throughout the meal I kept telling myself: "Now is the moment. You must say something." But all I said was: "More salad? Or do you want dessert now?" So the lunch passed and nothing happened. After I had finished my coffee I went into my bedroom and looked at myself in the large mirror. I saw my eyes trying to give their reflected brothers a little courage. As I stood there I heard a commotion in the other wing of the house: voices, bumpings, the sound of a scuffle. Above the noise came Gloria's sharp voice, imperious and excited: "No, mahn! Don't strike him!" And louder: "Peter, mahn, no!"

I went quickly toward the kitchen, where the trouble seemed to be, but on the way I was run into by Racky, who staggered into the hallway with his hands in front of his face.

"What is it, Racky?" I cried.

He pushed past me into the living room without moving his hands away from his face; I turned and followed him. From there he went into his own room, leaving the door open behind him. I heard him in his bathroom running the water. I was undecided what to do. Suddenly Peter appeared in the hall doorway, his hat in his hand. When he raised his head, I was surprised to see that his cheek was bleeding. In his eyes was a strange, confused expression of transient fear and deep hostility. He looked down again.

"May I please talk with you, sir?"

"What was all the racket? What's been happening?"

"May I talk with you outside, sir?" He said it doggedly, still not looking up.

In view of the circumstances, I humored him. We walked slowly up the cinder road to the main highway, across the bridge, and through the forest while he told me his story. I said nothing.

At the end he said: "I never wanted to, sir, even the first time, but after the first time I was afraid, and Mister Racky was after me every day."

I stood still, and finally said: "If you had only told me this the first time it happened, it would have been much better for everyone."

He turned his hat in his hands, studying it intently. "Yes, sir. But I didn't know what everyone was saying about him in Orange Walk until today. You know I al-

ways go to the beach at Saint Ives Cove with Mister
Racky on my free days. If I had known what they were
all saying I wouldn't have been afraid, sir. And I wanted
to keep on working here. I needed the money." Then
he repeated what he had already said three times. "Mister Racky said you'd see about it that I was put in the
jail. I'm a year older than Mister Racky, sir."

"I know, I know," I said impatiently; and deciding
that severity was what Peter expected of me at this point
I added: "You had better get your things together and
go home. You can't work here any longer, you know."

The hostility in his face assumed terrifying propor-
tions as he said: "If you killed me I would not work any
more at Cold Point, sir."

I turned and walked briskly back to the house, leaving
him standing there in the road. It seems he returned at
dusk, a little while ago, and got his belongings.

In his room Racky was reading. He had stuck some
adhesive tape on his chin and over his cheekbone.

"I've dismissed Peter," I announced. "He hit you,
didn't he?"

He glanced up. His left eye was swollen, but not yet
black.

"He sure did. But I landed him one, too. And I guess
I deserved it anyway."

I rested against the table. "Why?" I asked nonchalantly.

"Oh, I had something on him from a long time back
that he was afraid I'd tell you."

"And just now you threatened to tell me?"

"Oh, no! He said he was going to quit the job here,
and I kidded him about being yellow."

"Why did he want to quit? I thought he liked the
job."

"Well, he did, I guess, but he didn't like me." Racky's
candid gaze betrayed a shade of pique. I still leaned
against the table.

I persisted. "But I thought you two got on fine together. You seemed to."

"Nah. He was just scared of losing his job. I had something on him. He was a good guy, though; I liked him all right." He paused. "Has he gone yet?" A strange quaver crept into his voice as he said the last words, and I understood that for the first time Racky's heretofore impeccable histrionics were not quite equal to the occasion. He was very much upset at losing Peter.

"Yes, he's gone," I said shortly. "He's not coming back, either." And as Racky, hearing the unaccustomed inflection in my voice, looked up at me suddenly with faint astonishment in his young eyes, I realized that this was the moment to press on, to say: "What did you have on him?" But as if he had arrived at the same spot in my mind a fraction of a second earlier, he proceeded to snatch away my advantage by jumping up, bursting into loud song, and pulling off all his clothes simultaneously. As he stood before me naked, singing at the top of his lungs, and stepped into his swimming trunks, I was conscious that again I should be incapable of saying to him what I must say.

He was in and out of the house all afternoon: some of the time he read in his room, and most of the time he was down on the diving board. It is strange behavior for him; if I could only know what is in his mind. As evening approached, my problem took on a purely obsessive character. I walked to and fro in my room, always pausing at one end to look out the window over the sea, and at the other end to glance at my face in the mirror. As if that could help me! Then I took a drink. And another. I thought I might be able to do it at dinner, when I felt fortified by the whisky. But no. Soon he will have gone to bed. It is not that I expect to confront him with any accusations. That I know I never can do. But I must find a way to keep him from his wanderings, and I must offer a reason to give him, so that he will never suspect that I know.

We fear for the future of our offspring. It is ludicrous, but only a little more palpably so than anything else in life. A length of time has passed; days which I am content to have known, even if now they are over. I think

that this period was what I had always been waiting for
life to offer, the recompense I had unconsciously but
firmly expected, in return for having been held so closely
in the grip of existence all these years.

That evening seems long ago only because I have recalled its details so many times that they have taken on
the color of legend. Actually my problem already had
been solved for me then, but I did not know it. Because
I could not perceive the pattern, I foolishly imagined
that I must cudgel my brains to find the right words with
which to approach Racky. But it was he who came to
me. That same evening, as I was about to go out for a
solitary stroll which I thought might help me hit upon a
formula, he appeared at my door.

"Going for a walk?" he asked, seeing the stick in my
hand.

The prospect of making an exit immediately after
speaking with him made things seem simpler. "Yes," I
said, "but I'd like to have a word with you first."

"Sure. What?" I did not look at him because I did not
want to see the watchful light I was sure was playing in
his eyes at this moment. As I spoke I tapped with my
stick along the designs made by the tiles in the floor.
"Racky, would you like to go back to school?"

"Are you kidding? You know I hate school."

I glanced up at him. "No, I'm not kidding. Don't look
so horrified. You'd probably enjoy being with a bunch of
fellows your own age." (That was not one of the arguments I had meant to use.)

"I might like to be with guys my own age, but I don't
want to have to be in school to do it. I've had school
enough."

I went to the door and said lamely: "I thought I'd get
your reactions."

He laughed. "No, thanks."

"That doesn't mean you're not going," I said over my
shoulder as I went out.

On my walk I pounded the highway's asphalt with
my stick, stood on the bridge having dramatic visions
which involved such eventualities as our moving back to

the States, Racky's having a bad spill on his bicycle and being paralyzed for some months, and even the possibility of my letting events take their course, which would doubtless mean my having to visit him now and then in the governmental prison with gifts of food, if it meant nothing more tragic and violent. "But none of these things will happen," I said to myself, and I knew I was wasting precious time; he must not return to Orange Walk tomorrow.

I went back toward the point at a snail's pace. There was no moon and very little breeze. As I approached the house, trying to tread lightly on the cinders so as not to awaken the watchful Ernest and have to explain to him that it was only I, I saw that there were no lights in Racky's room. The house was dark save for the dim lamp on my night table. Instead of going in, I skirted the entire building, colliding with bushes and getting my face sticky with spider webs, and went to sit a while on the terrace where there seemed to be a breath of air. The sound of the sea was far out on the reef, where the breakers sighed. Here below, there were only slight watery chugs and gurgles now and then. It was unusually low tide. I smoked three cigarettes mechanically, having ceased even to think, and then, my mouth tasting bitter from the smoke, I went inside.

My room was airless. I flung my clothes onto a chair and looked at the night table to see if the carafe of water was there. Then my mouth opened. The top sheet of my bed had been stripped back to the foot. There on the far side of the bed, dark against the whiteness of the lower sheet, lay Racky asleep on his side, and naked.

I stood looking at him for a long time, probably holding my breath, for I remember feeling a little dizzy at one point. I was whispering to myself, as my eyes followed the curve of his arm, shoulder, back, thigh, leg: "A child. A child." Destiny, when one perceives it clearly from very near, has no qualities at all. The recognition of it and the consciousness of the vision's clarity leave no room on the mind's horizon. Finally I turned off the light and softly lay down. The night was absolutely black.

He lay perfectly quiet until dawn. I shall never know whether or not he was really asleep all that time. Of course he couldn't have been, and yet he lay so still. Warm and firm, but still as death. The darkness and silence were heavy around us. As the birds began to sing, I sank into a soft, enveloping slumber; when I awoke in the sunlight later, he was gone.

I found him down by the water, cavorting alone on the springboard; for the first time he had discarded his trunks without my suggesting it. All day we stayed together around the terrace and on the rocks, talking, swimming, reading, and just lying flat in the hot sun. Nor did he return to his room when night came. Instead after the servants were asleep, we brought three bottles of champagne in and set the pail on the night table.

Thus it came about that I was able to touch on the delicate subject that still preoccupied me, and profiting by the new understanding between us, I made my request in the easiest, most natural fashion.

"Racky, would you do me a tremendous favor if I asked you?"

He lay on his back, his hands beneath his head. It seemed to me his regard was circumspect, wanting in candor.

"I guess so," he said. "What is it?"

"Will you stay around the house for a few days—a week, say? Just to please me? We can take some rides together, as far as you like. Would you do that for me?"

"Sure thing," he said, smiling.

I was temporizing, but I was desperate.

Perhaps a week later—(it is only when one is not fully happy that one is meticulous about time, so that it may have been more or less)—we were having breakfast. Isiah stood by, in the shade, waiting to pour us more coffee.

"I noticed you had a letter from Uncle Charley the other day," said Racky. "Don't you think we ought to invite him down?"

My heart began to beat with great force.

"Here? He'd hate it here," I said casually. "Besides,

there's no room. Where would he sleep?" Even as I heard myself saying the words, I knew that they were the wrong ones, that I was not really participating in the conversation. Again I felt the fascination of complete helplessness that comes when one is suddenly a conscious onlooker at the shaping of one's fate.

"In my room," said Racky. "It's empty."

I could see more of the pattern at that moment than I had ever suspected existed. "Nonsense," I said. "This is not the sort of place for Uncle Charley."

Racky appeared to be hitting on an excellent idea. "Maybe if I wrote and invited him," he suggested, motioning to Isiah for more coffee.

"Nonsense," I said again, watching still more of the pattern reveal itself, like a photographic print becoming constantly clearer in a tray of developing solution.

Isiah filled Racky's cup and returned to the shade. Racky drank slowly, pretending to be savoring the coffee.

"Well, it won't do any harm to try. He'd appreciate the invitation," he said speculatively.

For some reason, at this juncture I knew what to say, and as I said it, I knew what I was going to do.

"I thought we might fly over to Havana for a few days next week."

He looked guardedly interested, and then he broke into a wide grin. "Swell!" he cried. "Why wait till next week?"

The next morning the servants called "Good-bye" to us as we drove up the cinder road in the McCoigh car. We took off from the airport at six that evening. Racky was in high spirits; he kept the stewardess engaged in conversation all the way to Camagüey.

He was delighted also with Havana. Sitting in the bar at the Nacional, we continued to discuss the possibility of having C. pay us a visit at the island. It was not without difficulty that I eventually managed to persuade Racky that writing him would be inadvisable.

We decided to look for an apartment right there in Vedado for Racky. He did not seem to want to come back here to Cold Point. We also decided that living in Havana he would need a larger income than I. I am already having the greater part of Hope's estate transferred to his name in the form of a trust fund which I shall administer until he is of age. It was his mother's money, after all.

We bought a new convertible, and he drove me out to Rancho Boyeros in it when I took my plane. A Cuban named Claudio with very white teeth, whom Racky had met in the pool that morning, sat between us.

We were waiting in front of the landing field. An official finally unhooked the chain to let the passengers through. "If you get fed up, come to Havana," said Racky, pinching my arm.

The two of them stood together behind the rope, waving to me, their shirts flapping in the wind as the plane started to move.

The wind blows by my head; between each wave there are thousands of tiny licking and chopping sounds as the water hurries out of the crevices and holes; and a part-floating, part-submerged feeling of being in the water haunts my mind even as the hot sun burns my face. I sit here and I read, and I wait for the pleasant feeling of repletion that follows a good meal, to turn slowly, as the hours pass along, into the even more delightful, slightly stirring sensation deep within, which accompanies the awakening of the appetite.

I am perfectly happy here in reality, because I still believe that nothing very drastic is likely to befall this part of the island in the near future.

The Heart of the Artichoke

Herbert Gold

For Ed and Eileen Pols

My father, his horny hands black with sulphur, lit a cigar with a brief, modest, but spectacular one-handed gesture, his thumbnail crr-racking across the blue-headed kitchen match; when he described his first job in America, selling water to the men building the sky-scrapers, teetering across the girders for fifteen cents a pail, green flecks fumed and sailed in his yellowish Tartar eyes; he peeled an artichoke with both hands simultaneously, the leaves flying toward his mouth, crossing at the napkin politely tucked at the master juggler's collar, until with a groan that was the trumpet of all satisfaction he attained the heart; he—but he was a man of capabilities, such feats apart.

As my mother said of him before they married, "He's well-off. Lots of personality." Older than the other women of her family, she used the word *well-off* in a primitive sense, to signify a general relationship with the world, not subtracting from the term all but its usual financial refrain: "Well-off very, he's a Buick. . . ." But she took the word from Aunt Sarah and Aunt Ethel; it's important that the vocabulary derives from economic security to be extended outward only by an exceptional act of vitality. We, my brothers and I, could never eat enough for her. "Don't aggravate me. Eat. Eat," she would say.

"We already ate," I pointed out.

"But look at your father!"

He was eating. He ate with silent respect for food, a great deal, and not out of gluttony but with appreciation for his own labor in it. He knew the cost. In each spoonful of soup carried with music to his mouth I heard the winds whistling through the branches of the knaedloch trees; I saw the farmers' trucks, laden with chopped liver, musing in his crocodile eyes. "Eat," he pronounced at intervals, assuaging his love for us, "eat, eat."

We ate with a hunger in our bellies or in a filial loyalty while his was in his heart. Wearing a sheepskin coat which came as a gift from Mother and Pitkin's with the no-overhead, a silvery-pronged crate-hammer arming his back pocket, he climbed into the cab of his truck before dawn on market days, his wife's lips still parted against their single pillow while he checked off a list measured in gross over a breakfast of liver-and-onions with the other fruitmen in Solly's Market Tearoom. Perhaps at the earlier moment of supper, while we heedlessly digested, carloads of artichokes were coming in at the Food Terminal for the Thursday morning auction. He would get the best for Jack's Food & Vegetable: *The Best is the Best Buy.*

"Always," my mother piously breathed after him. She was proud of his slogan. "He made it up himself one day, I remember it, he was by the cooler sorting asparagus. Lots of personality, loads," she informed Aunt Ethel and Aunt Sarah. "Eat," she said to me. "The nice ovenbaked potato."

I once asked the address of the poor hungry man in China who would be glad to finish my potato. "I'll send it to him with Mr. Kennedy the mailman," I suggested.

"I need your backtalk like I need my own brother Morton's agar-agar oil for his constipation, Henry Ford should take him. A whole tablespoon," she said. "I need it." Repenting of my sarcasm, I never believed in the poor hungry man, although I had recently become convinced of China at least in Geography.

My father had the knowledge of things—how to hoist an orange crate in a movement like a dance, how to tell an honest farmer from one who will hide his bad Pascal or Iceberg under bravado and a show of good ones, whom to trust in the fleet meetings of money at a fruit auction; this is already a great deal. Only once was he famously tricked, and by Uncle Morton, a man who installed automatic sprinkling pipes in his lawn ("For show! for the neighbors!" my mother communicated, outraged) but spent his Sundays tightening the faucets and complaining that his daughters filled the bathtub too full. (How clean can you get?)

Well, this brother-in-law, exalted by cupidity in one federally sponsored moment, suggested a partnership in the property in order to eliminate my father's competition at an auction: Should brothers, or almost-brothers, bid each other up like cats and dogs? No, the answer.

Afterward, the deal secured, my father approached, tendering a hand-rolled cigar fraternally-in-law and saying, "Nu Mort, now about the partnership I think well we should let Henry there in the Republic Building, not that Hank from 105th Street, Henry a reliable man Hazelton Hotels uses him, draw up the papers—"

"Partners! hah!" Villainous Uncle Morton, performing for some secret inner croak of applause, permitted himself laughter at such innocence. "I'm partners me only with my wife"—and they haven't spoken since, nor have his daughters and I, cousins all.

But this was real estate, not food, which was the true sphere of my father's power; besides, such an error brings scope and savor to a legend of paternal infallibility. He could say, or let my mother say while above the broad cheekbones his eyes glittered like two long plump lima beans on sidewalk display in the sun: "The only time Jake got it but good, it was that time with the Woodward property, his own brother-in-law my brother, they run a house in the Heights and two cars—they need it?—a Buick sure and a Chevie for Yetta and the kids, may his breath turn sour in his old age—"

And his daughters' too. Amen.

As my mother talked my father measured us from under a vast biblical forehead which had sojourned in Kamenetz-Podolsk; it was a forehead that barely escaped the scars of reprisal for a tradesman's life given to a man who needed labor in the open air. He wrestled out this frozen compression, these knotty ravages, at the cost of an over-quickening in the work of the store, wielding cases with a plunging violence and mounting trucks like a burly fruit-store tomcat. Over-happiness too is a threat, Zarathustra said. The yellow flecks of his long narrow eyes fumed in contemplation. His sons were strange animals, born in America.

Question-shaped, my belly in advance of my thoughts, I had unnoticed by all but myself become skinny, pimply, shrewd, and poetic. I trained myself to wake at dawn, not for work like my father or to drink formula like my youngest brother, but because of the possibility that Pattie Donahue might feel my presence and stir in response to it; I believed in telepathy, tuning in on no messages because no one sent me any. I searched her face during Miss Baxter's Reading and The Library How To Use It for a sign of complicity (received no answer); I never spoke to her, for reasons of shyness and reasons of magic. She had aquarium eyes, profoundly green, profoundly empty, and a mouth like a two-cent Bull's Eye candy, and pale transparent fingers busy as fins. She powdered her nose in public, no longer picking it; she touched her ears to make sure of their presence on the beach of her head; patiently she plucked the angora from her mittens off the front of her cardigan, with this gesture of pale-boned fingers exploring herself and me. Together only abstractly, we were linked by both imagining atrocious ways to wish her well.

I let her swim again in my memory. She considered the future by judging it with the deliberate active forgetfulness of a fish floating asleep under ice: power through patience. Pattie Donahue wanted more than love, more than strength; she wanted mastery in denial, divinity in refusal of her own blood. Up the ladder to godhood or down to fishliness? That was her one risk in life. Seaweed is good for you! Lots of iodine! She had a repertory of head-tuckings, wiggles, peeps, curtseys, suckings, winks, herself charmed by herself; she was crippled for eternity, condemned to increase by parthenogenesis. She could not laugh with her body because her body could never move to another's, sway as it might under the seas of her ambition. Bemused, pious, she granted herself an adoring hand, fingers straddling to squeeze her sweater at the root of milk and psychology. Recall that princess who could undress before a slave because she did not regard him as a human being? We are all sometimes slaves.

Slavishly I kneeled for her chamois penwiper where it fell behind her desk in Music and Singing.

"Oh thank you," she said.

"Never mind, never mind"—me melting like March ice in a Spring pool of timidity and chagrin.

"Oh don't stop me, Daniel Berman. Thank you indeed. My mother says I need practice how to be gracious. Please let me do thank you. Oh thank you, Daniel Berman. . . ."

This too is a sort of excess!—and I let her take me under the green grasp of her greedy eyes. The fishy princess pouted, ducked, abstractly reached; I worshipped this body shivering and glistening under bracelets like scale. I saw her as age. Age during that time signifies secret power, secret passion, and the death which follows age is known only as the death which follows love. Girls, born queens, are older than boys, ten-thousand-eyed drones, living for love, empty-headed, precariously housebroken. "Oh thank you really," said Princess Pattie Donahue, her royal sardine, queen of the hive.

She was gracious on me.

One day, the talk of the Horace Greeley junior high playground, a pride for events beyond me took her; she wore a shiny black brassiere which hung in lank splendor beneath the faintly distended yarn of her sweater and the morning's accretion of pink angora. She plucked, she pinched; in my poems I never found a rhyme for Donahue. Desire for a girl with nipples like tapioca spots! She went out, it was alleged, with high school seniors.

It was at this era of sudden sweat and pubic rancor that the issue of working in the store afternoons or at least Saturdays became prominent. "To help out," my father said.

"To learn the value of a dollar," my mother said.

"To know what's what in life," my father said.

"To learn the value of a dollar," my mother said.

"To find out it's like something to be a man," my father said.

"To learn the value of a dollar," my mother said.

"To see how people—"

"To learn the value—"

"To help—"

"To learn—"

There always remained another word to propose on the subject. "I have homework to do?" I asked, making this a question because the whole world knew I did no homework.

"Your cousin Bernie works in his father's store," my mother said. "He's learning the value."

"Your cousin Irwin works in his father's store," my father said. "Very mature kit, grown-up. Knows what's what."

No fonder of my cousins, I began to work in the store. At first there were compensations besides learning the value and knowing what's what; for example, I quickly suspected the potentialities of stacking Jello. Its six delicious box colors made possible the development of a penchant toward baroque in counter displays. I gave over to fantasy in exercises of pure structure; I brought art to Dried Desserts (end of first aisle), evolving from a gothic striving and simplicity to a rococo exuberance, raspberry mounting lemon in commercial embrace. The Jello man beamed and said I had talent. He promised me an autographed photograph of Jack Benny from his sample case, the signature printed as good as original, the *same identical thing*. I stood off, narrow-eyed, architectural, three loose boxes in each hand. While orange buttresses flew and lime vaulted over naves of cherry, my father grew impatient. "Is that all you got on your mind, the playboy?" It was not all, but he was right: there is a limit to what one can do with Jello. And what finally happened to my dream of a celestial engineering? Bananas were sliced into it.

I knew that my friends were playing touch football in the street or perhaps, if it were late afternoon, amorously lobbing rocks onto Pattie Donahue's front porch. Pity the man with an unemployed throwing-arm! Aproned and earth-bound despite my Buster Brown aviator shoes, I stood in exile among the creak of shopping baskets and a cash-register clang, such matters unmusical where a rumor of roller skates on a girl's sidewalk pledges passion eternal and a well-placed rock portends an invitation to Rosalie Fallon's second annual traditional Hallowe'en party; these are suburban verities which held even in the prehistory before Mayor Cassidy's first reign, where I began my studies of how to pee in an enameled pot. A marksman now, I turned sullen despite my skill, sour as a strawberry plucked too early; my father knew their need to ripen wild in the sun, unfingered by ambitious farm-wives. I was a bad crop, green through, lazy for spite.

"Stop slouching," my mother said. "Stand up like a mench. Bernie *likes* the store. He stays and works even when Uncle Abe says go home, here's a quarter."

I learned contempt for my cousins, the submissive ones, who worked so that they could spend dimes like grownups instead of nickels in the Chippewa Lake slot machines. No amount of labor could harden their gluey hands. Irwin had flat feet, a mustache at fourteen because his mother did not tell him to shave, the habit of standing too close when he talked, and, as luck would have it, a talent for projecting his bad breath with such accuracy that any customer's sales resistance must have died in the first whiff. Later he learned to brush his tongue, shave his armpits, sprinkle himself with Johnson's Baby Powder, and rinse his mouth with spearmint mouthwash. Anything for a client. He gave up his soul, a pulpy one at that, which resided in the crevices of his teeth.

Bernie, Narcissus Gaynesbargh the Go-getter, developed an artist's pure love for illness, hospitals, and operations. He saved up enough—"All by his lonesome," bragged Aunt Sarah—for an operation which joined his ears more cunningly to his head. "Clark Gable can let himself go, he's a big man already, but not my Bernie," his mother proudly recounted. "Today he looks a million—stand frontways Bernie! And how tall is your Daniel?"

Bernie had enough left over in his account to have his piles removed during the after-Christmas slow spell. *Carpe Diem:* he obeyed our junior high motto, constantly improving himself, a medically made man, an expert on vitamin pills, eye exercises, and local anaesthesia. He was also judicially made; let us not omit the subtle alterations in the orthography of his name. Imagine the legal nightmare in which a Ginsberg-into-Gaynesbargh signifies more rebirth than immolation! The suicide was a complete success. Neither his ears nor his ancestors stuck out, although the stitching showed.

"*They* will marry nice rich girls from New York City, you'll see," my mother threatened me. Later both took Marital Engineering courses, one at Miami University and the other at Cornell, and it paid, because Bernie married a nice rich shoe business from Hartford and Irwin married a wholesale Divan & Studio Couch, a steady thing.

"But," as my mother said, "you can't measure happiness in dollars and cents. There are things more important especially with taxes these days. A sweet little wife, a nice little family . . ."

"Have a piece Sanders." Aunt Sarah consoled her with the Continental assortment. "I got it by Sanders Chocolates when I went downtown to look for my new Person Lamb yesterday. Purse-and-lamb, I mean. Who knows maybe I'll settle for a Shirt Beaver, the season's almost over."

Not even Aunt Sarah can distract my mother when philosophy comes over her. "You could marry in a low element, maybe he wouldn't really be rich only pretending, living high, that kind of a click—"

"My Irwin hm hm, you should know he sent me a this year's pillow direct from the factory to me," Aunt Sarah might remark. "He don't have to put birds in his vest, my Irwin."

"Don't tell me, I know," Mother groaned. "Some people are real type bigshots, some people have to make look big to themselves with escalator heels and Scotch shoelaces, who ever heard?"

"My Irwin—"

"What, you crazy? He's a nice steady boy your Irwin, clean-cut, a neat dresser. I'm mentioning it so happens one of those fast clicks, oh, oh."

"Ho," breathed Aunt Sarah.

They communed in silence over the family shame. They clopped the bitter memory from their outraged palates. They drew the lesson from what befell poor Cousin Bessie, who returned from a vacation—she had a nice job with the government, too—with pierced ears and coral earrings, a pair of chartreuse silk slacks, and a new man to replace the one who broke his head. "My new husband," she announced, indicating a plump individual with oily sunburned pouches under his eyes, Novelty-style shoelaces, and a sky-blue Kalifornia Kravate with a silver-lightning pin, the tie tucked into a Hickock Kowboy-type belt: "Roland, he's in the wholesale business in Los Angeles."

"Wholesale what?" Mother had asked, suspicious already.

"Just wholesale," Cousin Bessie said equably. Roland smiled to show the gap in his teeth bridged by invisible platinum. His little woman spoke for him: "He has the biggest outlet in Los Angeles."

"Ellay," he corrected her.

Later, after Uncle Moish from Indian River Drive discovered that this Roland was a bad-type thief off the legit, not a dealer in factory-to-you eliminate-the-middleman low-costs, they helped Bessie out again. She promised to be more careful next season. She was pushing thirty-five, although the family loyally counted only the last twenty-seven of them; she had combed the summertime mountains and the winter-time seaside since she bur-

ied Lester. Mother took three deep breaths and announced, addressing her in the ceremonial third person
while Bessie wept wholesale tears: "Next time she should
vacate a week ten days in Atlantic City on the Atlantic,
the sun, the salt-water taffy, she should meet a nice
steady New York type fella, she still got her health why
not? Knock on wood. Just he shouldn't have the biggest outlet in Ellay."

Still my cousins were generally nice, steady, and successful even at that early time. I was recalcitrant, a failure
in affairs.

"The whole world knows. Aunt Ethel and Aunt Sarah
know, it should happen to me I try to be a good mama to
you. The whole city knows."

Aunt Sarah encouraged my mother in her own way.
" 'Mama,' my Bernie tell me,"—and her eyes moistened
over such devotion—" 'Mama,' he says, 'you look like
sugar in the urine again. What did I tell you about those
two-dollar Sanders assortments?'. . . . So thoughtful,"
she concluded, folding her arms across a high stalwart
bone of her *garment*, leaning back, and waiting for my
mother to tell something good about me. I couldn't even
read an oral thermometer. After a while she sighed with
pity, yawned for contentment, and added soothingly,
"Your Danny working nice in the store these days
maybe? Just tell him about my Bernie, he'll learn, you got
to encourage."

"I look in the looking glass I ask myself why, I got no
answer. A son of mine, why? A thirteen-years-old lump,"
she encouraged.

It wasn't laziness. That's a maternal answer. I would
have worked in other ways, and did; if I could have remained at some comprehensible task, delivering orders
perhaps, building shelves, loading the truck, or manipulating the stock in the basement, I might have attained a
fulfillment equal in its way to Cousin Bernie's avarice
for operations. The constant pouring of commands from a
triumphant father shivered and shattered my sense for
work; he wanted me by his side, proud of an eldest son,

any eldest son. For good reasons of his own—he had been poor, he wanted me to see what he had done for himself and for us all—he urged me to learn the pleasure of a direct delicious manipulation of money, its worn old touch of cloth, its warmth of hands and pockets, its smell of sex and work, its color of economy or death in our world, signed in those days by Andrew W. Mellon. "Here! it says right here. Read it yourself. That's the secretary of the treasurer of the U.S.A., his own auto-graph."

"Oh for God's sake. Jake, you can notice such things?" —my mother discovering new depths, she a modest economist, my father not.

"Notice notice," he admitted virtuously. Money was poetry, a symbol of life and power on one side, economy and death for him with the White House on the other, but only a symbol—how could I understand such meta-physics, ungraduate-schooled in that epoch of despair with girls and ambitions of purity? My agile Tartar-eyed father made the distinction by enjoying both the earning and the spending, finding his truth higgledy-piggledy in an exploit of strapping a load-and-a-healthy-half on his 1928 White Motors truck or in giving himself to a snack of artichoke with Kraft's dressing, the heart his end but the money-colored leaves loved for what they were.

He wanted me to clerk, to *wait on trade*, then, to be an aproned catalyst toward the final term. How could I take money from Mrs. Donahue, whose daughter no one but Tom Moss knew I loved, while Pattie herself teased her mouth with an end of lipstick without glancing at me in my feminizing wraparound? My languishing yip should have betrayed me: "That'll be just three sixty-five, please," recited as I had been taught. It did not; no one saw me. The money joined money in the new Serv-a-slip cash register. *O love me, Pattie! look!*—and I feared that she would. I gave the cash to Hannah, the cashier, my father's deputy while he bargained with the Wheaties jobber for bonus Eversharps and an electric fan-flame wood-glow fireplace.

"Okay, Little Jack, you're picking up now. I'll tell your pa. Just keep the hands out of the pockets when you're making a sale. Say thank you to the customer." Hannah had a tongue cracked and ridged, mounds at the meaty sides and fissures among the yellowish scale, betrothed to dyspepsia. These wounds came of a continual talking confused with a continual eating. No one knew a remedy. She suffered unsilently, chewing Baseball Gum. "I said take hands out of pockets that's a boy. I said say thank you to the nice customer."

"Thank you, Mrs. Donahue," I mumbled miserably.

I carried Mrs. Donahue's order to her Hudson. Pattie moved ahead, her rump twitching like a snapdragon delicately pinched. I fled as she fumbled with her purse for a tip. The next Monday, inspecting my approach from her station at the side entrance to Horace Greeley junior high, without taking her eyes off mine she bent significantly to whisper into her friend Rosalie Fallon's ear. To stifle their laughter the two of them made paws of their silly adored hands at their mouths. This gesture insured politeness and (reward for a suburban virtue) the secret renewal of laughter when the grocery boy had passed. Sober and unblinking, Pattie nonchalantly rubbed her edible kneecap.

"Don't call me Little Jack," I told Hannah once more without hope. "Call me my name."

"Okay. . . . Little Jack," she said, humorously chewing.

Sometimes I carried a book to work, wearing it piously between my shirt and my chest, and then hid with it and a cigarette in the basement among the cases of Libby's Whole Sliced Pineapple and Hinz-zuzz Pork and Beans with Tomato Sauce. The white-washed walls sweated; the storeroom smelled of dampness, rat poison, cardboard packing cases, and a broken bottle of soy sauce. Here I was happy, the complicated atmosphere making me dizzy as I perched corrupt with one of Andy's Wing butts on a peak of pineapple under the dusty 40-watt bulb. Sometimes I put down the Poe (I had memorized *Ulalume* without being able to pronounce it) and moodily considered my childhood, before Pattie Donahue and before my parents had decided I was a man, when I had sometimes visited this range of cans and bottles to leap like a goat among it in my innocence. I practiced a tragic sigh, inhaling soy.

Always my father roared down the stairway to discover me. "YOU THINK YOU CAN KID ME, HAH? The A & P can't even kid me, I got a list of your tricks—"

I stood up with no answer, understanding that he would forever find me, silent in my wished chagrin. I could not explain to him the disgrace of working in a store in a neighborhood where boys had important unexplainable things to do, secret clubs and fatal loafing, while their fathers managed offices for Standard Machines or handled law cases for insurance companies downtown. I wanted him to commute instead of work, like the others; I could not tell either of us the reason for my stubborn reluctance to follow him to the market, racy and challenging though it was. I felt a justice in his despair with me. A coward, I hid each time.

"Your mother says today you'll be good, I say I'll find you sneaking off with a book."

I studied his boots on the cement and deeply assented. He had looked in the backroom to see if I were filling orders, giving me the benefit of a doubt and profligate hope which is still my debt.

"Nu, what do you say for yourself? I'm going crazy upstairs, it's a big one-cent-sale, the Saturday help's no good these days. . . . Hah?"

I said nothing.

"Why not tell me another lie, you'll be good like you promised I should be happy?"

I stared, Poe sweaty in my hands.

"So why don't you at least say you had to go the toilet, the mensroom?"—a treble note of exasperation hidden in his bass, wanting an excuse for me, loving his oldest.

I refused this. I was over-moral for a moment, going on thirteen, as he was over-happy; I despised anything but extreme commitments, surrender to his world or defiance of it.

"What's the matter, you constipated? You got stomach trouble?"—pretending that I had given us this excuse, unable to bear our misery together.

He watched the tears silently fill my eyes.

He relented; he appealed to me, trying to preserve his anger by shouting; he betrayed his helplessness by heavily sitting down beside me on the canned pineapple. "What's the matter, you hungry, you want your mother should make you a tomato and balonny sandwich with Kraft's Miracle Whip dressing?"

"I want to go upstairs and help out," I whispered at last.

Reconciled, unable to preserve animus, he bumped against me up the narrow steps. Instead of letting me sink into the crowd of customers reaching with their lists and their clippings of advertisements at the counters, he ordered me to go to lunch with him, knowing that I liked this. To have the Business Men's special with Dad in a restaurant was one of the compensations; choosing food is the act of a god—only gods and businessmen don't have mothers to tell them what to eat, filling their plates with it. It was a pure joy although a bad restaurant; we had to go there because Guy Mallin owed my father two hundred dollars, which he never paid and we couldn't eat through by the time he left his wife and ran off to Montreal with Stella, the waitress, and a week's receipts. (When this happened Dad tried, although he knew little about the restaurant business, to help out poor Mrs. Mallin, who had no children but only a thyroid condition to give her an interest in life.) Both of us would have preferred an egg roll and hamburger steak at Louie's, the Chinaman across the street, and our unity on this—winking across the table as fast-talking Guy Mallin approached—cleared the hatred of civilizations between father and son. I should insist on this: the storm confined itself to its direct object, my laziness, rising like an East wind to its peak on the busy day, Saturday or before holidays, then falling away. "You learn with meet people," he only said. "You learn with know their ways."

After we finished our lunch I hid in the basement of the store to read Edgar Allan Poe.

2

As the months went by, the ruses deepened and the anger swam like some exiled bull carp in the deepest pools of the natures of my mother, my father, and me. Pattie Donahue had definitively given up roller-skating in the street, and not only on bricked Pittsburg Road but also on the mellifluous asphalt of Chesterton Avenue. We were freshmen in junior high, seventh graders learning dignity from a Social Dancing teacher added to the curriculum by the Board of Education which decided that Grace and Poise (formerly Comportment) were as essential as geography and algebra to the Young Men & Women of Tomorrow, be they bond salesmen like their fathers or *homemakers* like their mothers. The Real Estate Taxpayers League issued a protest against educational frills; pioneering virtues that made our country great, assessment already excessive, it argued. Artichokes, bulky and hard to handle, were coming into season again.

Shamefully I pretended to be sleeping Saturday mornings when my father had got up at three or earlier. Mother was more violent, my father more deeply hurt— the denial, after all, was of him. She nagged constantly; yet on Saturdays when I stayed motionless slugabed, her pride in sleep—"It's very healthy"—protected me there. Later, my father telephoning to ask if I had arisen yet, he fell silent before her report, pressing the receiver to his ear amid the mob of shoppers importunate about fork-tongued Hannah's dais, and he darkly said nothing while Mother repeated, infuriated with me but stubborn in her allegiance to health: "Let the kid sleep just one more morning, kids need sleep. It's good for them."

Having vacuumed, she herself got ready to go to the store for *relief*. Out of some relic of pride I could not bring myself to feign until she would safely leave me among my angry bedclothes in the occult reproach of a house. "I'm up," I fatally admitted. I reached for a paltry revenge in wearing yesterday's socks. She edified me in a steady torrent on the streetcar to the store:

"No good! big lump! lazy good-for-nothing. You're thirteen already and look at you!"

"Twelve," I corrected her.

" 'Please Daddy I want to work in the store like a big man,' Bernie always says. Aunt Sarah says. Such a go-getter! But what do you say?—look ma the dog wet the rug I'm twelve years old. Aunt Sarah says I should stop aggravating myself. Please give a look my waricose weins from standing up." She had forgotten that the effect of threatening to telephone Aunt Sarah when I was *bad* had been dissipated years ago with the advent of Unlimited Calls. Sometimes I had even offered to dial the number for her.

"A big lump like you he should give me a rest, take the load off your feet Ma like Bernie, not trouble trouble all the time."

"Why is it you always say I'm thirteen when it's something you want me to do and you know I'm twelve?" I asked, a savant without rimless glasses: "And when I want to do something I can't because I'm not old enough, I'm only eleven? My birthday is July twentieth at six o'clock in the morning."

"I remember," she said morosely. "And a fine night I had with you in Mount Sinai all night too, they almost had to use force-its. Dr. Shapiro said my bones were so delicate close together. . . . Thirteen, going on now. Even Uncle Morton knows about you, I'm so ashamed in the family why I told Aunt Ethel I'll never hold my head high again, at least Morton he got daughters they keep themselves clean at least not so much aggravation, all right so worry a tiny bit they should marry nice, but not heartache a no-good like you day in day out—"

Outside the streetcar the first autumn leaves were burning in piles on the street, sending up an odor redolent of freedom in the open air. My friends flamboyantly loitered on the Saturday streets, chalk in their mouths, their hearts unfettered. Pattie Donahue was perhaps walking alone in Rocky River Park, just waiting for me telepathically to find her.

The store opened about us with the intense plushy smell of old vegetables. Hannah was comforting old Mrs. Simmons, a childless widow whose husband had been manager of the Guarantee Trust, Rocky River branch; she generally admitted herself among us with the distant face of someone who disliked the smell of the inside of her own nose, but now she claimed to have seen a spider in a hand of bananas. "It probably wasn't a deadly poisonous banana spider," Hannah said. "Did it have a lot of legs? Furry ones from Costo Rico?"

"A South American banana spider! oh!" Mrs. Simmons, realizing that it was a foreign element, rolled her eyes in search of a pleasant place to faint.

"Probably not deadly poisonous, though. Probably just a sleepy little old banana spider from the deadly jungles of Hatey." Mrs. Simmons fainted. That is, considering her dignity and the aristocratic unpaid bills in the drawer with Hannah's sandwiches, she *swooned*. "Anyway no one else saw it, the thousand-legger bug, the horrible deadly spider," Hannah mused on, rubbing Mrs. Simmons' without taking off her Ovaltine Birthstone & Goodluck Ring.

"Ouch, you're scratching," said Mrs. Simmons.

My father, harried but always expecting the best, greeted me with an order. Stack the oranges, wait on Mrs. Simmons, put on your apron, what's the matter with you? . . . . Could I confess the chief reason for my tardiness, a hope that telepathic pressure concentrated among my bedclothes might compel Mrs. Donahue to buy her Ohio State hothouse tomatoes and Swansdown ready-mix no-sift cake flour before my surrender to penance in a wrap-around? *Develop Your Will Increase Your Power. Sample Booklet Fool Your Friends. 25¢ Coin or Stamps.* No, I could not. My father's will developed, he spoke a language in which existed no vocabulary to explain that, among the people with whom he chose to bring me up, it was more important to run end in a pick-up touch football game, spinning craftily about the young trees planted by the Our Street Beautiful committee, than to fill orders in sour old orange crates on Saturday afternoons. We all paid, in our various ways, a price for those trees and for the privilege of overhead doors on our garages and colonial-style magazine racks for our Saturday Evening Posts. He did not draw the consequences of his ambition for me; if he judged our neighborhood to be better than that of his childhood, then our neighborhood would judge his world. In a develop-your-will (Fool Your Friends) like my father's the only lack was the will to find my will-less longing. He worked! Mother worked! Like dogs!—They were right, but they could not see through to my rightness, forgetting a child's hunger to belong. Ulalume might have been for the ages, but Rosalie Fallon and Pattie tongued their malicious pencils and wrote my fate in their Slam Books. He knew he was a foreigner, my father did; I had to discover it in pain, shame before my parents, and self-judgings. "I earned my own living when I was thirteen, and proud of it," he had said.

"Your father earned his own living when he was twelve," Mother remarked contentedly in explanation, "and he is proud of it. *Proud* of it."

"Thirteen he said," I said.

"Proud he said," she said.

He studied me in sorrow and silence, figuring with his short black-nailed thick-knuckled hands reaching for the silvery crating hammer in his back pocket. I was just a kid. I even looked like him. Hannah said so. Even Guy Mallin said I was a chip off the. Hey kid? You want a Business Men's plate with chocolate ice cream instead of the green peas with butter sauce? It should be easy to figure. . . . "Gravy on that there ice cream haw-haw yessir, hey kid? Gravy!" Guy Mallin roared. "A real chip if I ever saw one, Jake. I'm telling you listen to me now. Your eyes. Your chin. His mother's, a sweet little woman you got there, nose. Yessir. Your hair. Off the old block there Jake. Good material, hey? It won't be long before it's *Jake & Son,* what-do-you-say? I'm telling you now Jake you heard what I said."

"Maybe things are different these days," he told me. "You ain't the way I was."

My father had the gift of listening to the artichokes at the top of a load in such a way—they informed him in a language which only he and the artichokes spoke— that he always knew when their brothers at the bottom were defective, defeated, edged with rust or shriveled from a stingy soil. Silent in their hampers, they communicated by the violence of love, all knowing their role on this occasion as opportunities, each thick-leafed one, for a sociable debating between farmer and merchant, green, crisp, candid, and nutritive after a pleasant journeying into the hands of women. They accepted the gift of himself which my father made, their shoots curly for him, their unbaked hearts shy in a bra of ticklish felt. Buy us! sell us!—they asked nothing more. Artichokes understood my father, and his sympathy for vegetables arose to meet theirs for him. Devotion—he gave this freely. He accepted, too, being stuck with thorns.

Unfortunately I, even in those days, was not an artichoke—perhaps not so rewarding, my heart not luscious with a dab of miracle-whip, stunted in fact, even hornier, full of bad character and a brooding plant rust. "Lots of personality," my mother had said, feebly defending me when as a child I had refused to shell lima beans for the store with the rest of the family on Friday nights. "Everyone says he takes after your side, Jake. Ethel says, Sarah says."

"Since I was thirteen! I got scars on my back, the bucket cut me, the greenhorn I didn't get a pad cloth. Look at Irwin, look at Bernie born the same week like you in Mount Sinai, you was the first so I got your mother a semi-private. A healthy kid like you, he sleeps all morning Saturday."

"Since he was twelve years old a greenhorn," Mother mournfully intoned. "Who ever heard of it?"

Pattie Donahue plucked at her sweater and pouted with kiss-proof lipstick (maybe) over teeth lucky to serve her. Lewis Snyder, the sheik, told stories about Rosalie Fallon and Pattie. Tom Moss told me. "The liar," we agreed, ferociously believing him.

Such matters flowed in time; the store remained outside time, its claim ripening through the spines but as incredible to me as a heartless artichoke to my father. The store gulped me down. I evaded, I squirmed, I stubbornly bent, receded, and persisted like heartburn, taking all shapes but in fact knowing only itself, which has no shape and a mysterious matter.

"You don't want, what kind of a reason is that?" my mother demanded, fertile as Hera in argument. "No reason, that's what kind."

I couldn't explain to myself or to them, much less to Aunt Sarah or to Aunt Ethel, to Hannah, Guy Mallin, or Cousin Bernie the Smarty. Let him marry a nice rich girl from New York Queens in the clothing business, I don't care, I sacrilegiously insisted. My single purpose was love for Pattie Donahue, whose father carried a portfolio to work in his hairless pink little hands; she would love only the elaborate loungers, the conspicuous consumers—a little Veblenite she was! You Americans all long for the useless, the hymen no proper end; it feathers no beds, it fleshes no bellies—this Mother and Dad might have pointed out if they had argued philosophy. I sensed, too, that my father's agility and strength and love moving among the objects all his in the store were a threat to me, the more dangerous because—one of his few fatal thoughts outside the moment—he was beginning to see Jack's Fruit & Vegetable in terms of immortality for both of us. He asked only a sign of recognition for this gift to me.

I refused his gift daily now. Even the Jello counter fell into ruins. My ultimate denial lay outside morality, essential to character. My father was over-happy, over-moral. I crouched like a troll under a mushroom in the cellar, a troll who read *Ulalume* and murmured, "Pattie

Donahue!" with dilated eyes in the shadow of a shipment from Procter & Gamble. Poor Dad!

We can measure his desolation. He left his struggle and joyous head-on combat with farmers, jobbers, salesmen, Saturday help, policemen, wilting lettuce and pears which remained green until they rotted, competitors, the chain stores, the landlord, debtors, creditors, the delivery truck, the account books, the government, insects, rodents, spoilage, wastage, heat, cold, the margin of profit, draw items, push merchandise which he could not get, premiums, samplers, one-cent giveaways, Chrismas trees on January second and Easter candy in May, children who skated through a display of jars of olives (the olives lined up one by one in bottles shaped like a straw, optically illusive, expensive all the same), Mr. Jenkins who insisted on Aunt Mary's pancake mix and would not be content with Aunt Jemimah's or any other Aunt's because he wanted to honor in this way his poor dead old Aunt Mary his mother's sister, Mrs. Rawlings the klepto whose chauffeur dropped her off at the store every morning to slip a bottle of vanilla extract into her pink muff (her daughter paid, but we had to keep score), the charity ladies and the lottery girls, the kids selling advertisements in their parochial school bulletins, the beggars who claimed to have had a store just like his in Phoenix, Arizona, until they hit a run of bad luck back in '29 (he was unanimously elected to a directory circulated by a syndicate of beggars, Phoenix & Miami Beach Chapter), the faithful customers who tried to convert him to their religions, Mrs. Colonel Greenough who came with tears to tell him that her husband forbade her to shop at Jack's Fruit & Vegetable any longer because the colonel himself had given him three months to read a book on technocracy and he had not yet complied (she bought a farewell bouquet of cauliflower before she left), the high school teacher who wanted to pay an overdue bill in the privacy of her chamber, the judges asking support both moral and ah financial in the coming primaries, the tax collectors, the bill collectors, the garbage collectors, the health inspectors, the housing inspectors, the zoning inspectors, electricians, refrigerator repair men, insurance which only covered fires begun by safety matches when his fire had resulted from a cigar butt, illness among his clerks, jealousies, rivalries, romances, extended lunch hours, female troubles which (a gentleman) he could not publicly doubt, inventories, lentil soup in cans labeled liver pate, children who descended like locusts to remove all the tops from the Ralston boxes to send away as a mark of esteem for Tom Mix, the electric cash register playing Chopin in a short circuit, Hannah who had B.O., Andy who left his hair among the macaroons, Myrna who showed too much of her bosom in order to encourage Mr. Tramme to take an extra cantaloupe, and other problems which I'll not mention because I want to avoid making a list.

My father abandoned his direct response to these issues in order to *use psychology* on me. He appealed in subtle ways. He tried to *get me interested*. His Tartar eyes were made to squint for laughter and appetite, not cunning. My heart contracts with sadness for him now, sadness and regret. He came to me on the porch one Sunday afternoon, his great arms slack at his sides, saying, "Say!" in the way of a good fellow, and asked me to write a paragraph for his weekly advertisement in the neighborhood throwaway. I responded, too, working hard at a composition modeled on The Raven, sharpening three pencils into oblivion before I finished. Proudly I announced to Tom Moss the prospect of publication in the West Side Advertiser.

The work never appeared. Trochees had no place next to bargains in Crisco. The Crisco people paid half and supplied the engraving; the Spry people, not caught napping at the shortening, offered to pay sixty per cent and sent my mother a portable sunlamp for her sinuses. I wasn't even impregnated with Vitamin D or viosterol from Wisconsin, living by Poe and Pattie. Psychology failed; my father came as an alien to such maneuvers. Nevermore!

One day I sneaked out of the store at 4:30, made my own dinner of Laub's rye, Blue Moon pimento cheese with those taste-delightful little chopped-up pieces of real pimento, Krunchy peanut butter (kan't remember the brand), and Thursday's spoiled milk; then I went to an Edward G. Robinson with Tom Moss. The three of us stood off the coppers for a reel and a half, and when they finally got Edward G. the camera noticed a paper boat which sailed down the gutter in the symbolic rain. "Just like The Strange Case of Monsieur Whatsizname," I pedantically reminded Tom. We fought back our tears, magnificent to THE END, ate a dime's worth of ever-green mints, and went divvies on a Spicy Detective to read under the Jantzen's Swimsuit for That Lee-*uscious* Look billboard on the way home. I told him about Pattie and he told me about Rosalie Fallon. Our patient listening to each other was more than politesse; we learned through it although the histories remained classically similar, unmodified in months except for the time Rosalie kicked Tom in the shins when he complimented her by rubbing one of the last March snowballs in her face. He rolled up his pantleg to show me the wound once more. I accused him of preserving it with salt. He denied this. He accused me of envy. I lowered my eyes. Tom was a lady-killer, he was; I'll never understand how he did it.

"Well, good night Tom. Good luck with Rosalie."

"Well, good night Dan. I'll ask Lewis Snyder about Pattie. He took Virginia Thompson out on a date and maybe she knows something. He'll tell me if I ask him because I know something on him."

Good night. . . . Good night. . . . In that mid-world of childish seriousness and the first adult frivolity of passion Tom and I needed the sense of banding to-gether, our sufferings held in common while our sense of them remained untouchable, pariahs of glandular en-thusiasm in a structure built of economy. He gave me the Spicy to hide in the garage. I had often dreamed of moving through an atmosphere of glue, invisibly held from my family's home in an empty night. Empty?—full of unknown excess. Now I whistled, leaving Tom Moss an hour before midnight, forgetting that I had last seen my parents seven hours earlier when my father had said,

"Wait on trade!" and I had crept out the back door where Andy was boxing strawberries and beet greens were blackening in the sun.

The door to our house was locked. The windows were dark. There was no key under the mat. The crickets suddenly deafened me, like in the movies. I thought I knew, then, how Edward G. felt when the boys went over to the South Side mob, but found a basement window open, crawled through the coal chute, and significantly murmured Pattie's name out of the side of my mouth. Ulalume Donahue, Killer Berman's moll. . . . I'd have flipped a quarter with disdain except that it was too dark and I had no quarter. *Dad!* I thought. I worried about the gas stove upstairs. Maybe they were all dead and so I should bang on the door until they let me in to sleep in my own bed. What if there were rats in the basement? Big ones like in the Paris sewers with Gene Valgene? The washing machine opened its mouth at me in the darkness. *Mother!* I thought. If the water pipes broke and I got drowned they'd be sorry. They'd be sorry someday when I spit blood into my monogrammed handkerchief from sleeping all alone in a damp basement. They would be sorry. I was sorry. *Mother and Dad!* I thought.

While taking off my shoes I slept on the extra kitchen table in the basement, amid dirty laundry (my pillow) and old hatreds (my dreams).

3

Even this passed. The next Saturday I was as faithful as Irwin, as true as Bernie with his eyes like spoiled oysters. I tasted during one evening the delights of approval, staying up with Mother and Dad while we discussed the day's business, counted the receipts, and discussed the pros and cons of tangle displays against neat pyramids of cans or fruit. I spoke for tangle displays, Mother for order; Dad listened to us both, sipping his tea with little Ahs through his lump of sugar, and reserved decision. He tried to lasso my head as he used to in a ring of cigar smoke. "It's too big," he complained. "Just like mine, a size seven seven-eighths. So look who needs a hat! You want a Stetson?"

We had a long late supper, and before going to bed he slipped me three dollar bills in a secret conspiratorial gesture while Mother stacked the dishes.

"I saw! I saw!" she cried out, her eyes peeping bright in the mirror over the sink. We all giggled together.

Dad slapped her rump, yawned, and said, "Nothing like a good day's work, hey?" in his imitation of Guy Mallin.

"Jake, you crazy?" At peace with each other we parted. "And don't forget whose birthday is next month," my mother said: "Yours. You'll be thirteen, kiddel."

She had it right this time. It was a real truce; I knew its joys. But had anything been altered? As aphoristic Aunt Ethel might say, "A leopard coat can't change its spots."

A few days afterward I received a letter. The envelope carried my name on the outside, together with the smart-alecky title *Master,* all printed in green ink. I studied it, marveling, my first mail since the revolutionary discovery of INCREASE YOUR WILL POWER FOOL YOUR FRIENDS, and for that I had sent away a coupon and a quarter. I sniffed it. I licked the ink and made a smear of what our art teacher called *graded area.* I tasted my name in green, finding it more subtle than black but just as lucid. At last I decided to open the letter.

It was an invitation from Mr. B. Franklyn Wilkerson to go on a Nature Walk a week from Saturday. Mr. Wilkerson, who taught General Science to the seventh grade, had worked out a plan to augment his income during the summer vacation by conveying flower names and leaf shapes to suburban scholars. Small, swarthy, with three daughters and thin black hair artfully spaced and glued into place to cover his scalp, Mr. Wilkerson recited Science (general) with his neck petrified for fear a sudden breeze or emotion might betray his baldness. Zealous, he devoted himself to general science textbooks, turning the pages slowly to avoid drafts. A real scientist would have perforated the pages. He was but a general scientist, however, combining, as he thought, the virtues of the practical and the theoretical in Elevating the Young, an intellectual sort whose pink resentful mouth and clenched neck gave him the expression of someone who had swallowed a banana sideways.

The first walk, a free trial, would take place on a Saturday, and the Saturday before the Fourth, the third-busiest day of the year in the store. I decided not to go.

Tom Moss was going. Lewis Snyder, who had dates alone with girls, was going. I learned that several of them, including Rosalie Fallon and Pattie Donahue, would be botanically present. I decided to go.

We met, everyone carrying lunch but me, at eleven thirty. Mother didn't know about it; I had run away from the store, taking my cap from under the cash register and, for some last scruple, telling Hannah to tell my father that I had gone. "Where?"—but I disappeared without answering, subtle as a hungry tomcat unable to hide its rut, sneaking around corners with its yellow eyes scheming. Lewis Snyder had a scout canteen filled with near-beer left over after repeal. I suspected him of planning to offer Pattie some.

Pedantic, amorous, shifty-eyed general scientists, we followed Mr. Wilkerson into the Rocky River reservation. He wore a checkered golf cap, its band black with Sta-Neet, and showed how he taught his wife to wrap his lunch—cellophane insulated the deviled eggs each from each. "Practical. Sanitary germ-free. Vitamins spoil in the open air," he advised us.

Tom Moss, my friend the skeptic, whispered to me that he thought it was supposed to be *good* for you to be out in the fresh air, and then went to step on Rosalie Fallon's heels.

We penetrated the woods, already hungry. "Now right here on your left children we find an interesting phenomenon page one hundred and forty-eight in Brenner's figure sixteen that orange growth over there with the black spots now that's a wild spermaphore," Mr. Wilkerson remarked. "Ess. Pee. Ee. Arrh—"

"Looks like a toadstool to me," I said.

"Spermaphore. Silver spoons unreliable poor quality silver these days no workmanship. Damp places. Twenty-four on a picnic without a general scientist. Could have told them. Whole party dead in eight to ten hours. Horrible. Too bad. Ess, pee, ee—"

A voice occurred behind me, whispering, "Hello, Daniel Berman." It was Pattie. "Toadstools are very poisonous"—she leaned sociably. "Do you like—are you fond of mushrooms?"

I soared into paradise at her feet. "My mother cooks spermaphores with meat loaf," I said, "and stuffed peppers."

"Oh!"—a gasp of scandal. "She does not! You'll all be dead. . . . Does she?"

"Yes," I lied, death-defying—what could be a better beginning between lovers? All lies come true in a world of such supple twelve-year-old facts. It was cool here across the city from the store. Birds soon to be falsely named cocked their heads in the trees and lectured us. Some place customers swarmed amid the imperatives of telephones and the distance between my father and me widened past even the nine-month doubt separating an instant of giving from the birth of a son. Fatherhood, a metaphysical idea, was being taken from Dad as Mrs. Rawlings slipped her daily bottle of vanilla extract into her bosom, no one to distract her, and as Mr. Wilkerson bravely broke the perfidious spermaphore with a five-foot stick, no academician he, a man of general action in science. Rosalie Fallon gave her pressed-lip assent and moral outrage against hypocritical silver spoons while my thoughts fled back from the store to recall prepared speeches of passion for Miss Donahue, known by Killer Berman and Edward G. as Ulalume or The Lost Lenore.

"Oh-h-h," she was saying.

"Look the bug," I replied.

She pretended to be scared, not. I knew. Death and complicity—love is not a biological gesture in suburban children, O Mr. Wilkerson! I had forgotten my speeches and Ulalume.

Despite this meeting I again felt deserted, lunchless

at lunchtime. Tom Moss pretended not to notice: excuse him his hunger. "Where's yours?" Pattie asked, her
mouth full.

"Don't have any. My mother didn't. Not hungry anyway."

Girls always have enough to give. Suburban girls
(economical) always enough to invest. Sweetly she
murmured, "You can have one of my bacon and tomato-
motto sandwiches and a bite of cottage cheese with the
canopy, please do." Smiling, licking her lipstick, her eyes
calculating under the modest fluttering venereal lids,
she whispered intimately: "And a cookie the one with
the candied cherry in the middle, please do, really."

"Oh!" I protested.

Take take, my mother would have said.

"Really, I don't mind, please do," said dainty Miss Pa-
tricia Donahue.

I did.

Later, when we bid farewell to sporting, big-toothed,
intellectual (generally scientific) Mr. Wilkerson, and
thanked him for a lovely nice afternoon, and promised
to ask our parents to fork over five smackeroos for a Program of Nature Walks, Pattie Donahue allowed it to be
known that I was walking her home. Under the circumstances even Lewis Snyder had to count it a date with a
girl alone; the evidence whelmed, overwhelmed. I obeyed
the protocol. We had a coke and then an ice cream stick.
That Snyder must have been eating his heart out, at least
aggravated. All right then—I soliloquied with Tom
Moss *qua* Conscience & Scorekeeper—half-credit then
for a daytime date.

"Did you get a free one?" I asked.

She read her ice cream stick. "No," she said.

"Neither did I. Don't believe in luck anyway"—and
I expounded my philosophy of will power concentrate
your way to fame and/or fortune. I tried to recite *Ulalume* but forgot it.

My mother's arches were hurting in her Enna Jetticks,
but she avoided my father so that he would not order
her home. Andy was making off to the vegetable cooler

with a bagful of macaroons. Basketwood splintered under orders; customers fidgeted untended; my father wiped his forehead with a paper towel from the pine forests of Maine, leaving crumbs of lint, and mourned me.

"I never knew you were so smart," said Pattie Donahue.

We had fallen silent, sitting on the front steps of her house in the shadow of a bush where her mother could not see us. Up the street someone was hosing his car, an incontinent sound, in preparation for a Fourth of July trip. The afternoon was over. Pattie Donahue, an economical creature, an Indian giver, took back her gift in a way which expressed her genius. Business acumen. Operating costs and turnover. Appraising me with her turtle-round eyes, shrewd to calculate the value of an investment, she first created a bear market by sighing Ohh, rustling her dress, and accidentally touching my arm with her transparent turquoise-veined hands. Cologned and dusted with powder, she breathed on me.

"Yes!" I spilled out, naked in summer smells. "Do you like me, Pattie? I like you."

"Sure I like you"—disappointed and a pout that it had been so easy. Even economy becomes sport with such a housekeeper. "Sure I like you but you're too fat."

"Fat?" I repeated stupidly.

Her laughter tinkled in the July calm by the watered bush. "Fat I mean skinny. I mean you're just a *grocery* boy, you. You just grub around a certain store I could name all the Saturdays *I* ever heard about, except I suppose today—"

She was a sly old creature, that Pattie Donahue. The lips: *grocery boy*. The frozen iris: the same. Her laughter caroled forth, free, enterprising, resolute, the investment paying off in a Saturday afternoon dividend of power. Not all men are men, her laughter told her. This is a profit forever, my face told her.

"Oh but—oh but—oh but—" I said.

She put her little hand to her mouth and delicately closed it. Tee-hee. She looked at me, unblinking. My father, knowing he was a foreigner, could have accepted

this in the perspective of history. I had to discover a fact
without a past; it leapt out at me like some fierce fish
from the glittering shale of Pattie Donahue's economical eyes.

I stood up. "Thank you for the sandwich and the
cookie," I said. (The cookie with a preserved cherry on
it.)

"Oh me no," she said.

"I was hungry."

"Oh you're welcome really," she said. "Thank you
for the coke. Thank you for the ice cream."

"Good-by, Pattie."

"It was nice, Daniel Berman," she said, "truly very
nice."

4

I prowled, growing up fast that afternoon. I climbed a
fat hump of a mailbox for packages and, my hands hanging in front, or my elbows on my knees and my fists in
my cheeks, I watched the traffic on Parkside Boulevard. I
did not choose the sentimental places, the tree by the lake,
the woods where the river on which we skated in
winter spread out like a sheet. I began to understand
how the lost Lenore really got mislaid, without a dark
conversational bird, without a tomb, without even a long
metrical sigh. A heavy July sky lowered and thickened
above me. I perched on the box like an animal in a dream.

But I was no animal in no dream. I was wide-awake,
me, itchy, straddling a mailbox. Once someone mailed a
book between my legs. I did not stop to wonder whether
it were some quaint and curious volume, this being already forgotten lore. I studied the houses squatting like
fat-necked bullfrogs along the boulevard, puzzled over
the nay-saying mouths and step of the emerging stroll-
ers, celebrated and grieved for the crystallizing structure
of my judgment (my *complexes*), no longer contained by
sad and pretty words—grieved but did not cry.

Long after dark I finally went home. My parents were
in the kitchen, talking in low voices, the relieved haw-

ing of Saturday nights absent today. Entering at the street, I went directly to my room and lay down on the bed. I made none of the dramatic flourishes of locking the door or pushing the footstool in front of it.

"Daniel!"

Doltish, I wondered if this were what it felt like to be an adult. It was true that for weeks I had been awakening mornings with my bite clamped, my jaw aching, and my tongue plunged against my teeth. Was that the seeding for Pattie Donahue's educational crop? her economy predicted by my extravagance in sleep?

"Daniel!"—Mother's voice. I went. Mother stood by the kitchen table. Dad sat without looking at me, his head lowered, his hands about a bowl of soup. "You should come when I called you," she said.

"I did come."

"When I called you I said. Not whenever you please." She looked at my father and waited for him to speak. He did not. We all waited for him, the challenged one, amid the summer smell of flypaper in the kitchen and the buzzing of the wily flies.

Resentfully I broke the stillness: "I went on a naturewalk."

"What?—what?"

"I learned what's a toadstool and the names of birds. A naturewalk. Mr. Wilkerson general science from junior high, he—"

"And what about Mr. and Mrs. Slave-their-heads-off, I suppose your parents by the store?" my mother asked. The sarcasm gave me hope; it was, after all, only dialectic again. How soon hope returns! We dwell in it even after the exile to which Pattie Donahue's laughter and nibbling teeth send us.

Turning to my father, whose head bent over the table in a way I only remembered afterward—his brother had died and Mother said he was crying because he was sad and I didn't believe her because daddies don't cry—I appealed to him with a manly challenge: "Almost everyone I know went on the naturewalk."

He did not yet look up.

"It's educational. Mr. Wilkerson says. Tom Moss was there. Almost everyone in our grade Seven-B Seven-A was there—"

"Lookit my waricose from standing up all day working like a horse eating my heart out," Mother said. "You should take a load off my feet, not I should carry you like a baby you're going on fourteen."

"Thirteen," I said.

"Going on anyway," she insisted, "*going* on. That's what it means. Big lummox. Look at my waricose go on look lookit."

She could not know—my cruelty at twelve years, soon thirteen!—that my only concern was for surgery on the distended veins, as other women had, instead of wearing the lumpy corset that bulged about her calves under webbed brown stockings. My garment, she called it. Like taxes, Jake says. Teeth too, O! Sarah had the same trouble after Bernie and she took calcium. You ask me I think better injections in the arm, injections.

Dad listened watchfully over the soup in the evening heat. He hunched and studied vegetables in the bowl.

See how I admit the two of them to paper. Put my refusal of their world, which was their deepest gift to me, beside a son's longed-for and imagined love for his parents. Let me call myself a liar, but don't you be quick to do it. "Want to playboy around all your life dreaming smoke in the head?" my father used to ask me, and yet he loved me despite the law that we cannot love someone who refuses our gifts. I did not see the power and light of his world, in which the four causes were felt in action with my mother, vegetables, and the Saturday specials; I had looked for light and power in Pattie and Poe while all the Aristotelian potencies and more lay waiting for me with the combustible garbage swept into the backyard at closing time each evening. The backroom, emptied and cleaned, was filled and emptied of carrot tops, beet greens, and the furry blue glow of spoiled oranges. I stalled; my father waited. I looked; my father watched.

A week earlier I had overheard Mother murmuring

into the telephone, "So how's your Bernie? My Daniel shouldn't be better, he got a all-A report card and with a B plus in gymnistics, he gained two pounds by the scale but he's full of complexes, still a heart-ache in the store. . . . Yah. . . . I read in the paper it's complexes, Jake says he'll grow out. . . ."

But only the complexes kept growing out. It's because I really like my parents that it costs me so much to speak kindly of them. I remember how my father offered me his entire world and I threw it in his face like a rotten orange because he left out one little lump of an Atlantis, my own world.

"Listen to your father he's talking," my mother said. He had not yet spoken, but she knew him well and knew he now would. "You take his fifteen cents for a movie, don't you? Listen to your father."

Still sitting in his washed-out shirt crusted with salt under the armpits, in his old blue serge work pants, once dress-up with sharpy stripe down the legs, more generous than fathers have a right to be, he tried to help me expiate my sin in a ritual of reprimand. No ceremony could heal him this time, but he waited. This came before the beginning: "At your age I was a man," he said.

He was right.

He swayed over the soup, food breathing back into his body the prayers he had forgotten in leaving his own father. His swaying shoulders heavily sloped and remembered. His father had forbidden him to go to godless America, better to die than to be unfaithful. This too he had forgotten, his father struck down by a Cossack's rifle, but the chant in his voice and the dance of his shoulders remembered.

"Look at you"—he could not. "Are you a man?"

No. Right again.

"A playboy. A naturewalker. A eater of ice cream."

All true. I still like ice cream, especially with Hershey's chocolate syrup. He taught me quality in food, my father. I waited for him to force me to make myself what we both agreed I should be; no ceremony could

compel it though only ceremony could confirm it. Still
I had to choose. Untheological, without brand names, we
improvised ritual.

"A lollypop!" my mother shrilled, thinking she was
on her husband's side. Here she was wrong. I was not a
lollypop.

"Let me tell it, Rose," my father said softly, as if this
were an incident on their trip to South Haven. "It's my
turn to tell it, Rose."

"I don't care"—me turning in my pointed shoes perforated for ventilation and sweet beauty's sake under
the eyes of Pattie. I mourned her now, blaming my
birth. "I don't care about you." I lowered my gaze to my
father's stubby foreign feet in steel-backed boots. "None
of the kids have to do it. I don't care about you and your
store."

He needed an instant for this. I gave it to him over-
flowing. "And—your—store."

His hand floated up like a speck fuming on the eyes;
his fist crashed down on the enameled table like the
plunging claw of a crate-hammer. "Oh! Oh!"—Mother.
Soup splashed out on his pants and ran weeping with
little red carrot eyes.

His gaze was prophetic in mine. "*Some kits help out
in the store*," he said.

"We were practically supposed to go," I said, neither
retreating nor regretting, gaining time and learning patience. "Mr. Wilkerson is a teacher."

"*Some kits remember their father and mother.*"

Everyone knows where it hurts when you begin to
cry—that place at the back of the throat. Pins jabbed under my eyelids. My palate ached. The tears hurt most in
that instant before they break out. . . . And then I
imagined cologned Pattie's cool laughter at my father's
pronunciation of the *d* in *kits* ("—remember their father
and mother"), and then drunk with the idea of the murder of someone I loved, my belly awash at the thought, I
screamed him to his feet:

"I won't, I *won't* work in your store. I don't want it.
It's not my life. I hate it. I hate it!"

He stood huge over me, smelling of leafy vegetables and sweat, smelling of his strength and his terror because he would have to beat me. This is the reek of power, what the men at the Food Terminal understood when Ollie the Agent tried to shake down him first of the West Side men. . . . The opponents were uneven. He had wise muscles, protected by years of work, and good eating, the skills of use, the satisfactions of his time of life. He had three sons, only one of those baby brothers of mine lying awake to listen. His swaying body knew it loved me as his father had loved him, the woman carrying her child on a belly or breast, the man taking his son only at the eye or the fist. There must have been a great satisfaction in his fear and love at that moment.

My sole weapon was exactly my dissatisfaction. My father's arms swam with veins among the curled oily hairs on his light bluish freckled flesh. No bow-straight shoulders like Atlas the World's Most Perfect Develop It! No Culver Academy athlete calling for Pattie Donahue in his uniform at Christmastime! It was a body which had worked well and been used with pleasure, a happy body, soup on the pants, making its own purpose and content with this.

Mine, as I have said: discontented. I looked for a use for it. I said:

"And you and your grocery boys and everyone! *I hate you!*"

Mother was crying and stacking the dishes in the sink when his open hand—generous! open!—struck my shoulder. I flew back and then up at him, slipping past his collar rough as a dog's tongue. Mother screamed. I climbed him, flailing; he was planted on the floor and he rocked under my weight for a moment, both of us silently straining toward each other and apart, our sweat pouring together while Mother screamed on and on— the malignant smell of hate and fear becoming the myrrh of two men fighting, the sweet cunning of love and death. I clung to his great neck to strangle it. His beard scratched my arms. He hugged my ribs, forcing them up —cracking!—pushing my hair out, lengthening my bones, driving my voice deep. Savagely he told me his life, wringing my childhood from me. I took this after his long day and had nothing to give in return but my unfleshed arms roped about his neck. We embraced like this.

The broken blood fled for a window into my mouth. I felt myself fainting.

Abruptly I lunged down, perhaps permitted to beg free. His weighty old-country strength: my agile sporting slyness: as he glanced for pity at my mother I threw myself like a pole against his knees in a playground stunt performed without thinking. The trick uprooted his legs; he crashed; his forehead above the unsurprised Tartar eyes hit my mother's foot when he fell.

He sat up and started to his feet as she held him. I could not breathe, my chest frozen. I turned from his sprawling. I let him hear me choke and then ran to my room. Yes, I had wanted to win, but now, fatalistic, in an instant guessing ahead, I made the highest demand on a father: that he know he had beaten me too, only because he had let it happen.

"What's happening to us all?"—those first tears of old age. "What's happening to us?" Dad was crying in the bathroom with the door shut and the water running in the sink so that no one would hear an old man with an ingrate son. He had locked Mother out, who was dry-eyed now, figuring.

If I am bereaved of my sons, the first Jacob said, *then am I bereaved.* To fight back was all I needed; he had given too much. Economy in Pattie! my father a spendthrift!—such knowledge comes late to me now.

A Mother's Tale

James Agee

THE calf ran up the little hill as fast as he could and stopped sharp. "Mama!" he cried, all out of breath. "What *is* it! What are they *doing!* Where are they *going!*"

Other spring calves came galloping too.

They all were looking up at her and awaiting her explanation, but she looked out over their excited eyes. As she watched the mysterious and majestic thing they had never seen before, her own eyes became even more than ordinarily still, and during the considerable moment before she answered, she scarcely heard their urgent questioning.

Far out along the autumn plain, beneath the sloping light, an immense drove of cattle moved eastward. They went at a walk, not very fast, but faster than they could imaginably enjoy. Those in front were compelled by those behind; those at the rear, with few exceptions, did their best to keep up; those who were locked within the herd could no more help moving than the particles inside a falling rock. Men on horses rode ahead, and alongside, and behind, or spurred their horses intensely back and forth, keeping the pace steady, and the herd in shape; and from man to man a dog sped back and forth incessantly as a shuttle, barking, incessantly, in a hysterical voice. Now and then one of the men shouted fiercely, and this like the shrieking of the dog was tinily audible above a low and awesome sound which seemed to come not from the multitude of hooves but from the center of the world, and above the sporadic bawlings and bellowings of the herd.

From the hillside this tumult was so distant that it only made more delicate the prodigious silence in which the earth and sky were held; and, from the hill, the sight was as modest as its sound. The herd was virtually hidden in the dust it raised, and could be known, in general, only by the horns which pricked this flat sunlit dust like little briars. In one place a twist of the air revealed the trembling fabric of many backs; but it was only along the near edge of the mass that individual animals were discernible, small in a driven frieze, walking fast, stumbling and recovering, tossing their armed heads, or opening their skulls heavenward in one of those cries which reached the hillside long after the jaws were shut.

From where she watched, the mother could not be sure whether there were any she recognized. She knew that among them there must be a son of hers; she had not seen him since some previous spring, and she would not be seeing him again. Then the cries of the young ones impinged on her bemusement: "Where are they going?"

She looked into their ignorant eyes.

"Away," she said.

"Where?" they cried. "Where? Where?" her own son cried again.

She wondered what to say.

"On a long journey."

"But where *to?*" they shouted. "Yes, where *to?*" her son exclaimed, and she could see that he was losing his patience with her, as he always did when he felt she was evasive.

"I'm not sure," she said.

Their silence was so cold that she was unable to avoid their eyes for long.

"Well, not *really* sure. Because, you see," she said in her most reasonable tone, "I've never seen it with my own eyes, and that's the only way to *be* sure; isn't it."

They just kept looking at her. She could see no way out.

"But I've *heard* about it," she said with shallow cheerfulness, "from those who *have* seen it, and I don't suppose there's any good reason to doubt them."

She looked away over them again, and for all their interest in what she was about to tell them, her eyes so changed that they turned and looked, too.

The herd, which had been moving broadside to them, was being turned away, so slowly that like the turning of stars it could not quite be seen from one moment to the next; yet soon it was moving directly away from them, and even during the little while she spoke and they all watched after it, it steadily and very noticeably diminished, and the sounds of it as well.

"It happens always about this time of year," she said quietly while they watched. "Nearly all the men and horses leave, and go into the North and the West."

"Out on the range," her son said, and by his voice she knew what enchantment the idea already held for him.

"Yes," she said, "out on the range." And trying, impossibly, to imagine the range, they were touched by the breath of grandeur.

"And then before long," she continued, "everyone has been found, and brought into one place; and then . . . what you see, happens. All of them.

"Sometimes when the wind is right," she said more quietly, "you can hear them coming long before you can see them. It isn't even like a sound, at first. It's more as if something were moving far under the ground. It makes you uneasy. You wonder, why, what in the world can *that* be! Then you remember what it is and then you can really hear it. And then finally, there they all are."

She could see this did not interest them at all.

"But where are they *going?*" one asked, a little impatiently.

"I'm coming to that," she said; and she let them wait. Then she spoke slowly but casually.

"They are on their way to a railroad."

There, she thought; that's for that look you all gave me when I said I wasn't sure. She waited for them to ask; they waited for her to explain.

"A railroad," she told them, "is great hard bars of metal lying side by side, or so they tell me, and they go on and on over the ground as far as the eye can see. And great wagons run on the metal bars on wheels, like wagon wheels but smaller, and these wheels are made of solid metal too. The wagons are much bigger than any wagon you've ever seen, as big as, big as sheds, they say, and they are pulled along on the iron bars by a terrible huge dark machine, with a loud scream."

"Big as *sheds?*" one of the calves said skeptically.

"Big *enough*, anyway," the mother said. "I told you I've never seen it myself. But those wagons are so big that several of us can get inside at once. And that's exactly what happens."

Suddenly she became very quiet, for she felt that somehow, she could not imagine just how, she had said altogether too much.

"Well, *what* happens," her son wanted to know. "What do you mean, *happens.*"

She always tried hard to be a reasonably modern mother. It was probably better, she felt, to go on, than to leave them all full of imaginings and mystification. Besides, there was really nothing at all awful about what happened . . . if only one could know *why*.

"Well," she said, "it's nothing much, really. They just —why, when they all finally *get* there, why there are all the great cars waiting in a long line, and the big dark machine is up ahead . . . smoke comes out of it, they say . . . and . . . well, then, they just put us into the wagons, just as many as will fit in each wagon, and when everybody is in, why . . ." She hesitated, for again, though she couldn't be sure why, she was uneasy.

"Why then," her son said, "the train takes them away."

Hearing that word, she felt a flinching of the heart. Where had he picked it up, she wondered, and she gave him a shy and curious glance. Oh dear, she thought. I should never have even *begun* to explain. "Yes," she said, "when everybody is safely in, they slide the doors shut."

They were all silent for a little while. Then one of them asked thoughtfully, "Are they taking them somewhere they don't want to go?"

"Oh, I don't think so," the mother said. "I imagine it's very nice."

"*I* want to go," she heard her son say with ardor. "I want to go right now," he cried. "Can I, Mama? *Can* I? *Please?*" And looking into his eyes, she was overwhelmed by sadness.

"Silly thing," she said, "there'll be time enough for that when you're grown up. But what I very much hope," she went on, "is that instead of being chosen to go out on the range and to make the long journey, you will grow up to be very strong and bright so they will decide that you may stay here at home with Mother. And you, too," she added, speaking to the other little males; but she could not honestly wish this for any but her own, least of all for the eldest, strongest and most proud, for she knew how few are chosen.

She could see that what she said was not received with enthusiasm.

"But I want to go," her son said.

"Why?" she asked. "I don't think any of you realize that it's a great *honor* to be chosen to stay. A great privilege. Why, it's just the most ordinary ones are taken out onto the range. But only the very pick are chosen to stay here at home. If you want to go out on the range," she said in hurried and happy inspiration, "all you have to do is be ordinary and careless and silly. If you want to have even a chance to be chosen to stay, you have to try to be stronger and bigger and braver and brighter than anyone else, and that takes *hard work. Every day.* Do you see?" And she looked happily and hopefully from one to another. "Besides," she added, aware that they were not won over, "I'm told it's a very rough life out there, and the men are unkind.

"Don't you see," she said again; and she pretended to speak to all of them, but it was only to her son.

But he only looked at her. "Why do you want me to stay home?" he asked flatly; in their silence she knew the others were asking the same question.

"Because it's safe here," she said before she knew
better; and realized she had put it in the most unfortunate way possible. "Not safe, not just that," she fumbled.
"I mean . . . because here we *know* what happens, and
what's going to happen, and there's never any doubt
about it, never any reason to wonder, to worry. Don't
you see? It's just *Home*," and she put a smile on the
word, "where we all know each other and are happy and
well."

They were so merely quiet, looking back at her, that
she felt they were neither won over nor alienated. Then
she knew of her son that he, anyhow, was most certainly
not persuaded, for he asked the question she most
dreaded: "Where do they go on the train?" And hearing
him, she knew that she would stop at nothing to bring
that curiosity and eagerness, and that tendency toward
skepticism, within safe bounds.

"Nobody knows," she said, and she added, in just the
tone she knew would most sharply engage them, "Not
for sure, anyway."

"What do you mean, *not for sure*," her son cried. And
the oldest, biggest calf repeated the question, his voice
cracking.

The mother deliberately kept silence as she gazed out
over the plain, and while she was silent they all heard
the last they would ever hear of all those who were going away: one last great cry, as faint almost as a breath;
the infinitesimal jabbing vituperation of the dog; the
solemn muttering of the earth.

"Well," she said, after even this sound was entirely
lost, "there was one who came back." Their instant, trustful eyes were too much for her. She added, "Or so they
say."

They gathered a little more closely around her, for
now she spoke very quietly.

"It was my great-grandmother who told me," she said.
"She was told it by *her* great-grandmother, who claimed
she saw it with her own eyes, though of course I can't
vouch for that. Because of course I wasn't even dreamed
of then; and Great-grandmother was so very, very old,

you see, that you couldn't always be sure she knew quite *what* she was saying."

Now that she began to remember it more clearly, she was sorry she had committed herself to telling it.

"Yes," she said, "the story is, there was one, *just* one, who ever came back, and he told what happened on the train, and where the train went and what happened after. He told it all in a rush, they say, the last things first and every which way, but as it was finally sorted out and gotten into order by those who heard it and those they told it to, this is more or less what happened:

"He said that after the men had gotten just as many of us as they could into the car he was in, so that their sides pressed tightly together and nobody could lie down, they slid the door shut with a startling rattle and a bang, and then there was a sudden jerk, so strong they might have fallen except that they were packed so closely together, and the car began to move. But after it had moved only a little way, it stopped as suddenly as it had started, so that they all nearly fell down again. You see, they were just moving up the next car that was joined on behind, to put more of us into it. He could see it all between the boards of the car, because the boards were built a little apart from each other, to let in air."

Car, her son said again to himself. Now he would never forget the word.

"He said that then, for the first time in his life, he became very badly frightened, he didn't know why. But he was sure, at that moment, that there was something dreadfully to be afraid of. The others felt this same great fear. They called out loudly to those who were being put into the car behind, and the others called back, but it was no use; those who were getting aboard were between narrow white fences and then were walking up a narrow slope and the man kept jabbing them as they do when they are in an unkind humor, and there was no way to go but on into the car. There was no way to get out of the car, either: he tried, with all his might, and he was the one nearest the door.

"After the next car behind was full, and the door was shut, the train jerked forward again, and stopped again, and they put more of us into still another car, and so on, and on, until all the starting and stopping no longer frightened anybody; it was just something uncomfortable that was never going to stop, and they began instead to realize how hungry and thirsty they were. But there was no food and no water, so they just had to put up with this; and about the time they became resigned to going without their suppers (for by now it was almost dark), they heard a sudden and terrible scream which frightened them even more deeply than anything had frightened them before, and the train began to move again, and they braced their legs once more for the jolt when it would stop, but this time, instead of stopping, it began to go fast, and then even faster, so fast that the ground nearby slid past like a flooded creek and the whole country, he claimed, began to move too, turning slowly around a far mountain as if it were all one great wheel. And then there was a strange kind of disturbance inside the car, he said, or even inside his very bones. He felt as if everything in him was *falling*, as if he had been filled full of a heavy liquid that all wanted to flow one way, and all the others were leaning as he was leaning, away from this queer heaviness that was trying to pull them over, and then just as suddenly this leaning heaviness was gone and they nearly fell again before they could stop leaning against it. He could never understand what this was, but it too happened so many times that they all got used to it, just as they got used to seeing the country turn like a slow wheel, and just as they got used to the long cruel screams of the engine, and the steady iron noise beneath them which made the cold darkness so fearsome, and the hunger and the thirst and the continual standing up, and the moving on and on and on as if they would never stop."

"*Didn't* they ever stop?" one asked.

"Once in a great while," she replied. "Each time they did," she said, "he thought, Oh, now *at last! At last* we can get out and stretch our tired legs and lie down! *At last* we'll be given food and water! But they never let them out. And they never gave them food or water. They never even cleaned up under them. They had to stand in their manure and in the water they made."

"Why did the train stop?" her son asked; and with somber gratification she saw that he was taking all this very much to heart.

"He could never understand why," she said. "Sometimes men would walk up and down alongside the cars, and the more nervous and the more trustful of us would call out; but they were only looking around, they never seemed to do anything. Sometimes he could see many houses and bigger buildings together where people lived. Sometimes it was far out in the country and after they had stood still for a long time they would hear a little noise which quickly became louder, and then became suddenly a noise so loud it stopped their breathing, and during this noise something black would go by, very close, and so fast it couldn't be seen. And then it was gone as suddenly as it had appeared, and the noise became small, and then in the silence their train would start up again.

"Once, he tells us, something very strange happened. They were standing still, and cars of a very different kind began to move slowly past. These cars were not red, but black, with many glass windows like those in a house; and he says they were as full of human beings as the car he was in was full of our kind. And one of these people looked into his eyes and smiled, as if he liked him, or as if he knew only too well how hard the journey was.

"So by his account it happens to them, too," she said, with a certain pleased vindictiveness. "Only they were sitting down at their ease, not standing. And the one who smiled was eating."

She was still, trying to think of something; she couldn't quite grasp the thought.

"But didn't they *ever* let them out?" her son asked. The oldest calf jeered. "Of *course* they did. He came back, didn't he? How would he ever come back if he didn't get out?"

"They didn't let them out," she said, "for a long, long time."

"How long?"

"So long, and he was so tired, he could never quite be sure. But he said that it turned from night to day and from day to night and back again several times over, with the train moving nearly all of this time, and that when it finally stopped, early one morning, they were all so tired and so discouraged that they hardly even noticed any longer, let alone felt any hope that anything would change for them, ever again; and then all of a sudden men came up and put up a wide walk and unbarred the door and slid it open, and it was the most wonderful and happy moment of his life when he saw the door open, and walked into the open air with all his joints trembling, and drank the water and ate the delicious food they had ready for him; it was worth the whole terrible journey."

Now that these scenes came clear before her, there was a faraway shining in her eyes, and her voice, too, had something in it of the faraway.

"When they had eaten and drunk all they could hold they lifted up their heads and looked around, and everything they saw made them happy. Even the trains made them cheerful now, for now they were no longer afraid of them. And though these trains were forever breaking to pieces and joining again with other broken pieces, with shufflings and clashings and rude cries, they hardly paid them attention any more, they were so pleased to be in their new home, and so surprised and delighted to find they were among thousands upon thousands of strangers of their own kind, all lifting up their voices in peacefulness and thanksgiving, and they were so wonderstruck by all they could see, it was so beautiful and so grand.

"For he has told us that now they lived among fences as white as bone, so many, and so spiderishly complicated, and shining so pure, that there's no use trying even to hint at the beauty and the splendor of it to anyone who knows only the pitiful little outfittings of a ranch. Beyond these mazy fences, through the dark and bright smoke which continually turned along the sunlight, dark buildings stood shoulder to shoulder in a wall as huge and proud as mountains. All through the air, all the time, there was an iron humming like the humming of the iron bar after it has been struck to tell the men it is time to eat, and in all the air, all the time, there was that same strange kind of iron strength which makes the silence before lightning so different from all other silence.

"Once for a little while the wind shifted and blew over them straight from the great buildings, and it brought a strange and very powerful smell which confused and disturbed them. He could never quite describe this smell, but he has told us it was unlike anything he had ever known before. It smelled like old fire, he said, and old blood and fear and darkness and sorrow and most terrible and brutal force and something else, something in it that made him want to run away. This sudden uneasiness and this wish to run away swept through every one of them, he tells us, so that they were all moved at once as restlessly as so many leaves in a wind, and there was great worry in their voices. But soon the leaders among them concluded that it was simply the way men must smell when there are a great many of them living together. Those dark buildings must be crowded very full of men, they decided, probably as many thousands of them, indoors, as there were of us, outdoors; so it was no wonder their smell was so strong and, to our kind, so unpleasant. Besides, it was so clear now in every other way that men were not as we had always supposed, but were doing everything they knew how to make us comfortable and happy, that we ought to just put up with their smell, which after all they couldn't help, any more than we could help our own. Very likely men didn't like the way we smelled, any more than we liked theirs. They passed along these ideas to the others, and soon everyone felt more calm, and then the wind changed again, and the fierce smell no longer came to them, and the smell of their own kind was back again, very strong of course, in such a crowd, but ever so homey and comforting, and everyone felt easy again.

"They were fed and watered so generously, and treated so well, and the majesty and the loveliness of this place where they had all come to rest was so far beyond anything they had ever known or dreamed of, that many of the simple and ignorant, whose memories were short, began to wonder whether that whole difficult journey, or even their whole lives up to now, had ever really been. Hadn't it all been just shadows, they murmured, just a bad dream?

"Even the sharp ones, who knew very well it had all really happened, began to figure that everything up to now had been made so full of pain only so that all they had come to now might seem all the sweeter and the more glorious. Some of the oldest and deepest were even of a mind that all the puzzle and tribulation of the journey had been sent us as a kind of harsh trying or proving of our worthiness; and that it was entirely fitting and proper that we could earn our way through to such rewards as these, only through suffering, and through being patient under pain which was beyond our understanding; and that now at the last, to those who had borne all things well, all things were made known: for the mystery of suffering stood revealed in joy. And now as they looked back over all that was past, all their sorrows and bewilderments seemed so little and so fleeting that, from the simplest among them even to the most wise, they could feel only the kind of amused pity we feel toward the very young when, with the first thing that hurts them or they are forbidden, they are sure there is nothing kind or fair in all creation, and carry on accordingly, raving and grieving as if their hearts would break."

She glanced among them with an indulgent smile, hoping the little lesson would sink home. They seemed interested but somewhat dazed. I'm talking way over their heads, she realized. But by now she herself was too deeply absorbed in her story to modify it much. *Let* it be, she thought, a little impatient; it's over *my* head, for that matter.

"They had hardly before this even wondered that they were alive," she went on, "and now all of a sudden they felt they understood *why* they were. This made them very happy, but they were still only beginning to enjoy this new wisdom when quite a new and different kind of restiveness ran among them. Before they quite knew it they were all moving once again, and now they realized that they were being moved, once more, by men, toward still some other place and purpose they could not know. But during these last hours they had been so well that now they felt no uneasiness, but all moved forward calm and sure toward better things still to come; he has told us that he no longer felt as if he were being driven, even as it became clear that they were going toward the shade of those great buildings; but guided.

"He was guided between fences which stood ever more and more narrowly near each other, among companions who were pressed ever more and more closely against one another; and now as he felt their warmth against him it was not uncomfortable, and his pleasure in it was not through any need to be close among others through anxiousness, but was a new kind of strong and gentle delight, at being so very close, so deeply of his own kind, that it seemed as if the very breath and heartbeat of each one were being exchanged through all that multitude, and each was another, and others were each, and each was a multitude, and the multitude was one. And quieted and made mild within this melting, they now entered the cold shadow cast by the buildings, and now with every step the smell of the buildings grew stronger, and in the darkening air the glittering of the fences was ever more queer.

"And now as they were pressed ever more intimately together he could see ahead of him a narrow gate, and he was strongly pressed upon from either side and from behind, and went in eagerly, and now he was between two fences so narrowly set that he brushed either fence with either flank, and walked alone, seeing just one other ahead of him, and knowing of just one other behind him, and for a moment the strange thought came to him, that the one ahead was his father, and that the one behind was the son he had never begotten.

"And now the light was so changed that he knew he must have come inside one of the gloomy and enormous buildings, and the smell was so much stronger that it seemed almost to burn his nostrils, and the smell and the somber new light blended together and became some other thing again, beyond his describing to us except to say that the whole air beat with it like one immense heart and it was as if the beating of this heart were pure violence infinitely manifolded upon violence: so that the uneasy feeling stirred in him again that it would be wise to turn around and run out of this place just as fast and as far as ever he could go. This he heard, as if he were telling it to himself at the top of his voice, but it came from somewhere so deep and so dark inside him that he could only hear the shouting of it as less than a whisper, as just a hot and chilling breath, and he scarcely heeded it, there was so much else to attend to.

"For as he walked along in this sudden and complete loneliness, he tells us, this wonderful knowledge of be- ing one with all his race meant less and less to him, and in its place came something still more wonderful: he knew what it was to be himself alone, a creature separate and different from any other, who had never been be- fore, and would never be again. He could feel this in his whole weight as he walked, and in each foot as he put it down and gave his weight to it and moved above it, and in every muscle as he moved, and it was a pride which lifted him up and made him feel large, and a pleasure which pierced him through. And as he be- gan with such wondering delight to be aware of his own exact singleness in this world, he also began to under- stand (or so he thought) just why these fences were set so very narrow, and just why he was walking all by himself. It stole over him, he tells us, like the feeling of a slow cool wind, that he was being guided toward some still more wonderful reward or revealing, up ahead, which he could not of course imagine, but he was sure it was being held in store for him alone.

"Just then the one ahead of him fell down with a great sigh, and was so quickly taken out of the way that he did not even have to shift the order of his hooves as he walked on. The sudden fall and the sound of that sigh dismayed him, though, and something within him told him that it would be wise to look up: and there he saw Him.

"A little bridge ran crosswise above the fences. He stood on this bridge with His feet as wide apart as He could set them. He wore spattered trousers but from the belt up He was naked and as wet as rain. Both arms were raised high above His head and in both hands He held an enormous Hammer. With a grunt which was hardly like the voice of a human being, and with all His strength, He brought this Hammer down onto the forehead of our friend: who, in a blinding blazing, heard from his own mouth the beginning of a gasping sigh; then there was only darkness."

Oh, this is *enough!* it's *enough!* she cried out within herself, seeing their terrible young eyes. How *could* she have been so foolish as to tell so much!

"What happened then?" she heard, in the voice of the oldest calf, and she was horrified. This shining in their eyes: was it only excitement? no pity? no fear?

"What happened?" two others asked.

Very well, she said to herself. I've gone so far; now I'll go the rest of the way. She decided not to soften it, either. She'd teach them a lesson they wouldn't forget in a hurry.

"Very well," she was surprised to hear herself say aloud.

"How long he lay in this darkness he couldn't know, but when he began to come out of it, all he knew was the most unspeakably dreadful pain. He was upside down and very slowly swinging and turning, for he was hanging by the tendons of his heels from great frightful hooks, and he has told us that the feeling was as if his hide were being torn from him inch by inch, in one piece. And then as he became more clearly aware he found that this was exactly what was happening. Knives would sliver and slice along both flanks, between the hide and the living flesh; then there was a moment of most precious relief; then red hands seized his hide and there was a jerking of the hide and a tearing of tissue which it was almost as terrible to hear as to feel, turning his whole body and the poor head at the bottom of it; and then the knives again.

"It was so far beyond anything he had ever known unnatural and amazing that he hung there through several more such slicings and jerkings and tearings before he was fully able to take it all in: then, with a scream, and a supreme straining of all his strength, he tore himself from the hooks and collapsed sprawling to the floor and, scrambling right to his feet, charged the men with the knives. For just a moment they were so astonished and so terrified they could not move. Then they moved faster than he had ever known men could—and so did all the other men who chanced to be in his way. He ran down a glowing floor of blood and down endless corridors which were hung with the bleeding carcasses of our kind and with bleeding fragments of carcasses, among blood-clothed men who carried bleeding weapons, and out of that vast room into the open, and over and through one fence after another, shoving aside many an astounded stranger and shouting out warnings as he ran, and away up the railroad toward the West.

"How he ever managed to get away, and how he ever found his way home, we can only try to guess. It's told that he scarcely knew, himself, by the time he came to this part of his story. He was impatient with those who interrupted him to ask about that, he had so much more important things to tell them, and by then he was so exhausted and so far gone that he could say nothing very clear about the little he did know. But we can realize that he must have had really tremendous strength, otherwise he couldn't have outlived the Hammer; and that strength such as his—which we simply don't see these days, it's of the olden time—is capable of things our own strongest and bravest would sicken to dream of. But there was something even stronger than his strength. There was his righteous fury, which nothing could stand up against, which brought him out of that fearful place. And there was his high and burning and heroic purpose, to keep him safe along the way, and to guide him home, and to keep the breath of life in him until he could warn us. He did manage to tell us that he just followed the railroad, but how he chose one among the many which branched out from that place, he couldn't say. He told us, too, that from time to time he recognized shapes of mountains and other landmarks, from his journey by train, all reappearing backward and with a changed look and hard to see, too (for he was shrewd enough to travel mostly at night), but still recognizable. But that isn't enough to account for it. For he has told us, too, that he simply *knew* the way; that he didn't hesitate one moment in choosing the right line of railroad, or even think of it as choosing; and that the landmarks didn't really guide him, but just made him the more sure of what he was already sure of; and that whenever he *did* encounter human beings—and during the later stages of his journey, when he began to doubt he would live to tell us, he traveled day and night—they never so much as moved to make him trouble, but stopped dead in their tracks, and their jaws fell open.

"And surely we can't wonder that their jaws fell open. I'm sure yours would, if you had seen him as he arrived, and I'm very glad I wasn't there to see it, either, even though it is said to be the greatest and most momentous day of all the days that ever were or shall be. For we have the testimony of eyewitnesses, how he looked, and it is only too vivid, even to hear of. He came up out of the East as much staggering as galloping (for by now he was so worn out by pain and exertion and loss of blood that he could hardly stay upright), and his heels were so piteously torn by the hooks that his hooves doubled under more often than not, and in his broken forehead the mark of the Hammer was like the socket for a third eye.

"He came to the meadow where the great trees made shade over the water. 'Bring them all together!' he cried out, as soon as he could find breath. 'All!' Then he drank; and then he began to speak to those who were already there: for as soon as he saw himself in the water it was as clear to him as it was to those who watched him that there was no time left to send for the others. His hide was all gone from his head and his neck and his fore-legs and his chest and most of one side and a part of the other side. It was flung backward from his naked muscles by the wind of his running and now it lay around him in the dust like a ragged garment. They say there is no imagining how terrible and in some way how grand the eyeball is when the skin has been taken entirely from around it: his eyes, which were bare in this way, also burned with pain, and with the final energies of his life, and with his desperate concern to warn us while he could: and he rolled his eyes wildly while he talked, or looked piercingly from one to another of the listeners, interrupting himself to cry out, '*Believe* me! Oh, *believe* me!' For it had evidently never occurred to him that he might not be believed, and must make this last great effort, in addition to all he had gone through for us, to *make* himself believed; so that he groaned with sorrow and with rage and railed at them without tact or mercy for their slowness to believe. He had scarcely what you could call a voice left, but with this relic of a voice he shouted and bellowed and bullied us and insulted us, in the agony of his concern. While he talked he bled from the mouth, and the mingled blood and saliva hung from his chin like the beard of a goat.

"Some say that with his naked face, and his savage eyes, and that beard and the hide lying off his bare shoulders like shabby clothing, he looked almost human. But others feel this is an irreverence even to think; and others, that it is a poor compliment to pay the one who told us, at such cost to himself, the true ultimate purpose of Man. Some did not believe he had ever come from our ranch in the first place, and of course he was so different

from us in appearance and even in his voice, and so
changed from what he might ever have looked or sounded
like before, that nobody could recognize him for
sure, though some were sure they did. Others suspected
that he had been sent among us with his story for some
mischievous and cruel purpose, and the fact that they
could not imagine what this purpose might be, made
them, naturally, all the more suspicious. Some believed
he was actually a man, trying—and none too successfully, they said—to disguise himself as one of us; and
again the fact that they could not imagine why a man
would do this, made them all the more uneasy. There
were quite a few who doubted that anyone who could get
into such bad condition as he was in, was fit even to give
reliable information, let alone advice, to those in good
health. And some whispered, even while he spoke, that
he had turned lunatic; and many came to believe this.
It wasn't only that his story was so fantastic; there was
good reason to wonder, many felt, whether anybody
in his right mind would go to such trouble for others.
But even those who did not believe him listened intently, out of curiosity to hear so wild a tale, and out of
the respect it is only proper to show any creature who
is in the last agony.

"What he told, was what I have just told you. But his
purpose was away beyond just the telling. When
they asked questions, no matter how curious or suspicious or idle or foolish, he learned, toward the last, to
answer them with all the patience he could and in all
the detail he could remember. He even invited them to
examine his wounded heels and the pulsing wound in
his head as closely as they pleased. He even begged
them to, for he knew that before everything else, he
must be believed. For unless we could believe him,
wherever could we find any reason, or enough courage,
to do the hard and dreadful things he told us we must
do!

"It was only these things he cared about. Only for
these, he came back."

Now clearly remembering what these things were, she felt her whole being quail. She looked at the young ones quickly and as quickly looked away.

"While he talked," she went on, "and our ancestors listened, men came quietly among us; one of them shot him. Whether he was shot in kindness or to silence him is an endlessly disputed question which will probably never be settled. Whether, even, he died of the shot, or through his own great pain and weariness (for his eyes, they way, were glazing for some time before the men came), we will never be sure. Some suppose even that he may have died of his sorrow and his concern for us. Others feel that he had quite enough to die of, without that. All these things are tangled and lost in the disputes of those who love to theorize and to argue. There is no arguing about his dying words, though; they were very clearly remembered:

" 'Tell them! Believe!' "

After a while her son asked, "What did he tell them to do?"

She avoided his eyes. "There's a great deal of disagreement about that, too," she said after a moment. "You see, he was so very tired."

They were silent.

"So tired," she said, "some think that toward the end, he really *must* have been out of his mind."

"Why?" asked her son.

"Because he was so tired out and so badly hurt."

They looked at her mistrustfully.

"And because of what he told us to do."

"What did he tell us to do?" her son asked again.

Her throat felt dry. "Just . . . things you can hardly bear even to think of. That's all."

They waited. "Well, *what?*" her son asked in a cold, accusing voice.

" 'Each one is himself,' " she said shyly. " 'Not of the herd. Himself alone.' That's one."

"What else?"

" '*Obey nobody. Depend on none.*' "

"What else?"

She found that she was moved. " '*Break down the fences,*' " she said less shyly. " '*Tell everybody, everywhere.*' "

"Where?"

"Everywhere. You see, he thought there must be ever so many more of us than we had ever known."

They were silent. "What else?" her son asked.

" '*For if even a few do not hear me, or disbelieve me, we are all betrayed.*' "

"Betrayed?"

"He meant, doing as men want us to. Not for ourselves, or the good of each other."

They were puzzled.

"Because, you see, he felt there was no other way." Again her voice altered: " '*All who are put on the range are put onto trains. All who are put onto trains meet the Man With The Hammer. All who stay home are kept there to breed others to go onto the range, and so betray themselves and their kind and their children forever.*

" '*We are brought into this life only to be victims; and there is no other way for us unless we save ourselves.*'

"Do you understand?"

Still they were puzzled, she saw; and no wonder, poor things. But now the ancient lines rang in her memory, terrible and brave. They made her somehow proud. She began actually to want to say them.

" '*Never be taken,*' " she said. " '*Never be driven. Let those who can, kill Man. Let those who cannot, avoid him.*' "

She looked around at them.

"What else?" her son asked, and in his voice there was a rising valor.

She looked straight into his eyes. " '*Kill the yearlings,*' " she said very gently. " '*Kill the calves.*' "

She saw the valor leave his eyes.

"Kill us?"

She nodded. " '*So long as Man holds dominion over us,*' " she said. And in dread and amazement she heard herself add, " '*Bear no young.*' "

With this they all looked at her at once in such a way that she loved her child, and all these others, as never before; and there dilated within her such a sorrowful and marveling grandeur that for a moment she saw nothing, and heard nothing except her own inward whisper, "Why, *I* am one alone. And of the herd, too. Both at once. All one."

Her son's voice brought her back: "Did they do what he told them to?"

The oldest one scoffed, "Would we be here, if they had?"

"They say some did," the mother replied. "Some tried. Not all."

"What did the men do to them?" another asked.

"I don't know," she said. "It was such a very long time ago."

"Do you believe it?" asked the oldest calf.

"There are some who believe it," she said.

"Do *you?*"

"I'm told that far back in the wildest corners of the range there are some of us, mostly very, very old ones, who have never been taken. It's said that they meet, every so often, to talk and just to think together about the heroism and the terror of two sublime Beings, The One Who Came Back, and The Man With The Hammer. Even here at home, some of the old ones, and some of us who are just old-fashioned, believe it, or parts of it anyway. I know there are some who say that a hollow at the center of the forehead—a sort of shadow of the Hammer's blow—is a sign of very special ability. And I remember how Great-grandmother used to sing an old, pious song, let's see now, yes, 'Be not like dumb-driven cattle, be a hero in the strife.' But there aren't many. Not any more."

"Do *you* believe it?" the oldest calf insisted; and now she was touched to realize that every one of them, from the oldest to the youngest, needed very badly to be sure about that.

"Of course not, silly," she said; and all at once she was overcome by a most curious shyness, for it occurred to her that in the course of time, this young thing might be bred to her. "It's just an old, old legend." With a tender little laugh she added, lightly, "We use it to frighten children with."

By now the light was long on the plain and the herd was only a fume of gold near the horizon. Behind it, dung steamed, and dust sank gently to the shattered ground. She looked far away for a moment, wondering. Something—it was like a forgotten word on the tip of the tongue. She felt the sudden chill of the late afternoon and she wondered what she had been wondering about. "Come, children," she said briskly, "it's high time for supper." And she turned away; they followed.

The trouble was, her son was thinking, you could never trust her. If she said a thing was so, she was probably just trying to get her way with you. If she said a thing wasn't so, it probably was so. But you never could be sure. Not without seeing for yourself. I'm going to go, he told himself; I don't care *what* she wants. And if it isn't so, why then I'll live on the range and make the great journey and find out what *is* so. And if what she told was true, why then I'll know ahead of time and the one I will charge is The Man With The Hammer. I'll put Him and His Hammer out of the way forever, and that will make me an even better hero than The One Who Came Back.

So, when his mother glanced at him in concern, not quite daring to ask her question, he gave her his most docile smile, and snuggled his head against her, and she was comforted.

The littlest and youngest of them was doing double skips in his efforts to keep up with her. Now that he wouldn't be interrupting her, and none of the big ones would hear and make fun of him, he shyly whispered his question, so warmly moistly ticklish that she felt as if he were licking her ear.

"What is it, darling?" she asked, bending down.

"What's a train?"

Faq'

George P. Elliott

DURING the war my geographer was a lieutenant in the
Air Corps. On one of his trips to North Africa his plane
flew over the lower edge of the Atlas Mountains, where
they meet the Sahara. For long stretches the range was a
desolation, as he had expected, relieved only by a few ribbons of green. No doubt rivers from melting snows came
down these valleys and squandered themselves in the
desert, supplying just enough water to keep a strip of
trees and grasses alive on their banks. All this was what
he had learned in his studies. But he had also been
taught that no one lived on the south side of the mountains, and yet he was quite certain that in one of the
valleys he had seen a cluster of huts and some smoke
weaving up through the trees. The smoke could have
been mist—though it was a hot clear day—but the huts
were certainly human dwellings. His curiosity was
aroused. He resolved to satisfy it as soon as he was able.

After the war, when he was able to investigate, he discovered only two references to anything that could possibly be identified as his special valley. The first was in a
book written in 1837 by one Benjamin Huntley, *Exploring the Atlas Mountains*. Huntley mentions hearing
of the existence of a village somewhere south of Mount
Tizi, but he says he doubts if his informants were reliable. The other reference was in a twelfth-century Arabic
manuscript now in the Royal Library in Madrid, a report
on revenues from slave trading in Spain and Northwest
Africa. On a map in this manuscript a spot considerably
south and west of Mount Tizi is identified as Faq'. There

is nothing in the text to explain Faq'; there was nothing but the word itself on the old parchment map. There was nothing else at all anywhere. What was he to do?

If he sought the assistance of one of the learned societies, he would certainly lose much or all of the credit for the discovery—if discovery there was to be. But the expenses would probably come to more than his purse could bear, unless he risked making the explorations quite alone and with no further reconnaissance by air. And it was a risk—the region was a true wilderness, mountainous, arid, huge, and inhospitable even to plants. But he was young and a good mountaineer and he could speak Arabic, and for years he had been risking his life for a lesser cause—to him—than this. His is the sort that wants every place to be given its right name; for him the words terra incognita signify an admission of defeat or a region of impenetrable cold; error is his evil. It was clear what he must do: discover Faq'.

I will not tell you much about the adventures he had before he reached his goal, the delays caused by the suspicion and incredulity of small officials, the hostility of the hill people, the grandeur of that wilderness in which he wandered for weeks not even sure of the existence of his goal, the privation and fatigue and load of bad doubt which only his pride could support, the great good fortune by which he was saved from starvation by a wounded eagle dropping from the skies near to him—too weak to kill it outright, he had to suck its blood. But finally he stood at the brink of a fertile valley, a valley flat and broad for these mountains, but inaccessible from above because of the sheer rise of the range and from the sides because of the steep cliffs and, as he found, uninviting from below because it narrowed to a gorge that emptied the river out precipitously; but people lived here—it was Faq'. It took him three days to discover the tortuous route of access into the valley, and one whole day to get to the floor. Among rushes at the edge of the river he collapsed, one hand trailing in the water, flat on his belly, sunk at last into that weariness which his pride no longer needed to deny. He lay there for at least one day and perhaps two, he had no way of knowing. When he awoke he could scarcely roll over, and the hand which had fallen into the water was wrinkled white and seemed to be paralyzed. It was lucky for him that he was not discovered, for the women of Faq' would have killed him if they had found him asleep.

He finally rolled onto his back, and lay wondering whether he would ever be able to get up. But as he lay there in the soft rushes in the warmth of afternoon he began to notice, as though for the first time, that vast clean sky under which he had so long labored; and in his fatigue he could not resist the sudden fancy that the sky was not *over* him—he was not *below* its perfection, but rather he was a part of it. "For is not the blueness of the sky," he said to himself, "achieved only by the refraction of light on innumerable particles, which are about me here as well as out there, and maybe in me for all I know?" The longer he lay, looking not up but out, into, among, the more it seemed to him that the sky was not so absolute a blue as it had been on the days before. Yet there could be no mist, not here on this side of these mountains. He lay wondering whether so much blandness had deceived his senses, but he was swimming in that perfection all the same; and then suddenly an explanation for the seeming mistiness occurred to him. It was a light smoke haze. He remembered the curls of smoke he had seen from the airplane, and he observed that there was no wind. No doubt a nearly imperceptible film of smoke obscured his perfect vision. This saddened him for a moment, but then he thought, "Why is it not as absolute a perfection, the sky with this faint and even haze in it, as a clean sky? These smoke particles have been added, but thinly like the blue particles, perfectly distributed. They are not an adulteration, but a version of that other perfection, a part of it, distributed differently now than before; if it hadn't been for that tiny difference I would never have noticed the whole, huge sublimity, and who can say that one of these versions is truer than the other?" Full of these reflections he arose and went down the riverside in search of friends.

He had not gone far when he heard children's laughter in the woods across the river. The stream was neither very wide nor fast-flowing, and at its deepest it did not come over his chest; yet he thought he would never get across it alive. When he was ten yards from the opposite shore he fell in exhaustion into the stream, and floated on the current more dead than alive. But he was caught in an eddy where he lay with his nose and eyes just sticking above water, slowly revolving under the green shade of an hospitable tree like a log in the pool. All he had to do to save himself was to crawl up under the tree onto a pleasant bank. But it didn't seem worth the trouble. It was too lovely there to move, looking up into the twining imperfections of this tree, cool and still and spread out and wet, slowly going about in the eddy, finally without will, only a thing that once had been able to think and now was at peace in the enveloping water, in one complete embrace happy. He does not yet understand why he ever climbed out of the water. He was not conscious of making a decision. All of a sudden it came to him that the sun had gone down and it was time to come home; before he could reflect on this odd notion (where was home?) he found himself climbing out on the bank, a live man again. Never since then has he felt anything out of the ordinary about floating in a river or looking at the sky, and he doesn't know exactly how to explain the experiences of that day—his fatigue perhaps, or the special air and water there, or his relief at finding his goal. What he is sure of is this: while he didn't know what to expect from the people of Faq', he was prepared for it when it came.

It was dusk when he approached the huts. They were long and thin, and all of them pointed up the valley toward the mountains. There were no windows in them. They were interspersed among trees. At some distance he could see a large hut in which there were fire, cooking, noise, children. He crept up to the closest hut, and crouched on the dark side of it listening to the mutter coming from within. The muttering was fast and monotonous, in a man's voice. It seemed to be a praying in some Arabic dialect. He could make out some of the words, or thought he could; they seemed to be numerals. As he listened to that unflagging drone it occurred to him that this must be a machine, no man could do it; but then he heard a clearing of the throat and a slight pause, and he realized it was a man all right, but a man imitating a machine. A praying machine. He thought of hermits.

Footsteps approached. He glued himself to the wall. He heard a woman murmuring, a slight altercation, a moment of laughter, stirring sounds, and then footsteps going away. He looked carefully around the edge of the building and saw a well-built young man, not an old one as he had expected, and a young woman. Side by side they were approaching the building of light and noise. Others were coming to it also. There were no dogs around; at least none had smelled him out, none were barking. He crept nearer the communal house. The odor of cooking food nearly made him faint it was so pleasant. Nevertheless, he lay low a while, trying to understand what was going on. Everything about the scene appeared to be unexceptional and happy. There were several men and many more women and a good many children. Three old women came out into the darkness and on the way to their hut began singing quietly a song the like of which he had never heard. He saw a young man catch and embrace a struggling young woman at the door to the hut, to the general merriment, all with an openness which he had never so much as heard of among Mohammedans. He had no idea what would be best for him to do.

What he finally did was to walk straight toward the doorway crying as loud as he could, which was not very loud, "Food in the name of Allah!"

Well, they took care of him, fed him, and nursed him back to strength again. He learned later that he was the only outsider who had ever been allowed to live in Faq'—to stay alive, I mean, not just abide there. I think it was more than a matter of whim that he was allowed to stay. He was completely at their mercy and they could understand something of what he said, so much was in his favor; but mostly he helped himself with his own honest pride.

After he had eaten some of the vegetable stew which is their chief food, watched intently by a hundred dark, silent faces, the chief, Alfaleen, asked him in their dialect who he was. Now my geographer had noticed that no one had mentioned Allah and that the chief's style was very plain for Arabic, with none of those honorific courtesies universal among Mohammedans. He had noticed this, but hadn't known what to make of it. He answered, "Destroyer of boundaries." There was no response. Either they had not understood his accent or else they were not at all impressed. "Foe of all ignorance," he said. No response. "Seeker of truth."

Then Alfaleen said to him, "What must be?"

"What has always been will always be."

Alfaleen repeated, "What must be?"

"So long as there are hills the rain will flow down them in streams."

Alfaleen repeated, "What must be?"

"Each number will always have two neighbors."

But Alfaleen asked again, "What must be?"

And this time he gave the answer he would never before in his life have given: "Nothing." It saved him.

He has wondered a thousand times why he gave that unlikely answer. He had of course heard of the indeterminacy principle; he had heard, with fascination, that law is a matter of statistical probability and that truth is finally a matter of whichever of the many geometries best suits your needs. But since he had never been able to imagine such things he had not believed in them, and he certainly had never asked himself whether or not a stone *must* fall, two plus two *must* equal four. Yet he had said to Alfaleen, that black, cool, impersonal man, that nothing must be. He attributes this answer of his to the power of Alfaleen's mind. He was concentrating hard on understanding what was being said to him and on choosing the correct Arabic words for his answers, he was weak with fatigue, he sensed that much depended upon his answer, and he was alerted by the very strangeness of the question. Even so, he thinks it was the power of that other mind which put the answer into his mouth. He learned to respect that power.

For a week he convalesced. The women and children, among whom he stayed, treated him with all the friendliness in the world. Alfaleen had commanded him to tell them nothing about the place from which he had come, and had also commanded them not to ask him about it. He had nothing to do but to lie about listening to them, learning what their customs were and how they thought and what they were afraid of—not learning it so much as taking it in like the food and water and bright air. He observed that none of the mature men did any of the ordinary tasks, like gathering fuel, fishing, repairing the huts, irrigating the fields; they seemed to have some other work. The women did not resent this state of affairs; it had not occurred to them, apparently, that things could be otherwise arranged. The children were amazingly unrestricted and happy. There were at least twice as many girls as boys for some reason, but the women did not seem to treat the boys with any great reverence. The children were not allowed to go near the huts at the other end of the village (where he had heard the man praying like a machine). Every morning Alfaleen would take the boys over five off to school. The girls learned from the women. Boys were punished for being too rough, too "manly"; girls were punished for using a number over one hundred. The children had a game which they loved to play, with innumerable variations: a boy would sit in a special position and begin to count in a low regular voice, and a girl or perhaps two or three of them would try to distract him. They would use every means imaginable except hurting: shout in his ear, caress him, throw cold water on him, count backwards in his same rhythm, put food in his mouth. Some of the boys had developed amazing powers of concentration, but the wiles of the girls were irresistible. No boy could hold out for more than a quarter of an hour—but no ordinary boy would have held out against those girls for two minutes, whatever he was doing. One little girl, about eight or nine, who was particularly attached to him—a quiet thing with a clumsy, strong body, rather deliberate, rather grave—told him one morning that she had had a nightmare about the end of the world. She had dreamed, she said, that "they came to the end of the counting and I was one of the ones left over." A little boy who got angry with him once called him a "slow counter." From the awed silence and snickers with which the other children greeted this, he concluded that it was a serious insult. The women and children were the happiest he had ever seen; yet there was nothing intense about what they did. They seemed never to have suffered. He was too feeble, too contented to feel any strangeness about all this; while it lasted it seemed exactly the way things should be. But when he was strong again at the end of a week and Alfaleen removed him from his idyl he was glad it was over.

At first Alfaleen asked him questions about the world from which he had come. "Which men are most revered? Which have the greatest power? For what is a man put to death? What is God nowadays?" But the questioning did not go on for long. Alfaleen was feeling him out, determining just how to introduce him to the life which he was entering. To one who lives with beauty hourly, as to a man in love, the various semblances of beauty to which he may be exposed are all imperfect and not in the least interesting; he wants to be with the true beauty. Alfaleen's was the beauty of truth, and he wanted to share it. He tried tricks and deceptions in his questionings, but he was hopelessly honest; it was clear that no one had lied in Faq' for a long time.

Well, the upshot of it all was that he was deemed worthy to become a bearer of the mystery of the truth, a participant in it. He was taken to a hut of his own in the men's section of the village—a bare, dark, quiet hut— and there taught to count. One sat in a certain manner— the way the boys had sat in their game—weaved in a certain rhythm, closed one's senses to the outside world, thought only of the perfection of one's technique, and counted in a steady voice. He was given a block of numbers very high in the series, told certain permissible abbreviations and short cuts, and left each morning to his counting. Alfaleen instructed him each afternoon in the history and aims of Faq'. He understood it all in a way. He was quite good at counting. But then he had to be; anyone who fell below a certain monthly quota was put to death. So was any cheater. Alfaleen would prowl about outside the huts listening to the voices of the counters—two or three times a day he came by, so keen and trained that he could tell by the very cadences of the murmuring count whether the counter was in danger of falling behind. There were no cheaters.

In the tenth century, when the Arabs were conquerors of North Africa and Spain and were also developing advanced mathematical theories, a nobleman-mathematician named Alfaleen stopped in the province of Maraq' while en route to Spain to enter the faculty of the new college of mathematics. But he fell out with the theologians of Maraq' and was condemned for his heresy. Alfaleen had maintained that pure reason, and only pure reason, could ever achieve the truth, and that since thought was the greatest power in the universe then Allah must be thought. According to the theologians this was as much as to say that the Koran wasn't worth a couple of quadratic equations and that if God is idea then idea is God. To rescue the youth of Spain from such notions they recommended to the governor of Maraq' that he execute Alfaleen. But the governor was an old friend of Alfaleen's father; instead of executing him, he had him and all his party driven off into the granite wilderness to perish for heresy. And that would have been that; but by some hook or crook they fell in with a band of native blacks, founded Faq', and established a colony. Their descendants have lived there in peace ever since. They had no animals or tools, but none were needed. The outside world forgot they were there, and any stranger who happened to come to Faq' was put to death.

So far as their traditions tell, the constitution of Faq' has remained unaltered since its founding—the laws of reason are ageless. There is Alfaleen, the chief, the philosopher, the king; there are the men, who count; and there are the women, who do the work and tend to the men. The original Alfaleen, to whose genius Faq' owes its peace and its purpose, had by the exercise of pure reason seen the folly of racial distinctions; blacks and Arabs had intermingled as they desired, the third Alfaleen was himself pure black, and by now the blend of races is complete. He had seen the problem of keeping down the population; defectives, women who can no longer work, innovators, are all put to death. The ratio of women to men had been kept fairly constant at three to one. Though the women, having no souls, cannot be entrusted with the high mission of Faq', yet the actual survival of the colony has come more and more to rest upon them—they weed out the unfit, they maintain everyone physically, and they keep watch on the men. Indeed, though Alfaleen is the governor, it is the women who actually make and execute all the rules and customs —except, of course, those having to do with the only thing that matters, the exercise of pure reason, the counting.

For Alfaleen had set his people reason's purest problem: number. And each Alfaleen, chosen solely for his ability, spends his life in the contemplation of number and the attributes of number in the confidence that the penetration of this mystery, the final conquering of it, will lay bare the secret to all power. But not many men are capable of such true and ultimate endeavor; hence, as soon as the colony had stabilized itself, Alfaleen, like a good philosopher-king, had set his subjects to the accomplishment of a communal task, one which in its very nature surpasses any other that men have set themselves: counting. By hypothesis the highest nameable number is as far from the end as one is, and there is no end to counting. It is the function of Faq' to test this hypothesis in the only statistically verifiable fashion, actually by counting forever.

The women may not use a number greater than one hundred; the life of Faq' does not make larger numbers necessary and woman's reason would sully truth. Originally there was much defection from the strict regime, and at one time had the insurrectionists banded together they could have overthrown the rule of this godless theocracy, but Alfaleen won out. They have reached a very high number; they expect in our lifetime to reach the number beyond which numbers have no name. Into that darkness Alfaleen will shed the light of reason.

More and more in the past few centuries Alfaleen has come to believe that the core of the problem of number lies in its oneness-endlessness and that the original impulse which set the men of Faq' to telling the rosary of reason's mystery was by no means an expedient but rather an attempt to mechanize the mystery itself. For this, says Alfaleen, is not only the activity of reason, it is reason pure, this counting, because only incidentally does it correspond to anything outside man's mind. It becomes clearer and clearer that without this endless and exact demonstration of reason's truth all reason would be subverted and mankind go back to what it had been before.

Alfaleen said, and certainly he believes it, that there is a sense in which man's destiny hangs upon those counters in Faq', for that they do not reach the end of counting is the demonstration of all hypothesis. If they should reach the end, reason would have done what is impossible to it and the rest would be chess, for then they would have proved that reason too has its law—absolute positive correlation. But if they should quit counting—weary, exhausted, rebellious, defeated—then would you and I have succumbed at last to our weariness and rebellion and defeat, and the women would take over.

At first he was exhilarated by the novelty of the life and what seemed to be the importance of the counting. At the outset boredom was the dread at the back of his mind, but in fact he was never bored. The counting seemed to hypnotize him into a state of strange tranquillity. He was tranced, as it were, into reason's realm. So much so, indeed, that it was not many weeks before he quite lost interest in exercise and food and the evening conviviality. Then girls taunted and seduced him, with an innocent artfulness and a voluptuous naïveté which he found (as had the boys in the game) irresistible. One night he counted in his sleep, and all the next day he was required to play with children and make love to young women and lie in the sun. Everything was communal in Faq', property and love as well as the great task. It was a world of reason and sense and trance, and he found it far happier than the world of mystery and strong feeling from which he had come. But eventually he began to think.

Or perhaps not to think so much as to remember. He remembered the anxiety and injustice and despair and the huge splendors of this world—the poverty, the right and wrong, the power, the pain. Especially the pain. He told himself again and again that ten thousand sink that one may rise, that whole cities stink in ugliness that fifty men may make and enjoy only a little beauty. But not all the reasonableness he could muster, nor horror at his memories, nor the truth and high pleasantness of Faq' could drive the thought of pain from his mind. For it was pain, suffering, moral agony, that his memories revolved about. It became clearer and clearer to him that he could not live without pain, not even thus happily, not even thus participating in the great task of man's noblest faculty. He tried hurting himself physically; he had a large rock balanced precariously once, ready to roll onto his arm and smash it. But the absurdity of such an act here in this equable valley stopped him from doing it. And afterwards the indignity he felt at not having been able to prepare a greater pain for himself than this which any accident might provide, not having been able to go through with even this little thing made him resolve to leave Faq' as soon as he could. For a long time he had been dissembling at his counting, with great anxiety and guiltiness. Now that he had resolved to leave, all this counting suddenly seemed silly to him, and he dissembled without a qualm.

He sat day after day in his hut making the sounds of

counting, and often actually tranced into it—it had its own power. But most of the time he was planning his escape. It was necessarily an escape too, for anyone guilty of any defection, from bad health to rebelliousness, was without mercy or remorse killed. He collected food and water and made himself a substitute for shoes. He walked on rocky ground till his feet were horny. He played and swam very hard till he was strong and supple. He had no human ties to break; four of the women were pregnant at the time, one perhaps with his child, perhaps all four, perhaps none, he did not care. He would miss Alfaleen's cold, pure speculations, but never, he knew, so much as he now missed the pain of this world of ours. He lay in the sun till he was nearly as black as they, and in the middle of one stormy night he left. He was not pursued.

He returned to us after much difficulty. He is suffering with us now, and looking back at the bland perfection of Faq' with a sometimes acute nostalgia. But my geographer is determined never to go there again, for he is sure that though he does not know what is right for men ordered perfection is wrong, and that though suffering is bad the lack of suffering is much worse.

The Mattress by the Tomato Patch

Tennessee Williams

My landlady, Olga Kedrova, has given me a bowl of
ripe tomatoes from the patch that she lies next to, sunning herself in the great white and blue afternoons of
California. These tomatoes are big as my fist, bloody red
of color, and firm to the touch as a young swimmer's
pectoral muscles.

I said, Why, Olga, my God, it would take me a month
to eat that many tomatoes, but she said, Don't be a fool,
you'll eat them like grapes, and that was almost how I
ate them. It is now five o'clock of this resurrected day in
the summer of 1943, a day which I am recording in the
present tense although it is ten years past. Now there are
only a couple of the big ripe tomatoes left in the pale-
blue china bowl, but their sweetness and pride are un-
dimmed, for their heart is not in the bowl which is their
graveyard but in the patch that Olga lies next to, and the
patch seems to be inexhaustible. It remains out there in
the sun and the loam and in the consanguine presence
of big Olga Kedrova. She rests beside the patch all afternoon on a raggedy mattress retired from service in one
of her hotel bedrooms.

This resurrected day is a Saturday and all afternoon
pairs of young lovers have wandered the streets of Santa
Monica, searching for rooms to make love in. Each uni-
formed boy holds a small zipper bag and the sun-pinked-
or-gilded arm of a pretty girl, and they seem to be moving
in pools of translucent water. The girl waits at the foot

of steps which the boy bounds up, at first eagerly, then anxiously, then with desperation, for Santa Monica is literally flooded with licensed and unlicensed couples in this summer of 1943. The couples are endless and their search is unflagging. By sundown and long after, even as late as two or three in the morning, the boy will bound up steps and the girl wait below, sometimes primly pretending not to hear the four-letter word he mutters after each disappointment, sometimes saying it for him when he resumes his dogged hold on her arm. Even as daybreak comes they'll still be searching and praying and cursing with bodies that ache from pent-up longing more than fatigue.

Terrible separations occur at daybreak. The docile girl finally loses faith or patience; she twists violently free of the hand that bruises her arm and dashes sobbing into an all-night café to phone for a cab. The boy hovers outside, gazing fiercely through fog and window, his now empty fist opening and closing on itself. She sits between two strangers, crouches over coffee, sobbing, sniffing, and maybe after a minute she goes back out to forgive him and rests in his arms without hope of anything private, or maybe she is relentless and waits for the cab to remove her from him forever, pretending not to see him outside the fogged window until he wanders away, drunk now, to look for more liquor, turning back now and then to glare at the hot yellow pane that shielded her from his fury. Son of a bitch of a four-letter word for a part of her woman's body is muttered again and again as he stumbles across the car tracks into Palisades Park, under regal palm trees as tall as five-story buildings and over the boom of white breakers and into mist. Long pencils of light still weave back and forth through the sky in search of enemy planes that never come over and nothing else seems to move. But you never can tell. Even at this white hour he might run into something that's better than nothing before the paddy-wagon picks him up or he falls onto one of those cots for service men only at some place like the Elks' Lodge.

Olga knows all this, but what can she do about it?

Build more rooms single-handed? To look at Olga you'd almost believe that she could. She is the kind of woman whose weight should be computed not in pounds but in stones, for she has the look of a massive primitive sculpture. Her origin is the Middle East of Europe. She subscribes to the *Daily Worker*, copies of which she sometimes thrusts under my door with paragraphs boxed in red pencil, and she keeps hopefully handing me works by Engels and Veblen and Marx which I hold for a respectful interval and then hand back to her with the sort of vague comment that doesn't fool her a bit. She has now set me down as a hopelessly unregenerate prostitute of the capitalist class, but she calls me "Tennie" or "Villyums" with undiminished good humor and there is nothing at all that she doesn't tell me about herself and nothing about myself that she doesn't expect me to tell . . . When I first came to stay here, late in the spring, and it came out in our conversation that I was a writer at Metro's, she said, Ha ha, I know you studio people! She says things like this with an air of genial complicity which a lingering reserve in my nature at first inclined me to pretend not to understand. But as the summer wore on, my reserve dropped off, and at present I don't suppose we have one secret between us. Sometimes while we are talking, she will go in my bathroom and continue the conversation with the door wide open and her seated figure in full view, looking out at me with the cloudlessly candid eyes of a child who has not yet learned that some things are meant to be private.

This is a house full of beds and I strongly suspect that big Olga has lain in them all. These big old-fashioned brass or white iron beds are like the keyboard of a concert grand piano on which she is running up and down in a sort of continual arpeggio of lighthearted intrigues, and I can't much blame her when I look at her husband. It is sentimental to think that all sick people deserve our sympathy. Ernie is sick but I can't feel sorry for him. He is a thin, sour man whose chronic intestinal trouble was diagnosed eight years ago as cancer, but whose condition today is neither much worse nor better than when the

diagnosis was made, a fact that confirms the landlady's
contempt for all opinions that don't come through "The
Party."

Ernie does the woman's work around the apartment-
hotel, while Olga soaks up the sun on the high front
steps or from the mattress by the tomato patch out back.
From those front steps her lively but unastonished look
can comprehend the whole fantasy of Santa Monica
Beach, as far north as the "Gone with the Wind" mansion of former film star Molly Delancey and as far
south as the equally idiotic but somewhat gayer design of
the roller coasters at Venice, California.

Somehow it seems to me, because I like to think so,
that this is the summer hotel, magically transplanted
from the Crimean seacoast, where Chekhov's melancholy
writer, Trigorin, first made the acquaintance of Madame
Arcadina, and where they spent their first weekend together, sadly and wisely within the quiet sound of the
sea, a pair of middle-aged lovers who turn the lights off
before they undress together, who read plays aloud to
each other on heaps of cool pillows and sometimes find
that the pressure of a hand before falling asleep is all that
they really need to be sure they are resting together.

The Palisades is a big white wooden structure with
galleries and gables and plenty of space around it. It
stands directly over a municipal playground known as
"Muscle Beach." It is here that the acrobats and tumblers
work out in the afternoons, great powerful Narcissans
who handle their weightless girls and daintier male partners with a sort of tender unconsciousness under the
blare and activity of our wartime heavens.

While I am working at home, during my six-week lay-
off-without-pay from the studio (a punishment for in-
transigence that presages a short term of employment
and forces me to push my play anxiously forward), it is a
comfort now and then to notice Big Olga dreaming on
the front steps or sprawled on that old mattress in back
of the building.

I like to imagine how the mattress got out there . . .
This is how I see it.

On one of those diamond-bright mornings of early summer, Big Olga looms into an upstairs bedroom a soldier and his girl-friend have occupied for the week-end which has just passed. With nonchalant grunts, she looks at the cigarette stains and sniffs at the glasses on the bedside table. With only a token wrinkle or two of something too mild to be defined as disgust, she picks up the used contraceptives tossed under the bed, counts them and murmurs "My God" as she drops them into the toilet and comes back out of the bathroom without having bothered to wash her hands at the sink. The boy and the girl have plainly enjoyed themselves and Olga is not the kind to resent their pleasure and she is philosophical about little damages to beds and tables incurred in a storm of love-making. Some day one of them will fall asleep or pass out in bed with a lighted cigarette and her summer hotel will burn down. She knows this will happen some day but till it happens, oh, well, why worry about it.

She goes back to the bed and jerks off the crumpled sheets to expose the mattress.

My God, she cries out, the condition this mattress is in!

Bad? says Ernie.

Completely ruined, she tells him.

Pigs, says Ernie.

But Olga is not unhappy.

Pigs, pigs, pigs, says Ernie with almost squealing repugnance, but Olga says, Aw, shut up! A bed is meant to make love on, so why blow your stack about it?

This shuts Ernie up, but inwardly he boils and becomes short-winded.

Ernie, says Olga, you take that end of the mattress.

She picks up the other.

Where does it go? asks Ernie.

The little man backs toward the door but Olga thinks differently of it. She gives an emphatic tug toward the gallery entrance. This way, she says roughly, and Ernie, who rarely presumes anymore to ask her a question, tags along with his end of the mattress dragging the carpet.

She kicks the screen door open and with a joyous gasp she steps out into the morning above the ocean and beach. The white clocktower of downtown Santa Monica is looking out of the mist, and everything glistens. She sniffs like a dog at the morning, grins connivingly at it, and shouts, Around this way!

The mattress is lugged to the inland side of the gallery, and Ernie is still not aware of what she is up to.

Now let go, says Olga.

Ernie releases his end and staggers back to the scalloped white frame wall. He is broken and breathless, he sees pinwheels in the sky. But Olga is chuckling a little. While the pinwheels blinded him, Olga has somehow managed to gather both ends of the mattress into her arms and has rolled them together to make a great cylinder. Hmmm, she says to herself. She likes the feel of the mattress, exults in the weight of it on her. She stands there embracing the big inert thing in her arms and with the grip of her thighs. It leans against her, a big exhausted lover, that she has pressed upon his back and straddled and belabored and richly survived. She leans back with the exhausted weight of the mattress resting on her, and she is chuckling and breathing deeply now that she feels her power no longer contested. Fifteen, twenty, twenty-five years are in her of life still, not depleted more than enough to make her calm and easy. Time is no problem to her. Hugging the mattress, she thinks of a wrestler named "Tiger" who comes and goes all summer, remembers a sailor named Ed who has spent some liberties with her, thinks of a Marine Sergeant, brought up in a Kansas orphanage, who calls her Mama, feels all the weight of them resting lightly on her as the weight of one bird with various hurrying wings, staying just long enough to satisfy her and not a moment longer. And so she grips the big mattress and loves the weight of it on her. Ah, she says to herself, ah, hmmm . . .

She sees royal palm trees and the white clocktower of downtown Santa Monica, and possibly says to herself, Well, I guess I'll have a hot barbecue and a cold beer for lunch at the Wop's stand on Muscle Beach and I'll see if

Tiger is there, and if he isn't, I'll catch the five o'clock bus to L.A. and take in a good movie, and after that I'll walk over to Olivera Street and have some tamales with chili and two or three bottles of Carta Blanca and come back out to the beach on the nine o'clock bus. That will be after sundown, and three miles east of the beach, they turn the lights out in the bus (because of the war-time blackout), and Olga will have chosen a good seat-companion near the back of the bus, a sailor who's done two hitches and knows the scoop, so when the lights go out, her knees will divide and his will follow suit and the traveling dusk will hum with the gossamer wings of Eros. She'll nudge him when the bus slows toward the corner of Wilshire and Ocean. They'll get off there and wander hand-in-hand into the booming shadows of Palisades Park, which Olga knows like a favorite book never tired of. All along that enormously tall cliff, under royal palms and over the Pacific, are little summer houses and trellised arbors with benches where sudden acquaintances burst into prodigal flower.

All of these things, these prospects, too vivid to need any thought, are in her nerves as she feels the weight of the mattress between her breasts and thighs, and now she is ready to show the extent of her power. She tightens the grip of her arms on the soft-hard bulk and raises the mattress to the height of her shoulders.

Watch out, my God, says Ernie, you'll rupture yourself!

Not I! says Olga, I'll not rupture myself!

Ha ha, look here! she orders.

Her black eyes flash as she coils up her muscles.

One for the money, two for the show, three to get ready, and four to GO!

Christ Almighty, says Ernie without much breath or conviction, as the mattress sails, yes, almost literally sails above the rail of the gallery and out into the glistening air of morning. Fountains of delicate cotton fiber spurt out of at least a thousand ruptures in its cover the moment the wornout mattress plops to the ground.

Hmmm, says Olga.

The act has been richly completed. She grips the rail of the gallery with her hands that have never yet been fastened on anything they could not overwhelm if they chose to. The big brass bangles she has attached to her ears are jingling with silly but rapturous applause, and Ernie is thinking again, as he has thought so often, since death so thoughtlessly planted a slow seed in his body: How is it possible that I ever lay with this woman, even so long ago as that now is!

With an animal's sense of what goes on behind it, Olga knows what her invalid husband feels when she exhibits her power, and her back to him is neither friendly nor hostile. And if tonight he has a cramp in the bowels that doubles him up, she'll help him to the bathroom and sit yawning on the edge of the tub with a cigarette and a Hollywood fan-magazine, while he sweats and groans on the stool. She'll utter goodhumored "phews" and wave her cigarette at the stench of his anguish, sometimes extending a hand to cup his forehead. And if he bleeds and collapses, as he sometimes does, she'll pick him up and carry him back to bed and fall asleep with his hot fingers twitching in hers, doing it all as if God had told her to do it. There are two reasons: He is a mean and sick little beast that once mated with her and would have been left and forgotten a long time ago except for the now implausible circumstance that she bore two offspring by him—a daughter employed as "executive secretary to a big wheel at Warner's." (She has to stay at his place because he's a lush and needs her constant attention.) And this one, "My God, look at him." A blownup Kodachrome snapshot of a glistening wet golden youth on some unidentified beach that borders a jungle. He makes his nakedness decent by holding a mass of red flowers before his groin. Olga lifts the picture and gives it five kisses as fast as machine-gun fire, which leave rouge-stains on the glass, as bright as the blossoms the grinning boy covers his sex with.

So those are the circumstances she feels behind her in Ernie, and yet they cast no shadow over the present moment. What she is doing is what is usual with her, she's thinking in terms of comfort and satisfaction as she looks down at the prostrate bulk of the mattress. Her eyes are soaking up the possibilities of it. The past of the mattress was good. Olga would be the last to deny its goodness. It has lain beneath many summers of fornications in Olga's summer hotel. But the future of the mattress is going to be good, too. It is going to lie under Olga on afternoons of leisure and under the wonderful rocking-horse weather of Southern California.

That is what the veteran mattress has done for the past few summers. The rain and the sun have had their influence on it. Unable to dissolve and absorb it into themselves, the elements have invested it with their own traits. It is now all softness and odors of ocean and earth, and it is still lying next to the prodigal patch of tomatoes that make me think of a deck of green-backed cards in which everything but diamonds and hearts have been thrown into discard.

(What do you bid? demands the queen of hearts. But that is Olga, and Olga is bidding *forever!*)

On afternoons of leisure she lies out there on this over-blown mattress of hers and her slow-breathing body is steamed and relaxed in a one-piece sarong-type garment that a Hollywood pinup girl would hardly dare to appear in. The cocker spaniel named Freckles is resting his chin on her belly. He looks like a butterscotch pudding with whipped cream on it. And these two indolent creatures drift in and out of attention to what takes place in Olga's summer hotel. The quarrels, the music, the wailing receipt of bad news, the joyful shouting, everything that goes on is known and accepted. Without even feeling anything so strong as contempt, their glances take in the activities of the husband having words with a tenant about a torn window shade or sand in a bathtub or wet tracks on the stairs. Nobody pays much attention to poor little Ernie. The Ernies of the world are treated that way. They butt their heads against the walls of their indignation until their dry little brains are shaken to bits. There he goes now, I can see him out this window, trotting along the upstairs gallery of the projecting back wing of the building with some linen to air, some bedclothes on which young bodies have taken their pleasure, for which he hates them. Ernie treats everyone with the polite fury of the impotent cuckold, and they treat Ernie in such an offhand manner it turns him around like a top till he runs down and stops. Sometimes while he complains, they walk right past him dripping the brine of the ocean along the stairs, which Ernie must get down on his hands and knees to wipe up. Pigs, pigs, is what he calls them, and of course he is right, but his fury is too indiscriminate to be useful. Olga is also capable of fury, but she reserves it for the true beast which she knows by sight, sound, and smell, and although she has no name for it, she knows it is the beast of mendacity in us, the beast that tells mean lies, and Olga is not to be confused and thrown off guard by smaller adversaries. Perhaps all adversaries are smaller than Olga, for she is almost as large as the afternoons she lies under.

And so it goes and no one resists the going.

The wonderful rocking-horse weather of California goes rocking over our heads and over the galleries of Olga's summer hotel. It goes rocking over the acrobats and their slim-bodied partners, over the young cadets at the school for flyers, over the ocean that catches the blaze of the moment, over the pier at Venice, over the roller coasters and over the vast beach-homes of the world's most successful kept women—not only over those persons and paraphernalia, but over all that is shared in the commonwealth of existence. It has rocked over me all summer, and over my afternoons at this green and white checkered table in the yellow gelatine flood of a burlesque show. It has gone rocking over accomplishments and defeats; it has covered it all and absorbed the wounds with the pleasures and made no discrimination. For nothing is quite so cavalier as this horse. The giant blue rocking-horse weather of Southern California is rocking and rocking with all the signs pointing forward. Its plumes are smoky blue ones the sky can't hold and so lets grandly go of . . .

And now I am through with another of these afternoons so I push the chair back from the table, littered with paper, and stretch my cramped spine till it crackles and rub my fingers gently over a dull pain in my chest, and think what a cheap little package this is that we have been given to live in, some rubbery kind of machine not meant to wear long, but somewhere in it is a mysterious tenant who knows and describes its being. Who is he and what is he up to? Shadow him, tap his wires, check his intimate associates, if he has any, for there is some occult purpose in his coming to stay here and all the time watching so anxiously out of the windows . . .

Now I am looking out of a window at Olga who has been sunning herself on that smoking-car joke of a mattress the whole livelong afternoon, while she ages at leisure and laps up life with the tongue of a female bull. The wrestler Tiger has taken the room next to mine, that's why she keeps looking this way, placidly alert for the gleam of a purple silk robe through his window curtains, letting her know of his return from the beach, and before he has hung the robe on a hook on the door, the door will open and close as softly as an eyelid and Olga will have disappeared from her mattress by the tomato patch. Once the cocker spaniel had the impudence to sniff and bark outside Tiger's door and he was let in and tossed right out the back window, and another time I heard Tiger muttering, Jesus, you fat old cow, but only a few moments later the noises that came through the wall made me think of the dying confessions of a walrus.

And so it goes and no one resists the going.

The perishability of the package she comes in has cast on Olga no shadow she can't laugh off. I look at her now, before the return of Tiger from Muscle Beach, and if no thought, no knowledge has yet taken form in the protean jelly-world of brain and nerves, if I am patient enough to wait a few moments longer, this landlady by Picasso may spring up from her mattress and come running into this room with a milky-blue china bowl full of reasons and explanations for all that exists.

Angel Levine

Bernard Malamud

MANISCHEVITZ, a tailor, in his fifty-first year suffered many reverses and indignities. Previously a man of comfortable means, he overnight lost all he had, when his establishment caught fire and, after a metal container of cleaning fluid exploded, burned to the ground. Although Manischevitz was insured against fire, damage suits by two customers who had been hurt in the flames deprived him of every penny he had collected. At almost the same time, his son, of much promise, was killed in the war, and his daughter, without so much as a word of warning, married a lout and disappeared with him as off the face of the earth. Thereafter Manischevitz was victimized by excruciating backaches and found himself unable to work even as a presser—the only kind of work available to him—for more than an hour or two daily, because beyond that the pain from standing became maddening. His Fanny, a good wife and mother, who had taken in washing and sewing, began before his eyes to waste away. Suffering shortness of breath, she at last became seriously ill and took to her bed. The doctor, a former customer of Manischevitz, who out of pity treated them, at first had difficulty diagnosing her ailment but later put it down as hardening of the arteries at an advanced stage. He took Manischevitz aside, prescribed complete rest for her, and in whispers gave him to know there was little hope.

Throughout his trials Manischevitz had remained somewhat stoic, almost unbelieving that all this had descended upon his head, as if it were happening, let us say, to an acquaintance or some distant relative; it was in sheer quantity of woe incomprehensible. It was also ridiculous, unjust, and because he had always been a religious man, it was in a way an affront to God. Manischevitz believed this in all his suffering. When his burden had grown too crushingly heavy to be borne he prayed in his chair with shut hollow eyes: "My dear God, sweetheart, did I deserve that this should happen to me?" Then recognizing the worthlessness of it, he put aside the complaint and prayed humbly for assistance: "Give Fanny back her health, and to me for myself that I shouldn't feel pain in every step. Help now or tomorrow is too late. This I don't have to tell you." And Manischevitz wept.

Manischevitz's flat, which he had moved into after the disastrous fire, was a meager one, furnished with a few sticks of chairs, a table, and bed, in one of the poorer sections of the city. There were three rooms: a small, poorly-papered living room; an apology for a kitchen, with a wooden icebox; and the comparatively large bedroom where Fanny lay in a sagging secondhand bed, gasping for breath. The bedroom was the warmest room of the house and it was here, after his outburst to God, that Manischevitz, by the light of two small bulbs overhead, sat reading his Jewish newspaper. He was not truly reading, because his thoughts were everywhere; however the print offered a convenient resting place for his eyes, and a word or two, when he permitted himself to comprehend them, had the momentary effect of helping him forget his troubles. After a short while he discovered, to his surprise, that he was actively scanning the news, searching for an item of great interest to him. Exactly what he thought he would read he couldn't say—until he realized, with some astonishment, that he was expecting to discover something about himself. Manischevitz put his paper down and looked up with the distinct impression that someone had entered the apartment, though he could not remember having heard the sound of the door opening. He looked around: the room was very still, Fanny sleeping, for once, quietly. Half-frightened, he watched her until he was satisfied she wasn't dead; then, still disturbed by the thought of an unannounced visitor, he stumbled into the living room and there had the shock of his life, for at the table sat a Negro reading a newspaper he had folded up to fit into one hand.

"What do you want here?" Manischevitz asked in fright.

The Negro put down the paper and glanced up with a gentle expression. "Good evening." He seemed not to be sure of himself, as if he had got into the wrong house. He was a large man, bonily built, with a heavy head covered by a hard derby, which he made no attempt to remove. His eyes seemed sad, but his lips, above which he wore a slight mustache, sought to smile; he was not otherwise prepossessing. The cuffs of his sleeves, Manischevitz noted, were frayed to the lining and the dark suit was badly fitted. He had very large feet. Recovering from his fright, Manischevitz guessed he had left the door open and was being visited by a case worker from the Welfare Department—some came at night—for he had recently applied for relief. Therefore he lowered himself into a chair opposite the Negro, trying, before the man's uncertain smile, to feel comfortable. The former tailor sat stiffly but patiently at the table, waiting for the investigator to take out his pad and pencil and begin asking questions; but before long he became convinced the man intended to do nothing of the sort.

"Who are you?" Manischevitz at last asked uneasily.

"If I may, insofar as one is able to, identify myself, I bear the name of Alexander Levine."

In spite of all his troubles Manischevitz felt a smile growing on his lips. "You said Levine?" he politely inquired.

The Negro nodded. "That is exactly right."

Carrying the jest farther, Manischevitz asked, "You are maybe Jewish?"

"All my life I was, willingly."

The tailor hesitated. He had heard of black Jews but had never met one. It gave an unusual sensation.

Recognizing in afterthought something odd about the tense of Levine's remark, he said doubtfully, "You ain't Jewish anymore?"

Levine at this point removed his hat, revealing a very white part in his black hair, but quickly replaced it. He replied, "I have recently been disincarnated into an angel. As such, I offer you my humble assistance, if to offer is within my province and ability—in the best sense." He lowered his eyes in apology. "Which calls for added explanation: I am what I am granted to be, and at present the completion is in the future."

"What kind of angel is this?" Manischevitz gravely asked.

"A bona fide angel of God, within prescribed limitations," answered Levine, "not to be confused with the members of any particular sect, order, or organization here on earth operating under a similar name."

Manischevitz was thoroughly disturbed. He had been expecting something but not this. What sort of mockery was it—provided Levine was an angel—of a faithful servant who had from childhood lived in the synagogues, always concerned with the word of God?

To test Levine he asked, "Then where are your wings?"

The Negro blushed as well as he was able. Manischevitz understood this from his changed expression. "Under certain circumstances we lose privileges and prerogatives upon returning to earth, no matter for what purpose, or endeavoring to assist whosoever."

"So tell me," Manischevitz said triumphantly, "how did you get here?"

"I was transmitted."

Still troubled, the tailor said, "If you are a Jew, say the blessing for bread."

Levine recited it in sonorous Hebrew.

Although moved by the familiar words Manischevitz still felt doubt that he was dealing with an angel.

"If you are an angel," he demanded somewhat angrily, "give me the proof."

Levine wet his lips. "Frankly, I cannot perform either

miracles or near miracles, due to the fact that I am in a
condition of probation. How long that will persist or even
consist, I admit, depends on the outcome."

Manischevitz racked his brains for some means of causing Levine positively to reveal his true identity, when
the Negro spoke again:

"It was given me to understand that both your wife
and you require assistance of a salubrious nature?"

The tailor could not rid himself of the feeling that he
was the butt of a jokester. Is this what a Jewish angel
looks like? he asked himself. This I am not convinced.

He asked a last question. "So if God sends to me an
angel, why a black? Why not a white that there are so
many of them?"

"It was my turn to go next," Levine explained.

Manischevitz could not be persuaded. "I think you are
a faker."

Levine slowly rose. His eyes showed disappointment
and worry. "Mr. Manischevitz," he said tonelessly, "if
you should desire me to be of assistance to you any time
in the near future, or possibly before, I can be found"
—he glanced at his fingernails—"in Harlem."

He was by then gone.

The next day Manischevitz felt some relief from his
backache and was able to work four hours at pressing.
The day after, he put in six hours; and the third day
four again. Fanny sat up a little and asked for some hal-
vah to suck. But on the fourth day the stabbing, breaking ache afflicted his back, and Fanny again lay supine,
breathing with blue-lipped difficulty.

Manischevitz was profoundly disappointed at the return of his active pain and suffering. He had hoped for
a longer interval of easement, long enough to have some
thought other than of himself and his troubles. Day by
day, hour by hour, minute after minute, he lived in pain,
pain his only memory, questioning the necessity of it,
inveighing against it, also, though with affection, against
God. Why so much, Gottenyu? If He wanted to teach
His servant a lesson for some reason, some cause—the

nature of His nature—to teach him, say, for reasons of his weakness, his pride, perhaps, during his years of prosperity, his frequent neglect of God—to give him a little lesson, why then any of the tragedies that had happened to him, any *one* would have sufficed to chasten him. But *all together*—the loss of both his children, his means of livelihood, Fanny's health and his—that was too much to ask one frail-boned man to endure. Who, after all, was Manischevitz that he had been given so much to suffer? A tailor. Certainly not a man of talent. Upon him suffering was largely wasted. It went nowhere, into nothing: into more suffering. His pain did not earn him bread, nor fill the cracks in the wall, nor lift, in the middle of the night, the kitchen table; only lay upon him, sleepless, so sharply oppressively that he could many times have cried out yet not heard himself through this thickness of misery.

In this mood he gave no thought to Mr. Alexander Levine, but at moments when the pain wavered, slightly diminishing, he sometimes wondered if he had been mistaken to dismiss him. A black Jew and angel to boot —very hard to believe, but suppose he *had* been sent to succor him, and he, Manischevitz, was in his blindness too blind to comprehend? It was this thought that put him on the knife-point of agony.

Therefore the tailor, after much self-questioning and continuing doubt, decided he would seek the self-styled angel in Harlem. Of course he had great difficulty, because he had not asked for specific directions, and movement was tedious to him. The subway took him to 116th Street, and from there he wandered in the dark world. It was vast and its lights lit nothing. Everywhere were shadows, often moving. Manischevitz hobbled along with the aid of a cane, and not knowing where to seek in the blackened tenement buildings, looked fruitlessly through store windows. In the stores he saw people and *everybody* was black. It was an amazing thing to observe. When he was too tired, too unhappy to go farther, Manischevitz stopped in front of a tailor's store. Out of familiarity with the appearance of it, with some sadness he entered. The tailor, an old skinny Negro with a mop of woolly gray hair, was sitting cross-legged on his workbench, sewing a pair of full-dress pants that had a razor slit all the way down the seat.

"You'll excuse me, please, gentleman," said Manischevitz, admiring the tailor's deft, thimbled fingerwork, "but you know maybe somebody by the name Alexander Levine?"

The tailor, who Manischevitz thought, seemed a little antagonistic to him, scratched his scalp.

"Cain't say I ever heared dat name."

"Alex-ander Lev-ine," Manischevitz repeated it.

The man shook his head. "Cain't say I heared."

About to depart, Manischevitz remembered to say: "He is an angel, maybe."

"Oh *him*," said the tailor clucking. "He hang out in dat honky tonk down here a ways." He pointed with his skinny finger and returned to the pants.

Manischevitz crossed the street against a red light and was almost run down by a taxi. On the block after the next, the sixth store from the corner was a cabaret, and the name in sparkling lights was Bella's. Ashamed to go in, Manischevitz gazed through the neon-lit window, and when the dancing couples had parted and drifted away, he discovered at a table on the side, towards the rear, Levine.

He was sitting alone, a cigarette butt hanging from the corner of his mouth, playing solitaire with a dirty pack of cards, and Manischevitz felt a touch of pity for him, for Levine had deteriorated in appearance. His derby was dented and had a gray smudge on the side. His ill-fitting suit was shabbier, as if he had been sleeping in it. His shoes and trouser cuffs were muddy, and his face was covered with an impenetrable stubble the color of licorice. Manischevitz, though deeply disappointed, was about to enter, when a big-breasted Negress in a purple evening gown appeared before Levine's table, and with much laughter through many white teeth, broke into a vigorous shimmy. Levine looked straight at Manischevitz with a haunted expression, but the tailor was too paralyzed to move or acknowledge it. As Bella's gyrations continued, Levine rose, his eyes lit in excitement. She embraced him with vigor, both his hands clasped around her big restless buttocks and they tangoed together across the floor, loudly applauded by the noisy customers. She seemed to have lifted Levine off his feet and his large shoes hung limp as they danced. They slid past the windows where Manischevitz, white-faced, stood staring in. Levine winked slyly and the tailor left for home.

Fanny lay at death's door. Through shrunken lips she muttered concerning her childhood, the sorrows of the marriage bed, the loss of her children, yet wept to live. Manischevitz tried not to listen, but even without ears he would have heard. It was not a gift. The doctor panted up the stairs, a broad but bland, unshaven man (it was Sunday) and soon shook his head. A day at most, or two. He left at once, not without pity, to spare himself Manischevitz's multiplied sorrow; the man who never stopped hurting. He would someday get him into a public home.

Manischevitz visited a synagogue and there spoke to God, but God had absented himself. The tailor searched his heart and found no hope. When she died he would live dead. He considered taking his life although he knew he wouldn't. Yet it was something to consider. Considering, you existed. He railed against God— Can you love a rock, a broom, an emptiness? Baring his chest, he smote the naked bones, cursing himself for having believed.

Asleep in a chair that afternoon, he dreamed of Levine. He was standing before a faded mirror, preening small decaying opalescent wings. "This means," mumbled Manischevitz, as he broke out of sleep, "that it is possible he could be an angel." Begging a neighbor lady to look in on Fanny and occasionally wet her lips with a few drops of water, he drew on his thin coat, gripped his walking stick, exchanged some pennies for a subway token, and rode to Harlem. He knew this act was the last desperate one of his woe: to go without belief, seeking a black magician to restore his wife to invalidism. Yet if there was no choice, he did at least what was chosen.

He hobbled to Bella's but the place had changed hands. It was now, as he breathed, a synagogue in a store. In the front, towards him, were several rows of empty wooden benches. In the rear stood the Ark, its portals of rough wood covered with rainbows of sequins; under it a long table on which lay the sacred scroll unrolled, illuminated by the dim light from a bulb on a chain overhead. Around the table, as if frozen to it and the scroll, which they all touched with their fingers, sat four Negroes wearing skullcaps. Now as they read the Holy Word, Manischevitz could, through the plate glass window, hear the singsong chant of their voices. One of them was old, with a gray beard. One was bubble-eyed. One was hump-backed. The fourth was a boy, no older than thirteen. Their heads moved in rhythmic swaying. Touched by this sight from his childhood and youth, Manischevitz entered and stood silent in the rear.

"Neshoma," said bubble eyes, pointing to the word with a stubby finger. "Now what dat mean?"

"That's the word that means soul," said the boy. He wore glasses.

"Let's git on wid de commentary," said the old man.

"Ain't necessary," said the humpback. "Souls is immaterial substance. That's all. The soul is derived in that manner. The immateriality is derived from the substance, and they both, causally an' otherwise, derived from the soul. There can be no higher."

"That's the highest."

"Over de top."

"Wait a minute," said bubble eyes. "I don't see what is dat immaterial substance. How come de one gits hitched up to de odder?" He addressed the humpback.

"Ask me something hard. Because it is substanceless immateriality. It couldn't be closer together, like all the parts of the body under one skin—closer."

"Hear now," said the old man.

"All you done is switched de words."

"It's the primum mobile, the substanceless substance from which comes all things that were incepted in the idea—you, me and everything and body else."

"Now how did all dat happen? Make it sound simple."

"It de speerit," said the old man. "On de face of de water moved de speerit. An' dat was good. It say so in de Book. From de speerit ariz de man."

"But now listen here. How come it become substance if it all de time a spirit?"

"God alone done dat."

"Holy! Holy! Praise His Name."

"But has dis spirit got some kind of a shade or color?" asked bubble eyes, deadpan.

"Man of course not. A spirit is a spirit."

"Then how come we is colored?" he said with a triumphant glare.

"Ain't got nothing to do wid dat."

"I still like to know."

"God put the spirit in all things," answered the boy. "He put it in the green leaves and the yellow flowers. He put it with the gold in the fishes and the blue in the sky. That's how come it came to us."

"Amen."

"Praise Lawd and utter loud His speechless name."

"Blow de bugle till it bust the sky."

They fell silent, intent upon the next word. Manischevitz approached them.

"You'll excuse me," he said. "I am looking for Alexander Levine. You know him maybe?"

"That's the angel," said the boy.

"Oh, *him*," snuffed bubble eyes.

"You'll find him at Bella's. It's the establishment right across the street," the humpback said.

Manischevitz said he was sorry that he could not stay, thanked them, and limped across the street. It was already night. The city was dark and he could barely find his way.

But Bella's was bursting with the blues. Through the window Manischevitz recognized the dancing crowd and among them sought Levine. He was sitting loose-lipped at Bella's side table. They were tippling from an almost empty whiskey fifth. Levine had shed his old clothes, wore a shiny new checkered suit, pearl-gray derby, cigar, and big, two-tone button shoes. To the tailor's dismay, a drunken look had settled upon his formerly dignified face. He leaned toward Bella, tickled her ear lobe with his pinky, while whispering words that sent her into gales of raucous laughter. She fondled his knee.

Manischevitz, girding himself, pushed open the door and was not welcomed.

"This place reserved."

"Beat it, pale puss."

"Exit, Yankel, Semitic trash."

But he moved towards the table where Levine sat, the crowd breaking before him as he hobbled forward.

"Mr. Levine," he spoke in a trembly voice. "Is here Manischevitz."

Levine glared blearily. "Speak yo' piece, son."

Manischevitz shuddered. His back plagued him. Cold tremors tormented his crooked legs. He looked around, everybody was all ears.

"You'll excuse me. I would like to talk to you in a private place."

"Speak, Ah is a private pusson."

Bella laughed piercingly. "Stop it, boy, you killin' me."

Manischevitz, no end disturbed, considered fleeing but Levine addressed him:

"Kindly state the pu'pose of yo' communication with yo's truly."

The tailor wet cracked lips. "You are Jewish. This I am sure."

Levine rose, nostrils flaring. "Anythin' else yo' got to say?"

Manischevitz's tongue lay like stone.

"Speak now or fo'ever hold off."

Tears blinded the tailor's eyes. Was ever man so tried?

Should he say he believed a half-drunken Negro to be an angel?

The silence slowly petrified.

Manischevitz was recalling scenes of his youth as a wheel in his mind whirred: believe, do not, yes, no, yes, no. The pointer pointed to yes, to between yes and no, to no, no it was yes. He sighed. It moved but one had still to make a choice.

"I think you are an angel from God." He said it in a broken voice, thinking, If you said it it was said. If you believed it you must say it. If you believed, you believed.

The hush broke. Everybody talked but the music began and they went on dancing. Bella, grown bored, picked up the cards and dealt herself a hand.

Levine burst into tears. "How you have humiliated me."

Manischevitz apologized.

"Wait'll I freshen up." Levine went to the men's room and returned in his old clothes.

No one said goodbye as they left.

They rode to the flat via subway. As they walked up the stairs Manischevitz pointed with his cane at his door.

"That's all been taken care of," Levine said. "You best go in while I take off."

Disappointed that it was so soon over but torn by curiosity, Manischevitz followed the angel up three flights to the roof. When he got there the door was already padlocked.

Luckily he could see through a small broken window. He heard an odd noise, as though of a whirring of wings, and when he strained for a wider view, could have sworn he saw a dark figure borne aloft on a pair of magnificent black wings.

A feather drifted down. Manischevitz gasped as it turned white, but it was only snowing.

He rushed downstairs. In the flat Fanny wielded a dust mop under the bed and then upon the cobwebs on the wall.

"A wonderful thing, Fanny," Manischevitz said. "Believe me, there are Jews everywhere."

Good Country People

Flannery O'Connor

BESIDES the neutral expression that she wore when she
was alone, Mrs. Freeman had two others, forward and
reverse, that she used for all her human dealings. Her
forward expression was steady and driving like the advance of a heavy truck. Her eyes never swerved to left
or right but turned as the story turned as if they followed a yellow line down the center of it. She seldom
used the other expression because it was not often necessary for her to retract a statement, but when she did, her
face came to a complete stop, there was an almost imperceptible movement of her black eyes, during which
they seemed to be receding, and then the observer would
see that Mrs. Freeman, though she might stand there as
real as several grain sacks thrown on top of each other,
was no longer there in spirit. As for getting anything
across to her when this was the case, Mrs. Hopewell had
given it up. She might talk her head off. Mrs. Freeman
could never be brought to admit herself wrong on any
point. She would stand there and if she could be brought
to say anything, it was something like, "Well, I wouldn't
of said it was and I wouldn't of said it wasn't," or letting
her gaze range over the top kitchen shelf where there was
an assortment of dusty bottles, she might remark, "I see
you ain't ate many of them figs you put up last summer."

They carried on their most important business in the
kitchen at breakfast. Every morning Mrs. Hopewell got
up at seven o'clock and lit her gas heater and Joy's. Joy
was her daughter, a large blonde girl who had an
artificial leg. Mrs. Hopewell thought of her as a child
though she was thirty-two years old and highly educated.

Joy would get up while her mother was eating and lumber into the bathroom and slam the door, and before long, Mrs. Freeman would arrive at the back door. Joy would hear her mother call, "Come on in," and then they would talk for a while in low voices that were indistinguishable in the bathroom. By the time Joy came in, they had usually finished the weather report and were on one or the other of Mrs. Freeman's daughters, Glynese or Carramae. Joy called them Glycerin and Caramel. Glynese, a redhead, was eighteen and had many admirers; Carramae, a blonde, was only fifteen but already married and pregnant. She could not keep anything on her stomach. Every morning Mrs. Freeman told Mrs. Hopewell how many times she had vomited since the last report.

Mrs. Hopewell liked to tell people that Glynese and Carramae were two of the finest girls she knew and that Mrs. Freeman was a *lady* and that she was never ashamed to take her anywhere or introduce her to anybody they might meet. Then she would tell how she had happened to hire the Freemans in the first place and how they were a godsend to her and how she had had them four years. The reason for her keeping them so long was that they were not trash. They were good country people. She had telephoned the man whose name they had given as a reference and he had told her that Mr. Freeman was a good farmer but that his wife was the nosiest woman ever to walk the earth. "She's got to be into everything," the man said. "If she don't get there before the dust settles, you can bet she's dead, that's all. She'll want to know all your business. I can stand him real good," he had said, "but me nor my wife neither could have stood that woman one more minute on this place." That had put Mrs. Hopewell off for a few days.

She had hired them in the end because there were no other applicants but she had made up her mind beforehand exactly how she would handle the woman. Since she was the type who had to be into everything, then, Mrs. Hopewell had decided, she would not only let her be into everything, she would *see to it* that she was into everything—she would give her the responsibility of everything, she would put her in charge. Mrs. Hopewell had no bad qualities of her own but she was able to use other people's in such a constructive way that she never felt the lack. She had hired the Freemans and she had kept them four years.

Nothing is perfect. This was one of Mrs. Hopewell's favorite sayings. Another was: that is life! And still another, the most important, was: well, other people have their opinions too. She would make these statements, usually at the table, in a tone of gentle insistence as if no one held them but her, and the large hulking Joy, whose constant outrage had obliterated every expression from her face, would stare just a little to the side of her, her eyes icy blue, with the look of someone who has achieved blindness by an act of will and means to keep it.

When Mrs. Hopewell said to Mrs. Freeman that life was like that, Mrs. Freeman would say, "I always said so myself." Nothing had been arrived at by anyone that had not first been arrived at by her. She was quicker than Mr. Freeman. When Mrs. Hopewell said to her after they had been on the place awhile, "You know, you're the wheel behind the wheel," and winked, Mrs. Freeman had said, "I know it. I've always been quick. It's some that are quicker than others."

"Everybody is different," Mrs. Hopewell said.

"Yes, most people is," Mrs. Freeman said.

"It takes all kinds to make the world."

"I always said it did myself."

The girl was used to this kind of dialogue for breakfast and more of it for dinner; sometimes they had it for supper too. When they had no guest they ate in the kitchen because that was easier. Mrs. Freeman always managed to arrive at some point during the meal and to watch them finish it. She would stand in the doorway if it were summer but in the winter she would stand with one elbow on top of the refrigerator and look down on them, or she would stand by the gas heater, lifting the back of her skirt slightly. Occasionally she would stand against the wall and roll her head from side to side. At no time was she in any hurry to leave. All this was very trying on Mrs. Hopewell but she was a woman of great patience. She realized that nothing is perfect and that in the Freemans she had good country people and that if, in this day and age, you get good country people, you had better hang onto them.

She had had plenty of experience with trash. Before the Freemans she had averaged one tenant family a year. The wives of these farmers were not the kind you would want to be around you for very long. Mrs. Hopewell, who had divorced her husband long ago, needed someone to walk over the fields with her; and when Joy had to be impressed for these services, her remarks were usually so ugly and her face so glum that Mrs. Hopewell would say, "If you can't come pleasantly, I don't want you at all," to which the girl, standing square and rigid-shouldered with her neck thrust slightly forward, would reply, "If you want me, here I am—LIKE I AM."

Mrs. Hopewell excused this attitude because of the leg (which had been shot off in a hunting accident when Joy was ten). It was hard for Mrs. Hopewell to realize that her child was thirty-two now and that for more than twenty years she had had only one leg. She thought of her still as a child because it tore her heart to think instead of the poor stout girl in her thirties who had never danced a step or had any *normal* good times. Her name was really Joy but as soon as she was twenty-one and away from home, she had had it legally changed. Mrs. Hopewell was certain that she had thought and thought until she had hit upon the ugliest name in any language. Then she had gone and had the beautiful name, Joy, changed without telling her mother until after she had done it. Her legal name was Hulga.

When Mrs. Hopewell thought the name, Hulga, she thought of the broad blank hull of a battleship. She would not use it. She continued to call her Joy to which the girl responded but in a purely mechanical way.

Hulga had learned to tolerate Mrs. Freeman who saved

her from taking walks with her mother. Even Glynese and Carramae were useful when they occupied attention that might otherwise have been directed at her. At first she had thought she could not stand Mrs. Freeman for she had found that it was not possible to be rude to her. Mrs. Freeman would take on strange resentments and for days together she would be sullen but the source of her displeasure was always obscure; a direct attack, a positive leer, blatant ugliness to her face—these never touched her. And without warning one day, she began calling her Hulga.

She did not call her that in front of Mrs. Hopewell who would have been incensed but when she and the girl happened to be out of the house together, she would say something and add the name Hulga to the end of it, and the big spectacled Joy-Hulga would scowl and redden as if her privacy had been intruded upon. She considered the name her personal affair. She had arrived at it first purely on the basis of its ugly sound and then the full genius of its fitness had struck her. She had a vision of the name working like the ugly sweating Vulcan who stayed in the furnace and to whom, presumably, the goddess had to come when called. She saw it as the name of her highest creative act. One of her major triumphs was that her mother had not been able to turn her dust into Joy, but the greater one was that she had been able to turn it herself into Hulga. However, Mrs. Freeman's relish for using the name only irritated her. It was as if Mrs. Freeman's beady steel-pointed eyes had penetrated far enough behind her face to reach some secret fact. Something about her seemed to fascinate Mrs. Freeman and then one day Hulga realized that it was the artificial leg. Mrs. Freeman had a special fondness for the details of secret infections, hidden deformities, assaults upon children. Of diseases, she preferred the lingering or incurable. Hulga had heard Mrs. Hopewell give her the details of the hunting accident, how the leg had been literally blasted off, how she had never lost consciousness. Mrs. Freeman could listen to it any time as if it had happened an hour ago.

When Hulga stumped into the kitchen in the morning (she could walk without making the awful noise but she made it—Mrs. Hopewell was certain—because it was ugly-sounding), she glanced at them and did not speak. Mrs. Hopewell would be in her red kimono with her hair tied around her head in rags. She would be sitting at the table, finishing her breakfast and Mrs. Freeman would be hanging by her elbow outward from the refrigerator, looking down at the table. Hulga always put her eggs on the stove to boil and then stood over them with her arms folded, and Mrs. Hopewell would look at her—a kind of indirect gaze divided between her and Mrs. Freeman—and would think that if she would only keep herself up a little, she wouldn't be so bad looking. There was nothing wrong with her face that a pleasant expression wouldn't help. Mrs. Hopewell said that people who looked on the bright side of things would be beautiful even if they were not.

Whenever she looked at Joy this way, she could not help but feel that it would have been better if the child had not taken the Ph.D. It had certainly not brought her out any and now that she had it, there was no more excuse for her to go to school again. Mrs. Hopewell thought it was nice for girls to go to school to have a good time but Joy had "gone through." Anyhow, she would not have been strong enough to go again. The doctors had told Mrs. Hopewell that with the best of care, Joy might see forty-five. She had a weak heart. Joy had made it plain that if it had not been for this condition, she would be far from these red hills and good country people. She would be in a university lecturing to people who knew what she was talking about. And Mrs. Hopewell could very well picture her there, looking like a scarecrow and lecturing to more of the same. Here she went about all day in a six-year-old skirt and a yellow sweat shirt with a faded cowboy on a horse embossed on it. She thought this was funny; Mrs. Hopewell thought it was idiotic and showed simply that she was still a child. She was brilliant but she didn't have a grain of sense. It seemed to Mrs. Hopewell that every

year she grew less like other people and more like herself—bloated, rude, and squint-eyed. And she said such
strange things! To her own mother she had said—without warning, without excuse, standing up in the middle
of a meal with her face purple and her mouth half full—
"Woman! do you ever look inside? Do you ever look inside and see what you are *not*? God!" she had cried sinking down again and staring at her plate, "Malebranche
was right: we are not our own light. We are not our
own light!" Mrs. Hopewell had no idea to this day what
brought that on. She had only made the remark, hoping
Joy would take it in, that a smile never hurt anyone.

The girl had taken the Ph.D. in philosophy and this
left Mrs. Hopewell at a complete loss. You could say,
"My daughter is a nurse," "My daughter is a school
teacher," or even, "My daughter is a chemical engineer."
You could not say, "My daughter is a philosopher."
That was something that had ended with the Greeks
and Romans. All day Joy sat on her neck in a deep chair,
reading. Sometimes she went for walks but she didn't
like dogs or cats or birds or flowers or nature or nice
young men. She looked at nice young men as if she could
smell their stupidity.

One day Mrs. Hopewell had picked up one of the
books the girl had just put down and opening it at random, she read, "Science, on the other hand, has to assert
its soberness and seriousness afresh and declare that it is
concerned solely with what-is. Nothing—how can
it be for science anything but a horror and a phantasm?
If science is right, then one thing stands firm: science
wishes to know nothing of nothing. Such is after all the
strictly scientific approach to Nothing. We know it by
wishing to know nothing of Nothing." These words had
been underlined with a blue pencil and they worked
on Mrs. Hopewell like some evil incantation in gibber-
ish. She shut the book quickly and went out of the room
as if she were having a chill.

This morning when the girl came in, Mrs. Freeman
was on Carramae. "She thrown up four times after sup-

per," she said, "and was up twict in the night after three o'clock. Yesterday she didn't do nothing but ramble in the bureau drawer. All she did. Stand up there and see what she could run up on."

"She's got to eat," Mrs. Hopewell muttered, sipping her coffee, while she watched Joy's back at the stove. She was wondering what the child had said to the Bible salesman. She could not imagine what kind of a conversation she could possibly have had with him.

He was a tall gaunt hatless youth who had called yesterday to sell them a Bible. He had appeared at the door, carrying a large black suitcase that weighted him so heavily on one side that he had to brace himself against the door facing. He seemed on the point of collapse but he said in a cheerful voice, "Good morning, Mrs. Cedars!" and set the suitcase down on the mat. He was not a bad-looking young man though he had on a bright blue suit and yellow socks that were not pulled up far enough. He had prominent face bones and a streak of sticky-looking brown hair falling across his forehead.

"I'm Mrs. Hopewell," she said.

"Oh!" he said, pretending to look puzzled but with his eyes sparkling, "I saw it said 'The Cedars,' on the mailbox so I though you was Mrs. Cedars!" and he burst out in a pleasant laugh. He picked up the satchel and under cover of a pant, he fell forward into her hall. It was rather as if the suitcase had moved first, jerking him after it. "Mrs. Hopewell!" he said and grabbed her hand. "I hope you are well!" and he laughed again and then all at once his face sobered completely. He paused and gave her a straight earnest look and said, "Lady, I've come to speak of serious things."

"Well, come in," she muttered, none too pleased because her dinner was almost ready. He came into the parlor and sat down on the edge of a straight chair and put the suitcase between his feet and glanced around the room as if he were sizing her up by it. Her silver gleamed on the two sideboards; she decided he had never been in a room as elegant as this.

"Mrs. Hopewell," he began, using her name in a way that sounded almost intimate, "I know you believe in Chrustian service."

"Well yes," she murmured.

"I know," he said and paused, looking very wise with his head cocked on one side, "that you're a good woman. Friends have told me."

Mrs. Hopewell never liked to be taken for a fool. "What are you selling?" she asked.

"Bibles," the young man said and his eye raced around the room before he added, "I see you have no family Bible in your parlor, I see that is the one lack you got!"

Mrs. Hopewell could not say, "My daughter is an atheist and won't let me keep the Bible in the parlor." She said, stiffening slightly, "I keep my Bible by my bedside." This was not the truth. It was in the attic somewhere.

"Lady," he said, "the word of God ought to be in the parlor."

"Well, I think that's a matter of taste," she began. "I think . . ."

"Lady," he said, "for a Chrustian, the word of God ought to be in every room in the house besides in his heart. I know you're a Chrustian because I can see it in every line of your face."

She stood up and said, "Well, young man, I don't want to buy a Bible and I smell my dinner burning."

He didn't get up. He began to twist his hands and looking down at them, he said softly, "Well lady, I'll tell you the truth—not many people want to buy one nowadays and besides, I know I'm real simple. I don't know how to say a thing but to say it. I'm just a country boy." He glanced up into her unfriendly face. "People like you don't like to fool with country people like me!"

"Why!" she cried, "good country people are the salt of the earth! Besides, we all have different ways of doing, it takes all kinds to make the world go 'round. That's life!"

"You said a mouthful," he said.

"Why, I think there aren't enough good country people in the world!" she said, stirred. "I think that's what's wrong with it!"

His face had brightened. "I didn't inraduce myself," he said. "I'm Manley Pointer from out in the country around Willohobie, not even from a place, just from near a place."

"You wait a minute," she said. "I have to see about my dinner." She went out to the kitchen and found Joy standing near the door where she had been listening.

"Get rid of the salt of the earth," she said, "and let's eat."

Mrs. Hopewell gave her a pained look and turned the heat down under the vegetables. "I can't be rude to anybody," she murmured and went back into the parlor.

He had opened the suitcase and was sitting with a Bible on each knee.

"You might as well put those up," she told him. "I don't want one."

"I appreciate your honesty," he said. "You don't see any more real honest people unless you go way out in the country."

"I know," she said, "real genuine folks!" Through the crack in the door she heard a groan.

"I guess a lot of boys come telling you they're working their way through college," he said, "but I'm not going to tell you that. Somehow," he said, "I don't want to go to college. I want to devote my life to Chrustian service. See," he said, lowering his voice, "I got this heart condition. I may not live long. When you know it's something wrong with you and you may not live long, well then, lady . . ." He paused, with his mouth open, and stared at her.

He and Joy had the same condition! She knew that her eyes were filling with tears but she collected herself quickly and murmured, "Won't you stay for dinner? We'd love to have you!" and was sorry the instant she heard herself say it.

"Yes mam," he said in an abashed voice, "I would sher love to do that!"

Joy had given him one look on being introduced to him and then throughout the meal had not glanced at him again. He had addressed several remarks to her, which she had pretended not to hear. Mrs. Hopewell could not understand deliberate rudeness, although she lived with it, and she felt she had always to overflow with hospitality to make up for Joy's lack of courtesy. She urged him to talk about himself and he did. He said he was the seventh child of twelve and that his father had been crushed under a tree when he himself was eight year old. He had been crushed very badly, in fact, almost cut in two and was practically not recognizable. His mother had got along the best she could by hard working and she had always seen that her children went to Sunday School and that they read the Bible every evening. He was now nineteen year old and he had been selling Bibles for four months. In that time he had sold seventy-seven Bibles and had the promise of two more sales. He wanted to become a missionary because he thought that was the way you could do most for people. "He who losest his life shall find it," he said simply and he was so sincere, so genuine and earnest that Mrs. Hopewell would not for the world have smiled. He prevented his peas from sliding onto the table by blocking them with a piece of bread which he later cleaned his plate with. She could see Joy observing sidewise how he handled his knife and fork and she saw too that every few minutes, the boy would dart a keen appraising glance at the girl as if he were trying to attract her attention.

After dinner Joy cleared the dishes off the table and disappeared and Mrs. Hopewell was left to talk with him. He told her again about his childhood and his father's accident and about various things that had happened to him. Every five minutes or so she would stifle a yawn. He sat for two hours until finally she told him she must go because she had an appointment in town. He packed his Bibles and thanked her and prepared to leave, but in the doorway he stopped and wrung her hand and said that not on any of his trips had he met a lady as nice as her and he asked if he could come again.

She had said she would always be happy to see him.

Joy had been standing in the road, apparently looking at something in the distance, when he came down the steps toward her, bent to the side with his heavy valise. He stopped where she was standing and confronted her directly. Mrs. Hopewell could not hear what he said but she trembled to think what Joy would say to him. She could see that after a minute Joy said something and that then the boy began to speak again, making an excited gesture with his free hand. After a minute Joy said something else at which the boy began to speak once more. Then to her amazement, Mrs. Hopewell saw the two of them walk off together, toward the gate. Joy had walked all the way to the gate with him and Mrs. Hopewell could not imagine what they had said to each other, and she had not yet dared to ask.

Mrs. Freeman was insisting upon her attention. She had moved from the refrigerator to the heater so that Mrs. Hopewell had to turn and face her in order to seem to be listening. "Glynese gone out with Harvey Hill again last night," she said. "She had this sty."

"Hill," Mrs. Hopewell said absently, "is that the one who works in the garage?"

"Nome, he's the one that goes to chiropracter school," Mrs. Freeman said. "She had this sty. Been had it two days. So she says when he brought her in the other night he says, 'Lemme get rid of that sty for you,' and she says, 'How?' and he says, 'You just lay yourself down acrost the seat of that car and I'll show you.' So she done it and he popped her neck. Kept on a-popping it several times until she made him quit. This morning," Mrs. Freeman said, "she ain't got no sty. She ain't got no traces of a sty."

"I never heard of that before," Mrs. Hopewell said.

"He ast her to marry him before the Ordinary," Mrs. Freeman went on, "and she told him she wasn't going to be married in no *office*."

"Well, Glynese is a fine girl," Mrs. Hopewell said. "Glynese and Carramae are both fine girls."

"Carramae said when her and Lyman was married

Lyman said it sure felt sacred to him. She said he said he wouldn't take five hundred dollars for being married by a preacher."

"How much would he take?" the girl asked from the stove.

"He said he wouldn't take five hundred dollars," Mrs. Freeman repeated.

"Well we all have work to do," Mrs. Hopewell said.

"Lyman said it just felt more sacred to him," Mrs. Freeman said. "The doctor wants Carramae to eat prunes. Says instead of medicine. Says them cramps is coming from pressure. You know where I think it is?"

"She'll be better in a few weeks," Mrs. Hopewell said.

"In the tube," Mrs. Freeman said. "Else she wouldn't be as sick as she is."

Hulga had cracked her two eggs into a saucer and was bringing them to the table along with a cup of coffee that she had filled too full. She sat down carefully and began to eat, meaning to keep Mrs. Freeman there by questions if for any reason she showed an inclination to leave. She could perceive her mother's eye on her. The first round-about question would be about the Bible salesman and she did not wish to bring it on. "How did he pop her neck?" she asked.

Mrs. Freeman went into a description of how he had popped her neck. She said he owned a '55 Mercury but that Glynese said she would rather marry a man with only a '36 Plymouth who would be married by a preacher. The girl asked what if he had a '32 Plymouth and Mrs. Freeman said what Glynese had said was a '36 Plymouth.

Mrs. Hopewell said there were not many girls with Glynese's common sense. She said what she admired in those girls was their common sense. She said that reminded her that they had had a nice visitor yesterday, a young man selling Bibles. "Lord," she said, "he bored me to death but he was so sincere and genuine I couldn't be rude to him. He was just good country people, you know," she said, "—just the salt of the earth."

"I seen him walk up," Mrs. Freeman said, "and then

later—I seen him walk off," and Hulga could feel the slight shift in her voice, the slight insinuation, that he had not walked off alone, had he? Her face remained expressionless but the color rose into her neck and she seemed to swallow it down with the next spoonful of egg. Mrs. Freeman was looking at her as if they had a secret together.

"Well, it takes all kinds of people to make the world go 'round," Mrs. Hopewell said. "It's very good we aren't all alike."

"Some people are more alike than others," Mrs. Freeman said.

Hulga got up and stumped, with about twice the noise that was necessary, into her room and locked the door. She was to meet the Bible salesman at ten o'clock at the gate. She had thought about it half the night. She had started thinking of it as a great joke and then she had begun to see profound implications in it. She had lain in bed imagining dialogues for them that were insane on the surface but that reached below to depths that no Bible salesman would be aware of. Their conversation yesterday had been of this kind.

He had stopped in front of her and had simply stood there. His face was bony and sweaty and bright, with a little pointed nose in the center of it, and his look was different from what it had been at the dinner table. He was gazing at her with open curiosity, with fascination, like a child watching a new fantastic animal at the zoo, and he was breathing as if he had run a great distance to reach her. His gaze seemed somehow familiar but she could not think where she had been regarded with it before. For almost a minute he didn't say anything. Then on what seemed an insuck of breath, he whispered, "You ever ate a chicken that was two days old?"

The girl looked at him stonily. He might have just put this question up for consideration at the meeting of a philosophical association. "Yes," she presently replied as if she had considered it from all angles.

"It must have been mighty small!" he said triumphantly and shook all over with little nervous giggles, getting very red in the face, and subsiding finally into his gaze of complete admiration, while the girl's expression remained exactly the same.

"How old are you?" he asked softly.

She waited some time before she answered. Then in a flat voice she said, "Seventeen."

His smiles came in succession like waves breaking on the surface of a little lake. "I see you got a wooden leg," he said. "I think you're real brave. I think you're real sweet."

The girl stood blank and solid and silent.

"Walk to the gate with me," he said. "You're a brave sweet little thing and I liked you the minute I seen you walk in the door."

Hulga began to move forward.

"What's your name?" he asked, smiling down on the top of her head.

"Hulga," she said.

"Hulga," he murmured, "Hulga. Hulga. I never heard of anybody name Hulga before. You're shy, aren't you, Hulga?" he asked.

She nodded, watching his large red hand on the handle of the giant valise.

"I like girls that wear glasses," he said. "I think a lot. I'm not like these people that a serious thought don't ever enter their heads. It's because I may die."

"I may die too," she said suddenly and looked up at him. His eyes were very small and brown, glittering feverishly.

"Listen," he said, "don't you think some people was meant to meet on account of what all they got in common and all? Like they both think serious thoughts and all?" He shifted the valise to his other hand so that the hand nearest her was free. He caught hold of her elbow and shook it a little. "I don't work on Saturday," he said. "I like to walk in the woods and see what Mother Nature is wearing. O'er the hills and far away. Pic-nics and things. Couldn't we go on a pic-nic tomorrow? Say yes, Hulga," he said and gave her a dying look as if he felt his insides about to drop out of him. He had even seemed to sway slightly toward her.

During the night she had imagined that she seduced him. She imagined that the two of them walked on the place until they came to the storage barn beyond the two back fields and there, she imagined, that things came to such a pass that she very easily seduced him and that then, of course, she had to reckon with his remorse. True genius can get an idea across even to an inferior mind. She imagined that she took his remorse in hand and changed it into a deeper understanding of life. She took all his shame away and turned it into something useful.

She set off for the gate at exactly ten o'clock, escaping without drawing Mrs. Hopewell's attention. She didn't take anything to eat, forgetting that food is usually taken on a picnic. She wore a pair of slacks and a dirty white shirt, and as an afterthought, she had put some Vapex on the collar of it since she did not own any perfume. When she reached the gate no one was there.

She looked up and down the empty highway and had the furious feeling that she had been tricked, that he had only meant to make her walk to the gate after the idea of him. Then suddenly he stood up, very tall, from behind a bush on the opposite embankment. Smiling, he lifted his hat which was new and wide-brimmed. He had not worn it yesterday and she wondered if he had bought it for the occasion. It was toast-colored with a red and white band around it and was slightly too large for him. He stepped from behind the bush still carrying the black valise. He had on the same suit and the same yellow socks sucked down in his shoes from walking. He crossed the highway and said, "I knew you'd come!"

The girl wondered acidly how he had known this. She pointed to the valise and asked, "Why did you bring your Bibles?"

He took her elbow, smiling down on her as if he could not stop. "You can never tell when you'll need the word of God, Hulga," he said. She had a moment in which she doubted that this was actually happening and then they began to climb the embankment. They went down into the pasture toward the woods. The boy walked lightly by her side, bouncing on his toes. The valise did not seem to be heavy today; he even swung it. They crossed half the pasture without saying anything and then, putting his hand easily on the small of her back, he asked softly, "Where does your wooden leg join on?"

She turned an ugly red and glared at him and for an instant the boy looked abashed. "I didn't mean you no harm," he said. "I only meant you're so brave and all. I guess God takes care of you."

"No," she said, looking forward and walking fast, "I don't even believe in God."

At this he stopped and whistled. "No!" he exclaimed as if he were too astonished to say anything else.

She walked on and in a second he was bouncing at her side, fanning with his hat. "That's very unusual for a girl," he remarked, watching her out of the corner of his eye. When they reached the edge of the wood, he put his hand on her back again and drew her against him without a word and kissed her heavily.

The kiss, which had more pressure than feeling behind it, produced that extra surge of adrenalin in the girl that enables one to carry a packed trunk out of a burning house, but in her, the power went at once to the brain. Even before he released her, her mind, clear and detached and ironic anyway, was regarding him from a great distance, with amusement but with pity. She had never been kissed before and she was pleased to discover that it was an unexceptional experience and all a matter of the mind's control. Some people might enjoy drain water if they were told it was vodka. When the boy, looking expectant but uncertain, pushed her gently away, she turned and walked on, saying nothing as if such business, for her, were common enough.

He came along panting at her side, trying to help her when he saw a root that she might trip over. He caught and held back the long swaying blades of thorn vine until she had passed beyond them. She led the way and he came breathing heavily behind her. Then they came out on a sunlit hillside, sloping softly into another one a little smaller. Beyond, they could see the rusted top of the old barn where the extra hay was stored.

The hill was sprinkled with small pink weeds. "Then you ain't saved?" he asked suddenly, stopping.

The girl smiled. It was the first time she had smiled at him at all. "In my economy," she said, "I'm saved and you are damned but I told you I didn't believe in God."

Nothing seemed to destroy the boy's look of admiration. He gazed at her now as if the fantastic animal at the zoo had put its paw through the bars and given him a loving poke. She thought he looked as if he wanted to kiss her again and she walked on before he had the chance.

"Ain't there somewheres we can sit down sometime?" he murmured, his voice softening toward the end of the sentence.

"In that barn," she said.

They made for it rapidly as if it might slide away like a train. It was a large two-story barn, cool and dark inside. The boy pointed up the ladder that led into the loft and said, "It's too bad we can't go up there."

"Why can't we?" she asked.

"Yer leg," he said reverently.

The girl gave him a contemptuous look and putting both hands on the ladder, she climbed it while he stood below, apparently awestruck. She pulled herself expertly through the opening and then looked down at him and said, "Well, come on if you're coming," and he began to climb the ladder, awkwardly bringing the suitcase with him.

"We won't need the Bible," she observed.

"You never can tell," he said, panting. After he had got into the loft, he was a few seconds catching his breath. She had sat down in a pile of straw. A wide sheath of sunlight, filled with dust particles, slanted over her. She lay back against a bale, her face turned away, looking out the front opening of the barn where hay was thrown from a wagon into the loft. The two pink-speckled hillsides lay back against a dark ridge of woods.

The sky was cloudless and cold blue. The boy dropped down by her side and put one arm under her and the other over her and began methodically kissing her face, making little noises like a fish. He did not remove his hat but it was pushed far enough back not to interfere. When her glasses got in his way, he took them off of her and slipped them into his pocket.

The girl at first did not return any of the kisses but presently she began to and after she had put several on his cheek, she reached his lips and remained there, kissing him again and again as if she were trying to draw all the breath out of him. His breath was clear and sweet like a child's and the kisses were sticky like a child's. He mumbled about loving her and about knowing when he first seen her that he loved her, but the mumbling was like the sleepy fretting of a child being put to sleep by his mother. Her mind, throughout this, never stopped or lost itself for a second to her feelings. "You ain't said you loved me none," he whispered finally, pulling back from her. "You got to say that."

She looked away from him off into the hollow sky and then down at a black ridge and then down farther into what appeared to be two green swelling lakes. She didn't realize he had taken her glasses but this landscape could not seem exceptional to her for she seldom paid any close attention to her surroundings.

"You got to say it," he repeated. "You got to say you love me."

She was always careful how she committed herself. "In a sense," she began, "if you use the word loosely, you might say that. But it's not a word I use. I don't have illusions. I'm one of those people who see *through* to nothing."

The boy was frowning. "You got to say it. I said it and you got to say it," he said.

The girl looked at him almost tenderly. "You poor baby," she murmured. "It's just as well you don't understand," and she pulled him by the neck, face-down, against her. "We are all damned," she said, "but some of us have taken off our blindfolds and see that there's nothing to see. It's a kind of salvation."

The boy's astonished eyes looked blankly through the ends of her hair. "Okay," he almost whined, "but do you love me or don'tcher?"

"Yes," she said and added, "in a sense. But I must tell you something. There mustn't be anything dishonest between us." She lifted his head and looked him in the eye. "I am thirty years old," she said. "I have a number of degrees."

The boy's look was irritated but dogged. "I don't care," he said. "I don't care a thing about what all you done. I just want to know if you love me or don'tcher?" and he caught her to him and wildly planted her face with kisses until she said, "Yes, yes."

"Okay then," he said, letting her go. "Prove it."

She smiled, looking dreamily out on the shifty landscape. She had seduced him without even making up her mind to try. "How?" she asked, feeling that he should be delayed a little.

He leaned over and put his lips to her ear. "Show me where your wooden leg joins on," he whispered.

The girl uttered a sharp little cry and her face instantly drained of color. The obscenity of the suggestion was not what shocked her. As a child she had sometimes been subject to feelings of shame but education had removed the last traces of that as a good surgeon scrapes for cancer; she would no more have felt it over what he was asking than she would have believed in his Bible. But she was as sensitive about the artificial leg as a peacock about his tail. No one ever touched it but her. She took care of it as someone else would his soul, in private and almost with her own eyes turned away. "No," she said.

"I known it," he muttered, sitting up. "You're just playing me for a sucker."

"Oh no no!" she cried. "It joins on at the knee. Only at the knee. Why do you want to see it?"

The boy gave her a long penetrating look. "Because," he said, "it's what makes you different. You ain't like anybody else."

She sat staring at him. There was nothing about her face or her round freezing-blue eyes to indicate that this had moved her; but she felt as if her heart had stopped and left her mind to pump her blood. She decided that for the first time in her life she was face to face with real innocence. This boy, with an instinct that came from beyond wisdom, had touched the truth about her. When after a minute, she said in a hoarse high voice, "All right," it was like surrendering to him completely. It was like losing her own life and finding it again, miraculously, in his.

Very gently he began to roll the slack leg up. The artificial limb, in a white sock and brown flat shoe, was bound in a heavy material like canvas and ended in an ugly jointure where it was attached to the stump. The boy's face and his voice were entirely reverent as he uncovered it and said, "Now show me how to take it off and on."

She took it off for him and put it back on again and then he took it off himself, handling it as tenderly as if it were a real one. "See!" he said with a delighted child's face. "Now I can do it myself!"

"Put it back on," she said. She was thinking that she would run away with him and that every night he would take the leg off and every morning put it back on again. "Put it back on," she said.

"Not yet," he murmured, setting it on its foot out of her reach. "Leave it off for a while. You got me instead."

She gave a little cry of alarm but he pushed her down and began to kiss her again. Without the leg she felt entirely dependent on him. Her brain seemed to have stopped thinking altogether and to be about some other function that it was not very good at. Different expressions raced back and forth over her face. Every now and then the boy, his eyes like two steel spikes, would glance behind him where the leg stood. Finally she pushed him off and said, "Put it back on me now."

"Wait," he said. He leaned the other way and pulled the valise toward him and opened it. It had a pale blue spotted lining and there were only two Bibles in it. He took one of these out and opened the cover of it. It was hollow and contained a pocket flask of whiskey, a pack of cards, and a small blue box with printing on it. He laid these out in front of her one at a time in an evenly-spaced row, like one presenting offerings at the shrine of a goddess. He put the blue box in her hand. THIS PRODUCT TO BE USED ONLY FOR THE PRE-VENTION OF DISEASE, she read, and dropped it. The boy was unscrewing the top of the flask. He stopped and pointed, with a smile, to the deck of cards. It was not an ordinary deck but one with an obscene picture on the back of each card. "Take a swig," he said, offering her the bottle first. He held it in front of her, but like one mesmerized, she did not move.

Her voice when she spoke had an almost pleading sound. "Aren't you," she murmured, "aren't you just good country people?"

The boy cocked his head. He looked as if he were just beginning to understand that she might be trying to insult him. "Yeah," he said, curling his lip slightly, "but it ain't held me back none. I'm as good as you any day in the week."

"Give me my leg," she said.

He pushed it farther away with his foot. "Come on now, let's begin to have us a good time," he said coaxingly. "We ain't got to know one another good yet."

"Give me my leg!" she screamed and tried to lunge for it but he pushed her down easily.

"What's the matter with you all of a sudden?" he asked, frowning as he screwed the top on the flask and put it quickly back inside the Bible. "You just a while ago said you didn't believe in nothing. I thought you was some girl!"

Her face was almost purple. "You're a Christian!" she hissed. "You're a fine Christian! You're just like them all—say one thing and do another. You're a perfect Christian, you're . . ."

The boy's mouth was set angrily. "I hope you don't think," he said in a lofty indignant tone, "that I believe in that crap! I may sell Bibles but I know which end is up and I wasn't born yesterday and I know where I'm going!"

"Give me my leg!" she screeched. He jumped up so quickly that she barely saw him sweep the cards and the blue box back into the Bible and throw the Bible into the valise. She saw him grab the leg and then she saw it for an instant slanted forlornly across the inside of the suitcase with a Bible at either side of its opposite ends. He slammed the lid shut and snatched up the valise and swung it down the hole and then stepped through himself.

When all of him had passed but his head, he turned and regarded her with a look that no longer had any admiration in it. "I've gotten a lot of interesting things," he said. "One time I got a woman's glass eye this way. And you needn't to think you'll catch me because Pointer ain't really my name. I use a different name at every house I call at and don't stay nowhere long. And I'll tell you another thing, Hulga," he said, using the name as if he didn't think much of it, "you ain't so smart. I been believing in nothing ever since I was born!" and then the toast-colored hat disappeared down the hole and the girl was left, sitting on the straw in the dusty sunlight. When she turned her churning face toward the opening, she saw his blue figure struggling successfully over the green speckled lake.

Mrs. Hopewell and Mrs. Freeman, who were in the back pasture, digging up onions, saw him emerge a little later from the woods and head across the meadow toward the highway. "Why, that looks like that nice dull young man that tried to sell me a Bible yesterday," Mrs. Hopewell said, squinting. "He must have been selling them to the Negroes back in there. He was so simple," she said, "but I guess the world would be better off if we were all that simple."

Mrs. Freeman's gaze drove forward and just touched him before he disappeared under the hill. Then she returned her attention to the evil-smelling onion shoot she was lifting from the ground. "Some can't be that simple," she said. "I know I never could."

The Engines of Hygeia

John Phillips

At nine in the morning, when all was fresh, the starched uniforms of the nurses bustled more briskly, their curious caps sat more pertly, and the illusion of sanitation and good cheer bloomed on the fifth floor of the Private Pavilion more brightly than at any hour of the day. Through the high glass doors at either end of the corridor the summer sun poured over the linoleum carpeting. A force of scrub women in apricot-colored dresses, softly chattering in the rapid language of Puerto Ricans, was wetting down the last mote of infectious dust. And the hygienic odors of the great hospital were suffused with the building momentum of nurses, tray-bearing orderlies, and interns, freshly shaven.

Merril stood before the reception desk. Mrs. Dougherty was reading Look Magazine and had not noticed him. A big man with a heavy fretful face neither old nor still identifiably young. He held his thick calves and shoulders of an athlete tense underneath the wrinkle-proof Dacron suit of which he was rather proud.

"Mrs. Dougherty," he began presently. "I want to apologize for what I said last night. I've been on edge lately," and he added, "—in this hot weather," and now Merril judged he'd made his amends, formally enough, without obsequiousness or truckling.

Mrs. Dougherty, the Floor Supervisor, looked up and answered, as though she had been expecting this all morning. "I know you didn't mean it, Mr. Merril," she said.

Mrs. Dougherty, with whom he'd had the first of his

humiliating colloquies the night before, was bestowing a motherly look. Merril knew that no words, nor scarcely any contrite deed, could serve as penance this morning. He felt, for an instant against his harsh better judgment, greatly humbled.

He had made up his mind last night never again to speak to Mrs. Dougherty beyond the perfunctory limits of civility.

Last night, after he laid down the poetry book and started to take his leave of Ellen, he had opened both her windows wide. But the July night hung outside with a moist oppressiveness that refused quite to surrender itself to the catharsis of a thunder shower. Merril cursed inwardly, always inwardly, the antiseptic mediocrity of this room. It faced onto an air shaft and the grated windows of the Men's Ward. When Ellen was brought back to the hospital in June it had been the cheapest available, and yet Merril no longer dared to contemplate its pyramiding expense.

"At least they could get you a fan," he said.

"No."

"You can't expect to sleep this way, Ellen. God."

"No—" She broke off long enough for Merril to hear her swallow and then moisten her lips. "Darling—it's not worth it."

"You have to sleep. You know that, Ellen."

"Darling, don't bother."

"You'll burn up!" He realized that he had raised his voice and that his own mouth was dry, that it was his own brow tingling.

A rubber cord was looped over the bed's headstand, its button dangling by the bed table. Merril reached for it cautiously so as not to interfere with the intravenous feeding tube, not to upset the chromium basin that had been sheltered under a napkin almost two weeks now one foot from Ellen's pillow. But he pressed his thumb defiantly against the button, as though he were willing to break either one or both. He went to the doorway to satisfy himself that the light was functioning, a yellowish disc blinking over Ellen's door while a low buzz sounded in the nurses' sitting room two doors down. The sound of a radio came from afar. A shouting voice, then uproarious laughter and the applause of a studio audience. Merril glared down the dim corridor.

"Damn their souls," he said, not quite to himself.

"Hugh, the nurses work so hard."

"*Hard?*"

When, after a minute more, Mrs. Dougherty came by in a street dress, he'd signaled her.

"I'm off duty, Mr. Merril. The night nurse will be with you in two shakes."

"My wife is not comfortable" Merril said. "I want an electric fan in here."

Mrs. Dougherty, the whole competent bulk of her, brushed by him and approached the bed with an infuriating tenderness. "You real hot in here, dear?"

"Not hot." Merril again heard his wife's laborious swallowing. "I'm just a little warm." Ellen spoke so wearily.

Mrs. Dougherty, in her hospital way, was touching sheets and smoothing pillows. She secured the rubber tube to Ellen's vein with a fresh adhesive and glanced at the glass attached to the wall, safely out of Ellen's vision, looking like a vast inverted raindrop, whose dwindling sugary content Merril was reasonably sure, though every nurse denied it, was drugged.

"Say, darned if we're not almost through our supper," Mrs. Dougherty said.

The hygienic crudity of the remark made Merril catch a breath, and he knew how it must have sounded to Ellen.

For—however long ago?—when Neddy was just born . . . When Neddy was born, Ellen's father made them a present of a fancy trained nurse who was to stay a week or two, until Ellen became accustomed to the feedings. She'd been a fragile but authoritarian woman and for four days she dominated their lives. The fourth night, when she brought Neddy in to Ellen, clucking over the shrewd and wizened face, she cooed without a vestige of sensitivity, "Now Neddy, time to eat now. Time to go to

your cow." And next morning, Ellen telephoned her
father that she wouldn't need a nurse a day longer. She
and Neddy were going to have a long association and
they didn't want to begin in a state of mutual revulsion.

The episode, the recollection of it, belonged remote
and buried like most things associated with the birth of
Neddy, with rosy illusions, resolves and fiery beginnings.
Their presence was no more fitting in the here and now
than small sheltered children.

"Just about ten minutes, and you'll have it all drunk
up." Mrs. Dougherty snapped off the ceiling light.

"I'd like to have an electric fan in here," Merril said
furiously.

"The night nurse will pop in," Mrs. Dougherty went
on, "in case there's anything you'd like. Would you like a
nice windy fan, dear?"

"Don't worry about me," Ellen answered faintly.
"Please go home now."

"My yes, I'm going home." Mrs. Dougherty snapped
off the light by the bed, plunging them into darkness,
and said good night to Ellen and started for the door.

"I'd appreciate it if—" Merril started sarcastically, but
he was too late.

"Good night, darling," Ellen said, almost a whisper.

"Good night, Ellie," he said, going to the bed. "Sleep
tight." His voice quavered, protesting an unnatural imposition of his emotions. "Don't let the bedbugs bite."

Ellen spoke, a real whisper now in the stillness, "She
works . . . very hard. You mustn't scold her, Hugh."

Mechanically, he bent over the pillows, looking for the
dark pocket in which he could barely make out her head
in a trace of light from the corridor. He'd forgotten that
she would have a little smell of lavender.

"Do something pleasant this evening," Ellen whispered. "Don't sit at home alone."

When she unexpectedly turned her head, Merril
steeled himself (it was a dreadful thing she asked) and
with effort kissed her waiting lips and completed for this
day his gesture of expiation.

"ETH I DO INDEEDY DOLLY DEAR!"

The full volume of the radio struck Merril at the bedside. A woman shrieked something through her adenoids
to which the babytalking voice of the comedian replied
to bring on a thunderclap of applause and laughter.

Merril rushed to the corridor and down it like a bull
and burst into a lighted room. "Do you know that people
here are ill?" he heard himself shouting against the noise,
and suddenly there was nothing but his shouting. *"Desperately ill?"*

He was aware of two bony hands frantically grasping
at an array of plastic dials. And still it seemed an hour
before he recognized that he was bellowing against silence, or that Mrs. Dougherty was beside him, her hand
commandingly upon his arm. The culprit hung his
shaggy head and tugged at the bedclothing. In his polka
dot pajamas, he looked, like Penrod, like the idealized
cover of a woman's magazine, or, as he rolled his terrified
eyes at Merril, like Neddy.

"It was Red Skelton," the boy said.

"Red Skelton!"

"I have to have my tonsils out tomorrow," the boy
said.

Mrs. Dougherty was saying, "Will you just step
outside, Mr. Merril?"

"I never worked this kind of radio," said the boy.

"Try and keep it nice and low, honey. It's past eight
o'clock."

Mrs. Dougherty brushed past Merril, grazing his arm
this time with her great bosom. Merril followed, in
instinctive obedience. He followed Mrs. Dougherty
dumbly down the corridor, past Ellen, past the reception
desk and into the nurses' sitting room, where Mrs.
Dougherty turned.

"Mr. Merril, I don't mind saying I'm in charge of this
floor."

"It strikes me your supervision leaves much to be desired. I think if Dr. Dagget were to know—"

"You have the right to complain to Dr. Dagget, Mr.
Merril."

Mrs. Dougherty pulled on a black pair of gloves and

gathered up two swollen brownpaper bags that he was sure contained soiled foundation garments, facial creams, and unfinished knitting. He had seen a score of Mrs. Doughertys, clutching brownpaper parcels, traveling barren, manless, their faces tired under pancake makeup, valiant, wronged, champions of astrology. They shared their grievances in trolley cars, buzzing like hot summer bees. ("I sez, if that don't beat the band . . . I sez the *nerve* . . . and she sez . . . sez . . . sez")

"Mrs. Merril isn't the only sick person on the floor," Mrs. Dougherty said.

"In 517?" he demanded. She was about to brush past him, maddeningly, through yet another doorway, and therefore his question came louder and more helpless than he intended. "Well, when is *he* going to die?"

He stared passionately at Mrs. Dougherty's back. She looked back at him from the hall.

"You should take a rest, Mr. Merril. You know you make her all worn out too when she sees you like this. Every day the same way and not getting any rest."

"Thank you," Merril said. "I think this is hardly the time to take a vacation."

"You're a very selfish man. That's all your trouble," Mrs. Dougherty answered. "You say you come for her sake, but you don't. You come for your own. —So you won't feel so bad. For you hate sick people all the same. Yes you do, you hate them. I know *you.*"

Merril left Mrs. Dougherty outside the nurses' sitting room. She must have stood there, staring his full retreat down the corridor, for he felt her eyes on the nape of his neck. He shuddered once, hunching his shoulders, and walked quickly and quietly as he could, like a boy escaping a haunted house.

He did not feel better until out in his car driving home.

The apartment was cool in contrast to the night in the streets and it was musty. It smelled of camphor, having been sealed off for the summer. Ellen had been back in the hospital for two months, and Neddy was sent to camp, and Merril did not wish to commute in solitude

from the bungalow by the seashore that had belonged
to Ellen's father. He'd decided, with a satisfying twinge
of martyrdom, to suffer through the summer in the city.
He left the apartment each week-day morning to go to
work, and came back to it each night on his return from
the hospital. He remained in it over the weekends, and
by now he was scarcely aware of the airlessness or the
camphor balls.

When he opened the door and stepped into the entry-
way, he was greeted by an unusually large white light.
Ordinarily, he would not have permitted such an indulgence. For example, Ellen had liked to leave on the hall
light for Neddy when they went out for dinner.

Ellen said it was a harmless comfort. Merril said it was
an indulgence which, however harmless-seeming, was
in fact harmful to Neddy, who must learn, from a scroll
of tenets, self-reliance and that nothing was going to
hurt him in the dark.

It was a difficulty of Ellen's that she looked for disaster
wherever Neddy was concerned. It was something pathological in Ellen, a sort of contagious anxiety. She said her
father had had something to do with it. But Merril, with
due respect to the memory of that thunderous and acquis-
itive old Draco, knew this was nonsense. What had poisoned Ellen was the shelf of child psychology tomes she
held so dear—those, and an ebullient, bow-tie-sporting
drink of water named Brattle. Lester H. Brattle, Headmaster. *Dear Parent, This April as in Aprils past Merrivale appeals to your generosity. It is our hope that this
year's Easter Pageant will be the most memorable ever.
We have planned an unusually . . .* Merrivale Country
Day School, a suburban cluster of oddly angled, spacious-
windowed buildings. An embarrassing derivation from
Frank Lloyd Wright, to which Neddy was driven on winter mornings at half past eight with five scowling companions wearing mittens and ski caps in a maroon Ranch-
wagon with yellow acorns on its doors. Where Neddy
had not yet mastered his multiplication tables but had
learned to build a kayak and tended the progeny of two
guinea pigs Ellen had given him as a reward for good

table manners. "What could be more preposterous?" Merril used to say, "Sweetheart, I ask you." When *he* was Neddy's age, he had had to be content with the Pennsylvania public school system. If he spent his busfare on ice cream, he'd had to walk home, the full four miles. *He* hadn't had a rich, dead Granddaddy.

Merril shut his front door and looked up at the bulb, and was forced to close his eyes. Merril had not turned off the switch for a week. It was indulgence, extravagance, coddling. And yet as long as Ellen lived he could not imagine returning but to bathe at the day's end in this remorseless light. He found a coldness in the hall and a brilliance sharp enough to blind the saints. Merril had purchased the bulb a week ago to replace the smaller weakening one which unaccountably depressed him coming from the hospital, and made him think of death. Although that had been foolish enough, because death, he saw now, did not have to have a sickly yellow. It could as easily hide in glacial white, holy, of such radiance as he'd thought pertained to visions of archangels and other sanctities he was too infected to behold. A light that left you standing paralyzed at your own front door. (Merril fancied he had reached back and snatched from the face of time, which was probably a black winter sky at night, one insignificant particle of a star. And, finding it so very chilly in his hand, had stuck it to the ceiling to observe its heatless burning.)

Off the hall were the dark interiors of the family rooms. Merril's impulse took him into Neddy's, where he sat gingerly on the mattress, as though it were a pane of glass. Always when he went in Neddy's room he had this sense of trespassing, that this was the boy's domain and Ellen's. Ellen heard Neddy's prayers at bedtime here, Neddy shut himself up in here in the evenings, sometimes when friends came by for a drink Merril found Neddy hiding from them in this closet. Neddy slammed this door, once, in his father's face. That happened on a Sunday evening last December when Merril discovered his son playing with a yo-yo during the weekly Reading Aloud. *Around the World in Eighty Days* was slammed

to the floor, and Neddy had cried, "I was paying attention!" and Merril, moving after his son fast enough to be
aware of the air rushing by his cheeks, shouted too, and
then Neddy's door slammed, he remembered it clearly,
inches from his nose. A long silence, and finally Ellen
emerged from the kitchen with a gust of cooking smells,
wearing that look of patient wiltedness that drove him
wild, and unhesitatingly entered Neddy's room. More
silence and at length some murmuring. Merril put on his
coat, disgusted, and went out. He crossed the street, soaking his slippers in the sooty snow, and entered the drug
store and called up Mary Hagen.

"Tears again, I suppose?" Mary Hagen said. "Everybody's in tears," Merril answered desperately. She would
be smiling at him at the other end of the connection, and
he knew she was taking care that her voice revealed only
the faintest amusement. "This is awful," Merril told her.
"And now there's this business of Ellie and the doctors."
Mary Hagen said, "The trouble is as much in Ellie as
in you. We agreed on that." He said helplessly, "They
think she may be really sick. I can't find out from Dagget." She would be smiling all the harder. "I can reas-
sure you about Dagget, darling. My gynecologist tells me
he's absolutely tops." He said, "I don't know if you should
get into this, Mary. I'm not so sure it's right." And here
she permitted herself a light indulgent laugh. "Hugh,
you dumb bunny. I'll have to take you in hand."

That was December.

Dr. Dagget performed an exploratory operation in early
February and then kept Ellen in the hospital for six weeks
of X-ray treatment. Once in the hospital when Ellen inquired casually after Mary Hagen, Merril asked her to
please stop making mountains out of molehills.

Neddy's bed was bare. Merril sat on it stiffly, pluck-
ing at mattress buttons. Neddy's winter clothes were
piled on a chair, their pockets lined with mothballs that
Ellen had put in them in May. For she was out of the
hospital then for over a month. Merril brought her breakfast in bed. They had a day nurse who crooned, "Now
isn't that glorious?" when Ellen told her she could *feel*

her strength coming back. It was then they decided that Neddy should spend the summer in a different atmosphere. Mary Hagen, who could arrange anything, had been kind enough to arrange for a summer camp in Maine. "I won't send him there, if Mary's mixed up in it," Ellen firmly said. Merril entreated her not to make mountains out of molehills. But Ellen was well enough to enter Neddy in a camp in New Hampshire. She was well enough to manage the spring cleaning, and well enough to hire a maid and well enough to supervise, lying shyly on the sofa, the rolling of the rugs, the waxing of the floors, the draping of the furniture in sheets against dust, and well enough to see that Merril's clothes and Neddy's would be proof against moths. But Ellen had worn herself out by then.

Wily Dr. Dagget deemed it advisable that Ellen return, temporarily, just for convenience's sake, to the hospital, "That way we'll be sure she treats herself to a *real* rest," said Dr. Dagget. Said the experienced and tactful Dr. Dagget—by now Merril was calling him the Benign Healer. Thus cannily he lured Ellen back to the operating table upon which, he was later to confide majestically to Merril ("I don't want to be anything but absolutely on the level with you, Mr. M."), the Benign Healer hoped that she would die. The second incision the Benign Healer made in Ellen's abdomen relieved distension and she would be feeling better for a time. However, it had revealed no trace of the parent tumor, only the increase of dark grapelike things over the peritoneum. Further X-ray would be useless, useless and downright cruel. The Benign Healer shook his silver head and made a fist, as if to smite his responsibility-ridden breast. "I tell you, Mr. M., it's things like this make a man wonder why he wanted to be a surgeon. May I say I think your wife is one of the loveliest persons it's been my privilege in thirty years . . ." The Benign Healer had mastered the quavering basso. He addressed Merril as though from a pulpit. Even his carpeted Consultation Room with its early American furniture and photographs of strapping grandchildren took on a Gothic air.

With Ellen his tone was less awful, and fey at times. Hope. Hope springs eternal—he was delighted by the phrase. He had no right to thwart instinctive hope in any human creature, and there, with a pious lowering of the eyes and some pursing of the lips, he let the subject drop with such emphasis that Merril hesitated to revive it. So, it was determined to sustain Ellen with a series of ingenious cheery nothings as she grew weaker and the weeks dragged on. *Let her believe what she wants to believe,* quoth the Benign Healer. *Who are we to interfere in these questions?*

He was never better than at the bedside, pooh-poohing. One morning in early June he made a whole day blaze with specious promise. Ellen was recovering from the second operation and starting to say again that she could *feel* her strength returning. She was receiving visitors. The room was decked with flowers. Enter the Benign Healer, humming. "Dr. Dagget, am I going to die?" Ellen asked suddenly. And without an instant's pause there came a familiar peal of basso laughter. "Are you going to die, Mrs. M.? Why, I should hope to think! So am I going to die, and so's Mr. M., and so's Mrs. Dougherty here. Wouldn't we be a little piggish to ask otherwise? Gadzooks, smell those roses!" Merril fell against the wall in disbelief, and Ellen smiled as he hadn't seen her smile since Neddy was a baby.

On one wall hung a prize of Neddy's, a mounted barracuda caught by his grandfather off the Bahama Banks. The malevolent little eyes looked into the white light of the hall and were somehow dulled and baleful. On the desk was a walnut stained pipe rack that Neddy had fashioned in the Manual Arts Shop at Merrivale as a Father's Day present and then had reclaimed after a year's disuse as a receptacle for crayons and mechanical pencils. Merril considered these homely objects now with a corrosive kind of poignance; he'd felt the same while reading aloud the little toy soldier is red with rust and his musket moulds in his hands.

The telephone was on a table in the hall. Merril went to it eagerly and placed the call and was cheerful to the operator, twice spelling out for her phonetically the poly-syllabic Indian name of the camp. The call was answered by the wife of the Camp Director who maintained that her boys went to bed at half past nine. Merril pleaded on a note of sentimental urgency which overwhelmed that motherly heart. Neddy's voice, when it came on at last, was frightened.

"Hullo."

"Hello, old man. I thought I'd call up and say hello."

"Hullo—" and here the pause so bewildering to Merril, as Neddy thought what to call his father—"Dad."

"I suppose they have you out on that lake all day, swimming and canoeing and sailing a sailboat?"

"Sometimes."

"Your mother tells me they're teaching you to dive. I wish someone had taught me to dive when I was your age. I was always taking great big belly busters and knocking my wind out," Merril said rapidly, and managed to laugh.

"She called me up tonight," Neddy said.

"She did, did she? Well, that's great."

"I guess she's still in the hospital."

"She's doing fine and there isn't anything to worry about," Merril said.

"She's still in there."

"Just to get rested up," Merril said.

"She sounded tired."

"Well it was late. They probably gave her a sleeping pill."

"She talks as if it hurt her. She can hardly—"

"Now!" Merril said. "Now, we want her to be proud of us. You understand that, don't you? We've got to stick together."

His words, with which he had been faintly pleased, hung in a long silence. Merril saw his son standing on tip-toe in his pajamas to reach the wall telephone in the sitting room of a summer cottage in New Hampshire. No doubt the Camp Director and his wife, good soul, were taking in the scene. No doubt they wondered, as

Merril always wondered, what went on in the shaggy head, behind the wide eyes.

"You understand I'm not scolding you?" Merril said.

"No. I mean yes. I mean I understand."

"I didn't have a chance to get your birthday present. What would you say to a camera?"

"Sure," Neddy said. "Thank you very much."

"Maybe you'd like a boy scout hatchet. I saw some of those in a hardware store."

"Mrs. Hagen sent me a hatchet."

"Mrs. Hagen?"

"She sent a letter. She said some stuff about me growing up and I ought to have a hatchet for the woods. It was a funny letter."

"I think you should write back and thank her."

"I was going to send her back that hatchet. I have a pretty good hatchet anyway."

Merril could not remember Neddy's being this positive before.

"I've been thinking you might want to go to Canada in September," Merril began. "We'd have a guide and a canoe for fishing and we'd sleep in a cabin. You could help cook. How would you like that? Would you like that?"

"If you would."

"I'm not going to bite you," Merril said.

In the silence Merril saw again the Camp Director and his good soul wife. They had devoted ruddy faces and simple kindly smiles and they would be sitting up there side by side on some sort of wicker sofa.

Neddy said, "If there's nothing the matter with her, you could make them let her out of the hospital."

"How can I *make* them?" Merril realized that he had shouted. "Oh God. God damn it," he said.

"I better hang up," Neddy said.

"Why can't you talk to me? What is it? I take the trouble to call you up and you refuse to—"

"Please, Dad. Somebody wants to use the phone."

"I can't help that."

"Please."

"I don't understand you," Merril said. "Not the first thing about you." He paused, whether from desperation or lethargy he could not tell, but on the far end of the wire there was no response.

Merril feared for a moment after he slammed down the receiver that he had cracked it. The black instrument was cooling beneath his palm as his own rage turned cold. He was back in himself, afraid of the white light once more, and the ridge of his fingers on his thick right palm began to smart as though he had finished a game of handball.

Merril went into the living room, and it too was partially lit by the light in the hall. He sat in the brass-studded leather chair that Ellen had inherited from her father. He enjoyed sitting here in the evenings, requiring silence from the household as he read manuscripts sent him in cardboard boxes by literary agents. Since his separation from the Navy in 1945 Merril had been employed as Associate Editor in the Trade Department of Benedict Burgess and Son, publishers. In the years ensuing, Merril derived a touch of vanity from his accomplishments—of "finding" a housewife touted as another Katherine Mansfield, of "getting" the memoirs of a disgruntled general, of "fixing" an historical novel rejected by five publishers which—no one was more stupefied than Merril—sold more than three hundred thousand copies. Sometimes when a big gun on the Burgess fiction list like Clarence Tolles came East, Merril took him to the theatre and afterwards, since Ellen never accompanied them, to Mary Hagen's apartment where there was liquor and a chosen circle of Tolles' admirers. And he had learned how to comport himself at salesmen's banquets and to address heartily by their first names stupid people whom he despised. Every now and again Merril made a hasty recapitulation of these achievements to justify his usurpation of that armchair in which Ellen's legendary and successful father used to sit.

In other moods he made excoriating judgments. He raged at the hypocrisy of a commercial enterprise which masqueraded as a cultural endeavor. "You would be amazed at the impotence of the printed word." (His audience, invariably, was Ellen.) "Did you ever stop to think how many perfectly intelligent adults can go through life without ever reading a book? And why shouldn't they? We turn them out like toothpaste, we try to sell them like toothpaste, but they don't matter as much as toothpaste. Did you ever think of the quantities of words, words, words the benighted writers struggle over every year? Of the fraction of those that are worth remembering, who *gives* a damn? All the promotion men and Book and Author luncheons since Gutenberg amount to exactly zero. I wish I *were* selling toothpaste!"

These tirades did not shock Ellen, though such may have been their purpose. Rather, they seemed to disgust her. "Hugh, if you really mean that, you should be ashamed of yourself. Why don't you get another job, if that's the way you feel?" Whereas Mary Hagen, to whom he voiced a similar lament, had laughed the sorry thought out of existence: "Poor dope, don't you think you're running off at the mouth a bit?"

The difference in their reactions was the difference in the women. Ellen was, she had been, somehow indisputably lovely. The memory of her as a bride bruised an old sense of unworthiness in Merril. She moved, she had moved, in an aura of blue eyes and mystery and it frightened him. In Ellen lay a shadowy and disturbing wisdom which struck out at him from unanticipated directions just when he told himself that it was all under control. With Mary Hagen he felt none of this. She was good looking—he found no other term for her standardized, furs-and-lipstick appearance—and approximately as pert as she had been when as a girl of twenty-four her middle-aged husband had strayed with a girl of nineteen and Mary Hagen, ever the realist, had settled for a short infinity of alimony. She had a brittleness which Merril could conveniently confuse with "guts." She could cajole him or tease him or openly deride him, but this was no more than he asked and he was at ease with her. He was never unsure. Merril recognized this difference often, as he recognized in himself a multitude of interwoven weaknesses. His father-in-law, a belaboring lip-worshiper of God, would have called them sins. Each night, and particularly in this dreadful time, Merril held his self-confessional, and peeled his spirit open like an onion, skin after skin.

Merril pressed his thumb against the swollen finger ridge of his right hand. Lately he had been slamming too many books and kitchen plates and telephones. He longed for the old schedule, to be stopping off at the gym in the evenings to work out in the handball court. He flailed a hard rubber ball against a scarred white wall. He used both hands, right, left, right, left, building a rhythm, approximating a machine. He played alone, a big man in tennis shorts, racing angrily about a vast cold room. It took only half an hour to achieve exhaustion. Afterwards Merril went into the showers, both palms sore and tingling, and stood under the hot water until the last particle of anger was washed away. Then he turned on the cold so hard that his chest felt pierced with needles. The relief came as he walked home from the gym. It was as though his feelings had been smelted out of existence. A brisk walk home in the cold night air and he was ready for anything—a drink with Ellen, a silent supper, a briefcaseful of wasted words. The old schedule, he thought, and nursed his damaged hand.

He rose from the chair and stood a moment among the ghostly sheet-covered forms of the furniture, smelling the camphor and dry dust. He walked across a rugless stretch of floor towards the desk where lay the typewritten manuscript of the Burgess Headliner for fall, *The Ethical Path to Dynamic Living*, by a radio clergyman in Southern California. He was about to snap on a lamp when the telephone started ringing in the hall and he knew who it would be by the persistence of the ring. He didn't want to answer.

"I knew it," Mary Hagen said. "Brooding in the dark."

Merril sighed for himself, pitifully. "I talked to Neddy," he said.

"Have you been sitting there in the dark?"

"I have a big light here."

"Have you had supper?" she said. "I don't see why you should go on dragging yourself through hell. I suppose you like it."

"Please," he said.

"I was merely about to suggest that we go somewhere and have a cool drink and a light dinner. Like two grown-up people."

"I didn't ask for sympathy. I'll get something from the icebox," Merril said.

"For five cents, I would gladly run over and wring your neck."

"Mary, I don't think this is a time for us to act selfishly. I won't do anything that would hurt Ellen."

"You are absolutely unbelievable," she said.

"I think this should be the last call for a while. I think it's only right."

"I'm not going to burst into tears, darling. Never fear. I'm not going to get red-eyed and sniffy. Or play Sweet Alice to your Ben Bolt."

"I wish you hadn't said that, Mary."

"Ellie's much too good for you but she trembled with fear at your frown. Do you remember Sweet Alice, Ben Bolt?"

"Shut up," he said. It was an old joke of hers and he had used to laugh at it. It was a sample of her peppery sense of humor. "And don't call her Ellie," he said sharply.

"I've known her longer than you have, my darling."

"I don't care."

"You've got to stop punishing yourself, Hugh. Ellie is not in pain. She is not going to be in pain," she said. "You're ruining yourself, Hugh. You must try and take an adult point of view."

"You've done enough," Merril answered. "You've done just about enough taking over. Why did you have to send a hatchet to Neddy?"

"O. K." She paused and then she snapped, "Good night, Hugh."

"I'll call you," he said, suddenly apprehensive.

"It's all right, Hugh."

"Mary?" he said desperately. "Mary?"

"Yes?"

"I have to think it all over by myself. Then I'll call you. When I've decided something."

"Decided something?" she laughed. "What could you conceivably decide?"

"I will." He retraced everything. He conceded her everything. "I will decide."

"Good-bye, Hugh. I'm getting tired myself."

"I apologize," Merril said.

"Good-bye."

"I'll call you later in the week."

"Good-bye."

"I'll call you Wednesday," he said. "Mary?"

Even after he found himself listening to the hum of the dead wire it was a full minute before he laid the receiver back in its black cradle and noticed that he had cracked it, after all, when he hung up on Neddy.

A draft blew under the apartment door. He watched a spidery ball of lint scudding out of the light across the dark parlor floor. Merril thought, now I've let her see too much. I have poisoned her too.

When soon the panic and the loss receded, he leaned against the wall, and blinking under the remorseless white light he experienced a sense of being naked. Merril went into the bedroom and straight to bed without washing. He lay rigidly, as though Ellen were there, on his alloted side of the bed and gradually it came to him that it was a sweltering night. The first distant rumbles of a thunderstorm sounded high above the city. He got up and opened a window.

"It's been real hot," Mrs. Dougherty was saying. "If I wasn't on duty this week-end I'd get *my*self out to the beach and take a good rest."

The big nurse set Look Magazine aside and continued to smile upon Merril. She had dismissed the subject of last night as deftly as if she were tucking a hospital corner.

It seemed to Merril that he had traveled to the edge of the universe since confronting Mrs. Dougherty last. The aftermath of that nightmare had not left him and even when he looked out the window onto the waving green trees in the park and the bursting summer morning he was weak.

At last he asked, "Will Dr. Dagget be with us today?"

"Not on Saturdays. Saturday he plays golf."

"Of course, forgive a stupid question," Merril started, and then withdrew his feeble shaft of irony.

"I think you'll find your missus feeling spry this fine morning." Mrs. Dougherty cheerfully got up.

Down the corridor, a short distance from the Reception Desk, Ellen's door opened to permit the emergence of a wheel-table laden with towels and metal bowls and pushed by a woman wearing the apricot uniform of the Pavilion.

"Now you can go right in. She's finished her bed bath," Mrs. Dougherty said. "She wants to look pretty because her sister's coming.—Mrs. Robert Gowan," she explained, noting Merril's surprise. "I think Mr. Gowan is coming too."

"They're not bringing their children?"

"Mrs. Gowan didn't mention it on the telephone."

"They can't bring the children," Merril said.

Ellen lay upon a bank of pillows, attempting to tie a blue ribbon into a bow on top of her brown hair and Merril went to her and tied the bow and kissed her piously on the forehead. "Isn't it a glorious morning?" Ellen said. "I thought I'd dress up a little because Georgica's coming, —oh, and Bob." Merril agreed it was a fine day for a visit. He said Ellen looked as though she'd had a good night's rest, she looked fine. He leaned over the bed and fussed the ribbon bow, knowing all it meant to her, and he kept bravely smiling into her face.

Ellen's face, what remained of her face, was a suggestion. The eyes were there, the lips, and nose, but the familiar skin once pliable beneath his fingers clung hungrily to the chin and cheekbones. The eyes were deeper and darker than Merril remembered and they gave the face a dreadful and abstracted beauty which he could look upon no longer.

"Darling?" she asked. "They're not going to bring the children?"

"I shouldn't think so," Merril answered.

"I couldn't let the children see me, Hugh."

"Ah, that's no way to talk."

Then Merril noticed that for the first time in days she was not taking intravenous feeding. The glass globe was gone from its rack above her head and a fresh strip of adhesive was stuck on her forearm, across a punctured vein. Both arms must be riddled now, he thought. A hundred tiny punctures done in the name of mercy. Once he'd overheard the nurses talking. There are just so many veins in the arm, one of the nurses said. Then we start the legs. But if phlebitis develops, it's almost always in the legs.

"But I *am* better," Ellen said. "Isn't it the darnedest thing, I can *feel* the strength coming back? I'm going to have some lunch today. Actually. Some poached egg."

"That's grand," he said.

Ellen smiled and strained her words with a sort of urgency. "Darling, why don't you do something *pleasant?* It's the loveliest day."

He pretended to be looking out the window, to be lost in thought.

"Georgica will be here after all. Please go to the beach, darling. Darling Hugh."

"If I wanted to go to the beach I would go to the beach," he answered carefully.

"*Please* have a pleasant day. Why don't you call Mary Hagen?"

"Really, Ellie."

"I don't mind. I'm not going to be bitchy," she said.

"Bitchy? Did I ever say you were bitchy?"

"I'm not afraid of her, Hugh. I don't think I even resent her any more. Since I've been sick and you've been here and I am just getting to know you. Now, I'm getting sentimental. I'm embarrassing you," she said.

"Of course you're not embarrassing me," Merril answered. He was looking out into the cramped air shaft. A bald man in candy striped pajamas sat on the edge of his bed in the Men's Ward and poured himself a glass of water.

"Go to the beach," Ellen pleaded. "Please go."

He turned and stared at her, bewilderingly thin and small in the bed, with the bowed blue ribbon in her hair. He felt for that moment capable of speaking out, of communicating in a spate of words. "I've wasted so much time, Ellie. We're getting middle-aged—" and there he stopped himself, wondering why he could not gather up his thoughts before they drifted off forever into muteness and confusion.

"You could have had anything you wanted if you hadn't been afraid. You could have had Mary," Ellen told him softly, "and you could have had me and Neddy, whichever you wanted. And you didn't dare have any of us. I wish you saw that, Hugh. It's foolish to punish yourself because I won't punish you. Please," she said gently, "you're so worn out. Call up somebody and find something pleasant to do when it's a nice day."

"I'm not going to call Mary. We're not going to mention her name again," he answered. "I want to make that perfectly clear. I hate her and that's the truth, Ellie."

"Don't you understand? Darling, I used to mind dreadfully but I don't care about Mary Hagen any more and if after I'm gone—"

"Ellie!" He took a wild step towards her and checked himself. "That's a fine way to talk," he said. "That *is* sentimental. Who's being silly now?" He went on this way in monologue, prattling and coaxing, until he discovered that he was merely imitating the Benign Healer and that she wasn't listening at all.

"I don't care any more," Ellen said, from the depths of her daydream, "about any of it." She made a small motion of one arm that took in, in their cruel sequence, the hospital, this room, and herself in the bed.

"Ellie, don't," Merril said.

"I wanted to divorce you."

"You had every right," he said.

"And since I've been ill, you've been here always—feeling guilty and making rows." She smiled at him.

"I've been a brick," he said.

"It doesn't matter," Ellen said. "I loved you better than I loved anybody in the world."

"Don't, Ellie."

She smiled at Merrill, knowingly, as though she meant to ask him, what was so frightening about that? He fell silent for a time, toiling within himself. "I can't help making rows," he said and he spoke painfully, his lips atremble like a schoolboy's. "Ellie, I want to say that I love you—and I always will love you."

Ellen asked him to read aloud. He took up the Oxford Book of American Verse and read to her from "The Song of the Open Road" as he sat in a wooden armchair by the bed. In less than half an hour the door was flung open and Ellen's younger sister Georgica burst in. Bob Gowan, an habitually smiling, secondary figure hovered behind his wife. He held awkwardly in one hand the handle of a bell jar which contained a nourishing broth that Georgica had made at home, and he embraced in his arms a vast spray of gladioli.

"Hello, hello," Georgica said, making straight for the bed. Her navy blue dress gave her the appearance of being fatter than she was because it was sleeveless and Georgica made much use of a fleshy pair of freckled arms. "What a divine hair ribbon!"

"Hugh tied it," Ellen said.

Georgica Gowan talked on breathlessly until noon about the outrageous costs of living, and then Merril descended with her and the ever-smiling Bob for a hasty lunch in the basement cafeteria. He picked at a codfish cake and listened in snatches to his sister-in-law, who attached herself to him like a delirious bobby-soxer: "Hugh, you poor *angel!* . . . There is *no* justice on earth. I said to Bob last night, 'Bob . . .'"

They found that Ellen had not done well with her lunch. A cup of Georgica's beef broth sat untouched on the tray. One of the poached eggs was untouched. "We don't have much sympathy for each other, that egg and

I," she told them as a joke, and Georgica looked smitten and Bob gave one high and frenzied laugh. Ellen was tiring; the noontime sedatives were claiming her. So Merril walked the Gowans to the elevators and said good-bye and Georgica was crying and beside her Bob, wearing that inobliterable smile, hesitatingly offered her his arm. Merril did not wait with them for the car to come.

Because he found the room very warm, he turned on the fan trademarked Tropik-Breeze. Ellen hated its sucking noise. She asked him to switch it off, and fighting against sleep she tried to tell Merril of her dreams about being in a submarine. Last night she dreamed of going down down, all by herself with that whirring machine to breathe by, to the bottom of the ocean and she knew that, because it was only a machine, it could not whir forever. And she had been frightened because she knew that sooner or later the whirring would end in a grating, clattering sound like the morning she stripped the gears of the Plymouth. ("You were terribly angry, Hugh. I can't forget.") She woke in a panic and rang for the night nurse to turn off that ghastly Tropik-Breeze.

So Merril opened the window instead, optimistically, since the freshness of the morning was long past and the sun's heat hung dead in the air shaft. He lowered the shade and turned to smile at Ellen, but she had gone off by then. Her mouth lay slightly open and she was already breathing the long shuddering breaths he had taught himself not to hear. One day he'd inquired of Dr. Dagget what the Cheyne-Stokes breathing was going to sound like and the Benign Healer frowned ponderously and replied that it was just a medical term.

Merril sat and dozed and perspired in the wooden chair by the bed for the remainder of the afternoon. A pair of houseflies, somehow bound to this room like he and Ellen, described lonely circles beyond his reach, returned to buffet themselves against the windowscreen, finally to drop to the sill and recoup themselves, their wings twitching malevolently, black, in an intense patch of sun. One fly careened off Merril's temple. He swung after it hopelessly with his big hand, but he was surprised at not being angry, because the presence of insects was intolerable here. Movie stars and senators and foreign chiefs of state flocked here to humble themselves before the gods of Antisepsis, to beseech them their wonders to perform amid the neurosurgical clinics and therapy programs and biopsy labs, with the twenty-four million volt betatron which had almost, with accidental mercy, killed Ellen last month. All the engines of Hygeia. And here, in the heart of the Temple, a microbe-ridden insect had left a track of invisible filth across his hot forehead. He would raise hell, complain to Dr. Dagget. Oh, Lord, whatever for? He felt himself worn and powerless, complacent. Even the hearty indispensable sense of outrage had left him. He did not care.

Ellen slept with her head deep in a pillow. Merril made out the edge of this morning's blue ribbon nearly lost in the brown, disordered hair. She lay motionless, but for the hands which rose from her sides at the start of each long breath. The fingers clutched in spasms, and yet with what seemed a conscious intricacy, as if on a phantom rosary. It struck Merril, watching, that a sleeping infant has no control of its hands. They grasp, assert, protest, surrender, in obedience to life's first mystery; so then, to face life's last, we are brought back full circle to the same precise obedience.

Later Ellen startled him by rising in the bed.

"I don't want them to force Neddy," she said, looking him full in the eyes.

"What?" He was so taken aback by her literal tone that his reaction was to accept her statement querulously. "What are you talking about?"

"At the camp."

"Yes, at the camp." He collected himself.

"They've no right forcing him to dive high dives if he doesn't want to."

"They won't force him. I'll see to it," Merril said.

"That's very deep water," Ellen said.

"I know it is," he told her. "Don't you worry."

She sank back into the pillow mumbling. When the room was darker and the translucent window shade had

turned dull with the receding of the sun, Merril was
aware of the old man's cry repeating itself in the air shaft.
Hah-mah! Hah-maree! Hah-mah! Hah-mah! Hah-maree!
Sometimes there was a pause long enough for Merril to
think it was over, that some emotional doctor had rushed
in with a hypodermic full of air. But no one was emotional here—in the Temple. *Hah-mah!* Merril suspected
there was a common language among the cruelly dying.
When the aircraft carrier on which he served took on a
Kamikaze, three men had burned to death within yards
of him. The two seamen who were eighteen years old
and fresh out of boot camp had not surprised him by
calling for their mothers, but the Captain, an Annapolis
man, had bellowed rhythmic monosyllables so unbearable that the Executive Officer asked for a .45 and blew
the top off the Captain's head. *Hah-mah! Hah-maree!*
And now finally a nurse must have gone in there, be-
case he was quieting down.

The long stalks of Georgica Gowan's gladioli were
crushed into a small vase of hospital crockery. Their
husky odorless blossoms bulking with good intentions
drooped and dominated the bedtable. Merril smiled at the
uplifting brochures which the hospital Chaplain had
left on the shelf below. When she was up to holding a
book Ellen had read only The Book of Common Prayer,
according to the use of the Protestant Episcopal Church.
At the age of fourteen she was confirmed and her father
had presented it, with a distant inscription on the flyleaf.
The Lord is my Shepherd, therefore shall I lack nothing
—neither Emmet Fox nor get-well-quick-cards nor
gladioli. And Ellen had liked to look through the yellow
photographs on the black pages of her album. There
were pictures of Neddy in various phases of growth, of
herself getting older, of Merril in his lieutenant-com-
mander's uniform, and in various subsequent phases
of stagnation. Ellen had written the captions, in white
ink. "Like father, like son"—Merril pretending to balance Neddy on a lopsided seesaw. "I become domestic"
—Ellen in a makeshift bandanna beating rugs on a
clothesline. The earliest snapshots were taken abroad

before Merril's day. (*Où sont les neiges d'antan?*) Ellen
and her father at low tide before Mont Saint Michel. Ellen
and Georgica on the Acropolis, smiling upon the carya-
tids of the Erectheum. Merril snapped the album shut
and replaced it hastily. Doing so, he knocked open at
his foot the Oxford Book of American Verse; he retrieved
it and began to read:

> "Hope is the thing with feathers
> That perches in the soul,
> And sings the tune without the words,
> And never stops at all."

Ellen had murmured, "I'm glad I wasn't Emily Dickin-
son," one afternoon when her lips were hot and very
dry. Merril had stared at her, startled; for that moment
it seemed as though she were already dead. The
thought plunged him more deeply into herself than he
had ever gone. He felt only the dumb struggling of his
heart and afterwards as in a damp cave of memory he
came upon the lurking spectre of himself, The Oaf.

> "Do you remember Sweet Alice, Ben Bolt?
> Sweet Alice, whose hair was so brown,
> Who wept with delight when you gave her a smile,
> And trembled with fear at your frown!"

There was no ceiling to his grief, and not the weari-
est recognition of sentimentality. Merril sat in the stiff
chair and gazed across an abyss at his wife. He felt the
hundred angers cooling since last night flowing through
him in an infinite cloudy stream, making him a conduit
for all the tears shed since time began.

When it was over, he left the room and went into the
corridor where a young doctor was examining charts.

"Is it hot enough for you?" the young man asked. He
was no more than thirty years old and though he was
some sort of assistant of the Benign Healer's, Merril had
decided to like this boy. He would make a real doctor
some day, Merril would swear it by the shy pop eyes and
the pale fat face.

"They run you pretty ragged?"

"I guess that's what we're here for," the doctor said.

"Meantime the good Dr. Dagget is out on the golf course."

"He's a fine surgeon, Dr. Dagget." He looked at Merril uneasily.

"My wife's asleep now," Merril said abruptly.

"That's the best thing."

"I suppose you see this kind of thing all the time."

"Not all the time."

"I don't envy you taking up medicine. It isn't the answer."

"It's part of the answer."

"You people have no right to claim miracles."

"We don't," the young doctor said.

"Well, tell me this, is she going to feel as much as that old man?"

"I would doubt it. He came much too late."

"You can drug him."

"We have to go slowly."

Merril grinned. "So he'll last as long as possible?"

"If you like to put it that way."

"I appreciate that you people have to be pretty cold-blooded."

"Sometimes. We don't enjoy being."

"I know," Merril said. "You can't be murderers. Mustn't demean Hippocrates."

The doctor turned his young, moon face into a smile of such sad dignity and forgiveness that Merril was shamed by it

"I guess you know what's going to happen," the doctor said. "I doubt she'll be in any bad pain. You can feel that tumor in her abdomen like a salad bowl, and it will get bigger. She's in the best place she could be anyway. The comforting thing is she's already started on drugs and so we can build up gradually."

"Sweet Jesus," Merril said. A suggestion of formalde-hyde seeped up from some laboratory on a floor below. He looked vaguely down the corridor where two ward boys were pushing an empty stretcher. The afternoon was waning. Mrs. Dougherty had long since gone home on a trolley car carrying her girdle in a brownpaper bag. Down at the western end where the porch was, the sunlight fell in at an angle making slender shadows of the iron grill against the linoleum floor.

The doctor said, "What you have to remember about these patients is that they'll fight like wildcats out of corners to keep from going under. When I was an intern there was a physician who when he couldn't stomach it any more would go in to a patient and say, 'Tonight I'm going to trust you with these pills. Be sure you take only a couple because if you take a handful by accident you won't be here in the morning!' And when I'd go in in the morning the pills were always right there by the bed —a little white pile with only two missing. Why, I could bet you dollars to little round doughnuts that if we were to go in to that fellow tonight and leave him a dozen seconals . . ."

"Say," Merril said, "Are you tied up?"

"No," the doctor said. "No more than usual."

"I mean right now?"

"Well not any more than usual."

"Maybe we could go out for a few minutes and get a cigarette in the park. Perhaps I could interest you in letting me buy you a drink." Merril spoke quickly. "You see, I'm alone all the time."

But he knew before he finished that it was a ridiculous request to make of an unknown doctor on his rounds, and he knew that he could never leave the brown tundra of his spirit, that he was beyond communion or confidence of any sort.

Merril left the hospital by himself and made his way to the street where his car was parked. Some small boys on roller skates were playing with toy hockey sticks and a dirty tennis ball. As he went through them a gust of hot wind blew across the littered sidewalk and lodged a fragment in his eye. He paused a moment from the sting and as he was wiping at the eye with a handkerchief one of the boys crashed against his leg, fell, righted himself and, to the shrill delight of his companions, shouted and gestured obscenely at Merril's back.

The green Plymouth sedan was fifteen feet away, its windows heavy with soot and a scarlet parking ticket on its windshield. He patiently untied the ticket from the wiper and studied the formidable language of the summons before he unlocked the car. He got behind the wheel, unrolled the window, and was rereading the ticket when a policeman rapped on the door.

"What's on *your* mind?"

Merril noticed first the policeman's dark shirt well sweated through at the collar, the stomach, and deep under the arms. The policeman's face was streaked and grimy and angry from walking all the hot days away on filthy streets. It reminded Merril of his own.

"I asked a simple question, Georgie." The policeman pointed to a sign.

"Loading Zone. No Standing or Parking. Eight A. M. to Seven P. M. Monday through Friday," Merril read aloud. "Per Order Police Department."

"Let me advise you, don't snot me. It so happens this is a warehouse. There has to be free access, and you've been sittin' on it all day. I can impound your car, you know it. So have a care. I'll bag you, Georgie."

"You're right, Officer, and I'm wrong and I apologize."

"That's nice. So you can come to court with a clear conscience."

"I'll pay my fine, Officer."

"Hey, what's the matter? There anything the matter?"

Merril said nothing and rolled up the window. It was like an oven inside the car. The policeman moved off indifferently while Merril stared after him. Suddenly he felt an irresistible weariness. For a moment he fought against it with tightened wrists, but his moist hands were already slipping on the plastic steering wheel and he let himself slump forward. He was aware of his eyes pressed tight together, his mouth opened, and his shoulders heaving—up and down up and down. Then his cheeks were cool and off the backs of his hands he tasted his own tears. Very slowly he began to hear the sound of the horn blaring steadily under the weight of his chest. Recoiling from the steering wheel, he had a glimpse of the policeman turning and looking back at him with a startled frown. Merril was a big and powerful man who two seasons had played right tackle at the University of Pennsylvania. He sobbed in great spasms and whimpered at the end of every breath.

Pages from an Abandoned Journal

Gore Vidal

I

April 30, 1948

AFTER last night, I was sure they wouldn't want to see
me again but evidently I was wrong because this morning I had a call from Steven . . . he spells it with a "v"
. . . asking me if I would like to come to a party at
Elliott Magren's apartment in the *Rue du Bac*. I should
have said no but I didn't. It's funny: when I make up my
mind *not* to do something I always end up by doing it,
like meeting Magren, like seeing any of these people
again, especially after last night. Well, I guess it's experience. What was it Pascal wrote? I don't remember
what Pascal wrote . . . another sign of weakness: I
should look it up when I don't remember . . . the book
is right here on the table but the thought of leafing
through all those pages is discouraging so I pass on.

Anyway, now that I'm in Paris I've got to learn to be
more adaptable and I do think, all in all, I've handled
myself pretty well. . . until last night in the bar when
I told everybody off. I certainly never thought I'd see
Steven again . . . that's why I was so surprised to get
his call this morning. Is he still hopeful after what I said?
I can't see how. I was *ruthlessly* honest. I said I wasn't
interested, that I didn't mind what other people did,
etc., just as long as they left me alone, that I was getting
married in the fall when I got back to the States

267

(WRITE HELEN) and that I don't go in for any of that, never did and never will. I also told him in no uncertain terms that it's very embarrassing for a grown man to be treated like some idiot girl surrounded by a bunch of seedy, middle-aged Don Juans trying to get their hooks into her . . . him. Anyway, I really let him have it before I left. Later, I felt silly but I was glad to go on record like that once and for all: now we know where we stand and if they're willing to accept me on *my* terms, the way I am, then there's no reason why I can't see them sometimes. That's really why I agreed to meet Magren who sounds very interesting from what everybody says, and everybody talks a lot about him, at least in those circles which must be the largest and busiest circles in Paris this spring. Well, I shouldn't complain: this is the Bohemian life I wanted to see. It's just that there aren't many girls around, for fairly obvious reasons. In fact, except for running into Hilda Devendorf at American Express yesterday, I haven't seen an American girl to talk to in the three weeks I've been here.

My day: after the phone call from Steven, I worked for two and a half hours on Nero and the Civil Wars . . . I wish sometimes I'd picked a smaller subject for a doctorate, not that I don't like the period but having to learn German to read a lot of books all based on sources available to anybody is depressing: I could do the whole thing from Tacitus but that would be cheating, no bibliography, no footnotes, no scholastic quarrels to record and judge between. Then, though the day was cloudy, I took a long walk across the river to the Tuileries where the gardens looked fine. Just as I was turning home into the *Rue de l'Université* it started to rain and I got wet. At the desk Madame Revenel told me Hilda had called. I called her back and she said she was going to Deauville on Friday to visit some people who own a hotel and why didn't I go too? I said I might and wrote down her address. She's a nice girl. We were in high school together back in Toledo; I lost track of her when I went to Columbia.

Had dinner here in the dining room (veal, french

fried potatoes, salad and something like a pie but very good . . . I like the way Madame Revenel cooks). She talked to me all through dinner, very fast, which is good because the faster she goes the less chance you have to translate in your head. The only other people in the dining room were the Harvard professor and his wife. They both read while they ate. He's supposed to be somebody important in the English Department but I've never heard of him . . . Paris is like that: everyone's supposed to be somebody important only you've never heard of them. The Harvard professor was reading a mystery story and his wife was reading a life of Alexander Pope. . . .

I got to the *Rue du Bac* around ten-thirty. Steven opened the door, yelling: "The beautiful Peter!" This was about what I expected. Anyway, I got into the room quickly . . . if they're drunk they're apt to try to kiss you and there was no point in getting off on the wrong foot again . . . but luckily he didn't try. He showed me through the apartment, four big rooms one opening off another . . . here and there an old chair was propped against a wall and that was all the furniture there was till we got to the last room where, on a big bed with a torn canopy, Elliott Magren lay, fully dressed, propped up by pillows. All the lamps had red shades. Over the bed was a paining of a nude man, the work of a famous painter I'd never heard of (read Berenson!).

There were about a dozen men in the room, most of them middle-aged and wearing expensive narrow suits. I recognized one or two of them from last night. They nodded to me but made no fuss. Steven introduced me to Elliott who didn't move from the bed when he shook hands; instead, he pulled me down beside him. He had a surprisingly powerful grip, considering how pale and slender he is. He told Steven to make me a drink. Then he gave me a long serious look and asked me if I wanted a pipe of opium. I said I didn't take drugs and he said nothing which was unusual: as a rule they give you a speech about how good it is for you or else they start defending themselves against what they feel is moral censure. Personally, I don't mind what other people do. As a matter of fact, I think all this is very interesting and I sometimes wonder what the gang back in Toledo would think if they could've seen me in a Left-Bank Paris apartment with a male prostitute who takes drugs. I thought of those college boys who sent T. S. Eliot the record "You've Come a Long Way From St Louis".

Before I describe what happened, I'd better write down what I've heard about Magren since he is already a legend in Europe, at least in these circles. First of all, he is not very handsome. I don't know what I'd expected but something glamorous, like a movie star. He is about five foot ten and weighs about a hundred sixty pounds. He has dark straight hair that falls over his forehead; his eyes are black. The two sides of his face don't match, like Oscar Wilde's, though the effect is not as disagreeable as Wilde's face must've been from the photographs. Because of drugs, he is unnaturally pale. His voice is deep and his accent is still Southern; he hasn't picked up that phoney English accent so many Americans do after five minutes over here. He was born in Galveston, Texas about thirty-six years ago. When he was sixteen he was picked up on the beach by a German baron who took him to Berlin with him. (I always wonder about details in a story like this: what did his parents say about a stranger walking off with their son? was there a scene? did they know what was going on?) Elliot then spent several years in Berlin during the twenties which were the great days, or what these people recall now as the great days . . . I gather the German boys were affectionate: It all sounds pretty disgusting. Then Elliott had a fight with the Baron and he walked, with no money, nothing but the clothes he was wearing, from Berlin to Munich. On the outskirts of Munich, a big car stopped and the chauffeur said that the owner of the car would like to give him a lift. The owner turned out to be a millionaire ship-owner from Egypt, very fat and old. He was intrigued with Elliott and he took him on a yachting tour of the Mediterranean. But Elliott couldn't stand him and when the ship got to Naples, Elliott and a Greek sailor skipped ship together after first stealing two thousand dollars from the Egyptian's stateroom. They went to Capri where they moved into the most expensive hotel and had a wonderful time until the money ran out and the sailor deserted Elliott for a rich American woman. Elliott was about to be taken off to jail for not paying his bill when Lord Glenellen, who was just checking in the hotel, saw him and told the police to let him go, that *he* would pay his bill . . . here again: how would Glenellen know that it would be worth his while to help this stranger? I mean you can't tell by looking at him that Elliott is queer. Suppose he hadn't been? Well, maybe that soldier I met on Okinawa the night of the hurricane was right: they can always tell about each other, like Masons. Glenellen kept Elliott for a number of years. They went to England together and Elliott rose higher and higher in aristocratic circles until he met the late King Basil who was then a Prince. Basil fell in love with him and Elliott went to live with him until Basil became king. They didn't see much of each other after that because the war started and Elliott went to California to live. Basil died during the war, leaving Elliott a small trust fund which is what he lives on now. In California, Elliott got interested in Vedanta and tried to stop taking drugs and lead a quiet . . . if not a normal . . . life. People say he was all right for several years but when the war ended he couldn't resist going back to Europe. Now he does nothing but smoke opium, his courtesan life pretty much over. This has been a long account but I'm glad I got it all down because the story is an interesting one and I've heard so many bits and pieces of it since I got here that it helps clarify many things just writing this down in my journal. . . . It is now past four o'clock and I've got a hangover already from the party but I'm going to finish, just as discipline. I never seem to finish anything which is a bad sign, God knows.

While I was sitting with Elliott on the bed, Steven brought him his opium pipe, a long painted wooden affair with a metal chimney. Elliott inhaled deeply, holding the smoke in his lungs as long as he could; then he

exhaled the pale medicinal-scented smoke, and started
to talk. I can't remember a word he said. I was aware,
though, that this was probably the most brilliant conversation I'd ever heard. It might have been the setting
which was certainly provocative or maybe I'd inhaled
some of the opium which put me in a receptive mood
but, no matter the cause, I sat listening to him, fascinated, not wanting him to stop. As he talked, he kept
his eyes shut and I suddenly realized why the lamp
shades were red: the eyes of drug addicts are hypersensi-
tive to light; whenever he opened his eyes he would
blink painfully and the tears would streak his face,
glistening like small watery rubies in the red light. He
told me about himself, pretending to be a modern Can-
dide, simple and bewildered but actually he must have
been quite different, more calculating, more resource-
ful. Then he asked me about myself and I couldn't tell
if he was really interested or not because his eyes were
shut and it's odd talking to someone who won't look at
you. I told him about Ohio and high school and the
University and now Columbia and the doctorate I'm
trying to get in History and the fact I want to teach, to
marry Helen . . . but as I talked I couldn't help but
think how dull my life must sound to Elliott. I cut it
short. I couldn't compete with him . . . and didn't
want to. Then he asked me if I'd see him some evening, alone, and I said I would like to but . . . and this
was completely spur of the moment . . . I said I was
going down to Deauville the next day, with a girl. I
wasn't sure he'd heard any of this because at that moment Steven pulled me off the bed and tried to make me
dance with him which I wouldn't do, to the amusement
of the others. Then Elliott went to sleep so I sat and
talked for a while with an interior decorator from New
York and, as usual, I was floored by the amount these
people know: painting, music, literature, architecture
. . . where do they learn it all? I sit like a complete
idiot, supposedly educated, almost a Ph.D. while they
talk circles around me: Fragonard, Boucher, Leonore
Fini, Gropius, Sacheverell Sitwell, Ronald Firbank,

Jean Genet, Jean Giono, Jean Cocteau, Jean Brown's body
lies a'mouldering in Robert Graves. God damn them
all. I have the worst headache and outside it's dawn. Remember to write Helen, call Hilda about Deauville, study
German two hours tomorrow instead of one, start bon-
ing up on Latin again, read Berenson, get a book on modern art (what book?), read Firbank. . . .

II

May 21, 1948

Another fight with Hilda. This time about religion.
She's a Christian Scientist. It all started when she saw
me taking two aspirins this morning because of last
night's hangover. She gave me a lecture on Christ—
Scientist and we had a long fight about God on the
beach (which was wonderful today, not too many people, not too hot). Hilda looked more than ever like a
great golden seal. She is a nice girl but like so many
who go to Bennington feels she must continually be alert
to the life about her. I think tonight we'll go to bed together. Remember to get suntan oil, change money at
hotel, finish Berenson, study German grammar! See if
there's a Firbank in a paper edition.

May 22, 1948

It wasn't very successful last night. Hilda kept talking
all the time which slows me down, also she is a good deal
softer than she looks and it was like sinking into a feather
mattress. I don't think she has bones, only elastic web-
bing. Well, maybe it'll be better tonight. She seemed
pleased but then I think she likes the idea better than
the actual thing. She told me she had her first affair at
fourteen. We had another argument about God. I told
her the evidence was slight, etc. but she said evidence
had nothing to do with faith. She told me a long story
about how her mother had cancer last year but wouldn't
see a doctor and the cancer went away. I didn't have the
heart to tell her that Mother's days are unpleasantly num-

bered. We had a wonderful dinner at that place on the
sea, lobster, *moules*. Write Helen.

May 24, 1948

A fight with Hilda, this time about Helen whom she
hardly knows. She felt that Helen was pretentious. I said
who isn't? She said many people weren't. I said name
me one. She said *she* wasn't pretentious. I then told her
all the pretentious things she'd said in the past week
starting with that discussion about the importance of an
aristocracy and ending with atonalism. She then told
me all the pretentious things I'd said, things I either
didn't remember saying or she had twisted around. I got
so angry I stalked out of her room and didn't go back:
just as well. Having sex with her is about the dullest
past-time I can think of. I went to my room and read
Tacitus in Latin, for practice.

My sunburn is better but I think I've picked up some
kind of liver trouble. Hope it's not jaundice: a burning
feeling right where the liver is.

May 25, 1948

Hilda very cool this morning when we met on the
beach. Beautiful day. We sat on the sand a good yard
between us, and I kept thinking how fat she's going to
be in a few years, only fit for child-bearing. I also
thought happily of those agonizing "painless" child-
births she'd have to endure because of Christian Science. We were just beginning to quarrel about the pronunciation of a French word when Elliott Magren appeared . . . the last person in the world I expected to
see at bright noon on that beach. He was walking slowly,
wearing sunglasses and a pair of crimson trunks. I noticed
with surprise how smooth and youthful his body was,
like a boy. I don't know what I'd expected: something
gaunt and hollowed out I suppose, wasted by drugs.
He came up to me as though he'd expected to meet me
right where I was. We shook hands and I introduced
him to Hilda who fortunately missed the point to him
from the very beginning. He was as charming as ever. It
seems he had to come to Deauville alone . . . he hated

the sun but liked the beach . . . and, in answer to the
golden Hilda's inevitable question, no, he was not married. I wanted to tell her everything, just to see what
would happen, to break for a moment that beaming com-
placency, but I didn't . . .

May 27, 1948

Well, this afternoon Hilda decided it was time to go
back to Paris. I carried her bag to the station and we didn't
quarrel once. She was pensive but I didn't offer the usual
small change for her thoughts. She didn't mention Elliott
and I have no idea how much she suspects; in any
case, it's none of her business, none of mine either. I
think, though, I was nearly as shocked as she was when
he came back to the hotel this morning with that fourteen year old boy. We were sitting on the terrace having
coffee when Elliott, who must've got up very early, appeared with this boy. Elliott even introduced him to us
and the little devil wasn't faintly embarrassed, assuming,
I guess, that we were interested in him, too. Then Elliott whisked him off to his room and, as Hilda and I sat
in complete silence, we could hear from Elliott's room
on the first floor the hoarse sound of the boy's laughter.
Not long after, Hilda decided to go back to Paris.

Wrote a long letter to Helen, studied Latin grammar.
. . . I'm more afraid of my Latin than of anything else
in either the written or the orals: can't seem to concentrate, can't retain all those irregular verbs. Well, I've
come this far. I'll probably get through all right.

May 28, 1948

This morning I knocked on Elliott's door around
eleven o'clock. He'd asked me to pick him up on my way
to the beach. When he shouted come in I did and
found both Elliott and the boy on the floor together,
stark naked, putting together a Meccano set. Both were
intent on building an intricate affair with wheels and
pulleys, a blueprint between them. I excused myself
hurriedly but Elliott told me to stay . . . they'd be finished in a moment. The boy who was the color of a terra-
cotta pot gave me a wicked grin. Then Elliott, completely

unself-conscious, jumped to his feet and pulled on a pair
of trunks and a shirt. The boy dressed, too, and we went
out on the beach where the kid left us. I was blunt. I
asked Elliott if this sort of thing wasn't very dangerous
and he said yes it probably was but life was short and he
was afraid of nothing, except drugs. He told me then that
he had had an electrical shock treatment at a clinic
shortly before I'd first met him. Now, at last, he was off
opium and he hoped it was a permanent cure. He described the shock treatment, which sounded terrible. Part
of his memory was gone: he could recall almost nothing of his childhood . . . yet he was blithe even about
this: after all, he believed only in the present. . . . Then
when I asked him if he always went in for young boys he
said yes and he made a joke about how, having lost all
memory of his own childhood, he would have to live out
a new one with some boy.

May 29, 1948

I had a strange conversation with Elliott last night.
André went home to his family at six and Elliott and I
had an early dinner on the terrace. A beautiful evening:
the sea green in the last light . . . a new moon. Eating
fresh sole from the Channel, I told Elliott all about
Jimmy, told him things I myself had nearly forgotten,
had wanted to forget. I told him how it had started at
twelve and gone on, without plan or thought or even
acknowledgment until, at seventeen, I went to the army
and he to the Marines and a quick death. After the army,
I met Helen and forgot him completely; his death, like
Elliott's shock treatment, took with it all memory, a
thousand summer days abandoned on a coral island. I
can't think now why on earth I told Elliott about Jimmy,
not that I'm ashamed but it was, after all, something intimate, something nearly forgotten . . . anyway, when
I finished, I sat there in the dark, not daring to look at
Elliott, shivering as all in a rush the warmth left the
sand about us and I had that terrible feeling I always
have when I realize too late I've said too much. Finally,
Elliott spoke. He gave me a strange disjointed speech

about life and duty to oneself and how the moment is all one has and how it is dishonorable to cheat oneself of that. . . . I'm not sure that he said anything very useful or very original but sitting there in the dark, listening, his words had a peculiar urgency for me and I felt, in a way, that I was listening to an oracle. . . .

June 1, 1948

Shortly before lunch, the police came and arrested Elliott. Luckily, I was down on the beach and missed the whole thing. . . . The hotel's in an uproar and the manager's behaving like a mad man. It seems André stole Elliott's camera. His parents found it and asked him where he got it. He wouldn't tell. When they threatened him, he said Elliott gave him the camera and then, to make this story credible, he told them that Elliott had tried to seduce him. . . . The whole sordid business then proceeded logically: parents to police. . . police to Elliott . . . arrest. I sat down shakily on the terrace and wondered what to do. I was . . . I am frightened. While I was sitting there, a gendarme came out on the terrace and told me Elliott wanted to see me, in prison. Meanwhile, the gendarme wanted to know what I knew about Mr Magren. It was only too apparent what his opinion of *me* was: another *pédérast américain*. My voice shook and my throat dried up as I told him I hardly knew Elliott . . . I'd only just met him . . . I new nothing about his private life. The gendarme sighed and closed his note book: the charges against Elliott were *très grave, très grave,* but I would be allowed to see him tomorrow morning. Then, realizing I was both nervous and uncooperative, the gendarme gave me the address of the jail and left. I went straight to my room and packed. I didn't think twice. All I wanted was to get away from Deauville, from Elliott, from the crime . . . and it *was* a crime, I'm sure of that. I was back in Paris in time for supper at the hotel.

June 4, 1948

Ran into Steven at the Café Flore and I asked him if

there'd been any news of Ellott. Steven took the whole thing as a joke: yes, Elliott had called a mutual friend who was a lawyer and everything was all right. Money was spent; the charges were dropped and Elliott was staying on in Deauville for another week . . . doubtless to be near André. I was shocked but relieved to hear this. I'm not proud of my cowardice but I didn't want to be drawn into something I hardly understood.

Caught a glimpse of Hilda with some college boy, laughing and chattering as they left the brasserie across the street. I stepped behind a kiosk, not wanting Hilda to see me. Write Helen. See the doctor about wax in ears, also liver. Get tickets for Roland Petit ballet.

III

December 26, 1953

The most hideous hangover! How I hate Christmas, especially this one. Started out last night at the *Caprice* where the management gave a party, absolutely packed. The new room is quite stunning, to my surprise: black walls, white driftwood but not artsy-craftsy, a starlight effect for the ceiling . . . only the upholstery is really *mauvais goût*: tufted velveteen in SAFFRON! . . . but then Piggy has no sense of color and why somebody didn't stop him I'll never know. All the tired old faces were there. Everyone was going to the ballet except me and there was all the usual talk about who was sleeping with whom, such a bore . . . I mean who cares who . . . whom dancers sleep with? Though somebody did say that Niellsen was having an affair with Dr Bruckner which is something of a surprise considering what a mess there was at Fire Island last summer over just that. Anyway, I drank too many vodka martinis and, incidentally, met Robert Gammadge the English playwright who isn't at all attractive though he made the biggest play for me. He's supposed to be quite dreary but makes tons of money. He was with that awful Dickie Mallory whose whole life is devoted to meeting celebrities, even

the wrong ones. Needless to say, he was in seventh heaven
with his playwright in tow. I can't understand people
like Dickie: what fun do they get out of always being
second fiddle? After the *Caprice* I went over to Steven's
new apartment on the river: it's in a remodeled tenement
house and I must say it's fun and the Queen Anne desk
I sold him looks perfect heaven in his living room. I'll
say one thing for him: Steven is one of the few people
who has the good sense simply to let a fine piece go in a
room. There were quite a few people there and we had
New York champagne which is drinkable when you're
already full of vodka. Needless to say, Steven pulled me
off to one corner to ask about Bob. I wish people
wouldn't be so sympathetic not that they really are of
course but they feel they must *pretend* to be: actually,
they're only curious. I said Bob *seemed* all right when I
saw him last month. I didn't go into any details though
Steven did his best to worm the whole story out of me.
Fortunately, I have a good grip on myself nowadays and
I am able to talk about the break-up quite calmly. I
always tell everybody I hope Bob will do well in his new
business and that I like Sydney very much . . . actually,
I hear things are going badly, that the shop is doing *no*
business and that Bob is drinking again which means
he's busy cruising the streets and getting into trouble.
Well, I'm out of it and any day now I'll meet somebody
. . . though it's funny how seldom you see anyone who's
really attractive. There was a nice young Swede at
Steven's but I never did get his name and anyway he is
being kept by that ribbon clerk from the Madison Avenue Store. After Steven's I went to a real brawl in the
Village: a studio apartment, packed with people, dozens
of new faces, too. I wish now I hadn't got so drunk because there were some really attractive people there. I
was all set, I thought, to go home with one but the friend
intervened at the last moment and it looked for a moment
like there was going to be real trouble before our host
separated us . . . I never did get the host's name, I
think he's in advertising. So I ended up alone. Must call
doctor about hepatitis pills, write Leonore Fini, check

last month's invoices (re. missing Sheraton receipt), call
Mrs. Blaine-Smith about sofa.

December 27, 1953

I finally had tea with Mrs Blaine-Smith today . . .
one of the most beautiful women I've ever met, so truly
chic and well-dressed. . . . I'm hopelessly indebted to
Steven for bringing us together: she practically keeps the
shop going. She had only six or seven people for tea,
very much *en famille* and I couldn't've been more surprised and pleased when she asked me to stay on. (I expect she knows what a discount I gave her on that Hep-
pelwhite sofa.) Anyway, one of her guests was an Italian
Count who was terribly nice though unattractive. We
sat next to each other on that delicious ottoman in the
library and chatted about Europe after the war: what a
time that was! I told him I hadn't been back since 1948
but even so we knew quite a few people in common.
Then, as always, the name Elliott Magren was mentioned. He's practically a code-word . . . if you know
Elliott, well, you're on the inside and of course the
Count (as I'd expected all along) knew Elliott and we
exchanged bits of information about him, skirting carefully drugs and small boys because Mrs Blaine-Smith
though she knows everyone (and everything) *never*
alludes to that sort of thing in any way, such a relief
after so many of the queen bees you run into. Hilda, for
instance, who married the maddest designer in Los Angeles and gives, I am told, the crudest parties with everyone drunk from morning till night. (Must stop drinking so much: nothing *after* dinner, that's the secret . . .
especially with my liver.) We were discussing Elliott's
apartment in the *Rue du Bac* and that marvelous Tcheli-
chew that hangs over his bed when a little Englishman
whose name I never did get, turned and said: did you
know that Elliott Magren died last week? I must say it
was stunning news, sitting in Mrs Blaine-Smith's library
so far, far away. . . . The Count was even more upset
than I (could he have been one of Elliott's numerous
admirers?) I couldn't help recalling then that terrible

time at Dauville when Elliott was arrested and I had
had to put up bail for him and hire a lawyer, all
in French! Suddenly everything came back to me in a
flood: that summer, the affair with Hilda . . . and
Helen (incidentally, just this morning got a Christmas
card from Helen, the first word in years: a photograph
of her husband and three ghastly children, all living
in Toledo: well, I suppose she's happy). But what an
important summer that was, the chrysalis burst at last
which, I think, prepared me for all the bad luck later
when I failed my doctorate and had to go to work in
Steven's office. . . . And now Elliott's dead. Hard to
believe someone you once knew is actually dead, not like
the war where sudden absences in the roster were taken
for granted. The Englishman told us the whole story. It
seems Elliott was rounded up in a police raid on dope
addicts in which a number of very famous people were
caught, too. He was told to leave the country; so he piled
everything into two taxicabs and drove to the Gare St
Lazare where he took a train for Rome. He settled down
in a small apartment off the Via Veneto. Last fall he underwent another series of shock treatments, administered
by a quack doctor who cured him of drugs but lost his
memory for him in the process. Aside from this, he was
in good health and looked as young as ever except that
for some reason he dyed his hair red . . . too mad!
Then, last week, he made a date to go to the opera with
a friend. The friend arrived . . . the door was open but,
inside, there was no Elliott. The friend was particularly
annoyed because Elliott often would not show up at
all if, enroute to an appointment, he happend to see
someone desirable in the street. I remember Elliott telling me once that his greatest pleasure was to follow a
handsome stranger for hours on end through the
streets of a city. It was not so much the chase which interested him as the identification he had with the boy he
followed: he would become the other, imitating his
gestures, his gait, becoming himself young, absorbed in
a boy's life. But Elliott had followed no one that day.
The friend finally found him face down in the bath-

room, dead. When the autopsy was performed, it was discovered that Elliott had had a malformed heart, an extremely rare case, and he might have died as suddenly at any moment in his life . . . the drugs, the shock treatments and so on had contributed nothing to his death. He was buried Christmas day in the Protestant cemetery close to Shelley, in good company to the end. I must say I can't imagine him with red hair. . . . The Count asked me to have dinner with him tomorrow at the Colony (!) and I said I'd be delighted. Then Mrs Blaine-Smith told the most devastating story about the Duchess of Windsor in Palm Beach.

Find out about Helen Gleason's sphinxes. Call Bob about the keys to the back closet. Return Steven's copy of "Valmouth." *Find out the Count's name before dinner tomorrow.*

Sonny's Blues

James Baldwin

I READ about it in the paper, in the subway, on my way to work. I read it, and I couldn't believe it, and I read it again. Then perhaps I just stared at it, at the newsprint spelling out his name, spelling out the story. I stared at it in the swinging lights of the subway car, and in the faces and bodies of the people, and in my own face, trapped in the darkness which roared outside.

It was not to be believed and I kept telling myself that as I walked from the subway station to the high school. And at the same time I couldn't doubt it. I was scared, scared for Sonny. He became real to me again. A great block of ice got settled in my belly and kept melting there slowly all day long, while I taught my classes algebra. It was a special kind of ice. It kept melting, sending trickles of ice water all up and down my veins, but it never got less. Sometimes it hardened and seemed to expand until I felt my guts were going to come spilling out or that I was going to choke or scream. This would always be at a moment when I was remembering some specific thing Sonny had once said or done.

When he was about as old as the boys in my classes his face had been bright and open, there was a lot of copper in it; and he'd had wonderfully direct brown eyes, and great gentleness and privacy. I wondered what he looked like now. He had been picked up, the evening before, in a raid on an apartment downtown, for peddling and using heroin.

I couldn't believe it: but what I mean by that is that I couldn't find any room for it anywhere inside me. I had kept it outside me for a long time. I hadn't wanted to know. I had had suspicions, but I didn't name them, I kept putting them away. I told myself that Sonny was wild, but he wasn't crazy. And he'd always been a good boy, he hadn't ever turned hard or evil or disrespectful, the way kids can, so quick, so quick, especially in Harlem. I didn't want to believe that I'd ever see my brother going down, coming to nothing, all that light in his face gone out, in the condition I'd already seen so many others. Yet it had happened and here I was, talking about algebra to a lot of boys who might, every one of them for all I knew, be popping off needles every time they went to the head. Maybe it did more for them than algebra could.

I was sure that the first time Sonny had ever had horse, he couldn't have been much older than these boys were now. These boys, now, were living as we'd been living then, they were growing up with a rush and their heads bumped abruptly against the low ceiling of their actual possibilities. They were filled with rage. All they really knew were two darknesses, the darkness of their lives, which was now closing in on them, and the darkness of the movies, which had blinded them to that other darkness, and in which they now, vindictively, dreamed, at once more together than they were at any other time, and more alone.

When the last bell rang, the last class ended, I let out my breath. It seemed I'd been holding it for all that time. My clothes were wet—I may have looked as though I'd been sitting in a steam bath, all dressed up, all afternoon. I sat alone in the classroom a long time. I listened to the boys outside, downstairs, shouting and cursing and laughing. Their laughter struck me for perhaps the first time. It was not the joyous laughter which—God knows why—one associates with children. It was mocking and insular, its intent was to denigrate. It was disenchanted, and in this, also, lay the authority of their curses. Perhaps I was listening to them because I was thinking about my brother and in them I heard my brother. And myself.

One boy was whistling a tune, at once very complicated and very simple, it seemed to be pouring out of him
as though he were a bird, and it sounded very cool and
moving through all that harsh, bright air, only just holding its own through all those other sounds.

I stood up and walked over to the window and looked
down into the courtyard. It was the beginning of the
spring and the sap was rising in the boys. A teacher
passed through them every now and again, quickly, as
though he or she couldn't wait to get out of that courtyard, to get those boys out of their sight and off their
minds. I started collecting my stuff. I thought I'd better get home and talk to Isabel.

The courtyard was almost deserted by the time I got
downstairs. I saw this boy standing in the shadow of a
doorway, looking just like Sonny. I almost called his
name. Then I saw that it wasn't Sonny, but somebody we
used to know, a boy from around our block. He'd been
Sonny's friend. He'd never been mine, having been too
young for me, and, anyway, I'd never liked him. And
now, even though he was a grown-up man, he still hung
around that block, still spent hours on the street corner,
was always high and raggy. I used to run into him from
time to time and he'd often work around to asking me for
a quarter or fifty cents. He always had some real good
excuse, too, and I always gave it to him, I don't know
why.

But now, abruptly, I hated him. I couldn't stand the
way he looked at me, partly like a dog, partly like a cunning child. I wanted to ask him what the hell he was doing in the school courtyard.

He sort of shuffled over to me, and he said, "I see you
got the papers. So you already know about it."

"You mean about Sonny? Yes, I already know about
it. How come they didn't get you?"

He grinned. It made him repulsive and it also brought
to mind what he'd looked like as a kid. "I wasn't there. I
stay away from them people."

"Good for you." I offered him a cigarette and I

watched him through the smoke. "You come all the way down here just to tell me about Sonny?"

"That's right." He was sort of shaking his head and his eyes looked strange, as though they were about to cross. The bright sun deadened his damp dark brown skin and it made his eyes look yellow and showed up the dirt in his conked hair. He smelled funky. I moved a little away from him and I said, "Well, thanks. But I already know about it and I got to get home."

"I'll walk you a little ways," he said. We started walking. There were a couple of kids still loitering in the courtyard and one of them said good night to me and looked strangely at the boy beside me.

"What're you going to do?" he asked me. "I mean, about Sonny?"

"Look. I haven't seen Sonny for over a year, I'm not sure I'm going to do anything. Anyway, what the hell *can* I do?"

"That's right," he said quickly, "ain't nothing you can do. Can't much help old Sonny no more, I guess."

It was what I was thinking and so it seemed to me he had no right to say it.

"I'm surprised at Sonny, though," he went on—he had a funny way of talking, he looked straight ahead as though he were talking to himself—"I thought Sonny was a smart boy, I thought he was too smart to get hung."

"I guess he thought so too," I said sharply, "and that's how he got hung. And how about you? You're pretty goddamn smart, I bet."

Then he looked directly at me, just for a minute. "I ain't smart," he said. "If I was smart, I'd have reached for a pistol a long time ago."

"Look. Don't tell *me* your sad story, if it was up to me, I'd give you one." Then I felt guilty—guilty, probably, for never having supposed that the poor bastard *had* a story of his own, much less a sad one, and I asked, quickly, "What's going to happen to him now?"

He didn't answer this. He was off by himself some place. "Funny thing," he said, and from his tone we might have been discussing the quickest way to get to

Brooklyn, "when I saw the papers this morning, the first thing I asked myself was if I had anything to do with it. I felt sort of responsible."

I began to listen more carefully. The subway station was on the corner, just before us, and I stopped. He stopped, too. We were in front of a bar and he ducked slightly, peering in, but whoever he was looking for didn't seem to be there. The juke box was blasting away with something black and bouncy and I half watched the bar maid as she danced her way from the juke box to her place behind the bar. And I watched her face as she laughingly responded to something someone said to her, still keeping time to the music. When she smiled one saw the little girl, one sensed the doomed, still-struggling woman beneath the battered face of the semi-whore.

"I never *give* Sonny nothing," the boy said finally, "but a long time ago I come to school high and Sonny asked me how it felt." He paused, I couldn't bear to watch him, I watched the barmaid, and I listened to the music which seemed to be causing the pavement to shake. "I told him it felt great." The music stopped, the barmaid paused and watched the juke box until the music began again. "It did."

All this was carrying me some place I didn't want to go. I certainly didn't want to know how it felt. It filled everything, the people, the houses, the music, the dark, quicksilver barmaid, with menace; and this menace was their reality.

"What's going to happen to him now?" I asked again.

"They'll send him away some place and they'll try to cure him." He shook his head. "Maybe he'll even think he's kicked the habit. Then they'll let him loose"—he gestured, throwing his cigarette into the gutter. "That's all."

"What do you mean, that's all?"

But I knew what he meant.

"I *mean*, that's *all*." He turned his head and looked at me, pulling down the corners of his mouth. "Don't you know what I mean?" he asked, softly.

"How the hell *would* I know what you mean?" I almost whispered it, I don't know why.

"That's right," he said to the air, "how would *he* know what I mean?" He turned toward me again, patient and calm, and yet I somehow felt him shaking, shaking as though he were going to fall apart. I felt that ice in my guts again, the dread I'd felt all afternoon; and again I watched the barmaid, moving about the bar, washing glasses, and singing. "Listen. They'll let him out and then it'll just start all over again. That's what I mean."

"You mean—they'll let him out. And then he'll just start working his way back in again. You mean he'll never kick the habit. Is that what you mean?"

"That's right," he said, cheerfully. "*You* see what I mean."

"Tell me," I said at last, "why does he want to die? He must want to die, he's killing himself, why does he want to die?"

He looked at me in surprise. He licked his lips. "He don't want to die. He wants to live. Don't nobody want to die, ever."

Then I wanted to ask him—too many things. He could not have answered, or if he had, I could not have borne the answers. I started walking. "Well, I guess it's none of my business."

"It's going to be rough on old Sonny," he said. We reached the subway station. "This is your station?" he asked. I nodded. I took one step down. "Damn!" he said, suddenly. I looked up at him. He grinned again. "Damn if I didn't leave all my money home. You ain't got a dollar on you, have you? Just for a couple of days, is all."

All at once something inside gave and threatened to come pouring out of me. I didn't hate him any more. I felt that in another moment I'd start crying like a child.

"Sure," I said. "Don't sweat." I looked in my wallet and didn't have a dollar, I only had a five. "Here," I said. "That hold you?"

He didn't look at it—he didn't want to look at it. A terrible, closed look came over his face, as though he were keeping the number on the bill a secret from him and me. "Thanks," he said, and now he was dying to see me go. "Don't worry about Sonny. Maybe I'll write him or something."

"Sure," I said. "You do that. So long."

"Be seeing you," he said. I went on down the steps.

And I didn't write Sonny or send him anything for a long time. When I finally did, it was just after my little girl died, he wrote me back a letter which made me feel like a bastard.

Here's what he said:

Dear brother,

You don't know how much I needed to hear from you. I wanted to write you many a time but I dug how much I must have hurt you and so I didn't write. But now I feel like a man who's been trying to climb up out of some deep, real deep and funky hole and just saw the sun up there, outside. I got to get outside.

I can't tell you much about how I got here. I mean I don't know how to tell you. I guess I was afraid of something or I was trying to escape from something and you know I have never been very strong in the head (smile). I'm glad Mama and Daddy are dead and can't see what's happened to their son and I swear if I'd known what I was doing I would never have hurt you so, you and a lot of other fine people who were nice to me and who believed in me.

I don't want you to think it had anything to do with me being a musician. It's more than that. Or maybe less than that. I can't get anything straight in my head down here and I try not to think about what's going to happen to me when I get outside again. Sometime I think I'm going to flip and *never* get outside and sometime I think I'll come straight back. I tell you one thing, though, I'd rather blow my brains out than go through this again. But that's what they all say, so they tell me. If I tell you when I'm coming to New York and if you could meet me, I sure would appreciate it. Give my love to Isabel and the kids and I was sure sorry to hear about little

Gracie. I wish I could be like Mama and say the Lord's will be done, but I don't know it seems to me that trouble is the one thing that never does get stopped and I don't know what good it does to blame it on the Lord. But maybe it does some good if you believe it.

Your brother,
SONNY

Then I kept in constant touch with him and I sent him whatever I could and I went to meet him when he came back to New York. When I saw him many things I thought I had forgotten came flooding back to me. This was because I had begun, finally, to wonder about Sonny, about the life that Sonny lived inside. This life, whatever it was, had made him older and thinner and it had deepened the distant stillness in which he had always moved. He looked very unlike my baby brother. Yet, when he smiled, when we shook hands, the baby brother I'd never known looked out from the depths of his private life, like an animal waiting to be coaxed into the light.

"How you been keeping?" he asked me.

"All right. And you?"

"Just fine." He was smiling all over his face. "It's good to see you again."

"It's good to see you."

The seven years' difference in our ages lay between us like a chasm: I wondered if these years would ever operate between us as a bridge. I was remembering, and it made it hard to catch my breath, but I had been there when he was born; and I had heard the first words he had ever spoken. When he started to walk, he walked from our mother straight to me. I caught him just before he fell when he took the first steps he ever took in this world.

"How's Isabel?"

"Just fine. She's dying to see you."

"And the boys?"

"They're fine, too. They're anxious to see their uncle."

"Oh, come on. You know they don't remember me."

"Are you kidding? Of course they remember you."

He grinned again. We got into a taxi. We had a lot to say to each other, far too much to know how to begin.

As the taxi began to move, I asked, "You still want to go to India?"

He laughed. "You still remember that. Hell, no. This place is Indian enough for me."

"It used to belong to them," I said.

And he laughed again. "They damn sure knew what they were doing when they got rid of it."

Years ago, when he was around fourteen, he'd been all hipped on the idea of going to India. He read books about people sitting on rocks, naked, in all kinds of weather, but mostly bad, naturally, and walking barefoot through hot coals and arriving at wisdom. I used to say that it sounded to me as though they were getting away from wisdom as fast as they could. I think he sort of looked down on me for that.

"Do you mind," he asked, "if we have the driver drive alongside the park? On the west side—I haven't seen the city in so long."

"Of course not," I said. I was afraid that I might sound as though I were humoring him, but I hoped he wouldn't take it that way.

So we drove along, between the green of the park and the stony, lifeless elegance of hotels and apartment buildings, toward the vivid, killing streets of our childhood. These streets hadn't changed, though housing projects jutted up out of them now like rocks in the middle of a boiling sea. Most of the houses in which we had grown up had vanished, as had the stores from which we had stolen, the basements in which we had first tried sex, the rooftops from which we had hurled tin cans and bricks. But houses exactly like the houses of our past yet dominated the landscape, boys exactly like the boys we once had been found themselves smothering in these houses, came down into the streets for light and air and found themselves encircled by disaster. Some escaped the trap, most didn't. Those who got out always left something of themselves behind, as some animals amputate a leg and leave it in the trap. It might be said, perhaps, that I had escaped, after all, I was a school teacher; or that Sonny had, he hadn't lived in Harlem for years. Yet, as the cab moved uptown through streets which seemed, with a rush, to darken with dark people, and as I covertly studied Sonny's face, it came to me that what we both were seeking through our separate cab windows was that part of ourselves which had been left behind. It's always at the hour of trouble and confrontation that the missing member aches.

We hit 110th Street and started rolling up Lenox Avenue. And I'd known this avenue all my life, but it seemed to me again, as it had seemed on the day I'd first heard about Sonny's trouble, filled with a hidden menace which was its very breath of life.

"We almost there," said Sonny.

"Almost." We were both too nervous to say anything more.

We live in a housing project. It hasn't been up long. A few days after it was up it seemed uninhabitably new, now, of course, it's already rundown. It looks like a parody of the good, clean, faceless life—God knows the people who live in it do their best to make it a parody. The beat-looking grass lying around isn't enough to make their lives green, the hedges will never hold out the streets, and they know it. The big windows fool no one, they aren't big enough to make space out of no space. They don't bother with the windows, they watch the TV screen instead. The playground is most popular with the children who don't play at jacks, or skip rope, or roller skate, or swing, and they can be found in it after dark. We moved in partly because it's not too far from where I teach, and partly for the kids; but it's really just like the houses in which Sonny and I grew up. The same things happen, they'll have the same things to remember. The moment Sonny and I started into the house I had the feeling that I was simply bringing him back into the danger he had almost died trying to escape.

Sonny has never been talkative. So I don't know why

I was sure he'd be dying to talk to me when supper was over the first night. Everything went fine, the oldest boy remembered him, and the youngest boy liked him, and Sonny had remembered to bring something for each of them; and Isabel, who is really much nicer than I am, more open and giving, had gone to a lot of trouble about dinner and was genuinely glad to see him. And she's always been able to tease Sonny in a way that I haven't. It was nice to see her face so vivid again and to hear her laugh and watch her make Sonny laugh. She wasn't, or, anyway, she didn't seem to be, at all uneasy or embarrassed. She chatted as though there were no subject which had to be avoided and she got Sonny past his first, faint stiffness. And thank God she was there, for I was filled with that icy dread again. Everything I did seemed awkward to me, and everything I said sounded freighted with hidden meaning. I was trying to remember everything I'd heard about dope addiction and I couldn't help watching Sonny for signs. I wasn't doing it out of malice. I was trying to find out something about my brother. I was dying to hear him tell me he was safe.

"Safe!" my father grunted, whenever Mama suggested trying to move to a neighborhood which might be safer for children. "Safe, hell! Ain't no place safe for kids, nor nobody."

He always went on like this, but he wasn't, ever, really as bad as he sounded, not even on weekends, when he got drunk. As a matter of fact, he was always on the lookout for "something a little better," but he died before he found it. He died suddenly, during a drunken weekend in the middle of the war, when Sonny was fifteen. He and Sonny hadn't ever got on too well. And this was partly because Sonny was the apple of his father's eye. It was because he loved Sonny so much and was frightened for him, that he was always fighting with him. It doesn't do any good to fight with Sonny. Sonny just moves back, inside himself, where he can't be reached. But the principal reason that they never hit it off is that they were so much alike. Daddy was big and rough and loud-talking, just the opposite of Sonny, but they both had—that same privacy.

Mama tried to tell me something about this, just after Daddy died. I was home on leave from the army.

This was the last time I ever saw my mother alive. Just the same, this picture gets all mixed up in my mind with pictures I had of her when she was younger. The way I always see her is the way she used to be on a Sunday afternoon, say, when the old folks were talking after the big Sunday dinner. I always see her wearing pale blue. She'd be sitting on the sofa. And my father would be sitting in the easy chair, not far from her. And the living room would be full of church folks and relatives. There they sit, in chairs all around the living room, and the night is creeping up outside, but nobody knows it yet. You can see the darkness growing against the windowpanes and you hear the street noises every now and again, or maybe the jangling beat of a tambourine from one of the churches close by, but it's real quiet in the room. For a moment nobody's talking, but every face looks darkening, like the sky outside. And my mother rocks a little from the waist, and my father's eyes are closed. Everyone is looking at something a child can't see. For a minute they've forgotten the children. Maybe a kid is lying on the rug, half asleep. Maybe somebody's got a kid in his lap and is absent-mindedly stroking the kid's head. Maybe there's a kid, quiet and big-eyed, curled up in a big chair in the corner. The silence, the darkness coming, and the darkness in the faces frightens the child obscurely. He hopes that the hand which strokes his forehead will never stop—will never die. He hopes that there will never come a time when the old folks won't be sitting around the living room, talking about where they've come from, and what they've seen, and what's happened to them and their kinfolk.

But something deep and watchful in the child knows that this is bound to end, is already ending. In a moment someone will get up and turn on the light. Then the old folks will remember the children and they won't talk any more that day. And when light fills the room, the child is filled with darkness. He knows that every time this happens he's moved just a little closer to that darkness outside. The darkness outside is what the old folks have been talking about. It's what they've come from. It's what they endure. The child knows that they won't talk any more because if he knows too much about what's happened to *them*, he'll know too much too soon, about what's going to happen to *him*.

The last time I talked to my mother, I remember I was restless. I wanted to get out and see Isabel. We weren't married then and we had a lot to straighten out between us.

There Mama sat, in black, by the window. She was humming an old church song, *Lord, you brought me from a long ways off*. Sonny was out somewhere. Mama kept watching the streets.

"I don't know," she said, "if I'll ever see you again, after you go off from here. But I hope you'll remember the things I tried to teach you."

"Don't talk like that," I said, and smiled. "You'll be here a long time yet."

She smiled, too, but she said nothing. She was quiet for a long time. And I said, "Mama, don't you worry about nothing. I'll be writing all the time, and you be getting the checks. . . ."

"I want to talk to you about your brother," she said, suddenly. "If anything happens to me he ain't going to have nobody to look out for him."

"Mama," I said, "ain't nothing going to happen to you *or* Sonny. Sonny's all right. He's a good boy and he's got good sense."

"It ain't a question of his being a good boy," Mama said, "nor of his having good sense. It ain't only the bad ones, nor yet the dumb ones that gets sucked under." She stopped, looking at me. "Your Daddy once had a brother," she said, and she smiled in a way that made me feel she was in pain. "You didn't never know that, did you?"

"No," I said, "I never knew that," and I watched her face.

"Oh, yes," she said, "your Daddy had a brother." She looked out of the window again. "I know you never saw your Daddy cry. But I did—many a time, through all these years."

I asked her, "What happened to his brother? How come nobody's ever talked about him?"

This was the first time I ever saw my mother look old.

"His brother got killed," she said, "when he was just a little younger than you are now. I knew him. He was a fine boy. He was maybe a little full of the devil, but he didn't mean nobody no harm."

Then she stopped and the room was silent, exactly as it had sometimes been on those Sunday afternoons. Mama kept looking out into the streets.

"He used to have a job in the mill," she said, "and, like all young folks, he just liked to perform on Saturday nights. Saturday nights, him and your father would drift around to different places, go to dances and things like that, or just sit around with people they knew, and your father's brother would sing, he had a fine voice, and play along with himself on his guitar. Well, this particular Saturday night, him and your father was coming home from some place, and they were both a little drunk and there was a moon that night, it was bright like day. Your father's brother was feeling kind of good, and he was whistling to himself, and he had his guitar slung over his shoulder. They was coming down a hill and beneath them was a road that turned off from the highway. Well, your father's brother, being always kind of frisky, decided to run down this hill, and he did, with that guitar banging and clanging behind him, and he ran across the road, and he was making water behind a tree. And your father was sort of amused at him and he was still coming down the hill, kind of slow. Then he heard a car motor and that same minute his brother stepped from behind the tree, into the road, in the moonlight. And he started to cross the road. And your father started to run down the hill, he says he don't know why. This car was full of white men. They was all drunk, and when they seen

your father's brother they let out a great whoop and hol-
ler and they aimed the car straight at him. They was
having fun, they just wanted to scare him, the way they
do sometimes, you know. But they was drunk. And I
guess the boy, being drunk, too, and scared, kind of lost
his head. By the time he jumped it was too late. Your
father says he heard his brother scream when the car
rolled over him, and he heard the wood of that guitar
when it give, and he heard them strings go flying, and
he heard them white men shouting, and the car kept on
a-going and it ain't stopped till this day. And, time your
father got down the hill, his brother weren't nothing but
blood and pulp."

Tears were gleaming on my mother's face. There
wasn't anything I could say.

"He never mentioned it," she said, "because I never let
him mention it before you children. Your Daddy was
like a crazy man that night and for many a night thereafter. He says he never in his life seen anything as dark
as that road after the lights of that car had gone away.
Weren't nothing, weren't nobody on that road, just your
Daddy and his brother and that busted guitar. Oh, yes.
Your Daddy never did really get right again. Till the day
he died he weren't sure but that every white man he saw
was the man that killed his brother."

She stopped and took out her handkerchief and dried
her eyes and looked at me.

"I ain't telling you all this," she said, "to make you
scared or bitter or to make you hate nobody. I'm telling
you this because you got a brother. And the world ain't
changed."

I guess I didn't want to believe this. I guess she saw
this in my face. She turned away from me, toward the
window again, searching those streets.

"But I praise my Redeemer," she said at last, "that He
called your Daddy home before me. I ain't saying it to
throw no flowers at myself, but, I declare, it keeps me
from feeling too cast down to know I helped your father
get safely through this world. Your father always acted

like he was the roughest, strongest man on earth. And everybody took him to be like that. But if he hadn't had *me* there—to see his tears!"

She was crying again. Still, I couldn't move. I said, "Lord, Lord, Mama, I didn't know it was like that."

"Oh, honey," she said, "there's a lot that you don't know. But you are going to find it out." She stood up from the window and came over to me. "You got to hold on to your brother," she said, "and don't let him fall, no matter what it looks like is happening to him and no matter how evil you gets with him. You going to be evil with him many a time. But don't you forget what I told you, you hear?"

"I won't forget," I said. "Don't you worry, I won't forget. I won't let nothing happen to Sonny."

My mother smiled as though she were amused at something she saw in my face. Then, "You may not be able to stop nothing from happening. But you got to let him know you's *there*."

Two days later I was married, and then I was gone. And I had a lot of things on my mind and I pretty well forgot my promise to Mama until I got shipped home on a special furlough for her funeral.

And, after the funeral, with just Sonny and me alone in the empty kitchen, I tried to find out something about him.

"What do you want to do?" I asked him.

"I'm going to be a musician," he said.

For he had graduated, in the time I had been away, from dancing to the juke box to finding out who was playing what, and what they were doing with it, and he had bought himself a set of drums.

"You mean, you want to be a drummer?" I somehow had the feeling that being a drummer might be all right for other people but not for my brother Sonny.

"I don't think," he said, looking at me very gravely, "that I'll ever be a good drummer. But I think I can play a piano."

I frowned. I'd never played the role of the older brother quite so seriously before, had scarcely ever, in fact, *asked* Sonny a damn thing. I sensed myself in the presence of something I didn't really know how to handle, didn't understand. So I made my frown a little deeper as I asked: "What kind of musician do you want to be?"

He grinned. "How many kinds do you think there are?"

"Be *serious*," I said.

He laughed, throwing his head back, and then looked at me. "I *am* serious."

"Well, then, for Christ's sake, stop kidding around and answer a serious question. I mean, do you want to be a concert pianist, you want to play classical music and all that, or—or what?" Long before I finished he was laughing again. "For Christ's *sake*, Sonny!"

He sobered, but with difficulty. "I'm sorry. But you sound so—*scared!*" and he was off again.

"Well, you may think it's funny now, baby, but it's not going to be so funny when you have to make your living at it, let me tell you *that*." I was furious because I knew he was laughing at me and I didn't know why.

"No," he said, very sober now, and afraid, perhaps, that he'd hurt me, "I don't want to be a classical pianist. That isn't what interests me. I mean"—he paused, looking hard at me, as though his eyes would help me to understand, and then gestured helplessly, as though perhaps his hand would help—"I mean, I'll have a lot of studying to do, and I'll have to study *everything*, but, I mean, I want to play *with*—jazz musicians." He stopped. "I want to play jazz," he said.

Well, the word had never before sounded as heavy, as real, as it sounded that afternoon in Sonny's mouth. I just looked at him and I was probably frowning a real frown by this time. I simply couldn't see why on earth he'd want to spend his time hanging around night clubs, clowning around on band-stands, while people pushed each other around a dance floor. It seemed—beneath him, somehow. I had never thought about it before, had never been forced to, but I suppose I had always put jazz musicians in a class with what Daddy called "good-time people."

"Are you *serious?*"

"Hell, *yes*, I'm serious."

He looked more helpless than ever, and annoyed, and deeply hurt.

I suggested, helpfully: "You mean—like Louis Armstrong?"

His face closed as though I'd struck him. "No. I'm not talking about none of that old-time, down home crap."

"Well, look, Sonny, I'm sorry, don't get mad. I just don't altogether get it, that's all. Name somebody—you know, a jazz musician you admire."

"Bird."

"Who?"

"Bird! Charlie Parker! Don't they teach you nothing in the goddamn army?"

I lit a cigarette. I was surprised and then a little amused to discover that I was trembling. "I've been out of touch," I said. "You'll have to be patient with me. Now. Who's this Parker character?"

"He's just one of the greatest jazz musicians alive," said Sonny, sullenly, his hands in his pockets, his back to me. "Maybe *the* greatest," he added, bitterly, "that's probably why *you* never heard of him."

"All right," I said, "I'm ignorant. I'm sorry. I'll go out and buy all the cat's records right away, all right?"

"It don't," said Sonny, with dignity, "make any difference to me. I don't care what you listen to. Don't do me no favors."

I was beginning to realize that I'd never seen him so upset before. With another part of my mind I was thinking that this would probably turn out to be one of those things kids go through and that I shouldn't make it seem important by pushing it too hard. Still, I didn't think it would do any harm to ask: "Doesn't all this take a lot of time? Can you make a living at it?"

He turned back to me and half leaned, half sat, on the

kitchen table. "Everything takes time," he said, "and— well, yes, sure, I can make a living at it. But what I don't seem to be able to make you understand is that it's the only thing I want to do."

"Well, Sonny," I said, gently, "you know people can't always do exactly what they *want* to do—"

"*No*, I don't know that," said Sonny, surprising me. "I think people *ought* to do what they want to do, what else are they alive for?"

"You getting to be a big boy," I said desperately, "it's time you started thinking about your future."

"I'm thinking about my future," said Sonny, grimly. "I think about it all the time."

I gave up. I decided, if he didn't change his mind, that we could always talk about it later. "In the meantime," I said, "you got to finish school." We had already decided that he'd have to move in with Isabel and her folks. I knew this wasn't the ideal arrangement because Isabel's folks are inclined to be dicty and they hadn't especially wanted Isabel to marry me. But I didn't know what else to do. "And we have to get you fixed up at Isabel's."

There was a long silence. He moved from the kitchen table to the window. "That's a terrible idea. You know it yourself."

"Do you have a *better* idea?"

He just walked up and down the kitchen for a minute. He was as tall as I was. He had started to shave. I suddenly had the feeling that I didn't know him at all.

He stopped at the kitchen table and picked up my cigarettes. Looking at me with a kind of mocking, amused defiance, he put one between his lips. "You mind?"

"You smoking already?"

He lit the cigarette and nodded, watching me through the smoke. "I just wanted to see if I'd have the courage to smoke in front of you." He grinned and blew a great cloud of smoke to the ceiling. "It was easy." He looked at my face. "Come on, now. I bet you was smoking at my age, tell the truth."

I didn't say anything but the truth was on my face,

and he laughed. But now there was something very strained in his laugh. "Sure. And I bet that ain't all you was doing."

He was frightening me a little. "Cut the crap," I said. "We already decided that you was going to go and live at Isabel's. Now what's got into you all of a sudden?"

"*You* decided it," he pointed out. "*I* didn't decide nothing." He stopped in front of me, leaning against the stove, arms loosely folded. "Look, brother. I don't want to stay in Harlem no more, I really don't." He was very earnest. He looked at me, then over toward the kitchen window. There was something in his eyes I'd never seen before, some thoughtfulness, some worry all his own. He rubbed the muscle of one arm. "It's time I was getting out of here."

"Where do you want to *go*, Sonny?"

"I want to join the army. Or the navy, I don't care. If I say I'm old enough, they'll believe me."

Then I got mad. It was because I was so scared. "You must be crazy. You goddamn fool, what the hell do you want to go and join the *army* for?"

"I just told you. To get out of Harlem."

"Sonny, you haven't even finished *school*. And if you really want to be a musician, how do you expect to study if you're in the *army*?"

He looked at me, trapped, and in anguish. "There's ways. I might be able to work out some kind of deal. Anyway, I'll have the G.I. Bill when I come out."

"*If* you come out." We stared at each other. "Sonny, please. Be reasonable. I know the setup is far from perfect. But we got to do the best we can."

"I ain't learning nothing in school," he said. "Even when I go." He turned away from me and opened the window and threw his cigarette out into the narrow alley. I watched his back. "At least, I ain't learning nothing you'd want me to learn." He slammed the window so hard I thought the glass would fly out, and turned back to me. "And I'm sick of the stink of these garbage cans!"

"Sonny," I said, "I know how you feel. But if you don't finish school now, you're going to be sorry later that you didn't." I grabbed him by the shoulders. "And you only got another year. It ain't so bad. And I'll come back and I swear I'll help you do *whatever* you want to do. Just try to put up with it till I come back. Will you please do that? For me?"

He didn't answer and he wouldn't look at me.

"Sonny. You hear me?"

He pulled away. "I hear you. But you never hear anything *I* say."

I didn't know what to say to that. He looked out of the window and then back at me. "OK," he said, and sighed. "I'll try."

Then I said, trying to cheer him up a little, "They got a piano at Isabel's. You can practice on it."

And as a matter of fact, it did cheer him up for a minute. "That's right," he said to himself. "I forgot that." His face relaxed a little. But the worry, the thoughtfulness, played on it still, the way shadows play on a face which is staring into the fire.

But I thought I'd never hear the end of that piano. At first, Isabel would write me, saying how nice it was that Sonny was so serious about his music and how, as soon as he came in from school, or wherever he had been when he was supposed to be at school, he went straight to that piano and stayed there until suppertime. And, after supper, he went back to that piano and stayed there until everybody went to bed. He was at that piano all day Saturday and all day Sunday. Then he bought a record player and started playing records. He'd play one record over and over again, all day long sometimes, and he'd improvise along with it on the piano. Or he'd play one section of the record, one chord, one change, one progression, then he'd do it on the piano. Then back to the record. Then back to the piano.

Well, I really don't know how they stood it. Isabel finally confessed that it wasn't like living with a person at all, it was like living with sound. And the sound didn't make any sense to her, didn't make any sense to any of them—naturally. They began, in a way, to be afflicted by this presence that was living in their home. It was as though Sonny were some sort of god, or monster. He moved in an atmosphere which wasn't like theirs at all. They fed him and he ate, he washed himself, he walked in and out of their door; he certainly wasn't nasty or unpleasant or rude, Sonny isn't any of those things; but it was as though he were all wrapped up in some cloud, some fire, some vision all his own; and there wasn't any way to reach him.

At the same time, he wasn't really a man yet, he was still a child, and they had to watch out for him in all kinds of ways. They certainly couldn't throw him out. Neither did they dare to make a great scene about that piano because even they dimly sensed, as I sensed, from so many thousands of miles away, that Sonny was at that piano playing for his life.

But he hadn't been going to school. One day a letter came from the school board and Isabel's mother got it— there had, apparently, been other letters but Sonny had torn them up. This day, when Sonny came in, Isabel's mother showed him the letter and asked where he'd been spending his time. And she finally got it out of him that he'd been down in Greenwich Village, with musicians and other characters, in a white girl's apartment. And this scared her and she started to scream at him and what came up, once she began—though she denies it to this day—was what sacrifices they were making to give Sonny a decent home and how little he appreciated it.

Sonny didn't play the piano that day. By evening, Isabel's mother had calmed down but then there was the old man to deal with, and Isabel herself. Isabel says she did her best to be calm but she broke down and started crying. She says she just watched Sonny's face. She could tell, by watching him, what was happening with him. And what was happening was that they penetrated his cloud, they had reached him. Even if their fingers had been a thousand times more gentle than human fingers ever are, he could hardly help feeling that they had stripped him naked and were spitting on that nakedness. For he also had to see that his presence, that music, which was life or death to him, had been torture for them and that they had endured it, not at all for his sake, but only for mine. And Sonny couldn't take that. He can take it a little better today than he could then but he's still not very good at it and, frankly, I don't know anybody who is.

The silence of the next few days must have been louder than the sound of all the music ever played since time began. One morning, before she went to work, Isabel was in his room for something and she suddenly realized that all of his records were gone. And she knew for certain that he was gone. And he was. He went as far as the navy would carry him. He finally sent me a postcard from some place in Greece and that was the first I knew that Sonny was still alive. I didn't see him any more until we were both back in New York and the war had long been over.

He was a man by then, of course, but I wasn't willing to see it. He came by the house from time to time, but we fought almost every time we met. I didn't like the way he carried himself, loose and dreamlike all the time, and I didn't like his friends, and his music seemed to be merely an excuse for the life he led. It sounded just that weird and disordered.

Then we had a fight, a pretty awful fight, and I didn't see him for months. By and by I looked him up, where he was living, in a furnished room in the Village, and I tried to make it up. But there were lots of other people in the room and Sonny just lay on his bed, and he wouldn't come downstairs with me, and he treated these other people as though they were his family and I weren't. So I got mad and then he got mad, and then I told him that he might just as well be dead as live the way he was living. Then he stood up and he told me not to worry about him any more in life, that he *was* dead as far as I was concerned. Then he pushed me to the door and the other people looked on as though nothing were happening, and he slammed the door behind me. I stood in the hallway, staring at the door. I heard somebody laugh in the room and then the tears came to my eyes.

I started down the steps, whistling to keep from crying,
I kept whistling to myself, *You going to need me, baby,
one of these cold, rainy days.*

I read about Sonny's trouble in the spring. Little Grace
died in the fall. She was a beautiful little girl. But she
only lived a little over two years. She died of polio and
she suffered. She had a slight fever for a couple of days,
but it didn't seem like anything and we just kept her in
bed. And we would certainly have called the doctor, but
the fever dropped, she seemed to be all right. So we
thought it had just been a cold. Then, one day, she was
up, playing, Isabel was in the kitchen fixing lunch for
the two boys when they'd come in from school, and she
heard Grace fall down in the living room. When you
have a lot of children you don't always start running
when one of them falls, unless they start screaming or
something. And, this time, Grace was quiet. Yet, Isabel
says that when she heard that *thump* and then that silence, something happened in her to make her afraid.
And she ran to the living room and there was little Grace
on the floor, all twisted up, and the reason she hadn't
screamed was that she couldn't get her breath. And when
she did scream, it was the worst sound, Isabel says, that
she'd ever heard in all her life, and she still hears it sometimes in her dreams. Isabel will sometimes wake me up
with a low, moaning, strangled sound and I have to be
quick to awaken her and hold her to me and where Isabel
is weeping against me seems a mortal wound.
    I think I may have written Sonny the very day that
little Grace was buried. I was sitting in the living room
in the dark, by myself, and I suddenly thought of Sonny.
My trouble made his real.

    One Saturday afternoon, when Sonny had been living
with us, or, anyway, been in our house, for nearly two
weeks, I found myself wandering aimlessly about the living room, drinking from a can of beer, and trying to work
up the courage to search Sonny's room. He was out, he
was usually out whenever I was home, and Isabel had

taken the children to see their grandparents. Suddenly I was standing still in front of the living room window, watching Seventh Avenue. The idea of searching Sonny's room made me still. I scarcely dared to admit to myself what I'd be searching for. I didn't know what I'd do if I found it. Or if I didn't.

On the sidewalk across from me, near the entrance to a barbecue joint, some people were holding an old-fashioned revival meeting. The barbecue cook, wearing a dirty white apron, his conked hair reddish and metallic in the pale sun, and a cigarette between his lips, stood in the doorway, watching them. Kids and older people paused in their errands and stood there, along with some older men and a couple of very tough-looking women who watched everything that happened on the avenue, as though they owned it, or were maybe owned by it. Well, they were watching this, too. The revival was being carried on by three sisters in black, and a brother. All they had were their voices and their Bibles and a tambourine. The brother was testifying and while he testified two of the sisters stood together, seeming to say, Amen, and the third sister walked around with the tambourine outstretched and a couple of people dropped coins into it. Then the brother's testimony ended and the sister who had been taking up the collection dumped the coins into her palm and transferred them to the pocket of her long black robe. Then she raised both hands, striking the tambourine against the air, and then against one hand, and she started to sing. And the two other sisters and the brother joined in.

It was strange, suddenly, to watch, though I had been seeing these street meetings all my life. So, of course, had everybody else down there. Yet, they paused and watched and listened and I stood still at the window. *"Tis the old ship of Zion,"* they sang, and the sister with the tambourine kept a steady, jangling beat, *"it has rescued many a thousand!"* Not a soul under the sound of their voices was hearing this song for the first time, not one of them had been rescued. Nor had they seen much in the way of rescue work being done around them. Nei-

ther did they especially believe in the holiness of the
three sisters and the brother, they knew too much about
them, knew where they lived, and how. The woman
with the tambourine, whose voice dominated the air,
whose face was bright with joy, was divided by very little
from the woman who stood watching her, a cigarette between her heavy, chapped lips, her hair a cuckoo's nest,
her face scarred and swollen from many beatings, and
her black eyes glittering like coal. Perhaps they both
knew this, which was why, when, as rarely, they addressed each other, they addressed each other as Sister. As
the singing filled the air the watching, listening faces
underwent a change, the eyes focusing on something
within; the music seemed to soothe a poison out of them;
and time seemed, nearly, to fall away from the sullen,
belligerent, battered faces, as though they were fleeing
back to their first condition, while dreaming of their last.
The barbecue cook half shook his head and smiled, and
dropped his cigarette and disappeared into his joint. A
man fumbled in his pockets for change and stood holding it in his hand impatiently, as though he had just remembered a pressing appointment further up the avenue.
He looked furious. Then I saw Sonny, standing on the
edge of the crowd. He was carrying a wide, flat notebook
with a green cover, and it made him look, from where I
was standing, almost like a schoolboy. The coppery
sun brought out the copper in his skin, he was very
faintly smiling, standing very still. Then the singing
stopped, the tambourine turned into a collection plate
again. The furious man dropped in his coins and vanished, so did a couple of the women, and Sonny
dropped some change in the plate, looking directly at the
woman with a little smile. He started across the avenue,
toward the house. He has a slow, loping walk, something like the way Harlem hipsters walk, only he's im-
posed on this his own half-beat. I had never really noticed it before.

I stayed at the window, both relieved and apprehensive. As Sonny disappeared from my sight, they began

singing again. And they were still singing when his key turned in the lock.

"Hey," he said.

"Hey, yourself. You want some beer?"

"No. Well, maybe." But he came up to the window and stood beside me, looking out. "What a warm voice," he said.

They were singing *If I could only hear my mother pray again!*

"Yes," I said, "and she can sure beat that tambourine."

"But what a terrible song," he said, and laughed. He dropped his notebook on the sofa and disappeared into the kitchen. "Where's Isabel and the kids?"

"I think they went to see their grandparents. You hungry?"

"No." He came back into the living room with his can of beer. "You want to come some place with me tonight?"

I sensed, I don't know how, that I couldn't possibly say No. "Sure. Where?"

He sat down on the sofa and picked up his notebook and started leafing through it. "I'm going to sit in with some fellows in a joint in the Village."

"You mean, you're going to play, tonight?"

"That's right." He took a swallow of his beer and moved back to the window. He gave me a sidelong look. "If you can stand it."

"I'll try," I said.

He smiled to himself and we both watched as the meeting across the way broke up. The three sisters and the brother, heads bowed, were singing *God be with you till we meet again*. The faces around them were very quiet. Then the song ended. The small crowd dispersed. We watched the three women and the lone man walk slowly up the avenue.

"When she was singing before," said Sonny, abruptly, "her voice reminded me for a minute of what heroin feels like sometimes—when it's in your veins. It makes you feel sort of warm and cool at the same time. And distant.

And—and sure." He sipped his beer, very deliberately not looking at me. I watched his face. "It makes you feel —in control. Sometimes you've got to have that feeling."

"Do you?" I sat down slowly in the easy chair.

"Sometimes." He went to the sofa and picked up his notebook again. "Some people do."

"In order," I asked, "to play?" And my voice was very ugly, full of contempt and anger.

"Well"—he looked at me with great, troubled eyes, as though, in fact, he hoped his eyes would tell me things he could never otherwise say—"they *think* so. And *if* they think so—!"

"And what do *you* think?" I asked.

He sat on the sofa and put his can of beer on the floor. "I don't know," he said, and I couldn't be sure if he were answering my question or pursuing his thoughts. His face didn't tell me. "It's not so much to *play*. It's to *stand* it, to be able to make it at all. On any level." He frowned and smiled: "In order to keep from shaking to pieces."

"But these friends of yours," I said, "they seem to shake themselves to pieces pretty goddamn fast."

"Maybe." He played with the notebook. And something told me that I should curb my tongue, that Sonny was doing his best to talk, that I should listen. "But of course you only know the ones that've gone to pieces. Some don't—or at least they haven't *yet* and that's just about all *any* of us can say." He paused. "And then there are some who just live, really, in hell, and they know it and they see what's happening and they go right on. I don't know." He sighed, dropped the notebook, folded his arms. "Some guys, you can tell from the way they play, they on something *all* the time. And you can see that, well, it makes something real for them. But of course," he picked up his beer from the floor and sipped it and put the can down again, "they *want* to, too, you've got to see that. Even some of them that say they don't— *some*, not all."

"And what about you?" I asked—I couldn't help it. "What about you? Do *you* want to?"

He stood up and walked to the window and remained

silent for a long time. Then he sighed. "Me," he said. Then: "While I was downstairs before, on my way here, listening to that woman sing, it struck me all of a sudden how much suffering she must have had to go through—to sing like that. It's *repulsive* to think you have to suffer that much."

I said: "But there's no way not to suffer—is there, Sonny?"

"I believe not," he said, and smiled, "but that's never stopped anyone from trying." He looked at me. "Has it?" I realized, with this mocking look, that there stood between us, forever, beyond the power of time or forgiveness, the fact that I had held silence—so long!—when he had needed human speech to help him. He turned back to the window. "No, there's no way not to suffer. But you try all kinds of ways to keep from drowning in it, to keep on top of it, and to make it seem—well, like *you*. Like you did something, all right, and now you're suffering for it. You know?" I said nothing. "Well you know," he said, impatiently, "why *do* people suffer? Maybe it's better to do something to give it a reason, *any* reason."

"But we just agreed," I said, "that there's no way not to suffer. Isn't it better, then, just to—take it?"

"But nobody just takes it," Sonny cried, "that's what I'm telling you! *Everybody* tries not to. You're just hung up on the *way* some people try—it's not *your* way!"

The hair on my face began to itch, my face felt wet. "That's not true," I said, "that's not true. I don't give a damn what other people do, I don't even care how they suffer. I just care how *you* suffer." And he looked at me. "Please believe me," I said, "I don't want to see you—die—trying not to suffer."

"I won't," he said, flatly, "die trying not to suffer. At least, not any faster than anybody else."

"But there's no need," I said, trying to laugh, "is there? in killing yourself."

I wanted to say more, but I couldn't. I wanted to talk about will power and how life could be—well, beautiful. I wanted to say that it was all within; but was it? or, rather, wasn't that exactly the trouble? And I wanted to promise that I would never fail him again. But it would all have sounded—empty words and lies.

So I made the promise to myself and prayed that I would keep it.

"It's terrible sometimes, inside," he said, "that's what's the trouble. You walk these streets, black and funky and cold, and there's not really a living ass to talk to, and there's nothing shaking, and there's no way of getting it out—that storm inside. You can't talk it and you can't make love with it, and when you finally try to get with it and play it, you realize *nobody's* listening. So *you've* got to listen. You got to find a way to listen."

And then he walked away from the window and sat on the sofa again, as though all the wind had suddenly been knocked out of him. "Sometimes you'll do *anything* to play, even cut your mother's throat." He laughed and looked at me. "Or your brother's." Then he sobered. "Or your own." Then: "Don't worry. I'm all right now and I think I'll *be* all right. But I can't forget—where I've been. I don't mean just the physical place I've been, I mean where I've *been*. And *what* I've been."

"What have you been, Sonny?" I asked.

He smiled—but sat sideways on the sofa, his elbow resting on the back, his fingers playing with his mouth and chin, not looking at me. "I've been something I didn't recognize, didn't know I could be. Didn't know anybody could be." He stopped, looking inward, looking helplessly young, looking old. "I'm not talking about it now because I feel *guilty* or anything like that—maybe it would be better if I did, I don't know. Anyway, I can't really talk about it. Not to you, not to anybody," and now he turned and faced me. "Sometimes, you know, and it was actually when I was most *out* of the world, I felt that I was in it, that I was *with* it, really, and I could play or I didn't really have to *play*, it just came out of me, it was there. And I don't know how I played, thinking about it now, but I know I did awful things, those times, sometimes, to people. Or it wasn't that I *did* anything to them—it was that they weren't real." He picked up the beer can; it was empty; he rolled it between his palms: "And other times—well, I needed a fix, I needed to find a place to lean, I needed to clear a space to *listen*—and I couldn't find it, and I—went crazy, I did terrible things to *me*, I was terrible *for* me." He began pressing the beer can between his hands, I watched the metal begin to give. It glittered, as he played with it, like a knife, and I was afraid he would cut himself, but I said nothing. "Oh well. I can never tell you. I was all by myself at the bottom of something, stinking and sweating and crying and shaking, and I smelled it, you know? *my* stink, and I thought I'd die if I couldn't get away from it and yet, all the same, I knew that everything I was doing was just locking me in with it. And I didn't know," he paused, still flattening the beer can, "I didn't know, I still *don't* know, something kept telling me that maybe it was good to smell your own stink, but I didn't think that *that* was what I'd been trying to do—and—who can stand it?" and he abruptly dropped the ruined beer can, looking at me with a small, still smile, and then rose, walking to the window as though it were the lodestone rock. I watched his face, he watched the avenue. "I couldn't tell you when Mama died—but the reason I wanted to leave Harlem so bad was to get away from drugs. And then, when I ran away, that's what I was running from—really. When I came back, nothing had changed, *I* hadn't changed, I was just—older." And he stopped, drumming with his fingers on the windowpane. The sun had vanished, soon darkness would fall. I watched his face. "It can come again," he said, almost as though speaking to himself. Then he turned to me. "It can come again," he repeated. "I just want you to know that."

"All right," I said, at last. "So it can come again, All right."

He smiled, but the smile was sorrowful. "I had to try to tell you," he said.

"Yes," I said. "I understand that."

"You're my brother," he said, looking straight at me, and not smiling at all.

"Yes," I repeated, "yes. I understand that."

He turned back to the window, looking out. "All that hatred down there," he said, "all that hatred and misery and love. It's a wonder it doesn't blow the avenue apart."

We went to the only night club on a short, dark street, downtown. We squeezed through the narrow, chattering, jam-packed bar to the entrance of the big room, where the bandstand was. And we stood there for a moment, for the lights were very dim in this room and we couldn't see. Then, "Hello, boy," said a voice and an enormous black man, much older than Sonny or myself, erupted out of all that atmospheric lighting and put an arm around Sonny's shoulder. "I been sitting right here," he said, "waiting for you."

He had a big voice, too, and heads in the darkness turned toward us.

Sonny grinned and pulled a little away, and said, "Creole, this is my brother. I told you about him."

Creole shook my hand. "I'm glad to meet you, son," he said, and it was clear that he was glad to meet me *there*, for Sonny's sake. And he smiled, "You got a real musician in *your* family," and he took his arm from Sonny's shoulder and slapped him, lightly, affectionately, with the back of his hand.

"Well. Now I've heard it all," said a voice behind us. This was another musician, and a friend of Sonny's, a coal-black, cheerful-looking man, built close to the ground. He immediately began confiding to me, at the top of his lungs, the most terrible things about Sonny, his teeth gleaming like a lighthouse and his laugh coming up out of him like the beginning of an earthquake. And it turned out that everyone at the bar knew Sonny, or almost everyone; some were musicians, working there, or nearby, or not working, some were simply hangers-on, and some were there to hear Sonny play. I was introduced to all of them and they were all very polite to me. Yet, it was clear that, for them, I was only Sonny's brother. Here, I was in Sonny's world. Or, rather: his kingdom. Here, it was not even a question that his veins bore royal blood.

They were going to play soon and Creole installed me, by myself, at a table in a dark corner. Then I watched them, Creole, and the little black man, and Sonny, and the others, while they horsed around, standing just below the bandstand. The light from the bandstand spilled just a little short of them and, watching them laughing and gesturing and moving about, I had the feeling that they, nevertheless, were being most careful not to step into that circle of light too suddenly: that if they moved into the light too suddenly, without thinking, they would perish in flame. Then, while I watched, one of them, the small, black man, moved into the light and crossed the bandstand and started fooling around with his drums. Then—being funny and being, also, extremely ceremonious—Creole took Sonny by the arm and led him to the piano. A woman's voice called Sonny's name and a few hands started clapping. And Sonny, also being funny and being ceremonious, and so touched, I think, that he could have cried, but neither hiding it nor showing it, riding it like a man, grinned, and put both hands to his heart and bowed from the waist.

Creole then went to the bass fiddle and a lean, very bright-skinned brown man jumped up on the bandstand and picked up his horn. So there they were, and the atmosphere on the bandstand and in the room began to change and tighten. Someone stepped up to the microphone and announced them. Then there were all kinds of murmurs. Some people at the bar shushed others. The waitress ran around, frantically getting in the last orders, guys and chicks got closer to each other, and the lights on the bandstand, on the quartet, turned to a kind of indigo. Then they all looked different there. Creole looked about him for the last time, as though he were making certain that all his chickens were in the coop, and then he—jumped and struck the fiddle. And there they were.

All I know about music is that not many people ever really hear it. And even then, on the rare occasions when something opens within, and the music enters, what we mainly hear, or hear corroborated, are personal, private

vanishing evocations. But the man who creates the music
is hearing something else, is dealing with the roar rising
from the void and imposing order on it as it hits the air.
What is evoked in him, then, is of another order, more
terrible because it has no words, and triumphant, too,
for that same reason. And his triumph, when he triumphs, is ours. I just watched Sonny's face. His face
was troubled, he was working hard, but he wasn't with
it. And I had the feeling that, in a way, everyone on
the bandstand was waiting for him, both waiting for
him and pushing him along. But as I began to watch
Creole, I realized that it was Creole who held them all
back. He had them on a short rein. Up there, keeping the
beat with his whole body, wailing on the fiddle, with
his eyes half closed, he was listening to everything, but
he was listening to Sonny. He was having a dialogue
with Sonny. He wanted Sonny to leave the shore line
and strike out for the deep water. He was Sonny's
witness that deep water and drowning were not the
same thing—he had been there, and he knew. And he
wanted Sonny to know. He was waiting for Sonny to
do the things on the keys which would let Creole know
that Sonny was in the water.

And, while Creole listened, Sonny moved, deep
within, exactly like someone in torment. I had never before thought of how awful the relationship must be between the musician and his instrument. He has to fill it,
this instrument, with the breath of life, his own. He has
to make it do what he wants it to do. And a piano is just
a piano. It's made out of so much wood and wires and
little hammers and big ones, and ivory. While there's
only so much you can do with it, the only way to find this
out is to try to try and make it do everything.

And Sonny hadn't been near a piano for over a year.
And he wasn't on much better terms with his life, not
the life that stretched before him now. He and the piano
stammered, started one way, got scared, stopped; started
another way, panicked, marked time, started again; then
seemed to have found a direction, panicked again, got
stuck. And the face I saw on Sonny I'd never seen be-

fore. Everything had been burned out of it, and, at the same time, things usually hidden were being burned in, by the fire and fury of the battle which was occurring in him up there.

Yet, watching Creole's face as they neared the end of the first set, I had the feeling that something had happened, something I hadn't heard. Then they finished, there was scattered applause, and then, without an instant's warning, Creole started into something else, it was almost sardonic, it was *Am I Blue*. And, as though he commanded, Sonny began to play. Something began to happen. And Creole let out the reins. The dry, low, black man said something awful on the drums, Creole answered, and the drums talked back. Then the horn insisted, sweet and high, slightly detached perhaps, and Creole listened, commenting now and then, dry, and driving, beautiful and calm and old. Then they all came together again, and Sonny was part of the family again. I could tell this from his face. He seemed to have found, right there beneath his fingers, a damn brand-new piano. It seemed that he couldn't get over it. Then, for awhile, just being happy with Sonny, they seemed to be agreeing with him that brand-new pianos certainly were a gas.

Then Creole stepped forward to remind them that what they were playing was the blues. He hit something in all of them, he hit something in me, myself, and the music tightened and deepened, apprehension began to beat the air. Creole began to tell us what the blues were all about. They were not about anything very new. He and his boys up there were keeping it new, at the risk of ruin, destruction, madness, and death, in order to find new ways to make us listen. For, while the tale of how we suffer, and how we are delighted, and how we may triumph is never new, it always must be heard. There isn't any other tale to tell, it's the only light we've got in all this darkness.

And this tale, according to that face, that body, those strong hands on those strings, has another aspect in every country, and a new depth in every generation. Lis-

ten, Creole seemed to be saying, listen. Now these are
Sonny's blues. He made the little black man on the drums
know it, and the bright, brown man on the horn. Creole
wasn't trying any longer to get Sonny in the water. He
was wishing him Godspeed. Then he stepped back, very
slowly, filling the air with the immense suggestion that
Sonny speak for himself.

Then they all gathered around Sonny and Sonny
played. Every now and again one of them seemed to
say, Amen. Sonny's fingers filled the air with life, his
life. But that life contained so many others. And Sonny
went all the way back, he really began with the spare,
flat statement of the opening phrase of the song. Then
he began to make it his. It was very beautiful because it
wasn't hurried and it was no longer a lament. I seemed
to hear with what burning he had made it his, with what
burning we had yet to make it ours, how we could cease
lamenting. Freedom lurked around us and I understood,
at last, that he could help us to be free if we would listen, that he would never be free until we did. Yet, there
was no battle in his face now. I heard what he had gone
through, and would continue to go through until he
came to rest in earth. He had made it his: that long line,
of which we knew only Mama and Daddy. And he was
giving it back, as everything must be given back, so
that, passing through death, it can live forever. I saw my
mother's face again, and felt, for the first time, how the
stones of the road she had walked on must have bruised
her feet. I saw the moonlit road where my father's brother
died. And it brought something else back to me, and
carried me past it, I saw my little girl again and felt
Isabel's tears again, and I felt my own tears begin to
rise. And I was yet aware that this was only a moment,
that the world waited outside, as hungry as a tiger, and
that trouble stretched above us, longer than the sky.

Then it was over. Creole and Sonny let out their
breath, both soaking wet, and grinning. There was a lot
of applause and some of it was real. In the dark, the girl
came by and I asked her to take drinks to the bandstand. There was a long pause, while they talked up

there in the indigo light and after awhile I saw the girl put a Scotch and milk on top of the piano for Sonny. He didn't seem to notice it, but just before they started playing again, he sipped from it and looked toward me, and nodded. Then he put it back on top of the piano. For me, then, as they began to play again, it glowed and shook above my brother's head like the very cup of trembling.

Venus, Cupid, Folly and Time

Peter Taylor

THEIR house alone would not have made you think
there was anything so awfully wrong with Mr. Dorset or
his old maid sister. But certain things about the way both
of them dressed had, for a long time, annoyed and disturbed everyone. We used to see them together at the
grocery store, for instance, or even in one of the big department stores downtown, wearing their bedroom slippers. Looking more closely we would sometimes see the
cuff of a pyjama top or the hem of a hitched up night-
gown showing from underneath their ordinary daytime
clothes. Such slovenliness in one's neighbors is so unpleasant that even husbands and wives in West Vesey
Place, which was the street where the Dorsets lived, had
got so they didn't like to joke about it with each other.
Were the Dorsets, poor old things, losing their minds? If
so, what was to be done about it? Some neighbors got
so they would not even admit to themselves what they
saw. And a child coming home with an ugly report on
the Dorsets was apt to be told that it was time he learned
to curb his imagination.

Mr. Dorset wore tweed caps and sleeveless sweaters.
Usually he had his sweater stuffed down inside his
trousers with his shirt tails. To the women and young
girls in West Vesey Place this was extremely distasteful.
It made them feel as though Mr. Dorset had just come
from the bathroom and had got his sweater inside his
trousers by mistake. There was, in fact, nothing about
Mr. Dorset that was not offensive to the women. Even
the old touring car he drove was regarded by most of

them as a disgrace to the neighborhood. Parked out in front of his house, as it usually was, it seemed a worse violation of West Vesey's zoning than the house itself. And worst of all was seeing Mr. Dorset wash the car.

Mr. Dorset washed his own car! He washed it not back in the alley or in his driveway but out there in the street of West Vesey Place. This would usually be on the day of one of the parties which he and his sister liked to give for young people or on a day when they were going to make deliveries of the paper flowers or the home grown figs which they sold to their friends. Mr. Dorset would appear in the street carrying two buckets of warm water and wearing a pair of skin-tight coveralls. The skin-tight coveralls, of khaki material but faded almost to flesh color, were still more offensive to the women and young girls than his way of wearing his sweaters. With sponges and chamois cloths and a large scrub brush (for use on the canvas top) the old fellow would fall to and scrub away, gently at first on the canvas top and more vigorously as he progressed to the hood and body, just as though the car were something alive. Neighbor children felt that he went after the headlights exactly as if he were scrubbing the poor car's ears. There was an element of brutality in the way he did it and yet an element of tenderness too. An old lady visiting in the neighborhood once said that it was like the cleansing of a sacrificial animal. I suppose it was some such feeling as this that made all women want to turn away their eyes whenever the spectacle of Mr. Dorset washing his car presented itself.

As for Mr. Dorset's sister, her behavior was in its way just as offensive as his. To the men and boys in the neighborhood it was she who seemed quite beyond the pale. She would come out on her front terrace at mid-day clad in a faded flannel bathrobe and with her dyed black hair all undone and hanging down her back like the hair of an Indian squaw. To us whose wives and mothers did not even come downstairs in their negligees, this was very unsettling. It was hard to excuse it even on the grounds that the Dorsets were too old and lonely and hardpressed to care about appearances any more.

Moreover, there was a boy who had gone to Miss Dorset's house one morning in the early fall to collect for his paper route and saw this very Miss Louisa Dorset pushing a carpet sweeper about one of the downstairs rooms without a stitch of clothes on. He saw her through one of the little lancet windows that opened on the front loggia of the house, and he watched her for quite a long while. She was clearing the house in preparation for a party they were giving for young people that night, and the boy said that when she finally got hot and tired she dropped down in an easy chair and crossed her spindly, blue veined, old legs and sat there completely naked, with her legs crossed and shaking one scrawny little foot, just as unconcerned as if she didn't care that somebody was likely to walk in on her at any moment. After a little bit the boy saw her get up again and go and lean across a table to arrange some paper flowers in a vase. Fortunately he was a nice boy, though he lived only on the edge of the West Vesey Place neighborhood, and he went away without ringing the doorbell or collecting for his paper that week. But he could not resist telling his friends about what he had seen. He said it was a sight he would never forget! And she an old lady more than sixty years old who, had she not been so foolish and self-willed, might have had a house full of servants to push that carpet sweeper for her!

This foolish pair of old people had given up almost everything in life for each other's sake. And it was not at all necessary. When they were young they could have come into a decent inheritance, or now that they were old they might have been provided for by a host of rich relatives. It was only a matter of their being a little tolerant—or even civil—toward their kinspeople. But this was something that old Mr. Dorset and his sister could never consent to do. Almost all their lives they had spoken of their father's kin as "Mama's in-laws" and of their mother's kin as "Papa's in-laws." Their family name was Dorset, not on one side but on both sides. Their parents had been distant cousins. As a matter of fact, the Dorset family in the city of Mero had once been so large and was so long established there that it would have been hard to estimate how distant the kinship might be. But still it was something that the old couple never liked to have mentioned. Most of their mother's close kin had, by the time I am speaking of, moved off to California, and most of their father's people lived somewhere up east. But Miss Dorset and her old bachelor brother found any contact, correspondence, even an exchange of Christmas cards with these in-laws intolerable. It was a case, so they said, of the in-laws respecting the value of the dollar above all else, whereas they, Miss Louisa and Mr. Alfred Dorset, placed importance on other things.

They lived in a dilapidated and curiously mutilated house on a street which, except for their own house, was the most splendid street in the entire city. Their house was one that you or I would have been ashamed to live in—even in the lean years of the early thirties. In order to reduce taxes the Dorsets had had the third story of the house torn away, leaving an ugly, flat-topped effect without any trim or ornamentation. Also they had had the south wing pulled down and had sealed the scars not with matching brick but with a speckled stucco that looked raw and naked. All this the old couple did in violation of the strict zoning laws of West Vesey Place, and for doing so they would most certainly have been prosecuted except that they were the Dorsets and except that this was during the depression when zoning laws weren't easy to enforce in a city like Mero.

To the young people whom she and her brother entertained at their house once each year Miss Louisa Dorset liked to say: "We have given up everything for each other. Our only income is from our paper flowers and our figs." The old lady, though without showing any great skill or talent for it, made paper flowers. During the winter months her brother took her in that fifteen-year-old touring car of theirs, with its steering wheel on the wrong side and with isinglass side-curtains that were never taken down, to deliver these flowers to her customers. The flowers looked more like sprays of tinted potato-chips than like any real flowers. Nobody could possibly have wanted to buy them except that she charged next to nothing for them and except that to people with children it seemed important to be on the Dorsets' list of worthwhile people. Nobody could really have wanted Mr. Dorset's figs either. He cultivated a dozen little bushes along the back wall of their house, covering them in the wintertime with some odd looking boxes which he had had constructed for the purpose. The bushes were very productive, but the figs they produced were dried up little things without much taste. During the summer months he and his sister went about in their car, with the side-curtains still up, delivering the figs to the same customers who bought the paper flowers. The money they made could hardly have paid for the gas it took to run the car. It was a great waste and it was very foolish of them.

And yet, despite everything, this foolish pair of old people, this same Miss Louisa and Mr. Alfred Dorset, had become social arbiters of a kind in our city. They had attained this position entirely through their fondness for giving an annual dancing party for young people. To *young* people—to *very* young people—the Dorsets' hearts went out. I don't mean to suggest that their hearts went out to orphans or to the children of the poor, for they were not foolish in that way. The guests at their little dancing parties were the thirteen- and fourteen-year-olds from families like the one they had long ago set themselves against, young people from the very houses to which, in season, they delivered their figs and their paper flowers. And when the night of one of their parties came round, it was in fact the custom for Mr. Alfred to go in the same old car and fetch all the invited guests to his house. His sister might explain to reluctant parents that this saved the children the embarrassment of being taken to their first dance by mommy and daddy. But the parents knew well enough that for twenty years the Dorsets had permitted no adult person, besides themselves, to put foot inside their house.

At those little dancing parties which the Dorsets gave, peculiar things went on—unsettling things to the boys and girls who had been fetched round in the old car. Sensible parents wished to keep their children away. Yet what could they do? For a Mero girl to have to explain, a few years later, why she never went to a party at the Dorsets' was like having to explain why she had never been a debutante. For a boy it was like having to explain why he had not gone up East to school or even why his father hadn't belonged to the Mero Raquet Club. If when you were thirteen or fourteen you got invited to the Dorsets' house, you went; it was the way of letting people know from the outset who you were. In a busy, modern city like Mero you cannot afford to let people forget who you are—not for a moment, not at any age. Even the Dorsets knew that.

Many a little girl, after one of those evenings at the Dorsets', was heard to cry out in her sleep. When waked, or half waked, her only explanation might be: "It was just the fragrance from the paper flowers." Or: "I dreamed I could really smell the paper flowers." Many a boy was observed by his parents to seem "different" afterward. He became "secretive." The parents of the generation that had to attend those parties never pretended to understand what went on at the Dorsets' house. And even to those of us who were in that unlucky generation it seemed we were half a lifetime learning what really took place during our one evening under the Dorsets' roof. Before our turn to go ever came round we had for years been hearing about what it was like from older boys and girls. Afterward, we continued to hear about it from those who followed us. And, looking back on it, nothing about the one evening when you were actually there ever seemed quite so real as the glimpses and snatches which you got from those people before and after you—the second-hand impressions of the Dorsets' behavior, of things they said, of looks that passed between them.

Since Miss Dorset kept no servants she always
opened her own door. I suspect that for the guests at her
parties the sight of her opening her door, in her astonish-
ing attire, came as the most violent shock of the whole
evening. On these occasions she and her brother got themselves up as we had never seen them before and never
would again. The old lady invariably wore a modish
white evening gown, a garment perfectly fitted to her
spare and scrawny figure and cut in such high fashion
that it must necessarily have been new that year. And
never to be worn but that one night! Her hair, long and
thick and newly dyed for the occasion, would be swept
upward and forward in a billowy mass which was topped
by a corsage of yellow and coral paper flowers. Her
cheeks and lips would be darkly rouged. On her long bony
arms and her bare shoulders she would have applied
some kind of sun-tan powder. Whatever else you had
been led to expect of the evening, no one had ever
warned you sufficiently about the radical change to be
noted in her appearance—or in that of her brother, either. By the end of the party Miss Louisa might look as
dowdy as ever, and Mr. Alfred a little worse than usual.
But at the outset, when the party was assembling in
their drawing room, even Mr. Alfred appeared resplendent in a nattily tailored tuxedo, with exactly the shirt,
the collar, and the tie which fashion prescribed that
year. His grey hair was nicely trimmed, his puffy old face
freshly shaven. He was powdered with the same dark
powder that his sister used. One felt even that his cheeks
had been lightly touched with rouge.

A strange perfume pervaded the atmosphere of the
house. The moment you set foot inside, this awful fragrance engulfed you. It was like a mixture of spicy incense and sweet attar of roses. And always, too, there
was the profusion of paper flowers. The flowers were
everywhere—on every cabinet and console, every inlaid
table and carved chest, on every high, marble mantelpiece, on the book shelves. In the entrance hall special
tiers must have been set up to hold the flowers, because
they were there in overpowering masses. They were in

such abundance that it seemed hardly possible that Miss
Dorset could have made them all. She must have spent
weeks and weeks preparing them, even months, perhaps even the whole year between parties. When she
went about delivering them to her customers, in the
months following, they were apt to be somewhat faded
and dusty; but on the night of the party the colors of
the flowers seemed even more impressive and more unlikely than their number. They were fuchsia, they were
chartreuse, they were coral, aqua-marine, brown, they
were even black.

Everywhere in the Dorsets' house too were certain curious illuminations and lighting effects. The source of the
light was usually hidden and its purpose was never
obvious at once. The lighting was a subtler element
than either the perfume or the paper flowers, and ultimately it was more disconcerting. A shaft of lavender
light would catch a young visitor's eye and lead it, seem-
ingly without purpose, in among the flowers. Then just
beyond the point where the strength of the light would
begin to diminish, the eye would discover something. In
a small aperture in the mass of flowers, or sometimes in
a larger grotto-like opening, there would be a piece of
sculpture—in the hall a plaster replica of Rodin's *The
Kiss*, in the library an antique plaque of Leda and the
Swan. Or just above the flowers would be hung a picture, usually a black and white print but sometimes a
reproduction in color. On the landing of the stairway
leading down to the basement ballroom was the only
picture that one was likely to learn the title of at the
time. It was a tiny color print of Bronzino's *Venus,
Cupid, Folly and Time*. This picture was not even
framed. It was simply tacked on the wall, and it had obviously been torn—rather carelessly, perhaps hurriedly—
from a book or magazine. The title and the name of the
painter were printed in the white margin underneath.

About these works of art most of us had been warned
by older boys and girls; and we stood in painful dread of
that moment when Miss Dorset or her brother might
catch us staring at any one of their pictures or sculptures.

We had been warned, time and again, that during the course of the evening moments would come when she or he would reach out and touch the other's elbow and indicate, with a nod or just the trace of a smile, some guest whose glance had strayed among the flowers.

To some extend the dread which all of us felt of that evening at the Dorsets' cast a shadow over the whole of our childhood. Yet for nearly twenty years the Dorsets continued to give their annual party. And even the most sensible of parents were not willing to keep their children away.

But a thing happened finally which could almost have been predicted. Young people, even in West Vesey Place, will not submit forever to the prudent counsel of their parents. Or some of them won't. There was a boy named Ned Meriwether and his sister Emily Meriwether, who lived with their parents in West Vesey Place just one block away from the Dorsets' house. In November Ned and Emily were invited to the Dorsets' party, and because they dreaded it they decided to play a trick on everyone concerned—even on themselves, as it turned out. . . . They got up a plan for smuggling an un-invited guest into the Dorsets' party.

The parents of this Emily and Ned sensed that their children were concealing something from them and suspected that the two were up to mischief of some kind. But they managed to deceive themselves with the thought that it was only natural for young people— "mere children"—to be nervous about going to the Dorsets' house. And so instead of questioning them during the last hour before they left for the party, these sensible parents tried to do everything in their power to calm their two children. The boy and the girl, seeing that this was the case, took advantage of it.

"You must not go down to the front door with us when we leave," the daughter insisted to her mother. And she persuaded both Mr. and Mrs. Meriwether that after she and her brother were dressed for the party they should all wait together in the upstairs sitting room until Mr. Dorset came to fetch the two young people in his car.

When, at eight o'clock, the lights of the automobile appeared in the street below, the brother and sister were still upstairs—watching from the bay window of the family sitting room. They kissed Mother and Daddy goodbye and then they flew down the stairs and across the wide, carpeted entrance hall to a certain dark recess where a boy named Tom Bascomb was hidden. This boy was the uninvited guest whom Ned and Emily were going to smuggle into the party. They had left the front door unlatched for Tom, and from the upstairs window just a few minutes ago they had watched him come across their front lawn. Now in the little recess of the hall there was a quick exchange of overcoats and hats between Ned Meriwether and Tom Bascomb; for it was a feature of the plan that Tom should attend the party as Ned and that Ned should go as the uninvited guest.

In the darkness of the recess Ned fidgeted and dropped Tom Bascomb's coat on the floor. But the boy, Tom Bascomb, did not fidget. He stepped out into the light of the hall and began methodically getting into the overcoat which he would wear tonight. He was not a boy who lived in the West Vesey Place neighborhood (he was in fact the very boy who had once watched Miss Dorset cleaning house without any clothes on), and he did not share Emily's and Ned's nervous excitement about the evening. The sound of Mr. Dorset's footsteps outside did not disturb him. When both Ned and Emily stood frozen by that sound, he continued buttoning the unfamiliar coat and even amused himself by stretching forth one arm to observe how high the sleeve came on his wrist.

The doorbell rang, and from his dark corner Ned Meriwether whispered to his sister and to Tom: "Don't worry. I'll be at the Dorsets' in plenty of time."

Tom Bascomb only shrugged his shoulders at this reassurance. Presently when he looked at Emily's flushed face and saw her batting her eyes like a nervous monkey, a crooked smile played upon his lips. Then, at a sign from Emily, Tom followed her to the entrance door and permitted her to introduce him to old Mr. Dorset as her brother.

From the window of the upstairs sitting room the Meriwether parents watched Mr. Dorset and this boy and this girl walking across the lawn toward Mr. Dorset's peculiar looking car. A light shone bravely and protectively from above the entrance of the house, and in its rays the parents were able to detect the strange angle at which Brother was carrying his head tonight and how his new fedora already seemed too small for him. They even noticed that he seemed a bit taller tonight.

"I hope it's all right," said the mother.

"What do you mean 'all right'?" the father asked petulantly.

"I mean—," the mother began, and then she hesitated. She did not want to mention that the boy out there did not look like their own Ned. It would have seemed to give away her feelings too much. "I mean that I wonder if I should have put Sister in that long dress at this age and let her wear my cape. I'm afraid the cape is really inappropriate. She's still young for that sort of thing."

"Oh," said the father, "I thought you meant something else."

"Whatever else did you think I meant, Edwin?" the mother said, suddenly breathless.

"I thought you meant the business we've discussed before," he said although this was of course not what he had thought she meant. He had thought she meant that the boy out there did not look like their Ned. To him it had seemed even that the boy's step was different from Ned's. "The Dorsets' parties," he said, "are not very nice affairs to be sending your children off to, Muriel. That's all I thought you meant."

"But we *can't* keep them away," the mother said defensively.

"Oh, it's just that they are growing up faster than we

realize," said the father, glancing at his wife out of the corner of his eye.

By this time Mr. Dorset's car had pulled out of sight, and from downstairs Muriel Meriwether thought she heard another door closing. "What was that?" she said, putting one hand on her husband's.

"Don't be so jumpy," her husband said irritably, snatching away his hand. "It's the servants closing up in the kitchen."

Both of them knew that the servants had closed up in the kitchen long before this. Both of them had heard quite distinctly the sound of the side door closing as Ned went out. But they went on talking and deceiving themselves in this fashion during most of that evening.

Even before she opened the door to Mr. Dorset, little Emily Meriwether had known that there would be no difficulty about passing Tom Bascomb off as her brother. In the first place, she knew that without his spectacles Mr. Dorset could hardly see his hand before his face and knew that due to some silly pride he had he never put on his spectacles except when he was behind the wheel of his automobile. This much was common knowledge. In the second place, Emily knew from experience that neither he or his sister ever made any real pretense of knowing one child in their general acquaintance from another. And so, standing in the doorway and speaking almost in a whisper, Emily had merely to introduce first herself and then her pretended brother to Mr. Dorset. After that the three of them walked in silence from her father's house to the waiting car.

Emily was wearing her mother's second best evening wrap, a white lapin cape which, on Emily, swept the ground. As she walked between the boy and the man, the touch of the cape's soft silk lining on her bare arms and on her shoulders spoke to her silently of a strange girl she had seen in her looking glass upstairs tonight. And with her every step toward the car the skirt of her long taffeta gown whispered her own name to her: *Emily . . . Emily.* She heard it distinctly, and yet the name

sounded unfamiliar. Once during this unreal walk from
house to car she glanced at the mysterious boy, Tom
Bascomb, longing to ask him—if only with her eyes—
for some reassurance that she was really she. But Tom
Bascomb was absorbed in his own irrelevant observa-
tions. With his head tilted back he was gazing upward
at the nondescript winter sky where, among drifting
clouds, a few pale stars were shedding their dull light
alike on West Vesey Place and on the rest of the world.
Emily drew her wrap tightly about her, and when presently Mr. Dorset held open the door to the back seat
of his car she shut her eyes and plunged into the pitch-
blackness of the car's interior.

Tom Bascomb was a year older than Ned Meriwether
and he was nearly two years older than Emily. He had
been Ned's friend first. He and Ned had played baseball
together on Saturdays before Emily ever set eyes on him.
Yet according to Tom Bascomb himself, with whom
several of us older boys talked just a few weeks after
the night he went to the Dorsets, Emily always insisted
that it was she who had known him first. On what she
based this false claim Tom could not say. And on the
two or three other occasions when we got Tom to talk
about that night, he kept saying that he didn't understand what it was that had made Emily and Ned quarrel
over which of them knew him first and knew him
better.

We could have told him what it was, I think. But we
didn't. It would have been too hard to say to him that
at one time or another all of us in West Vesey had
had our Tom Bascombs. Tom lived with his parents in
an apartment house on a wide thoroughfare known as
Division Boulevard, and his only real connection with
West Vesey Place was that that street was included in his
paper route. During the early morning hours he rode
his bicycle along West Vesey and along other quiet
streets like it, carefully aiming a neatly rolled paper
at the dark loggia, at the colonnaded porch, or at the
ornamented doorway of each of the palazzos and cha-
teaux and manor houses that glowered at him in the

dawn. He was well thought of as a paper boy. If by mistake one of his papers went astray and lit on an upstairs balcony or on the roof of a porch, Tom would always take more careful aim and throw another. Even if the paper only went into the shrubbery, Tom got off his bicycle and fished it out. He wasn't the kind of boy to whom it would have occurred that the old fogies and the rich kids in West Vesey could very well get out and scramble for their own papers.

Actually a party at the Dorsets' house was more a grand tour of the house than a real party. There was a half hour spent over very light refreshments (fruit jello, English tea biscuits, lime punch). There was another half hour ostensibly given to general dancing in the basement ballroom (to the accompaniment of victrola music). But mainly there was the tour. As the party passed through the house, stopping sometimes to sit down in the principal rooms, the host and hostess provided entertainment in the form of an almost continuous dialogue between themselves. This dialogue was famous and was full of interest, being all about how much the Dorsets had given up for each other's sake and about how much higher the tone of Mero society used to be than it was nowadays. They would invariably speak of their parents, who had died within a year of each other when Miss Louisa and Mr. Alfred were still in their teens; they even spoke of their wicked in-laws. When their parents died, the wicked in-laws had first tried to make them sell the house, then had tried to separate them and send them away to boarding schools, and had ended by trying to marry them off to "just anyone." Their two grandfathers had still been alive in those days and each had had a hand in the machinations, after the failure of which each grandfather had disinherited them. Mr. Alfred and Miss Louisa spoke also of how, a few years later, a procession of "young nobodies" had come of their own accord trying to steal the two of them away from each other. Both he and she would scowl at the very recollection of those "just anybodies" and those "nobodies," those "would-be suitors" who always turned out to be misguided fortune-hunters and had to be driven away.

The Dorsets' dialogue usually began in the living room the moment Mr. Dorset returned with his last collection of guests. (He sometimes had to make five or six trips in the car.) There, as in other rooms afterward, they were likely to begin with a reference to the room itself or perhaps to some piece of furniture in the room. For instance, the extraordinary length of the drawing room —or reception room, as the Dorsets called it—would lead them to speak of an even longer room which they had had torn away from the house. "It grieved us, we wept," Miss Dorset would say, "to have Mama's French drawing room torn away from us."

"But we tore it away from ourselves," her brother would add, "as we tore away our in-laws—because we could not afford them." Both of them spoke in a fine declamatory style, but they frequently interrupted themselves with a sad little laugh which expressed something quite different from what they were saying and which seemed to serve them as an aside not meant for our ears.

"That was one of our greatest sacrifices," Miss Dorset would say, referring still to her mother's French drawing room.

And her brother would say: "But we knew the day had passed in Mero for entertainments worthy of that room."

"It was the room which Mama and Papa loved best, but we gave it up because we knew, from our upbringing, which things to give up."

From this they might go on to anecdotes about their childhood. Sometimes their parents had left them for months or even a whole year at a time with only the housekeeper or with trusted servants to see after them. "You could trust servants then," they explained. And: "In those days parents could do that sort of thing, because in those days there was a responsible body of people within which your young people could always find proper companionship."

In the library, to which the party always moved from

the drawing room, Mr. Dorset was fond of exhibiting snap-shots of the house taken before the south wing was pulled down. As the pictures were passed around, the dialogue continued. It was often there that they told the story of how the in-laws had tried to force them to sell the house. "For the sake of economy!" Mr. Dorset would exclaim, adding an ironic, "Ha ha!"

His sister would repeat the exclamation, "For the sake of economy!" and also the ironic "Ha ha!"

"As though money—" he would begin.

"As though money ever took the place," his sister would come in, "of living with your own kind."

"Or of being well born," said Mr. Dorset.

After the billiard room, where everyone who wanted it was permitted one turn with the only cue that there seemed to be in the house, and after the dining room, where it was promised refreshments would be served later, the guests would be taken down to the ballroom —purportedly for dancing. Instead of everyone's being urged to dance, however, once they were assembled in the ballroom, Miss Dorset would announce that she and her brother understood the timidity which young people felt about dancing and that all that she and he intended to do was to set the party a good example. . . . It was only Miss Louisa and Mr. Alfred who danced. For perhaps thirty minutes, in a room without light excepting that from a few weak bulbs concealed among the flowers, the old couple danced; and they danced with such grace and there was such perfect har-mony in all their movements that the guests stood about in stunned silence, as if hypnotized. The Dorsets waltzed, they two-stepped, they even fox-trotted, stopping only long enough between dances for Mr. Dorset, amid general applause, to change the victrola record.

But it was when their dance was ended that all the effects of the Dorsets' careful grooming that night would have vanished. And, alas, they made no effort to restore themselves. During the remainder of the evening Mr. Dorset went about with his bow tie hanging limply on his damp shirtfront, a gold collar button shining above it. A strand of grey hair, which normally covered his bald spot on top, now would have fallen on the wrong side of his part and hung like fringe about his ear. On his face and neck the thick layer of powder was streaked with perspiration. Miss Dorset was usually in an even more dishevelled state, depending somewhat upon the fashion of her dress that year. But always her powder was streaked, her lipstick entirely gone, her hair falling down on all sides, and her corsage dangling somewhere about the nape of her neck. In this condition they led the party upstairs again, not stopping until they had reached the second floor of the house.

On the second floor we—the guests—were shown the rooms which the Dorsets' parents had once occupied (the Dorsets' own rooms were never shown). We saw, in glass museum cases along the hallway, the dresses and suits and hats and even the shoes which Miss Louisa and Mr. Alfred had worn to parties when they were very young. And now the dialogue, which had been left off while the Dorsets danced, was resumed. "Ah, the happy time," one of them would say, "was when we were *your* age!" And then, exhorting us to be happy and gay while we were still safe in the bosom of our own kind and before the world came crowding in on us with its ugly demands, the Dorsets would recall the happiness they had known when they were very young. This was their *pièce de résistance*. With many a wink and blush and giggle and shake of the forefinger—and of course standing before the whole party—they each would remind the other of his or her naughty behavior in some old fashioned parlor game or of certain silly little flirtations which they had long ago caught each other in.

They were on their way downstairs again now, and by the time they had finished with this favorite subject they would be downstairs. They would be in the dark, flower bedecked downstairs hall and just before entering the dining room for the promised refreshments: the fruit jello, the English tea biscuits, the lime punch.

And now for a moment Mr. Dorset bars the way to the dining room and prevents his sister from opening the closed door. "Now, my good friends," he says, "let us eat, drink and be merry!"

"For the night is yet young," says his sister.

"Tonight you must be gay and carefree," Mr. Dorset enjoins.

"Because in this house we are all friends," Miss Dorset says. "We are all young, we all love one another."

"And love can make us all young forever," her brother says.

"Remember!"

"Remember this evening always, sweet young people!"

"Remember!"

"Remember what our life is like here!"

And now Miss Dorset, with one hand on the knob of the great door which she is about to throw open, leans a little toward the guests and whispers hoarsely: "This is what it is like to be young forever!"

Ned Meriwether was waiting behind a big japonica shrub near the sidewalk when, about twenty minutes after he had last seen Emily, the queer old touring car drew up in front of the Dorsets' house. During the interval, the car had gone from the Meriwether house to gather a number of other guests, and so it was not only Emily and Tom who alighted on the sidewalk before the Dorsets' house. The group was just large enough to make it easy for Ned to slip out from his dark hiding place and join them without being noticed by Mr. Dorset. And now the group was escorted rather unceremoniously up to the door of the house, and Mr. Dorset departed to fetch more guests.

They were received at the door by Miss Dorset. Her eyesight was no doubt better than her brother's, but still there was really no danger of her detecting an uninvited guest. Those of us who had gone to that house in the years just before Ned and Emily came along, could remember that during a whole evening, when their house was full of young people, the Dorsets made no introductions and made no effort to distinguish which of their guests was which. They did not even make a count of

heads. Perhaps they did vaguely recognize some of the
faces, because sometimes when they had come delivering
figs or paper flowers to a house they had of necessity encountered a young child there, and always they smiled
sweetly at it, asked its age, and calculated on their old
fingers how many years must pass before the child
would be eligible for an invitation. Yet at those moments
something in the way they had held up their fingers
and in the way they had gazed at the little face instead
of into it had revealed their lack of interest in the individual child. And later when the child was finally old
enough to receive their invitation he found it was still
no different with the Dorsets. Even in their own house it
was evidently to the young people as a group that the
Dorsets' hearts went out; while they had the boys and
girls under their roof they herded them about like so
many little thoroughbred calves. Even when Miss Dorset opened the front door she did so exactly as though
she were opening a gate. She pulled it open very slowly,
standing half behind it to keep out of harm's way.
And the children, all huddled together, surged in.

How meticulously this Ned and Emily Meriwether
must have laid their plans for that evening! And the
whole business might have come out all right if only
they could have foreseen the effect which one part of
their plan—rather a last minute embellishment of it—
would produce upon Ned himself. Barely ten minutes
after they entered the house Ned was watching Tom as
he took his seat on the piano bench beside Emily.
Ned probably watched Tom closely, because certainly
he knew what the next move was going to be. The moment Miss Louisa Dorset's back was turned Tom Bascomb
slipped his arm gently about Emily's little waist and
commenced kissing her all over her pretty face. It was
almost as if he were kissing away tears.

This spectacle on the piano bench, and others like it
which followed, had been an inspiration of the last day
or so before the party. Or so Ned and Emily maintained
afterward when defending themselves to their parents.
But no matter when it was conceived, a part of their plan

it was, and Ned must have believed himself fully prepared for it. Probably he expected to join in the round of
giggling which it produced from the other guests. But
now that the time had come—it is easy to imagine—the
boy Ned Meriwether found himself not quite able to join
in the fun. He watched with the others, but he was not
quite infected by their laughter. He stood a little apart,
and possibly he was hoping that Emily and Tom would
not notice his failure to appreciate the success of their
comedy. He was no doubt baffled by his own feelings,
by the failure of his own enthusiasm, and by a growing
desire to withdraw himself from the plot and from the
party itself.

It is easy to imagine Ned's uneasiness and confusion
that night. And I believe the account which I have given
of Emily's impressions and her delicate little sensations
while on the way to the party has the ring of truth about
it, though actually the account was supplied by girls who
knew her only slightly, who were not at the party, who
could not possibly have seen her afterward. It may, after
all, represent only what other girls imagined she would
have felt. As for the account of how Mr. and Mrs. Meriwether spent the evening, it is their very own. And they
did not hesitate to give it to anyone who would listen.

It was a long time, though, before many of us had a
clear picture of the main events of the evening. We
heard very soon that the parties for young people were to
be no more, that there had been a wild scramble and
chase through the Dorsets' house, and that it had ended
by the Dorsets locking some boy—whether Ned or Tom
was not easy to determine at first—in a queer sort of
bathroom in which the plumbing had been disconnected,
and even the fixtures removed, I believe. (Later I learned
that there was nothing literally sinister about the bathroom itself. By having the pipes disconnected to this,
and perhaps other bathrooms, the Dorsets had obtained
further reductions in their taxes.) But a clear picture
of the whole evening wasn't to be had—not without
considerable searching. For one thing, the Meriwether
parents immediately, within a week after the party,

packed their son and daughter off to boarding schools. Accounts from the other children were contradictory and vague—perversely so, it seemed. Parents reported to each other that the little girls had nightmares which were worse even than those which their older sisters had had. And the boys were secretive and elusive, even with us older boys when we questioned them about what had gone on.

One sketchy account of events leading up to the chase, however, did go the rounds almost at once. Ned must have written it back to some older boy in a letter, because it contained information which no one but Ned could have had. The account went like this: When Mr. Dorset returned from his last round-up of guests, he came hurrying into the drawing room where the others were waiting and said in a voice trembling with excitement: "Now, let us all be seated, my young friends, and let us warm ourselves with some good talk."

At that moment everyone who was not already seated made a dash for a place on one of the divans or love seats or even in one of the broad window seats. (There were no individual chairs in the room.) Everyone made a dash, that is, except Ned. Ned did not move. He remained standing beside a little table rubbing his fingers over its polished surface. And from this moment he was clearly an object of suspicion in the eyes of his host and hostess. Soon the party moved from the drawing room to the library, but in whatever room they stopped Ned managed to isolate himself from the rest. He would sit or stand looking down at his hands until once again an explosion of giggles filled the room. Then he would look up just in time to see Tom Bascomb's cheek against Emily's or his arm about her waist.

For nearly two hours Ned didn't speak a word to anyone. He endured the Dorsets' dialogue, the paper flowers, the perfumed air, the works of art. Whenever a burst of giggling forced him to raise his eyes he would look up at Tom and Emily and then turn his eyes away. Before looking down at his hands again he would let his eyes travel slowly about the room until they came to rest on the figures of the two Dorsets. That, it seems, was how he happened to discover that the Dorsets understood, or thought they understood, what the giggles meant. In the great mirror mounted over the library mantel he saw them exchanging half suppressed smiles. Their smiles lasted precisely as long as the giggling continued, and then, in the mirror, Ned saw their faces change and grow solemn when their eyes—their identical, tiny, dull, amber colored eyes—focussed upon himself.

From the library the party continued on the regular tour of the house. At last when they had been to the ballroom and watched the Dorsets dance, had been up-stairs to gaze upon the faded party clothes in the museum cases, they descended into the downstairs hall and were just before being turned into the dining room. The guests had already heard the Dorsets teasing each other about the silly little flirtations and about their naughtiness in parlor games when they were young and had listened to their exhortations to be gay and happy and carefree. Then just when Miss Dorset leaned toward them and whispered, "This is what it is like to be young forever," there rose a chorus of laughter, breathless and shrill, yet loud and intensely penetrating.

Ned Meriwether, standing on the bottom step of the stairway, lifted his eyes and looked over the heads of the party to see Tom and Emily half hidden in a bower of paper flowers and caught directly in a ray of mauve light. The two had squeezed themselves into a little niche there and stood squarely in front of the Rodin statuary. Tom had one arm placed about Emily's shoulders and he was kissing her lightly first on the lobe of one ear and then on the tip of her nose. Emily stood as rigid and pale as the plaster sculpture behind her and with just the faintest smile on her lips. Ned looked at the two of them and then turned his glance at once on the Dorsets.

He found Miss Louisa and Mr. Alfred gazing quite openly at Tom and Emily and frankly grinning at the spectacle. It was more than Ned could endure. "Don't you *know?*" he fairly wailed, as if in great physical pain.

"Can't you *tell?* Can't you see who they *are?* They're *brother* and *sister!*"

From the other guests came one concerted gasp. And then an instant later, mistaking Ned's outcry to be something he had planned all along and probably intended —as they imagined—for the very cream of the jest, the whole company burst once again into laughter—not a chorus of laughter this time but a volley of loud guffaws from the boys, and from the girls a cacophony of separately articulated shrieks and trills.

None of the guests present that night could—or would—give a satisfactory account of what happened next. Everyone insisted that he had not even looked at the Dorsets, that he, or she, didn't know how Miss Louisa and Mr. Alfred reacted at first. Yet this was precisely what those of us who had gone there in the past *had* to know. And when finally we did manage to get an account of it, we knew that it was a very truthful and accurate one. Because we got it, of course, from Tom Bascomb.

Since Ned's outburst came after the dancing exhibition, the Dorsets were in their most dishevelled state. Miss Louisa's hair was fallen half over her face, and that long, limp strand of Mr. Alfred's was dangling about his left ear. Like that, they stood at the doorway to the dining room grinning at Tom Bascomb's antics. And when Tom Bascomb, hearing Ned's wail, whirled about, the grins were still on the Dorsets' faces even though the guffaws and the shrieks of laughter were now silenced. Tom said that for several moments they continued to wear their grins like masks and that you couldn't really tell how they were taking it all until presently Miss Louisa's face, still wearing the grin, began turning all the queer colors of her paper flowers. Then the grin vanished from her lips and her mouth fell open and every bit of color went out of her face. She took a step backward and leaned against the doorjamb with her mouth still open and her eyes closed.

If she hadn't been on her feet, Tom said he would have thought she was dead. Her brother didn't look at her, but his own grin had vanished just as hers did, and his face, all drawn and wrinkled, momentarily turned a dull copperish green.

Presently, though, he too went white, not white in faintness but in anger. His little brown eyes now shone like rosin. And he took several steps toward Ned Meriwether. "What we know is that you are not one of us," he croaked. "We have perceived that from the beginning! We don't know how you got here or who you are. But the important question is, What are you doing here among these nice children?"

The question seemed to restore life to Miss Louisa. Her amber eyes popped wide open. She stepped away from the door and began pinning up her hair which had fallen down on her shoulders, and at the same time addressing the guests who were huddled together in the center of the hall. "Who is he, children? He is an intruder, that we know. If you know who he is, you must tell us."

"Who *am* I? Why, I am Tom Bascomb!" shouted Ned, still from the bottom step of the stairway. "I am Tom Bascomb, your paper boy!"

Then he turned and fled up the stairs toward the second floor. In a moment Mr. Dorset was after him.

To the real Tom Bascomb it had seemed that Ned honestly believed what he had been saying; and his own first impulse was to shout a denial. But being a level-headed boy and seeing how bad things were, Tom went instead to Miss Dorset and whispered to her that Tom Bascomb was a pretty tough guy and that she had better let *him* call the police for her. She told him where the telephone was in the side hall, and he started away.

But Miss Dorset changed her mind. She ran after Tom telling him not to call. Some of the guests mistook this for the beginning of another chase. Before the old lady could overtake Tom, however, Ned himself had appeared in the doorway toward which she and Tom were moving. He had come down the back stairway and he was calling out to Emily, "We're going *home*, Sis!"

A cheer went up from the whole party. Maybe it was this that caused Ned to lose his head, or maybe it was simply the sight of Miss Dorset rushing at him that did it. At any rate, the next moment he was running up the front stairs again, this time with Miss Dorset in pursuit.

When Tom returned from the telephone, all was quiet in the hall. The guests—everybody except Emily—had moved to the foot of the stairs and they were looking up and listening. From upstairs Tom could hear Ned saying, "All right. All right. All right." The couple had cornered him.

Emily was still standing in the little niche among the flowers. And it is the image of Emily Meriwether standing among the paper flowers that tantalizes me whenever I think or hear someone speak of that evening. That, more than anything else, can make me wish that I had been there. I shall never cease to wonder what kind of thoughts were in her head to make her seem so oblivious to all that was going on while she stood there, and, for that matter, what had been in her mind all evening while she endured Tom Bascomb's caresses. When, in years since, I have had reason to wonder what some girl or woman is thinking—some Emily grown older— my mind nearly always returns to the image of that girl among the paper flowers. Tom said that when he returned from the telephone she looked very solemn and pale still but that her mind didn't seem to be on any of the present excitement. Immediately he went to her and said, "Your dad is on his way over, Emily." For it was the Meriwether parents he had telephoned, of course, and not the police.

It seemed to Tom that so far as he was concerned the party was now over. There was nothing more he could do. Mr. Dorset was upstairs guarding the door to the strange little room in which Ned was locked up. Miss Dorset was serving lime punch to the other guests in the dining room, all the while listening with one ear for the arrival of the police whom Tom pretended he had called. When the doorbell finally rang and Miss Dorset hurried to answer it, Tom slipped quietly out through the pantry and through the kitchen and left the house by the back door as the Meriwether parents entered by the front.

There was no difficulty in getting Edwin and Muriel Meriwether, the children's parents, to talk about what happened after they arrived that night. Both of them were sensible and clear-headed people, and they were not so conservative as some of our other neighbors in West Vesey. Being fond of gossip of any kind and fond of reasonably funny stories on themselves, they told how their children had deceived them earlier in the evening and how they had deceived themselves later. They tended to blame themselves more than the children for what had happened. They tried to protect the children from any harm or embarrassment that might result from it by sending them off to boarding school. In their talk they never referred directly to Tom's reprehensible conduct or to the possible motives that the children might have had for getting up their plan. They tried to spare their children and they tried to spare Tom, but fortunately it didn't occur to them to try to spare the poor old Dorsets.

When Miss Louisa opened the door, Mr. Meriwether said, "I'm Edwin Meriwether, Miss Dorset. I've come for my son, Ned."

"And for your daughter Emily, I hope," his wife whispered to him.

"And for my daughter Emily."

Before Miss Dorset could answer him Edwin Meriwether spied Mr. Dorset descending the stairs. With his wife, Muriel, sticking close to his side Edwin now strode over to the foot of the stairs. "Mr. Dorset," he began, "my son Ned—"

From behind them, Edwin and Muriel now heard Miss Dorset saying, "All the invited guests are gathered in the dining room." From where they were standing the two parents could see into the dining room. Suddenly they turned and hurried in there. Mr. Dorset and his sister of course followed them.

Muriel Meriwether went directly to Emily who was standing in a group of girls. "Emily, where is your brother?"

Emily said nothing, but one of the boys answered: "I think they've got him locked up upstairs somewhere."

"Oh, no!" said Miss Louisa, a hairpin in her mouth—for she was still rather absent-mindedly working at her hair. "It is an intruder that my brother has upstairs."

Mr. Dorset began speaking in a confidential tone to Edwin. "My dear neighbor," he said, "our paper boy saw fit to intrude himself upon our company tonight. But we recognized him as an outsider from the start."

Muriel Meriwether asked: "Where *is* the paper boy? Where is the paper boy, Emily?"

Again one of the boys volunteered: "He went out through the back door, Mrs. Meriwether."

The eyes of Mr. Alfred and Miss Louisa searched the room for Tom. Finally their eyes met and they smiled coyly. "*All* the children are being mischievous tonight," said Miss Louisa, and it was quite as though she had said, "all *we* children." Then, still smiling, she said, "Your tie has come undone, Brother. Mr. and Mrs. Meriwether will hardly know what to think."

Mr. Alfred fumbled for a moment with his tie but soon gave it up. Now with a bashful glance at the Meriwether parents, and giving a nod in the direction of the children, he actually said, "I'm afraid we've all decided to play a trick on Mr. and Mrs. Meriwether."

Miss Louisa said to Emily: "We've hidden our brother somewhere, haven't we?"

Emily's mother said firmly: "Emily, tell me where Ned is."

"He's upstairs, Mother," said Emily in a whisper.

Emily's father said: "I wish you to take me to the boy upstairs, Mr. Dorset."

The coy, bashful expressions vanished from the two Dorsets' faces. Their eyes were little dark pools of incredulity, growing narrower by the second. And both of them were now trying to put their hair in order. "Why, *we* know nice children when we see them," Miss Louisa said peevishly. There was a pleading quality in her voice, too. "We knew from the beginning that that boy upstairs didn't belong amongst us," she said. "Dear neighbors, it isn't just the money, you know." All at once she sounded like a little girl about to burst into tears.

"It isn't just the money?" Edwin Meriwether repeated.

"Miss Dorset," said Muriel with new gentleness in her tone, as though she had just sensed that she was talking to a little girl, "there has been some kind of mistake—a misunderstanding."

Mr. Alfred Dorset said: "Oh, we wouldn't make a mistake of that kind! People *are* different. It isn't something you can put your finger on, but it isn't the money."

"I don't know what you're talking about," Edwin said, exasperated. "But I'm going upstairs and find that boy." He left the room with Mr. Dorset following him with quick little steps—steps like those of a small boy trying to keep up with a man.

Miss Louisa now sat down in one of the high-backed dining chairs which were lined up along the oak wainscot. She was trembling, and Muriel came and stood beside her. Neither of them spoke, and in almost no time Edwin Meriwether came downstairs again with Ned. Miss Louisa looked at Ned, and tears came into her eyes. "Where is my brother?" she asked accusingly, as though she thought possibily Ned and his father had locked Mr. Dorset in the bathroom.

"I believe he has retired," said Edwin. "He left us and disappeared into one of the rooms upstairs."

"Then I must go up to him," said Miss Louisa. For a moment she seemed unable to rise. At last she pushed herself up from the chair and walked from the room with the slow, steady gait of a somnambulist. Muriel Meriwether followed her into the hall and as she watched the old woman ascending the steps, leaning heavily on the rail, her impulse was to go and offer to assist her. But something made her turn back into the dining room. Perhaps she imagined that her daughter, Emily, might need her now.

The Dorsets did not reappear that night. After Miss Louisa went upstairs, Muriel promptly got on the telephone and called the parents of some of the other boys and girls. Within a quarter of an hour half a dozen parents had arrived. It was the first time in many years that any adult had set foot inside the Dorset house. It was the first time that any parent had ever inhaled the perfumed air or seen the masses of paper flowers and the illuminations and the statuary. In the guise of holding consultations over whether or not they should put out the lights and lock up the house the parents lingered much longer than was necessary before taking the young people home. Some of them even tasted the lime punch. But in the presence of their children they made no comment on what had happened and gave no indication of what their own impressions were—not even their impressions of the punch. At last it was decided that two of the men should see to putting out the lights everywhere on the first floor and down in the ballroom. They were a long time in finding the switches for the indirect lighting. In most cases they simply resorted to unscrewing the bulbs. Meanwhile the children went to the large cloak closet behind the stairway and got their wraps. When Ned and Emily Meriwether rejoined their parents at the front door to leave the house, Ned was wearing his own overcoat and held his own fedora in his hand.

Miss Louisa and Mr. Alfred Dorset lived on for nearly ten years after that night, but they gave up selling their figs and paper flowers and of course they never entertained young people again. I often wonder if growing up in Mero can ever have seemed quite the same since. Some of the terror must have gone out of it. Half the dread of coming of age must have vanished with the dread of the Dorsets' parties.

After that night, their old car would sometimes be observed creeping about town, but it was never parked in front of their house any more. It stood usually at the side entrance where the Dorsets could climb in and out of it without being seen. They began keeping a servant too—mainly to run their errands for them, I imagine. Sometimes it would be a man, sometimes a woman, never the same one for more than a few months at a time. Both of the Dorsets died during the Second World War while many of us who had gone to their parties were away from Mero. But the story went round— and I am inclined to believe it—that after they were dead and the house was sold, Tom Bascomb's coat and hat were found still hanging in the cloak closet behind the stairs.

Tom himself was a pilot in the War and was a considerable hero. He was such a success and made such a name for himself that he never came back to Mero to live. He found bigger opportunities elsewhere I suppose, and I don't suppose he ever felt the ties to Mero that people with Ned's kind of upbringing do. Ned was in the War too, of course. He was in the navy and after the War he did return to Mero to live, though actually it was not until then that he had spent much time here since his parents bundled him off to boarding school. Emily came home and made her debut just two or three years before the War, but she was already engaged to some boy in the East; she never comes back any more except to bring her children to see their grandparents for a few days during Christmas or at Easter.

I understand that Emily and Ned are pretty indifferent to each other's existence nowadays. I have been told this by Ned Meriwether's own wife. Ned's wife maintains that the night Ned and Emily went to the Dorsets' party marked the beginning of this indifference, that it marked the end of their childhood intimacy and the beginning of a shyness, a reserve, even an animosity between them that was destined to be a sorrow forever to the two sensible parents who had sat in the upstairs sitting room that night waiting until the telephone call came from Tom Bascomb.

Ned's wife is a girl he met while he was in the navy.

She was a Wave, and her background isn't the same as his. Apparently she isn't too happy with life in what she refers to as "Mero proper." She and Ned have recently moved out into a suburban development, which she doesn't like either and which she refers to as "greater Mero." She asked me at a party one night how Mero ever got its absurd name, and when I told her that it was named for the last Spanish governor of Louisiana she burst out laughing. I don't know why exactly. But what interests me most about her is that after a few drinks she likes to talk about Ned and Emily and Tom Bascomb and the Dorsets. Tom Bascomb has become a kind of hero—and I don't mean a wartime hero—in her eyes, though of course not having grown up in Mero she has never seen him in her life. But she is a clever girl, and there are times when she will say to me, "Tell me about Mero. Tell me about the Dorsets." And I try to tell her. I tell her to remember that Mero looks upon itself as a rather old city. I tell her to remember that it was one of the first English-speaking settlements west of the Alleghenies and that by the end of the American Revolution, when veterans began pouring westward over the Wilderness Road or down the Ohio River, Mero was often referred to as a thriving village. Then she tells me that I am being dull, because it is hard for her to concentrate on any aspect of the story that doesn't center around Tom Bascomb and that night at the Dorsets'.

But I make her listen. Or at least one time I did. The Dorset family, I insisted on saying, was in Mero even in those earliest times right after the Revolution, but they had come here under somewhat different circumstances from those of the other early settlers. How could that really matter, Ned's wife asked, after a hundred and fifty years? How could distinctions between the first settlers matter after the Irish had come to Mero, after the Germans, after the Italians? Well, in West Vesey Place it could matter. It had to. If the distinction was false, it mattered all the more and it was all the more necessary to make it.

But let me interject here that Mero is located in a

state about whose history most Mero citizens—not new-comers like Ned's wife, but old timers—have little interest and less knowledge. Most of us, for instance, are never even quite sure whether during the 1860's our state did secede or didn't secede. As for the city itself, some of us hold that it is geographically Northern and culturally Southern. Others say the reverse is true. We are all apt to want to feel misplaced in Mero, and so we are not content merely to say that it is a border city. How you stand on this important question is apt to depend entirely on whether your family is one of those with a good Southern name or one that had its origin in New England, because those are the two main categories of old society families in Mero.

But truly—I told Ned's wife—the Dorset family was never in either of those categories. The first Dorset had come, with his family and his possessions and even a little capital, direct from a city in the English Midlands to Mero. The Dorsets came not as pioneers, but paying their way all the way. They had not bothered to stop for a generation or two to put down roots in Pennsylvania or Virginia or Massachusetts. And this was the distinction which some people wished always to make. Apparently those early Dorsets had cared no more for putting down roots in the soil of the New World than they had cared for whatever they had left behind in the Old. They were an obscure mercantile family who came to invest in a new western city. Within two generations the business—no, the industry!—which they established made them rich beyond any dreams they could have had in the beginning. For half a century they were looked upon, if any family ever was, as our first family.

And then the Dorsets left Mero—practically all of them except the one old bachelor and the one old maid—left it just as they had come, not caring much about what they were leaving or where they were going. They were city people, and they were Americans. They knew that what they had in Mero they could buy more of in other places. For them Mero was an investment that had paid off. They went to live in Santa Barbara and Laguna Beach, in Newport and on Long Island. And the truth which it was so hard for the rest of us to admit was that, despite our family memories of Massachusetts and Virginia, we were all more like the Dorsets—those Dorsets who left Mero—than we were *un*like them. Their spirit was just a little closer to being the very essence of Mero than ours was. The obvious difference was that we had to stay on here and pretend that our life had a meaning which it did not. And if it was only by a sort of chance that Miss Louisa and Mr. Alfred played the role of social arbiters among the young people for a number of years, still no one could honestly question their divine right to do so.

"It may have been their right," Ned's wife said at this point, "but just think what might have happened."

"It's not a matter of what might have happened," I said. "It is a matter of what did happen. Otherwise, what have you and I been talking about?"

"Otherwise," she said with an irrepressible shudder, "I would not be forever getting you off in a corner at these parties to talk about my husband and my husband's sister and how it is they care so little for each other's company nowadays?"

And I could think of nothing to say to that except that probably we had now pretty well exhausted our subject.

The Time of Her Time

Norman Mailer

I

I WAS living in a room one hundred feet long and twenty-five feet wide, and it had nineteen windows staring at me from three of the walls and part of the fourth. The floor planks were worn below the level of the nails which held them down, except for the southern half of the room where I had laid a rough linoleum which gave a hint of sprinkled sand, conceivably an aid to the footwork of my pupils. For one hundred dollars I had the place whitewashed; everything; the checkerboard of tin ceiling plates one foot square with their fleurs-de-lis stamped into the metal, the rotted sashes on the window frames (it took twelve hours to scrape the calcimine from the glass), even parts of the floor had white drippings (although that was scuffed into dust as time went on) and yet it was worth it: when I took the loft it stank of old machinery and the paint was a liverish brown— I had tried living with that color for a week, my old furniture, which had been moved by a mover friend from the Village and me, showed the scars of being bumped and dragged and flung up six flights of stairs, and the view of it sprawled over twenty-five hundred feet of living space, three beat old day beds, some dusty cushions, a broken-armed easy chair, a cigarette-scarred coffee table made from a door, a kitchen table, some peeled enamel chairs which thumped like a wooden-legged pirate when one sat in them, the bookshelves of unfinished pine butted by bricks, yes, all of this, my

purview, this grand vista, the New York sunlight
greeting me in the morning through the double filter
of the smog-yellow sky and the nineteen dirt-frosted windows, inspired me with so much content, especially
those liver-brown walls, that I fled my pad like the
plague, and in the first week, after a day of setting the
furniture to rights, I was there for four hours of sleep a
night, from five in the morning when I maneuvered
in from the last closed Village bar and the last coffee-
klatsch of my philosopher friends' for the night to let
us say nine in the morning when I awoke with a partially destroyed brain and the certainty that the sore vicious growl of my stomach was at least the onset of an
ulcer and more likely the first gone cells of a thorough-
going cancer of the duodenum. So I lived in that way
for a week, and then following the advice of a bar-type
who was the friend of a friend, I got myself up on the
eighth morning, boiled my coffee on a hot-plate while
I shivered in the October air (neither the stove nor the
gas heaters had yet been bought) and then I went
downstairs and out the front door of the warehouse onto
Monroe Street, picking my way through the garbage-
littered gutter which always made me think of the gangs
on this street, the Negroes on the east end of the block,
the Puerto Ricans next to them, and the Italians and
Jews to the west—those gangs were going to figure a
little in my life, I suspected that, I was anticipating
those moments with no quiet bravery considering how
hung was my head in the morning, for the worst clue
to the gangs was the six-year-olds. They were the de-
filers of the garbage, knights of the ordure, and here, in
this province of a capital Manhattan, at the southern
tip of the island, with the overhead girders of the Manhattan and Brooklyn bridges the only noble structures
for a mile of tenement jungle, yes here the barbarians
ate their young, and any type who reached the age of
six without being altogether mangled by father, mother,
family or friends, was a pint of iron man, so tough, so
ferocious, so sharp in the teeth that the wildest alley

cat would have surrendered a freshly caught rat rather than contest the meal. They were charming, these six-year-olds, as I told my uptown friends, and they used to topple the overloaded garbage cans, strew them through the street, have summer snowball fights with orange peel, coffee grounds, soup bones, slop, they threw the discus by scaling the raw tin rounds from the tops of cans, their pillow fights were with loaded socks of scum, and a debauch was for two of them to scrub a third around the inside of a twenty-gallon pail still warm with the heat of its emptied treasures. I heard that the Olympics took place in summer when they were out of school and the streets were so thick with the gum of old detritus, alluvium and dross that the mash made by passing car tires fermented in the sun. Then the parents and the hoods and the debs and the grandmother dowagers cheered them on and promised them murder and the garbage flew all day, but I was there in fall and the scene was quiet from nine to three. So I picked my way through last night's stew of rubble on this eighth morning of my hiatus on Monroe Street, and went half down the block to a tenement on the boundary between those two bandit republics of the Negroes and the Puerto Ricans, and with a history or two of knocking on the wrong door, and with a nose full of the smells of the sick over-peppered bowels of the poor which seeped and oozed out of every leaking pipe in every communal crapper (only as one goes north does the word take on the Protestant propriety of john), I was able finally to find my man, and I was an hour ahead of him—he was still sleeping off his last night's drunk. So I spoke to his wife, a fat masculine Negress with the face and charity of a Japanese wrestler, and when she understood that I was neither a junk-peddler nor fuzz, that I sold no numbers, carried no bills, and was most certainly not a detective (though my Irish face left her dubious of that) but instead had come to offer her husband a job of work, I was admitted to the first of three dark rooms, face to face with the gray luminescent eye of the television set going its way in a dark room on a bright morning, and through the hall curtains I could hear them talking in the bedroom.

"Get up, you son of a bitch," she said to him.

He came to work for me, hating my largesse, lugging his air compressor up my six flights of stairs, and after a discussion in which his price came down from two hundred to one, and mine rose from fifty dollars to meet his, he left with one of my twenty-dollar bills, the air compressor on the floor as security, and returned in an hour with so many sacks of whitewash that I had to help him up the stairs. We worked together that day, Charley Thompson his name was, a small lean Negro maybe forty years old, and conceivably sixty, with a scar or two on his face, one a gouge on the cheek, the other a hairline along the bridge of his nose, and we got along not too badly, working in sullen silence until the hangover was sweated out, and then starting to talk over coffee in the Negro hashhouse on the corner where the bucks bridled a little when I came in, and then ignored me. Once the atmosphere had become neutral again, Thompson was willing to talk.

"Man," he said to me, "what you want all that space for?"

"To make money."

"Out of which?"

I debated not very long. The people on the block would know my business sooner or later—the reward of living in a slum is that everyone knows everything which is within reach of the senses—and since I would be nailing a sign over my mailbox downstairs for the pupils to know which floor they would find me on, and the downstairs door would have to be open since I had no bell, the information would be just as open. But for that matter I was born to attract attention; given my height and my blond hair, the barbarians would notice me, they noticed everything, and so it was wiser to come on strong than to try to sidle in.

"Ever hear of an *Escuela de Torear?*" I asked him without a smile.

He laughed with delight at the sound of the words, not even bothering to answer.

"That's a bullfighter's school," I told him. "I teach bullfighting."

"You know that?"

"I used to do it in Mexico."

"Man, you can get killed."

"Some do." I let the exaggeration of a cooled nuance come into my voice. It was true after all; some do get killed. But not so many as I was suggesting, maybe one in fifty of the successful, and one in five hundred of the amateurs like me who fought a few bulls, received a few wounds, and drifted away.

Charley Thompson was impressed. So were others— the conversation was being overheard after all, and I had become a cardinal piece on the chaotic chessboard of Monroe Street's sociology—I felt the clear bell-like adrenalins of clean anxiety, untainted by weakness, self-interest, neurotic habit, or the pure yellows of the liver. For I had put my poker money on the table, I was the new gun in a frontier saloon, and so I was asking for it, not today, not tomorrow, but come sooner, come later, something was likely to follow from this. The weak would leave me alone, the strong would have respect, but be it winter or summer, sunlight or dark, there would come an hour so cold or so hot that someone, somebody, some sexed-up head, very strong and very weak, would be drawn to discover a new large truth about himself and the mysteries of his own courage or the lack of it. I knew. A year before, when I had first come to New York, there was a particular cat I kept running across in the bars of the Village, an expert with a knife, or indeed to maintain the salts of accuracy, an expert with two knives. He carried them everywhere—he had been some sort of hophead instructor in the Marines on the art of fighting with the knife, and he used to demonstrate nice fluid poses, his elbows in, the knives out, the points of those blades capering free of one another—he could feint in any direction with either hand, he was an artist, he believed he was better with a knife than any man

in all of New York, and night after night in bar after bar
he sang the love-song of his own prowess, begging for
the brave type who would take on his boast, and leave
him confirmed or dead.

It is mad to take on the city of New York, there is too
much talent waiting on line; this cat was calling for every hoodlum in every crack gang and clique who fancies
himself with the blade, and one night, drunk and on the
way home, he was greeted by another knife, a Puerto
Rican cat who was defective in school and spent his
afternoons and nights shadow-knifing in the cellar club-
house of his clique, a real contender, long-armed for a
Latin, thin as a Lehmbruck, and fast as a hungry wolf;
he had practiced for two months to meet the knife of
New York.

So they went into an alley, the champion drunk, a
fog of vanity blanketing the point of all his artistic reflexes, and it turned out to be not too much of a fight:
the Puerto Rican caught it on the knuckles, the lip, and
above the knee, but they were only nicks, and the champion was left in bad shape, bleeding from the forearm,
the belly, the chest, the neck, and the face: once he was
down, the Puerto Rican had engraved a double oval,
labium majorum and minorum on the skin of the cheek,
and left him there, having the subsequent consideration
or fright to make a telephone call to the bar in which
our loser had been drinking. The ex-champion, a bloody
cat, was carried to his pad which was not far away (a
bit of belated luck) and in an hour, without undue
difficulty the brother-in-law doctor of somebody or
other was good enough to take care of him. There were
police reports, and as our patois goes, the details were a
drag, but what makes my story sad is that our ex-champion was through. He mended by sorts and shifts, and
he still bragged in the Village bars, and talked of finding
the Puerto Rican when he was sober and in good shape,
but the truth was that he was on the alcoholic way, and
the odds were that he would stay there. He had been one
of those gamblers who saw his life as a single bet, and he
had lost. I often thought that he had been counting on a

victory to put some charge below his belt and drain his mouth of all that desperate labial libido.

Now I was following a modest parallel, and as Thompson kept asking me some reasonable if openly ignorant questions about the nature of the bullfight, I found myself shaping every answer as carefully as if I were writing dialogue, and I was speaking particularly for the black-alerted senses of three Negroes who were sitting behind me, each of them big in his way (I had taken my glimpse as I came in) with a dull, almost Chinese, sullenness of face. They could have been anything. I had seen faces like theirs on boxers and ditch diggers, and I had seen such faces by threes and fours riding around in Cadillacs through the Harlem of the early-morning hours. I was warning myself to play it carefully, and yet I pushed myself a little further than I should, for I became ashamed of my caution and therefore was obliged to brag just the wrong bit. Thompson, of course, was encouraging me—he was a sly old bastard—and he knew even better than me the character of our audience.

"Man, you can take care of yourself," he said with glee.

"I don't know about that," I answered, obeying the formal minuet of the *macho*. "I don't like to mess with anybody," I told him. "But a man messes with me—well, I wouldn't want him to go away feeling better than he started."

"Oh, yeah, ain't that a fact. I hears just what you hear." He talked like an old-fashioned Negro—probably Southern. "What if four or five of them comes on and gangs you?"

We had come a distance from the art of the *corrida.* "That doesn't happen to me," I said. "I like to be careful about having some friends." And part for legitimate emphasis, and part to fulfill my image of the movie male lead—that blond union of the rugged and the clean-cut (which would after all be *their* image as well)—I added, "Good friends, you know."

There we left it. My coffee cup was empty, and in the slop of the saucer a fly was drowning. I was thinking idly and with no great compassion that wherever this fly had been born it had certainly not expected to die in a tan syrupy ring-shaped pond, struggling for the greasy hot-dogged air of a cheap Negro hashhouse. But Thompson rescued it with a deft flip of his fingers.

"I always save," he told me seriously. "I wouldn't let nothing be killed. I'm a preacher."

"Real preacher?"

"Was one. Church and devoted congregation." He said no more. He had the dignified sadness of a man remembering the major failure of his life.

As we got up to go, I managed to turn around and get another look at the three spades in the next booth. Two of them were facing me. Their eyes were flat, the whites were yellow and flogged with red—they stared back with no love. The anxiety came over me again, almost nice—I had been so aware of them, and they had been so aware of me.

2

That was in October, and for no reason I could easily discover, I found myself thinking of that day as I awoke on a spring morning more than half a year later with a strong light coming through my nineteen windows. I had fixed the place up since then, added a few more pieces of furniture, connected a kitchen sink and a metal stall shower to the clean water outlets in the john, and most noticeably I had built a wall between the bullfight studio and the half in which I lived. That was more necessary than one might guess—I had painted the new wall red; after Thompson's job of whitewash I used to feel as if I were going snowblind; it was no easy pleasure to get up each morning in a white space so blue with cold that the chill of a mountain peak was in my blood. Now, when I opened my eyes, I could choose the blood of the wall in preference to the ice slopes of Mt. O'Shaughnessy, where the sun was always glinting on the glaciers of the windows.

But on this particular morning, when I turned over a little more, there was a girl propped on one elbow in the bed beside me, no great surprise, because this was the year of all the years in my life when I was scoring three and four times a week, literally combing the pussy out of my hair, which was no great feat if one knew the Village and the scientific temperament of the Greenwich Village mind. I do not want to give the false impression that I was one of the lustiest to come adventuring down the pike—I was cold, maybe by birth, certainly by environment: I grew up in a Catholic orphanage—and I had had my little kinks and cramps, difficulties enough just a few years ago, but I had passed through that, and I was going now on a kind of disinterested but developed competence; what it came down to was that I could go an hour with the average girl without destroying more of the vital substance than a good night's sleep could repair, and since that sort of stamina seems to get advertised, and I had my good looks, my blond hair, my height, build, and bullfighting school, I suppose I became one of the Village equivalents of an Eagle Scout badge for the girls. I was one of the credits needed for a diploma in the sexual humanities, I was par for a good course, and more than one of the girls and ladies would try me on an off-evening like comparison-shoppers to shop the value of their boy friend, lover, mate, or husband against the certified professionalism of Sergius O'Shaugnessy.

Now if I make this sound bloodless, I am exaggerating a bit—even an old habit is livened once in a while with color, and there were girls I worked to get and really wanted, and nights when the bull was far from dead in me. I even had two women I saw at least once a week, each of them, but what I am trying to emphasize is that when you screw too much and nothing is at stake, you begin to feel like a saint. It was a hell of a thing to be holding a nineteen-year-old girl's ass in my hands, hefting those young kneadables of future power, while all the while the laboratory technician in my brain was deciding that the experiment was a routine success— routine because her cheeks looked and felt just about the way I had thought they would while I was sitting beside her in the bar earlier in the evening, and so I still had come no closer to understanding my scientific compulsion to verify in the retort of the bed how accurately I had predicted the form, texture, rhythm and surprise of any woman who caught my eye.

Only an ex-Catholic can achieve some of the rarer amalgams of guilt, and the saint in me deserves to be recorded. I always felt an obligation—some noblesse oblige of the kindly cocksman—to send my women away with no great wounds to their esteem, feeling at best a little better than when they came in, I wanted to be friendly (What vanity of the saint!). I was the messiah of the one-night stand, and so I rarely acted like a pig in bed, I wasn't greedy, I didn't grind all my tastes into their mouths, I even abstained from springing too good a lay when I felt the girl was really in love with her man, and was using me only to give love the benefit of new perspective. Yes, I was a good sort, I probably gave more than I got back, and the only real pains for all those months in the loft, for my bullfighting classes, my surprisingly quiet time (it had been winter after all) on Monroe Street, my bulging portfolio of experiments— there must have been fifty girls who spent at least one night in the loft—my dull but doggedly advancing scientific data, even the cold wan joys of my saintliness demanded for their payment only one variety of the dead hour: when I woke in the morning, I could hardly wait to get the latest mouse out of my bed and out of my lair. I didn't know why, but I would awaken with the deadliest of depressions, the smell of the woman had gone very stale for me, and the armpits, the ammonias and dead sea life of old semen and old snatch, the sour fry of last night's sweat, the whore scent of overexercised perfume, became an essence of the odious, all the more remarkable because I clung to women in my sleep, I was one Don John who hated to sleep alone, I used to feel as if my pores were breathing all the maternal (because sleeping) sweets of the lady, wet or dry, firm or flaccid, plump, baggy, or lean who was handled by me while we dreamed. But on awakening, hung with my head—did I make love three times that year without being drunk? —the saint was given his hour of temptation, for I would have liked nothing more than to kick the friendly ass out of bed, and dispense with the coffee, the good form, my depression and often hers, and start the new day by lowering her in a basket out of my monk-ruined retreat six floors down to the garbage pile (now blooming again in the freshets of spring), wave my hand at her safe landing and get in again myself to the blessed isolations of the man alone.

But of course that was not possible. While it is usually a creep who generalizes about women, I think I will come on so heavy as to say that the cordial tone of the morning after is equally important to the gymkhana of the night before—at least if the profit made by a nice encounter is not to be lost. I had given my working hours of the early morning to dissolving a few of the inhibitions, chilled reflexes and dampened rhythms of the corpus before me, but there is not a restraint in the world which does not have to be taken twice—once at night on a steam-head of booze, and once in daylight with the grace of a social tea. To open a girl up to the point where she loves you or It or some tremor in her sexual baggage, and then to close her in the morning is to do the disservice which the hateful side of women loves most— you have fed their cold satisfied distrust of a man. Therefore my saint fought his private churl, and suffering all the detail of abusing the sympathetic nervous system, I made with the charm in the daylight and was more of a dear than most.

It was to be a little different this morning, however. As I said, I turned over in my bed, and looked at the girl propped on her elbow beside me. In her eyes there was a flat hatred which gave no ground—she must have been staring like this at my back for several minutes, and when I turned, it made no difference—she continued to examine my face with no embarrassment and no delight.

That was sufficient to roll me around again, my shoulder blades bare to her inspection, and I pretended that the opening of my eyes had been a false awakening. I felt deadened then with all the diseases of the dull— making love to her the night before had been a little too

much of a marathon. She was a Jewish girl and she was
in her third year at New York University, one of those
harsh alloys of a self-made bohemian from a middle-class
home (her father was a hardware wholesaler), and I
was remembering how her voice had irritated me each
time I had seen her, an ugly New York accent with a cul-
tured overlay. Since she was still far from formed, there
had been all sorts of Lesbian hysterias in her shrieking
laugh and they warred with that excess of strength, com-
placency and deprecation which I found in many Jewish
women—a sort of "Ech" of disgust at the romantic and
mysterious All. This one was medium in size and she had
dark long hair which she wore like a Village witch in two
extended braids which came down over her flat breasts,
and she had a long thin nose, dark eyes, and a kind of
lean force, her arms and square shoulders had shown
the flat thin muscles of a wiry boy. All the same, she
was not bad, she had a kind of Village chic, a certain
snotty elegance of superiority, and when I first came to
New York I had dug girls like her—Jewesses were strange
to me—and I had even gone with one for a few months.
But this new chick had been a mistake—I had met
her two weeks ago at a party, she was on leave from her
boy friend, and we had had an argument about T. S.
Eliot, a routine which for me had become the quintes-
sence of corn, but she said that Eliot was the apotheosis
of manner, he embodied the ecclesiasticism of classical
and now futureless form, she adored him she said, and I
was tempted to tell her how little Eliot would adore the
mannerless yeasts of the Brooklyn from which she came,
and how he might prefer to allow her to appreciate his
poetry only in step to the transmigration of her voice
from all urgent Yiddish nasalities to the few high English analities of relinquished desire. No, she would not
make that other world so fast—nice society was not cutting her crumpets thus quickly because she was gone on
Thomas Stearns Eeeee. Her college-girl snobbery, the
pity for me of eighty-five other honey-pots of the Village aesthetic whose smell I knew all too well, so in-
flamed the avenger of my crotch, that I wanted to prong

her then and there, right on the floor of the party, I was a primitive for a prime minute, a gorged gouge of a working-class phallus, eager to ram into all her nasty little tensions. I had the message again, I was one of the millions on the bottom who had the muscles to move the sex which kept the world alive, and I would grind it into her, the healthy hearty inches and the sweat of the cost of acquired culture when you started low and you wanted to go high. She was a woman, what! she sensed that moment, she didn't know if she could handle me, and she had the guts to decide to find out. So we left the party and we drank and (leave it to a Jewish girl to hedge the bet) she drained the best half of my desire in conversation because she was being psychoanalyzed, what a predictable pisser! and she was in that stage where the jargon had the totalitarian force of all vocabularies of mechanism, and she could only speak of her infantile relations to men, and the fixations and resistances of unassimilated penis-envy with all the smug gusto of a female commissar. She was enthusiastic about her analyst, he was also Jewish (they were working now on Jewish self-hatred), he was really an integrated guy, Stanford Joyce, he belonged to the same mountain as Eliot, she loved the doers and the healers of life who built on the foundationless prevalence of the void those islands of proud endeavor.

"You must get good marks in school," I said to her.

"Of course."

How I envied the jazzed-up grain of the Jews. I was hot for her again. I wanted the salts of her perspiration in my mouth. They would be acrid perhaps, but I would digest them, and those intellectual molecules would rise to my brain.

"I know a girl who went to your bullfighting school," she said to me. She gave her harsh laugh. "My friend thought you were afraid of her. She said you were full of narcissistic anxieties."

"Well, we'll find out," I said.

"Oh, you don't want me. I'm very inadequate as a lover." Her dark hard New York eyes, bright with appetite, considered my head as if I were a delicious and particularly sour pickle.

I paid the check then, and we walked over to my loft. As I had expected, she made no great fuss over the back-and-forth of being seduced—to the contrary. Once we were upstairs, she prowled the length of my loft twice, looked at the hand-made bullfighting equipment I had set up along one wall of the studio, asked me a question or two about the killing machine, studied the swords, asked another question about the cross-guard on the descabellar, and then came back to the living-room—bedroom—dining-room—kitchen of the other room, and made a face at the blood-red wall. When I kissed her she answered with a grinding insistence of her mouth upon mine, and a muscular thrust of her tongue into my throat, as direct and unfeminine as the harsh force of her voice.

"I'd like to hang my clothes up," she said.

It was not all that matter-of-fact when we got to bed. There was nothing very fleshy about the way she made love, no sense of the skin, nor smell, nor touch, just anger, anger at her being there, and another anger which was good for my own, that rage to achieve . . . just what, one cannot say. She made love as if she were running up an inclined wall so steep that to stop for an instant would slide her back to disaster. She hammered her rhythm at me, a hard driving rhythm, an all but monotonous drum, pound into pound against pound into pound until that moment when my anger found its way back again to that delayed and now recovered Time when I wanted to prong her at the party. I had been frustrated, had waited, had lost the anger, and so been taken by her. That finally got me—all through the talk about T. S. Eliot I had been calculating how I would lay waste to her little independence, and now she was alone, with me astride her, going through her paces, teeth biting the pillow, head turned away, using me as the dildoe of a private gallop. So my rage came back, and my rhythm no longer depended upon her drive, but found its own life, and we made love like two club fighters in an open exchange, neither giving ground, rhythm to rhythm, even to even, hypnotic, knowing neither the pain of punishment nor the pride of pleasure, and the equality of this, as hollow as the beat of the drum, seemed to carry her into some better deep of desire, and I had broken through, she was following me, her muscular body writhed all about me with an impersonal abandon, the wanton whip-thrash of a wounded snake, she was on fire and frozen at the same time, and then her mouth was kissing me with a rubbery greedy compulsion so avid to use all there was of me, that to my distant surprise, not in character for the saint to slip into the brutal, my hand came up and clipped her mean and openhanded across the face which brought a cry from her and broke the piston of her hard speed into something softer, wetter, more sly, more warm, I felt as if her belly were opening finally to receive me, and when her mouth kissed me again with a passing tender heat, warm-odored with flesh, and her body sweetened into some feminine embrace of my determination driving its way into her, well, I was gone, it was too late, I had driven right past her in that moment she turned, and I had begun to come, I was coming from all the confluences of my body toward that bud of sweetness I had plucked from her, and for a moment she was making it, she was a move back and surging to overtake me, and then it was gone, she made a mistake, her will ordered all temptings and rhythms to mobilize their march, she drove into the hard stupidities of a marching-band's step, and as I was going off in the best for many a month, she was merely going away, she had lost it again. As I ebbed into what should have been the contentments of a fine after-pleasure, warm and fine, there was one little part of me remaining cold and murderous because she had deprived me, she had fled the domination which was liberty for her, and the rest of the night was bound to be hell.

Her face was ugly. "You're a bastard, do you know that?" she asked of me.

"Let it go. I feel good."

"Of course you feel good. Couldn't you have waited one minute?"

I disliked this kind of thing. My duty was reminding me of how her awakened sweets were souring now in the belly, and her nerves were sharpening into the gone electric of being just nowhere.

"I hate inept men," she said.

"Cool it." She could, at least, be a lady. Because if she didn't stop, I would give her back a word or two.

"You did that on purpose," she nagged at me, and I was struck with the intimacy of her rancor—we might as well have been married for ten years to dislike each other so much at this moment.

"Why," I said, "you talk as if this were something unusual for you."

"It is."

"Come on," I told her, "you never made it in your life."

"How little you know," she said. "This is the first time I've missed in months."

If she had chosen to get my message, I could have been preparing now for a good sleep. Instead I would have to pump myself up again—and as if some ghost of the future laid the squeak of a tickle on my back, I felt an odd dread, not for tonight so much as for some ills of the next ten years whose first life was stirring tonight. But I lay beside her, drew her body against mine, feeling her trapped and irritable heats jangle me as much as they roused me, and while I had no fear that the avenger would remain asleep, still he stirred in pain and in protest, he had supposed his work to be done, and he would claim the wages of overtime from my reserve. That was the way I thought it would go, but Junior from New York University, with her hard body and her passion for proper poetry, gave a lewd angry old grin as her face stared boldly into mine, and with the practical bawdiness of the Jew she took one straight utilitarian finger, smiled a deceptive girlish pride, and then she jabbed, fingernail and all, into the tight defended core of my clenched buttocks. One wiggle of her knuckle and I threw her off, grunting a sound between rage and surprise, to which she laughed and lay back and waited for me.

Well, she had been right, that finger tipped the balance, and three-quarters with it, and one-quarter hung with the mysteries of sexual ambition, I worked on her like a beaver for forty-odd minutes or more, slapping my tail to build her nest, and she worked along while we made the round of the positions, her breath sobbing the exertions, her body as alive as a charged wire and as far from rest.

I gave her all the Time I had in me and more besides, I was weary of her, and the smell which rose from her had so little of the sea and so much of the armpit, that I breathed the stubborn wills of the gymnasium where the tight-muscled search for grace, and it was like that, a hard punishing session with pulley weights, stationary bicycle sprints, and ten breath-seared laps around the track. Yes, when I caught that smell, I knew she would not make it, and so I kept on just long enough to know she was exhausted in body, exhausted beyond the place where a ten-minute rest would have her jabbing that finger into me again, and hating her, hating women who could not take their exercise alone, I lunged up over the hill with my heart pounding past all pleasure, and I came, but with hatred, tight, electric, and empty, the spasms powerful but centered in my heart and not from the hip, the avenger taking its punishment even at the end, jolted clear to the seat of my semen by the succession of rhythmic blows which my heart drummed back to my feet.

For her, getting it from me, it must have been impressive, a convoluted, smashing, and protracted spasm, a hint of the death throe in the animal male which cannot but please the feminine taste for the mortal wound. "Oh, you're lucky," she whispered in my ear as I lay all collapsed beside her, alone in my athlete's absorption upon the whisperings of damage in the unlit complexities of my inner body. I was indeed an athlete, I knew my body was my future, and I had damaged it a

bit tonight by most certainly doing it no good. I disliked
her for it with the simple dislike we know for the stupid.

"Want a cigarette?" she asked.

I could wait, my heart would have preferred its rest,
but there was something tired in her voice beyond the
fatigue of what she had done. She too had lost after all.
So I came out of my second rest to look at her, and her
face had the sad relaxation (and serenity) of a young
whore who has finished a hard night's work with the
expected lack of issue for herself, content with no more
than the money and the professional sense of the hard job
dutifully done.

"I'm sorry you didn't make it," I said to her.

She shrugged. There was a Jewish tolerance for the
expected failures of the flesh. "Oh, well, I lied to you before," she said.

"You never have been able to, have you?"

"No." She was fingering the muscles of my shoulder,
as if in unconscious competition with my strength.
"You're pretty good," she said grudgingly.

"Not really inept?" I asked.

"*Sans façons*," said the poetess in an arch change of
mood which irritated me. "Sandy has been illuminating
those areas where my habits make for destructive impulses."

"Sandy is Doctor Joyce?" She nodded. "You make him
sound like your navigator," I told her.

"Isn't it a little obvious to be hostile to psychoanalysis?"

Three minutes ago we had been belaboring each other
in the nightmare of the last round, and now we were
close to cozy. I put the sole of my foot on her sharp little
knee.

"You know the first one we had?" she asked of me.
"Well, I wanted to tell you. I came close—I guess I came
as close as I ever came."

"You'll come closer. You're only nineteen."

"Yes, but this evening has been disturbing to me.
You see I get more from you than I get from my lover."

Her lover was twenty-one, a senior at Columbia, also
Jewish—which lessened interest, she confessed readily.

Besides, Arthur was too passive—"Basically, it's very comprehensible," said the commissar, "an aggressive female and a passive male—we complement one another, and that's no good." Of course it was easy to find satisfaction with Arthur, "via the oral perversions. That's because, vaginally, I'm anaesthetized—a good phallic narcissist like you doesn't do enough for me."

In the absence of learned credentials, she was setting out to bully again. So I thought to surprise her. "Aren't you mixing your language a little?" I began. "The phallic narcissist is one of Wilhelm Reich's categories."

"Therefore?"

"Aren't you a Freudian?"

"It would be presumptuous of me to say," she said like a seminar student working for his pee-aitch-dee. "But Sandy is an eclectic. He accepts a lot of Reich—you see, he's very ambitious, he wants to arrive at his own synthesis." She exhaled some smoke in my face, and gave a nice tough little grin which turned her long serious young witch's face into something indeed less presumptuous. "Besides," she said, "you are a phallic narcissist. There's an element of the sensual which is lacking in you."

"But Arthur possesses it?"

"Yes, he does. And you . . . you're not very juicy."

"I wouldn't know what you mean."

"I mean this." With the rich cruel look of a conquistador finding a new chest of Indian gold, she bent her head and gave one fleeting satiric half-moon of a lick to the conjugation of my balls. "That's what I mean," she said, and was out of bed even as I was recognizing that she was finally not without art. "Come back," I said.

But she was putting her clothes on in a hurry. "Shut up. Just don't give me your goddamned superiority."

I knew what it was: she had been about to gamble the reserves which belonged to Arthur, and the thought of possibly wasting them on a twenty-seven-year-old connoisseur like myself was too infuriating to take the risk.

So I lay in bed and laughed at her while she dressed—I did not really want a go at things again—and besides, the more I laughed, the angrier she would be, but the anger would work to the surface, and beneath it would be resting the pain that the evening had ended on so little.

She took her leisure going to the door, and I got up in time to tell her to wait—I would walk her to the subway. The dawn had come, however, and she wanted to go alone, she had had a bellyful of me, she could tell me that.

My brain was lusting its own private futures of how interesting it would be to have this proud, aggressive, vulgar, tense, stiff and arrogant Jewess going wild on my bottom—I had turned more than one girl on, but never a one of quite this type. I suppose she had succeeded instead of me; I was ready to see her again and improve the message.

She turned down all dates, but compromised by giving me her address and the number of her telephone. And then glaring at me from the open door, she said, "I owe you a slap in the face."

"Don't go away feeling unequal."

I might have known she would have a natural punch. My jaw felt it for half an hour after she was gone and it took another thirty minutes before I could bring myself back to concluding that she was one funny kid.

All of that added up to the first night with the commissar, and I saw her two more times over this stretch, the last on the night when she finally agreed to sleep over with me, and I came awake in the morning to see her glaring at my head. So often in sex, when the second night wound itself up with nothing better in view than the memory of the first night, I was reminded of Kafka's *Castle*, that tale of the search of a man for his apocalyptic orgasm: in the easy optimism of a young man, he almost captures the castle on the first day, and is never to come so close again. Yes, that was the saga of the nervous system of a man as it was bogged into the defeats, complications, and frustrations of middle age. I still had my future before me of course—the full engagement of my will in some go-for-broke I considered worthy of myself was yet to come, but there were times in that loft when I knew the psychology of an old man, and my second night with Denise—for Denise Gondelman was indeed her name—left me racked for it amounted to so little that we could not even leave it there—the hangover would have been too great for both of us—and so we made a date for a third night. Over and over in those days I used to compare the bed to the bullfight, sometimes seeing myself as the matador and sometimes as the bull, and this second appearance, if it had taken place, in the Plaza Mexico, would have been a *fracaso* with kapok seat cushions jeering down on the ring, and a stubborn cowardly bull staying in *querencia* before the doubtful prissy overtures, the gloomy trim technique of a veteran and mediocre *torero* on the worst of days when he is forced to wonder if he has even his *pundonor* to sustain him. It was a gloomy deal. Each of us knew it was possible to be badly worked by the other, and this seemed so likely that neither of us would gamble a finger. Although we got into bed and had a perfunctory ten minutes, it was as long as an hour in a coffee shop when two friends are done with one another.

By the third night we were ready for complexities again; to see a woman three times is to call on the dialectic of an affair. If the waves we were making belonged less to the viper of passion than the worm of inquiry, still it was obvious from the beginning that we had surprises for one another. The second night we had been hoping for more, and so got less; this third night, we each came on with the notion to wind it up, and so got involved in more.

For one thing, Denise called me in the afternoon. There was studying she had to do, and she wondered if it would be all right to come to my place at eleven instead of meeting me for drinks and dinner. Since that would save me ten dollars she saw no reason why I should complain. It was a down conversation. I had been planning to lay siege to her, dispense a bit of elixir from my vast reservoirs of charm, and instead she was going to keep it *in camera*. There was a quality about her I could not locate, something independent—abruptly, right there, I knew what it was. In a year she would have no memory of me, I would not exist for her unless . . . and then it was clear . . . unless I could be the first to carry her stone of no-orgasm up the cliff, all the way, over and out into the sea. That was the kick I could find, that a year from now, five years from now, down all the seasons to the hours of her old age, I would be the one she would be forced to remember, and it would nourish me a little over the years, thinking of that grudged souvenir which could not die in her, my blond hair, my blue eyes, my small broken nose, my clean mouth and chin, my height, my boxer's body, my parts —yes, I was getting excited at the naked image of me in the young-old mind of that sour sexed-up dynamo of black-pussied frustration.

A phallic narcissist she had called me. Well, I was phallic enough, a Village stickman who could muster enough of the divine It on the head of his will to call forth more than one becoming out of the womb of feminine Time, yes a good deal more than one from my fifty new girls a year, and when I failed before various prisons of frigidity, it mattered little. Experience gave the cue that there were ladies who would not be moved an inch by a year of the best, and so I looked for other things in them, but this one, this Den-of-Ease, she was ready, she was entering the time of her Time, and if not me, it would be another—I was sick in advance at the picture of some bearded Negro cat who would score where I had missed and thus cuckold me in spirit, deprive me of those telepathic waves of longing (in which I obviously believed) speeding away to me from her over the years to balm the hours when I was beat, because I had been her psychic bridegroom, had plucked her ideational diddle, had led her down the walk of her real wedding night. Since she did not like me, what a feat to pull it off.

In the hours I waited after dinner, alone, I had the sense—which I always trusted—that tonight this little victory or defeat would be full of leverage, magnified beyond its emotional matter because I had decided to bet on myself that I would win, and a defeat would bring me closer to a general depression, a fog bank of dissatisfaction with myself which I knew could last for months or more. Whereas a victory would add to the panoplies of my ego some peculiar (but for me, valid) ingestion of her arrogance, her stubbornness, and her will—those necessary ingredients of which I could not yet have enough for my own ambition.

When she came in she was wearing a sweater and dungarees which I had been expecting, but there was a surprise for me. Her braids had been clipped, and a short cropped curled Italian haircut decorated her head, moving her severe young face half across the spectrum from the austerities of a poetess to a hint of all those practical and promiscuous European girls who sold their holy hump to the Germans and had been subsequently punished by shaved heads—how attractive the new hair proved; once punished, they were now free, free to be wild, the worst had happened and they were still alive with the taste of the first victor's flesh enriching the sensual curl of the mouth.

Did I like her this way? Denise was interested to know. Well, it was a shock, I admitted, a pleasant shock. If it takes you so long to decide, you must be rigid, she let me know. Well, yes, as a matter of fact I was rigid, rigid for her with waiting.

The nun of severity passed a shade over her. She hated men who were uncool, she thought she would tell me.

"Did your analyst tell you it's bad to be uncool?"

She had taken off her coat, but now she gave me a look as if she were ready to put it on again. "No, he did not tell me that." She laughed spitefully. "But he told me a couple of revealing things about you."

"Which you won't repeat."

"Of course not."

"I'll never know," I said, and gave her the first kiss of the evening. Her mouth was heated—it was the best kiss I had received from her, and it brought me on too quickly

—"My fruit is ready to be plucked," said the odors of her mouth, betraying that perfume of the ducts which, against her will no doubt, had been plumping for me. She was changed tonight. From the skin of her face and the glen of her neck came a new smell, sweet, sweaty, and tender, the smell of a body which had been used and had enjoyed its uses. It came to me nicely, one of the nicest smells in quite some time, so different from the usual exudations of her dissatisfied salts that it opened a chain of reflexes in me, and I was off in all good speed on what Denise would probably have called the vertical foreplay. I suppose I went at her like a necrophiliac let loose upon a still-warm subject, and as I gripped her, grasped her, groped her, my breath a bellows to blow her into my own flame, her body remained unmoving, only her mouth answering my call, those lips bridling hot adolescent kisses back upon my face, the smell almost carrying me away—such a fine sweet sweat.

Naturally she clipped the rhythm. As I started to slip up her sweater, she got away and said a little huskily, "I'll take my own clothes off." Once again I could have hit her. My third eye, that athlete's inner eye which probed its vision into all the corners, happy and distressed of my body whole, was glumly cautioning the congestion of the spirits in the coils of each teste. They would have to wait, turn rancid, maybe die of delay.

Off came the sweater and the needless brassière, her economical breasts swelled just a trifle tonight, enough to take on the convexities of an Amazon's armor. Open came the belt and the zipper of her dungarees, zipped from the front which pleased her not a little. Only her ass, a small masterpiece, and her strong thighs, justified this theatre. She stood there naked, quite psychically clothed, and lit a cigarette.

If a stiff prick has no conscience, it has also no common sense. I stood there like a clown, trying to coax her to take a ride with me on the bawdy car, she out of her clothes, I in all of mine, a muscular little mermaid to melt on my knee. She laughed, one harsh banker's snort —she was giving no loans on my idiot's collateral.

"You didn't even ask me," Denise thought to say, "of how my studying went tonight."

"What did you study?"

"I didn't. I didn't study." She gave me a lovely smile, girlish and bright. "I just spent the last three hours with Arthur."

"You're a dainty type," I told her.

But she gave me a bad moment. That lovely flesh-spent smell, scent of the well used and the tender, that avatar of the feminine my senses had accepted so greedily, came down now to no more than the rubbings and the sweats of what was probably a very nice guy, passive Arthur with his Jewish bonanzas of mouth-love.

The worst of it was that it quickened me more. I had the selfish wisdom to throw such evidence upon the mercy of my own court. For the smell of Arthur was the smell of love, at least for me, and so from man or woman, it did not matter—the smell of love was always feminine —and if the man in Denise was melted by the woman in Arthur, so Arthur might have flowered that woman in himself from the arts of a real woman, his mother?—it did not matter—that voiceless message which passed from the sword of the man into the cavern of the woman was carried along from body to body, and if it was not the woman in Denise I was going to find tonight, at least I would be warmed by the previous trace of another.

But that was a tone poem to quiet the toads of my doubt. When Denise—it took five more minutes—finally decided to expose herself on my clumped old mattress, the sight of her black pubic hair, the feel of the foreign but brotherly liquids in her unembarrassed maw, turned me into a jackrabbit of pissy tumescence, the quicks of my excitement beheaded from the resonances of my body, and I wasn't with her a half-minute before I was over, gone, and off. I rode not with the strength to reap the harem of her and her lover, but spit like a pinched little boy up into black forested hills of motherly contempt, a passing picture of the nuns of my childhood to drench my piddle spurtings with failures of gloom.

She it was who proved stronger than me, she the he to my silly she.

All considered, Denise was nice about it. Her harsh laugh did not crackle over my head, her hand in passing me the after-cigarette settled for no more than a nudge of my nose, and if it were not for the contempt of her tough grin, I would have been left with no more than the alarm to the sweepers of my brain to sweep this failure away.

"Hasn't happened in years," I said to her, the confession coming out of me with the cost of the hardest cash.

"Oh, shut up. Just rest." And she began to hum a mocking little song. I lay there in a state, parts of me jangled for forty-eight hours to come, and yet not altogether lost to peace. I knew what it was. Years ago in the air force, as an enlisted man, I had reached the light-heavyweight finals on my air base. For two weeks I trained for the championship, afraid of the other man all the way because I had seen him fight and felt he was better than me; when my night came, he took me out with a left hook to the liver which had me conscious on the canvas but unable to move, and as the referee was counting, which I could hear all too clearly, I knew the same kind of peace, a swooning peace, a clue to that kind of death in which an old man slips away—nothing mattered except that my flesh was vulnerable and I had a dim revery, lying there with the yells of the air force crowd in my ears, there was some far-off vision of green fields and me lying in them, giving up all ambition to go back instead to another, younger life of the senses, and I remember at that moment I watered the cup of my boxer's jock, and then I must have slipped into something new, for as they picked me off the canvas the floor seemed to recede from me at a great rate as if I were climbing in an airplane.

A few minutes later, the nauseas of the blow to my liver had me retching into my hands, and the tension of three weeks of preparation for that fight came back. I knew through the fading vistas of my peace, and the oncoming spasms of my nausea, that the worst was yet to come, and it would take me weeks to unwind, and then years, and maybe never to overcome the knowledge that I had failed completely at a moment when I wanted very much to win.

A ghost of this peace, trailing intimations of a new nausea, was passing over me again, and I sat up in bed abruptly, as if to drive these weaknesses back into me. My groin had been simmering for hours waiting for Denise, and it was swollen still, but the avenger was limp, he had deserted my cause, I was in a spot if she did not co-operate.

Co-operate she did. "My God, lie down again, will you," she said, "I was thinking that finally I had seen you relax."

And then I could sense that the woman in her was about to betray her victory. She sat over me, her little breasts budding with their own desire, her short hair alive and flowering, her mouth ready to taste her gentleman's defeat. I had only to raise my hand, and push her body in the direction she wished it to go, and then her face was rooting in me, her angry tongue and voracious mouth going wild finally as I had wished it, and I knew the sadness of sour timing, because this was a prize I could not enjoy as I would have on the first night, and yet it was good enough—not art, not the tease and languor of love on a soft mouth, but therapy, therapy for her, the quick exhaustions of the tension in a harsh throat, the beseechment of an ugly voice going down into the expiation which would be its beauty. Still it was good, practically it was good, my ego could bank the hard cash that this snotty head was searching me, the act served its purpose, anger traveled from her body into mine, the avenger came to attention, cold and furious, indifferent to the trapped doomed pleasure left behind in my body on that initial and grim piddle spurt, and I was ready, not with any joy nor softness nor warmth nor care, but I was ready finally to take her tonight, I was going to beat new Time out of her if beat her I must, I was going to teach her that she was only a child, because if at last I could not take care of a nineteen-year-old, then I was gone indeed. And so I took her with a cold calculation, the rhythms of my body corresponding to no more than a metronome in my mind, tonight the driving mechanical beat would come from me, and blind to nerve-raddlings in my body, and blood pressures in my brain, I worked on her like a riveter, knowing her resistances were made of steel, I threw her a fuck the equivalent of a fifteen-round fight, I wearied her, I brought her back, I drove my fingers into her shoulders and my knees into her hips. I went, and I went, and I went, I bore her high and thumped her hard, I sprinted, I paced, I lay low, eyes all closed, under sexual water, like a submarine listening for the distant sound of her ship's motors, hoping to steal up close and trick her rhythms away.

And she was close. Oh, she was close so much of the time. Like a child on a merry-go-round the touch of the colored ring just evaded the tips of her touch, and she heaved and she hurdled, arched and cried, clawed me, kissed me, even gave a shriek once, and then her sweats running down and her will weak, exhausted even more than me, she felt me leave and lie beside her. Yes, I did that with a tactician's cunning, I let the depression of her failure poison what was left of her will never to let me succeed, I gave her slack to mourn the lost freedoms and hate the final virginity for which she fought, I even allowed her baffled heat to take its rest and attack her nerves once more, and then, just as she was beginning to fret against me in a new and unwilling appeal, I turned her over suddenly on her belly, my avenger wild with the mania of the madman, and giving her no chance, holding her prone against the mattress with the strength of my weight, I drove into the seat of all stubbornness, tight as a vise, and I wounded her, I knew it, she thrashed beneath me like a trapped little animal, making not a sound, but fierce not to allow me this last of the liberties, and yet caught, forced to give up millimeter by millimeter the bridal ground of her symbolic and therefore real vagina. So I made it, I made it all the way—it took ten minutes and maybe more, but as the avenger rode down to his hilt and tunneled the threshold of sexual home all those inches closer into the bypass of the womb, she gave at last a little cry of farewell, and I could feel a new shudder which began as a ripple and rolled into a wave, and then it rolled over her, carrying her along, me hardly moving for fear of damping this quake from her earth, and then it was gone, but she was left alive with a larger one to follow.

So I turned her once again on her back, and moved by impulse to love's first hole. There was an odor coming up, hers at last, the smell of the sea, and none of the arm-pit or a dirty sock, and I took her mouth and kissed it, but she was away, following the wake of her own waves which mounted, fell back, and in new momentum mounted higher and should have gone over, and then she was about to hang again, I could feel it, that mo-ment of hesitation between the past and the present, the habit and the adventure, and I said into her ear, "You dirty little Jew."

That whipped her over. A first wave kissed, a second spilled, and a third and a fourth and a fifth came break-ing over, and finally she was away, she was loose in the water for the first time in her life, and I would have liked to go with her, but I was blood-throttled and numb, and as she had the first big moment in her life, I was nothing but a set of aching balls and a congested cock, and I rode with her wistfully, looking at the contortion of her face and listening to her sobbing sound of "Oh, Jesus, I made it, oh Jesus, I did."

"Compliments of T. S. Eliot," I whispered to myself, and my head was aching, my body was shot. She curled against me, she kissed my sweat, she nuzzled my eyes and murmured in my ear, and then she was slipping away into the nicest of weary sweet sleep.

"Was it good for you too?" she whispered half-awake, having likewise read the works of The Hemingway, and I said, "Yeah, fine," and after she was asleep, I disen-gaged myself carefully, and prowled the loft, accepting the hours it would take for my roiled sack to clean its fatigues and know a little sleep. But I had abused myself too far, and it took till dawn and half a fifth of whiskey before I dropped into an unblessed stupor. When I awoke, in that moment before I moved to look at her, and saw her glaring at me, I was off on a sluggish masculine debate as to whether the kick of studying this Denise for another few nights—now that I had turned the key—would be worth the danger of deepening into some small real feeling. But through my hangover and the knowledge of the day and the week and the month it would take the different parts of all of me to repair, I was also knowing the taste of a reinforced will—finally, I had won. At no matter what cost, and with what luck, and with a piece of charity from her, I had won nonetheless, and since all real pay came from victory, it was more likely that I would win the next time I gambled my stake on something more appropriate for my ambition.

Then I turned, saw the hatred in her eyes, turned over again, and made believe I was asleep while a dread of the next few minutes weighed a leaden breath over the new skin of my ego.

"You're awake, aren't you?" she said.

I made no answer.

"All right, I'm going then. I'm getting dressed." She whipped out of bed, grabbed her clothes, and began to put them on with all the fury of waiting for me to get the pronouncement. "That was a lousy thing you did last night," she said by way of a start.

In truth she looked better than she ever had. The severe lady and the tough little girl of yesterday's face had put forth the first agreements on what would yet be a bold chick.

"I gave you what you could use," I made the mistake of saying.

"Just didn't you," she said, and was on her way to the door. "Well, cool it. You don't do anything to me." Then she smiled. "You're so impressed with what you think was such a marvelous notch you made in me, listen, Buster, I came here last night thinking of what Sandy Joyce told me about you, and he's right, oh man is he right." Standing in the open doorway, she started to light a cigarette, and then threw the matches to the floor.

From thirty feet away I could see the look in her eyes, that unmistakable point for the kill that you find in the eyes of very few bullfighters, and then having created her pause, she came on for her moment of truth by saying, "He told me your whole life is a lie, and you do nothing but run away from the homosexual that is you."

And like a real killer, she did not look back, and was out the door before I could rise to tell her that she was a hero fit for me.

Everything Under the Sun

James Purdy

"I don't like to make things hard for you," Jesse said to Cade, "but when you act like this I don't know what's going to happen. You don't like nothing I do for you anyhow."

The two boys, Jesse and Cade, shared a room over the south end of State Street. Jesse had a job, but Cade, who was fifteen, seldom could find work. They were both down to their last few dollars.

"I told you a man was coming up here to offer me a job," Cade said.

"You can't wait for a man to come offering you a job," Jesse said. He laughed. "What kind of a man would that be anyhow."

Cade laughed too because he knew Jesse did not believe anything he said.

"This man did promise me," Cade explained, and Jesse snorted.

"Don't pick your nose like that," Jesse said to Cade. "What if the man seen you picking."

Cade said the man wouldn't care.

"What does this man do?" Jesse wondered.

"He said he had a nice line of goods I could sell for him and make good money," Cade replied.

"Good money selling," Jesse laughed. "My advice to you is go out and look for a job, any job, and not wait for no old man to come to teach you to sell."

"Well nobody else wants to hire me due to my face," Cade said.

"What's wrong with your face?" Jesse wanted to

know. "Outside of you picking your nose all the time, you have as good a face as anybody's."

"I can't look people in the eye is what," Cade told him.

Jesse got up and walked around the small room.

"Like I told you," Jesse began the same speech he always gave when Cade was out of work, "I would do anything for you on account of your brother. He saved my life in the goddam army and I ain't never going to forget that."

Cade made his little expression of boredom which was to pinch the bridge of his nose.

"But you got to work sometimes!" Jesse exploded. "I don't get enough for two!"

Cade grimaced, and did not let go the bridge of his nose because he knew this irritated Jesse almost as much as his picking did, but Jesse could not criticize him for just holding his nose, and that made him all the angrier.

"And you stay out of them arcades too!" Jesse said to Cade. "Spending the money looking at them pictures," Jesse began. "For the love of. . . ." Suddenly Jesse stopped short.

"For the love of what?" Cade jumped him. He knew the reason that Jesse did not finish the sentence with a swear word was he went now to the Jesus Saves Mission every night, and since he had got religion he had quit being quite so friendly to Cade as before, cooler and more distant, and he talked, like today, about how good work is for everybody.

"That old man at the trucking office should have never told you you had a low IQ," Jesse returned to this difficulty of Cade's finding work.

But this remark did not touch Cade today.

"Jesse," Cade said, "I don't care about it."

"You don't care!" Jesse flared up.

"That's right," Cade said, and he got up and took out a piece of cigarette from his pants cuff, and lit a match to the stub. "I don't believe in IQ's," Cade said.

"Did you get that butt off the street?" Jesse wanted to know, his protective manner making his voice soft again.

"I ain't answering that question," Cade told him.

"Cade, why don't you be nice to me like you used to be," Jesse said.

"Why don't *I* be nice to *you!*" Cade exclaimed with savagery.

Suddenly frightened, Jesse said, "Now simmer down." He was always afraid when Cade suddenly acted too excited.

"You leave me alone," Cade said. "I ain't interferin' with your life and don't you interfere with mine. The little life I have, that is." He grunted.

"I owe something to you and that's why I can't just let you be any old way you feel like being," Jesse said.

"You don't owe me a thing," Cade told him.

"I know who I owe and who I don't," Jesse replied.

"You always say you owe me on account of my brother saved your life just before he got hisself blowed up."

"Cade, you be careful!" Jesse warned, and his head twitched as he spoke.

"I'm glad he's gone," Cade said, but without the emotion he usually expressed when he spoke of his brother. He had talked against his brother so long in times past in order to get Jesse riled up that it had lost nearly all meaning for both of them. "Yes, sir, I don't care!" Cade repeated.

Jesse moved his lips silently and Cade knew he was praying for help.

Jesse opened his eyes wide then and looking straight at Cade, twisted his lips, trying not to let the swear words come out, and said: "All right, Cade," after a long struggle.

"And if religion is going to make you close with your money," Cade began looking at Jesse's mouth, "close and *mean,* too, then I can clear out of here. I don't need you, Jesse."

"What put the idea into your head religion made me close with my money?" Jesse said, and he turned very pale.

"You need me here, but you don't want to pay what it takes to keep me," Cade said.

Jesse trembling walked over to Cade very close and stared at him.

Cade watched him, ready.

Jesse said, "You can stay here as long as you ever want to. And no questions asked." Having said this, Jesse turned away, a glassy look on his face, and stared at the cracked calcimine of their wall.

"On account of my old brother I can stay!" Cade yelled.

"All right then!" Jesse shouted back, but fear on his face. Then softening with a strange weakness he said, "No, Cade, that's not it either," and he went over and put his arm on Cade's shoulder.

"Don't touch me," Cade said. "I don't want none of that *brother* love. Keep your distance."

"You behave," Jesse said, struggling with his emotion.

"Ever since you give up women and drinking you been picking on me," Cade said. "I do the best I can."

Cade waited for Jesse to say something.

"And you think picking on me all the time makes you get a star in heaven, I suppose," Cade said weakly.

Jesse, who was not listening, walked the length of the cramped little room. Because of the heat of the night and the heat of the discussion, he took off his shirt. On his chest was tattooed a crouched black panther, and on his right arm above his elbow a large unfolding flower.

"I did want to do right by you, but maybe we *had* better part," Jesse said, crossing his arms across his chest. He spoke like a man in his sleep, but immediately he had spoken, a scared look passed over his face.

Cade suddenly went white. He moved over to the window.

"I can't do no more for you!" Jesse cried, alarmed but helpless at his own emotion. "It ain't in me to do no more for you! Can't you see that, Cade. Only so much, no more!"

When there was no answer from Cade, Jesse said, "Do you hear what I say?"

Cade did not speak.

"Fact is," Jesse began again, as though explaining now to himself, "I don't seem to care about nothing. I just want somehow to sit and not move or do nothing. I don't know what it is."

"You never did give a straw if I lived or died, Jesse," Cade said, and he just managed to control his angry tears.

Jesse was silent, as on the evenings when alone in the dark, while Cade was out looking for a job, he had tried to figure out what he should do in his trouble.

"*Fact* is," Cade now whirled from the window, his eyes brimming with tears, "It's all the other way around. I don't need you except for money, but you need me *to tell you who you are!*"

"What?" Jesse said, thunderstruck.

"You know goddam well *what*," Cade said, and he wiped the tears off his face with his fist. "On account of you don't know who you are, that's why."

"You little crumb," Jesse began, and he moved threateningly, but then half remembering his nights at the Mission, he walked around the room, muttering.

"Where are my cigarettes?" Jesse said suddenly. "Did you take them?"

"I thought you swore off when you got religion," Cade said.

"Yeah," Jesse said in the tone of voice more like his old self, and he went up to Cade, who was smoking another butt.

"Give me your smoke," he said to Cade.

Cade passed it to him, staring.

"I don't think you heard what I said about leaving," Cade told Jesse.

"I heard you," Jesse said.

"Well, I'm going to leave you, Jesse. God damn you."

Jesse just nodded from where he now sat on a crate they used as a chair. He groaned a little like the smoke was disagreeable for him.

"Like I say, Jesse," and Cade's face was dry of tears now. "It may be hard for me to earn money, but I know who I am. I may be dumb, but I'm *all together!*"

"Cade," Jesse said sucking on the cigarette furiously. "I

didn't mean for you to go. After all, there is a lot between us."

Jesse's fingers moved nervously over the last tiny fragment of the cigarette.

"Do you have any more smokes in your pants cuff or anywhere?" Jesse asked, as though he were the younger and the weaker of the two now.

"I have, but I don't think I should give any to a religious man," Cade replied.

Jesse tightened his mouth.

Cade handed him another of the butts.

"What are you going to offer me, if I do decide to stay," Cade said suddenly. "On account of this time I'm not going to stay if you don't give me an offer!"

Jesse stood up suddenly, dropping his cigarette, the smoke coming out of his mouth as though he had all gone to smoke inside himself.

"What am I going to offer you?" Jesse said like a man in a dream. "What?" he said sleepily.

Then waving his arms, Jesse cried, "All right! Get out!"

And suddenly letting go at last he struck Cade across the mouth, bringing some blood. "Now you git," he said. "Git out."

Jesse panted, walking around the room. "You been bleedin' me white for a year. That's the reason I'm the way I am. I'm bled white."

Cade went mechanically to the bureau, took out a shirt, a pair of shorts, a toothbrush, his straight razor, and a small red box. He put these in a small bag such as an athlete might carry to his gym. He walked over to the door and went out.

Below, on the sidewalk, directly under the room where he and Jesse had lived together a year, Cade stood waiting for the streetcar. He knew Jesse was looking down on him. He did not have to wait long.

"Cade," Jesse's voice came from the window. "You get back here, Cade, goddam you." Jesse hearing the first of his profanity let loose at last, swore a lot more then, as though he had found his mind again in swearing.

A streetcar stopped at that moment.

"Don't get on that car, Cade," Jesse cried. "Goddam it."

Cade affected impatience.

"You wait now, goddam you," Jesse said putting on his rose-colored shirt.

"Cade," Jesse began when he was on the street beside his friend. "Let's go somewhere and talk this over. . . . See how I am," he pointed to his trembling arm.

"There ain't nowhere to go since you give up drinking," Cade told him.

Jesse took Cade's bag for him.

"Well if it makes you unhappy, I'll drink with you," Jesse said.

"I don't mind being unhappy," Cade said. "It's *you* that minds, Jesse."

"I want you to forgive me, Cade," Jesse said, putting his hand on Cade's arm.

Cade allowed Jesse's arm to rest there.

"Well, Jesse," Cade said coldly.

"You see," Jesse began, pulling Cade gently along with him as they walked toward a tavern. "You see, I don't know what it is, Cade, but you know everything."

Cade watched him.

They went into the tavern and although they usually sat at the bar, today they chose a table. They ordered beer.

"You see, Cade, I've lied to you, I think, and you're right. Of course your brother did save my life, but you saved it again. I mean you saved it more. You saved me," and he stretched out his trembling arm at Cade.

Jesse seeing the impassive look on Cade's face stopped and then going on as though he did not care whether anybody heard him or not, he said: "You're all I've got, Cade."

Cade was going to say *all right now* but Jesse went on speaking frantically and fluently as he had never spoken before. "You know ever since the war, I've been like I am . . . And Cade, I need you that's why . . . I know you don't need me," he nodded like an old man now. "But I don't care now. I ain't proud no more about it."

Jesse stopped talking and a globule of spit rested thickly on his mouth.

"I'm cured of being proud, Cade."

"Well, all right then," Cade finally said, folding his arms and compressing his mouth.

"All right?" Jesse said, a silly look on his face, which had turned very young again.

"But you leave me alone now if I stay," Cade said.

"I will," Jesse said, perhaps not quite sure what it was Cade meant. "You can do anything you want, Cade. All I need is to know you won't really run out. No matter what I might some day say or do, you stay, Cade!"

"Then I don't want to hear no more about me getting just any old job," Cade said, drinking a swallow of beer.

"All right," Jesse said. "All right, all right."

"And you quit going to that old Mission and listening to that religious talk."

Jesse nodded.

"I ain't living with no old religious fanatic," Cade said.

Jesse nodded again.

"And there ain't no reason we should give up drinking and all the rest of it at night."

Jesse agreed.

"Or women," Cade said, and he fumbled now with the button of his shirt. It was such a very hot night his hand almost unconsciously pushed back the last button which had held his shirt together, exposing the section of his chest on which rested the tattooed drawing of a crouched black panther, the identical of Jesse's.

"And I don't want to hear no more about me going to work at all for a while," Cade was emphatic.

"All right, then, Cade," Jesse grinned, beginning to giggle and laugh now.

"Well I should say *all right*," Cade replied, and he smiled briefly, as he accepted Jesse's hand which Jesse proffered him then by standing up.

Under the Rose

Thomas Pynchon

As the afternoon progressed, yellow clouds began to
gather over Place Mohammed Ali, casting a tendril or
two back toward the Libyan desert. A wind from the
southwest swept quietly up rue Ibrahim and across the
square, bringing the chill of the desert into the city.

Then let it rain, Porpentine thought: rain soon. He sat
at a small wrought-iron table in front of a café, smoking
Turkish cigarettes with a third cup of coffee, ulster
thrown over the back of an adjoining chair. Today he
wore light tweeds and a felt hat with muslin tied round
it to protect his neck from the sun; he was leery of the
sun. Clouds moved in now to dim it out. Porpentine
shifted in his seat, took a watch from his waistcoat
pocket, consulted it, replaced it. Turned once more to
look out at the Europeans milling about the square: some
hurrying into the Banque Impériale Ottomane, others
lingering by shopwindows, seating themselves at cafés.
His face was carefully arranged: nerveless, rakish-ex-
pectant; he might have been there to meet a lady.

All for the benefit of anyone who cared. God knew
how many there were. In practice it narrowed down to
those in the employ of Moldweorp, the veteran spy. One
somehow always tacked on "the veteran spy." It might
have been a throwback to an earlier time, when such
epithets were one reward for any proof of heroism or
manhood. Or possibly because now, with a century rushing headlong to its end and with it a tradition in
espionage where everything was tacitly on a gentlemanly
basis, where the playing-fields of Eton had conditioned

392

(one might say) premilitary conduct as well, the label was a way of fixing identity in this special *haut monde* before death—individual or collective—stung it to stillness forever. Porpentine himself was called *"il semplice inglese"* by those who cared.

Last week in Brindisi their compassion had been relentless as always; it gave them a certain moral advantage, realizing as they did that Porpentine was somehow incapable of returning it. Tender and sheepish, therefore, they wove their paths to cross his own at random. Mirrored, too, his private tactics: living in the most frequented hotels, sitting at the tourist cafés, traveling always by the respectable, public routes. Which surely upset him most; as if, Porpentine once having fashioned such proper innocence, any use of it by others—especially Moldweorp's agents—involved some violation of patent right. They would pirate if they could his child's gaze, his plump angel's smile. For nearly fifteen years he'd fled their sympathy; since the lobby of the Hotel Bristol, Naples, on a winter evening in '83, when everyone you knew in spying's free-masonry seemed to be waiting. For Khartum to fall, for the crisis in Afghanistan to keep growing until it could be given the name of sure apocalypse. There he had come, as he'd known he must at some stage of the game, to face the already aged face of Moldweorp himself, the prizeman or maestro, feel the old man's hand solicitous on his arm and hear the earnest whisper: "Things are reaching a head; we may be for it, all of us. Do be careful." What response? What possible? Only a scrutiny, almost desperate, for any fine trace of insincerity. Of course he'd found none there; and so turned, quickly, flaming, unable to cover a certain helplessness. Hoist thus by his own petard at every subsequent encounter as well, Porpentine by the dogdays of '98 seemed, in contrast, to have grown cold, unkind. They would continue to use so fortunate an engine: would never seek his life, violate The Rules, forbear what had become for them pleasure.

He sat now wondering if either of the two at Brindisi had followed him to Alexandria. Certain he had seen no one on the Venice boat, he reviewed possibilities. An Austrian Lloyd steamer from Trieste also touched at Brindisi; was the only other they would have taken. To-day was Monday. Porpentine had left on a Friday. The Trieste boat left on Thursday and arrived late Sunday. So that (a) at second-worst he had six days, or (b) at worst, they knew. In which case they had left the day before Porpentine and were already here.

He watched the sun darken and the wind flutter the leaves of acacias around Place Mohammed Ali. In the distance his name was being called. He turned to watch Goodfellow, blond and jovial, striding toward him down rue Cherif Pacha, wearing a dress suit and a pith helmet two sizes too large. "I say," Goodfellow cried. "Porpentine, I've met a remarkable young lady." Porpentine lit another cigarette and closed his eyes. All of Goodfellow's young ladies were remarkable. After two and a half years as partners one got used to an incidental progress of feminine attachments to Goodfellow's right arm: as if every capital of Europe were Margate and the promenade a continent long. If Goodfellow knew half his salary was sent out every month to a wife in Liverpool he showed none of it, rollicking along unperturbed, cock-a-hoop. Porpentine had seen his running mate's dossier but decided some time ago that the wife at least was none of his affair. He listened now as Goodfellow drew up a chair and summoned a waiter in wretched Arabic: "*Hat fingan kahwa bisukkar, ya weled.*"

"Goodfellow," Porpentine said, "you don't have to—"

"*Ya weled, ya weled,*" Goodfellow roared. The waiter was French and did not understand Arabic. "Ah," Goodfellow said, "coffee then. *Café,* you know."

"How are the digs?" asked Porpentine.

"First-rate." Goodfellow was staying at the Hotel Khedival, seven blocks away. There being a temporary hitch in finances, only one could afford the usual accommodations. Porpentine was staying with a friend in the Turkish quarter. "About this girl," Goodfellow said. "Party tonight at the Austrian Consulate. Her escort, Goodfellow: linguist, adventurer, diplomat . . ."

"Name," said Porpentine.

"Victoria Wren. Traveling with family, *videlicet*: Sir Alastair Wren, F.R.C.O., sister Mildred. Mother deceased. Departing for Cairo tomorrow. Cook's tour down the Nile." Porpentine waited. "Lunatic archaeologist," Goodfellow seemed reluctant. "One Bongo-Shaftsbury. Young, addlepated. Harmless."

"Aha."

"Tch-tch. Too highly strung. Should drink less café-fort."

"Possibly," Porpentine said. Goodfellow's coffee arrived. Porpentine continued: "You know we'll end up chancing it anyway. We always do." Goodfellow grinned absently and stirred his coffee.

"I have already taken steps. Bitter rivalry for the young lady's attentions between myself and Bongo-Shaftsbury. Fellow is a perfect ass. Is mad to see the Theban ruins at Luxor."

"Of course," Porpentine said. He arose and tossed the ulster around his shoulders. It had begun to rain. Goodfellow handed him a small white envelope with the Austrian crest on the back.

"Eight, I suppose," said Porpentine.

"Right you are. You must see this girl."

It was then that one of Porpentine's seizures came upon him. The profession was lonely and in constant though not always deadly earnest. At regular intervals he found need to play the buffoon. "A bit of skylarking," he called it. It made him, he believed, more human. "I will be there with false mustaches," he now informed Goodfellow, "impersonating an Italian count." He stood gaily at attention, pressed an imaginary hand: "*Carissima signorina.*" He bowed, kissed the air.

"You're insane," from Goodfellow, amiable.

"*Pazzo son!*" Porpentine began to sing in a wavering tenor. "*Guardate, come io piango ed imploro . . .*" His Italian was not perfect. Cockney inflections danced through. A group of English tourists, hurrying in out of the rain, glanced back at him, curious.

"Enough," Goodfellow winced. "'Twas Turin, I re-

member. Torino. Was it not? '93. I escorted a marche-
sina with a mole on her back and Cremonini sang Des
Grieux. You, Porpentine, desecrate the memory."

But the antic Porpentine leaped in the air, clicked his
heels; stood posturing, fist on chest, the other arm outstretched. "*Come io chiedo pietà!*" The waiter looked on
with a pained smile; it began to rain harder. Goodfellow
sat in the rain sipping his coffee. Drops of rain rattled
on the pith helmet. "The sister isn't bad," he observed as
Porpentine frolicked out in the square. "Mildred, you
know. Though only eleven." At length it occurred to him
that his dress suit was becoming soaked. He arose, left a
piastre and a millième on the table and nodded to Porpentine, who now stood watching him. The square was
empty except for the equestrian statue of Mohammed
Ali. How many times had they faced each other this way,
dwarfed horizontal and vertical by any plaza's late-after-
noon landscape? Could an argument from design be
predicated on that moment only, then the two must have
been displaceable, like minor chess-pieces, anywhere
across the board of Europe. Both of a color (though
one hanging back diagonal in deference to his chief),
both scanning any embassy's parquetry for signs of the
Opposition, any statue's face for a reassurance of self-
agency (perhaps, unhappily, self-humanity), they would
try not to remember that every city's square, however
you cut it, remains inanimate after all. Soon the two men
turned almost formally, to part in opposite directions:
Goodfellow back toward the hotel, Porpentine into rue
Raset-Tin and the Turkish quarter. Until 8:00 he
would ponder the Situation.

At the moment it was a bad job all round. Sirdar
Kitchener, England's newest colonial hero, recently
victorious at Khartum, was just now some four hundred
miles further down the White Nile, foraging about in the
jungle. A General Marchand was also rumored to be in
the vicinity. Britain wanted no part of France in the
Nile Valley. M. Delcassé, Foreign Minister of a newly
formed French cabinet, would as soon go to war as
not if there were any trouble when the two detachments

met. As meet, everyone realized by now, they would. Kitchener had been instructed not to take any offensive and to avoid all provocation. Russia would support France in case of war, while England had a temporary rapprochement with Germany, which of course meant Italy and Austria as well.

Moldweorp's chief amusement, Porpentine reflected, had always been to harass. All he asked was that eventually there be a war. Not just a small incidental skirmish in the race to carve up Africa, but one pip-pip, jolly-ho, up-goes-the-balloon Armageddon for Europe. Once Porpentine might have been puzzled that his opposite number should desire war so passionately. Now he took it for granted that at some point in these fifteen years of hare-and-hounds he himself had conceived the private mission of keeping off Armageddon. An alignment like this, he felt, could only have taken place in a Western World where spying was becoming less an individual than a group enterprise, where the events of 1848 and the activities of anarchists and radicals all over the Continent seemed to proclaim that history was being made no longer through the virtu of single princes but rather by man in the mass; by trends and tendencies and impersonal curves on a lattice of pale blue lines. So it was inevitably single combat between the veteran spy and *il semplice inglese.* They stood alone—God knew where —on deserted lists. Goodfellow knew of the private battle, as doubtless did Moldweorp's subordinates. They all took on the roles of solicitous seconds, attending to the strictly national interests while their chiefs circled and parried above them on some unreachable level. It happened that Porpentine worked nominally for England and Moldweorp for Germany, but this was accident: they would probably have chosen the same sides had their employments been reversed. For he and Moldweorp, Porpentine knew, were cut from the same pattern: comrade Machiavellians, still playing the games of Renaissance Italian politics in a world that had outgrown them. The self-assumed roles became only, then, assertions of a kind of pride, first of all in a profession which still remembered the freebooting agility of Lord Palmerston. Fortunately for Porpentine the Foreign Office had enough of the old spirit left to give him nearly a free hand. Although if they did suspect he'd have no way of knowing. Where his personal mission coincided with diplomatic policy, Porpentine would send back a report to London, and no one ever seemed to complain.

The key man now for Porpentine seemed to be Lord Cromer, the British Consul-General at Cairo, an extremely able diplomat and cautious enough to avoid any rash impulses: war, for example. Could Moldweorp have an assassination in the works? A trip to Cairo seemed in order. As innocent as possible; that went without saying.

The Austrian Consulate was across the street from the Hotel Khedival, the festivities there unexceptional. Goodfellow sat at the bottom of a wide flight of marble steps with a girl who could not have been more than eighteen and who, like the gown she wore, seemed awkwardly bouffant and provincial. The rain had shrunken Goodfellow's formal attire; his coat looked tight under the armpits and across the stomach; the blond hair had been disarranged by the desert wind, the face was flushed, uncomfortable. Watching him, Porpentine came aware of his own appearance: quaint, anomalous, his evening clothes purchased the same year General Gordon was done in by the Mahdi. Hopelessly passé at gatherings like this, he often played a game in which he was, say, Gordon returned from the dead and headless; that odd, at least, among a resplendent muster of stars, ribbons, and exotic Orders. That out of date, certainly: the Sirdar had retaken Khartum, the outrage was avenged, but people had forgotten. He'd seen the fabled hero of the China wars once, standing on the ramparts at Gravesend. At the time Porpentine had been ten or so and likely to be dazzled; he was. But something had happened between there and the Hotel Bristol. He had thought about Moldweorp that night and about the likelihood of some apocalypse; perhaps a little too on his own sense of estrangement. But not at all about Chinese

Gordon, lonely and enigmatic at the mouth of that boy-hood Thames; whose hair it was said had turned white in the space of a day as he waited for death in the besieged city of Khartum.

Porpentine looked about the Consulate, checking off diplomatic personnel: Sir Charles Cookson, Mr. Hewat, M. Girard, Hr. von Hartmann, Cav. Romano, Comte de Zogheb, &c., &c. Right ho. All present and accounted for. Except for the Russian Vice-Consul, M. de Villiers. And oddly enough one's host, Count Khevenhüller-Metsch. Could they be together?

He moved over to the steps where Goodfellow sat desperate, yarning about nonexistent adventures in South Africa. The girl regarded him breathless and smiling. Porpentine wondered if he should sing: It isn't the girl I saw you with in Brighton; who, who, who's your lady friend? He said:

"I say." Goodfellow, relieved and more enthusiastic than necessary, introduced them.

"Miss Victoria Wren."

Porpentine smiled, nodded, searched all over for a cigarette. "How do you do, Miss."

"She's been hearing about our show with Dr. Jame-son and the Boers," said Goodfellow.

"You were in the Transvaal together," the girl mar-veled. Porpentine thought: he can do whatever he wants with this one. Whatever he asks her.

"We've been together for some time, Miss." She bloomed, she billowed; Porpentine, shy, withdrew be-hind pale cheeks, pursed lips. As if her glow were a re-minder of any Yorkshire sunset, or at least some vestige of a vision of Home which neither he nor Goodfellow could afford—or when you came down to it, cared—to remember, they did share in her presence this common evasiveness.

A low growl sounded behind Porpentine. Goodfellow cringed, smiled weakly, introduced Sir Alastair Wren, Victoria's father. It became clear almost immediately that he was not fond of Goodfellow. With him was a robust, myopic girl of eleven; the sister. Mildred was in

Egypt, she soon informed Porpentine, to gather rock specimens, being daft for rocks in the same way Sir Alastair was for large and ancient pipe-organs. He had toured Germany the previous year, alienating the populations of various cathedral towns by recruiting small boys to toil away half-days at a clip keeping the bellows going: and then underpaying. Frightfully, added Victoria. There was, he continued, no decent pipe-organ anywhere on the African continent (which Porpentine could hardly doubt). Goodfellow mentioned an enthusiasm for the barrel-organ, and had Sir Alastair ever tried his hand at one. The peer growled ominously. Out of the corner of his eye Porpentine saw Count Khevenhüller-Metsch come out of an adjoining room, steering the Russian vice-consul by the arm and talking wistfully; M. de Villiers punctuated the conversation with mirthful little barks. Aha, Porpentine thought. Mildred had produced from her reticule a large rock, which she now held up to Porpentine for inspection. She had found it out near the site of the ancient Pharos, it contained trilobite fossils. Porpentine could not respond; it was his old weakness. A bar was set up on the mezzanine; he loped up the marble stairs after promising to bring punch (lemonade, of course, for Mildred).

Someone touched his arm as he waited at the bar. He turned and saw one of the two from Brindisi, who said: "Lovely girl." It was the first word he could remember any of them speaking to him directly in fifteen years. He only wondered, uneasy, if they reserved such artifice for times of singular crisis. He picked up the drinks, smiled all angelic; turned, started down the stairs. On the second step he tripped and fell: proceeded whirling and bouncing, followed by sounds of glass breaking and a spray of Chablis punch and lemonade, to the bottom. He'd learned in the army how to take falls. He looked up bashful at Sir Alastair Wren, who nodded in approval.

"Saw a fellow do that in a music-hall once," he said. "You're much better, Porpentine. Really."

"Do it again," Mildred said. Porpentine extracted a cigarette, lay there for a bit smoking. "How about late supper at the Fink," Goodfellow suggested. Porpentine got to his feet. "You remember the chaps we met in Brindisi." Goodfellow nodded, impassive, betraying no tics or tightenings; one of the things Porpentine admired him for. But: "Going home," Sir Alastair muttered, yanking fiercely at Mildred's hand. "Behave yourselves." So Porpentine found himself playing chaperon. He proposed another try for punch. When they got to the mezzanine Moldweorp's man had disappeared. Porpentine wedged one foot between the balusters and looked down, surveying rapidly the faces below. "No," he said. Goodfellow handed him a cup of punch.

"I can't wait to see the Nile," Victoria had been saying, "the pyramids, the Sphinx."

"Cairo," Goodfellow added.

"Yes," Porpentine agreed, "Cairo."

Directly across rue de Rosette was the Fink restaurant. They dashed across the street through the rain, Victoria's cloak ballooning about her; she laughed, delighted with the rain. The crowd inside was entirely European. Porpentine recognized a few faces from the Venice boat. After her first glass of white Vöslauer the girl began to talk. Blithe and so green, she pronounced her *o*'s with a sigh, as if fainting from love. She was Catholic; had been to a convent school near her home, a place called Lardwick-in-the-Fen. This was her first trip abroad. She talked a great deal about her religion: had, for a time, considered the son of God as a young lady will consider any eligible bachelor. But had realized eventually that of course he was not but maintained instead an immense harem clad in black, decked with rosaries. She would never stand for such competition, had therefore left the novitiate after a matter of weeks but not the Church: that, with its sad-faced statuary, its odor of candles and incense, formed along with an uncle Evelyn the twin foci of her serene orbit. The uncle, a wild or renegade sundowner, would arrive from Australia once a year bringing no gifts but prepared to weave as many yarns as the sisters could cope with. As far as Victoria remembered, he had never repeated himself.

So she was given enough material to evolve between visits a private and imaginary sphere of influence, which she played with and within constantly: developing, exploring, manipulating. Especially during Mass: for here was the stage, the dramatic field already prepared, serviceable to a seedtime fancy. And so it came about that God wore a wide-awake hat and fought skirmishes with an aboriginal Satan out at the antipodes of the firmament, in the name and for the safekeeping of any Victoria.

Now the desire to feel pity can be seductive; it was always so for Porpentine. At this point he could only flick a rapid glance at Goodfellow's face and think with the sort of admiration pity once foundered in makes detestable: a stroke of genius, the Jameson raid. He chose that, he knew. He always knows. So do I.

One had to. He'd realized long before that women had no monopoly on what is called intuition; that in most men the faculty was latent, only becoming developed or painfully heightened at all in professions like this. But men being positivists and women more dreamy, having hunches still remained at base a feminine talent; so that like it or not they all—Moldweorp, Goodfellow, the pair from Brindisi—had to be part woman. Perhaps even in this maintenance of a threshold for compassion one dared not go beneath was some sort of recognition.

But like a Yorkshire sunset, certain things could not be afforded. Porpentine had realized this as a fledgling. You do not feel pity for the men you have to kill or the people you have to hurt. You do not feel any more than a vague *esprit de corps* toward the agents you are working with. Above all, you do not fall in love. Not if you want to succeed in espionage. God knew what preadolescent agonies were responsible; but somehow Porpentine had remained true to that code. He had grown up possessing a sly mind and was too honest not to use it. He stole from streethawkers, could stack a deck at fifteen, would run away whenever fighting was useless. So that at some point, prowling any mews or alley in mid-century London, the supreme rightness of "the game for its own sake" must have occurred to him, and acted as an irresistible vector aimed toward 1900. Now he would say that any itinerary, with all its doublings-back, emergency stops, and hundred-kilometer feints remained transitory or accidental. Certainly it was convenient, necessary; but never gave an indication of the deeper truth that all of them operated in no conceivable Europe but rather in a zone forsaken by God, between the tropics of diplomacy, lines they were forbidden forever to cross. One had consequently to play that idealized colonial Englishman who, alone in the jungle, shaves every day, dresses for dinner every night, and is committed to St. George and no quarter as an article of love. Curious irony in that, of course. Porpentine grimaced to himself. Because both sides, his and Moldweorp's, had each in a different way done the unforgivable: had gone native. Somehow it had come about that one day neither man cared any longer which government he was working for. As if that prospect of a Final Clash were unable by men like them, through whatever frenzied twists and turns, to be evaded. Something had come to pass: who could guess what, or even when? In the Crimea, at Spicheren, at Khartum; it could make no difference. But so suddenly that there was a finite leap or omission in the maturing process—one fell asleep exhausted among immediacies: F.O. dispatches, Parliamentary resolutions; and awakened to find a tall specter grinning and gibbering over the foot of the bed, know that he was there to stay—hadn't they seen the apocalypse as an excuse for a glorious beano, a grand way to see the old century and their respective careers go out?

"You are so like him," the girl was saying, "my uncle Evelyn: tall, and fair, and oh! not really Lardwick-in-the-Fenish at all."

"Haw, haw," Goodfellow replied.

Hearing the languishment in that voice, Porpentine wondered idly if she were bud or bloom; or perhaps a petal blown off and having nothing to belong to any more. It was difficult to tell—getting more so every year —and he did not know if this were old age beginning to creep up on him at last or some flaw in the generation itself. His own had budded, bloomed, and, sensing some blight in the air, folded its petals up again like certain flowers at sunset. Would it be any use asking her?

"My God," Goodfellow said. They looked up to see an emaciated figure in evening clothes whose head seemed that of a nettled sparrow-hawk. The head guffawed, retaining its fierce expression. Victoria bubbled over in a laugh. "It's Hugh!" she cried, delighted.

"Indeed," echoed a voice inside. "Help me get it off, someone." Porpentine, obliging, stood on a chair to tug off the head.

"Hugh Bongo-Shaftsbury," said Goodfellow, ungracious.

"Harmakhis." Bongo-Shaftsbury indicated the hollow ceramic hawk-head. "God of Heliopolis and chief deity of Lower Egypt. Utterly genuine, this: a mask used in the ancient rituals." He seated himself next to Victoria. Goodfellow scowled. "Literally Horus on the horizon, also represented as a lion with the head of a man. Like the Sphinx."

"Oh," Victoria sighed, "the Sphinx." Enchanted, which did puzzle Porpentine: for this was a violation, was it not, so much rapture over the mongrel gods of Egypt? Her ideal should rightfully have been pure manhood or pure hawkhood; hardly the mixture.

They decided not to have liqueurs but to stay with the Vöslauer, which was off-vintage but only went for ten piastres.

"How far down the Nile do you intend to go?" asked Porpentine. "Mr. Goodfellow has mentioned your interest in Luxor."

"I feel it is fresh territory, sir," replied Bongo-Shaftsbury. "No first-rate work around the area since Grébaut discovered the tomb of the Theban priests back in 'ninety-one. Of course one should have a look round the pyramids at Gizeh, but that is pretty much old hat since Mr. Flinders Petrie's painstaking inspection of sixteen or seventeen years ago."

"I imagine," murmured Porpentine. He could have got the data, of course, from any Baedeker. At least there was a certain intensity or single-minded concern with matters archaeological which Porpentine was sure would drive Sir Alastair to frenzy before the Cook's tour was completed. Unless, like Porpentine and Goodfellow, Bongo-Shaftsbury intended to go no further than Cairo.

Porpentine hummed the aria from *Manon Lescaut* as Victoria poised prettily between the other two, attempting to keep equilibrium. The crowd in the restaurant had thinned out and across the street the Consulate was dark, save two or three lights in the upstairs rooms. Perhaps in a month all the windows would be blazing; perhaps the world would be blazing. Projected, the courses of Marchand and Kitchener would cross near Fashoda, in the district of Behr el-Abyad, some forty miles above the source of the White Nile. Lord Lansdowne, Secretary of State for War, had predicted 25 September as meeting-date in a secret dispatch to Cairo: a message both Porpentine and Moldweorp had seen. All at once a tic came dancing across Bongo-Shaftsbury's face; there was a time-lag of about five seconds before Porpentine—either intuitively or because of his suspicions about the archaeologist—reckoned who it was that stood behind his chair. Goodfellow nodded, sick and timid; said, civilly enough: "Lepsius, I say. Tired of the climate in Brindisi?" Lepsius. Porpentine hadn't even known the name. Goodfellow would have, of course. "Sudden business called me to Egypt," the agent hissed. Goodfellow sniffed at his wine. Soon: "Your traveling companion? I had rather hoped to see him again."

"Gone to Switzerland," Lepsius said. "The mountains, the clean winds. One can have enough, one day, of the sordidness of that South." They never lied. Who was his new partner?

"Unless you go far enough south," Goodfellow said. "I imagine far enough down the Nile one gets back to a kind of primitive cleanness."

Porpentine had been watching Bongo-Shaftsbury

closely, since the tic. The face, lean and ravaged like the body, remained expressionless now; but that initial lapse had set Porpentine on his guard.

"Doesn't the law of the wild beast prevail down there?" Lepsius said. "There are no property rights, only fighting; and the victor wins all. Glory, life, power and property, all."

"Perhaps," Goodfellow said. "But in Europe, you know, we are civilized. Fortunately. Jungle-law is inadmissible."

Soon Lepsius took his leave, expressing the hope they would meet again at Cairo. Goodfellow was certain they would. Bongo-Shaftsbury had continued to sit unmoving and unreadable.

"What a queer gentleman," Victoria said.

"Is it queer," Bongo-Shaftsbury said, deliberately reckless, "to favor the clean over the impure?"

So. Porpentine had wearied of self-congratulation ten years go. Goodfellow looked embarrassed. So: cleanness. After the deluge, the long famine, the earthquake. A desert-region's cleanness: bleached bones, tombs of dead cultures. Armageddon would sweep the house of Europe so. Did that make Porpentine champion only of cobwebs, rubbish, offscourings? He remembered a night-visit in Rome, years ago, to a contact who lived over a bordello near the Pantheon. Moldweorp himself had followed, taking station near a street-lamp to wait. In the middle of the interview Porpentine chanced to look out the window. A street-walker was propositioning Moldweorp. They could not hear the conversation, only see a slow and unkind fury recast his features to a wrath-mask; only watch him raise his cane and begin to slash methodically at the girl until she lay ragged at his feet. Porpentine was first to break out of that paralysis, open the door, and race down to the street. When he reached her Moldweorp was gone. His comfort was automatic, perhaps out of some abstract sense of duty, while she screamed into the tweed of his coat. "*Mi chiamava sozzura,*" she could say: he called me filth. Porpentine had tried to forget the incident. Not because it was ugly

but because it showed his terrible flaw so clear: reminding him it was not Moldweorp he hated so much as a
perverse idea of what is clean; not the girl he sympa-
thized with so much as her humanity. Fate, it occurred
to him then, chooses weird agents. Moldweorp somehow
could love and hate individually. The roles being, it
seemed, reversed, Porpentine found it necessary to believe if one appointed oneself savior of humanity that
perhaps one must love that humanity only in the abstract.
For any descent to the personal level can make a purpose less pure. Whereas a disgust at individual human
perversity might as easily avalanche into a rage for
apocalypse. He could never bring himself to hate the
Moldweorp crew, any more than they could avoid genuine anxiety over his welfare. Worse, Porpentine could
never make a try for any of them; would remain instead
an inept Cremonini singing Des Grieux, expressing certain passions by calculated musical covenant, would
never leave a stage where vehemences and tendresses
are merely forte and piano, where the Paris gate at Ami-
ens foreshortens mathematically and is illuminated by
the precise glow of calcium light. He remembered his
performance in the rain that afternoon: he like Victoria
needed the proper setting. Anything intensely European, it seemed, inspired him to heights of inanity.

It got late; only two or three tourists left scattered
about the room. Victoria showed no signs of fatigue,
Goodfellow and Bongo-Shaftsbury argued politics. A
waiter lounged two tables away, impatient. He had the
delicate build and high narrow skull of the Copt, and
Porpentine realized this had been the only non-Euro-
pean in the place, all along. Any such discord should
have been spotted immediately: Porpentine's slip. He
had no use for Egypt, had sensitive skin and avoided
its sun as if any tinge of it might make part of him the
East's own. He cared about regions not on the Continent only so far as they might affect its fortunes and no
further; the Fink restaurant could as well have been an
inferior Voisin's.

At length the party arose, paid, left. Victoria skipped

ahead across rue Cherif Pacha to the hotel. Behind them a closed carriage came rattling out of the drive beside the Austrian Consulate and dashed away hell-for-leather down rue de Rosette, into the wet night.

"Someone is in a hurry," Bongo-Shaftsbury noted.

"Indeed," said Goodfellow. To Porpentine: "At the Gare du Caire. The train leaves at eight." Porpentine gave them all good night and returned to his *pied-à-terre* in the Turkish quarter. Such choice of lodgings violated nothing; for he considered the Porte part of the Western World. He fell asleep reading an old and mutilated edition of *Antony and Cleopatra* and wondering if it were still possible to fall under the spell of Egypt: its tropic unreality, its curious gods.

At 7:40 he stood on the platform of the Gare, watching the porters from Cook's and Gaze's pile boxes and trunks. Across the double line of tracks was a small park, green with palms and acacias. Porpentine kept to the shadow of the station-house. Soon the others arrived. He noticed the tiniest flicker of communication pass between Bongo-Shaftsbury and Lepsius. The morning express pulled in, amid sudden commotion on the platform. Porpentine turned to see Lepsius in pursuit of an Arab, who had apparently stolen his valise. Goodfellow had already gone into action. Sprinting across the platform, blond mane flapping wild, he cornered the Arab in a doorway, took back the valise and surrendered his quarry to a fat policeman in a pith helmet. Lepsius watched him snake-eyed and silent as he handed back the valise.

Aboard the train they split up into two adjoining compartments, Victoria, her father, and Goodfellow sharing the one next the rear platform. Porpentine felt that Sir Alastair would have been less miserable in his company, but wanted to be sure of Bongo-Shaftsbury. The train pulled out at five past eight, heading into the sun. Porpentine leaned back and let Mildred ramble on about mineralogy. Bongo-Shaftsbury kept silent until the train had passed Sidi Gaber and swung toward the southeast.

He said: "Did you play with dolls, Mildred?" Porpentine gazed out the window. He felt something unpleasant was about to happen. He could see a procession of dark-colored camels with their drivers, moving slowly along the embankments of a canal. Far down the canal were the small white sails of barges.

"When I'm not out after rocks," said Mildred.

Bongo-Shaftsbury said: "I'll wager you do not have any dolls that walk, or speak, or are able to jump rope. Now do you."

Porpentine tried to concentrate on a group of Arabs who lazed about far down the embankment, evaporating part of the water in Lake Mareotis for salt. The train was going at top speed. He soon lost them in the distance.

"No," said Mildred, doubtful.

Bongo-Shaftsbury said: "But have you never seen dolls like that? Such lovely dolls, and clockwork inside. Dolls that do everything perfectly, because of the machinery. Not like real little boys and girls at all. Real children cry, and act sullen, and won't behave. These dolls are much nicer."

On the right now were fallow cotton-fields and mud huts. Occasionally one of the fellahin would be seen going down to the canal for water. Almost out of his field of vision Porpentine saw Bongo-Shaftsbury's hands, long and starved-nervous, lying still, one on each knee.

"They sound quite nice," said Mildred. Though she knew she was being talked down to her voice was unsteady. Possibly something in the archaeologist's face frightened her.

Bongo-Shaftsbury said: "Would you like to see one, Mildred?" It was going too far. For the man had been talking to Porpentine, the girl was being used. For what? Something was wrong.

"Have you one with you," she wondered, timid. Despite himself Porpentine moved his head away from the window to watch Bongo-Shaftsbury.

Who smiled: "Oh yes." And pushed back the sleeve of his coat to remove a cuff-link. He began to roll back the cuff of his shirt. Then thrust the naked underside of his forearm at the girl. Porpentine recoiled, thinking: Lord love a duck. Bongo-Shaftsbury is insane. Shiny and black against the unsunned flesh was a miniature electric switch, single-pole, double-throw, sewn into the skin. Thin silver wires ran from its terminals up the arm, disappearing under the sleeve.

The young often show a facile acceptance of the horrible. Mildred began to shake. "No," she said, "no: you are not one."

"But I am," protested Bongo-Shaftsbury, smiling, "Mildred. The wires run up into my brain. When the switch is closed like this I act the way I do now. When it is thrown the other—"

The girl shrank away. "Papa," she cried.

"Everything works by electricity," Bongo-Shaftsbury explained, soothing. "And it is simple, and clean."

"Stop it," Porpentine said.

Bongo-Shaftsbury whirled to him. "Why?" he whispered. "Why? For her? Touched by her fright, are you? Or is it for yourself?"

Porpentine retreated, bashful. "One doesn't frighten a child, sir."

"General principles. Damn you." He looked petulant, ready to cry.

There was noise out in the passageway. Goodfellow had been shouting in pain. Porpentine leaped up, shoving Bongo-Shaftsbury aside, and rushed out into the passageway. The door to the rear platform was open: in front of it Goodfellow and an Arab fought, tangled and clawing. Porpentine saw the flash of a pistol-barrel. He moved in cautiously, circling, choosing his point. When the Arab's throat was exposed sufficiently Porpentine kicked, catching him across the windpipe. He collapsed rattling. Goodfellow took the pistol. Pushed back his forelock, sides heaving. "Ta."

"Same one?" Porpentine said.

"No. The railroad police are conscientious. And it is possible, you know, to tell them apart. This is different."

"Cover him, then." To the Arab: "*Auz e. Ma ikhafsh minni.*" The Arab's head rolled toward Porpentine, he tried to grin but his eyes were sick. A blue mark was ap-

pearing on his throat. He could not talk. Sir Alastair and
Victoria had appeared, anxious.

"May have been a friend of the fellow I caught back
at the Gare," Goodfellow explained easily. Porpentine
helped the Arab to his feet. "*Ruh*. Go back. Don't let us
see you again." The Arab moved off.

"You're not going to let him go?" Sir Alastair rumbled.
Goodfellow was magnanimous. He gave a short speech
about charity and turning the other cheek which was
well received by Victoria but which seemed to nauseate
her father. The party resumed their places in the compartments, though Mildred had decided to stay with
Sir Alastair.

Half an hour later the train pulled into Damanhur.
Porpentine saw Lepsius get off two cars ahead and go
inside the station-house. Around them stretched the
green country of the Delta. Two minutes water the Arab
got off and cut across on a diagonal to the buffet entrance; met Lepsius coming out with a bottle of red wine.
He was rubbing the mark on his throat and apparently
wanted to speak to Lepsius. The agent glared and cuffed
him across the head. "No bakshish," he announced. Porpentine settled back, closed his eyes without looking at
Bongo-Shaftsbury. Without even saying aha. The train
began to move. So. What did they call clean, then? Not
observing The Rules, surely. If so they had reversed
course. They'd never played so foul before. Could it
mean that this meeting at Fashoda would be important:
might even be The One? He opened his eyes to watch
Bongo-Shaftsbury, engrossed in a book: Sidney J. Webb's
Industrial Democracy. Porpentine shrugged. Time was
his fellow professionals became adept through practice.
Learned ciphers by breaking them, customs officials by
evading them, some opponents by killing them. Now the
new ones read books: young lads, full of theory and (he'd
decided) a faith in nothing but the perfection of their
own internal machinery. He flinched, remembering the
knife-switch, fastened to Bongo-Shaftsbury's arm like a
malignant insect. Moldweorp must have been the oldest

spy active but in professional ethics he and Porpentine did belong to the same generation. Porpentine doubted if Moldweorp approved of the young man opposite.

Their silence continued for twenty-five miles. The express passed by farms which began to look more and more prosperous, fellahin who worked in the fields at a faster pace, small factories and heaps of ancient ruin and tall flowering tamarisks. The Nile was in flood: stretching away from them, a glittering network of irrigation canals and small basins caught the water, conducted it through wheat and barley fields which extended to the horizon. The train reached the Rosetta arm of the Nile; crossed high over it by a long, narrow iron bridge, entered the station at Kafr ez-Zaiyat, where it stopped. Bongo-Shaftsbury closed the book, arose and left the compartment. A few moments later Goodfellow entered, holding Mildred by the hand.

"He felt you might want to get some sleep," Goodfellow said. "I should have thought. I was preoccupied with Mildred's sister." Porpentine snorted, shut his eyes and fell asleep before the train started to move. He awoke half an hour out of Cairo. "All secure," Goodfellow said. The outlines of the pyramids were visible off to the west. Closer to the city gardens and villas began to appear. The train reached Cairo's Principal Station about noon.

Somehow, Goodfellow and Victoria managed to be in a phaeton and away before the rest of the party got on the platform. "Damme," Sir Alastair puzzled, "what are they doing, eloping?" Bongo-Shaftsbury looked properly outwitted. Porpentine, having slept, felt rather in a holiday mood. "*Arabiyeh*," he roared, gleeful. A dilapidated pinto-colored barouche came clattering up and Porpentine pointed after the phaeton: "A double paistre if you catch them." The driver grinned; Porpentine hustled everyone into the carriage. Sir Alastair protested, muttering about Mr. Conan Doyle. Bongo-Shaftsbury guffawed and away they galloped, around a sharp curve to the left, over the el-Lemun bridge and pell-mell down Sharia Bab el-Hadid. Mildred made faces at other tourists on foot or riding donkeys, Sir Alastair smiled tentatively. Ahead Porpentine could see Victoria in the phaeton tiny and graceful, holding Goodfellow's arm and leaning back to let the wind blow her hair.

The two carriages arrived at Shepheard's Hotel in a dead heat. All but Porpentine alighted and moved toward the hotel. "Check me in," he called to Goodfellow, "I must see a friend." The friend was a porter at the Hotel Victoria, four blocks south and west. While Porpentine sat in the kitchen discussing game birds with a mad chef he had known at Cannes, the porter crossed the street to the British Consulate, going in by the servants' entrance. He emerged after fifteen minutes and returned to the hotel. Soon an order for lunch was brought in to the kitchen. "*Crème*" had been misspelled to read "*chem.*"; "*Lyonnaise*" was spelled without an *e*. Both were underlined. Porpentine nodded, thanked everyone, and left. He caught a cab and rode up Sharia el-Maghrabi, through the luxurious park at the end; soon arrived at the Crédit Lyonnais. Nearby was a small pharmacy. He entered and asked about the prescription for laudanum he had brought in to be filled the day before. He was handed an envelope whose contents, once more in the cab, he checked. A raise of £50 for him and Goodfellow: good news. They would both be able to stay at Shepheard's.

Back at the hotel they set about decoding their instructions. F.O. knew nothing about an assassination plot. Of course not. No reason for one, if you were thinking only about the immediate question of who would control the Nile Valley. Porpentine wondered what had happened to diplomacy. He knew people who had worked under Palmerston, a shy, humorous old man for whom the business was a jolly game of blindman's-buff, where every day one reached out and touched, and was touched by, the Specter's cold hand.

"We're on our own, then," Goodfellow pointed out.

"Ah," Porpentine agreed. "Suppose we work it this way: set a thief to catch one. Make plans to do Cromer in ourselves. Go through the motions only, of course. That way whenever they get an opportunity, we can be right on the spot to prevent them."

"Stalk the Consul-General," Goodfellow grew enthusiastic, "like a bloody grouse. Why we haven't done that since—"

"Never mind," Porpentine said.

That night Porpentine commissioned a cab and roved about the city until early morning. The coded instructions had told them nothing more than to bide time: Goodfellow was taking care of that, having escorted Victoria to an Italian summer-theater performance at the Ezbekiyeh Garden. In the course of the night Porpentine visited a girl who lived in the Quartier Rosetti and was the mistress of a junior clerk in the British Consulate; a jewel merchant in the Muski who had lent financial support to the Mahdists and did not wish now that the movement was crushed to have his sympathies known; a minor Esthetic who had fled England on a narcotics charge to the land of no extradition and who was a distant cousin of the valet to Mr. Raphael Borg, the British Consul; and a pimp named Varkumian who claimed to know every assassin in Cairo. From this fine crew Porpentine returned to his room at three in the morning. But hesitated at the door, having heard movement behind it. Only one thing for it: at the end of the corridor was this window with a ledge outside. He grimaced. But then everyone knew that spies were continually crawling about window-ledges, high above the streets of exotic cities. Feeling an utter fool, Porpentine climbed out and got on the ledge. He looked down: there was a drop of about fifteen feet into some bushes. Yawning he made his way quickly but clumsily toward the corner of the building. The ledge became narrower at the corner. As he stood with each foot on a different side and the edge of the building bisecting him from eyebrows to abdomen he lost his balance and fell. On the way down it occurred to him to use an obscene word; he hit the shrubbery with a crash, rolled, and lay there tapping his fingers. After he had smoked half a cigarette he got to his feet

and noticed a tree next his own window, easily climb-
able. He ascended puffing and cursing; crawled out on
a limb, straddled it, and peered inside.

Goodfellow and the girl lay on Porpentine's bed, white
and exhausted-looking by street-light: her eyes, mouth,
and nipples were little dark bruises against the flesh. She
cradled Goodfellow's white head in a net or weaving of
fingers while he cried, streaking her breasts with tears.
"I'm sorry," he was saying, "the Transvaal, a wound.
They told me it was not serious." Porpentine, having no
idea how this sort of thing worked, fell back on alterna-
tives: (a) Goodfellow was being honorable, (b) was
truly impotent and had therefore lied to Porpentine
about a long list of conquests, (c) simply had no intention of getting involved with Victoria. Whichever it was,
Porpentine felt as always an alien. He swung down by
one arm from the limb, nonplused, until the stub of the
cigarette burned down to his fingers and made him swear
softly; and because he knew it was not really the burn
he cursed he began to worry. It was not only seeing
Goodfellow weak. He dropped into the bushes and lay
there thinking about his own threshold, sustained
proudly for twenty years of service. Though it had been
hammered at before, he suspected this was the first time
it had shown itself truly vulnerable. A pang of supersti-
tious terror caught him flat on his back in the bushes. It
seemed he knew, for a space of seconds, that this indeed
was The One. Apocalypse would surely begin at Fashoda
if for no other reason than that he felt his own so at hand.
But soon: gradually, with each lungful of a fresh cigarette's smoke, the old control seeped back to him; and he
got at last to his feet, still shaky, walked around to the
hotel entrance and up to his room. This time he pretended to've lost his key, making bewildered noises to
cover the girl as she gathered her clothing and fled
through connecting doors to her own room. All he felt by
the time Goodfellow opened was embarrassment, and
that he had lived with for a long time.

The theater had presented *Manon Lescaut*. In the
shower next morning Goodfellow attempted to sing

"Donna non vidi mai." "Stop," said Porpentine. "Would you like to hear how it should be done?" Goodfellow howled. "I doubt you could sing Ta-ra-ra-boom-di-ay without mucking it up."

But Porpentine could not resist. He thought it a harmless compromise. *"A dirle io t'amo,"* he caroled, *"a nuova vita l'alma mia si desta."* It was appalling; one got the impression he had once worked in a music-hall. He was no Des Grieux. Des Grieux knows, soon as he sees that young lady just off the diligence from Arras, what will happen. He does not make false starts or feints, this chevalier, has nothing to decode, no double game to play. Porpentine envied him. As he dressed he whistled the aria. Last night's moment of weakness bloomed again behind his eyes. He thought: if I step below the threshold, you know, I shall never get back again.

At two that afternoon the Consul-General emerged from the front door of the Consulate and entered a carriage. Porpentine watched from a deserted room on the third floor of the Hotel Victoria. Lord Cromer was a perfect target but this vantage at least was unavailable to any hired assassin-in-opposition as long as Porpentine's friends kept on the alert. The archaeologist had taken Victoria and Mildred to tour the bazaars and the Tombs of the Khalifs. Goodfellow was sitting in a closed landau directly under the window. Unobtrusive (as Porpentine watched) he started off behind the carriage, keeping at a safe distance. Porpentine left the hotel, strolled up Sharia el-Maghrabi. At the next corner he noticed a church off to his right; heard loud organ music. On a sudden whim he entered the church. Sure enough, it was Sir Alastair, booming away. It took the unmusical Porpentine some five minutes to come aware of the devastation Sir Alastair was wreaking on the keys and pedals. Music laced the interior of the tiny, Gothic house with certain intricate veinings, weird petal-shapes. But it was violent and somehow Southern foliage. Head and fingers uncontrollable for a neglect of his daughter's or any purity, for the music's own shape, for Bach—was it Bach?—himself? Foreign and a touch shabby, uncomprehending, how could

Porpentine say. But was yet unable to pull away until the music stopped abruptly, leaving the church's cavity to reverberate. Only then did he withdraw unseen out into the sun, adjusting his neck-cloth as if it were all the difference between wholeness and disintegration.

Lord Cromer was doing nothing to protect himself, Goodfellow reported that night. Porpentine, having re-checked with the valet's cousin, knew the word had gone through. He shrugged, calling the Consul-General a nit-wit: tomorrow was 25 September. He left the hotel at eleven and went by carriage to a *Brauhaus* a few blocks north of the Ezbekiyeh Garden. He sat alone at a small table against the wall, listening to maudlin accordion music which must surely have been old as Bach; closed his eyes, letting a cigarette droop from his lips. A waitress brought Munich beer.

"Mr. Porpentine." He looked up. "I followed you." He nodded, smiled; Victoria sat down. "Papa would die if he ever found out," gazing at him defiant. The accordion stopped. The waitress left two Krugers.

He pursed his lips, ruthful in that quiet. So she'd sought out and found the woman in him; the very first civilian to do so. He did not go through any routine of asking how she knew. She could not have seen him through the window. He said:

"He was sitting in the German church this afternoon, playing Bach as if it were all he had left. So that he may have guessed."

She hung her head, a mustache of foam on her upper lip. From across the canal came the faint whistle of the express for Alexandria. "You love Goodfellow," he haz-arded. Never had he been down so far: he was a tourist here. Could have used, at the moment, any Baedeker of the heart. Almost drowned in a fresh wailing of the ac-cordion her whisper came: yes. Then had Goodfellow told her. . . . He raised his eyebrows, she shook her head no. Amazing, the knowing of one another, these wordless flickerings. "Whatever I may think I have guessed," she said. "Of course you can't trust me, but I have to say it. It's true." How far down could one go, before . . . Desperate, Porpentine: "What do you want me to do, then." She, twisting ringlets round her fingers, would not look at him. Soon: "Nothing. Only understand." If Porpentine had believed in the devil he would have said: you have been sent. Go back and tell him, them, it is no use. The accordionist spotted Porpentine and the girl, recognized them as English. "Had the devil any son," he sang mischievous in German, "it was surely Palmerston." A few Germans laughed, Porpentine winced: the song was fifty years old at least. But a few still remembered.

Varkumian came weaving his way among tables, late. Victoria saw him and excused herself. Varkumian's report was brief: no action. Porpentine sighed. It left only one thing to do. Throw a scare into the Consulate, put them on their guard.

So next day they began "stalking" Cromer in earnest. Porpentine woke up in a foul mood. He donned a red beard and a pearl-gray morning hat and visited the Consulate, posing as an Irish tourist. The staff weren't having any: he got ejected forcibly. Goodfellow had a better idea: "Lob a bomb," he cried. Happily his knowledge of munitions was faulty as his aim. The bomb, instead of falling safely on the lawn, soared in through a window of the Consulate, sending one of the proverbial charwomen into hysterics (though it proved of course to be a dud) and nearly getting Goodfellow arrested.

At noon Porpentine visited the kitchen of the Hotel Victoria to find the place in a turmoil. The meeting at Fashoda had taken place. The Situation had turned to a Crisis. Upset, he dashed out into the street, commandeered a carriage, and tore off in search of Goodfellow. He found him two hours later sleeping in his hotel room where Porpentine had left him. In a rage he emptied a pitcher of ice-water over Goodfellow's head. Bongo-Shaftsbury appeared in the doorway grinning. Porpentine hurled the empty pitcher at him as he vanished down the corridor. "Where's the Consul-General?" Goodfellow inquired, amiable and sleepy. "Get dressed," bellowed Porpentine.

They found the clerk's mistress lying lazy in a patch of sunlight, peeling a mandarin orange. She told them Cromer was planning to attend the opera at eight. Up to then, she could not say. They went to the shop of the chemist, who had nothing for them. Barreling through the Garden Porpentine asked about the Wrens. They were at Heliopolis, as far as Goodfellow knew. "What the bloody hell is wrong with everyone?" Porpentine wanted to know. "Nobody knows anything." They could do nothing till eight; so sat in front of a cafe in the Garden and drank wine. Egypt's sun beat down, somehow threatening. There was no shade. The fear that had found him night before last now crawled along the flanks of Porpentine's jaw and up his temples. Even Goodfellow seemed nervous.

At a quarter to eight they strolled along the path to the theater, purchased tickets in the orchestra, and settled down to wait. Soon the Consul-General's party arrived and sat near them. Lepsius and Bongo-Shaftsbury drifted in from either side and stationed themselves in boxes; forming, with Lord Cromer as vertex, an angle of 120 degrees. "Bother," said Goodfellow. "We should have got some elevation." Four policemen came marching down the center aisle, glanced up at Bongo-Shaftsbury. He pointed to Porpentine. "My Gawd," Goodfellow moaned. Porpentine closed his eyes. He'd blown it, all right. This was what happened when one blundered right in. The policemen surrounded them, stood at attention. "All right," Porpentine said. He and Goodfellow arose and were escorted out of the theater. "We shall desire your passports," one of them said. Behind them on the breeze came the first sprightly chords of the opening scene. They marched down a narrow path, two police behind, two in front. Signals had, of course, been arranged years before. "I shall want to see the British Consul," Porpentine said and spun, drawing an old single-shot pistol. Goodfellow had the other two covered. The policeman who had asked for their passports glowered. "No one said they would be armed," another protested. Methodically, with four raps to the skull, the policemen

were neutralized and rolled into the underbrush. "A
fool trick," Goodfellow muttered: "we were lucky." Porpentine was already running back toward the theater.
They took the stairs two at a time and searched for an
empty box. "Here," Goodfellow said. They edged into
the box. It was almost directly across from Bongo-Shaftsbury's. That would put them next to Lepsius. "Keep
down," Porpentine said. They crouched, peering between small golden balusters. On stage Edmondo and
the students chaffed the Romantic, horny Des Grieux.
Bongo-Shaftsbury was checking the action of a small
pistol. "Stand by," Goodfellow whispered. The postilion
horn of the diligence was heard. The coach came rattling
and creaking into the inn courtyard. Bongo-Shaftsbury
raised his pistol. Porpentine said: "Lepsius. Next door."
Goodfellow withdrew. The diligence bounced to a halt.
Porpentine centered his sights on Bongo-Shaftsbury,
then let the muzzle drift down and to the right until it
pointed at Lord Cromer. It occurred to him that he could
end everything for himself right now, never have to
worry about Europe again. He had a sick moment of un-
certainty. Now how serious had anyone ever been? Was
aping Bongo-Shaftsbury's tactics any less real than oppos-
ing them? Like a bloody grouse, Goodfellow had said.
Manon was helped down from the coach. Des Grieux
gaped, was transfixed, read his destiny on her eyes. Someone was standing behind Porpentine. He glanced back,
quickly in that moment of hopeless love, and saw Moldweorp there looking decayed, incredibly old, face set in a
hideous though compassionate smile. Panicking, Porpentine turned and fired blindly, perhaps at Bongo-Shaftsbury, perhaps at Lord Cromer. He could not see and
would never be sure which one he had intended as target.
Bongo-Shaftsbury shoved the pistol inside his coat and
disappeared. A fight was on out in the corridor. Porpentine pushed the old man aside and ran out in time to see
Lepsius tear away from Goodfellow and flee toward the
stairs. "Please, dear fellow," Moldweorp gasped. "Don't
go after them. You are outnumbered." Porpentine had
reached the top step. "Three to two," he muttered.

"More than three. My chief and his, and staff person-nel . . ."

Which stopped Porpentine dead. "Your—"

"I have been under orders, you know." The old man sounded apologetic. Then, all in a nostalgic rush: "The Situation, don't you know, it is serious this time, we are all for it—"

Porpentine looked back, exasperated. "Go away," he yelled, "go away and die." And was certain only in a dim way that the interchange of words had now, at last, been decisive.

"The big chief himself," Goodfellow remarked as they ran down the stairs. "Things must be bad." A hundred yards ahead Bongo-Shaftsbury and Lepsius leaped into a carriage. Surprisingly nimble, Moldweorp had taken a short cut. He emerged from an exit to the left of Porpentine and Goodfellow and joined the others. "Let them go," Goodfellow said.

"Are you still taking orders from me?" Without wait-ing for an answer Porpentine found a phaeton, got in and swung around to pursue. Goodfellow grabbed on and hauled himself up. They galloped down Sharia Kamel Pasha, scattering donkeys, tourists, and drag-omans. In front of Shepheard's they nearly ran down Vic-toria, who had come out into the street. They lost ten seconds while Goodfellow helped her aboard. Porpen-tine could not protest. Again she had known. Something had passed out of his hands. He was only beginning to recognize, somewhere, a quite enormous betrayal.

It was no longer single combat. Had it ever been? Lep-sius, Bongo-Shaftsbury, all the others, had been more than merely tools or physical extensions of Moldweorp. They were all in it; all had a stake, acted as a unit. Un-der orders. Whose orders? Anything human? He doubted: like a bright hallucination against Cairo's night-sky he saw (it may have been only a line of cloud) a bell-shaped curve, remembered perhaps from some younger F.O. operative's mathematics text. Unlike Con-stantine on the verge of battle, he could not afford, this late, to be converted at any sign. Only curse himself, si-

lent, for wanting so to believe in a fight according to the
duello, even in this period of history. But they—no, it—
had not been playing those rules. Only satistical odds.
When had he stopped facing an adversary and taken on
a Force, a Quantity?

The bell curve is the curve for a normal or Gaussian
distribution. An invisible clapper hangs beneath it. Porpentine (though only half-suspecting) was being tolled
down.

The carriage ahead took a sharp left, moving toward
the canal. There it turned left again, and raced alongside the thin ribbon of water. The moon had risen, half
of it, fat and white. "They're going for the Nile Bridge,"
Goodfellow said. They passed the Khedive's palace and
clattered over the bridge. The river flowed dark and
viscous under them. On the other side they turned south
and sped through moonlight between the Nile and the
grounds of the viceregal palace. Ahead the quarry swung
right. "Damned if it isn't the road to the pyramids," Goodfellow said. Porpentine nodded: "About five and a half
miles." They made the turn and passed the prison and
the village of Gizeh, hit a curve, crossed the railroad
tracks and headed due west. "Oh," Victoria said quietly,
"we're going to see the Sphinx."

"In the moonlight," Goodfellow added, wry. "Leave
her alone," Porpentine said. They were silent for the rest
of the way, making little gain. Around them irrigation
ditches interlaced and sparkled. The two carriages passed
fellahin villages and water-wheels. No sound at all in
the night save wheels and hoofbeats. And the wind of
their passage. As they neared the edge of the desert Goodfellow said, "We're catching up." The road began to
slope upward. Protected from the desert by a wall five
feet high, it wound around to the left, ascending. Ahead
of them suddenly the other carriage lurched and crashed
into the wall. The occupants scrambled out and climbed
the rest of the way on foot. Porpentine continued on
around the curve, stopping about 100 yards from the
great pyramid of Kheops. Moldweorp, Lepsius, and
Bongo-Shaftsbury were nowhere in sight.

"Let's have a look about," Porpentine said. They rounded the corner of the pyramid. The Sphinx crouched 600 yards to the south. "Damn," Goodfellow said. Victoria pointed. "There," she cried: "going toward the Sphinx." They moved over the rough ground at a dead run. Moldweorp had apparently twisted his ankle. The other two were helping him. Porpentine drew his pistol. "You are for it, old man," he shouted. Bongo-Shaftsbury turned and fired. Goodfellow said: "What are we going to do with them anyway? Let them go." Porpentine did not answer. A moment or so later they brought the Moldweorp agents to bay against the right flank of the great Sphinx.

"Put it down," Bongo-Shaftsbury wheezed. "That is a single-shot, I have a revolver." Porpentine had not reloaded. He shrugged, grinned, tossed the pistol into the sand. Beside him Victoria looked up rapt at the lion, man, or god towering over them. Bongo-Shaftsbury pushed up his shirt-cuff, opened the switch and closed it the other way. A boyish gesture. Lepsius stood in the shadows, Moldweorp smiled. "Now," Bongo-Shaftsbury said. "Let them go," Porpentine said. Bongo-Shaftsbury nodded. "It is no concern of theirs," he agreed. "This is between you and the Chief, is it not?" Ho, ho, thought Porpentine: couldn't it have been? Like Des Grieux he must have his delusion even now; could never admit himself entirely a gull. Goodfellow took Victoria's hand and they moved away, back toward the carriage, the girl gazing back restless, eyes glowing at the Sphinx.

"You screamed at the Chief," Bongo-Shaftsbury announced. "You said: go away and die."

Porpentine put his hands behind his back. Of course. Had they been waiting for this, then? For fifteen years? He'd crossed some threshold without knowing. Mongrel now, no longer pure. He turned to watch Victoria move away, all tender and winsome for her Sphinx. Mongrel, he supposed, is only another way of saying human. After the final step you could not, nothing could be, clean. It was almost as if they'd tried for Goodfellow because he had stepped below the threshold that morning at the Gare du Caire. Now Porpentine had performed his own fatal act of love or charity by screaming at the Chief. And found out, shortly after, what he'd really screamed at. The two—act and betrayal—canceled out. Canceled to zero. Did they always? Oh God. He turned again to Moldweorp.

His Manon?

"You have been good enemies," he said at last. It sounded wrong to him. Perhaps if there had been more time, time to learn the new role . . .

It was all they needed. Goodfellow heard the shot, turned in time to see Porpentine fall to the sand. He cried out; watched the three turn and move away. Perhaps they would walk straight out into the Libyan desert and keep walking till they reached the shore of some sea. Soon he turned to the girl, shaking his head. He took her hand and they went to find the phaeton. Sixteen years later, of course, he was in Sarajevo, loitering among crowds assembled to greet the Archduke Francis Ferdinand. Rumors of an assassination, a possible spark to apocalypse. He must be there to prevent it if he could. His body had become stooped and much of his hair had fallen out. From time to time he squeezed the hand of his latest conquest, a blonde barmaid with a mustache who described him to her friends as a simple-minded Englishman, not much good in bed but liberal with his money.

Current Events

James Schuyler

A BEWILDERING scene met the eye of pedestrians in front
of the bus depot on the south-east corner of Main and
Cheektowaga on a recent Saturday morning April the
twenty-third. Dominating the orderly throng, gradually
assembled from about 7:30 A.M., was the retiring figure
of Miss Bellowes, home-room teacher and class-advisor
who kept well in the background due to conducting the
excursion along democratic lines with elected officers
chosen by secret ballot Tuesday last. Notable for their
absence were Priscilla Jones, Pauline Hutchy and Joseph Magoratoro, latest victims claimed by German mea-
sles.

Welcome back to class Priscilla and Pauline and a
quick recovery to Joe. Your absence was sincerely noted
and deeply felt by one and all.

While assigned seating was efficiently dispatched by
Richmond Crane, Class Treasurer in charge of alpha-
betical seating to avoid hard feelings with seat exchange
on the return for better views, your historian interviewed
Mr. Olson, our capable driver.

Mr. Olson, of Swedish descent on both sides, migrated
to this country at the early age of two where he grew up
attending Vocational High in this city. After gaining
experience around Army trucks during the Great War
in which he did not go overseas he subsequently became a driver for Inter-State Bus Lines not missing a
day's work since for which higher-ups singled him out for
an award. His specialty is driving charter buses including pilgrimages gotten up by civic groups for which he is

well acquainted with historic sights all over our land, such as Monticello, historic home of Thomas Jefferson. The scar some may have noted under the visor of Mr. Olson's cap dates from a fall through a greenhouse at the age of three and one half. Mr. Olson's father was in the greenhouse business at the time. He is since retired.

All present and accounted for except the above mentioned at 7:45 sharp Mr. Olson shut the pneumatic door and set his powerful bus in motion. It was off on another never to be forgotten excursion for the Eighth Grade Classmates of School Thirty-Six. Under the skilled leadership of Gloria Honig all joined in singing the National Anthem, the School Anthem and the Class Song, words by Gloria Honig, music by Percy Grainger.

At the intersection of Main and North Dakota Boulevard the group met with a mishap. To spare the feelings of present company your historian will skip details, familiar to all, and merely remark in passing that if you incline to car sickness it is the better part of wisdom to get out at the beginning and not suffer the whole live long day. As the bus rolled out into open country a vote of sympathy was taken for the hastily departed. The motion was made by Marilyn Skinker, seconded by Joel Price and unanimously passed.

No notable occurrences happened before reaching the State Capitol and the two hour and eighteen minute trip slipped by unheeded in conversations, group singing, games and bird watching by members of the Audubon Club.

First impressions of the capitol city of our state got interrupted when one of our number took a bad spill getting off the bus. No serious injury was sustained beyond having the wind knocked out of him and losing a button off his mackinaw. In a subsequent interview your reporter learned the button was about due to come off anyhow. This unforseen mishap brought to the attention of all the controversial subject of shoving. Officers of the Class Council report they intend giving the matter their close scrutiny and undivided attention.

Popular opinion among those who never saw the city

before was voiced by Marilyn Skinker inadvertently exclaiming, "It's so small!" and the fact a city of such im-
port is one-tenth the size of our home city and a good
deal less counting suburbs in the total metropolitan area
takes some getting used to. An anonymous bystander reports Miss Bellowes was overheard to aver that appearances are deceiving. It is true that all they have got to do
there is govern things and as Washington D. C. is not as
big as New York, Chicago or numerous other cities it is
probably big enough as it is.

First stop before taking in any sights was milk-break at
the Capitol Luncheonette. General comportment having
been discussed well in advance our class president, Morris Milkopper reports he is happy to state straw fights,
napkin raids and sugar snitching for souvenirs kept to a
mininum if at all. Some Indian wrestling between the
boys did not degenerate into rowdyness.

During a lull before setting out your historian gar-
nered on-the-spot opinions as to what it is like living in a
state capitol from Miss Bock, waitress at the Capitol Luncheonette. Miss Bock is in daily contact with legislators
of all classes and finds our leaders much the same as
other people except for the voice. The voice in general
she says is bigger and deeper. She says you cannot make
out the words as there is not any shouting but when they
are in all the booths talking it sets up a heavy hum. Sometimes the glassware rattles. Miss Bock definitely prefers
living where she is to moving some place else.

Owing to the informal occasion classmates and your
historian did not form into files after roll call outside the
Capitol Luncheonette. Instead, profiting by Miss Bellowes previous experience, all moved in a homogenous
mass across State Street, principal shopping street of the
city lined with shops, through Courthouse Square and
around the corner to Capitol Heights. All paused to marvel at the floral lay-out. It shows the state flag flanked by
the state arms in a design composed entirely of living
plants that later on will burst into a riot of bloom.

Then all turned to marvel at the Capitol itself an imposing edifice built entirely out of native materials mostly

red sandstone and composite. The cornerstone of the vast structure was laid in 1902 following the total destruction of the earlier historic capitol in a conflagration. The dome alone is one-third higher than the one on the National Capitol and made out of cast-iron. It is topped by an effigy. Plans to coat the dome with solid gold leaf fell though owing to the vast expense. Otherwise it would be the biggest gold dome in the world. As it is it dwarfs all surroundings.

After making the ascent of the fifty-two steps from the top of which new governors make their gubernatorial speeches more marvels met the startled gaze within. Mere words alone cannot summon up the unforgettable spectacle of Thaddeus Boroughman's masterpiece *Peace and Plenty* carved out of a single block of alabaster lit from within revolving slowly on its bronze base depicting scenes from the early history of the state in the awe-inspiring gloom under the vast dome. After a respectful silence Joel Price, who read up on it in advance, explained what the different figures mean and how as well as being the best you can do in sculpture it was also an engineering feat and triumph of science just getting it in place.

Around the hall in niches plaster casts of ancient statuary such as the Discus Thrower recalled Olympic days and invited comparison with the city our State Capitol is the most like, also built on hills.

As per previous arrangement, Mr. Carl Krause, one of the five official Capitol guides took over group leadership. Your historian will not attempt listing the sights he pointed out in the multitudinous halls since one and all will never forget them anyhow. The cases of tomahawks and ante-bellum firearms proved of greater interest to the boys while the Anne Chatfield room of relics such as clothing of the wife of the first governor found favor with the girls.

En route to the balcony overlooking the State Senate Chambers which was in session your historian elicited the following comments from Mr. Krause.

All five of the guides got their start in state civil service and do guiding for income supplement to their pensions. Mr. Krause is of the opinion pensions need looking into. He went on to say pensions could be bigger without the average taxpayer feeling it in his pocket book. Mr. Krause rates the State Capitol as the most imposing structure on the continent previous to Boulder Dam. He holds it superior to any known skyscraper since skyscrapers do not have domes. Mr. Krause and the other four guides are native born in that city of remote German descent as are most of the people there the original settlers being off-shoots of Lutheranism. Mr. Krause also holds there is more heavy eating than any other place he ever was. Dumplings are a feature of almost any meal in the typical home and Mr. Krause singlehanded eats a pound of farmer cheese for breakfast.

The balcony of the State Senate Chamber commands a fine view of what is going on. At time of arrival not much was. Each senator has his own leather chair and a desk for papers facing the rostrum decked with flags. The subject under discussion was what to do about some hot springs that turned up on a tract a public spirited farmer left the state for a beaver and duck preserve. This could be made into a park and general recreation area for people to visit and relax in except that might attract hunters, vandals and other thoughtless persons who would scare away the ducks and beavers from land rightfully theirs. On the other hand who is going to pay for watching it and looking out for the beavers' best interests and so on? Right now we are and while the expense is not incalculable these things add up the distinguished balding senator who had the floor pointed out. A side issue is a private enterprise that wants to benefit people by making the most out of the hot springs. It says beavers do not mind people watching them and furthermore what is now a total loss could become a source of revenue lightening the taxpayers' burden without hurting the wilderness any. Then a very old senator got the floor and started telling about the role of the beaver in building up our country from next to nothing. He was an orator of the old school and used his hands a lot. That is out of

date but when he stopped for breath you could hear a
pin drop. That is an advantage of old style oratory. You
can drown people out and really make them listen.

Sitting in on democracy in action was the high point
of the excursion for the civic minded class. Since the
issue wasn't such a burning one not so many senators
were in evidence. Some observers noted with surprise
how senators talked and got up and walked around while
one of their number was speaking. Being a senator is a
high pressure job and the remuneration is not as great as
in other lines of endeavor. People should think about
this at the polls. Perhaps if senators got a raise they could
concentrate more.

This enlightening visit was cut short by the lunch
hour. Many already felt yearnings in that direction and
began casting suspicious glances at Beverly Elder, official excursion time keeper. But the ever punctual Beverly gave the signal right on the dot of one when the historic carillons began their daily concert. At her signal
hungry excursionists happily adjourned to the Colonial
Inn casting a reluctant glance at the Senate Chamber
which many may never see again though who knows
what the future holds in store?

The Colonial Inn surpassed expectations. Completely
restored to its original state in 1933, it includes waitresses
in period costume and a fireplace big enough to roast an
ox in. Only native foods produced by the state are fea-
tured on the regional menu a copy of which was presented to each diner for a souvenir. Foods included
chicken, native grown vegetables, corn bread and cherry
cobbler. The latter was accompanied by the thick cream
produced by the cows for which the north of our state is
justly renowned.

In an off-the-record interview your historian gleaned
some interesting sidelights on what running such a far-
famed hostelry is like from Mr. Keal, permanent manager
in residence at the Colonial Inn. Mr. Keal gained wide
experience in the hotel field before taking on the Inn, his
most challenging position to date. For instance, at the
start uncompromising plans for serving only colonial

foods came up against present day food tastes and dietet-ics. People eat less nowadays, Mr. Keal cited, and con-sider gorging bad for health while way back then nobody thought of drinking the indispensable orange juice or even invented grapefruit. So they compromised by fea-turing state food with supplementaries. Radiators also presented a jarring note but that was solved in a number of ingenious ways. In his experienced opinion the Inn is much more than just a place to eat and sleep. It is living history, he stressed. All who visited it will concur.

Mounted photographs of the excursionists at lunch taken by Mrs. Parker, official Colonial Inn photog-rapher, are available at one dollar, suitable for framing. Interested parties please contact Richmond Crane.

Following the photographing a post-prandial tour around nearby streets filled in the time before bus de-parture. Classmates noted with surprise that first-run movies are a good three weeks behind our own and as-certained they only have two first-run movie houses. More unique was a sight of the governor's mansion well protected by its typical iron fence and gates. As the party filed by an older woman thought to be the first lady of the state got into a chauffeur driven limousine along with a man rumored to be governor's son, the distinguished at-torney.

Back at the Capitol Luncheonette which sees double duty as bus stop the group rejoined driver Olson and his bus at 2:45 P.M. sharp. Loading was conducted with dispatch and without incident when checking the roll just previous to departure the alarming discovery was made that two of our party were missing! Speculations were rife and energetic plans afoot for a search party when the two in question appeared out of a drugstore down the street. It developed half the couple finds cherry cobbler indigestible and the other gallantly squired her in a sundae. As democracy was the order of the day the incident passed without reprimand although the self-conscious pair did not escape jocular thrusts and some good natured ribbing.

The return trip was enlivened by a cloud burst.

Tired but happy the excursionists adjourned home a few assembling at Sweet's for discussion and opinion-comparing. The beaver and duck preserve issue received especially hot debate demonstrating the lively interest our generation takes in state, national and civic issues. Although not put to the vote opinion weighed heavily in favor of the wild life. Level heads felt a marked possibility of compromise since the question of how the animals feel about having a lot of people around is at present unresolved.

Your historian feels he voices the opinion of one and all in pronouncing the State Capitol excursion an unparalleled success. Considering the distance and quantity of people it is without precedent in class history it should have gone off almost 100% smoothly. The committee in charge rates a resounding vote of confidence but I see my time is up and so will not name them individually. On behalf of classmates I will simply say, thanks.

An announcement. Subject of next week's panel discussion following regular Current Events Club business is, could the stock market crash of 1920 have been averted, and if so, how? Open discussion will follow the debate and those wishing to take an informed part had better read up on it, so be prepared.

Novotny's Pain

Philip Roth

In the early months of the Korean War, a young man who had been studying to be a television cameraman in a night school just west of the Loop in Chicago was drafted into the Army and almost immediately fell ill. He awoke one morning with a pain on the right side of his body, directly above the buttock. When he rolled over, it was as though whatever bones came together inside him there were not meeting as they should. The pain, however, was not what had awakened him; his eyes always opened themselves five minutes before the appearance in the barracks of the Charge of Quarters. Though there was much of Army life that he had to grit his teeth to endure, he did not have to work at getting up on time; it simply happened to him. When it was necessary to grit his teeth, he gritted them and did what he was told. In that way, he was like a good many young men who suffered military life alongside him or had suffered it before him. His sense of shame was strong, as was his sense of necessity; the two made him dutiful.

Also, he was of foreign extraction, and though his hard-working family had not as yet grown fat off the fat of the land, it was nevertheless in their grain to feel indebted to this country. Perhaps if they had been a little fatter they would have felt less indebted. As it was, Novotny believed in fighting for freedom, but because what he himself wanted most from any government was that it should let him alone to live his life. His patriotism, then—his commitment to wearing this republic's uniform and carrying this republic's gun—was seriously qualified by his feeling of confinement and his feeling of loss, both of which were profound.

When the C.Q. got around to Novotny's bed that morning, he did not shine his flashlight into the soldier's eyes; he simply put a hand to his arm and said, "You better get yourself up, young trooper." Novotny was appreciative of this gentleness, and though, as he stepped from his bunk, the pain across his back was momentarily quite sharp, he met the day with his usual decision. Some mornings, making the decision required that he swallow hard and close his eyes, but he never failed to make it: *I am willing.* He did not know if any of those around him had equivalent decisions to make, because he did not ask. He did not mull much over motive. People were honest or dishonest, good or bad, himself included.

After dressing, he moved off with four others to the mess hall, where it was their turn to work for the day. It was still dark, and in the barracks the other recruits slept on. The previous day, the entire company had marched fifteen miserable miles with full packs, and then, when it was dark, they had dropped down on their stomachs and fired at pinpoints of light that flickered five hundred yards away and were supposed to be the gunfire of the enemy. Before they had climbed into trucks at midnight, they were ordered to attention and told in a high, whiny voice by their captain, a National Guardsman recently and unhappily called back to duty, that only one out of every fifty rounds they had fired had hit the targets. This news had had a strong effect upon the weary recruits, and the trucks had been silent all the way to the barracks, where it had been necessary for them to clean their rifles and scrape the mud from their boots before they flung themselves onto the springs of their bunks for a few hours' rest.

At the mess hall, the K.P.s were each served two large spoonfuls of Army eggs and a portion of potatoes. The potatoes had not been cooked long enough, and the taste they left on the palate was especially disheartening at such an early hour, with no light outdoors and a cold wind blowing. But Novotny did not complain. For one

thing, he was occupied with finding a comfortable position in which to sit and eat—he had the pain only when
he twisted the wrong way. Besides, the food was on his
tray to give him strength, not pleasure. Novotny did not
skip meals, no matter how ill-prepared they were, for he
did not want to lose weight and be unequal to the tasks
assigned him.

Before entering the Army, Novotny had worked for
several years as an apprentice printer with a company
that manufactured telephone books in Chicago. It had
turned out to be dull work, and because he considered
himself a bright and ambitious young man, he had looked
around for a night school where he might learn a job
with a future. He had settled on television, and for over
a year he had been attending classes two evenings a
week. He had a girl friend and a mother, to both of
whom he had a strong attachment; his girl friend he
loved, his mother he took care of. Novotny did not want
to cause any trouble. On the other hand, he did not want
to be killed. With his girl friend, he had been a man of
passion; he dreamed of her often. He was thrifty, and
had four hundred dollars in a savings account in the First
Continental Bank on LaSalle Street in Chicago. He
knew for a fact that he had been more adept at his work
than anyone else in his television course. He hated the
Army because nothing he did there was for himself.

The labors of the K.P.s began at dawn, and at midnight—light having come and gone—they were still at
it. The cooks had ordered the men around all day until
five in the afternoon, when the Negro mess sergeant
showed up. He hung his Eisenhower jacket on a hook,
rolled up the sleeves of his shirt, and said, "As there is a
regimental inspection tomorrow morning, we will now
get ourselves down to the fine points of housecleaning,
gentlemens." The K.P.s had then proceeded to scrub the
mess hall from floor to ceiling, inside and out.

A little after midnight, while Novotny was working
away at the inside of a potato bin with a stiff brush and a
bucket of hot, soapy water, the man working beside him
began to cry. He said the sergeant was never going to let

them go to sleep. The sergeant would be court-martialled for keeping them up like this. They would all get weak and sick. All Novotny knew of the fellow beside him was that his name was Reynolds and that he had been to college. Apparently, the mess sergeant only knew half that much, but that was enough; he came into the store-room and saw Reynolds weeping into the empty potato bins. "College boy," he said, "wait'll they get you over in Korea." The sergeant delivered his words standing over them, looking down, and for the moment Novotny stopped feeling sorry for himself.

When the scrubbing was finished, Novotny and Reyn-olds had to carry back the potatoes, which were in gar-bage cans, and dump them into the bins. Reynolds be-gan to explain to Novotny that he had a girl friend whom he was supposed to have called at ten-thirty. For some reason, Reynolds said, his not having been able to get to a phone had made him lose control. Novotny had, till then, been feeling superior to Reynolds. For all his re-senting of the stupidity that had made them scrub out bins one minute so as to dump dirty potatoes back into them the next, he had been feeling somewhat in league with the sergeant. Now Reynolds' words broke through to his own unhappiness, and he was about to say a kind word to his companion when the fellow suddenly started crying again. Reynolds threw his hand up to cover his wet cheeks and dropped his end of the can. Novotny's body stiffened; with a great effort he yanked up on the can so that it wouldn't come down on Reynolds' toes. Pain cut deep across the base of Novotny's spine.

Later, he limped back to the barracks. He got into bed and counted up the number of hours he had spent scrub-bing out what hadn't even needed to be scrubbed. At a dollar and a quarter an hour, he would have made over twenty dollars. Nineteen hours was as much night-school time as he had been able to squeeze into three weeks. He had known Rose Anne, his girl, for almost a year, but never had he spent nineteen consecutive hours in her company. Though once they had had twelve hours. . . . He had driven in his Hudson down to Champaign, where she was a freshman at the University of Illinois, and they had stayed together, in the motel room he had rented, from noon to midnight, not even going out for meals. He had driven her back to her dormitory, his shoe-laces untied and wearing no socks. Never in his life had he been so excited.

The following week, he had been drafted.

After completing his eight weeks of basic training, Novotny was given a week's leave. His first evening home, his mother prepared a large meal and then sat down opposite him at the table and watched him eat it. After dinner, he stood under the hot shower for twenty minutes, letting the water roll over him. In his bedroom, he carefully removed the pins from a new white-on-white shirt and laid it out on the bedspread, along with a pair of Argyles, a silver tie clasp, cufflinks, and his blue suit. He polished his shoes—not for the captain's pleasure, but for his own—and chose a tie. Then he dressed for his date as he had learned to dress for a date from an article he had read in a Sunday picture magazine, while in high school, that he kept taped to the inside of his closet door. He had always collected articles having to do with how to act at parties, or dances, or on the job; his mother had never had any reason not to be proud of Novotny's behavior. She kissed him when he left the house, told him how handsome he looked, and then tears moved over her eyes as she thanked him for the government checks—for always having been a good son.

Novotny went to a movie with Rose Anne, and afterward he drove to the forest preserve where they remained until 2 A.M. In bed, later, he cursed the Army. He awoke the following morning to find that the pain, which had not troubled him for some weeks, had returned. It came and went through the next day and the following night, when once again he saw Rose Anne. Two days later, he visited the family doctor, who said Novotny had strained a muscle, and gave him a diathermy treatment. On their last night together, Rose Anne said that if writing would help, she would write not just twice a day, as was her habit, but three times a day, even four. In the dark of the forest preserve, she told Novotny that she dreamed about his body; in the dark, he told her that he dreamed of hers.

He left her weeping into a Kleenex in her dim front hallway, and drove home in a mood darker than any he had ever known. He would be killed in Korea and never see Rose Anne again, or his mother. And how unfair— for he *had* been a good son. Following his father's death, he had worked every day after school, plus Wednesday nights and Saturdays. When he had been drafted, he had vowed he would do whatever they told him to do, no matter how much he might resent it. He had kept his mouth shut and become proficient at soldiering. The better he was at soldiering, the better chance he had of coming out alive and in one piece. But that night when he left Rose Anne, he felt he had no chance at all. He would leave some part of his body on the battlefield, or come home to Rose Anne in a box. Good as he had been —industrious, devoted, stern, sacrificing—he would never have the pleasure of being a husband, or a television cameraman, or a comfort to his mother in her old age.

Five days after his return to the post—where he was to receive eight weeks of advanced infantry training, preparatory to being shipped out—he went on sick call. He sat on a long bench in the barren waiting room, and while two sullen prisoners from the stockade mopped the floor around his feet, he had his temperature taken. There were thirteen men on sick call, and they all watched the floor being washed and held thermometers under their tongues. When Novotny got to see the medic, who sat outside the doctor's office, he told him that every time he twisted or turned or stepped down on his right foot, he felt a sharp pain just above the buttock on the right side of his body. Novotny was sent back to duty with three inches of tape across his back, and a packet of APC pills.

At mail call the following morning, Novotny received a letter from Rose Anne unlike any he had ever received

from her before. It was not only that her hand was larger
and less controlled than usual; it was what she said. She
had written down, for his very eyes to see, all those things
she dreamed about when she dreamed about his body. He
saw, suddenly, scenes of passion that he and she were
yet to enact, moments that would not merely repeat the
past but would be even deeper, even more thrilling. Oh
Rose Anne—how had he found her?

Novotny's company spent the afternoon charging
around with fixed bayonets—crawling, jumping up, racing ahead, through fences, over housetops, down into
trenches—screaming murderously all the while. At one
point, leaping from a high wall, Novotny almost took his
eye out with his own bayonet; he had been dreaming of
his beautiful future.

The next morning, he walked stiffly to sick call and
asked to see the doctor. When, in response to a question,
he said it was his back that hurt him, the medic who was
interviewing him replied sourly, "Everybody's back
hurts." The medic told Novotny to take off his shirt so
that he could lay on a few more inches of tape. Novotny
asked if he could please see the doctor for just a minute.
He was informed that the doctor was only seeing men
with temperatures of a hundred or more. Novotny had
no temperature, and he returned to his unit, as directed.

On the seventh weekend, with only one more week of
training left, Novotny was given a seventy-two-hour pass.
He caught a plane to Chicago and a bus to Champaign,
carrying with him only a small ditty bag and Rose Anne's
impassioned letter. Most of Friday, most of Saturday,
and all day Sunday, Rose Anne wept, until Novotny was
more miserable than he had ever imagined a man could
be. On Sunday night, she held him in her arms and he
proceeded to tell her at last of how he had been mis-
treated by the medic; till then he had not wanted to
cause her more grief than she already felt. She stroked
his hair while he told how he had not even been allowed
to see a doctor. Rose Anne wept and said the medic
should be shot. They had no right to send Novotny to
Korea if they wouldn't even look after his health here at

home. What would happen to him if his back started to act up in the middle of a battle? How could he take care of himself? She raised many questions—rational ones, irrational ones, but none that Novotny had not already considered himself.

Novotny travelled all night by train so as to be back at the base by reveille. He spent most of the next day firing a Browning automatic, and the following morning, when he was to go on K.P., he could not even lift himself from his bed, so cruel was the pain in his back.

In the hospital, the fellow opposite Novotny had been in a wheelchair for two years with osteomyelitis. Every few months, they shortened his legs; nevertheless, the disease continued its slow ascent. The man on Novotny's right had dropped a hand grenade in basic training and blown bits of both his feet off. Down at the end of Novotny's aisle lay a man who had had a crate full of ammunition tip off a truck onto him, and the rest of the men in the ward, many of whom were in the hospital to learn to use prosthetic devices, had been in Korea.

The day after Novotny was assigned to the ward, the man the crate had fallen on was wheeled away to be given a myelogram. He came back to the ward holding his head in his hands. As soon as Novotny was able to leave his bed, he made his way over to this fellow's bed, and because he had heard that the man's condition had been diagnosed as a back injury, he asked him how he was feeling. He got around to asking what a myelogram was, and why he had come back to the ward holding his head. The fellow was talkative enough, and told him that they had injected a white fluid directly into his spine and then X-rayed him as the fluid moved down along the vertebrae, so as to see if the spinal discs were damaged. He told Novotny that apparently it was the stuff injected into him that had given him the headache, but then he added that, lousy as he had felt, he considered himself pretty lucky. He had heard of cases, he said, where the needle had slipped. Novotny had himself heard of instances where doctors had left towels and sponges inside patients, so he could believe it. The man said that all the needle had to do was go off by a hair-breadth and it would wind up in the tangle of nerves leading into the spine. Two days later, two damaged discs were cut out of the man with the injured back, and three of his vertebrae were fused together. All through the following week he lay motionless in his bed.

One evening earlier, while Novotny was still restricted to bed, he had been visited by Reynolds. Reynolds had come around to say goodbye; the entire outfit was to be flown out the next day. Since Reynolds and Novotny hardly knew each other, they had been silent after Reynolds spoke of what was to happen to him and the others the following day. Then Reynolds had said that Novotny was lucky to have developed back trouble when he did; he wouldn't have minded a touch of it himself. Then he left.

When Novotny was out of bed and walking around, X-rays were taken of his back, and the doctors told him they showed no sign of injury or disease; there was a slight narrowing of the intervertebral space between what they referred to on the pictures as L-1 and L-2, but nothing to suggest damage to the disc—which was what Novotny had worked up courage to ask them about. The doctors took him into the examination room and bent him forward and backward. They ran a pin along his thigh and calf and asked if he felt any sensation. They laid him down on a table and, while they slowly raised his leg, asked if he felt any pain. When his leg was almost at a ninety-degree angle with his body, Novotny thought that he did feel his pain—he did, most certainly, remember the pain, and remembered the misery of no one's taking it seriously but himself. Then he thought of all the men around him who hobbled on artificial limbs during the day and moaned in their beds at night, and he said nothing. Consequently, they sent him back to duty.

He was shunted into an infantry company that was in its seventh week of advanced training. Two days before the company was to be shipped out, he awoke in the morning to discover that the pain had returned. He was able to limp to sick call, where he found on duty the unsympathetic medic, who, almost immediately upon seeing Novotny, began to unwind a roll of three-inch tape. Novotny raised an objection, and an argument ensued, which was settled when the doctor emerged from behind his door. He ordered Novotny into his office and had him strip. He told him to bend forward and touch his toes. Novotny tried, but could come only to within a few inches of them. The doctor looked over Novotny's medical record and then asked if he expected the Army to stand on its head because one soldier couldn't touch his toes. He asked him what he expected the Army to do for him. The doctor said there were plenty of G.I.s with sore backs in Korea. And with worse. Plenty worse.

Though the pain diminished somewhat during the day, it returned the next morning with increased severity. Novotny could by this time visualize his own insides—he saw the bone as white, and the spot where the pain was located as black. At breakfast, he changed his mind three times over, then went off to the first sergeant to ask permission to go on sick call. He had decided finally that if he did not go and have the condition taken care of within the next few days it would simply get worse and worse; surely there would be no time for medical attention, no proper facilities, while they were in transit to Korea. And, once in Korea, those in charge would surely be even more deaf to his complaints than they were here; there they would be deafened by the roar of cannons. The first sergeant asked Novotny what the matter was this time, and he answered that his back hurt. The first sergeant said what the medic had said the first day: "Everybody's back hurts." But he let him go.

At sick call, the doctor sat Novotny down and asked him what *he* thought was wrong with him. What the suffering soldier had begun to think was that perhaps he had cancer or leukemia. It was really in an effort to minimize his complaint that he said that maybe he had a slipped disc. The doctor said that if Novotny had slipped a disc he wouldn't even be able to walk around. Novotny suddenly found it difficult to breathe. What had he done in life to deserve this? What had he done, from the day he had grown out of short pants, but everything that was asked of him? He told the doctor that all he knew was that he had a pain. He tried to explain that taping it up didn't seem to work; the pain wasn't on the surface but deep inside his back. The doctor said it was deep inside his head. When the doctor told him to go back to duty like a man, Novotny refused.

Novotny was taken to the hospital, and to the office of the colonel in charge of orthopedics. He was a bald man with weighty circles under his eyes and a very erect carriage, who looked to have lived through a good deal. The colonel asked Novotny to sit down and tell him about the pain. Novotny, responding to a long-suffering quality in the man that seemed to him to demand respect, told him the truth: he had rolled over one morning during his basic training, and there it had been, deep and sharp. The colonel asked Novotny if he could think of anything at all that might have caused the pain. Novotny recounted what had happened on K.P. with Reynolds. The doctor asked if that had occurred before the morning he had awakened with the pain, or after it. Novotny admitted that it was after. But surely, he added, that must have aggravated the pain. The doctor said that that did not clear up the problem of where the pain had come from in the first place. He reminded Novotny that the X-rays showed nothing. He ordered Novotny to take off his hospital blues and stretch out on the examination table. By this time, of course, Novotny knew all the tests by heart; once, in fact, he anticipated what he was about to be asked to do, and the colonel gave him a strange look.

When the doctor was finished, he told Novotny that he had a lumbosacral strain with some accompanying muscle spasm. Nothing more. It was what they used to call a touch of lumbago. Novotny stood up to leave, and the colonel informed him that when he was released from the hospital he would have to appear at a summary court-martial for having refused to obey the doctor's order to return to duty. Novotny felt weak enough to faint. He was suddenly sorry he had ever opened his mouth. He was ashamed. He heard himself explaining to the colonel that he had refused to obey only because he had felt too sick to go back to duty. The colonel said it was for a trained doctor to decide how sick or well Novotny was. But, answered Novotny—hearing the gates to the stockade slamming shut behind him, imagining prison scenes so nasty even he couldn't endure them—but the doctor had made a mistake. As the colonel said, he *did* have a lumbosacral strain, and muscle spasm, too. In a steely voice, the colonel told him that there were men in Korea who had much worse. That was the statement to which Novotny had no answer; it was the statement that everyone finally made to him.

When they put him in traction, he had further premonitions of his court-martial and his subsequent internment in the stockade. He, Novotny, who had never broken a law in his life. What was happening? Each morning, he awoke at the foot of the bed, pulled there by the weights tied to his ankles and hanging to the floor. His limbs and joints ached day in and day out from being stretched. More than once, he had the illusion of being tortured for a crime he had not committed, although he knew that the traction was therapeutic. At the end of a week, the weights were removed and he was sent to the physical-therapy clinic, where he received heat treatments and was given a series of exercises to perform. Some days, the pain lessened almost to the point of disappearing. Other days, it was as severe as it had ever been. Then he believed that they would have to cut him open, and it would be the doctor at sick call who would be court-martialled instead of himself. When the pain was at its worst, he felt vindicated; but then, too, when it was at its worst he was most miserable.

He was only alone when he was in the bathroom, and it was there that he would try to bend over and touch his toes. He repeated and repeated this, as though it were a key to something. One day, thinking himself alone, he had begun to strain toward his toes when he was turned around by the voice of the osteomyelitis victim, who was sitting in the doorway in his wheelchair. "How's your backache, buddy?" he said, and wheeled sharply away. Everybody in the ward somehow knew bits of Novotny's history; nobody, nobody knew the whole story.

Nobody he didn't know liked him; and he stopped liking those he did know. His mother appeared at the hospital two weeks after his admittance. She treated him like a hero, leaving with him a shoebox full of baked goods and a Polish sausage. He could not bring himself to tell her about his court-martial; he could not disappoint her—and that made him angry. He was even glad to see her go, lonely as he was. Then, the following weekend, Rose Anne arrived. Everybody whistled when she walked down the ward. And he was furious at her—but for what? For being so desirable? So perfect? They argued, and Rose Anne went back to Champaign, bewildered. That night, the Negro fellow next to Novotny, who had lost his right leg in the battle of Seoul, leaned over the side of his bed and said to him, with a note in his voice more dreamy than malicious, "Hey, man, you got it made."

The next day, very early, Novotny went to the hospital library and searched the shelves until he found a medical encyclopedia. He looked up "slipped disc." Just as he had suspected, many of his own symptoms were recorded there. His heart beat wildly as he read of the difficulties of diagnosing a slipped disc, even with X-rays. Ah yes, only the myelogram was certain. He read on and on, over and over, symptoms, treatments, and drugs. One symptom he read of was a tingling sensation that ran down the back of the leg and into the foot, caused by pressure of the herniated disc on a nerve. The following morning, he awoke with a tingling sensation that ran down the back of his right leg and into his foot. Only momentarily was he elated; then it hurt.

On his weekly ward rounds, the colonel, followed by

the nurse and the resident, walked up to each bed and talked to the patient; everyone waited his turn silently as in formation. The colonel examined stumps, incisions, casts, prosthetic devices, and then asked each man how he felt. When he reached Novotny, he asked him to step out of bed and into the aisle, and there he had him reach down and touch his toes. Novotny tried, bending and bending. Someone in the ward called out, "Come on, Daddy, you can do it." Another voice called, "Push, Polack, *push*"—and then it seemed to him that all the patients in the ward were shouting and laughing, and the colonel was doing nothing to restrain them. "Ah, wait'll they get you in Korea"—and then suddenly the ward was silent, for Novotny was straightening up, his face a brilliant red. "I can't do it, sir," he said. "Does your back feel better?" the colonel asked. "Yes, sir." "Do you think we should send you back to duty?" "I've had a tingling sensation down the back of my right leg," Novotny said. "So?" the colonel asked. The ward was silent; Novotny decided not to answer.

In the afternoon, Novotny was called to the colonel's office. He walked there without too much difficulty— but then it was not unusual for the pain to come and go and come back again, with varying degrees of severity. Sometimes the cycle took hours, sometimes days, sometimes only minutes. It was enough to drive a man crazy.

In the colonel's office, Novotny was told that he was going to get another chance. Novotny was too young, the Colonel said, not to be extended a little forgiveness for his self-concern. If he went back to duty, the charges against him would be dismissed and there would be no court-martial. The colonel said that with a war on there was nothing to be gained by putting a good soldier behind bars. The colonel let Novotny know that he was impressed by his marksmanship record, which he had taken the trouble to look up in the company files.

When it was Novotny's turn to speak, he could only think to ask if the colonel believed the tingling sensation in his leg meant nothing at all. The colonel, making it

obvious that it was patience he was displaying, asked
Novotny what *he* thought it meant. Novotny said he understood it to be a symptom of a slipped disc. The
colonel asked him how he knew that, and Novotny—
hesitating only a moment, then going on with the truth,
on and on with it—said that he had read it in a book.
The colonel, his mouth turning down in disgust, asked
Novotny if he was that afraid of going to Korea.
Novotny did not know what to answer; he truly had not
thought of it that way before. The colonel then asked
him if he ever broke out in a cold sweat at night.
Novotny said no—the only new symptom he had was
the tingling in the leg. The colonel brought a fist down
on his desk and told Novotny that the following day he
was sending him over to see the psychiatrist. He could
sit out the rest of the war in the nuthouse.

What to do? Novotny did not know. It was not a cold
but a hot sweat that he was in all through dinner. In the
evening, he walked to the Coke machine in the hospital
basement, as lonely as he had ever been. A nurse passed
him in the hall and smiled. She thought he was sick. He
drank his Coke, but when he saw two wheelchairs headed
his way he turned and moved up the stairs to the hospital
library. He began to perspire again, and then he set
about looking through the shelves for a book on psychology. Since he knew as little about psychology as he
did about medicine, he had to look for a very long time.
He did not want to ask for the help of the librarian, even
though she was a civilian. At last he was able to pick out
two books, and he sat down on the floor between the
stacks, where nobody could see him.

Much of what he read he did not completely follow,
but once in a while he came upon an anecdote, and in
his frustration with the rest of the book, he would read
that feverishly. He read of a woman in a European
country who had imagined that she was pregnant. She
had swelled up, and then, after nine months, she had
had labor pains—but no baby. Because it had all been
in her imagination. *Her imagination had made her*

swell up! Novotny read this over several times. He was respectful of facts, and believed what he found in books. He did not believe that a man would take the time to sit down and write a book so as to tell other people lies.

When he walked back to the ward, his back seemed engulfed in flames. It was then that he became absorbed in the fantasy of reaching inside himself and cutting out of his body the offending circle of pain. He saw himself standing over his own naked back and twisting down on an instrument that resembled the little utensil that is sold in dime stores to remove the core of a grapefruit. In his bed, he could not find a position in which the pain could be forgotten or ignored. He got up and went to the phone booth, where he called long distance to Rose Anne. He could barely prevent himself from begging her to get on a plane and fly down to him that very night. And yet—the darkness, his fright, his fatigue were taking their toll—if it wasn't his back that was causing the pain, was it Rose Anne? Was he being punished for being so happy with her? Were they being punished for all that sex? Unlike his mother, he was not the kind of Catholic who believed in Hell; he was not the kind who was afraid of sex. All he wanted was his chance at life. That was all.

In the washroom, before he returned to bed, he tried to touch his toes. He forced himself down and down and down until his eyes were cloudy from pain and his fingers had moved to within an inch of the floor. But he could not keep his brain from working, and he did not know what to think. If a woman could imagine herself to be in labor, then for him, too, anything was possible. He leaned over the sink and looked into the mirror. With the aid of every truthful cell in his pained body, he admitted to his own face that he was—yes, he was—frightened of going to Korea. Terribly frightened. But wasn't everybody? He wondered if nothing could be wrong with him. He wondered if nothing he knew was so.

The next day, the psychiatrist asked Novotny if he felt nervous. He said he didn't. The psychiatrist asked if he had felt nervous before he had come into the Army.

Novotny said no, that he had been happy. He asked if Novotny was afraid of high places, and if he minded being in crowds; he asked if he had any brothers and sisters, and which he liked better, his mother or his father. Novotny answered that his father was dead. He asked which Novotny had liked better before his father died. Novotny did not really care to talk about this subject, particularly to someone he didn't even know, but he had decided to be as frank and truthful with the psychiatrist as it was still possible for him to be—at least, he meant to tell him what he *thought* was the truth. Novotny answered that his father had been lazy and incompetent, and the family was finally better off with him gone. The psychiatrist then asked Novotny about Rose Anne. Novotny was frank. He asked Novotny if his back hurt when he was being intimate with Rose Anne. Novotny answered that sometimes it did and sometimes it didn't. He asked Novotny if, when it did hurt, they ceased being intimate. Novotny dropped his head. It was with a searing sense that some secret had been uncovered, something he himself had not even known, that he admitted that they did not. He simply could not bring himself, however, to tell the psychiatrist what exactly they did do when Novotny's back was at its worst. He said quickly that he planned to marry Rose Anne—that he had always known he would marry her. The psychiatrist asked where the couple would live, and Novotny said with his mother. When he asked Novotny why, Novotny said because he had to take care of her, too.

The psychiatrist made Novotny stand up, close his eyes, and try to touch the tips of his index fingers together. While Novotny's eyes were closed, the psychiatrist leaned forward and, in a whisper, asked if Novotny was afraid of dying. The weight of all that he had been put through in the past weeks came down upon the shoulders of the young soldier. He broke down and admitted to a fear of death. He began to weep and to say that he didn't want to die. The psychiatrist asked him if he hated the Army, and he admitted that he did.

The psychiatrist's office was across the street from the main hospital, in the building the colonel had called the nuthouse. Novotny, full of shame, was led out of the building by an attendant with a large ring of keys hooked to his belt; he had to unlock three doors before Novotny got out to the street. He went out the rear door, just in sight of a volleyball game that was being played within a wire enclosure at the back of the building. To pull himself together before returning to the hostile cripples in the ward, Novotny watched the teams bat the ball back and forth over the net, and then he realized that they were patients who spent their days and nights inside the building from which he had just emerged. It occurred to him that the doctors were going to put him into the psychiatric hospital. Not because he was making believe he had a pain in his back—which, he had come to think, was really why they had been going to put him in the stockade—but precisely because he was *not* making believe. He was feeling a pain for which there was no cause. He had a terrible vision of Rose Anne having to come here to visit him. She was only a young girl, and he knew that it would frighten her so much to be led through three locked doors that he would lose her. He was about to begin to lose things.

He pulled himself straight up—he had been stooping —and clenched his teeth and told himself that in a certain number of seconds the pain would be gone for good. He counted to thirty, and then took a step. He came down upon his right foot with only half his weight, but the pain was still there, so sharp that it made his eyes water. The volleyball smashed against the fence through which he was peering, and, trying to walk as he remembered himself walking when he was a perfectly healthy young man, a man with nothing to fear—a man, he thought, who had not even begun to know of all the confusion growing up inside him—he walked away.

The colonel had Novotny called to his office the following day. The night before, Novotny had got little sleep, but by dawn he had reached a decision. Now, though he feared the worst, he marched to the colonel's

office with a plan of action held firmly in mind. When
Novotny entered, the colonel asked him to sit down, and
proceeded to tell him of his own experiences in the Second World War. He had flown with an airborne division
at a time when he was only a little more than Novotny's
age. He had jumped from a plane over Normandy and
broken both his legs, and then been shot in the chest by
a French farmer for a reason he still did not understand.
The colonel said that he had returned from Korea only
a week before Novotny had entered the hospital. He
wished that Novotny could see what the men there were
going through—he wished Novotny could be witness to
the bravery and the courage and the comradery, and, too,
to the misery and suffering. The misery of our soldiers
and of those poor Koreans! He was not angry with Novotny personally; he was only trying to tell him something
for his own good. Novotny was too young to make a decision that might disgrace him for the rest of his life. He
told the young soldier that if he walked around with
that back of his for a few weeks, if he just stopped *thinking* about it all the time, it would be as good as new.
That, in actual fact, it was almost as good as new right
now. He said that Novotny's trouble was that he was a
passive-aggressive.

Novotny's voice was very thin when he asked the
colonel what he meant. The colonel read to him what the
psychiatrist had written. It was mostly the answers that
Novotny had given to the psychiatrist's questions; some
of it had to do with the way Novotny had sat, and the
tone of his voice, and certain words he had apparently
used. In the end, the report said that Novotny was a passive-aggressive and recommended he be given an administrative separation from the Army, and the appropriate discharge. Novotny asked what that meant. The colonel replied that the appropriate discharge as far as he
was concerned was "plain and simple;" he took down
a book of regulations from a shelf behind him, and
after flipping past several pages read to Novotny in a loud
voice. "'An undesirable discharge is an administrative
separation from the service under conditions other than

honorable. It is issued for unfitness, misconduct, or security reasons.'" He looked up, got no response, and, fiery-eyed, read further. "'It is recognized that all enlisted personnel with behavior problems cannot be rehabilitated by proper leadership and/or psychiatric assistance. It is inevitable that a certain percentage of individuals entering the service subsequently will demonstrate defective moral habits, irresponsibility, inability to profit by experience—'" He paused to read the last phrase again, and then went on—"'untrustworthiness, lack of regard for the rights of others, and inability to put off pleasures and impulses of the moment.'" He engaged Novotny's eye. "'Often,'" he said, returning to the regulation, "'these individuals show poor performance despite intelligence, superficial charm, and a readiness to promise improvement. The effective leader is able to rehabilitate only the percentage of persons with behavior problems who are amenable to leadership.'" He stopped. "You can say that again," he mumbled, and pushed the book forward on his desk so that it faced Novotny. "Unfitness, soldier," he said, tapping his finger on the page. "It's what we use to get the crackpots out—bed-wetters, homos, petty thieves, malingerers, and so on." He waited for Novotny to take in the page's contents, and while he did, the colonel made it clear that such a discharge followed a man through life. Novotny, raising his head slightly, asked again what a passive-aggressive was. The colonel looked into his eyes and said, "Just another kind of coward."

What Novotny had decided in bed the night before was to request a myelogram. Of course, there lived still in his imagination the man who had said that all the needle had to do was be off by a hairbreadth; he was convinced, in fact, that something like that was just what would happen to him, given the way things had begun to go in his life. But though such a prospect frightened him, he did not see that he had any choice. The truth had to be known, one way or the other. But when the colonel finished and waited for him to speak, he remained silent.

"What do you have against the Army, Novotny?" the colonel asked. "What makes you so special?"

Novotny did not mention the myelogram. Why *should* he? Why should he have to take so much from people when he had an honest-to-God pain in his back? He was not imagining it, he was not making it up. He had practically ruptured himself when Reynolds had dropped the end of the can of potatoes. Maybe he had only awakened with a simple strain that first morning, but trying to keep the can from dropping on Reynolds' toes, he had done something serious to his back. That all the doctors were unable to give a satisfactory diagnosis did not make his pain any less real.

"You are a God-damned passive-aggressive, young man, what do you think of that?" the colonel said.

Novotny did not speak.

"You know how many people in America have low back pain?" the colonel demanded. "Something like fifteen per cent of the adult population of this country has low back pain—and what do you think they do, quit? Lay down on the job? What do you think a man does who has a family and responsibilities—stop supporting them? You know what your trouble is, my friend? You think life owes you something. You think something's coming to you. I spotted you right off, Novotny. You're going to get your way in this world. Everybody else can to to hell, just so long as you have your way. Imagine if all those men in Korea, if they all gave in to every little ache and pain. Imagine if that was what our troops had done at Valley Forge, or Okinawa. Then where would we all be? Haven't you ever heard of self-sacrifice? The average man, if you threatened him with this kind of discharge, would do just about anything he could to avoid it. But not you. Even if you have a pain, haven't you got the guts to go ahead and serve like everybody else? Well, answer me, yes or no?"

But Novotny would not answer. All he had done was answer people and tell them the truth, and what had it got him? What good was it, being good? What

good was it, especially if at bottom you were bad anyway? What good was it, acting strong, if at bottom you
were weak and couldn't *be* strong if you wanted to?
With the colonel glaring across at him, the only solace
Novotny had was to think that nobody knew any more
about him than he himself did. Whatever anybody chose
to call him didn't really mean a thing.

"Ah, get out of my sight," the colonel said. "People
like you make me sick. Go ahead, join the bed-wetters
and the queers. Get the hell out of here."

Within six days, the Army had rid itself of Novotny.
It took Novotny, however, a good deal more than six days
to rid himself of infirmity—if he can be said ever to have
rid himself of infirmity—or, at least, the threat of infirmity. During the next year, he missed days of work
and evenings of night school, and spent numerous weekends on a mattress supported by a bedboard, where he
rested and nursed away his pain. He went to one doctor
who prescribed a set of exercises, and another who prescribed a steel brace, which Novotny bought but found so
uncomfortable that he finally had to stick it away in the
attic, though it had cost forty-five dollars. Another doctor, who had been recommended to him, listened to his
story, then simply shrugged his shoulders; and still another told Novotny what the colonel had—that many
Americans had low back ailments, that they were frequently of unknown origin, and that he would have to
learn to live with it.

That, finally, was what he tried to do. Gradually, over
the years, the pain diminished in severity and frequency,
though even today he has an occasional bad week, and
gets a twinge if he bends the wrong way or picks up
something he shouldn't. He is married to Rose Anne and
is employed as a television cameraman by an educational channel in Chicago. His mother lives with him and
his wife in Park Forest. For the most part, he leads a
quiet, ordinary sort of life, though his attachment to Rose
Anne is still marked by an unusual passion. When the
other men in Park Forest go bowling on Friday nights,

Novotny stays home, for he tries not to put strains upon his body to which he has decided it is not equal. In a way, all the awfulness of those Army days has boiled down to that—no bowling. There are nights, of course, when Novotny awakens from a dead sleep to worry in the dark about the future. What will happen to him? What won't? But surely those are questions he shares with all men, sufferers of low back pain and non-sufferers alike. Nobody has ever yet asked to see his discharge papers, so about that the colonel was wrong.

Margins

Donald Barthelme

EDWARD was explaining to Carl about margins. "The *width* of the margin shows culture, aestheticism and a sense of values or the lack of them," he said. "A very wide left margin shows an impractical person of culture and refinement with a deep appreciation for the best in art and music. Whereas," Edward said, quoting his handwriting analysis book, "whereas, narrow left margins show the opposite. No left margin at all shows a practical nature, a wholesome economy and a general lack of good taste in the arts. A very wide *right* margin shows a person afraid to face reality, oversensitive to the future and generally a poor mixer."

"I don't believe in it," Carl said.

"Now," Edward continued, "with reference to your sign there, you have an *all-around wide margin* which shows a person of extremely delicate sensibilities with love of color and form, one who holds aloof from the multitude and lives in his own dream world of beauty and good taste."

"Are you sure you got that right?"

"I'm communicating with you," Edward said, "across a vast gulf of ignorance and darkness."

"*I* brought the darkness, is that the idea?" Carl asked.

"You brought the darkness, you black mother," Edward said. "Funky, man."

"Edward," Carl said, "for God's sake."

"Why did you write all that jazz on your sign, Carl? Why? It's not true, is it? Is it?"

"It's kind of true," Carl said. He looked down at his brown sandwich boards, which said: *I Was Put in Jail in Selby County Alabama for Five Years for Stealing A Dollar and A Half Which I Did Not Do. While I Was In Jail My Brother Was Killed & My Mother Ran Away When I Was Little. In Jail I Began Preaching & I Preach to People Wherever I Can Bearing the Witness of Eschatological Love. I Have Filled Out Papers for Jobs But Nobody Will Give Me a Job Because I Have Been In Jail & The Whole Scene Is Very Dreary, Pepsi Cola. I Need Your Offerings to Get Food. Patent Applied For & Deliver Us From Evil.* "It's true," Carl said, "with a kind of *merde*-y inner truth which shines forth as the objective correlative of what actually did happen, back home."

"Now, look at the way you made that 'm' and that 'n' there," Edward said. "The tops are pointed rather than rounded. That indicates aggressiveness and energy. The fact that they're also pointed rather than rounded at the bottom indicates a sarcastic, stubborn and irritable nature. See what I mean?"

"If you say so," Carl said.

"Your capitals are very small," Edward said, "indicating humility."

"My mother would be pleased," Carl said, "if she knew."

"On the other hand, the excessive size of the loops in your 'y' and your 'g' display exaggeration and egoism."

"That's always been one of my problems," Carl answered.

"What's your whole name?" Edward asked, leaning against a building. They were on Fourteenth Street, near Broadway.

"Carl Maria von Weber," Carl said.

"Are you a drug addict?"

"Edward," Carl said, "you *are* a swinger."

"Are you a Muslim?"

Carl felt his long hair. "Have you read *The Mystery of Being*, by Gabriel Marcel? I really liked that one. I thought that one was fine."

"No, c'mon Carl, answer the question," Edward insisted. "There's got to be frankness and honesty between the races. Are you one?"

"I think an accommodation can be reached and the government is doing all it can at the moment," Carl said. "I think there's something to be said on all sides of the question. This is not such a good place to hustle, you know that? I haven't got but two offerings all morning."

"People like people who look neat," Edward said. "You look kind of crummy, if you don't mind my saying so."

"You really think it's too long?" Carl asked, feeling his hair again.

"Do you think I'm a pretty color?" Edward asked. "Are you envious?"

"No," Carl said. "Not envious."

"See? Exaggeration and egoism. Just like I said."

"You're kind of boring, Edward. To tell the truth."

Edward thought about this for a moment. Then he said: "But I'm white."

"It's the color of choice," Carl said. "I'm tired of talking about color, though. Let's talk about values or something."

"Carl, I'm a fool," Edward said suddenly.

"Yes," Carl said.

"But I'm a *white* fool," Edward said. "That's what's so lovely about me."

"You *are* lovely, Edward," Carl said. "It's true. You have a nice look. Your aspect is good."

"Oh, hell," Edward said despondently. "You're very well-spoken," he said. "I noticed that."

"The reason for that is," Carl said, "I read. Did you read *The Cannibal* by John Hawkes? I thought that was a hell of a book."

"Get a haircut, Carl," Edward said. "Get a new suit. Maybe one of those new Italian suits with the tight coats. You could be upwardly mobile, you know, if you just put your back into it."

"Why are you worried, Edward? Why does my situation distress you? Why don't you just walk away and talk to somebody else?"

"You bother me," Edward confessed. "I keep trying to

penetrate your inner reality, to find out what it is. Isn't that curious?"

"John Hawkes also wrote *The Beetle Leg* and a couple of other books whose titles escape me at the moment," Carl said. "I think he's one of the best of our younger American writers."

"Carl," Edward said, "*what is* your inner reality? Blurt it out, baby."

"It's mine," Carl said quietly. He gazed down at his shoes, which resembled a pair of large dead brownish birds.

"Are you sure you didn't steal that dollar and a half mentioned on your sign?"

"Edward, I *told* you I didn't steal that dollar and a half." Carl stamped up and down in his sandwich boards. "It sure is *cold* here on Fourteenth Street."

"That's your imagination, Carl," Edward said. "This street isn't any colder than Fifth, or Lex. Your feeling that it's colder here probably just arises from your marginal status as a despised person in our society."

"Probably," Carl said. There was a look on his face. "You know I went to the government, and asked them to give me a job in the Marine Band, and they wouldn't do it?"

"Do you blow good, man? Where's your axe?"

"They wouldn't *give* me that cotton-pickin' job," Carl said. "What do you think of that?"

"This eschatological love," Edward said, "what kind of love is that?"

"That is later love," Carl said. "That's what I call it, anyhow. That's love on the other side of the Jordan. The term refers to a set of conditions which . . . It's kind of a story we black people tell to ourselves to make ourselves happy."

"Oh me," Edward said. "Ignorance and darkness."

"Edward," Carl said, "you don't *like* me."

"I do too like you, Carl," Edward said. "Where do you steal your books, mostly?"

"Mostly in drugstores," Carl said. "I find them good

because mostly they're long and narrow and the clerks tend to stay near the prescription counters at the back of the store, whereas the books are usually in those little revolving racks near the front of the store. It's normally pretty easy to slip a couple in your overcoat pocket, if you're wearing an overcoat."

"But . . ."

"Yes," Carl said, "I know what you're thinking. If I'll steal books I'll steal other things. But stealing books is metaphysically different from stealing like money. Villon has something pretty good to say on the subject I believe."

"Is that in 'If I Were King'?"

"Besides," Carl added, "haven't *you* ever stolen anything? At some point in your life?"

"My life," Edward said. "Why do you remind me of it?"

"Edward, you're not satisfied with your life! I thought white lives were *nice!*" Carl said, surprised. "I love that word 'nice.' It makes me so happy."

"Listen Carl," Edward said, "why don't you just concentrate on improving your handwriting."

"My character, you mean."

"No," Edward said, "don't bother improving your character. Just improve your handwriting. Make larger capitals. Make smaller loops in your 'y' and your 'g.' Watch your word-spacing so as not to display disorientation. Watch your margins."

"It's an idea. But isn't that kind of a superficial approach to the problem?"

"Be careful about the spaces between the lines," Edward went on. "Spacing of lines shows clearness of thought. Pay attention to your finals. There are twenty-two different kinds of finals and each one tells a lot about a person. I'll lend you the book. Good handwriting is the key to advancement, or if not *the* key, at least *a* key. You could be the first man of your race to be Vice-President."

"That's something to shoot for, all right."

"Would you like me to go get the book?"

"I don't think so," Carl said, "no thanks. It's not that

I don't have any faith in your solution. What I *would* like is to take a leak. Would you mind holding my sandwich boards for a minute?"

"Not at all," Edward said, and in a moment had slipped Carl's sandwich boards over his own slight shoulders. "Boy, they're kind of heavy, aren't they?"

"They cut you a bit," Carl said with a malicious smile. "I'll just go into this men's store here."

When Carl returned the two men slapped each other sharply in the face with the back of the hand, that beautiful part of the hand where the knuckles grow.

Judging Keller

Gilbert Rogin

KELLER writes in his notebook, "I am sitting on a dunce's stool at the kitchen counter, being defeated in war by my son, who keeps dropping the cards on the floor. If it is a game of luck, why do I always lose? My daughter is in her room. I can hear her playing a popular love song on the Hum-A-Zoo I bought her at the Feast of St. Anthony, a street fair. She is not playing for me but for Barbie and Ken and Barbie's best friend, Midge, the dolls that are advertised on television. My son tells me, with a wonder I have mislaid, that it is snowing out."

In fact, Keller is sitting beneath an awning in a launch. There are three launches drifting as one in the lagoon of the atoll; they are held together by hands on the gunwales. In the boat with Keller is a child who he believes is dying of meningitis. With her are her parents, her brothers and sisters, and a group of friends and relations. The two other launches are similarly loaded. Everyone is waiting for the flying boat that will take the girl to the hospital. In respect for the occasion, the natives are dressed as though they were going to church. The men are wearing shirts, and several have woollen sports jackets on, too, despite the heat; the women wear dresses printed with flowers they have never seen. Keller has gathered that someone must have radioed for the plane, as it normally comes only on Thursdays and Sundays and today, he is quite sure, is Saturday. Keller is not at all clear about what is going on; he does not speak either French or Polynesian. For instance, they still think he is a doctor.

Keller's incertitude began, in one sense, when he examined the hydrographic chart of the archipelago before arriving at the atoll three days ago. In another sense, indecision, bafflement, and unease had been Keller's company for some years. The chart was full of cautionary and foreboding notations. Stirred by these disquieting auguries, Keller made a list of them:

The geographic positions are approximate.
The north point lies 3 miles further west.
Reported to be 2 miles closer than charted.
Soundings in fathoms reduced to approximately Lowest Low Water.
The lights are reported to be unreliable.
Disappeared 1938.
Very strong currents.
Remarkable gap.
Dangerous.

He felt, besides, that if someone had sounded and surveyed *him* he would, no doubt, have published just such indeterminate and apprehensive findings. But then, weren't they always fumbling over him with a plumb line and transit? Why was he so frequently assailed and indicted by moralistic cabdrivers and unrepentant relief doormen, reproached by the sullen glances of subway change clerks? Not long ago, a cabdriver had told him, full of condescending sorrow, that he, Keller . . . Well, he had said, after Keller had criticized him for missing a light, "Mister, you're a mean man." Then he had explained that at sixty-seven he was twice Keller's age, that his reactions were no longer as quick as Keller's, and that he had, only the other day, buried his wife of forty-three years. Keller would never forgive him for the last, gratuitous blow. What right had that anonymous old man in a madras cap—no doubt he was wearing matching Bermuda shorts as well—to involve him in his anguish? He *buried* her! *That* was an achievement! Had he shovelled the clods in with his own hands? A final presumption.

Shortly after that judgment, Keller had been con-

fronted by Mr. Gallagher. Mr. Gallagher had owned a
laundry called Mrs. Gallagher's French Hand Laundry &
Dry Cleaning. From time to time, Mr. Gallagher would
post a sign in the window announcing that the laundry
was moving to a new and larger location, but the new
store was always darker, more cramped, and meaner than
the old one. Keller often found occasion, in one store or
another, to reprove Mr. Gallagher—buttons were
missing or broken, a shirt was torn or had phenomenally
shrunk. Mr. Gallagher would tell him, with wrath,
righteousness, and fatigue mixed in his rasping voice,
that the laundry business was not what it once was, that
help these days was indifferent and clumsy and demanded not only higher wages but hospitalization—and,
at last, that he, Mr. Gallagher, would make it up to him.
Mr. Gallagher would then punch the "No Sale" key
on his rickety cash register as though he were detonat-
ing a charge that would mercifully blow him to bits. The
cash drawer was generally empty, so Mr. Gallagher
would next grub in his pockets—he wore, like a scarecrow, ill-fitting and unlikely garments abandoned by
customers—until he came up with, besides the tatters
and rubble of ancient Kleenexes, a few soiled bills that
he would tediously smooth out. At least he didn't tell
Keller what had happened to Mrs. Gallagher.

Exhausted and unnerved by this ritual, Keller sur-
reptitiously switched to a Chinese laundry. One day, walking by Mr. Gallagher's latest store, he noticed that it
was empty and that there was a "For Rent" sign in the
window instead of the usual doomed prophecy. A few
weeks later, Keller came home on a Monday night and
found a new relief doorman sitting on a bench in
the lobby. He was wearing a uniform that was much too
small for him, and he had drawn his visored hat over his
eyes as though he were ashamed to admit his identity.
His feet, however, were thrust contemptuously forward,
revealing white cotton socks and extraordinarily pale,
venous legs expressive of age and hard times. The doorman was, of course, Mr. Gallagher. He did not get up or
greet Keller as Keller walked to the elevator, only stared

at him with disdain, anger, and ponderous suffering before turning away. Keller ascended, assailed by rage and guilt, hardly relieved by the thought that he would not have to face Mr. Gallagher until the following Sunday. No, this man hiding bitterly in the shadow of a borrowed hat had been pulled down so harshly by circumstance that he had been stripped even of "Mr." and of "Gallagher." Now he had only a first name—Keller wondered what it would turn out to be—like, say, a draft horse.

But their next encounter never came about; several days later, Keller was flying toward the South Pacific, encumbered, as he often was on planes—was it a factor of altitude?—with sentimental wellings and constrictions. He smelled strange soaps and toilet waters on his hands and tenderly inspected them. What had he been doing last night, stumbling up and down the withered hills among the eucalyptus that emitted the odor of urine, of fear and childhood, amorously holding a sleeping child in his arms? On his stopover in Los Angeles, he had taken out this little girl's mother. They had left the child at a neighbor's, and afterward he was carrying her in the dark to her bedroom, where a dusky cat sat on the sill; he remembered climbing the stairs, frightened that he would drop her—he was really very drunk and she had become terribly heavy—or that her lolling head would hit the banister. As he climbed, he thought, at the same time aware of his pretension, of Abraham burdened and tormented by Isaac. Was the soap, then, the child, the toilet water the mother? Their sweet, confiding traces consoled him. He wished he could be mapped at that benevolent moment. He would even lay back his skin and tissue and expose the soft machinery, each organ brightly and childishly colored like the different countries on a tin globe.

Keller writes in his notebook, "I am sitting against the wall in the smoking section of the Leroy Street pool, facing the sun. I would be no more dazed and acquiescent if a firing squad should march casually out of the men's locker room and, turning, confront me. I gather I have done something wrong—or not done something, an act of neglect that was just as much a fundamental crime or error—and eventually I am to be punished. I have been callous and lofty; self-righteous, too, I suppose. I cannot confess, either to commissions or omissions, for I am not sure what it is they expect of me. But I am so agitated when faced with only the *possibility* that I have offended that I simply accept my doom and give up. I know I exaggerate, but in this mood the water in the pool seems as viscid and murky as that in which hippopotamuses might lurk, where stones knocked together underwater would not be heard. One hippopotamus, two hippopatamus, three hippopatamus. Several kids are playing a game in front of me. They have dropped a book of matches—the cover advertises the Valley of the Estancia Ranchettes—on the concrete and are trying, without success, to spit on it. My left arm is about my son, my right arm is about my daughter. When they judge me with rifles, they will have to judge us all. But, for the moment, we are talking intimately, conspirators three, about our new apartment.

"My daughter says, 'My room is going to have either pink or lemon-yellow walls, depending on whether I get a pink-and-white or yellow-and-white canopy bed. The yellow has to be lemon yellow, but the pink can be just pink. I think I'd rather have it lemon yellow and with curtains that come all the way down to the floor. It's going to be my house on rainy days and my brother can't make it dirty. If I let him inside, he has to clean his feet first.'

"My son says, 'I'm getting awfully sick of the word "lemon yellow." '

"I want to say, 'Can I hide in there with you?'

"My son says, 'In *my* room I want a little modern desk and a little modern typewriter, one little toy cupboard—because I'm going to give most of my toys away to little kids—one medium-sized window and my light, my little light, my light.' "

Keller looks about him at the ring of dark, committed faces. Oppressed by their trust and reverence, he takes the child's wrist. Her pulse is faint and rapid. He lays his head upon her chest as though he were lowering a great, unwanted weight, and wishes he could reside, obscurely penitent, on that hard, hot, ribbed casket. The flutter of her heart intrudes and he looks at his watch. Her pulse must be two hundred. He sits up and futilely examines the empty sky. The others obediently follow his gaze. The girl cries out. What was it they called it in "Introduction to Neurological Medicine"? The hydrocephalic cry? Now the rest are watching him again. Simon says write in your notebook or you will lose your mind. Keller feels the intolerable burden of his upper lip upon his lower.

Keller did not like islands, but he was drawn passionately to them the way the salmon is tugged upstream. He had once met a penniless alcoholic who had drifted infallibly from San Francisco to Miami one summer, vaguely searching for an ex-wife. This man could not have told you the purpose of his pilgrimage; the ex-wife was the same sort of perhaps sentimental goal as a grave is, or a mountaintop. As it turned out, by the time he got to Miami his ex-wife was in Ohio, but he found instead, although he had spied it from afar and it had been his target all along, a half bottle of Marie-Brizard crème de menthe hidden behind a giant box of Tide in the cupboard beneath the kitchenette sink. He finished it, replaced the empty bottle in a flourish of guilt, and presumably returned, without solace, to San Francisco. Another time, in the same vein, Keller had crossed paths with an elderly Chinese. He had seen this solitary three times in as many months, pausing, in pensive regard, hands clasped behind him, bent slightly forward as though at a high window: in Geneva, before a bed of plants growing in the image of a swan; considering flounders and soles in an aquarium in Göteborg; in Rome, scrutinizing a statue of a hermaphrodite. Keller imagined that the Chinese was undertaking a vast and penitential journey. Behind him, in the distance, there was death in a hall bedroom, disorder in the kitchen garden.

The more remote and the smaller the island was, the more desperately Keller sought it out; once it was achieved, he settled into melancholy and desolation, tranced by the imposition of his austerities. He was an admirer of St. Simeon Stylites, who dwelt on higher and higher pillars. Many years ago, Keller had observed in a restaurant a large, grave, and somehow ecclesiastical trout that maintained itself by cursory strokes of its fins in the exact center of a fish tank. The tank was too small to permit the trout to advance or retreat more than an inch, or to turn around—and, of course its destiny was assured and imminent, and Keller envied it its equilibrium.

On this occasion, Keller was visiting the most populous of the islets that, configured like a jawbone, made up the atoll. In the afternoon, he would walk through the coconut palms to the bleak esplanade of the reef and moon about it in his tennis shoes, at times stooping to examine a sea urchin or a turbinate shell, at others gazing sententiously at the Pacific. He would often speculate about the intricate foundations upon which he was standing. He understood that the reef was a great mausoleum composed of the skeletons of innumerable animals, but he wondered whether the coral was still silently dying beneath his feet, whether he was, at this moment, precariously balanced and uplifted by rapid generations.

Death and its relics, though they were less monumental and ingenious than the coral reef, seemed to be impinging upon Keller in recent months. While packing for this trip, for instance, he had come across an artificial pink egret plume that had been hidden under some shirts that still bore the mark, or stigma, of Mrs. Gallagher's French Hand Laundry. The plume came from the scanty costume of a French dancer; it had fallen, too light and gaudy to be a presentiment, into Keller's lap during a lounge show in Las Vegas and he had saved it. He had later read that the dancer had asphyxiated both herself and her toy poodle—also dyed pink, the paper reported—in her efficiency unit in the Paradise Valley Apartments. The plume retained, years afterward, the not wholly agreeable odor of her makeup.

There were, too, Sylvia's letters, which he kept in a shoebox, along with old Christmas cards, on an all but unattainable shelf at the top of his hall closet. Sylvia had, over the years, glanced across Keller's life like a stone shied across water, but it was only when she sank —in reality, leaping from a hotel window in, of all places, Baltimore—that she became lodged in his consciousness. The last time he saw her, he was standing on a dim platform in Pennsylvania Station; they had just said goodbye. Looking through the window of the parlor car Miles Standish, he had watched her revolving gravely in her chair. He waved, but she was turning faster and faster, as though on a carrousel, and apparently did not notice him.

One day, Keller took the letters down and read them over, copying passages in his notebook that underscored his irreparable failure and default.

I have been thinking [she had written] that I'll take your abominable overcoat to the cleaners, so that you'll look more like the sterling young man you are when you get back. Would you please send me a valentine. Since fifth grade I have never gotten one except from Ginger [Sylvia's daughter] and she usually makes me make the one she sends me. Ginger says she would like to work in your office because she likes your sliding door, also the music in the elevator. Thus is youth moulded. (Brit. sp.) . . .

Last night sitting under an arctic moon and eating bean soup, I thought of you. Aren't you the lucky boy to inspire such, ah, er, I can't think of the right word, but something like a religious fervor springing from base carnality. I have managed to fake the morning away and, lo, it is time for lunch. But my mid-morning jelly doughnut lies heavy on my heart, so maybe I'll just walk. Today spring seems to have come to New York. I have an over-powering urge to buy a hyacinth. . . .

My social life has been proscribed by a variety of cir-cumstances that are nauseating to me. I can't do anything with Mitchell because he might try to break another coffee table with my head and/or he is violently on the make, a combination of danger and flattery that I'd rather watch on TV. Henry Lansdorf is not only a fink but ab-solutely rotten right down to the worm at the core of his being, besides being a pothead and a lush, among other things. I don't like him very much, either. I went to a party last night. A man who is probably an assistant buyer told really dirty, non-funny jokes. The walls were covered with burlap, which makes me sneeze, and I was introduced to a man who once painted a portrait of the Pope and owns all the postcard rights. Diana went to the opening of the new El Morocco. Some of the wait-ers are Pinkerton men, she thinks. I wish I had somebody to talk to. . . .

Yesterday I washed your telephone and vacuumed your lampshade. Agnes [Keller's maid] says you are out of Mr. Clean. The only mail was from your Daitch Shop-well. Kel, I miss you. . . .

Olivio, the man who feels his own paintings, called just now. "How's your aesthetic boy friend?" he asked. It made me visualize you, chiaroscuro on a beach. Send me a swatch of your skin so I can see how brown you are. I will send you a plastic giraffe filled with bubble bath that is in the window of the Commodore drugstore. I had a long look at myself in a triple mirror the other day and decided that if I don't do something I will soon look like M. Pneu. I think I am going to a track meet. What does one wear? I have never been to a track meet. . . .

Tell me a joke please, a funny one. . . .

There was another letter, the contents of which he could hardly recall, which he had not copied out pas-sages from, and which stirred him like the strong move-ments and sentiments of a forgotten dream. It was not a

letter in the strict sense, having never been sent. Sylvia
had typed it in Keller's apartment; she had gone there on
a winter afternoon to water his philodendron. He found
it when he returned from one island or another with
plastic sandwich bags full of shells. He was not certain
where the letter was now. After Sylvia killed herself, he
mailed it to a mutual friend; it described scenes of her
childhood, something about an immense tree that she
climbed and hid in, inconspicuous and vulnerable. The
tone was both morose and mocking, and Keller felt that
in some fashion the letter expiated him; that is why he
forwarded it. At the time, this friend was living in Ar-
kansas, in the Ozarks. He wrote back about the taran-
tula that had its hole in one of the earthen steps that
led to the spring, and the soft-shelled turtles that his
neighbor killed; he cut off their heads and hung the
turtles upside down from boughs along the stream to
drain. It was then spring. Sylvia was not mentioned.
Months later, Keller got a postcard from a motel in Chi-
huahua; the friend was pushing south. Keller thought
of him walking in the desert, heavy with reproof, Sylvia's letter crumpled in his pocket like one of Mr.
Gallagher's dollar bills.

Sylvia asked Keller to marry her while they were driving to Key West in an air-conditioned Hertz car with
tinted windows which he had rented in Miami. He told
her—if he could no longer remember what she said
without looking at his notes, or even what she looked
like, except that she had a brilliant nose like Petrarch's,
he could still hear his own dreadful, commonplace sentence; it groaned in his ear like the artificial ocean in the
conch with "Greetings from Key West, Fla." painted
upon it which Sylvia bought for her daughter—"It's
not that I don't want to marry you, Sylvia; it's only that
I just don't want to get married now." She moved away
from him and stared out through the windshied at the
dark, stormy colors of the sea and roadside; the cold,
continuous rush of air blew between them; they might
have been standing on a platform between railway
coaches passing through the Alps. Instead of turning

back, they continued to Key West—a shabby dénouement. In the afternoon, they swam in their motel pool; the water was as hot as blood and filmed with suntan lotion. In the evening, they ate in a seafood restaurant that had comically illustrated maps of Key West as placemats. Sylvia kept going to the ladies' room to cry; "Mermaids" was written on the door. That night, they lay under a bas-relief: two snowy egrets and several stalks of bamboo beaten out of copper. She gripped him and implored him to marry her, and he heard himself, carefully selecting his words. . . . Many years before, Keller had walked barefoot to the end of the rocky mole that extends into the Adriatic at Venice. It was an unreasonable undertaking, but this lack of purpose or profit was, in a way, its justification. Without actually doping it out in these words, Keller wanted to see—and not very badly, at that—what it was like at the end, although he knew from experience that it would not be dissimilar to the beginning or the middle; all he would find there was the way back. It was July; Italy was suffering a heat wave; the rocks were hot, and their fragments cut into his bare soles. But Keller's discomfort was alleviated by the fact that with each step he was getting closer to his indifferent goal—the light and the fishermen, who had rowed out, sitting about it. The return, however, was entirely an ordeal. It was a reversion, and every step carried him nearer to a place that he had been to, and back to attitudes, briefly suspended, that brought him no comfort. Now, as he spoke to Sylvia, fair-minded and conciliatory, he felt he was picking his way slowly back along the rocks, searching for a smooth foothold, putting his foot down gingerly in the expectation of pain, at turns grieving, bored, and philosophical, the shore appallingly distant.

There was a radio in the wall of the motel room which could not be turned off. Faint, tinny, and incomprehensible voices seeped out of the grille. A man in the room next door was singing "Lady of Spain." As she held him, Sylvia trembled so that he disengaged her arms and legs, got out of bed, and turned the air-conditioner down to "L," for "Low."

When they returned to New York, Keller continued to see Sylvia on and off out of a sense of guilt and pity and, rarely, desire. He knew he was being irresponsible; he had wantonly led her out and now, instead of abandoning her, he was dragging her back. She asked him to marry her several more times, they had tearful scenes, and, finally, she took the train to Baltimore. She said she was going to visit an aunt. When she died, Keller owed her nine dollars. He thought of cancelling the debt by buying a present for her daughter, who was living with her grandparents in Cedarhurst, but he was not sure whether it would be in good taste, and in time he forgot the particulars of his obligation. Keller came to blame himself for Sylvia's death, a position that was not without an element of self-gratification; it gave him, like the fur and skeleton of the slain mouse in the owl's crop, a substantive ache about which he could wind and justify his doubt and discontent. The owl shortly coats and eliminates this sharp, indigestible relic, but Keller preserved his memory of Sylvia as though, in a secret and uncharted crypt, she and his shameful forebear, the sterling young man, lay side by side.

On his third morning on the reef, Keller heard someone shouting and, looking up, saw a young man in a red *pareu* jogging toward him. He beckoned to Keller and shouted again, "Kel-lair!" For a moment, Keller thought he had run all the way from the village to ask the time. Keller watched him approach with disbelief; he had come to regard the reef as his garden. If he had a garden, Keller thought, it would be like this—bitter and weedy. The intruder tugged at Keller's arm. "Kel-lair," he repeated in an almost sweet, despairing voice, and Keller realized, with wonder and relief, that he was saying his name, and what he wanted was Keller to return with him to the village. As though he felt the draw and agency of fate, Keller submissively followed. To keep up, he had to run. The native led him to a house shaded by breadfruit trees. It seemed to Keller that the entire population of the village was squatting on the front lawn. What had *he* done? Or what was he about to do, more like it. Or was it doomsday or a revolution? The young man took him by the hand and drew him through the silent and ambiguous crowd. Keller stooped as he entered the house, although the doorway was high enough; he felt extraordinarily tall and condemned to make unnecessary adjustments. Curtains hanging from fishing line divided the interior into a series of cubicles and blocked the light. The windows must have been open, for every so often the curtains, which were unevenly drawn, giving the effect of an elaborate maze, billowed theatrically. Keller was led this way and that, baffled and apprehensive. Once, he blundered into a chicken; it plunged into a curtain as though beheaded. At times, he lost sight of his guide as he preceded him around corners; the only sign of his presence was the pressure of his hand. At times, too, a curtain would abruptly part, someone would stare at Keller without expression and then would pull the curtain to. At last, the guide stopped and stepped aside. Before Keller was his reward, a girl of five or six lying on a bed as high as an altar. She was breathing rapidly and held her head in an odd, stiff position. Keller laid his hand on her forehead; she was burning up. He tried to move her head, and she screamed. Appalled and intimidated, Keller stepped back and found his way obstructed by people who had followed him in and stood behind him on tiptoe. He now noticed that there were others crouching on the floor about the bed.

"I'm not a doctor," Keller said fatuously.

There was no reply.

"You don't understand," he pleaded. "I'm sorry, but you're mistaken. I'm really not a doctor. What do you want of me?"

As though in response, a chair was brought to the head of the bed and Keller was gently pushed into it. He did not want to look at the child, but neither could he look at the supplicant and reliant faces of those who surrounded him. They, not she, were to be his clement nemeses. They must have discovered somehow that he had once gone to medical school. Were there clues or ruins in his face, manner, and belongings—the spoor of old declinations? Was it true that hunters could tell by the depth and temperature of the pool of urine how large an elephant had passed how long ago? But did they know, further, that he had left medical school because (he told himself, no doubt falsely) he was unable to endure the pain of strangers—that vast, abstract, public suffering and, more to the point, the infinite and irrational trust? He could not just sit there, eyes cast down, however, for the little girl had begun to twitch spasmodically; he could feel it through his knee, which was inadvertently touching the bed. He yearned to be elevated like St. Simeon Stylites, who was finally sixty feet tall, governing and forgiving by signs. Perhaps, he thought, if she died here and now he could say—but who would listen?—they came for him too late. No, she was moaning. Keller was fairly trapped. He leaned forward and carefully bent the child's neck. Her legs flexed in response. He pushed one of her thighs against her abdomen, then extended it. She cried out—a cry high-pitched and piteous like that of birds that follow a ship far at sea—and her other leg flexed quickly while the one he held strained against his hand. The signs of Kernig and Brudzinski. She had the classical symptoms of acute meningitis, the lecturer would say, lifting his voice in that high, dingy hall that seemed a place of departures, like a railway terminal. "Hallucinations, delirious states, maniacal episodes, and restlessness." He called them out as though they were stations down the line. Who were Kernig and Brudzinski anyway? Keller pictured them standing on a snowy corner by the great, dark loom of a hospital near the North Sea, waiting for the last bus. They were identically dressed in long overcoats with fur collars upon which the snow did not melt but built up about their dispassionate faces. Keller forced himself to take the child's pulse. It was a hundred and eighty.

"We've got to get her to the hospital," he announced.

Why were all his sentences so banal? It's not that I don't want to marry you, Sylvia. . . . He could have said that, for all they knew, for all that it mattered.

Keller took out his notebook and drew, without perspective, a building with many windows and a cross on it, then a seaplane; a dotted line ending in an arrow connected them. He felt like adding a chimney and a coil of smoke, Kernig and Brudzinski waiting for the bus. He tore out the page and they passed it among then. When it was handed to the last, who was the young man they had sent to bring him here, he nodded and left. The others made lifting motions with their arms. What did they want of him now? Or was it a dance? But celebrating what—or carry her where? He bent and picked her up, and all the curtains suddenly shot back and Keller saw that he was only a few feet from the door. The crowd on the lawn rose as he stepped out and parted with ceremony to allow him to pass. Some went before on the road, and he followed them; looking back, he saw the rest bringing up the rear, joined now by the village's abused and crippled dogs. He felt like a prisoner under escort. They were walking by the harbor. He recalled carrying that other sleeping child through the fragrant and treacherous hills. How many nights ago? Abraham and Isaac, too—that effrontery. The road went by the lagoon. Keller could see the black sea slugs on the bottom; kindred, these. He wanted to withdraw, like the hermit crab, into a tenement of shade. Balancing his trust in his arms, he remembered, imperfectly, the movie about Frankenstein. Wasn't there a scene where a dead girl was being borne through a town? There was round dancing in the street. It must have been a holiday. The rounds broke up as the solemn man and the girl passed through them. Who was it that was carrying the child, the father or the monster? At any rate, wasn't the monster a kindly person who had been misjudged? I mean, Keller thought, he had been treated badly, misunderstood; they had all turned against him, hadn't they?

Keller writes in his notebook: "My daughter has run away from home. Beneath the lemon-yellow-and-white canopy, her covers are smooth and empty. No one has ever slept there. I look in my son's room. He lies sprawled upon his bed as though he had been flung down from a great height. I go into the kitchen and hear the refrigerator's reassuring hum. On the counter is an unfinished jigsaw puzzle we were working on, once upon a time, the three of us. We were looking one evening for the dancing green men with the flat bottoms that made up a corner and Benjamin Franklin's coat."

Keller never married and he does not have any children. He writes, with fraudulence and innocence, in his notebook because he feels those in the launch expect him to do something professional—and to remember what never happened or to forget what has. How often can he take the child's vanishing pulse, feel her head? What is left? External cardiac massage? Mouth-to-mouth breathing? Tracheotomy? A drop of sweat falls and lodges along the gold rim at the bottom of one of the lenses of his sunglasses. It shimmers there, creating a spectrum. Keller is diverted. Refraction makes the rim appear to be a chain of gold coins; a sunken treasure, Keller thinks. He knows the child has died, but it is still his secret.

Keller writes in his notebook: "I love you."

He drops the notebook overboard. He hears several splashes and sees that the boats have drifted apart and men are diving into the lagoon like Greeks after the cross. No. I did it on purpose. I don't want it. I don't need it any longer. Please don't bring it back to me. It doesn't make any difference. Why do you all have to be so kind? He has seen these people dive and imagines them kicking powerfully toward the bright bottom, the notebook sinking beyond them into the sea's high, inviolate vault. They will never recover it. If the hydrographic chart is right, it is fifteen fathoms deep where the flying boat lands.

Keller continues to hear splashes and opens his eyes; he had not known they were shut. The men are swimming on the surface. The notebook was too light and gaudy to sink. One of them has it now and is returning to the launch. Had they radioed for the flying boat, after all? They had been waiting for him to drop it over the side, throw it away like a murder weapon, and now they are bringing it back—he has it between his teeth—to comfort and condemn him with.

Oh, The Wonder!

Jeremy Larner

I

ON a warm evening in May, Willie McBain telephoned his friend Lickens, who lived not far away on the Lower East Side of New York City.

"For me the worst time is after supper," he told Lickens. "It gets worse every minute. I try to keep from sleeping so I won't dream. I make sure that even if I do fall out I've got the lights and the radio on."

"But just what is it?" Lickens wanted to know.

"That's it, that's it: I don't know. Nothing! I'm going out of my box!"

"Afraid of getting married?"

"Of course! I'm afraid of everything. Oh the wonder of it, Lickens! Oh the wonder of it all. Life is unbearable. How can you be alive without going out of your box?"

"There are ways," Lickens said.

"Not with my stomach. I can't keep anything inside me, Lickens. I vomit before dinner and I vomit after dinner. I'm even afraid to go to the docaroony."

"Then that's what you're afraid of."

"Sure! But the reason I'm afraid is that if I keep talking to him I might really find out what I'm afraid of."

"So you're not only afraid, you're afraid of finding out what you're afraid of?"

"Oh the wonder of it all!"

"Me, too." Lickens sighed.

"Lickens!"

"Um?"

"Come over here and go me sock for sock!"

Lickens demurred. His arms had not yet recovered from the last time. He suggested they go for a beer.

"Can't," said Willie. "I've got to work."

"But you won't work. You know that. Take a break and then maybe things will be better."

"Then maybe things will be tomorrow, that's all! But why not? No, fuck it Lickens, this has got to be done to-night, so get thee the hell away from me. I've got to hang up."

"Good luck."

Willie McBain was a graduate student in Philosophy at Columbia University. He had set aside that night —just as he had set aside the eleven nights previous—to finish a paper that had been due in January. Within a week his extensions would be up on two more papers from the Fall semester, and he had not even begun research on one of them. When those were finished, he would have three fun-packed weeks in which to write his Master's paper and pass his language examinations. He complied with the mickeymouse because he wanted to teach; he thought he had a new way of teaching. Willie wanted to account for man's unpleasant psy-chology in philosophic terms. Specifically, he was im-pressed by the problem of aggression. From all that he felt and saw, he knew that to live was to hurt oneself. Could the pattern be undone? Could men come to know the score and do what they could for themselves? Or were his thoughts merely personal? These were the questions he would make his students answer, the very questions that had been neatly avoided by the spinners of spiritual and political systems. Because they were afraid: it's al-ways so much easier to write things out neatly when you don't have to care how they really are. Willie was going to make them see. He would hunt them down remorse-lessly, cutting off every avenue of transcendental escape. He didn't have the answers, he knew; but he could make a start by insisting on the real questions.

But sooner or later he would have to write a book, and

for the moment Willie McBain could not even manage to read a book. He would plot his time and settle carefully in the rubble of his railroad flat, only to find himself staring for hours at a single page. He could concentrate for a paragraph or two, then twenty minutes would disappear and he would come back to himself with a start, furious, without the slightest idea where he had been. The psychiatrist agreed that it was more than a matter of will-power. But still it made Willie angry. No matter what the doctor said, sooner or later he had to control himself, that was what it boiled down to, or else they might as well start padding the walls and removing sharp objects.

He pawed for the phone, and called Philadelphia where his fiancée was finishing her last year at college.

"I can't work," he told her. "I'm like that machine that turns itself off. Why don't you go out and find someone worthwhile?"

"Because I've got someone," she said. "Someone who turns *me* on. Willie, if you could only relax for a while. It doesn't make any difference if you can't do what you want right this minute. You'll do your work when you're really and truly ready, and tearing at yourself won't help."

"Sure I'll do my work! What if I don't? There's no law says I will. What's the difference between me and thousands of pretentious half-wits in this city who gas about what they are going to do some day?"

"There is a difference; I can't prove it to you but there is. I know it and so does everyone who ever met you."

Willie laughed. "Don't be a goddam girl-friend!"

She didn't answer. "What's the matter?" he said. "Are you hurt?"

"I guess so," she said. "I'm sorry."

"Look," he said. "I'm going to flunk out of school. I'll be drafted and you'll never see me again."

"I wouldn't like that. I'd go to the Army and make them give you back."

"What are you doing?" he asked her. "Get anything done tonight?"

JEREMY LARNER

She giggled. "Oh, I'm supposed to be studying for my Sosh finals tomorrow. But I think I know the material pretty well—I've just been sitting up talking with Francine . . ."

"Francine! That flaccid ass!"

"Shhhhhhhhh."

"Don't shhh me! I thought you promised not to see her anymore."

"I didn't promise."

"Oh, I get it, you just let me *think* you promised!"

"I can't talk about it now."

"Why not, 'cause she'll hear? Screw that! Who's more important to you anyway, me or her! Are you going to waste your whole life on namby-pamby gushing fawning half-wits? People who might challenge you you avoid like the plague! What's going to become of you, goddammit?"

He was nearly out of his box with rage. He shouted at her until she cried. When it was over he felt worse than ever. She promised to send Francine away and go back to studying, and he said, choking, that it didn't really matter what she did. He said if only he had her in his bed right that very instant—that was all that could make any difference. When he hung up he took a dish and slammed it against the wall.

Sarah was really not the girl for him. Perhaps he only loved her because she loved him. She was so utterly dependent on him, couldn't make a move without him, no plans, no ambitions, no nothing of her own . . . She wanted to be pregnant: he had to make damn sure every time that she got her diaphragm in. The ready-made identity! She would marry him and attach her life to his like a leech. But wasn't that what a woman was supposed to do? Was it wrong for a bright young girl to think of nothing but babies? Or was he so far out of his box he couldn't see straight?

But how would she become a person? Sarah wanted to think their life together was a lovey-dovey-duckywucky dreamaroony, and that wasn't what life was like! Life was too goddam unbearable, you had to be ready to fight! He, at least, had the guts to go to the doctor.

He paced the room thinking of his prize-fighting days. Maybe he should have turned pro. The new light-heavy-weight champ was a punk. Willie had a theory about how he could be set up. He cracked his fists into the porcelain of the fridgaroony, feeling it dent and spring out again. Neighbors pounded on the thin wall, loosening bits of plaster, and Willie pounded back, pound for pound, till the ceiling shook and he heard crashes on the other side.

He heard someone running down the stairs. Maybe the cops would come. Willie had never quite hit a cop. He coveted that pleasure; to sink a fist in one's massive blue frontage. He didn't care if they killed him.

He sat on the bed to watch a movie he had started in his mind. He was putting the slug to one cop after another while they pumped bullets into him and the whole block poured out to watch in love and fascination. Everyone loved him, he knew it—no matter if he brought the roach-infested house down. Even Sarah, whose teary face in the movie gave him a laugh. No babies now. No comfy for Sarah. Bitterly he thought how she would be the only one to miss the splendour of his gesture. She would feel cheated, and even think him foolish.

The hell with her, he would be dead. He laughed out loud and shook his head. He couldn't understand why when he was depressed he thought so little of dying. Normally the fear of death overtook him in every happiness, ran him down like a wolfhound. He was pondering this when the phone rang . . .

Ten minutes later he phoned Lickens.

"Luscious Louise called," he reported.

"Um," said Lickens.

"She wants me to come over. She's lonely. She wants me to talk to her. Let's be friends, she says."

"You going?"

"I shouldn't. But I was thinking what the hell I can't work anyway, maybe after this I'll come back, take a benny, stay up all night and it will be all out of my system, see?"

"So why call me?"

"You're supposed to talk me out of it."

"That's not fair. . . . but if you want, I'll go in your place."

"No," answered Willie, still sad, though the fact was that Lickens' offer had clinched it for him. "I'm going. Trouble is, I've got this itch in the old groinaroony . . ."

". . . and when Ah itches, Ah scratches!" Lickens drawled.

Luscious Louise made it difficult for about half an hour. She really did want to talk. She didn't know what to do with herself. She was too bright; she was tired of being a secretary. She had this idea that she would go to law school and she wanted Willie McBain to love her for it. Willie knew what her trouble was.

"I know what your trouble is," he said. "You want a penis. But you can't get one by going to law school. The only way is to use mine while you have a chance."

She tried to get on her high horse, but he wouldn't let her. He knew she wanted to.

"You know you want to," Willie said.

She sighed.

Making love to Louise was like riding the white horse in the circus. Where was she taking him, slick nervous antelope with such strange interior muscles?! She could play a tune on him like a piccolo. Sarah was tamer and didn't shriek so much—well, why should she? He loved her, she knew it . . . he wasn't even thinking of Luscious Louise except when she . . . wow! . . . she was going out of her box . . . he had never . . . now why couldn't Sarah be more like

this!

?

When she saw it was all up with him she snuggled close and closed her eyes in contentment. But Willie lay with his fists clenched and teeth jammed together like nails. He couldn't stand it; he wanted to get up and rush out on the fire escape and throw himself over. If he relaxed a single muscle he would plunge headfirst down the brickface wall and crunch powerfully through the sidewalk miles deep beneath the candy store.

Louise was clutching at his arms. "Willie, Willie-baby . . ."

"Let me go!"

He stood facing her, pathetic in his undershirt, his back against the wall while she made absurd calming motions.

"Get out of bed and I'll slam you one!"

She lay where she was. As he pulled on his clothes he heard her sniffling. Only when he was safely down in the street and running did he realize he had been tearing his hair and ears.

He ran six blocks down Avenue B and thumped three-at-a-time up the wooden steps of Lickens' tenement.

He knocked and from within heard the sounds of Lickens grumbling and rolling out of bed. Then the striking of a match.

"You!" said Lickens. "G'morning, silly bastard!"

Willie saw that Lickens' eyes were not quite open.

"Now Lickens, sorry to wake you, man, just get back in bed, fall out, land of nod, forget and forgive, Lickens, that's it, easy there . . ."

"Peckerhead!" Lickens mumbled, as Willie eased him back onto his mattress. The keys were on the night table where Willie could palm them without any trouble. He stood for a while watching Lickens drop back to sleep and right next to him Lickens' beautiful wife sleeping in a band of moonlight, her face calm and womanly, her long hair strewn lightly on the pillow. Her features were more relaxed than in her waking hours. And her mouth closed. He bent close to admire her full lips and long dark lashes. She breathed sweetly as a doe. And look at Lickens lying there, snorting and twisting! What a jackass to be thumping himself around so and sticking his silly head under the pillow! Lickens didn't have any problems. His only problem was he thought he had problems. Lucky Lickens!

But no luckier than he, Willie McBain, might be! He

had no debts, no job, no cancer. Nothing to lose but worry and time.

The junkpiley Lickensmobile sat right around the corner. Willie unlocked it, started it up and set off for Philadelphia.

He bit his nails at eighty miles an hour down the New Jersey turnpike. He didn't know it, but he was worried that he would arrive to find Sarah gone. Hung around his mind like an albatross was a picture of her with Roger Stennis. Stennis was the most respected student in Sarah's graduating class—an alert young man with quick lips and clean eyes. Stennis was going to be an historian, and one of the best: he had won a fellowship to Oxford and Willie was certain that Roger would like nothing better than to take Willie's Sarah along with him. And it was logical—why shouldn't she go? Wouldn't a cottage on the green and a well-bordered life and a creative, productive, attentive husband be far, far preferable to a stinking slum-hole in New York and a hung-up, hateful husband off screwing with Luscious Louise and even when with her flailing and cursing, climbing up by tearing her down, desperately clutching and snapping at every weakness in sight in his last-ditch efforts to punish the world for his own shortcomings? A sweet, bright girl like her, so long abused? She should have been long gone already. Without seeing it he saw in his mind a bed with Sarah and Roger Stennis well-sheeted together.

He would never forget what had happened when he took off on his canoe trip the summer before. On principle he had insisted that Sarah not refuse dates with other men, but when she wrote him she had gone out with Roger Stennis he nearly went out of his box. Stennis had been in love with her a long time—no doubt about that. Sure, going out he didn't mind, but Stennis was a betrayal! He would kill the bastard. He would blast his head open with a hard right.

There was blood in his mouth from where he had chewed into his cheek. Glancing at his gas gauge, he saw the needle stuck on empty, and, dressed hurriedly as he was in workshirt and jeans, his rummagings produced a mere quarter. His headlights picked up a sign announcing a rest stop. He had to think of something. Fifteen minutes later he found himself sitting over an empty coffee cup in a Howard Johnson's. He tried to remember the waitress bringing him the coffee: had she been friendly? Perhaps he had gotten it himself. He was sitting alone at a little table, and the only other people in the place were a clutch of fifteen-sixteen-year-old boys at the counter.

Damned if they weren't giggling!

They were staring at him and trying to puzzle him out and giggling because they had never seen anything like him in their part of New Jersey.

Willie glared back with a vicious eyeblast intensity utterly unequal to their intentions and sending them into gales of laughter.

Willie's standing silenced them, until a brave one voiced the single word they knew for him: "Hey Mister, you a beatnik or sompin!"

Willie said, "No, are you?" A volcano of giggles.

"What's your name?" Willie said. "You!"

The boy was stumped for a second. "Puddentane!" he said triumphantly, and put his comrades in convulsions.

"Well look, Puddentane, you look like a beatnik to me, with all that acne and that grease on your hair. How about it?"

"I'm just a normal American boy," Puddentane replied. The laughter this time was uneasy; the boys poked each other, shifted, whispered.

"What do normal American boys do with themselves, Puddentane? Hang around Howard Johnson's all night and stare at customers?"

"If we feel like it," said Puddentane. "We're not big-time like you."

"Don't you masturbate?"

The boys giggled in shock and broke out in very loud laughter and finally hoots. "Oh, brother!" said Puddentane. "You *are* a weird one!"

"It's weird to talk about sex, isn't it? You normal

American boys don't like it, do you? It embarrasses you,
huh?"

"Oh sure," someone said. No one was laughing.

"If it doesn't embarrass you, why are you turning red,
Puddentane?"

Puddentane didn't know why he was turning red, but
he did know, at last, that he had hated Willie's guts the
moment he saw him. The boys shrunk back like snakes,
their eyes fixed on Willie.

"Why don't you go back to Russia?" one of them inquired.

"You want to fight?" said Willie instantly.

He caught them unprepared. The five of them working together could have taken him, but separately
they couldn't decide. Time out for consultation.

"I'll leave you normal American boys to your circle-
jerk." Willie took his departure.

As he went out the door, he heard behind him the
shout, "Goodbye, beatnik!"—and then a chorus of
shouts: "Goodbye, Communist, Goodbye, orang-utang,
Goodbye, pigpen!" The five trailed behind as he walked
toward the Lickensmobile and came close as he started
it, shouting, jeering, thumping on the fenders and windows.

A mile later Willie remembered his gas gauge. Since
traffic was light he was able to back carefully up the
turnpike till he reached the Howard Johnson's again.
There was a souped-up Ford in back which obviously
belonged to the blackhead set. Willie took Lickens' al-
ways-ready rubber tube from the back seat and siphoned
off the gasoline from the jutting Fordaroony into
the thirsty tank of the Lickensmobile. As he was finishing
the boys came out and spotted him. The Ford gave hot
pursuit and undoubtedly would have caught him had it
not run out of gas in three minutes.

But Willie had forgotten his new-found enemies in
two minutes. He was remembering Sarah: "Roger?
Why, he's only a *boy!*"

"Did you kiss him?" he had asked.

"Yes," she had said, flaring up. "I think so. So what?"

I *think so? So what!* How had he put up with her solid brass evasiveness? He was eating on his tongue. It was obvious she was gone; he knew it now. He was driving full speed ahead into a tunnel that receded as fast as he came. But if he could encounter anything at all in the tunnel he would destroy it, or destroy himself trying.

He swung into Philadelphia and drove straight to the apartment where Sarah lived with her roommate, charged up the stairs and knocked three hard knocks at the door. In a matter of seconds he expected to be back in the Lickensmobile, racing for every last inch of justice he could extract. There was no answer to his knock. But he had forgotten that it was six o'clock in the morning. He had stormed down two landings when he heard the door open; he rushed back up and there was the anxious, bewildered, asleep face of his Sarah peering out from behind the door. There was no questinn of her not being there; it did not even occur to him. They sat in the kitchen having breakfast, she delighted and asleep, he at last relaxed. He had not remembered the depth or the sureness of her brown eyes, the charming rumple of her cotton bathrobe, her little breasts peeping out at him like baby birds. Relaxed: the new sun rippled on the kitchen wall, toilets flushed, radios came on. The dread night had vanished and Willie might curl the warm day around him and sleep.

Sarah tucked him into her bed all odorous of woman and he tumbled down a well, his thoughts behind him. He was up by noon, before she got back from her last final exam, in time to shower and wash all the Lusciousness of Louise from his stomach, chest and groin. Sarah's roommate was up and made bacon-lettuce-and-tomato sandwiches smothered in mayonnaise and rye bread (because she loved Willie, too, naturally—it was a problem). Willie ate two huge BLT's, laughed, joked, drank his beer, pinched Sarah's ass and the roommate's too. After lunch he went into Sarah's room and into bed with Sarah, quickly, voraciously, because the instant he was through Willie jumped up and sat down at the typewriter and from memory resumed his paper at the point where he had left off and finished it without even stopping to hesitate. There was no doubt in his mind, nor of anything else at the moment. If he did not go out of his box at an early age, he was going to be quite a man.

In only an hour he was through, and out of steam anyway, and collapsed back in bed with Sarah, where for a full five minutes he watched her sweet, spirited eyes dart back and forth along the book she was reading. Then his watching was too much for her and she turned to him. Until suppertime they stuck close, each to the other's skin, and talked about what they would make of their life together. Willie stretched out as he talked, and watched the afternoon sun come bouncing off the upturned venetian blinds and sparkle slowly across the ceiling.

More than anything, Sarah wanted to be his and to bear his children. But she had decided to take a degree in Social Psychology; for she had to be a person in her own right, and this meant having work of her own to last her whole life long and keep her from bringing to her children that desperate clutch which her own mother even now could not relax. Willie nodded, basked in her completeness. There was nothing unbeautiful in her, she fitted together in every part and thought: when he was not out of his box he saw this truly and wondered at his incredible luck in having her. What had he done, he whispered, caressing her trim thigh, interrupting her, to deserve someone so perfect? Just being you, she answered to his most private ear, pulling him close and delighting him with a gesture they had never before dared or even imagined.

Their final plans, as the light wobbled orange on the ceiling: in the morning they would drive to New York, take out a license and get married by a justice of the peace. Or why get married at all? he wondered idly —but she shyly confessed it meant something to her, she still had that much of the middle class in her. Or maybe it really wasn't that at all, she insisted, growing more confident, but simply that she wanted to feel him hers, the full weight of their promise to each other. Promise? Willie laughed, but he was flattered, pleased, touched . . . She thought him capable of keeping a promise!

Even so her parents would be shocked, but never mind . . . they would get over it, and she would never in all eternity get over him. Her parents would say how can you live? But what did they know about living? Willie and Sarah would live all right, just watch them.

They did not need the things their parents had needed. They would be too alive for the buying-earning routine through which they were expected to stumble and excuse their lives away. They had no use for empty job-working. They would live simply in an old barn in the country, changing it over with the love of their own hands, making it belong to them and the pulsing life they would bring to it. Life was possible, really possible, for those who had the gift of loving.

II

Willie came back to himself like an object sucking into a vacuum. Without warning, the room was dark. Night had pushed the sun down out of the sky and crept over the land looking for Willie. It got worse every minute, as it had the day before and the day before that, as it did on days when he loved and days when he was removed from his love. Sarah was sleeping nestled in his shoulder; he looked at her, felt of her . . . and could not stand her breathing there. He stroked her hair, trying, trying—he thrust her roughly away. He did not wake her. She looked like a goddam child. What had she ever done in her life to make him believe she could be a woman? He couldn't have a woman, not him, not yet: he was too weak and too young. They made an absurd spectacle, Sarah and he—two overgrown babies hugging each other and playing big people in a dream world. Disgusting! She was so soft he could hardly fuck her. Why did he need this? His moment with Luscious Louise seemed infinitely more honest.

It was getting worse and he couldn't face it. Headlights shot into the room and raced across the ceiling. He lay petrified. He wanted to sleep, to conk out and stay out—but he was afraid of his dreams. His fists clamped tight to his groin, he tried grimly to focus on the hayloft in that mythical barn, where he would have rigged a punching-bag. Of course there would be no barn. No morning, either, nothing but a grubby, scroungy life of night after night. The doctor couldn't cure him —what nonsense for her to count on that! There was nothing to cure him of, his sickness was life. He was not out of his box; it was just that he could not fool himself. He was not a woman, he could not lie all warm and smelly and dream of babies and houses: the night was there and he saw it, and there was nothing he or anyone could do about it.

If he could not sleep he had to act, to move. Or else it would all be up. He must rise now and turn on the lights and the radio. Get up, get out of bed, turn on lights and radio. He strained against his body until he broke out in a violent sweat. Lying paralyzed and unblinking in the soaking sheets he saw himself pulled as if by a magnet, sucked to the window and through the slats of the venetian blinds, through the shivered glass and through the crusted streets like so many sheets of paper, cutting clean as a knife-blade into the grave.

He rose at last, lurching heavily, a landlubber coming on deck in a hurricane and stumbling for the rail . . . arms stiff as boards, he snapped on the lights, snapped on the radio.

Got to the bathroom as his insides came rushing out, and lay with his head in the toilet-bowl while his lungs and stomach heaved in dry spasms. He was dying, surely dying, oh merciful God, just let it be quick, he prayed to himself. Later he knew that Sarah must have woken up; she clung to his back, soothing him, still asleep and moaning for his hurt. With a twitch of his shoulders he shrugged her away, so that she banged her head on the sink and cried like a little girl. He threw up again, this time with relief; lay weak with his head in the toilet, purged, subsiding; and he loved her and everyone with all his heart, mixing his own happy tears with the vomit.

They went out to eat—showered, dressed up, holding hands and feeling large and good as an opera. It should have worked. The restaurant was something special: linen napkins, silver three-foot menus, two kinds of waiters, and so many plates there was no room for your elbows. Maybe it was too much for them. They ate extremely well, but there was nothing to say. Sarah simply sat there. Willie made a few remarks on his work, then hers, and she made routine answers, but she had nothing to say, nothing to start on her own. She was nervous and did not want to talk at all, just sit there and enjoy being with him. He saw she felt only for him; it was he who had to begin any thought that might connect them to the outside world, to life. She was competent to follow; it was up to him to begin and she would follow wherever he led. Willie saw more clearly than ever that his love for Sarah could bring him into no new relations with the world. Hardly! Difficult as it was to keep himself alive he would henceforth be expected to pull for two.

He sat on the back of his neck with his meat and potatoes, bread and tomatoes bombing him to his chair, while the chair itself sank slowly to the bottom of the ocean. As the depths closed over him he saw her smile, waveringly. Oh the tentativity of her; she could scarcely keep herself afloat! Her hand drifted toward him apologetically. Hardly daring to touch, she walked her fingers on the back of his hand.

"You have nothing to say for yourself, do you?"

She was hurt. "Am I on trial?"

He belched. "Oh what the hell!" he said.

"Look, it's been a long day," she said, biting her lip. If only she would lose her temper!

"And a hard day?" he needled hopefully.

"A hard day but a very good day," she said quietly. "Willie, I'm so tired. Please don't be hard on me."

He couldn't even bring himself to look at her. "I'm not

being *hard* on you," he muttered. He ordered a globular heap of ice creams, which impacted themselves together about halfway down.

They walked down one of the streets bordering campus, where all the little stores were still open and brightly lit. Neat pressed suits could be had, and notebooks. He shoveled through a used-book stack while she looked on absently, as though all books were alike to her. He walked her rapidly down the street to one of the movie-houses. They were playing a sophisticated comedy with titillating risqué dialogue, the kind of picture he would see only in an emergency. He stopped with her in front of the posters.

"Well?" he said. She smiled, ready to go either way. "Do you want to see it?"

"If you do, Willie."

"The hell with whether I do! You're a person! This is a movie—either you want to see it, deep down *here* (poking her), or you don't. But don't do it just for me, baby —don't let yourself get away with that!"

She stuck her lip out and walked away. He ran after her, grabbed her roughly.

"No, goddammit! I'm not going to let you be hurt. That's too easy, Sarah. I just want to know a simple thing: do you or don't you want to see the movie? It's only a decision, baby, it's got nothing to do with me. You just say yes or no and it's all over."

She tried to jerk away, hatefully, but he held her fast. "You absolute bastard!" she cried. She began to weep. Willie relaxed. She was his small, tender girl, and he wanted only to love her and soothe her hurt. While he held her and caressed her she blubbered that she didn't know, didn't care about the movie—she knew he was nervous and would be happy doing anything that helped him relax, that's all, because she loved him. She didn't think of going to a harmless movie as a decision, she wasn't thinking of wasting her valuable time or building her valuable life. She was with him, and did it make much difference what they did?

Okay, okay, he said. Please don't cry. Here: he kissed

away a tear. She cried happily now, with her head sniffling on his chest. People were looking. I feel so foolish, she said, standing like this in the middle of the sidewalk.

They walked on; he couldn't blame her. It was his twisted-up way of seeing things. But he had nothing left to say to her. Had they really said all they ever had to say in one afternoon? They walked on in silence past the little shops and the dressy college people, and Willie wanted desperately to be alone.

He felt like dashing up the street and around the corner. Just standing by himself in his own body would be so free and fine. No little one to tow along beside him. Just to be himself in his own skin, smelling the night air and doing whatever, moving wherever, his desires took him. Himself alone.

But that was not to be. They met some friends of Sarah's on the street and had to stand babbling. Willie said little—the people were schmucks as far as he was concerned. He watched Sarah; she was giggling of all things, like a teenager. That was because the people had joked about marriage, and she didn't know what to say: she was giggling and looking up at him. He scowled and saw her eyes fill up with hurt. The inquiring young man & woman, when they got no reply from Sarah and no attention from Willie, smiled as if to shrug, and moved on.

"Maybe next week!" he called after them, like a fool.

Once more in a pinch she had lapsed into girlishness and made him look the brute.

"I only want you to respect yourself," he said.

She turned in anger—"Must you *watch* me like that!" —but the anger soon faded into a kind of bewilderment that was exasperating but really, when he thought about it, did her credit. She knew what he meant, why he was forced to watch. She was not by any means dead or done.

She took his arm.

"I'm sorry," she said. "I don't know what gets into me. My poor Willie, you certainly have a lot to put up with . . ."

But it was too late, Roger Stennis was upon them,

looking five years older, bolstered by two grinning syc-
ophants, handsome as the devil and dressed like the
Duke of Wales. "Sarah!" he announced, in his bulletin-
board baritone. He shook Willie's hand with a single
pump, European style. He introduced his entourage,
who followed suit.

"Well, old man!" Roger said.

"Well, old man!" mocked Willie.

Roger took the mockery fondly. Good old basically
lovable, irascible Willie. We know you.

"How are things down at Columbia? Department all
right?"

Okay, Willie guessed.

"Be through in another year, I suppose?"

"Through?"

"Phd, I mean. The old union card."

"Well, I don't know," Willie said, though he knew
very well and the answer was no. "Three years would be
a pretty short trip."

But it seemed that Roger would have it in three. After
his year at Oxford on the Fulbright, he would enter the
new three-year program at Harvard. He had an understanding with the department there.

"Nice," Willie said.

"Yes, but it's just the externals," Roger confessed.

"What really matters is what you do with it."

"Yes."

There was a difficult pause, as though Roger had inquired what Willie had done with his two years since
college, and Willie had not been able to answer. But
Roger didn't have to ask. Willie would have been almost brilliant, if he were not so hopelessly hungup . . .

They all shook hands again.

"I envy you Paris," said Willie, honestly. What he
might not learn in Paris!

"I envy you something more than Paris, Willie." Roger
smiled down at Sarah, the sad, knowing smile of one
who has loved well and lost, but lost only after the loving was finished and he had moved on to better things.

Dear old Sarah, his smile was saying, how I hope you'll be happy. I'm really quite fond of you, you know.

And Sarah, to Willie's horror, was blushing, grinning like a little half-wit, nestling into his lapels!

Roger shook Willie's hand one more time. "Good luck, old man . . . the best." He meant it, too, really meant it, and Willie liked him, always had, for at least a full second.

"Oh the wonder of it all!" Willie mumbled inanely, then swung with all his might, smashing Roger Stennis right in the smile, knocking him off his feet and dribbling blood into his costly tie.

Sarah clung petrified to his right arm as he stood with fists clenched, waiting for Stennis to rise so he could knock him down again. But Stennis was in no hurry to rise. His friends dragged him away, heels trailing, Stennis holding a folded handkerchief to his lips and shaking his head groggily at the madness of Willie McBain, who watched after him ferocious, fists cocked, rigid and trembling in rage.

Willie and Sarah went home weeping and ashamed, and might have been good to one another had it not been for the cops waiting at the door. It seemed that the maniac Lickens had reported the Lickensmobile stolen, and suggested that the police might inquire for the thief in Philadelphia. Was this his idea of a joke? As Willie was led off furious between two brass bellies he thought for a moment of burying his elbows one to a pot and making a break for it. Alone at last! But why die? Life was awful but he was damned if he would give them the satisfaction.

Betrayed twice over, he stewed two hours in a jail cell before the stately Lickens phoned to confirm his identity. He was thinking mostly of Sarah by that time, and his thoughts swung round and round on a well-worn track. He wasn't sorry about Roger Stennis—why should he be? That had been his first clean act in months. No, it was Sarah—there was something wrong, deeper than tears could plumb, and this time he meant to have it out with her.

498 JEREMY LARNER

When he got back she was in her room with the lights
out. She was still as stone but he could tell by her breathing she was not asleep. All the better. He snapped on
the light and saw her stare back dry-eyed and cold, not
moving a muscle.

"You're a coward," he said.

No answer.

"Well? Have anything to say for yourself? Has it been
a long day?"

"It's been a miserable day." She was glaring at him as
if she'd never seen him before. "It's always a miserable
day when you have to humiliate yourself at every opportunity."

"What do you want from me!" she burst out. "Humiliate! Yes, I was humiliated all right. I've never been
so humiliated in my life. I was humiliated by a man who
can no more control himself . . . no more . . . who
strikes out like a little boy!"

"You mean, who strikes out to protect his so-called
woman when she lets herself be turned into a ten-year-
old girl, and likes it, revels in it! Is this what I have to
expect from you? That every time there's a test you'll
snuggle away like a child! Is it? Is it?"

She was crying now and yelling through her tears.
"I a child! I a child! Why I felt sorry for that boy, I felt
sorry and embarrassed for him! He was trying his hardest to impress you, don't you see, but you thought it was
a test. You think everything's a test. You're still back in
grade school, taking tests. That's what you want life to
be for me, one test after another. Well I can't stand it,
you hear? I don't want that kind of life! I want someone
I can love and who loves me and who can live with me
and be proud of me; yes, and take care of me too. I'm a
woman, I'm not your boxing-partner!"

"Boxing-partner?! What does that mean? Shit! What
in God's name does that mean? You want someone to be
proud? Listen to me! I'll be proud of you when you can
be proud of yourself. Take care of you, sure, you telling
me I don't take care of you? But as a man takes care of
his woman, not as a father his baby girl! I'll respect you

when you have something to say for yourself, as one adult to another, when you can stand up and look people in the eye!"

"You mean *punch* people in the eye!"

"I MEAN WHAT I SAY! AND THAT'S ALL! I'M UPSET. I'M UPSET, I'M TERRIFICALLY UPSET AND YOU'RE DISTORTING EVERYTHING I SAY!"

He stepped back. He thought he was through shouting. "It's really very simple," he said. "God, how you upset me . . ."

She sat on the edge of the bed. She had stopped crying, and sat looking at him, eyes narrowed with hate.

"Get out," she said.

He stopped pacing. "What's that?"

"I said get out. I don't love you anymore. I loathe you. You're not a man, you're a bad-tempered little boy. You don't want me as a woman, you want me as a roughneck sidekick to help you bully the other kids on the block."

"Listen," he said. "Some of what you say is right. OK. But what I say is very simple. I want you to be yourself. I want you to be your best. I want you to be proud so I can be proud too, of us. Because I love you. Believe me. I love you."

"You love yourself. You're talking to yourself now, you've got it all worked out. Get out of here. You disgust me." Suddenly she lost control. "I LOATHE YOU I LOATHE YOU I LOATHE YOU," she screamed, and fell weeping hysterically to the floor.

Her hysteria calmed him. He leaned to take her shoulder in his gentle hand and cupping her head smoothe her hair but she screamed GET AWAY FROM ME GET AWAY I LOATHE YOU GET AWAY!

And she twisted from him, squirmed violently, ugly, her face contorted, crawling for the door . . . A red screen came down before his eyes.

"DON'T YOU TALK TO ME THAT WAY!" he yelled. "DON'T YOU DARE, DON'T YOU EVER!" Before he knew he would he hit her, then when he knew hit her again, not out of malice but pure blind rage:

clubbed the crawling girl clumsy blows on the head and then to the ribs, knocking her over.

He leaned back against the wall and screamed. She lay on the floor and screamed. She got to her feet, flashed him a look of indomitable hatred, ran to the bathroom and locked herself in.

When next he could speak he bellowed COME OUT OF THERE OR I'LL KNOCK YOUR GODDAM DOOR IN! At which she shouted, vulgar as a whore, FUCK YOU YOU BASTARD GO AWAY I HATE YOU. And he said, choking, "How lovely you are!"

Then, in a little while, he called to her, "Please come out, Sarah. I'm sorry. I do love you, very much. I'm sorry for what I said." He heard no sound but her desperate weeping.

Methodically, in a cold fury, he began to pummel the wall. And even as he smashed one ruined fist after the other weeping and swearing he knew she would love him again, she would forgive him, they would love and be together for the rest of their lives and oh how he would hate her for it.

In the Heart of the Heart
of the Country

William H. Gass

a place

So I have sailed the seas and come . . .

to B . . .

a small . . .

town fastened to a field in Indiana. Twice there have
been twelve hundred people here to answer to the census.
The town is outstandingly neat and shady, and always
puts its best side to the highway. On one lawn there's
even a wood or plastic iron deer.

You can reach us by crossing a creek. In the spring
the lawns are green, the forsythia is singing, and even the
railroad that guts the town has straight bright rails which
hum when the train is coming, and the train itself has a
welcome horning sound.

Down the back streets the asphalt crumbles into
gravel. There's Westbrook's, with the geraniums, Horse-
fall's, Mott's. The sidewalk shatters. Gravel dust rises like
breath behind the wagons. And I am in retirement from
love.

weather

In the Midwest, around the lower Lakes, the sky in the
winter is heavy and close, and it is a rare day, a day to remark on, when the sky lifts and allows the heart up. I
am keeping count, and as I write this page, it is eleven
days since I have seen the sun.

my house

There's a row of headless maples behind my house, cut to free the passage of electric wires. High stumps, ten feet tall, remain, and I climb these like a boy to watch the country sail away from me. They are ordinary fields, a little more uneven than they should be, since in the spring they puddle. The topsoil's thin, but only moderately stony. Corn is grown one year, soybeans another. At dusk starlings darken the single tree—a larch—which stands in the middle. When the sky moves, fields move under it. I feel, on my perch, that I've lost my years. It's as though I were living at last in my eyes, as I have always dreamed of doing, and I think then I know why I've come here: to see, and so to go out against new things—oh god how easily—like air in a breeze. It's true there are moments—foolish moments, ecstasy on a tree stump—when I'm all but gone, scattered I like to think like seed, for I'm the sort now in the fool's position of having love left over which I'd like to lose; what good is it now to me, candy ungiven after Halloween?

a person

There are vacant lots on either side of Billy Holsclaw's house. As the weather improves, they fill with hollyhocks. From spring through fall, Billy collects coal and wood and puts the lumps and pieces in piles near his door, for keeping warm is his one work. I see him most often on mild days sitting on his doorsill in the sun. I noticed he's squinting a little, which is perhaps the reason he doesn't cackle as I pass. His house is the size of a single garage, and very old. It shed its paint with its youth, and its boards are a warped and weathered gray. So is Billy. He wears a short lumpy faded black coat when it's cold, otherwise he always goes about in the same loose, grease-spotted shirt and trousers. I suspect his galluses were yellow once, when they were new.

wires

These wires offend me. Three trees were maimed on their account, and now these wires deface the sky. They

cross like a fence in front of me, enclosing the crows
with the clouds. I can't reach in, but like a stick, I throw
my feelings over. What is it that offends me? I am on my
stump, I've built a platform there and the wires prevent my going out. The cut trees, the black wires, all the
beyond birds therefore anger me. When I've wormed
through a fence to reach a meadow, do I ever feel the
same about the field?

people

Their hair in curlers and their heads wrapped in loud
scarves, young mothers, fattish in trousers, lounge about
in the speedwash, smoking cigarettes, eating candy,
drinking pop, thumbing magazines, and screaming at
their children above the whirr and rumble of the machines.

At the bank a young man freshly pressed is letting
himself in with a key. Along the street, delicately teetering, many grandfathers move in a dream. During the
murderous heat of summer, they perch on window
ledges, their feet dangling just inside the narrow shelf of
shade the store has made, staring steadily into the street.
Where their consciousness has gone I can't say. It's not
in the eyes. Perhaps it's diffuse, all temperature and skin,
like an infant's, though more mild. Near the corner there
are several large overalled men employed in standing.
A truck turns to be weighed at the Feed and Grain. Images drift on the drugstore window. The wind has blown
the smell of cattle into town. Our eyes have been driven
in like the eyes of the old men. And there's no one to
have mercy on us.

vital data

There are two restaurants here and a tearoom. two
bars. one bank. three barbers. one with a green shade
with which he blinds his window. two groceries. a dealer
in Fords. one drug, one hardware, and one appliance
store. several that sell feed, grain, and farm equipment. an
antique shop. a poolroom. a laundromat. three doctors. a
dentist. a plumber. a vet. a funeral home in elegant re-

pair the color of a buttercup. numerous beauty parlors which open and shut like night-blooming plants. a tiny dime and department store of no width but several floors. a hutch, homemade, where you can order, after lying down or squirming in, furniture that's been fashioned from bent lengths of stainless tubing, glowing plastic, metallic thread, and clear shellac. an American Legion Post and a root beer stand. little agencies for this and that: cosmetics, brushes, insurance, greeting cards and garden produce—anything—sample shoes—which do their business out of hats and satchels, over coffee cups and dissolving sugar. a factory for making paper sacks and pasteboard boxes that's lodged in an old brick building bearing the legend, OPERA HOUSE, still faintly golden, on its roof. a library given by Carnegie. a post office. a school. a railroad station. fire station. lumber yard. telephone company. welding shop. garage . . . and spotted through the town from one end to the other in a line along the highway—gas stations to the number five.

business

One side section of street is blocked off with saw-horses. Hard, thin, bitter men in blue jeans, cowboy boots and hats, untruck a dinky carnival. The merchants are promoting themselves. There will be free rides, raucous music, parades and coneys, pop, popcorn, candy, cones, awards and drawings, with all you can endure of pinch, push, bawl, shove, shout, scream, shriek, and bellow. Children pedal past on decorated bicycles, their wheels a blur of color, streaming crinkled paper and excited dogs. A little later there's a pet show for a prize—dogs, cats, birds, sheep, ponies, goats—none of which wins. The whirlabouts whirl about. The ferris wheel climbs dizzily into the sky as far as a tall man on tiptoe might be persuaded to reach, and the irritated operators measure with sour eyes the height and weight of every child to see if they are safe for the machines. An electrical megaphone repeatedly trumpets the names of the generous sponsors. The following day they do not allow the refuse to remain long in the street.

my house, this place and body

I have met with some mischance, wings withering, as Plato says obscurely, and across the breadth of Ohio, like heaven on a table, I've fallen as far as the poet, to the sixth sort of body, this house in B, in Indiana, with its blue and gray bewitching windows, holy magical insides. Great thick evergreens protect its entry. And I live *in.*

Lost in the corn rows, I remember feeling just another stalk, and thus this country takes me over in the way I occupy myself when I am well . . . completely—to the edge of both my house and body. No one notices, when they walk by, that I am brimming in the doorways. My house, this place and body, I've come in mourning to be born in. To anybody else it's pretty silly: love. Why should I feel a loss? How am I bereft? She was never mine; she was a fiction, always a golden tomgirl, barefoot, with an adolescent's slouch and a boy's taste for sports and fishing, a figure out of Twain, or worse, in Riley. Age cannot be kind.

There's little hand in hand here . . . not in B. No one touches except in rage. Occasionally girls will twine their arms about each other and lurch along, school out, toward home and play. I dreamed my lips would drift down your back like a skiff on a river. I'd follow a vein with the point of my finger, hold your bare feet in my naked hands.

the same person

Billy Holsclaw lives alone—how alone it is impossible to fathom. In the post office he talks greedily to me about the weather. His head bobs on a wild flood of words, and I take this violence to be a measure of his eagerness for speech. He badly needs a shave, coal dust has layered his face, he spits when he speaks, and his fingers pick at his tatters. He wobbles out in the wind when I leave him, a paper sack mashed in the fold of his arm, the leaves blowing past him, and our encounter drives me sadly home to poetry—where there's no answer. Billy closes his door and carries coal or wood to his fire and closes his eyes, and there's simply no way of knowing how lonely and empty he is or whether he's as vacant and barren and loveless as the rest of us are—here in the heart of the country.

weather

For we're always out of luck here. That's just how it is—for instance in the winter. The sides of the buildings, the roofs, the limbs of the trees are gray. Streets, sidewalks, faces, feelings—they are gray. Speech is gray, and the grass where it shows. Every flank and front, each top is gray. Everything is gray: hair, eyes, window glass, the hawkers' bills and touters' posters, lips, teeth, poles and metal signs—they're gray, quite gray. Cars are gray. Boots, shoes, suits, hats, gloves are gray. Horses, sheep, and cows, cats killed in the road, squirrels in the same way, sparrows, doves, and pigeons, all are gray, everything is gray, and everyone is out of luck who lives here.

A similar haze turns the summer sky milky, and the air muffles your head and shoulders like a sweater you've got caught in. In the summer light, too, the sky darkens a moment when you open your eyes. The heat is pure distraction. Steeped in our fluids, miserable in the folds of our bodies, we can scarcely think of anything but our sticky parts. Hot cyclonic winds and storms of dust crisscross the country. In many places, given an indifferent push, the wind will still coast for miles, gathering resource and edge as it goes, cunning and force. According to the season, paper, leaves, field litter, seeds, snow fill up the fences. Sometimes I think the land is flat because the winds have leveled it, they blow so constantly. In any case, a gale can grow in a field of corn that's as hot as a draft from hell, and to receive it is one of the most dismaying experiences of this life, though the smart of the same wind in winter is more humiliating, and in that sense even worse. But in the spring it rains as well, and the trees fill with ice.

place

Many small Midwestern towns are nothing more than rural slums, and this community could easily become one. Principally during the first decade of the century, though there were many earlier instances, well-to-do farmers moved to town and built fine homes to contain them in their retirement. Others desired a more social life, and so lived in, driving to their fields like storekeepers to their businesses. These houses are now dying like the bereaved who inhabit them; they are slowly losing their senses . . . deafness, blindness, forgetfulness, mumbling, an insecure gait, an uncontrollable trembling has overcome them. Some kind of Northern Snopes will occupy them next: large-familied, Catholic, Democratic, scrambling, vigorous, poor; and since the parents will work in larger, nearby towns, the children will be loosed upon themselves and upon the hapless neighbors much as the fabulous Khan loosed his legendary horde. These Snopes will undertake makeshift repairs with materials that other people have thrown away; paint halfway round their house, then quit; almost certainly maintain an ugly loud cantankerous dog and underfeed a pair of cats to keep the rodents down. They will collect piles of possibly useful junk in the backyard, park their cars in the front, live largely leaning over engines, give not a hoot for the land, the old community, the hallowed ways, the established clans. Weakening widow-ladies have already begun to hire large rude youths from families such as these to rake and mow and tidy the grounds they will inherit.

people

In the cinders at the station boys sit smoking steadily in darkened cars, their arms bent out the windows, white shirts glowing behind the glass. Nine o'clock is the best time. They sit in a line facing the highway—two or three or four of them—idling their engines. As you walk by a machine may growl at you or a pair of headlights flare up briefly. In a moment one will pull out, spinning cinders behind it, to stalk impatiently up and down the dark streets or roar half a mile into the country before returning to its place in line and pulling up.

my house, my cat, my company

I must organize myself. I must, as they say, pull myself together, dump this cat from my lap, stir—yes, resolve, move, do. But do what? My will is like the rosy dustlike light in this room: soft, diffuse, and gently comforting. It lets me do . . . anything . . . nothing. My ears hear what they happen to; I eat what's put before me; my eyes see what blunders into them; my thoughts are not thoughts, they are dreams. I'm empty or I'm full . . . depending; and I cannot choose. I sink my claws in Tick's fur and scratch the bones of his back until his rear rises amorously. Mr. Tick, I murmur, I must organize myself. I must pull myself together. Mr. Tick rolls over on his belly, all ooze.

I spill Mr. Tick when I've rubbed his stomach. Shoo. He steps away slowly, his long tail rhyming with his paws. How beautifully he moves, I think; how beautifully, like you, he commands his loving, how beautifully he accepts. So I rise and wander from room to room, up and down, gazing through most of my forty-one windows. How well this house receives its loving too. Let out like Mr. Tick, my eyes sink in the shrubbery. I am not here; I've passed the glass, passed second-story spaces, flown by branches, brilliant berries, to the ground, grass high in seed and leafage every season; and it is the same as when I passed above you in my aged, ardent body; it's, in short, a kind of love; and I am learning to restore myself, my house, my body, by paying court to gardens, cats, and running water, and with neighbors keeping company.

Mrs. Desmond is my right-hand friend; she's eighty-five. A thin white mist of hair, fine and tangled, manifests the climate of her mind. She is habitually suspicious, fretful, nervous. Burglars break in at noon. Children trespass. Even now they are shaking the pear tree, stealing rhubarb, denting lawn. Flies caught in the screens and numbed by frost awake in the heat to buzz and scrape the metal cloth and frighten her, though she is deaf to me, and consequently cannot hear them. Boards creak, the wind whistles across the chimney-mouth, drafts cruise like fish through the hollow rooms. It is herself she hears, her own flesh failing, for only death will preserve her from those daily chores she climbs like stairs, and all that anxious waiting. Is it now, she wonders. No? Then: is it now?

We do not converse. She visits me to talk. My task to murmur. She talks about her grandsons, her daughter who lives in Delphi, her sister or her husband—both gone—obscure friends—dead—obscurer aunts and uncles—lost—ancient neighbors, members of her church or of her clubs—passed or passing on; and in this way she brings the ends of her life together with a terrifying rush: she is a girl, a wife, a mother, widow, all at once. All at once—appalling—but I believe it; I wince in expectation of the clap. Her talk's a fence—a shade drawn, window fastened, door that's locked—for no one dies taking tea in a kitchen; and as her years compress and begin to jumble, I really believe in the brevity of life; I sweat in my wonder; death is the dog down the street, the angry gander, bedroom spider, goblin who's come to get her; and it occurs to me that in my listening posture I'm the boy who suffered the winds of my grandfather with an exactly similar politeness, that I am, right now, all my ages, out in elbows, as angular as badly stacked cards. Thus was I, when I loved you, every man I could be, youth and child—far from enough—and you, so strangely ambiguous a being, met me, heart for spade, play after play, the whole run of our suits.

Mr. Tick, you do me honor. You not only lie in my lap, but you remain alive there, coiled like a fetus. Through your deep nap, I feel you hum. You are, and are not, a machine. You are alive, alive exactly, and it means nothing to you—much to me. You are a cat—you cannot understand—you are a cat so easily. Your nature is not something you must rise to. You, not I, live in: in house, in skin, in shrubbery. Yes. I think I shall hat my head with a steeple; turn church; devour people. Mr. Tick, though, has a tail he can twitch, he need not fly his Fancy. Claws, not metrical schema, poetry his paws; while smoothing . . . smoothing . . . smoothing roughly, his tongue laps its neatness. O Mr. Tick, I know you; you are an electrical penis. Go on now, shoo. Mrs. Desmond doesn't like you. She thinks you will tangle yourself in her legs and she will fall. You murder her birds, she knows, and walk upon her roof with death in your jaws. I must gather myself together for a bound. What age is it I'm at right now, I wonder. The heart, don't they always say, keeps the true time. Mrs. Desmond is knocking. Faintly, you'd think, but she pounds. She's brought me a cucumber. I believe she believes I'm a woman. Come in, Mrs. Desmond, thank you, be my company, it looks lovely, and have tea. I'll slice it, crisp, with cream, for luncheon, each slice as thin as me.

more vital data

The town is exactly fifty houses, trailers, stores, and miscellaneous buildings long, but in places no streets deep. It takes on width as you drive south, always adding to the east. Most of the dwellings are fairly spacious farmhouses in the customary white, with wide wraparound porches and tall narrow windows, though there are many of the grander kind—fretted, scalloped, turreted, and decorated with clapboards set at angles or on end, with stained glass windows at the stair landings and lots of wrought iron full of fancy curls—and a few of these look like castles in their rarer brick. Old stables serve as garages now, and the lots are large to contain them and the vegetable and flower gardens which, ultimately, widows plant and weed and then entirely disappear in. The shade is ample, the grass is good, the sky a glorious fall violet; the apple trees are heavy and red, the roads are calm and empty; corn has sifted from the chains of tractored wagons to speckle the streets with gold and with the russet fragments of the cob, and a man would be a fool who wanted, blessed with this, to live anywhere else in the world.

education

Buses like great orange animals move through the early light to school. There the children will be taught to read and warned against Communism. By Miss Janet Jakes. That's not her name. Her name is Helen something—Scott or James. A teacher twenty years. She's now worn fine and smooth, and has a face, Wilfred says, like a mail-order ax. Her voice is hoarse, and she has a cough. For she screams abuse. The children stare, their faces blank. This is the thirteenth week. They are used to it. You will all, she shouts, you will all draw pictures of me. No. She is a Mrs.—someone's missus. And in silence they set to work while Miss Jakes jabs hairpins in her hair. Wilfred says an ax, but she has those rimless tinted glasses, graying hair, an almost dimpled chin. I must concentrate. I must stop making up things. I must give myself to life; let it mold me: that's what they say in Wisdom's Monthly Digest every day. Enough, enough—you've been at it long enough; and the children rise formally a row at a time to present their work to her desk. No, she wears rims; it's her chin that's dimpleless. So she grimly shuffles their sheets, examines her reflection crayoned on them. I would not dare . . . allow a child . . . to put a line around me. Though now and then she smiles like a nick in the blade, in the end these drawings depress her. I could not bear it—how can she ask?—that anyone . . . draw me. Her anger's lit. That's why she does it: flame. There go her eyes; the pink in her glasses brightens, dims. She is a pumpkin, and her rage is breathing like the candle in. No, she shouts, no—the cartoon trembling—no, John Mauck, John Stewart Mauck, this will not do. The picture flutters from her fingers. You've made me too muscular.

I work on my poetry. I remember my friends, associates, my students, by their names. Their names are Maypop, Dormouse, Upsydaisy. Their names are Gladiolus, Callow Bladder, Prince and Princess Oleo, Hieronymus, Cardinal Mummum, Mr. Fitchew, The Silken Howdah, Spot. Sometimes you're Tom Sawyer, Huckleberry Finn;

it is perpetually summer; your buttocks are my pillow; we are adrift on a raft; your back is our river. Sometimes you are Major Barbara, sometimes a goddess who kills men in battle, sometimes you are soft like a shower of water; you are bread in my mouth.

I do not work on my poetry. I forget my friends, associates, my students, and their names: Gramophone, Blowgun, Pickle, Serenade . . . Marge the Barge, Arena, Uberhaupt . . . Doctor Dildoe, The Fog Machine. For I am now in B, in Indiana: out of job and out of patience, out of love and time and money, out of bread and out of body, in a temper, Mrs. Desmond, out of tea. So shut your fist up, bitch, you bag of death; go bang another door; go die, my dearie. Die, life-deaf old lady. Spill your breath. Fall over like a frozen board. Gray hair grows from the nose of your mind. You are a skull already—*memento mori*—the foreskin retracts from your teeth. Will your plastic gums last longer than your bones, and color their grinning? And is your twot still hazel-hairy, or are you bald as a ditch? . . . bitch . . . . . . bitch . . . . bitch. I wanted to be famous, but you bring me age—my emptiness. Was it *that* which I thought would balloon me above the rest? Love? where are you? . . . love me. I want to rise so high, I said, that when I shit I won't miss anybody.

business

For most people, business is poor. Nearby cities have siphoned off all but a neighborhood trade. Except for feed and grain and farm supplies, you stand a chance to sell only what one runs out to buy. Chevrolet has quit, and Frigidaire. A locker plant has left its afterimage. The lumber yard has been, so far, six months about its going. Gas stations change hands clumsily, a restaurant becomes available, a grocery closes. One day they came and knocked the cornices from the watch repair and pasted campaign posters on the windows. Torn across, by now, by boys, they urge you still to vote for half an orange beblazoned man who as a whole one failed two years ago to win at his election. Everywhere, in this manner, the past speaks, and it mostly speaks of failure. The empty stores, the old signs and dusty fixtures, the debris in alleys, the flaking paint and rusty gutters, the heavy locks and sagging boards: they say the same disagreeable things. What do the sightless windows see, I wonder, when the sun throws a passerby against them? Here a stair unfolds toward the street—dark, rickety, and treacherous—and I always feel, as I pass it, that if I just went carefully up and turned the corner at the landing, I would find myself out of the world. But I've never had the courage.

that same person

The weeds catch up with Billy. In pursuit of the hollyhocks, they rise in coarse clumps all around the front of his house. Billy has to stamp down a circle by his door like a dog or cat does turning round to nest up, they're so thick. What particularly troubles me is that winter will find the weeds still standing stiff and tindery to take the sparks which Billy's little mortarless chimney spouts. It's true that fires are fun here. The town whistle, which otherwise only blows for noon (and there's no noon on Sunday), signals the direction of the fire by the length and number of its blasts, the volunteer firemen rush past in their cars and trucks, houses empty their owners along the street every time like an illustration in a children's book. There are many bikes, too, and barking dogs, and sometimes—hallelujah—the fire's right here in town—a vacant lot of weeds and stubble flaming up. But I'd rather it weren't Billy or Billy's lot or house. Quite selfishly I want him to remain the way he is—counting his sticks and logs, sitting on his sill in the soft early sun—though I'm not sure what his presence means to me . . . or to anyone. Nevertheless, I keep wondering whether, given time, I might not someday find a figure in our language which would serve him faithfully, and furnish his poverty and loneliness richly out.

weather

I would rather it were the weather that was to blame for what I am and what my friends and neighbors are—we who live here in the heart of the country. Better the weather, the wind, the pale dying snow . . . the snow —why not the snow? There's never much really, not around the lower Lakes anyway, not enough to boast about, not enough to be useful. My father tells how the snow in the Dakotas would sweep to the roofs of the barns in the old days, and he and his friends could sled on the crust that would form because the snow was so fiercely driven. In Bemidji trees have been known to explode. That would be something—if the trees in Davenport or Francisville or Terre Haute were to go blam some winter—blam! blam! blam! all the way down the gray, cindery, snow-sick streets.

A cold fall rain is blackening the trees or the air is like lilac and full of parachuting seeds. Who cares to live in any season but his own? Still I suspect the secret's in this snow, the secret of our sickness, if we could only diagnose it, for we are all dying like the elms in Urbana. This snow—like our skin it covers the country. Later dust will do it. Right now—snow. Mud presently. But it is snow without any laughter in it, a pale gray pudding thinly spread on stiff toast, and if that seems a strange description, it's accurate all the same. Of course soot blackens everything, but apart from that, we are never sufficiently cold here. The flakes as they come, alive and burning, we cannot retain, for if our temperatures fall, they rise promptly again, just as, in the summer, they bob about in the same feckless way. Suppose though . . . suppose they were to rise some August, climb and rise, and then hang in the hundreds like a hawk through December, what a desert we could make of ourselves—from Chicago to Cairo, from Gary to Columbus—what beautiful Death Valleys.

place

I would rather it were the weather. It drives us in upon ourselves—an unlucky fate. Of course there is enough

to stir our wonder anywhere; there's enough to love, anywhere, if one is strong enough, if one is diligent enough,
if one is perceptive, patient, kind enough—whatever it
takes; and surely it's better to live in the country, to live
on a prairie by a drawing of rivers, in Iowa or Illinois or
Indiana, say, than in any city, in any stinking fog of
human beings, in any blooming orchard of machines.
It ought to be. The cities are swollen and poisonous with
people. It ought to be better. Man has never been a fit
environment for man—for rats, maybe, rats do nicely, or
for dogs or cats and the household beetle.

A man in the city has no natural thing by which to
measure himself. His parks are potted plants. Nothing
can live and remain free where he resides but the pigeon, starling, sparrow, spider, cockroach, mouse, moth,
fly, and weed, and he laments the existence of even these
and makes his plans to poison them. The zoo? There *is*
the zoo. Through its bars the city man stares at the great
cats and dully sucks his ice. Living, alas, among men
and their marvels, the city man supposes that his happiness depends on establishing, somehow, a special kind of
harmonious accord with others. The novelists of the city,
of slums and crowds, they call it love—and break their
pens.

Wordsworth feared the accumulation of men in cities.
He foresaw their "degrading thirst after outrageous stim-
ulation," and some of their hunger for love. Living in a
city, among so many, dwelling in the heat and tumult of
incessant movement, a man's affairs are touch and go—
that's all. It's not surprising that the novelists of the
slums, the cities, and the crowds, should find that sex is
but a scratch to ease a tickle, that we're most human
when we're sitting on the john, and that the justest image of our life is in full passage through the plumbing.

Come into the country, then. The air nimbly and
sweetly recommends itself unto our gentle senses. Here,
growling tractors tear the earth. Dust roils up behind
them. Drivers sit jouncing under bright umbrellas. They
wear refrigerated hats and steer by looking at the tracks
they've cut behind them, their transistors blaring. Close

to the land, are they? good companions to the soil? Tell me: do they live in harmony with the alternating seasons?

It's a lie of old poetry. The modern husbandman uses chemicals from cylinders and sacks, spike-ball-and-claw machines, metal sheds, and cost accounting. Nature in the old sense does not matter. It does not exist. Our farmer's only mystical attachment is to parity. And if he does not realize that cows and corn are simply different kinds of chemical engine, he cannot expect to make a go of it.

It isn't necessary to suppose our cows have feelings; our neighbor hasn't as many as he used to have either; but think of it this way a moment, you can correct for the human imputations later: how would it feel to nurse those strange tentacled calves with their rubber, glass, and metal lips, their stainless eyes?

people

Aunt Pet's still able to drive her car—a high square Ford—even though she walks with difficulty and a stout stick. She has a watery gaze, a smooth plump face despite her age, and jet black hair in a bun. She has the slowest smile of anyone I ever saw, but she hates dogs, and not very long ago cracked the back of one she cornered in her garden. To prove her vigor she will tell you this, her smile breaking gently while she raises the knob of her stick to the level of your eyes.

house, my breath and window

My window is a grave, and all that lies within it's dead. No snow is falling. There's no haze. It is not still, not silent. Its images are not an animal that waits, for movement is no demonstration. I have seen the sea slack, life bubble through a body without a trace, its spheres impervious as soda's. Downwound, the whore at wagtag clicks and clacks. Leaves wiggle. Grass sways. A bird chirps, pecks the ground. An auto wheel in penning circles keeps its rigid spokes. These images are stones; they are memorials. Beneath this sea lies sea: god rest it . . . rest the world beyond my window, me in front of my reflection, above this page, my shade. Death is not so still, so silent, since silence implies a falling quiet, stillness a stopping, containing, holding in; for death is time in a clock, like Mr. Tick, electric . . . like wind through a windup poet. And my blear floats out to visible against the glass, befog its country and bespill myself. The mist lifts slowly from the fields in the morning. No one now would say: the Earth throws back its covers; it is rising from sleep. Why is the feeling foolish? The image is too Greek. I used to gaze at you so wantonly your body blushed. Imagine: wonder: that my eyes could cause such flowering. Ah, my friend, your face is pale, the weather cloudy; a street has been felled through your chin, bare trees do nothing, houses take root in their rectangles, a steeple stands up in your head. You speak of loving; then give me a kiss. The pane is cold. On icy mornings the fog rises to greet me (as you always did); the barns and other buildings, rather than ghostly, seem all the more substantial for looming, as if they grew in themselves while I watched (as you always did). Oh, my approach, I suppose, was like breath in a rubber monkey. Nevertheless, on the road along the Wabash in the morning, though the trees are sometimes obscured by fog, their reflection floats serenely on the river, reasoning the banks, the sycamores in French rows. Magically, the world tips. I'm led to think that only those who grow down live (which will scarcely win me twenty-five from Wisdom's Monthly Digest), but I find I write that only those who live down grow; and what I write, I hold, whatever I really know. My every word's inverted, or reversed—or I am. I held you, too, that way. You were so utterly provisional, subject to my change. I could inflate your bosom with a kiss, disperse your skin with gentleness, enter your vagina from within, and make my love emerge like a fresh sex. The pane is cold. Honesty is cold, my inside lover. The sun looks, through the mist, like a plum on the tree of heaven, or a bruise on the slope of your belly. Which? The grass crawls with frost. We meet on this window, the world and I, inelegantly, swimmers of the glass; and swung wrong way round to one another, the world seems in. The world—how grand, how monumental, grave and deadly, that word is: the world, my house and poetry. All poets have their inside lovers. Wee penis does not belong to me, or any of this foggery. It is *his* property which he's thrust through what's womanly of me to set down this. These wooden houses in their squares, gray streets and fallen sidewalks, standing trees, your name I've written sentimentally across my breath into the whitening air, pale birds: they exist in me now because of him. I gazed with what intensity. . . . A bush in the excitement of its roses would not have bloomed so beautifully as you did then. It was a look I'd like to give this page. For that is poetry: to bring within about, to change.

politics

Sports, politics, and religion are the three passions of the badly educated. They are the Midwest's open sores. Ugly to see, a source of constant discontent, they sap the body's strength. Appalling quantities of money, time, and energy are wasted on them. The rural mind is narrow, passionate, and reckless on these matters. Greed, however shortsighted and direct, will not alone account for it. I have known men, for instance, who for years have voted squarely against their interests. Nor have I ever noticed that their surly Christian views prevented them from urging forward the smithereening, say, of Russia, China, Cuba, or Korea—Vietnam. And they tend to back their country like they back their local team: they have a fanatical desire to win; yelling is their forte; and if things go badly, they are inclined to sack the coach. All in all, then, Birch is a good name. It stands for the bigot's stick, the wild-child-tamer's cane.

final vital data

The Modern Homemakers' Demonstration Club. The Prairie Home Demonstration Club. The Night-outers' Home Demonstration Club. The IOOF, FFF, VFW,

WCTU, WSCS, 4-H, 40 and 8, Psi Iota Chi, and PTA. The Boy and Girl Scouts. Rainbows, Masons, Indians and Rebekah Lodge. Also the Past Noble Grand Club of the Rebekah Lodge. As well as the Moose and the Ladies of the Moose. The Elks, the Eagles, the Jaynettes, and the Eastern Star. The Women's Literary Club, the Hobby Club, the Art Club, the Sunshine Society, the Dorcas Society, the Pythian Sisters, the Pilgrim Youth Fellowship, the American Legion, the American Legion Auxiliary, the American Legion Junior Auxiliary, the Gardez Club, the What-can-you-do? Club, the Get Together Club, the Coterie Club, the Worthwhile Club, the No Name Club, the Forget-me-not Club, the Merry-go-round Club . . . . . .

education

Has a quarter disappeared from Paula Frosty's pocketbook? Imagine the landscape of that face: no crayon could engender it; soft wax is wrong; thin wire in trifling snips might do the trick. Paula Frosty and Christopher Roger accuse the pale and splotchy Cheryl Pipes. But Miss Jakes, I *saw* her. Miss Jakes is so extremely vexed she snaps her pencil. What else is missing? I appoint you a detective, John: search her desk. Gum, candy, paper, pencils, marble, round eraser—whose? A thief. I can't watch her all the time, I'm here to teach. Poor pale fossetted Cheryl, it's determined, can't return the money because she took it home and spent it. Cindy, Janice, John, and Pete—you four who sit around her—you will be detectives this whole term to watch her. A thief. In all my time. Miss Jakes turns, unfists, and turns again. I'll handle you, she cries. To think. A thief. In all my years. Then she writes on the blackboard the name of Cheryl Pipes and beneath that the figure twenty-five with a large sign for cents. Now Cheryl, she says, this won't be taken off until you bring that money out of home, out of home straight up to here, Miss Jakes says, tapping her desk.

Which is three days.

another person

I was raking leaves when Uncle Halley introduced himself to me. He said his name came from the comet, and that his mother had borne him prematurely in her fright of it. I thought of Hobbes, whom fear of the Spanish Armada had hurried into birth, and so I believed Uncle Halley to honor the philosopher, though Uncle Halley is a liar, and neither the one hundred twenty-eight nor the fifty-three he ought to be. That fall the leaves had burned themselves out on the trees, the leaf-lobes had curled, and now they flocked noisily down the street and were broken in the wires of my rake. Uncle Halley was himself (like Mrs. Desmond and history generally) both deaf and implacable, and he shooed me down his basement stairs to a room set aside there for stacks of newspapers reaching to the ceiling, boxes of leaflets and letters and programs, racks of photo albums, scrapbooks, bundles of rolled up posters and maps, flags and pennants and slanting piles of dusty magazines devoted mostly to motoring and the Christian ethic. I saw a birdcage, a tray of butterflies, a bugle, a stiff straw boater, and all kinds of tassels tied to a coat tree. He still possessed and had on display the steering lever from his first car, a linen duster, driving gloves and goggles, photographs along the wall of himself, his friends, and his various machines, a shell from the first war, a record of Ramona nailed through its hole to a post, walking sticks and fanciful umbrellas, shoes of all sorts (his baby shoes, their counters broken, were held in sorrow beneath my nose— they had not been bronzed, but he might have them done someday before he died, he said), countless boxes of medals, pins, beads, trinkets, toys, and keys (I scarcely saw—they flowed like jewels from his palms), pictures of downtown when it was only a path by the railroad station, a brightly colored globe of the world with a dent in Poland, antique guns, belt buckles, buttons, souvenir plates and cups and saucers (I can't remember all of it— I won't), but I recall how shamefully, how rudely, how abruptly, I fled, a good story in my mouth but death in my nostrils; and how afterward I busily, righteously, burned my leaves as if I were purging the world of its years. I still wonder if this town—its life, and mine now —isn't really a record like the one of Ramona that I used to crank around on my grandmother's mahogany Victrola through lonely rainy days as a kid.

the first person

Billy's like the coal he's found: spilled, mislaid, discarded. The sky's no comfort. His house and his body are dying together. His windows are boarded. And now he's reduced to his hands. I suspect he has glaucoma. At any rate he can scarcely see, and weeds his yard of rubble on his hands and knees. Perhaps he's a surgeon cleansing a wound or an ardent and tactile lover. I watch, I must say, apprehensively. Like mine-war detectors, his hands graze in circles ahead of him. Your nipples were the color of your eyes. Pebble. Snarl of paper. Length of twine. He leans down closely, picks up something silvery, holds it near his nose. Foil? cap? coin? He has within him—what? I wonder. Does he know more now because he fingers everything and has to sniff to see? It would be romantic cruelty to think so. He bends the down on your arms like a breeze. You wrote me: something is strange when we don't understand. I write in return: I think when I loved you I fell to my death.

Billy, I could read to you from Beddoes; he's your man perhaps; he held with dying, freed his blood of its arteries; and he said that there were many wretched love-ill fools like me lying alongside the last bone of their former selves, as full of spirit and speech, nonetheless, as Mrs. Desmond, Uncle Halley and the ferris wheel, Aunt Pet, Miss Jakes, Ramona or the megaphone; yet I reverse him finally, Billy, on no evidence but braggadocio, and I declare that though my inner organs were devoured long ago, the worm which swallowed down my parts still throbs and glows like a crystal palace.

Yes, you were younger. I was Uncle Halley, the museum man and infrequent meteor. Here is my first piece of ass. They weren't so flat in those days, had more round, more juice. And over here's the sperm I've spilled, nicely jarred and clearly labeled. Look at this tape like lengths of intestine where I've stored my spew, the endless worm of words I've written, a hundred million emissions or more: oh I was quite a man right from the start; even when unconscious in my cradle, from crotch to cranium, I was erectile tissue; though mostly, after the manner approved by Plato, I had intercourse by eye. Never mind, old Holsclaw, you are blind. We pull down darkness when we go to bed; put out like Oedipus the actually offending organ, and train our touch to lies. All cats are gray, says Mr. Tick; so under cover of glaucoma you are sack gray too, and cannot be distinguished from a stallion.

I must pull myself together, get a grip, just as they say, but I feel spilled, bewildered, quite mislaid. I did not restore my house to its youth, but to its age. Hunting, you hitch through the hollyhocks. I'm inclined to say you aren't half the cripple I am, for there is nothing left of me but mouth. However, I resist the impulse. It is another lie of poetry. My organs are all there, though it's there where I fail—at the roots of my experience. Poet of the spiritual, Rilke, weren't you? yet that's what you said. Poetry, like love, is—in and out—a physical caress. I can't tolerate any more of my sophistries about spirit, mind, and breath. Body equals being, and if your weight goes down, you are the less.

household apples

I knew nothing about apples. Why should I? My country came in my childhood, and I dreamed of sitting among the blooms like the bees. I failed to spray the pear tree too. I doubled up under them at first, admiring the sturdy low branches I should have pruned, and later I acclaimed the blossoms. Shortly after the fruit formed there were falls—not many—apples the size of goodish stones which made me wobble on my ankles when I walked about the yard. Sometimes a piece crushed by a heel would cling on the shoe to track the house. I gathered a few and heaved them over the wires. A slingshot would have been splendid. Hard, an unattractive green, the worms had them. Before long I realized the worms had them all. Even as the apples reddened, lit their tree, they were being swallowed. The birds preferred the pears, which were small—sugar pears I think they're called—with thick skins of graying green that ripen on toward violet. So the fruit fell, and once I made some applesauce by quartering and pairing hundreds; but mostly I did nothing, left them, until suddenly, overnight it seemed, in that ugly late September heat we often have in Indiana, my problem was upon me.

My childhood came in the country. I remember, now, the flies on our snowy luncheon table. As we cleared away they would settle, fastidiously scrub themselves and stroll to the crumbs to feed where I would kill them in crowds with a swatter. It was quite a game to catch them taking off. I struck heavily since I didn't mind a few stains; they'd wash. The swatter was a square of screen bound down in red cloth. It drove no air ahead of it to give them warning. They might have thought they'd flown headlong into a summered window. The faint pink dot where they had died did not rub out as I'd supposed, and after years of use our luncheon linen would faintly, pinkly, speckle.

The country became my childhood. Flies braided themselves on the flypaper in my grandmother's house. I can smell the bakery and the grocery and the stables and the dairy in that small Dakota town I knew as a kid; knew as I dreamed I'd know your body, as I've known nothing, before or since; knew as the flies knew, in the honest, unchaste sense: the burned house, hose-wet, which drew a mist of insects like the blue smoke of its smolder, and gangs of boys, moist-lipped, destructive as its burning. Flies have always impressed me; they are so persistently alive. Now they were coating the ground beneath my trees. Some were ordinary flies; there were the large blue-green ones; there were swarms of fruit flies too, and the red-spotted scavenger beetle; there were a few wasps, several sorts of bees and butterflies—checkers, sulphers, monarchs, commas, question marks—and delicate dragonflies . . . but principally houseflies and horseflies and bottleflies, flies and more flies in clusters around the rotting fruit. They loved the pears. Inside, they fed. If you picked up a pear, they flew, and the pear became skin and stem. They were everywhere the fruit was: in the tree still—apples like a hive for them— or where the fruit littered the ground, squashing itself as you stepped . . . there was no help for it. The flies droned, feasting on the sweet juice. No one could go near the trees; I could not climb; so I determined at last to labor like Hercules. There were fruit baskets in the barn. Collecting them and kneeling under the branches, I began to gather remains. Deep in the strong rich smell of the fruit, I began to hum myself. The fruit caved in at the touch. Glistening red apples, my lifting disclosed, had families of beetles, flies, and bugs, devouring their rotten undersides. There were streams of flies; there were lakes and cataracts and rivers of flies, seas and oceans. The hum was heavier, higher, than the hum of the bees when they came to the blooms in the spring, though the bees were there, among the flies, ignoring me—ignoring everyone. As my work went on and juice covered my hands and arms, they would form a sleeve, black and moving, like knotty wool. No caress could have been more indifferently complete. Still I rose fearfully, ramming my head in the branches, apples bumping against me before falling, bursting with bugs. I'd snap my hand sharply but the flies would cling to the sweet. I could toss a whole cluster into a basket from several feet. As the pear or apple lit, they would explosively rise, like monads for a moment, windowless, certainly, with respect to one another, sugar their harmony. I had to admit, though, despite my distaste, that my arm had never been more alive, oftener or more gently kissed. Those hundreds of feet were light. In washing them off, I pretended the hose was a pump. What have I missed? Childhood is a lie of poetry.

the church

Friday night. Girls in dark skirts and white blouses

sit in ranks and scream in concert. They carry funnels loosely stuffed with orange and black paper which they shake wildly, and small megaphones through which, as drilled, they direct and magnify their shouting. Their leaders, barely pubescent girls, prance and shake and whirl their skirts above their bloomers. The young men, leaping, extend their arms and race through puddles of amber light, their bodies glistening. In a lull, though it rarely occurs, you can hear the squeak of tennis shoes against the floor. Then the yelling begins again, and then continues; fathers, mothers, neighbors joining in to form a single pulsing ululation—a cry of the whole community—for in this gymnasium each body becomes the bodies beside it, pressed as they are together, thigh to thigh, and the same shudder runs through all of them, and runs toward the same release. Only the ball moves serenely through this dazzling din. Obedient to law it scarcely speaks but caroms quietly and lives at peace.

business

It is the week of Christmas and the stores, to accommodate the rush they hope for, are remaining open in the evening. You can see snow falling in the cones of the street lamps. The roads are filling—undisturbed. Strings of red and green lights droop over the principal highway, and the water tower wears a star. The windows of the stores have been bedizened. Shamelessly they beckon. But I am alone, leaning against a pole—no . . . there is no one in sight. They're all at home, perhaps by their instruments, tuning in on their evenings, and like Ramona, tirelessly playing and replaying themselves. There's a speaker perched in the tower, and through the boughs of falling snow and over the vacant streets, it drapes the twisted and metallic strains of a tune that can barely be distinguished—yes, I believe it's one of the jolly ones, it's Joy to the World. There's no one to hear the music but myself, and though I'm listening, I'm no longer certain. Perhaps the record's playing something else.